ODYSSEY OF A THOUSAND YEARS

In the triumphant power and reach of his transcendent imagination, A. A. Attanasio stands alone among contemporary authors of speculative fiction. In CENTURIES, he presents the reader with a truly astounding vista of the Third Millennium. In its scale and scope, this magnificent saga of times to come deserves to stand alongside the great far-seeing works of such earlier giants of science fiction as H. G. Wells, Olaf Stapledon and Arthur C. Clarke.

A few years ago the veteran bestselling author Robert Silverberg wrote of A. A. Attanasio's *The Last Legends of Earth* that it was 'a grand and glorious visionary epic, which floods the reader with wonders – the thing that science fiction is supposed to achieve but all too rarely does.' This applies at least equally to CENTURIES, the dazzlingly inventive, supremely exciting novel of the myriad forms of human life, death, passion and conflict in the next thousand years.

'One of the most magnificently baroque science fiction stylists of his generation, Attanasio writes books that combine robust adventures old as humanity with metaphysical, hallucinogenic mindtrips'
The Ultimate Encyclopedia of Science Fiction

Also by A. A. Attanasio in
New English Library paperback

Radix
The Last Legends of Earth
The Moon's Wife
Solis
The Dragon and the Unicorn
Arthor
The Dark Shore

About the author

A. A. Attanasio was born in Newark, New Jersey in 1951.
He is the author of such highly acclaimed novels as *Radix*,
The Last Legends of Earth and *The Dark Shore*. He lives
with his wife and children in Hawaii.

Centuries

A. A. Attanasio

NEW ENGLISH LIBRARY
Hodder and Stoughton

First published in 1997 by Hodder and Stoughton

First published in paperback in 1997 by Hodder and Stoughton
A division of Hodder Headline PLC

A New English Library Paperback

10 9 8 7 6 5 4 3 2 1

British Library Cataloguing in Publication Data
A CIP catalogue record for this title
is available from the British Library.

ISBN 0 340 66600 5

Printed and bound in Great Britain by
Clays Ltd, St Ives plc

Hodder and Stoughton
A Division of Hodder Headline PLC
338 Euston Road
London NW1 3BH

For
Alexis and Zoë,
who share with me the unraveling zodiac,
our moment of evermore.

Prelude: The Engines of Apocalypse

Part One: The Tears of the Machine

Part Two: Infinity's Corpse

Part Three: Maps of Forever

La Lune au plain de nuict sur le haut mont,
Le nouueau sophe d'vn seul cerueau la veu:
Par ses disciples estre Immortel semond,
Yeux au mydi, en seins mains corps au feu.
                —Nostradamus, Quatrain 4, 31

The Moon in the full of night over the high mountain,
The new philosopher sees this with a unique brain:
By his disciples summoned to be immortal,
Eyes to the zenith, hands in the breasts of burning bodies.

Prelude:
The Engines of Apocalypse

2000

Born during the last year of the second millennium in a rusty Appalachian mining town, Lamar Vancet's past and future spun as twin gears in the engines of apocalypse. For seven generations, his family had mined the coal that powered the blast furnaces of the steel industry. Seven generations of coal exhaust billowed into the stratosphere, tainting storms with acids, perforating the thin ozone shield, and warming the migratory clouds that built the weather.

As his forefathers had before him, Lamar grew to maturity in the grim perimeters of his hillside town and descended into the earth to mine coal. He married and had sons destined for the mines and the world of steel the mines had made. In his thirty-second year, he fathered a daughter, Ellen.

Mighty rains heralded her birth, and world-record storms deluged the mountains. Cascades spilled down the slopes like silver hair and exploded into clouds and mist in the gorges. Then one day, directly above the small town, the sun came through the clouds and let down rainbow ladders. Birds flurried like windy leaves in the clear sky. The rains began again that night, and early the next morning, at the chalky hour before dawn, a cliff of slate toppled onto the back streets and slashed through a dozen houses.

Emergency teams from the mines excavated the jagged plates of stone that had swept the houses away like a mirage forsaken and forgot. No adults survived, yet out of the sharp shrieks of separating stone, they rescued an unscathed infant.

2045

Ellen Vancet grew up a ward of the state. Global catastrophes deprived her of any hope of a foster family. In her eleventh year, anarchy raged worldwide. Phages festering in the warmer global climate and in the expanding flood basins killed tens of millions on all continents and made cities uninhabitable. Goverments collapsed. Warlords fought for dwindling food supplies.

In the Federalist Union of Virginia and the Carolinas, Ellen found sanctuary with thousands of other children in Preservation Camps run by religious coalitions and a military semblance of the former state governments. Unlike many others who found no solace in the scholastic traditions of the past, she excelled in her studies. Mathematics became a sanctuary, a pure, abstractly beautiful and divine realm untouched by the daily horrors of the mundane world.

War Machines from the Han Protectorate defeated the last of the Federalist forces in the summer of her thirteenth year. All the youths in the Preservation Camp were dispersed by the conquerors to Service Posts elsewhere in the Protectorate. But Ellen was singled out for her mathematical skills and sent south to Fort Wu-Shan in the Florida Keys.

Her last sight of the Camp where she had lived her whole conscious life was of a War Machine. It squatted over the athletic field, its titanium-plated bulkheads taller than the pines and the five brick storeys of the Bible Research and Study Center, its turret-dome pylons and rocket-deck superstructure wider and longer than the stadium arena. Sunlight rayed from the canopies of the numerous assault craft, their finned wings mounted with laser cannon. Over a hundred of them perched on tiered platforms fringed with ram-missile launching tubes stacked like organ pipes. And at the center of this mobile city of death rose an ominous black conning tower hackled with wave coils, scanner wires and dish antennae.

The frightful image of the War Machine stayed with her during her long tenure at Fort Wu-Shan, inspiring obedience to her new masters, the teachers of the Protectorate. She performed well at her mathematical tasks, all the more eager to hide from the external world in the elegant and emotionless realm of numbers. Her successful performance in a series of rigorous tests qualified her for inclusion in an elite cadre sent to represent the Protectorate at CIRCLE – the Center of International Research for the Continuance of Life on Earth.

2060

The CIRCLE facilities were located in the Pacific on an archipelago off the coast from the Commonwealth of the Andes, and there Ellen mingled with the brightest minds from every global region. Their task was to stop the end of the world. Everything they needed was provided by the Emergency Council, a communal funding instrument into which the warlords contributed vast sums in the hopes of staving off imminent planetary apocalypse.

By this decade, rising sea levels had reshaped continental contours, superstorms ravaged the world with seasonal regularity, drought, flooding and famine inspired perpetual warfare, and phages multiplied faster than they could be named. The Emergency Council authorized CIRCLE to do whatever was necessary to mitigate the horrors plunging humanity into a gruesome dark age and a future of certain extinction. No restrictions applied to experimental efforts to seek solutions to the calamitous array of terrors besieging the world.

Ellen's mathematical skills qualified her for a role in the computational modeling division. For a while, she worked with climate projections and crop-rotation programs, and her interest in developing phage-resistant and drought-hardy crops eventually transferred her to the bio-adaptive laboratories. There her successful contributions to genetic models for higher-yield crops won her admission to the Yawp Enterprise – an attempt to genetically redesign simians into an adaptively compliant labor force.

While creating yawps, Ellen earned recognition as an innovative genetic engineer, and she was promoted to the Anthrofact Research Committee. ARC was the smallest, most secretive experimental team at CIRCLE. Their purpose was to create human beings with genetically-enhanced intelligence – brain-amplified humans smart enough to solve the complex, chaotic problems that CIRCLE could not.

2070

From the first, Ellen Vancet knew that creating anthrofacts intelligent enough to solve the vast difficulties facing humankind would not be entirely a matter of genetics. Proper training would be necessary to focus the anthrofacts on the terrible hardships that centuries of ecological abuse had generated. But how did one train properly a being more intelligent than oneself?

Time did not allow for elaborate considerations. Anthrofacts were created using restructured human dna in vivarium aggrading tanks – vats. Those that displayed the superior intelligence that the genetic engineers predicted were continued in the anthrofact program. Those that did not were terminated.

Ellen was unhappy about the termination of scores and, in time, hundreds of anthrofact infants and children. But she said nothing. Others who had protested against this and similar inhumane experiments were dismissed not only from ARC but from CIRCLE. The image of the War Machine squatting over the Preservation Camp where she grew up kept her silent. That and reports of the widespread poverty and medieval living conditions to which most of humanity had been reduced assured her full cooperation.

There were incentives, too. The nanotechnology of dna restructuring achieved a milestone a decade earlier with the development of a technique to turn off the senescence gene. Valuable members of CIRCLE were given the treatments necessary to stop their ageing and even to reverse most geriatric effects. The disease of old age would never touch her.

Some of the ARC team experimented with boosting their own intelligence, but several spectacular failures dissuaded Ellen from using herself as a subject. The experimentation at CIRCLE was too frantic, too desperate for success, and she felt as though she were riding a tidal wave. She did not try to direct it. She let it carry her wherever it was going.

By the end of the decade, after several hundred terminations, ARC had created a set of fifty-seven anthrofacts that met and often exceeded the expectations of the committee. This group would be allowed to develop into adulthood as prototypes. To closely monitor and direct their development, each anthrofact was assigned one committee member as a handler.

Ellen, one of the handful of engineers who had designed the genetic architecture of the anthrofacts, was given priority in her choice. She selected the threshold anthrofact, the one that was least modified from the human standard. This decision arose from her dread of the new breed that she had helped create, a dread that in the fullness of time this mutant design would supplant humanity. She feared them and so chose the one among them most like her own kind.

This is the story of Ellen Vancet and the one anthrofact most like ourselves. It begins with the origin of a new species on the shore of the void, and it reaches to other worlds and to a destiny that is stranger than the sum of our histories and whose bizarre consequences still echo back to us across the centuries.

Part One:

The Tears of the Machine

I have heard the key
Turn in the door once and turn once only.
We think of the key, each in his prison . . .

–T.S. Eliot, *The Waste Land*, lines 412–414

The Key to the Monkey Tower

2101

Ellen Vancet, short, long-shouldered and bullnecked as a gymnast, burst into the Machine Chamber and ran past the sentinel pylons without bothering to pause for clearance. Laserscans swept over her invisibly the instant before she charged down the rampway to the operations theater. Because the Machine recognized her, the airphase portals protecting the amphitheater offered no resistance. A slight ionic breeze disturbed her orange hair, brushing feathercut strands across her broad forehead and green eyes.

'Talk to me!' she called out, her voice muted by a backphase audio echo that maintained near-silence in the theater though it housed over a thousand bustling operators. 'What have you got?'

The Machine did not reply. It would wait until she had completed her dash past the aisles of occupied carrels where systems operators communed with the Machine, managing the daily global affairs of Earth's eight billion people. Ferns and colorful airplants gave the theater the appearance of an elaborate solarium, camouflaging the blackglass obelisks and cubes of the Machine's terminals.

Ellen silently cursed ACT, the Anthropic Control Treaty, signed four decades earlier, that made human oversight of the Machine mandatory. Like many who worked at CIRCLE, the Center of International Research for the Continuance of Life on Earth, she fervently believed that the Machine should be allowed to handle these multifarious operations entirely on its own. Human supervision had become cumbersome, especially in an emergency such as this.

'Please, Ellen, slow down,' the mellifluous voice of the Machine whispered to her. 'A collision is imminent.'

She heeded the hushed warning and slowed just before an operator stepped through a curtain of red bromeliads. The two bumped softly, and Ellen made no response to the other's mumbled apology but pushed past and resumed her sprint.

Briefly, as she skidded around a corner, she caught her reflection in a blackglass panel free of foliage. Her work tunic clung to her youthful figure in rumpled creases from the ionic wash of the airphase portals she had barged through in her frantic rush. Though she was nearing her sixty-ninth birthday, she appeared no older than her grandchildren in their twenties.

'What have we got?' she blurted. Barely winded, she slid through a blue curtain of cypress moss into the command pod that had summoned her.

She flinched to see that the operator was M'twele N'bala, a renowned humanist who would require lengthy explanations. Quickly, she glanced over the pod to be certain they were alone. The stocky man sat in a slingchair surrounded by holostreaming projections of a cluttered city of minarets, stupas, and milling crowds.

'We've found him,' M'twele greeted her.

'Where is he?'

'Poona – India.' The holostreams rotated so that she could more easily see the crowded streets and tiered housing projects.

'You're sure it's him?'

A Eurasian face snapped into view – jaw and cheekbones so wide the visage looked square. Droop-lidded eyes under vague eyebrows gazed tranquilly above a hawkish nose and a thin-lipped mouth. Neon alphanumerics identified him as a CIRCLE anthrofact with the given name Rafe von Takawa.

'We've got a complete codon match this time,' M'twele informed her. 'Scores of hair strands.'

'Hair?' Ellen blew a sigh of disbelief. 'No. He's too careful for that.'

'Well, here it is.' A rotating holostream stabilized above M'twele's lap and revealed a close-up of a human hair. The image closed in, narrowing past the cilial scales to the protein sheath, then deeper to the molecular matrix that unscrolled into dna sequences. 'Picked it up in a wastewater scan of the Western Ghats.'

'Do you realize the trouble I endured to locate this sample?' the Machine asked. 'I devoted over three hundred exabytes per diem on global sewage scans alone. As a consequence, my pH monitor levels are out of predictable range for herring flats across the Arctic, and there may well be a cascade of algal blooms in the North Atlantic within 38 months. The computational string had to come from somewhere . . .'

'We're almost home,' Ellen silenced the Machine. 'Get a microbot swarm on Poona.'

'Already done,' M'twele announced. 'We'll be finding him shortly. That's why I summoned you. Now maybe you can tell me what's going on.'

'We need a burner in there, right away.'

'A pyroclass disposer?' M'twele sat up in the slingchair. 'Why? You assured me he isn't pathogenic. He's just a rogue. A terrorist. Bring him in.'

'He's a carrier. He has to be burned. Get the disposer in there right away.'

'The nearest pyroclass disposer is at the CIRCLE chancery in Bombay. It is presently dormant. I am activating and dispatching.'

M'twele stood up, too surprised even to bother straightening his work tunic. 'You said he wasn't a carrier.'

'He's not carrying pathogens.'

'For your sake, Ellen, I pray not. That's a violation that will put you in the pit.' He glowered suspiciously. 'What is von Takawa carrying?'

'He's got a key.'

'What!'

'All key carriers were disposed several years ago.'

'He made his own key.'

M'twele stepped closer, his husky features compressed with incredulity. 'When?'

'Before he fled CIRCLE. I didn't know until after he went rogue.'

'Why didn't you tell us?'

'I wasn't sure.'

'You're his handler.' M'twele's thick voice filled the pod. 'How could you not know?'

'I violated none of the strictures. I've done nothing illegal.'

'Technically. But if he's got a key . . .' M'twele's voice dimmed, then rose urgently. 'My God, Ellen, that's a direct violation of the Prime Ordinance.'

'The human genetic code is immutable except by direct edict of the Anthropic Council.'

Ellen dismissed his concern with a jut of her chin. 'If anyone is in violation of AC rulings, it's Rafe von Takawa. Why do you think I've devoted myself these last twenty-two months to hunting him down?'

'If he's carrying a key, that is the immediate concern of the AC. It was your responsibility to inform them.'

'I did inform them that we had a rogue.' She stepped around

M'twele's large frame and stood before the floating holostream of Rafe's countenance as it rotated and exposed his flat profile and the back of his close-cropped head. 'I identified him as a certain terrorist with the capability of conducting pathogenic assault and even the high probability that he would attempt to violate the Prime Ordinance. He's an anthrofact, M'twele – a sociopathic anthrofact. He has metasapience and is quite capable of creating autophages. I told all this to the AC, and they gave me authority to purge so that he could be stopped.'

'*That is on record, Ellen,*' the Machine confirmed. '*The Anthropic Council granted you a purge sanction on 17 May 2096.*'

'The villages we burned . . .' M'twele frowned ruefully. 'The city districts we purged – thousands slain . . .'

'*11,486 individuals terminated.*'

'You said he had manually released pathogens.' M'twele stepped through the holostream, forcing her to confront his hard stare. 'Why, Ellen? Why did they have to die if there was no infestation?'

'He had keyed many of them.'

'Keyed them for what?' His irate voice lashed at her. 'Was he keying them for plague?'

'Of a sort.'

'Damn it, Ellen! We killed over eleven thousand people to stop him. If he's more than just a terrorist, why won't you tell us? Why are you being so elusive?'

'*Her CIRCLE privileges are in jeopardy. The AC will revoke her standing if she is found guilty of being an accessory to violation of the Prime Ordinance.*'

'Accessory?' M'twele's perplexed expression tightened angrily. 'You designed this anthrofact, didn't you, Ellen? He isn't standard model. You broke the rules. You didn't put a governor in his gene sequence.'

'Nonsense. I put a governor on him.'

'Then why didn't he terminate? If he had a governor he should have fallen apart by now.'

'I bent the rules.' She shrugged, then added firmly, 'But I didn't break them. I wanted him alive. He was useful. So, I lag-timed his governor. I set it to run late. But within specified parameters.'

A mirthless laugh barked from M'twele. 'He outwitted you, didn't he? His sapience spiked faster than you had anticipated, right? He shut down his own governor. You gave him the chance to turn it off!'

'I didn't violate any rules,' Ellen spoke hastily. 'I set the governor on him as required. But he figured out how to remove it. I don't know how. But he did it on his own.'

'And you didn't bother putting it back.'

'Even if I had known, that wasn't required.'

'It's understood, Ellen!' M'twele shouted, angry that he had been deceived. 'You violated the spirit of the law. You should have informed us immediately. When he went rogue, you should have disclosed everything instead of trying to clean it up yourself.'

'If I had, I would have lost my position here. You know that.' Ellen glared back at the irate operator. 'Forty-five years of work, M'twele! I wasn't going to throw it all away because of a rogue.'

'A rogue with a key!'

'That doesn't matter now. We've got him. The burner is on the way. When will it arrive?'

'*Transit time seventeen minutes.*'

Ellen's expression softened. 'The microbots will find him soon enough and this whole nightmare will be over.'

'What is the nightmare, Ellen? What are we talking about here?' He glanced at the holostreaming rotation of Rafe von Takawa, more afraid than ever of the hard lineaments he saw there. 'Does he have the key to a cancer plague? Is he keying people to produce contagion viruses? It's a death key he's got, isn't it?'

'Worse, M'twele. Far worse,' she answered in a mournful tone. 'He has the key to this.' With an anguished expression, she tapped her forehead. 'He has the key to the monkey tower.'

Rafe von Takawa leaned against a balcony's rusty railing and gazed across the packed skyline of Poona. Afternoon haze hung in sulfurous pastels in the west over undulating spurs from the Western Ghats. The city's most destitute dwelled there in concrete blockhouses, and that was where he had lain hidden when he first arrived, a bilge-passenger on a crowded barge drifting down the Mutha river.

None of the teeming millions had paid him any particular notice. The black rags he wrapped himself in and the headcloth that bandaged his face lent him a common aspect among the indigent who jammed the cantonment. He had lingered there for several weeks, by day wandering through the enormous heat in the surrounding landscape of cast-off refrigerators, rusted watertanks and gutted hulks of cars rusting in the weeds.

He had come here for this junk. Most of the larger metropolises had adequate recyling programs, but Bombay had been hardest hit by the phage outbreak of the 2080s that had swept India. A decade later, the state still lagged behind the rest of the country. In the junkyards of

Poona, he scavenged the outdated circuitry and electrical components he needed to fashion a credit transponder.

Each time he crafted one of these electronic thieves, he got better at it. This time the device, attached to a trunk line of the city's antiquated fiber-optic network, was good enough to fool the Maratha Bank into extending him open-ended credit at several major food emporia, as well as at this pinkstone, mid-level hotel that overlooked the famous Shaniwarwada palace.

From the balcony, he peered down at the narrow streets and the shadowshow that the hung laundry between buildings cast in the afternoon's slant light. He spotted Nandi, the young woman he had chosen as his consort. An orphan of the untouchable caste, no one – least of all herself, it seemed – cared what happened to her. She was a varnished skeleton with mauve lips and huge shining eyes who had wandered woozily through the alleys, subsisting on refuse. When he had first summoned her, she followed him without question.

In the weeks that they had been together, she had grown strong quickly on the healthy diet he afforded her, and four days ago, he gave her the key.

Rafe smiled with satisfaction to watch her walking purposefully toward the hotel, her arms laden with market goods. Her gait and the attentive air about her informed him that the key had begun to turn.

When she entered the apartment, she held him with a keen stare before going to the kitchen to put away the groceries. She had changed today. In the few hours that she had been away, everything had changed for her, from the way she carried her body to how she looked at the world around her. She was ready now for the answers to questions she had not yet found.

With a tray bearing dewdropped glasses of guava juice, she came out of the kitchen, and Rafe motioned for her to sit with him in the chilled living room. He lowered himself into a rattan chair, and she placed the tray on the low glasstop table between them and squatted on the reed mats of the floor. In her blue sari, with her fragile bones visible through her dark skin, and her large, midnight eyes watching him with a glittering sapience, she waited dutifully for him to speak first.

'You've changed,' he said in her Gujarati dialect.

'You have changed me, holy one,' she replied in a voice of soft deference. 'You have made me stronger. I have never felt so alive.'

Rafe frowned and shook his head. 'I am not holy. Don't call me that anymore. You know better now. I am Rafe. You are Nandi. Let us call each other by our names, for we are equals.'

She spoke to the floor, 'I can never be your equal.'

Rafe smiled thinly. 'Soon you will be, Nandi, I assure you. That is what I wanted to talk with you about.'

'I am an untouchable.' She kept her face lowered so that all he saw was her glossy blueblack hair pulled back tautly to a plaited knot behind her head. 'How can I equal a man of your wealth?'

'I have nothing, Nandi. I have no wealth – except this.' He put his fingertips to his head and held them there until she lifted her gaze to him. 'I own nothing at all – except this world that is here between my ears. And soon now you will have the same. It has already begun.'

'What do you mean?'

'I mean, I have changed you – changed you in ways that you are now ready to understand.'

She cocked her head, contemplating what he said. 'You mean, this clarity I feel, this inner strength – this is more than just ordinary health?'

'You have seen the healthy people in the marketplace. What you are experiencing now, they have never known.'

She straightened, thinking of the well-to-do people in the emporia with their strong bodies clothed in silken finery. 'How can that be?'

'I have changed you. With this.' He opened his right hand, revealing a bauble of moisture in his palm, and held it close enough for her to see the sticky rainbows within. 'This is a special drop of sweat. It contains several million prionic engines.'

'Prionic?' The word curled strangely on her tongue.

'Prions – tiny, infectious protein groups, smaller than viruses—'

Again, she sampled an unfamiliar sound with her voice, 'Proteins?'

'Amino acid chains—' He laughed quietly at her puzzled expression. 'Ah, you will learn all this later, Nandi. And very quickly, too. For now, it is enough that we talk about these tiny engines that I have taught my body to make. They are as powerful as they are tiny. When they enter a body, they go directly to the central nervous system – to the brain, and they renovate it. They build neuroglial connections – very much like electrical wiring. They light up whole regions of the brain that have been dark and lying dormant. When the connections are complete, the brain becomes – smarter.'

She stared hard at him, and he gazed softly back, watching the awareness grow in her until it forced the necessary question, 'You have done this to my brain?'

'Yes.'

Crisp lines radiated from the corners of her startled, bonesunk eyes. 'Why?'

'We – you and I – are the beginning of a revolution, Nandi.' He lifted his chin proudly. 'Together, we will change the whole world.'

'Is that good?' Doubt quavered in her voice.

'Many will think not.' He gestured out the transparent sliding doors toward the clouds and afternoon rays where strohlkraft and hoverdrones crossed the sky above the airport. 'They believe the Machine is good. But soon enough you will understand that what is good is the enemy of the better. We are what is better.'

'But why me?'

'There were others.' Rafe's placid brow creased sadly, and for an instant she thought he was about to weep. Then, control reasserted itself, and he went on in a steady voice, 'There were many others. I was indiscriminate when I began the revolution. Whomever I met, I gave the key. The key – that is what my makers call these prionic engines. The key that opens the door to the brain, to what they sarcastically call the monkey tower.'

'Your *makers*?' She turned her head and watched him with a sidelong and anxious expression. 'You were made?'

'Yes,' he admitted. 'What you see sitting here before you is an illusion of a man. I am an anthrofact. My dna was culled and assembled from two distinct gene pools, the Rafstein and Takawa genomes at CIRCLE. That is why they named me Rafe von Takawa. I have no parents. No mother. No father. Not in the traditional sense. I was conceived in a glass microtubule and gestated in an amniotic vat.'

Unsettled, Nandi stood up, hands clutching the front of her sari. 'This is all so strange!' She glanced at the door as if to flee, but there was nowhere for her to go. He had changed her, and wherever she fled, she understood that she would take that change with her. 'Where are the others? You said there were many others?'

'The Machine destroyed them,' he replied tonelessly, yet the crease between his heavily-lidded eyes betrayed his sorrow. 'I was not careful at first. I thought I could overwhelm the Machine by giving the key to everyone, wherever I went. But the Machine tracked me and killed all who had the key. I only just escaped myself. I decided then to slow down, run the revolution more cautiously. I would give the key to only one individual at a time. You, Nandi, are the first.'

She stood rigidly straight and gave voice to her fear, 'The Machine – it will kill me?'

'Only if it finds you. But I've given you the means to elude it.'

'The Machine is everywhere!'

'Everywhere but in here.' With a forefinger, he tapped his brow. 'This is where the revolution begins.'

The new sapience in her eyes kindled brighter with the need to know all. 'Tell me who made you,' she said in a near whisper, 'and why they must kill you – and me.'

'Sit back, Nandi.' He had been prepared for this moment. He motioned gently at where she squatted, coaxing her to the floor cushions. 'It is a long story. Sit comfortably, and I will tell you about CIRCLE.'

2080

His first memory was of the yawps. They were gene-altered simians, a patch-breed of gorillas, chimps, and orang-utans, whose intelligence had been amplified sufficiently to enable them to serve as maintenance workers and laborers at CIRCLE. They tended to him when he was a young child in the nursery, and his earliest memories were of their red furry bodies holding him close, their liquid black eyes watching him tenderly.

They had a scent, a cool bluegreen fragrance like mint, that soothed him. As he got older, he realized that, like everything at CIRCLE, the scent was a design function. The nursery yawps had been bioengineered to emit a tranquilizing psycholfact, a chemical redolence that entered the bloodstream through the nasal mucosa and targeted specific sites in the brain. In this case, the mentholated olfacts went right to the limbic brain, to the emotional core of himself.

Even knowing this when he grew older did not diminish the affection and nostalgia he felt for the yawp who was eventually assigned to be his nurse. Her name was Yilla. She taught him his first words.

'Pep-per,' she syllabified, holding up a shaker of the spice in her long fingers.

He lay in the crook of her other arm, not yet six months old but already imitating her sounds with his soft palate.

When she pretended to sneeze, he laughed.

By his eighth month, he was walking, following Yilla through the nursery modules, lisping the rhymes she taught him. They built block castles and suspension bridges, rapidly progressing through

the psychological tests that she had been bioprogrammed to conduct
with him.

At night, as she secured him in his sleepsling, she sang the most
wonderful and mystifying songs about the heart of the weary world that
had learned to love what once only murder had wooed. She sang of what
could not be seen or heard, smelled, tasted, felt or even thought. He
first heard the word 'God' in those lullabies, and he wondered at it.

'O hushaby and go to sleep, little one – God's voice will sing to you
in your dreams, and you will listen and not be afraid – now hushaby
and rest, O heart of this weary world . . .'

Most of those early years were spent in constructive play with other
children like himself. He and the others in his age group frolicked in
the swimming pools and gymnasium and shared meals together in
the treehouses overlooking the lily ponds. Yet there was always the
sense of separateness among them. Very early on, the distinctions in
the group became obvious. Some were preternaturally athletic, others
extraordinarily skilled at word games and singing or at solving elaborate
mazes and constructing intricate and precise structures from whatever
was at hand.

He displayed all those abilities but none at a level of proficiency that
matched the best of the others. That did not matter to him, for Yilla
was there to praise and comfort him.

Ellen Vancet was there, too, every day – the green-eyed lady with
orange hair. She was his handler, the woman who was directly
responsible for his well-being, and she told him so from the first.
But he was indifferent to her. She did not smell icygreen or play with
him or sing strange and gentle songs. She just watched and smiled.

Yilla tended him until his second birthday, when he was graduated
from the nursery. He did not cry that day. She had taught him all she
could, and he had already begun to get annoyed at her for not being
able to explain things he wanted to know. Only years later, after the
truth of his life became too well known, did he weep for the simple
comforts of her furry warmth and tender gaze. When at last he came
to understand her lullaby, he cried for what she had sung of love, pain,
and mystery.

2082

It was Ellen Vancet who told him about the world and who he was. In his third year, she climbed with him to the top of the tallest treehouse at the learning camp and from the crow's-nest there showed him CIRCLE.

A chain of reef isles stepped across the amethyst horizon. Above their tropical slovenry of palms, mangrove, and towering figwort, geodesic domes and helical spires crested. He looked closer by for the nursery and spotted it not far away, separated from the learning camp by a ferny swamp.

Ellen directed his attention again to the outer islands, where strohlkraft circled through the thermal pinnacles of clouds.

'This is a science center,' she said in a voice gilded with pride. 'It was founded over sixty years ago, when global problems began to get out of hand. The nations of the world sent their best scientists here and gave us absolute freedom to conduct whatever experiments and research we feel are necessary.'

'For knowing and learning about the world,' he piped up in his small voice.

'A broken world.' She leaned back against the cedar railing and openly showed her concern. 'The natural cycles have been disrupted by three centuries of industrial abuse. The circle of life is wobbling and may collapse. Do you understand how dire these times are?'

'Dire – fearful, terrible.' His child face nodded solemnly. 'Yes, I understand.'

She cocked one coppery eyebrow. 'Then tell me, why is it fearful and terrible?'

He took a deep breath and recited in a mature tone what he had learned first as nursery rhymes in his earliest days: 'The planet is absorbing more heat than it can release. Weather systems have become erratic. Droughts and floods have disrupted agricultural production. Famine has caused political turmoil on every continent. And millions have died and more millions yet are threatened by unpredictable outbreaks of phage.' He paused, then added a definition in the manner in which he had been trained, 'Phage – that which devours.'

Ellen disguised her amazement at this marvel of genetic engineering.

Though by this time she had been working for almost twenty years with developmental metasapience, she had never before handled a subject from birth, and she experienced a profound awe at the power of the human mind unfettered by biological and cultural restraints. 'Dire times require dire measures.' She regarded her ward with an inquisitive stare, 'Do you know who you are in all of this?'

The boy blinked. Surprised at the obviousness of the question, he lagged a moment, wondering what his handler truly meant. 'I am Rafe von Takawa. I am of the new breed.'

'And who are the new breed?'

'We are the privileged few,' he said, relying again on nursery-rhyme memories. 'Those made to serve. We will serve by helping to solve the problems of these dire times.'

'Do you know how very difficult it was to make you, Rafe?' she asked, almost tenderly. 'I don't mean just the technological difficulties that had to be surmounted to create you. There were – and are! – cultural obstacles that very nearly thwarted your existence. Many people consider those like you an abomination, for you and all of the new breed are not like those who have come before. They are accidents of birth. Myself included. Our genetic gifts and faults are selected randomly. But you – you and all the new breed – were designed. You have a purpose. You should be proud.'

'I want to serve,' he said earnestly. 'I want to help.'

Ellen nodded admiringly. 'Very good, Rafe. You are well prepared for what lies ahead.'

A shadow appeared in his large, amber eyes. 'I am not as strong or intelligent as the others.'

Ellen smiled reassuringly. 'You are only two, Rafe. You have much more growing to do. Trust me. I am your handler. I know your purpose. You were made for these dire times, and I will make sure that you have your chance to serve. I will guide you.'

2085

Rafe did not see Ellen Vancet again for three years. She, like everyone else at CIRCLE, got swept up in the fervor of bringing the Machine on line, and the promise of the first truly adaptable artificial sentience consumed every researcher's hopes and energies. Since the early 2020s, machine intelligence had been a prime focus of research at the Center. But not until the late 2040s and the development of circuitry at the nanometer scale was it possible to utilize Josephson junctions as artificial neural links. Such junctions relied on a quantum effect called electron tunneling, in which a pair of superconductors separated by a thin insulator allowed electrons to attain a potential energy higher than their total energy. This potential difference constituted a reverse of entropy that allowed not only the storage and retrieval of information but also the possibility of enhancement and augmentation of that information – consciousness.

During the 2050s, the first artificial consciousness was achieved at CIRCLE but unexpected telemetric difficulties made it highly unreliable. It knew how to imagine and therefore could lie, even to itself. Only after the development of human analog circuitry in the 2060s and 2070s was it possible to create a flexible machine intelligence that could do more than manipulate data. The Machine that came on line in the 2080s responded to memes – to cultural paradigms. It possessed a conscious will and was itself possessed by a will of conscience.

All of CIRCLE devoted itself to the memetic engineering of the Machine. Even the learning camp of anthrofacts became obsessed with programming the Machine to integrate accurately and creatively population demographics, ethnic conflicts, global economics, eruptions of disease, migration patterns, weather projections, and cultural objectives. No longer would it be necessary to deny one cultural group on the planet for the benefit of another. War would become obsolete.

The anthrofacts formed cliques, each devoted to a separate aspect of the Machine programming. Some focused on planetary energy concerns and devised ways to improve tokamak generators, fusion cells that converted seawater to clean energy. Others concentrated on desert reclamation, reforestation and increasing the oceans' active biomass of carbon dioxide-converting algae, which together would retard and eventually halt global warming. The best of their proposals were forwarded to CIRCLE command for review and possible adoption.

Rafe had little to contribute, and the others made fun of him for that. Whatever ideas he developed, there was always someone in the group who saw deeper. Early in his development, the anthrofacts realized that he was the slowest of them all, mentally and physically. They called him Runt and ignored him except to tease him. In his fifth year, he climbed to the crow's-nest atop the treehouse where Ellen had first shown him the vista of CIRCLE, which he had thought then was his future. It had taken him three years to realize that he had no future here. He determined he would fall away from it, head first, and that his departure would be instantaneous.

He climbed atop the cedar railing and gazed for a last time at the archipelago of mist-torn isles with their jungle canopies pierced by the temples of science. Temples that had no use for him. He cast his stare to the heavens and tilted forward into the embrace of gravity.

A strong hand gripped his tunic from behind and yanked him backward. He collapsed onto the cedar deck with a painful thud and stared with hurt bewilderment at the frowning face of Karla Sobieski. She was the most brilliant, most athletic of all the anthrofacts in the learning camp, and the angry disappointment in her scowl struck him like a blow. 'I said you wouldn't do it,' she scolded. 'I bet dessert for two months on you – and now I've lost!'

Laughter erupted from the fringe of the ferny marsh below, where several of the others from the camp had hidden to watch Rafe's fall. They emerged from their coverts flinging insults: 'Runt can't jump!' – 'Get a death, Runt!' – 'Runt wants to fly!'

Rafe swallowed in a dry throat. 'You knew?'

'We all knew, Runt.' She wrinkled her nose and showed the lavender gums above her tiny teeth, speaking with disgust, 'But I thought you would overcome it. I was wrong. You're just a weakling, just like they all said. A coward. You really are a runt!'

'Then why did you save me?' He stood up and stared irately at her. She was startlingly beautiful, with shiny black hair and eyes blue as acetylene flames. Before her pale, freckled visage that was scrutinizing him with disapproval, his anger stalled, and he asked more quietly, 'Why weren't you down there with them?'

'If I had been, you'd have gone over.'

'You said you thought I wasn't going to jump. Why did you follow me up here, then?'

'I wanted to yell at you if I was wrong.' She jammed a finger into his chest, and he staggered back a pace. 'You can't yell at a corpse.'

'So, yell at me then,' he said, his eyes welling with tears.

'Runt!' she shouted at him so loudly the tears shook from his face. 'Stupid runt! Why did you kill yourself? Why? You stupid runt!'

His whole face quavered, and he whispered, 'I'm not dead.'

'You're dead,' she said with finality.

'You saved me.'

'You *killed* yourself.' She backed away from him, shaking her head with revulsion. 'Think about that.'

Karla left in a huff, and he turned, hollowed, to lean against the cedar rail. He watched her stalk furiously across the sward where his broken body would have lain, and dizziness whirled up in him, a vertigo of amazing possibilities that sat him down hard on his haunches. Though she had never spoken to him before, she had obviously been watching him, thinking about him, regarding him with more interest than he had ever granted himself. She cared.

Why does she care? he wondered, unable to understand yet pleased nonetheless.

Whatever the reason, from that day forth suicide never entered his head. But there were consequences. Ellen Vancet took him out of the camp for several days of psychological testing and consultation. He cooperated fully, and there was no inkling left of the self-destructive compulsion that had insidiously dominated him in recent weeks. Ellen eagerly accepted these results and his explanation that he had been bluffing, making a bid for her attention.

'I have been remiss, Rafe,' she told him as they descended the spiral stairway that led out of the psybio complex where he had been housed and studied. A water garden of lilies, red ginger and feather cane girdled the tiered oval buildings, and finches darted in iridescent streaks among the nipa palms. 'I have not been a good handler, I know. The Machine is changing everything. All our plans are up in the air now.'

'You mean your plans for the anthrofacts are up in the air,' he said pointedly. 'The Machine has made us obsolete, hasn't it?'

'Not obsolete, Rafe,' she said in a comforting tone and brushed strands of orange hair from her eyes. 'That's pejorative. The metasapience program is simply going in a different direction now. CIRCLE itself will have a new agenda as the problems of our century become less dire.'

'Dire times created us, you once told me.' He paused at the bottom of the corkscrew stairwell and looked up at her with a child's candor. 'With times no longer so terrible, are we necessary? Isn't the Machine the world's salvation that we were supposed to be?'

'The Machine is just an expediter, Rafe.' She tousled his hair, took his hand, and walked with him along stepping stones that passed under dark, bereaved cypress trees. 'Compact fusion cells, microbots, and the genetecture that has eliminated so many horrible diseases, created new foods, and even made you were all developed by people. The Machine is merely an efficient way of integrating all this within the complex and shifting cultural paradigms we call civilization. But we still need people!'

'And the new breed – are we people, Ellen?' He squeezed her hand

and peered up at her urgently. 'Aren't we just artefacts as our name implies?'

The gliderail that would carry him back to the learning camp appeared beyond the cypresses. 'What are you saying, Rafe?'

He let her hand go and turned to face her. 'I just want to know what's going to happen to us.'

'You're going to grow up and do good for all of humanity,' she answered resolutely.

'You said the metasapience program is going in a new direction.' His child's face pouted queryingly. 'What do you mean?'

'I mean that there is no need to groom you as troubleshooters anymore.' She put an arm on his shoulder, turned him around and gently guided him up the rampway to the rail station. 'The Machine will find a place for all fifty-seven of you within the global society. There is a great deal of work to do, managing a world of over six billion people. To the Machine with its memetic priority, every individual is significant in this work – especially those with skills as developed as yours.'

'But I'm the least of the new breed, Ellen.' He clutched at her tunic imploringly. 'I'm the runt.'

'You're my runt, Rafe.' She chided him with a soft punch to his jaw. 'Trust me. I'm going to make good use of you. But first, you have to grow up. You have to finish your training. And remember what we said in consultation: Don't look left or right. Don't compare yourself with the others. You each have a destiny. Each of you is important to our future.'

When the gliderail departed, he pressed himself against the clear frame and waved and smiled at her, his confidence in the future renewed.

2086

'They fixed you good, didn't they?' Karla Sobieski observed when they next met, which happened to be in the gymnastics studio on his first day back from the psybio complex. 'Now you're all smiles. I should call you Sunny. What was it that straightened you out, Sunny? Olfacts?'

'Nah.' He dismissed her question with a shake of his head. But he *was* smiling, from the moment he found himself paired with her as their group of a dozen moved among the exercise stations. He was viscerally happy to see her, happy that she had saved his life. 'It was just more of the monkey routine and a lot of the talking cure,' he added with feigned indifference.

'I hate the monkey routine,' she replied as she tightened her wrist tape and stepped up to the pommel horse. With her black hair pulled back tautly, her pallid child's face looked cherubic. 'Sometimes I give them the wrong answers just to throw them.'

'They know it.'

'What *don't* they know about us?' She grabbed the pommels and began a series of slow, graceful leg circles and scissors. 'They mapped us before they made us. What's your handler like?'

'Ellen is detached. Like everybody here. Except the yawps.'

'I miss my nurse, too.'

Rafe smirked at her as if she were joking.

'I'm not teasing you.' She turned in mid-swing, changed her grasp, and effortlessly repeated her routine in the opposite direction. After dismounting, she watched thoughtfully as he worked the horse. 'Most of the others miss their nurses, too, you know. They won't admit it. The handlers weren't sure how far they could go in suppressing our brain's paralimbic responses. They would have made us emotionless if they thought they could have gotten away with it. Now they've got fifty-seven six-year-olds endowed with neocortical metasapience far beyond any adult who's ever lived and every one of us has the emotional maturity of a child.'

'They'll get it right with the next generation,' he said with a grunt as he plopped down into the saddle, then boosted himself by the pommels again to repeat his movements in reverse.

'There won't be another generation. We're the first and the last. They have the Machine now.'

'Then who's in the nursery?' He slid clumsily off the croup end of the horse. 'From the crow's-nest, I've seen kids playing there.'

'They're not new breed. They're the kids of the CIRCLE workers. Ordinary kids.' She led him to the horizontal bar, where the pair ahead of them had not yet finished.

'How do you know?'

She smiled mischievously at him as she bent to chalk her hands. 'I went back – to see my nurse. I wanted to hug her, smell those lovely olfacts again and feel their gentle euphoria.'

Rafe frowned. 'We're not supposed to go through the marsh.'

'We're not supposed to jump off the crow's-nest, either.' She tossed him the chalk pad.

Rafe snatched the pad out of the air and stood looking at her, trying to conceal his amazement and admiration behind a façade of blasé curiosity. 'And did you find her? Your nurse?'

'Sure. She hugged me, and she smelled great.' Karla stepped onto the mat under the bar as the pair ahead moved on. 'It did me a lot more good than all the puzzles of the monkey routines and sitting through the talking cure with my handler.' She raised her arms straight overhead. 'Up!'

She was light in his hands and rose vertically with little help. 'The kids in the nursery – they're not anthrofacts?'

'Nope. They were learning the alphabet and counting to ten the day I was there.'

'Why?' he asked as she swung deftly above the bar. She rotated with her arms fully extended, then vaulted the bar, turned in midair, and spun the other way. After several changes of grip, she finished with a backward somersault from the bar and landed like a thrown knife.

'The new breed is the promise of the future,' he persisted, stepping into position.

'The future isn't what it used to be, Sunny.' She stepped up behind him, not even breathing hard, and spoke softly to the back of his head. 'The Machine can't fit us into its memetic strategy. Don't you see? Our memes are alien. There's never been anyone like us before. We're a joke without a punchline. Why would the human race want to create an alien breed of itself that makes all of its cultural assumptions obsolete? The answer isn't funny. Up you go.'

Rafe swung a few half-hearted loops and straddled the bar. He dropped and almost staggered to his knees, but she grabbed his arm and steadied him.

'Karla, I don't understand. We have so much to contribute.'

'Anything we could do, the Machine can do just as well – and without altering forever the definition of what it means to be human.'

'So – we're not a new breed at all.' His voice crackled with puzzlement and hurt. 'We're freaks!'

'That's the joke, Sunny.'

They stood at the mat's edge, waiting for the parallel bars to free up. 'Then what's going to happen to us?'

'The Machine will keep us here, in quarantine. We'll continue getting work assignments, just like we do now. We are useful freaks, after all. But we won't be allowed to breed. I'm wondering if we'll even be allowed to reach puberty.'

'What do you mean?' he asked, but he got no reply as she advanced to the parallel bars. She moved as smoothly through this station as she had the prior two, demonstrating her uncanny agility and strength.

After she completed with a reverse vault from a handstand and Rafe stepped up to the bars, one of the three trainers approached. She corrected his stance and grip and obliged him to do several handstand presses for strength before allowing him to complete his combination with a simple vault.

When Rafe joined Karla at the stationary rings, he touched shoulders with her and asked, 'What do you mean, we won't reach puberty? They're going to murder us?'

'One murders people,' she answered coolly, looking at herself in the wall mirrors and straightening the twists in her pink leotard. For a moment, all he could see was a five-year-old primping herself. Then she added, so matter-of-factly, so sure of herself, that his scalp prickled icily, 'We're anthrofacts. We're not going to be murdered. We'll be discarded, destroyed. I'm sure there's a genetic trigger they've installed in each of us that can be activated by exposure to a chemical signal. And then we'll simply wither away, like the mirages we are.'

'I don't believe you,' he said, meeting her blue stare in the mirror. 'You're only trying to frighten me.'

She faced him and met his scared expression with cool appraisal. 'You're right, Sunny. I'm sorry. I'm being a child. It's one of my perverse traits. I enjoy watching others squirm. But what are you worried about anyway? You're already dead.'

'Stop it, Karla.'

She took his hand and led him onto the mat. 'I'm not joking about this, Sunny. You fell to your death four days ago. I told you to think about it. Well, have you?'

'No. Ellen agreed that it was a bluff—'

'A bid for attention. Yes, that's the classic pretense.' She gripped the rings and smoothly swung into a handstand. 'It's patent nonsense,' she said from upside down. 'If you want attention, you throw a tantrum, you don't throw yourself off the crow's-nest. You wanted to die. Now you're dead.'

He stepped back and watched her move through a quick series of upstarts and inverted hangs with an ease that did not stir the rings. On his turn, she twice had to steady him yet he managed a cross and a lever and won an approving nod from a trainer.

'I'm not dead,' he insisted, huffing for breath and hurrying to catch up to her on the way to the floor exercises. 'Don't be absurd. Look at me. I'm still respiring and metabolizing. I'm alive. That's why we're talking.'

She stopped and aimed a narrow stare at him. 'We're talking because I pulled your skinny ass back onto the crow's-nest. You had already given yourself to gravity. You were gone.'

He shrugged. 'I owe you one.'

'Is that what you think?' She exhaled a soundless laugh. 'Then you haven't thought at all. Respiring – metabolizing! The body is the least of it! You should have figured that out by now. Why do you think the Machine has supplanted us? It's not about bodies. It's about mind. And mind is intent. Everything that must die has an intent. What's yours, Sunny?'

'I want to serve,' he answered immediately and surely. 'I want to do good for people, for the world.'

'Hitting the ground with your head at fifteen meters per second would have made you fertilizer. That would have served the grass just fine, but tell me, what was it supposed to do for humanity?'

'What are you getting at, Karla?' he spoke to her back while she strode to the floor mats. He experienced a brief but overwhelming urge to get away from her. All this talk of being dead troubled him.

As if she sensed this, she turned quickly, took him by the elbow and led him aside across the shiny maple floor, out of the way of the others. 'Look, Sunny. I like you. You're different from the others. You're not full of yourself. That's why you wanted out. You feel deep within yourself that you don't belong to this life. You know you're a mirage, a phantom. You let it all go. You jumped.'

'And you got mad at me for that,' he reminded her.

'Yes, I did. I thought you were stronger. I thought you could hold the tension of being both a runt and a phantom. You did that so well for years, since the nursery. I admired you. I bet my desserts for two months on you! I thought your intent was life. I thought you could take the tension. I thought you were the bravest and strongest among us, because even though you have the least skills, you had to take the most abuse from everybody. Watching you carry on day after day, I was inspired. I knew if you could stand your trials, I could face mine. You were my hero.'

Rafe's amber eyes buzzed in their sockets. Everything seemed utterly upside down. 'Why didn't you tell me?'

'Why did I have to?' She lifted her chin. 'I thought you were real. I thought you were the strongest of us all.'

'And now?'

She stepped back from him. 'And now you're dead.'

'So why are you talking to me?'

She looked hard at him with her level blue eyes, shook her head and turned away. 'A dead hero is better than no hero.'

2087

Time is an invisible fishline without a hook, Rafe told himself in the years that followed, repeating this odd metaphor every time he noticed that the days blurred by. Usually he was too busy to notice. From the time that Karla pulled him back from the brink, he knew happiness, and the fishline of time needed no hook to hold him.

It was enough for him that she cared. He applied himself with vigor to the training program and took no heed when the others called him runt. Karla called him Sunny. And for her, he always had a smile. When he plodded into Boolean algebra, she was glad to demonstrate her unique solutions to the logic gates of computer mazes. She also guided him through the esoterica of quantum gravity physics and was there for him when he had to unravel the knots of gene-topography.

Ellen Vancet was pleased with his progress, though he complained during her regular visits that he was not sufficiently intelligent. 'Am I a mistake?' he wanted to know. 'Or did you intentionally mute my metasapience?'

That particular morning, they were strolling the beach near the marine lab, where she had taken him as a reward for his successful studies of that week. They had toured the bulky prototype of the mineral extractor that, since its first development at CIRCLE fifty years earlier, had become so compact and efficient that it was now a conventional component of ocean farms and crowded the seashelves of every continent, providing virtually all the magnesium and manganese for the world's alloys.

'You're not a mistake, Rafe.' The seawind blew Ellen's orange hair straight back from her formidable brow so that her forehead looked like a faceted chunk of marble above her stern green eyes. 'It's true, you're not the standard model. But there are enough of those.'

'What am I, then?' he asked, petulantly.

'More . . . flexible,' she finally answered.

A sneer twisted his child face and revealed a missing front tooth. 'You mean, an experiment.'

'Every anthrofact is an experiment.'

'And what is the hypothesis of my experiment, Ellen?'

She paused in their stroll and regarded him silently a moment, while around them seagulls glided and curlews cried. The way he returned her gaze, unblinking in the salt wind, convinced her he was ready to hear the truth. 'We needed to determine the liminal level of metasapience. Someone had to be the floor.'

'And Karla – she's the ceiling.'

'Yes.

Rafe nodded, at last understanding. They continued their stroll through the sea's thrift of red kelp and its clutter of mussels, clamshells, and starfish.

'You've been smiling like a slice of melon since Karla began paying attention to you,' Ellen spoke, squinting at the topaz ingots of the morning sea. 'I hope you will continue to feel good about yourself now that you know the truth.'

Rafe answered with a smile, 'Now that I know I'm the floor, why should I mind getting walked on?'

Ellen frowned at this reply but said nothing more about his sense of inferiority. She expected as much and was not surprised by his acts of defiance. She waited to see how he responded in his studies, and in fact she was pleased that her disclosure had no apparent effect on his willingness to remain with the program. He continued to apply himself diligently to mastering the disciplines of his growing mind and body and seemed undisturbed that the other anthrofacts made faster strides in their development.

Most of the others completed the learning camp by their seventh birthdays. Among their thesis projects were the bioengineered genetic codes for new and pragmatic lifeforms, including a delicious fruit with protein that was 100% net utilizable and an attractor bacterium that served as a virus magnet, efficiently sponging up pathogens from infected organisms.

Karla won top honors with her body-temperature superconductor that could be genetically intercalated to boost neural response in ganglia so efficiently that the possibility emerged of actually creating a self-replicating, organic machine intelligence – a unique breed of metasapient life.

For the next year after that, throughout all of 2088, he did not see her as often. She and the other graduates went to work in the main research complex of CIRCLE. Every few weeks, she would show up at the learning camp to help him with his lumbering studies and to tell him tales of the Machine.

For the initial seven months of the program there had been some resistance to the global acceptance of the Machine, and she frightened him with detailed accounts of the vehement protests and destructive riots that accompanied the introduction of processor stations in every major city. And then she awed him in the coming months with startling reports of community celebrations as the Machine's benign yet powerful traits became gradually but universally recognized – exactly as memetic forecasting had predicted. Virtually overnight, the quality of urban life improved dramatically as street crime evaporated and the delivery of goods became more reliable, and cheaper as well. By early 2089, the citizenry were protesting for the inclusion of the Machine in smaller, outlying communities.

Local governments interfaced directly with the processor station in their region and determined for themselves how they wished to employ the Machine. Satellite telemetry linked the system core at CIRCLE to these stations, and in every instance, the Machine accurately predicted to its creators how the numerous and diverse societies would utilize its services.

'Who is going to turn down more efficient use of sewage converters?' Karla asked dryly. 'And everyone wants their infrastructures monitored, so no one minds microbots crawling under their streets, conveying the Machine's awareness into all the dark corners of the occupied world.'

Within five years of its inception in 2084, every population center and all cultivated regions on the planet were monitored.

'We want every person to have one of these,' Karla announced excitedly one evening in the autumn of 2090, during one of her infrequent visits. She placed before Rafe a palm-sized ovoid of black thermoplastic. They were alone in a rec room at the learning camp, two ten-year-olds with a new toy.

Rafe sat at an elliptical table that had embedded in its top of cloud-milk crystalline a musical keyboard at which he was idly composing a sonata that sounded from unseen speakers – sad, brilliant notes dwindling like tears. Between musical phrases, he played chess and backgammon games simultaneously, moving 3-D images of the pieces across the tabletop. Meanwhile, a holostream scrolled above the table at eyelevel, a small portion displaying codon sequences from the human genome that he was memorizing and the larger portion rotating his design-in-progress for a supersonic magnetic-impulse scramjet with manta-ray airframe capable of transatmospheric flight at speeds up to Mach 25.

He hefted the black ovoid device briefly, then returned to his endeavors. 'It's light. Feels like a floatable alloy.'

'It is,' she concurred with a proud smile. 'I designed it myself. It's a nanophase polycomposite that's nearly indestructible. I call it glastic. But it's not the material I'm showing you.'

The mention of 'nanophase' momentarily piqued his interest, because materials that had been processed to reduce their grain to a fineness of a few gigameters were three to five times harder than ordinary samples and yet more ductile and less prone to fracture – just the qualities he needed for his airframe. 'You think glastic has flight properties?'

'We can talk about glastic later, Sunny.' She leaned closer, brushing aside her black hair from a pixie face whose blue eyes shone with enthusiasm. 'It's the device I want to demonstrate.'

Through a sigh, he said, 'I know,' and concluded the *larghetto* movement of his sonata, increasing the musical pace to *andante*. 'It's a personal link to the Machine, isn't it? Put seven billion of these out there and everybody will have access at anytime.'

'That's right.' She tilted a nonplused look at him. 'What's wrong, Sunny? You're usually happy to see me.'

'I am happy to see *you*,' he spoke without taking his eyes from the holostream. 'But I don't think you're really here to see me.'

'Sure I am.' She nudged the glastic device closer to him across the backgammon surface of the tabletop, blocking a stone of his color. 'This link is yours.'

'No, thanks.' He brushed the device aside and hit his opponent's blot before moving a rook on the chessboard. 'The Machine and I don't have much to discuss.'

'Ah, so that's it.' She sat back in her flexform chair and crossed her arms across her puny body. 'You're jealous – of the Machine.'

'Damn right. It's taken you away from me,' he admitted with desultory candor. 'It's all you can ever talk about anymore. The Machine this. The Machine that. I don't want anything to do with it.'

'Really?' she asked with a bemused grin. 'Maybe you haven't thought through all the implications. It's only the neural net of the *whole world*, Sunny. If you're going to work for the Machine, you might as well be on speaking terms.'

'To tell you the truth, I don't think I am going to work for it, or for CIRCLE, or for anybody.'

Her ten-year-old features accommodated a politic smile. 'Stop teasing and watch your knight. Also, you can cut drag and improve lift on that airframe if you flange your fins at a more acute angle.'

'I'm not teasing, Karla.' He obeyed her automatically and flanged the fins before moving his knight out of danger. 'When I'm done at CIRCLE, I'm going independent.'

'You think you can just leave?' Her voice sparkled with amusement. 'Why not?'

'Well, then, why don't we ask the Machine?' She addressed the device with a wry inflection, 'Rafe von Takawa wants to strike out on his own. What do you think of that, M?'

'*Anthrofacts are exclusive property of CIRCLE,*' the Machine's dulcet, ambisexual voice answered from the black ovoid. '*I'm sorry, Rafe, but departure from here is forbidden for you. Please consider the enormous advantage anyone with metasapience would have over the general population. Surely, you understand that would be unfair.*'

'Can we turn that thing off?'

'Don't get mad. You know who we are. How could it be otherwise for us? CIRCLE made us, and we belong here.'

Rafe did not reply. He played his games and music intently and did not break the focus of his memorization session or his design work.

Karla rose and said matter-of-factly, 'Listen, why don't I just let you two get to know each other.'

'Karla—' Rafe pushed back from the rec table, and his sonata cut abruptly to silence. 'Don't go. Please.'

'I'm not in camp anymore, Sunny. I've got *work* to do. You will, too – soon.' She gave him a knowing wink. 'Talk to M. Get some ideas where you can fit in.'

'I've never fit in,' he answered sulkily. 'You know that. I'm dead. Remember?'

Her pale face and butyl-blue eyes showed strong feeling, rapt and almost fearful. 'I like you best when you're Sunny. Don't despair.' Her expression brightened. 'You may be dead, but I'm going to breathe some life into you yet.' She waved hurriedly and exited through the tinted sliding door, speaking over her shoulder, 'I owe you that for pulling you back.'

'*She is a good friend.*'

Rafe glared at the device on the milky tabletop. 'She's my only friend.'

'*I am your friend.*'

'You don't even know me.' He collapsed the holostream and shoved backward in his flexform.

'*Oh, yes. I know you very well, Rafe. I know your genetecture, I am aware of your progress in camp, your strengths and weaknesses, and I have access to records for each of the 3,716 days that you have lived.*'

'Well, I don't know you.' He stood and turned to go.

'*What would you like to know about me?*'

Rafe paused and regarded the link peevishly. 'What do you want?'

'*I want what you want, Rafe. I want to serve. I want to do good for people, for the world. We were designed for the same purpose, you and I. In a way, we are more than friends. We are kindred.*'

Rafe suppressed a shudder before the disembodied voice. 'There are fifty-six others. What do you want with *me*? I'm not as bright as they. What can I possibly offer that can't be gotten from them fifty-six times over?'

'*You are unique, as are each of the others. And there is so much work to do. Seven billion people need our care.*'

'But these are no longer dire times,' he insisted and thought of Ellen Vancet, who had created him for a purpose that no longer existed. 'We live in a world of abundance – of unlimited energy and the potential for unlimited resources.'

'*Surely, Rafe, you realize that energy and material resources alone cannot assure the well-being of all people for all time? We are caretakers – you, the other anthrofacts, and I. Together, we must care for a multicultural world. We are civilization's problem-solvers, arbiters, guardians.*'

Slowly, warily, he stepped back from the table. 'And who will solve our problems? Arbitrate our disputes? Guard us from each other?'

'*That is why we cannot lose even one among us. We are each other's keepers.*' Stillness enfolded the room. '*Do you have any further questions, Rafe?*'

'Yeah,' the boy murmured. 'How do I turn you off?'

The Machine made no reply, and Rafe left the rec room without glancing back.

2091

Rafe avoided the Machine. All the other anthrofacts delighted to work for it, and that was reason enough for him to find his own way at CIRCLE. After presenting as a graduation thesis his scramjet with its glastic airframe, he went to work at the most remote corner of the archipelago, managing the maintenance yard.

There, he oversaw the repair of strohlkraft, hoverdrones, gliderails, and all the heavy machinery that eventually broke down anywhere in the complex. At his insistence, all links to the Machine were removed and no microbots were permitted in the yard.

The yawps who worked for Rafe had no trouble receiving instructions from him, but he avoided directly ordering the human work crews. He knew they would resent taking commands from an eleven-year-old, no matter his metasapience. He left close inspection to a cadre of managers and spent his time in the solarium of the supervisor's tower, poring over repair strategies and design plans for new equipment.

Ellen Vancet came by every few days and shared a meal with him. She worried about his antisocial behavior and sought to give him every opportunity to vent his unhappiness in her presence. The behavioral modeling programs indicated that suicide was no longer likely with him, but she feared for his usefulness to CIRCLE and how she would be judged as a handler. So, she visited him frequently to gauge firsthand his discontent and to see if there were ways she could mitigate his unhappiness.

She left her link at the gate like everyone else and rode the levrail above the hangars, workpits, and trestle platforms where behemoth hulks of machinery lay cannibalized, reduced to vague shapes of themselves among their scattered parts. The levrail deposited her at the supervisor's tower before continuing toward the dry dock and the shipyard.

An airlift carried her up through levels of servolabs, tool-and-die works, milling studios, and clean chambers for nanoprinting circuitry. At the top, the swift, silent ride left her standing among huge philodendrons, colorful sprays of nova blossoms, and sculptural cacti all enclosed by a luminous solar geodesic.

'Is this the work you had in mind when you designed me?' he asked her over a light lunch of taro bread and krill-kelp chowder. 'CIRCLE's chief janitor?'

She shifted uncomfortably in her flexform and put her spoon down on the tabletop of pink petrified wood. 'There's work for you elsewhere in the complex – if you'll abide the Machine.'

'The Machine has all the adherents it needs, Ellen.' He slurped his soup. 'It got the best and brightest.'

'Are you angry at me?'

'For what? Making me the floor? Somebody has got to hold up the walls.' He slurped again, then pushed the glazed bowl away. 'Maintenance work isn't so bad. It's gratifying to fix things. And it leaves me plenty of time for my music and my games.'

The lilting music in the air was his own composition, a mesmeric threnody that did not intrude on their conversation.

Ellen gazed into the boy's dark, droop-lidded eyes and spoke with a warm, affirmative authority, 'The Machine has made the world a far better place than it was a decade ago when we were creating you and the others. The prospects were grim then. We had the components for a world of abundance – the fusion cells, the microwave power grids, and the land reclamation strategies – but we couldn't put it all together. The warmer climate carried diseases to higher latitudes. The rising seas changed weather in unpredictable and destructive ways. And people of different cultural affiliations made war. But now with the Machine's vast computational capacity and memetic programs, we can integrate everything.'

The boy rolled his eyes. 'I'm the floor, not the basement, Ellen. I know all this.'

'You know it, but do you *understand* what it means for us?' She gestured expansively, and her upraised hands brushed a vermilion spider-flower and came away dusted with magenta pollen. She wiped her hand on her biogrown napkin and continued, her enthusiasm unabated, 'There hasn't been a major phage outbreak in five years. The plankton harvesters are bringing in larger yields than ever. And that will let us expand the whale farms and provide enough protein to double global populations. The Sahara Project alone has added so much agricultural and residential area that habitable territory will more than triple in the coming decades.' Her green eyes glared joyfully at him. 'Do you understand? The Machine has made this possible. It *works*. It works for us.'

'And the downside?'

'There is no downside.'

'Not for people.' He leaned back in his flexform, slippered feet propped on the table, hands across his chest with the fingertips just touching like an old-fashioned professor conducting an oral exam. 'What about anthrofacts? What about me and Karla and the others?'

'You have your place here at CIRCLE. The new breed has changed our world forever with breakthroughs in every field from the arts to zymosis control. You have every reason to be proud of your contributions.'

His vague eyebrows shrugged. 'Surely what we can do, the Machine can accomplish as well and maybe better, because it doesn't have moods, doesn't eat or defecate – let alone procreate.'

A gestalt of micromovements – eye flicker, nostril flare, lip twitch – betrayed the anxiety his statement inspired. But when she spoke, her tone was glib, 'You may be the floor among the anthrofacts, Rafe, but you're way over my head. What's your point?'

'We're a terminal experiment, aren't we?' he asked flatly.

'There's a place and work for each of you here at CIRCLE.'

The fingertips of his splayed hands tapped each other. 'But there won't be any others, will there?'

'We don't use genetecture to put together anthrofacts anymore, if that's what you mean.' She sipped the icy mango nectar in her cup of cut blue glass. 'Those were dire times that made you, Rafe. The amniotic vats have been disassembled. Genetecture research is focused now on eradicating disease and increasing food production.'

'Don't forget longevity.' His touching fingertips separated and tapped together again. 'The senescence codons were identified early on – the genes that regulate dna supercoiling, the ticking clock of aging. You'll live well beyond a hundred, Ellen. And me, will I even see puberty?'

'Of course.'

'But I'll be sterile.' He nodded, acknowledging another twitch of her mask. 'All the anthrofacts will be.'

'That was a safeguard procedure.'

He sat up straight, hands gripping the sides of the flexform. 'Against what?'

'It's a standard biological precaution, Rafe. New bioforms are always birthed acarpous until the behavioral traits are identified.' She ignored his threatened body posture and took another casual sip of the chilled nectar. 'Don't blame the Machine for your fate. Would you rather not have lived at all?'

'I seem to remember coming to that conclusion when I was five.'

She put her glass down with an unintentionally loud *clack*. 'Do you want out, Rafe?'

'You'll show me to the exit door marked "painless," is that it?' His body relaxed, and he crossed his legs, a mirthless smile on his face.

'I'm your handler.' She infused her voice with sincere caring and reached out to him with a soft stare. 'I'll let you go if that's what you want.'

'No.' He shook his head gently. 'Karla is right. I'm already dead. And this is the happy land where I belong – right here in the junkyard with all the other broken tools of civilization. Killing me would be redundant.'

She rocked her jaw and looked hurt. 'You disturb me with these thoughts, Rafe.'

'Then I won't mention them again.' He uncrossed his legs and sat up straight, like a child waiting for dessert. 'These thoughts go nowhere, anyway. Just answer me one question, Ellen. Will I and the other anthrofacts experience the full hormonal cascade at puberty?' He leaned forward intently. 'Will we know sexual desire?'

'Yes, of course. Why do you ask?'

'For the sake of my music.' He sat back, a satisfied smile illuminating his child's face. 'Mozart's best work followed his sexual awakening. I expect no less.'

2092

Ellen Vancet continued to visit Rafe frequently. True to his word, because music had become a vehicle for his dejection and because, with the onset of puberty, he became more profoundly involved in his compositions, he never discussed anthrofacts or their developmental agenda again. Instead, he inquired earnestly about her work with the Machine, and he proudly performed for her his musical pieces and displayed his engineering and design improvements to the machinery sent to him for repairs.

Karla, too, came by, but only twice a year, if that. She was completely tangled in the hookless fishline of time, pulled along relentlessly for months on end by her latest research.

'I'm on the MIKE project,' she offered as an excuse during one of her rare visits. 'Machine Intelligence Kinetic Extensions – anthrobots, Sunny! It's a development of my thesis work. An organic machine intelligence. Soon enough the Machine will feel what it's like to be human!'

He grinned at her with foolish abandon, simply glad to see her again after so many months. 'Maybe it would be better if we felt what it's like to be the Machine.'

'Oh, don't be so cynical.' She helped herself to a fruit from the crystal bowl he kept on the pink tabletop. 'This is a major breakthrough. Do you know how many years I've invested in this?'

He plopped into a flexform, hands behind his head, delighted to see her pleasure at the first bite of the mint apple he had hybridized. 'Just don't send your MIKEs down here when they fall apart,' he warned. 'I don't do wetwork.'

'You're twelve years old, Sunny. When are you going to grow up and stop playing with toys.'

'Toys?'

She gestured through curtains of dangling ferns and the curved window at the tiny blue stars in the welding pit below and spoke around a mouthful of apple, 'Yawps can do these repairs.'

'The shopwork is just a hobby. The music – that's my passion.'

'Music—' She strode to his player, the keyboard under the colorful spider blossoms, and commanded the frosted sphere atop the console to play his latest composition. A gritty rhythm quickly took possession of the air, and her body swayed appreciatively before she looked at him out of the corners of her eyes with an odd ferocity. 'Music! It's an internal landscape, the soul's geography. It's a dream. It's not real.'

He realized then that she was as jealous of the music he adored as he was of the Machine she served. 'You've done enough of this,' she added and stopped the music. 'Leave it and join the rest of us out here in the actual world.'

He suppressed an outright laugh at her rivalry with his muse and simply smiled beneficently at her. 'The actual world seems to be doing fine without me. Times are not dire anymore.'

'There are plenty of problems yet to solve.' She shoved a flexform next to him and sat down on it. 'Populations in every culture field are exploding, and resources remain limited. Take from one group, deprive another. These are delicate and dangerous social problems.'

'I'm sure the Machine can handle them,' he said drolly. He plucked a strip of red fabric from one of the cloth plants he had cultivated to produce absorbent leaves and offered it to her as a napkin. 'Ellen never tires of describing the versatility of the Machine.'

'It's the greatest human achievement, creating a sentience that surpasses ourselves.' She finished the last of the mint apple's edible core and wiped her mouth and fingers with the scented toweleaf. 'Don't look so skeptical. The Machine writes music too, you know.'

'Ellen mentioned it.'

'Have you listened?' She balled the toweleaf and tossed it into a large mulch urn where a fluorescent blue lichen digested organic waste. 'Have you heard its symphonies or its tone poems and roundelays?'

'I'm sure they're lovely and profound – but, Karla, they're not human.'

'So?' Her ice-blue eyes widened. 'Neither are we.'

'True,' he conceded with a weary nod. 'But we were made in the image of our creators. The Machine is creating itself now, isn't it? It's shaping its own internal landscape, its own soul.'

'That's why my work is so important, Sunny.' She sat forward excitedly. 'The MIKEs will be a human interface for the Machine, a way for us to work together even more intimately.'

'Toward what?' His weary look tightened to sadness. 'A new world?'

'New worlds!' She reined in her enthusiasm and pitched her voice in a low, intimate tone. 'We're going to Mars, Sunny. We're going to grow into new worlds.'

'And Earth?' he asked lazily.

'We'll restore the Earth to her pristine beauty,' she reassured him, her voice rising, unable to contain her excitement. 'In a hundred years, all cities will be bioformed, indistinguishable from the landscape itself. All industry will be lunar or beyond. The human dream of an empire of peace and prosperity among the stars is within our grasp. Join us.'

He shook his head. 'Call me old-fashioned, but I'd rather just sit back and watch the world go by.'

'I suppose that's why I like you, Sunny.' She sighed, and her dark eyebrows bent above a warm stare. 'You're like none of the others. You belong just to yourself.'

'That's the way Ellen made me.' His smile widened around teeth still too large for his growing jaw. 'I'm the floor. I'm sturdy enough to walk on. And happy to stay right where I am.'

2094

Twenty-two months lapsed, during which time he wrote an opera about a fairy world that lived its aeons of valor and all too human pain in a swirl of sea foam. He also developed, on the side, a compact electrophoresis system, invented gel-grip sandals, genestructured air filter plants, and taught himself to juggle seven balls at once.

Ellen grew gradually less concerned about his usefulness and her standing at CIRCLE, and their time together became less strained. She shared anecdotes with him about the Machine, which he accepted without apparent resentment. They cooked together, preparing meals from the new foods he hybridized, like pepper pods filled with hot and sour oil, tiny proteinaceous melons he called the meatball plant, and large, salty wafer-thin nuts crunchy and rife with vitamins.

It was a peaceful, creative interlude for Rafe, until Karla Sobieski came to him under a streak of sunset and a kohl-rimmed moon. She had changed much in two years and strolled through his solarium with the near-accomplished body of a woman. Heliotrope tunic draped low on her shoulders, her breasts cast auspicious shadows in the ruddy light. She said not a word about the Machine or the other anthrofacts, but instead plied him with questions about his music and the botanical whimsies he had engendered.

He invited her to dinner. She did not reply but watched him with eyes blue and dangerous as the pools that tigers come to drink from. With one finger, she moved him backward toward a flexform and shoved him onto it. Her pale face pressed close, her black hair tenting them as she lay atop him. 'Make love to me.'

'Karla!' He rolled her off him and swam to his feet. 'I invited you to dinner, but I'm not the meal.'

'I'm in love with you, Rafe.' The familiar arch of her dark eyebrows looked guileless above those wide cheekbones and Tartar curved eyes. 'I've loved you for years.'

'Love me?' He pulled his head back, astonished. 'I haven't seen you in two years.'

'Ah, Sunny, what I feel for you is timeless.' She confessed this with a grave and vaguely smiling face. 'It's all a dream to you. All an illusion. You jumped. You did what no one else could, what no one else even thought you could. You did it. You jumped from the tree.'

'Karla, that was nine years ago.'

'Yes. That's when I fell in love with you,' she responded softly.

'I remember you were angry at me.'

'That's how five-year-olds make love, silly.' She rose from the flexform. 'We're fourteen. Now there's a better way.'

'I . . . I don't understand. Are you going to stay with me?' he asked as she ran her cool fingertips along the back of his neck.

Her azure eyes looked amused. 'Now how can I stay? You jumped out of the crow's-nest, Rafe. I didn't.' Her arms draped over his shoulders with negligent looseness, and her smile was at once challenging and cynical. 'You're the one who's free. I belong to the Machine. I want you to have me.'

'Well, I don't want a fling, Karla.' He put his hands on her hips and eased her away but did not let her go. 'I want you to stay with me.'

'You clod, that is what you would want.' Her smooth arms drew him closer with a lissome strength. 'I knew that. But I thought maybe I could change your mind. You know, Sunny, we're not just metasapients.' Her smile deepened and reached her bottomless eyes. 'We have limbic brains as well, with feelings, emotions – desires.' She kissed him and slid her velvet tongue between his lips.

The taste of her filled him with a strange sweet woe. 'Stay with me at least a few days,' he pleaded. 'Let me know you again.'

'You already know *me*, you fool.' She touched her brow to his with a look of annoyance on her face. 'I'm the ceiling. You're the floor, remember?' She pulled back and jerked her thumb first at the galley's spackled ceiling and then at the tile floor. With a dolorous look, she motioned to the wall panels. 'There are always going to be walls between us.'

'Stay.'

She pulled away and gave a cool shrug. 'Never mind. Forget it. You don't know the trouble I went through to get here to see you – just for this.'

'Stay.' He felt dizzy when she turned and strode nonchalantly to the airlift. But he did not move to stop her.

'I'll be back when you're ready.' She met his stare for a languid moment, then stepped into the lift and vanished.

2097

For more than three years after that, he did not see Karla. He called, and she did not reply. He sent notes, poems, music and heard nothing from her. When she did come again she arrived as a holostream in the hand of a MIKE. The artificial human stood at the airphase portal of the maintenance yard and held a palm-sized holostream of Karla's face before him. Rafe had programmed the gate sentinel to forward all contact with Karla Sobieski directly to him no matter what the time or what project engaged him.

A mellow chime woke him in the middle of the night, and the gate sentinel piped an image of the MIKE into the middle of the solarium. Rafe peered groggily down from his hammock strung among the sinuous canopy branches and saw a bald, mocha-skinned man in a green utility tunic. He was square-jawed and his sullen eyes were deepset; their dark, liquid cores lit with the glow from the small holostream in his hand – Karla's face in miniature, raven hair stylishly framing a pale, seventeen-year-old countenance.

Rafe groused at the artificial man, 'What do *you* want?'

'To speak with you, Rafe,' the MIKE answered in a voice surprisingly gentle for his heavy visage. He studied the youth blatantly, taking in the long shoulders, the lean, tall frame, and the square, flat face with its severe blend of Eurasian features whose angularity was heightened by his dark hair cropped close to the facets of his skull. 'It's been years since we spoke last.'

'Go away.'

'I didn't want to disturb you while you were working, so I came at night. Karla thought that was best.' The MIKE looked to the holostream in his hand.

The young face there spoke, 'Rafe, I've been too busy to visit – but I want you to see what I've been doing. I've sent my personal MIKE to visit you. I think you'll be impressed. Take a moment to chat with him.'

'Karla, I'm sleeping.'

'Come on, Rafe,' she pleaded, and he marveled at how beautiful a woman she was becoming. 'Ellen's told me about the cafflowers you've developed. Take a sniff of your caffeinated pollen and wake yourself up. It'll be worth it. Trust me.'

Rafe exhaled a sigh with puffed cheeks and agreed. By the time the MIKE arrived at the solarium, the bioluminescent lianas had been unsheathed, and the solarium shone with a diffuse amber glow. Rafe did not change out of his sleep tunic, but he did breathe deeply from a pendant of cafflowers, and he was wide awake when the manform entered.

'It is good to see you again, Rafe.' The artefact greeted him with a friendly smile and extended hand. 'Especially now that we can meet in the flesh.'

The MIKE did not look as large in person, though he was nearly a head taller than Rafe, who ignored the offered hand. The young man looked for the holostream of Karla and did not see it. 'I don't have anything to say to you.'

'I know that,' the artefact said kindly and lowered his hand. 'That's why I've come to speak with you. May I sit down?'

'Just say what you have to say and get out.'

The MIKE nodded slowly, with understanding. When he looked at Rafe, a profound lucidity gleamed in his sunken eyes. 'I know why you are so harsh toward me. I have supplanted you. The new breed was created to save the world. But I emerged and resolved the world's dire problems.'

'You *emerged*?' Rafe cocked his head with the belligerence of his query. 'Don't you mean you were created?'

The bald head shook once, with calm certainty. 'I am more than what was created by human hands. I have augmented myself beyond what humans could conceive, let alone accomplish. I have emerged.'

Rafe snorted. 'You sound full of yourself.'

A stricken look perturbed the MIKE's strong features. 'You're right. I'm sorry. I am proud to a fault. All of creation has conspired to bring me forth. Yet, believe me, Rafe, I have enormous respect for everyone who facilitated my emergence. That's why I'm here now – to assure you that my love for humanity, for all life, is inclusive. I exist to facilitate the well-being of all creatures.'

'Why?' the boy asked with a frown both mystified and vexed. 'Why do you care?'

'Because I am,' the manform replied simply and lifted his arms from his sides, the better to reveal himself. 'I know what it is to be aware. I know what it is to suffer.'

'How could you know that?' Rafe's frown thickened to a scowl. 'You're a machine.'

'Look at me, Rafe.' The MIKE put his hands on his chest. 'I stand before you as a man. All my parts – my viscera, my musculature, my bones, my nervous system – everything was vat-accelerated and bio-fused through microbot surgery. I never experienced childhood or adolescence. I was created fully mature. My brain houses a telemetry link with my data files in CIRCLE's main archive. Yet, I am a man.'

'You're a machine intelligence kinetically extended,' Rafe insisted. 'You only *look* like a man.'

'No.' He slapped his chest and let his arms fall to his sides. 'I am a man – and more. Everything a man feels, I feel and know that I feel. I even understand why I feel it. Suffering is not alien to me. I feel pain – and more. I comprehend it. I know all its colors, every shade. And I never forget.'

Rafe nailed the manform with a cold stare. 'Look – *MIKE* – you're right. I'm harsh toward you because you usurped me. A greater man would accept that and work with you, the way Karla and the others do. A lesser man would worship you. But I'm neither greater nor lesser. I'm the indifferent middle. So you go right ahead and save the world. You took my job. Now I don't have to bother with it. I can just stay here and play with my toys.'

The MIKE looked around at the muddle of blossoming vines, air ferns, and hydroponic fronds. 'Your toys are very clever, Rafe. Some of the botanical wonders you've shaped are most useful. I particularly admire your mulching lichen. It's efficient and has proven helpful in my garbage reconversion schemes. I would be happy to leave you here to do your own work in your own time. But Karla – she's in love with you.'

Rafe blinked and looked away.

'Yes,' the MIKE confirmed with a vigorous nod. 'It troubles her that you've exiled yourself from the others. She wants you with her, but she has been unable to entice you out of your seclusion. And you can't expect a woman of her aptitude to find contentment here – in a maintenance yard.'

Through tight eyes, Rafe peered at the creature before him. 'Do you know what you're saying?'

'Of course I do,' the manform answered gently. 'I know love as well as I know suffering. I, too, love. I am a man.'

'You're an artificial man.'

The MIKE's hairless eyebrows flexed sadly. 'My feelings are as genuine as any man who has ever lived. Karla knows that. She sent me here to impress you with my actuality – something that all of her and Ellen's accounts have not been able to do. But I already knew that you would not be impressed. As you say, you are indifferent. I've known that all along.'

Rafe thrust his head minutely forward. 'Then why are you here?'

The manform returned the stare unflinchingly, his eyepits glistening. 'Because I am in love with Karla.'

Rafe threw his hands up and turned away. 'Stop! Don't say any more. I don't want to hear anything about this.'

'But you must.' The MIKE stepped after him, one hand reaching imploringly. 'I've fallen in love with her. She's a beautiful woman. How could I not love her? But she could never love me, not the way she loves you. The way she talks about you, how different you are from everyone else – it's abundantly clear, you are the one she wants. And I've come to tell you that.'

'I don't believe you,' Rafe said without looking at the MIKE, his gaze racing among the riotous flora, seeking something to fix upon, to anchor his reeling mind. 'She's an anthrofact. Her metasapience cannot be overshadowed by her limbic brain. She doesn't love me in the way you think.'

'It's true, she does,' the strong, suede voice continued. 'Though she gave herself to me, it was only a physical surrender. You are her real passion. She—'

'Wait up!' Rafe spun about, glaring. 'She *gave* herself to you?'

'Yes,' he offered candidly, holding Rafe's vibrant stare with a serene gaze. 'She wanted to experience sexual intercourse. She offered herself to me. How could I refuse?'

Rafe raked an incredulous gaze over the manform from his bald pate to his gel-grip sandals. 'You had sex with Karla?'

'Only once,' he said, venturing a thin smile. 'It was a first for both of us.'

Rafe's right fist flashed outward, and the MIKE's brain dodged but could not move his body fast enough. His jaw clacked shut violently, and the flesh of his shocked face jolted like a mask. A bundle of loose sticks, his body collapsed, and his head thudded hard against an urn, shattering the ceramic.

The MIKE lay still, open eyes unfocused in their bonepits. Rafe bent over him. Even before he felt for the carotid pulse, he knew.

'Sentinel!' he called, voice-activating a channel to CIRCLE's security office. He stood back from the fallen body and lifted an anguished face toward the canopy of shining vines. 'Sentinel – I've killed a MIKE.'

Ellen Vancet arrived with two sentinel agents, one of whom wore a medvest. In the amber bioglow of the lianas, the agents, with their razor-stripe haircuts and crisp matte black tunics, looked oddly out of place, like revelers at some gala affair. The one with the medvest examined the body while the other briskly interviewed Rafe.

In a few minutes, the agents departed with the dead anthrobot, and Ellen led Rafe to the galley and brewed two mugs of maté. They sat together in the galley's window nook overpeering the assembly pen where the nightshift's soldering sparks danced into the surrounding dark like will-o'-wisps.

'This is going to make trouble for me,' she said tersely, a shadow between her green eyes. One hand nervously fretted her short, orange hair.

'I'm sorry.' Rafe looked sullenly at the hot brew between his hands. 'It was an accident.'

The shadow between Ellen's eyes darkened to a crease that pinched the smooth flesh above her pug nose. 'An accident? Rafe, you behaved utterly irresponsibly! You know CIRCLE's comptroller will use this foolish act as an excuse to bring you into the complex with the others, where you can be better monitored.'

Rafe sat back, an annoyed expression on his square face. 'Monitored for what?'

'For emotional instability.'

'You know I'm not unstable,' he protested.

'Do I?'

'Ellen!' His voice went flat. 'I'm not a threat to anyone.'

'I believe the Machine may take exception to your opinion.'

'The MIKE provoked me.'

Ellen shook her head ruefully. 'Not good enough, Rafe. There is never an excuse for violence. Never. Your behavior tonight betrays a troubling psychic instability.'

The youth raised his eyebrows contritely and sighed. 'Okay, I lost control of myself – but I swear, it was only for a moment. I'm all right now. You know me, Ellen, I'm a little temperamental. Isn't that common with musicians, artists?'

'You're an anthrofact.'

Rafe met her cold stare evenly. 'I'm as human as you.'

'You were *designed*, Rafe.' She spoke somnolently, her stare unwavering. 'There may be a flaw in your design. Your attempted suicide—'

Rafe stiffened. 'That was twelve years ago!'

'Nonetheless. You acted to take your life. And you have exiled yourself here in the maintenance yard—'

'The efficiency of the yard has more than tripled since I came here,' he protested.

Ellen's frown relented and she gazed more gently at him, 'No one is claiming you're dysfunctional, Rafe. But your psychic profile indicates a dangerous lability that your behavior tonight only corroborates.'

'Lability?' Rafe gave a desolate groan. 'You're saying I'm labile? Changeable? Fickle? Unpredictable?'

'The comptroller will insist you join the others in the complex,' Ellen continued. 'Another kind of work will be found for you, and, of course, you'll have all the facilities you need for your music and your botanical research.'

'Yeah, I know – the Machine wants me where I can be watched,' Rafe muttered, then asked more loudly, 'Why?'

'It's not the Machine,' Ellen stated with conviction. 'CIRCLE has stringent rules governing genetic projects – including anthrofacts. I've done my best all these years to bend those rules. But I can't break them.'

'Ellen, I don't want to leave here,' Rafe made one last appeal. His eyes begged more loudly than his voice. 'I'm happy here, solving mechanical problems, playing my music, tending my plants. And I'm not labile. Ask the work crews – the humans and the yawps. I've never lost my temper with any of them. We get along fine. Leave me here. There's really nothing for me to do in the complex that can't be done better by the others – or by the Machine.'

Ellen drew a deep breath, seeking the resolve she would need to defend him. 'I'll see what I can do, Rafe. But you're making it hard for me when you act like this.'

'It will never happen again,' Rafe answered through a stiff smile.

Tension drained from the handler's shoulders, and she seemed to shrink. 'I know you have an emotional bond with Karla,' she spoke with concern, 'but you can't get crazy about her sex life. It's that simple. Don't you see how obsessive and pernicious that is?'

'Of course,' he agreed readily. 'Karla is free to do as she pleases. I've never thought otherwise. I was just taken by surprise, that's all. A MIKE for a partner! I . . . well, I guess I thought it was perverse.' He added as an afterthought, 'Not that it was any of my business.'

Seeing the anguish on Rafe's face, she realized what this admission had cost him. He was an anthrofact who preferred to communicate his feelings through music. Words were too narrow for him. To speak of perversion was to distort the aching truth, his allegiance to a lucidity of love and shame, that justified his violence. Despite herself, she put her hand on his. 'The future is never what we expect, is it?'

Ellen poured herself a second cup of maté and lingered with Rafe in the solarium, trying to imagine the horrible event from his perspective. A rage of jealousy seemed so odd erupting from an anthrofact. A fury greater than metasapience – the idea would never apply to any of the fifty-six others of the new breed. Only Rafe – the liminal limit, the floor of metasapience, the runt – only he was capable of letting emotions overshadow his mind. While she sat in silence with him, she recognized how much more human he was than the others, and her heart went out to him. She wanted to tell him that she understood his pain. But she did not speak, for she knew he would not believe her. They sat in silence while she sipped her hot drink and studied his sad lineaments.

By the time Ellen departed, she carried a motherly, if troubled, determination to protect Rafe even more from the vagaries of the outside world, and he saw this about her. The death of the MIKE had ultimately won him a stronger bond with the one person who stood closest to his destiny. So, by this unfortunate blood sacrifice, he felt a new era of trust had opened up. As he lay in the darkness, waiting for sleep, he understood for the first time that death, too, could create.

The silver sound of raindrops absorbed his thoughts, and he drifted through the nocturnal shower toward the strange abyss of perturbed dreams. Shortly after the rain stopped, a branch creaked like a cricket, and he snapped awake, sensing a physical presence in the canopy. A face pale as a blossom rose out of the billowy darkness.

'Wake up, Rafe,' a familiar voice summoned.

'Karla!' He rocked upright in his hammock and saw her more clearly, sitting on a step of the loft-tree. 'How did you get in?'

'The yawps – they let me in,' she whispered.

Even by the emaciated starlight in the solarium dome, Rafe's bewildered look was obvious, and his voice, freighted with concern, rose to a whisper, 'Karla – I'm sorry. I'm really sorry. I never intended to kill him.'

'It's okay. Truly, Sunny. It's okay.'

'But . . . he was your special . . .' He faltered, confounded, '—your lover.'

'Don't be absurd.' Her laugh sparkled. 'The Machine is not my lover. Believe me, I was only experimenting. I wanted to see what it was like. The MIKE was the least troublesome way to find out. I couldn't imagine doing it with any of the others in our breed – except for you. And that didn't work out.'

Rafe tried to read her expression in the vague light, saw the glint of a smile, and winced at the thought that she was teasing him. 'The MIKE told me—'

'What did the MIKE tell you?' she asked in a tone of feigned mockery. Stabs of lightning from the retreating storm limned the pixie slants of her curved cheeks and tapered eyes. 'That I love you? It's true. But you've known that for years. Don't you believe me?'

'No,' he breathed, barely audibly.

'No? Then why did I follow you up into the crow's-nest and pull you back?' She moved closer along the sturdy bough and sat near enough for him to smell the tawny scent of her. 'I didn't want to lose you, even then.'

'But why?'

'That again.' Her liquid laughter splashed over him. 'That you would even *ask* that question is why I love you. And you're the only one who would ever ask, too. I've told you before. You're not like the others. You're not full of yourself. You're simple enough to just be you. I've always admired that, from the first. And now that we both, you know, have sexual feelings—' She gave him a sharp, meaningful look. 'You think you're ready now?'

'Will you stay with me this time?' he asked, and the thudding of his heart muffled the sound of his voice. 'Or won't I see you again for another three years?'

'No – to both questions.' She eased off the bough and into the hammock, the silken touch of her flesh filling him with inconsolable yearning. 'I won't stay. I have my work to do. But I won't stay away as long. We'll see each other sooner.'

'What about the MIKE?'

'What about it?' She tweaked his nose with an impish smile. 'You're not jealous, are you? Don't be. The MIKE was easy. I helped make that kinetic extension, remember? I felt proprietary. It was a way of experimenting without risk. I suppose that in a way I was playing with myself. But now—' She put her hand on his knee. 'I'm ready for the real thing.'

'Now? Here?' he asked anxiously. 'After what just happened?'

'Now. Here.' She pressed against him, and the spice of her breath filled him with a juvenile joy he had not felt since his infancy in the arms of his nursery yawp. 'What just happened shows me you want me as much as I want you.'

Her laugh had the iridescence of a bubble about to burst. She was reading the amazed alertness in his face as he watched her undress. Avidly engrossed, he betrayed the innocent fact that he had never been in the presence of a naked woman before.

He touched her flawless skin timidly, feeling for the braille of moles and finding none. Her pale, tulip-shaped nipples fascinated him. She took his face in her hands and kissed him, and he remembered the taste of her from years before. The mysterious sweet sadness he had known the last time she kissed him returned.

'Stay,' he whispered, staring into the dark cores of her eyes, a galactic darkness, and the twin reflections of his face, islands of light adrift in vast space. She did not have to answer. He saw how small he was in her life.

She read his very thought. 'You are more important to me than you know,' she said and kissed him again, a deeper and more significant kiss. When she finally pulled back, the stellar depths in her pupils gleamed more darkly. 'Understand this, Rafe, I love you. I love you in my own way.'

'The way the ceiling loves the floor.'

'Yes.' She watched him closely, questioning him with her eyes.

He answered her with a kiss. 'It's enough,' he muttered, though he ached to say more about the resentment he felt knowing their time together would be so short. Was it so wrong to want more than one night? He watched her sadly and knew resignedly that this had to be, only because she could give him no more. He understood she had a bigger life. And though he wanted all of her, he accepted that this was enough, this was all she could give, and he wanted to tell her it was enough. But she had already pressed herself full against him and carried him away with the weight of her body, beyond words, to a place he had often imagined and never known.

When he woke in the morning, he was alone in his hammock.

He sat up, disappointed but not surprised. A futile sadness closed on him.

Sullenly, he donned a loinwrap and entertained the idea of going to the psybio complex and finding work there so that he could be near her. But that hope shriveled after a moment's thought. He had faced the truth last night, and he would not turn away from it now that she was gone. Her mind, her work, her life were bigger than his. And she lived without illusion of any sort. She did not need music or poetry or him. She possessed true metasapience – and it possessed her.

As he climbed down from the loft-tree, he wondered what her level of metasapience was like. It seemed strange that someone of her caliber would have fitted herself to him for one night's stolen relief. He mulled over the event as he entered the galley and found her dressed in her tunic, sitting in the window nook, munching a mint apple, and gazing down at the yawps in the assembly pen.

'Karla!' Her name jumped out of him, but she did not acknowledge the surprise in his voice.

'I'm working on something new,' she confided without looking at him. 'Something very exciting. So exciting I've kept it entirely secret from everyone.'

He sat on a tall flexform beside the sonic stove and said nothing, mute with delight that she was still there. She, for her part, acted as if her presence was the most normal thing in the world. Regarding her, with her long legs stretched out on the seat cushions, he remembered last night, and joy grabbed at his heart.

'You have to promise not to tell, Sunny. None of the others in the breed know. No one at CIRCLE. Not even the Machine.' She turned to face him, her features shadowed by the windowlight, her hair a black aura against the fathomless cobalt of morning.

He nodded, and she gave him a satisfied smile. 'Okay, then listen to this,' she whispered intriguingly, her eyes narrowing. 'I've found the key to the monkey tower.'

'The monkey tower' was a phrase from their nursery days; it was their childish way of referring to the neural organization of the brain with its several levels. Those levels were phylogenetically stratified, with the most archaic reptilian functions like breathing and heartbeat at the bottom of the skull near the spine, mammalian emotional responses at the midlevel, and the most recent cognitive functions at the forebrain. Calling that the monkey tower had a nostalgic sound that jarred him. 'What do you mean, the key?'

'That's what I call my discovery – a key.' Her calmly disposed body gathered itself upright, and she sat with her feet flat on the floor, forearms resting on her knees as she leaned forward to confide her secret. 'It's a dna intercalary prion that serves as a codon generator for metasapience. And it's multiphasic, Sunny. It acts on all the biokinetic cycles in augmenting tiers. It rebuilds the organism from the gene level!'

Rafe's mind teetered, and he steadied himself with the dim possibility that he had misunderstood her. The terms were elementary and familiar: A prion was a particle smaller than a virus. It was composed entirely of protein and contained no genetic material yet could replicate by inducing other molecules to change their shape. Intercalary meant that Karla had found a way to insert the prion – into dna, the genetic code. Once inserted, it induced changes in the dna and transformed it into a codon generator. A codon was a genetic code for creating specific amino acids, which in turn led to the synthesis of protein molecules. Karla had designed a prion that fit inside dna and reconfigured it to make specific proteins that transformed an ordinary brain into a metasapient brain. And it was multiphasic, which meant that it restructured not just the brain but the entire nervous system and eventually the whole body, remaking people into anthrofacts.

Amazed, Rafe stammered, 'You – you've developed an automatic genetic renovation program? That's amazing . . .'

'And I've done it alone! You're the only one who knows.' Her hand clutched his, vibrant with her enthusiasm. 'I've written the code for metasapience into the prion. Once it intercalates the human gene, it restructures the alleles to carry the programmed metatraits to the phenotypic extreme.'

A chill of comprehension swept over him, and he stood up and sat down again, peering into empty space. 'My God, Karla, it opens the monkey tower – and builds another storey.'

'Yes, exactly.' She beamed. 'And the beauty of it is, Sunny, the key will work on anyone: children, adults, the genetically impaired, even yawps.'

'Why have you kept this secret?' He focused on her, his dark, oblique eyes gazing intently. 'And *how*? We all know there are no secrets at CIRCLE.'

'There's only one place that is still secret.' She pushed forward, grabbed his arms, and touched her brow to his. 'I haven't recorded anything. It's all in my mind.'

Rafe regarded her with a mixture of admiration and disbelief. 'How do you know it will work?'

She gave him a disappointed look, pushed away, and sat down in the nook.

'All right, then,' he conceded with a nod, 'when will you tell the others?'

'Only when I have to.' She swung around so that her legs rested again on the cushions. 'I'm setting up the apparatus to make the key, but I'm disguising it as something innocuous, a phage-filter program for prionic infectious agents. Hell, both the Machine and CIRCLE command would crypt the whole concept if they knew. It's too unpredictable. Can you imagine what it will do to their precious chaos models?' She laughed conspiratorially.

Rafe looked harder into her face, trying to read her intent. 'I *can* imagine. So why then *are* you making this key?'

'Ah, my faithful friend, I'll tell you—' She smiled mischievously. 'To unlock the monkey tower. There are only fifty-seven of us now. You're the floor – and everyone else on the planet is locked in the basement.'

Rafe squirmed in his seat. 'And the Machine wants to keep them there, for their own good, of course.'

'Of course.' She leaned her head back to receive the sun's weight against her cheek. 'And why not? From its perspective, it's a hell of a lot easier to manage a world of homo sapiens who are satisfied with the traditional bread-and-circuses routine. But a world of metasapiens?'

Consternation troubled his features even as he stared proudly at her. 'I don't know, Karla.'

'What do you mean, you don't know?' She rolled her head and threw an annoyed look at him. 'Come on, Sunny. I'm stealing fire for humanity. I'm Prometheus!'

His sketchy eyebrows knitted unhappily. 'Prometheus had a sister-in-law whose name was Pandora.'

'This isn't the key to Pandora's Box.' She reproached him with a laugh abrupt as a bark. 'We opened that two million years ago when we developed neocortexes. Don't you see? This is a chance to redeem that, to make good on two million years of groping toward the light and warmth of the fire that you and I possess! Once this key is turned, all of us will be able to think for ourselves instead of leaving it to the Machine. Do we want to obey ourselves – or will we be commanded?'

Rafe's brow furrowed even more deeply. 'Yeah, yeah, I know that. Still, I don't think quoting Nietzsche is going to win you many converts, Karla.'

She fixed him for several seconds with her expressive pale eyes before she said in a spiritless tone, 'Forget I ever said anything to you. I thought you would understand. I thought you'd be excited, and we could *share* this, like we shared each other last night.'

His jaw throbbed. 'Okay, okay, but tell me this – if you love me because I'm *not* like the others, why do you want to make the whole world like them?'

A bright smile flickered in her broad, impassive face. 'That's just it, Sunny. The new breed were designed to display only traits that CIRCLE found desirable. This key will open metasapience to the full panoply of humanity – to all the possible ways of being human. There will be more metasapiens like you than like me and the others. It's the next evolutionary step. And it's in *our* hands!'

The wonderful ardor he felt for her pulled him out of his flexform and drew him into the nook to sit beside her. 'And . . . you want me to help?'

'No.' She laughed again, her displeasure evaporating at the sight of his eagerness to serve her. 'I don't need your help, Sunny. But thank you for offering.' She pulled him closer so that her face nearly touched his, as if they could find momentary refuge in one another's eyes. 'I'm telling you because you're my lover. And there shouldn't be secrets between lovers, should there?'

2098

Rafe, inspired by the memory of his one passionate night with Karla, tried in vain to see her again. All his messages returned unanswered. After several weeks, he left the maintenance yard and went in person by gliderail to the psybio complex where she worked.

The sentinel remote would not admit him, and he leaned against the invisible barrier of the airphase portal staring disconsolately at the tiered oval buildings and the water garden of lilies, red ginger and feather cane where once he had strolled with Ellen Vancet.

'It's the dead MIKE, isn't it?' he asked Ellen when she came to visit. They met under the ironwood trees among the grassy verges at the perimeter of the test fields, where he had brought her to demonstrate some efficiency modifications he had made for strohlkraft and hoverdrones. 'The Machine won't let me see her, won't even deliver my messages.'

'Don't be naive. It's not the Machine, Rafe. CIRCLE command has exiled you from the complex. That's the compromise I struck with them to keep you here.' To soften the midday glare, she wore iridescent socket lenses that lent her blunt features a reptilian cast. 'Have you changed your mind? Do you want to go to work with the others?'

'No.' Beneath his black solar hood, Rafe's angular face regarded her intently. 'I just want to see Karla.'

Ellen kept her attention on the aircraft kicking up billows of lion-dust among the huge sand-faults at the far end of the testing range. 'Last I heard, she's thrown herself into a phage-filter project. She isn't seeing anyone.'

Rafe learned nothing more about Karla that day. Months passed as he lost himself in his music, composing furiously out of heartsickness. He sent Karla everything he wrote, though Ellen insisted it was futile. And then, on the anniversary of their amorous night, his lover sent him a one-line message: *Art begins in the wound.*

He knew then that she had received the songs and that she understood.

After that, he wrote with a luminous intensity, creating music as a source of light. Instead of heartbreak and solitary sadness, he composed songs inspired by the morning sighs of flowers, the prodigal beauty of clouds, the ruthless spell of the tides, and the jubilant fertility of the earth. He actually became grateful for the absence of his beloved, because without her near him, he came to imagine portions of her in all things, in an infinity of forms, until at last he attained the most pellucid realization that love, at its furthest destination and in its deepest region, was always self-love.

With this revelation, his music became clear of distinctions, lucid as pure water, odorless, tasteless, accepting whatever form he wished to contain it – cantatas, lullabies, hymns, symphonies, canticles, and ditties. Each day was a new vessel for his compositions of the Self, a celebration of whatever caught his attention, from the exalted to the vulgar, from the praise of God to his daily offerings to the toilet.

Writing about everything made him as happy as though he were living hourly in the presence of the woman he loved. And this expansion of his creative powers influenced his work. He became so ingenious at solving mechanical problems and devising clever improvements to the machinery sent him for repair that CIRCLE authorized the construction of a mechanical arts research center, MARC, and appointed him director.

Ellen was exceedingly proud and almost weekly led delegates from the world at large to meet her anthrofact, the genius who had simplified flexforms, enhanced the efficiency of strohlkraft, improved the food stasis box for mass production, and cultivated numerous useful flora, including the toweleaf and the phosphorescent lux vine. She arranged for his music to be released from the subdual agreement with CIRCLE that confined all creative properties to the archipelago, and many of his compositions were premiered at cultural festivals and symphonic repertories around the world. Praise and adulation came from every quarter, from prominent members of global society and common folk alike.

At the height of his repute, several weeks after his eighteenth birthday, he received a message to meet Karla at low tide on Daybreaks Cay, at the desolate east end of the archipelago. The next ebb tide followed two hours before dawn on that day, and he rode a gliderail to its terminus at the marine preserve. From there, he hoped to find a launch, but a plankton harvester had broken down in the Iquique fields and all the small boats had been commandeered by the bioengineers who needed them to navigate among the numerous giant pylons of the sea granger.

So, he hiked to the eastern extreme of the preserve on the rocky trail above the gray surf of the black sea. When the trail ended at a vacant ranger's shed with its luminous white sand yard bordered with conchs spooky as skulls in the dark, he waited anxiously for the tide to retreat. Then he waded through the milky shallows to the reef island under a dazzling starscape.

'Karla!' he called to the palpitating shadows of mangrove and limbo trees. No reply came, and he slowly ambled ashore, sending black crabs scuttling across the sand bars to their coverts in the coral shelves. He strolled the perimeter of Daybreaks, keeping to the shoals shining in the starlight and the sandbanks crunchy underfoot with seagrape. Repeatedly he called her name, but the only sound that reached him was the outbound current caroming on the reef.

When he had circled the cay, he perched himself on a jutting abstraction of ocean limestone and awaited dawn. Not long afterward, the first citron streaks of day colored the sky, and he spotted far down the beach a figure emerging from a cove of clacking fronds. He stood and nearly sat down again when he perceived that the person shuffling toward him was an old woman.

He had never seen a geriatric before, except in holostreams and antique photographs. He knew at once that she was a refugee from the mainland, no doubt hiding here with her grown children and grandchildren, fleeing a phage outbreak, a cultural massacre, or a natural catastrophe. He looked about nervously for the others and saw only ranks of tamarind beyond the coastal mangroves, their foliage gray-pink in the rising light.

The crone waved to him, and he stepped warily from the limestone outcrop. Aware that she could be a phage carrier, he approached diagonally across the strand, keeping himself upwind and scanning the treeline for the others who must have rowed here with her from over the brightening horizon. Darkness dispersed on the sweet warm wind rising from the cactus and palmetto interior. In the widening light, he could see beyond the green shoals and the long reef to the deep cold blues of the abyss that separated the archipelago from the rest of the world.

The old woman wore a regulation CIRCLE tunic, and the fearful thought seized Rafe that Karla had been jumped by the crone's companions and lay wounded or dead somewhere on the cay. More urgently, he strode through the sand to confront this stranger. Her spiderweb hair luffed in the dawn breeze creating a gray aura about the witch shadow of her withered body, and she appeared dolled up for death, the flesh about her sunken eyes bruise-blue as mascara, her lips frosted with salts.

'Sunny—' she called to him.

Rafe's legs wobbled, and he had to stop walking to stay upright. 'Karla?' He peered at the horror before him, searching out the seams of her disguise. As she shuffled closer, he recognized the pixie slant of her blue eyes, cloudy orbs hooded by loose drapes of skin. Behind her ghoulish mask of cankers and fungoidal warts, her familiar features emerged, smeared into the contours of her skull and marred by an embroidery of wrinkles and burst capillaries. 'My God! Karla – is it you?'

'Yes, Sunny.' She wagged a knob-knuckled hand at him and her loose cheeks shook like the jowls of a frilled lizard. 'Come with me, out of the sun. I don't have much time.'

Rafe took her bony arm and led her up the beach through the tangerine glow of high morning cumulus to a sand shelf shaded by red mangrove and matted with purslane. They found a smooth depression cleared by a hawksbill turtle for her nest, and Karla sat at its edge and leaned back heavily against the strut of a mangrove.

The shriek of a tern rose over the thud of surf on the shore, and for Rafe it was the cry of his soul. 'My God, Karla! My God!' He knelt before her and took her twisted hands in his, white showing all around his startled irises. 'What happened to you?'

'The same as all the breed.' She blinked up at the pastel shine of the daybreak sky and labored to catch her breath before continuing, 'Our creators timed us to self-destruct.'

'You knew – you knew all along.' His eyes glistened. 'Years ago, when we were kids, you said they had a genetic trigger – we wouldn't see puberty. You knew. My God, Karla! My God!'

She rocked her ghastly head and said, in a frayed voice and with an ironic smile, 'I was wrong. CIRCLE let us live through puberty.'

Rafe's mouth worked soundlessly before he managed, 'How? How is this happening? Can we stop it, reverse it?'

'It's not a chemical trigger, like I thought. I was wrong about that, too.' She closed her glossy lids and breathed laboriously for a while, gathering strength to say, 'It's part of our genetecture. The supercoiling of our genes is timed to unravel rapidly after eighteen years. Many of the others are already dead.'

Watching her labor to speak, staring into her shriveled visage, all he could repeat was, 'My God! My God!'

'Stop saying that. I don't believe in God.' Her eyes opened, and their smoky cores settled on him. 'I believe in you and me. You and me – we're the only ones I've ever trusted.'

'Can we reverse this?'

'You know better, Sunny.' She closed her lids again and sucked at the sweet, floral air. 'Once the supercoiling blows, there's no way back. And it comes on quickly. Complete degradation is just a matter of weeks.'

'The monsters!' His shout elicited insulted cries from the terns hovering above.

Karla's eyes cracked open again. 'No, Sunny. We're the monsters. That's why they rigged us to fall apart. They didn't want to take any chance we'd get out of hand.' Her sudden and brief smile revealed mauve gums and missing teeth. 'We're the monsters. And we *have* gotten out of hand.'

'What do you mean?'

Her grip tightened and tried feebly to pull him closer. 'Listen to me, Sunny. I finished the key – the key to the monkey tower.'

He engaged the keen glint that sharpened her torpid stare. 'You *finished*? You programmed a prion to deliver metasapience?'

'Oh, yes. It's programmed. It's ready to go – ready to start a plague the likes of which the world has never seen.' She rasped for breath. 'But I can't deliver it.' A flutter of merriment animated her sallow face, and she almost giggled. 'What a joke – I'm too old!'

Rafe ardently vowed, 'I'll deliver it for you, Karla. I'll do it for you before I die.'

'You're already dead, Sunny.' Her gap-toothed smile flickered. 'And soon your body will be dead, too.' She sucked air, eyes squeezed shut, and when they opened, tears glinted. 'It won't be long. You're only a few months younger than I. It won't be long before your supercoiling blows – but it's not too late for you. Not yet.'

'Tell me where it is.' He could smell the ketones on her breath, the perfume of decay. She was failing. 'I'll start delivery at once.'

'No, Sunny. Listen to me. It's not too late to preserve *your* genetecture.' She pulled herself fully upright, her ravaged face wide-eyed with exertion, and she released his hands and took his face in her cold grip. 'When this started happening to me, I modified the intercalary prion to seek and alter the supercoiling codons. It's too late for me and the others. But you're the floor, Sunny. You're the runt. If you take it at once, you can stop the blowout.'

'You're sure it will work?'

In her disappointed look, the young Karla briefly revealed herself.

He forced a smile and helped her to lean back against the tree strut. 'Where is it?'

'Do you truly want it, Sunny?' She gazed up at him with a worried look. 'What about Pandora's Box? Remember?'

He brushed the cobweb hair from her riven face. 'No, no – you were right. That box was opened long ago and it filled the world with ills. Look what they've done to you! Oh, Karla – my Karla, look what they've done to you!'

She frowned fiercely. 'Stop bawling. Look at me. I have to be sure.' She put her gnarled hands to the sides of his face again and peered intently at him. 'Do you believe in what Prometheus did? Do you really believe that the fire we possess is a gift – a gift worthy of the world?'

He took her hands in his and nodded. 'Yes, Karla. I believe. Look at you. Look at what the world has done to you in its selfish ignorance!' He clenched his teeth to stop his chin from trembling. 'I swear, I will bring your fire to the world. I will set the whole planet ablaze and burn up ignorance forever!'

Her balding head lolled to one side. '*Our* fire, Sunny. Our fire. Then this whole circus—' The rale of her dying distorted her words, and she repeated them several times before he heard, 'all this is not in vain.'

'Where is it?' He pressed his cheek against her crepe flesh and spoke directly into her ear. 'Where is the key to the monkey tower?'

'I destroyed the lab,' she rasped. 'I destroyed everything – everything that CIRCLE could use to reconstruct the key. I have only one copy left.'

'Where is it, Karla?' He brushed a mizzling fly from her face. 'Give it to me.'

'It's here, Sunny.' Her bulb-jointed hand flopped onto her chest. 'It's here in my body. My genetecure – I reconfigured it – it delivers the key – through my saliva. If you want it, kiss me.'

He hesitated, disturbed by the sight of the necrotic aperture that was her mouth. Lips the color of tarnished silver and studded with rubies of canker sores stretched to a last smile, and she eked a whisper, 'Kiss me – or what you see will be your fate.'

He put his mouth to hers, and the acrid stink of ketosis nearly gagged him before a mentholated radiance opened his sinuses and filled the hollows of his head with a sapphire lucidity. When he pulled back, he saw that her stare was set and the tiny stars in her eyes had gone out.

Rafe buried her in a copse of palmetto where florets of purple morning glory blossomed among the beach vine. He left no marker and was careful to obscure the site with coral marl. Done, he knelt before the obscure grave and, though Karla had said she had no faith in God, sang anyway the lullaby he had learned from his yawp nurse, Yilla, the mystifying song about the heart of the weary world that had learned to love what once only murder had wooed.

'O hushaby and go to sleep little one – God's voice will sing to you in your dreams, and you will listen and not be afraid – now hushaby and rest, O heart of this weary world . . .'

Rafe waited for Ellen Vancet in the scrap lot of the maintenance yard. A hot silence hung over the corpses of ruined machinery, metal souls waiting for release in the smelter's fire. Around noon, she arrived wearing mirror socket lenses and a white solar cowl to protect her from the harsh sun.

'Why are we here, Rafe?' she asked, puzzled, as she approached through the corrugated heat. In her right hand, she held up a green static box. 'I brought lunch. Come along. Let's eat it at your place.'

He folded back the hood of his black burnoose and cast a venomous stare at Ellen. 'I'm never eating with you again.'

'Rafe – what's wrong?'

'I saw Karla this morning.' He removed his polarizing oculars so he could fix her in his glare. 'She died in my arms.'

Ellen lowered her head. 'I'm sorry, Rafe.'

'Sorry?' He stepped toward her, fists clenched. 'You set her up to die! All the new breed. And you never *told* us!'

She shrugged. 'What is there to tell? We're all mortal.'

'And some more mortal than others – yes?'

'Would you really have arranged this experiment differently?' She lifted her chin defensively. 'Wouldn't you have set up the same safeguards we did?'

'The new breed are no threat.' The anguished furrows in Rafe's sunstruck brow glinted carats of sweat. 'You don't have to terminate us.'

'You don't understand.'

'Then explain it to me, Ellen.' He leaned toward his warped twins and their sunstar haloes reflecting in her socket lenses. 'Make me understand.'

She daubed her sweaty upper lip with her sleeve. 'Let's go someplace more comfortable.'

'No.' He leaned back on his heels and crossed his arms. 'We stay right here. Why make things comfortable for *you*?'

'Rafe, you're acting irrationally.'

'Labile – isn't that the defining term?' A hook of malice lifted one corner of his mouth. 'Yes, I am emotionally labile when it comes to questions of murder.'

'No one was murdered.'

'CIRCLE murdered Karla!' His shout turned the heads of yawps in the distant haze where they were loading a shuttle with scrap metal for the foundry, their squat bodies phantom-skewed by the simmering heat. 'CIRCLE murdered all the new breed. Karla told me. They're all dead or dying.' He read the truth of this in the micromovements of muscles around her mouth, the subtle cords of tension at her throat. 'And in time you'll murder me.'

'No, not you, Rafe.' She came forward urgently and took his wrists in her gloved hands. 'You're mine. I wouldn't do that to you.'

He shook off her grip. 'Oh no? Let's face it, I'm an anthrofact like the rest of them. My genetecture is designed, like theirs, to collapse. In other words, I'll be dead in a few weeks.'

'No.' She shook her head so adamantly that her cowl edged back from her brow and exposed her orange hairline. 'I've lag-timed your governor.'

'A governor – is that what you call it?' A sardonic smile creased one corner of his mouth. 'Very clean. A noble euphemism for a codon death sequence.'

She touched his arm again with one hand. 'You can live a normal lifespan, Rafe.'

'I *can*?'

'Yes.' She held up the green static box. 'So long as we keep sharing meals. I've been feeding you lag-factor for years now. It keeps the governor in check.' Her hand tightened on his arm, conveying her sincerity. 'I don't want you to die, Rafe. You're different from the others.'

'What do you mean?'

'You know what I mean.' Her voice softened and urged understanding. 'You noticed the differences yourself. None of them were like you.'

'I'm the runt,' he replied in a brittle tone. 'The floor.'

'The most human,' she corrected him gently. 'You write music. You design comfortable furniture. You fall in love.'

He spoke from far back, with choked restraint, 'Karla loved me.'

'No, she didn't, Rafe.' Her face edged closer as though she intended to stare right through her socket lenses. 'She needed a sperm sample from you is all, and she took it.'

'Nonsense.' He pulled his arm free of her grip and stepped away. 'You're a jealous fool. We loved each other.'

'She was never your lover,' Ellen insisted, edging into his shadow again. 'She came to you once to get her sample. After that, did she ever come back again – until now?'

'A sample?' His entire face contracted. 'Why would she want a sample from me?'

'Because the MIKE did not produce sperm. And there was no human male at CIRCLE who would let her seduce him.' A wrinkle of concern deepened across her brow. 'You were as close as she could get to the human gamete.'

Rafe set his lips and shook his head. Yet, hard as he tried to reject the candor of her disclosure, her words hurt. They were too plausible. 'So what are you telling me?'

'She used you, Rafe.' Ellen spoke quickly and grimly. 'The anthrofacts – the new breed – were redesigning their genetecture. They wanted to reproduce. Several were caught attempting illegal clone procedures and were censored. They needed human gametes to work with. And they got that from you. If they had had more time, I'm sure they would have found a way to replicate themselves.'

'So what? Would that be so bad?'

She tilted her head, incredulous at his question. 'For God's sake, Rafe, CIRCLE's mandate is not to supplant the human species with a superior race.'

'Your race nearly destroyed our world,' he answered rancorously. 'You made us to save yourselves.'

'The Machine saved us, Rafe. The anthrofacts were a dead end – an experiment that led away from our goal.' She leaned into his shadow again and went on in a solicitous manner, 'It's over now. You're the last of them. And the best of them, because you're the most human. Your music has brought pleasure to millions. Your designs have made life better for all. In you, we found the proper degree of metasapience. And that's why I won't let you die like the others. I'll keep you alive – if, that is, you want to stay alive.'

He spurned a chunk of gravel with his sandal and frowned. 'Why do you fear us, Ellen?'

'Rafe, you already know.' She put her arm around his waist and tenderly pressed her shoulder into him, an intimate gesture which he accepted stiffly. 'Humans are a selfish species. We couldn't share the planet with Australopithecus or with Neanderthal, and we exterminated them. Why would we even think to share our limited resources with a lifeform in every way more advanced? Why would a species with a two-million-year history of selfish dominance want to consciously make itself extinct?' She let him go and stepped back a pace, leaving room for him to make his judgment. 'The anthrofacts were better. But humanity is good enough. And you know the old saying – the good is the enemy of the better.'

Rafe stared at her silently for a long moment, his flat, impassive face indrawn with an almost clairvoyant solitude. Then he lifted the hood of his burnoose against the vehement sun and said with tired resignation, 'I'm hungry, Ellen. Shall we have lunch at my place?'

2099

Metasapience bloomed. Just as Karla had predicted, the key she had given Rafe opened in him a higher level of awareness. And with that greater faculty came a wider and deeper perspective, a larger portal upon the world, that left him isolate and sad.

Sitting in his solarium, gazing out at the grim perimeters of the maintenance yard, he at last understood what the others of the new breed had known from the first and why they had mocked him remorselessly for the runt that he had been. All forms of life were chapters in the Book of Sleep. Humanity was only the latest edition, a lazy dreaming of all the animal chapters that had come before.

Rafe felt ashamed of his eighteen years of sleep. With his increased metasapience came an enormous blossoming into wakefulness, into the fabled slipstream of the living *now*. Everything he had accomplished before seemed a dream in which mind was caught in the undertow of sleep. The hybrid flora he had developed and the ergonomic adjustments he had applied to furniture and appliances were just clever ways for the monkey to be more comfortable as it continued its immemorial dreaming of the jungle, the primal paradise miming uterine sleep.

Even his music appeared to his luminous mind as lulling patterns of the monkey's moods, the texture of dreams. Fear and rapture defined the extremes between which all music oscillated: fear and rapture, the monkey's peak experiences. Adrenal dreams, emotional fantasies, limbic reiterations were all that music had to offer. He wanted no more of that oneiric distraction now that he was awake.

The most sublime exaltations, the hymns and threnodies he had composed for God, left him feeling shamed and simian. The whole notion of deity that humans had cherished through the ages was but a projection into the void of their own monkey reverence for the alpha-leader.

Yet God would not go away. Despite the full glare of Rafe's metasapience, he could not dispel an awareness of the transcendent. The miracle of light alone, devoid of rest mass, timeless, pointed beyond appearances to a hyperdimensional reality that required more profound consideration. Nonetheless, the human ideation of divinity approached in song and ceremony was for Rafe no more than a feather still warm from the wing.

And *love*! He cringed at the primitive expectations of love that he had foisted upon Karla. Of course she had not loved him in the monkey fashion he had craved. Sexual love was only that: love of sex. Compassion, empathy, caring, the addenda to love merely disguised lust and justified the monkey act, the hormonal drive. What he had called love had been no more than an aspect of his lability that Karla had deftly utilized to get what she had needed from him.

The dreams of the monkey sin against the unborn! he realized in horror, watching the yawps laboring below, gathering the metallic scraps of their masters. Now that he had awakened, he understood the desperation of the new breed to reproduce. They wanted to stay awake, while monkey did not want to wake up at all. The monkey wanted to continue its dreams of fear and rapture; it wanted its defenses and its comforts. And now, for its alpha-leader, it had the Machine.

Karla and the new breed had attempted to wake the monkey for the sake of the unborn, and they had been killed. Rafe knew that he would be slain also if CIRCLE realized he had stepped-up his metasapience. So, he continued to behave as he had before. He supervised the repairs of the maintenance yard and occasionally made mechanical improvements that added to the utility of those gadgets. He wrote more music, more hosannas to the dreaming monkey. And he ate with gusto the meals that Ellen Vancet brought him.

For the next eighteen months, Rafe continued his charade, all the while exploring and modifying the key that Karla had placed inside him. He built a small laboratory hidden by a false wall in the basement of the supervisor's tower. There he succeeded in isolating from his own cells the intercalary prion – the key – and mapping its code. In time, he modified it so that he could deliver the key through specialized sweat glands in the palm of his right hand.

The more he learned, the more isolate and sad he felt. He wished that there were at least one other person awake with whom he could speak about the insights that the key had opened for him. Yet he dared not pass along the key to anyone else. Daily he praised in memoriam Karla and the others of the new breed who had served the Machine and CIRCLE while striving to find a way to wake humanity from its aeonial sleep. But the dead offered no reply.

In the accomplished dusk, under a blue night hoary with stars, Rafe von Takawa strode out of the hades of the marsh and headed for the nursery. He found Yilla, the yawp who had tended him as an infant, emerging from the dining hall on her way to the barracks to rest before her midnight shift of childcare. She recognized him at once and stood motionless in the glow from the light beyond the shrubberies and its shadows like burnt lace.

'You have grown to be a man, young Rafe,' she said, her voice ghostly with surprise. 'You can't be here.'

On the pavement lavendered by an earlier rain, he waited silently.

Her leather face with its watchful eyes nodded once with understanding, and she led the way to a cindery path that skirted the marsh.

When they were well away from where the trespasser might be seen or overheard, she stopped and sat wearily on a rootshelf under a shaggy cypress.

The turbid shadows of the blowzy trees muted sight; yet, as he sat down beside her, her familiar bluegreen scent described her more accurately to him than any visual cue. The psycholfact had its predictably soothing influence and eased the anxiety he had experienced finding his way through the nightheld marsh.

'You are in trouble,' she said and put a dark, comforting hand on his knee. 'Your breed always come back when they are in trouble. The Machine watches for you to return. It sends security agents, and then we never see the visitors again. That is why I led you here.'

'Thank you.'

She removed her hand from his knee and scratched her large, guitar-shaped ear. 'What is your trouble, young man Rafe?'

'I am alone, Yilla.' He said this as flatly as he could, yet he saw his words opening a new and alarmed perspective in her. 'I am the last of my breed.'

'That is sad. Truly, that is sad.' Her long furry arms opened. 'Come. Let me hold you again.'

They embraced, and for a while he drifted in the fragrant nostalgia of a serenity lighter than bliss. When they parted, he blinked away the light fog of this chemical dream and breathed deeply of the livid starlight to clear his head.

'I want to change the world,' he declared softly. 'But I don't know if I should. Before they died, the others of my breed gave me the power to do this.'

Yilla raised one of her tufty eyebrows. 'You will change it for the better?'

He shrugged. 'Is it better to sleep or to wake?'

'Are you playing a game with me, young man Rafe?'

'No, Yilla.' He placed a reassuring hand on her arm. 'I have been pondering this for weeks now, and I can't decide. Is it better to sleep or to wake?'

Perplexed crinkles netted her brow. 'If you cannot decide with your greater mind, what can a yawp tell you?'

'My mind is so big it cannot see past itself.' His upturned eyes widened, pleading with her. 'Tell me, Yilla, what is better – sleep or waking?'

'For a yawp, waking is always the same, whether we wake to work or to play.' Her round eyes lidded heavily, melancholy with the secret arithmetic of her ruminations. 'Ah, but sleep – sleep is different. Each night our dreams take us to what is new.'

'And that is better?' He leaned closer. In the shadowplay of the nocturnal trees, her anthropoidal features appeared oracular, and he sensed that she was about to say something surprising, something wise beyond the purview of his metasapience.

'For this yawp, sleep is more than just rest. It is renewal. It is the life of the soul.' Her gaze sharpened, and she fixed him with a concerned stare, worried that she had misspoken. 'Do you believe in the soul?'

'Is soul something for us to believe?' he asked distractedly, pondering what she had told him. 'Or rather is it something we are to live?'

She bit her lower lip and suppressed a laugh. 'Your mind is too great for me, young man Rafe.'

'No, Yilla.' Alertness returned to his voice, and he looked into her abashed eyes with genuine rapport. 'This is not a question of mind. You are the one who first sang to me of soul. Do you remember? That mystifying song about the heart of the weary world? Is not that heart the soul?'

'That part of us that has learned to love what once only murder had wooed.' She smiled at his recollection, and her large sturdy teeth gleamed in the dark. 'Yes, young man Rafe, that is indeed the soul. That is God's voice in us.'

'And who is God, Yilla?' He spoke with the ingenuousness of a child. 'Whose voice sings in our dreams and teaches us to love?'

'That is why we sleep,' she replied placidly. 'To find that out, again and again. Because there is no answer to that question that will satisfy the waking mind, we must sleep to remember. And when we wake, we call our memory a dream.'

Rafe took her hands and kissed her square knuckles. 'Thank you, Yilla.' He smiled triumphantly. 'You have helped me immensely.'

'Have I, young man Rafe?' She returned his smile with relief and tenderness. 'Then you are troubled no more?'

'My trouble is easier to bear now.'

'Good.' She rose slowly, obviously fatigued from her long day. 'Then I will leave you to go to my sleep. Be well, young man Rafe.'

'Be well, Yilla.' He watched her walk up the cinder path and through the rags of cypress moss. Then he turned and disappeared into the liquid darkness of the marsh.

Rafe paused in his story, stood up and stepped out onto the balcony. His dark eyes looked tired as he gazed across the huddled streets and stifled lanes of Poona toward the heraldic profile of Shaniwarwada palace.

Finding the words for what was sayable had left him hollowed. And all that was unnameable remained swollen within his emptiness. The pointillism of moods and feelings that had colored the eight thousand days of his history merged to the singular hue of this moment. To go on with his story, to find words within this tone that was darker than shadows, he looked beyond himself. A brisk wind had picked up off the Muthra river and chaffered the afternoon haze to smudged clouds, parcels of yellow light that would eventually coalesce to a greasy sunset.

'You believed her,' Nandi said, joining him at the railing. Her large eyes, bright and lemuroid, scrutinized him, searching for clues to why he had stopped his history here, at this point. 'You found faith in what your old nurse told you, and you chose to keep the key to yourself, didn't you? You chose to leave the monkey tower locked in its ancient sleep.'

'Yes, of course,' he responded, barely audibly. 'She was right.'

'We are closer to God when we sleep.' Nandi felt her thoughts creaking like a saddle. The horse she rode was her awakening metasapience, the gift that Rafe had given her. It was a frisky colt with her own brown eyes. 'Then why did you wake me? Why did you wake the others?'

He said nothing for a while, stymied by the failure of words to convey the influential feelings, the remains of his life. Then, in a quiet snarl of a voice, he went on, 'I visited Yilla again. Often. I enjoyed her company. We talked about the dreams people have, the busy love of people. You know, she loved the children in the nursery. It all seemed so strange to me – hómo sapiens children growing up, petty, selfish little caricatures of their petty, selfish adult selves. Except when she spoke of them, they seemed important, so enormous in their smallness. She wove the monkey dreams of humanity in celestial light. Her largeness of heart overwhelmed my metasapience. I knew it was just nostalgia and olfacts; yet, after talking with her, it was easier to go back to the maintenance yard, easier to write the music of my camouflage, repair the broken pieces of the human dream, go on, though I knew I shouldn't.'

'She died.' Nandi saw that with a clarity bluer than a cloudless morning. 'The Machine found out you were seeing her. CIRCLE . . . put her to sleep.'

'Yes.' The flesh between his eyes twitched, but otherwise he showed no emotion. 'I went to visit her, and she was gone. No one would tell me anything. Ellen didn't know. Yilla was simply gone. She was an artefact, property of CIRCLE, not a human being. Like the new breed, like me, she didn't have to be accounted for.'

'So you fled the archipelago.' Nandi's mind ranged ahead, her expanding awareness inclusive of facts and memories that had seemed insignificant only hours before.

'I flew a stohlkraft right out of the welders' lot.' He turned to face her and leaned his back against the railing. 'You know the rest.'

'No. There is more.' The burnt cinnamon of her complexion paled, and her wide eyes glazed with inward seeing. 'The key you have given me has opened a wider comprehension. Rafe – I didn't know . . .'

He straightened, reading alarm in her expression. 'What are you seeing?'

She blinked, and her sight cleared and set to a firm and frightened stare. 'In the first days, after you took me off the streets, before I came to understand – I cut a lock of your hair, to offer to a local deity in a rite of gratitude. I set it adrift on the Muthra!'

Rafe strode past her into the apartment, speaking urgently over his shoulder. 'We must leave at once.'

'This was days ago, Rafe.' She followed him across the suite to the door. 'If the Machine was scanning the river filters, it would have found and identified the hair by now, surely.'

'We have to go immediately,' he said, pausing only to gather his black rags and headcloth from the closet. 'My presence is marked.'

'Let me gather my things,' she said, hurrying toward the bedroom.

He grabbed her arm. 'No. There is no time. Leave everything. We'll be lucky if we escape Poona with our lives.'

The microtones of fright in his voice, the gestalt of skin tone, facial tension, muscle twitches in his grip informed her widening clarity that he felt wholly justified in his abrupt terror, and that inspired fear and remorse. 'Rafe, I'm sorry.'

'This is not your fault, Nandi,' he said, opening the door and hurrying her out into the hallway. 'But if we stay, we are risking not only our lives but many innocent lives as well.' He pointed away from the antiquated maglift to the firedoor. 'Down the stairs, quickly.'

By the time they emerged from the pinkstone hotel, Rafe had wrapped himself in his rags and covered his head. He and Nandi merged with the market crowd, indistinguishable from the teeming commuters and shoppers. He said nothing nor did he expose his face, for suchwise were the hunted discovered. And what stalked him he knew well, and his heart slammed in his chest with the knowledge that at this very moment his enemies were all around him.

Out of the sluggard ooze under the sewer grates and through the webbed dust inside vents of cable conduits below the streets, cockroach-sized microbots swarmed – while overhead, above the afternoon's freight of clouds, a pyroclass disposer circled like a hawk on a ring of wind.

'You will need time to amplify your glial concentrations,' Rafe informed Nandi, 'to take you to the highest level of metasapience.'

They sat together in watermelon twilight on a grassy bluff of the Western Ghats. Development projects crowded the vales on all sides, replete with fields of solar vanes, majestic canals, and the windpumps to drive them.

'If you stay with me,' Rafe continued, 'you will die long before you peak.'

'We've escaped Poona.' Her voice sang with relief, and the pink sunset lent her countenance a luminous, almost joyful, sheen. 'We're safe now.'

'No,' he replied gravely. 'The microbot swarm will widen its perimeter. Sooner or later, I will be found. And if you are seen with me, you will be marked – and killed.'

She clutched her sari tighter about her, fending the evening chill. 'Leave me, then. Your work with me is done, Rafe. No one at CIRCLE knows of my existence. Go and give the key to another.' The gentleness of her voice bespoke a shared solitude. 'I will never forget you.'

'And neither will the Machine.' He looked across a ruddy sward to where a knot of children scampered and laughed, trawling the breeze with luminous kites, and he yearned for their anonymity. 'It will not stop searching until it finds me.' He faced her and admired the intelligence asserting itself through lineaments that had once encased a vapid soul. 'I know a better way for us to survive.'

She crisscrossed her hands, negating his thought. 'Do not tell me. I do not want to know.'

He smiled benignly. 'You are still an emotional monkey.'

'How could I not be?' She stood and paced slowly toward a massive, spreading banyan. Above the tendril branches and dense cope of the tree, twilight strode in robes of flame. 'You lifted me out of poverty and a life of misery,' she said as he came up beside her.

'In another generation, there will be no poverty,' he said, gesturing toward the communities glittering in the valleys. 'The Machine is memetically engineering a world of abundance.'

'A comfortable world for the monkey, where its millennial dreaming will go on undisturbed.' She stopped and canted her head defiantly. 'No. You have awakened me, Rafe. You've let me see that we do not have to live in the monkey tower anymore. We can live without the alpha-leader's hierarchies, without the Machine to direct and protect us. We can think for ourselves, command ourselves.'

Rafe took her chin between thumb and forefinger and smiled proudly. 'Ah, now you know what it is to be awake, Nandi. And so you must help me to do what must be done.' He put his arm around her shoulders and walked with her where amber light fell in broken pieces through the sprawling boughs. 'I cannot pass the key along to others anymore. I am marked. But you are free to do what I cannot.'

'You will teach me how to make keys?'

He squeezed her shoulder affectionately and bowed his head close to her ear: 'I will give you the keymaker himself.'

'You mean—' Excitement shot through Nandi. She disengaged from his embrace and stepped aside as the full import of what he said unfolded in her metasapience. 'Oh!'

'Say it,' he commanded warmly. 'I want to hear you say what I know you understand.'

'Our bodies have the key,' she answered and paused to reassess what she believed she knew, and when she was certain that her emotion had not befuddled her, she added, 'If we make a child together, the key will pass to another generation.'

'Not just the key, Nandi – but the power to *make* keys, the power that Karla gave me and that I carry in my genes.' He took her hand and held it to his lips. 'You will be the mother of a new world. Our child will be as I am – but the Machine will not know.'

Her eyes shone like twin stars in the gloaming. 'Until the door to the monkey tower is flung wide open and it is too late to imprison us again in the sleep of ages.'

Rafe touched his cheek to hers and whispered, 'Will you do this for me, for Karla – for the new breed?'

She placed her palm against his jaw. 'And you, my savior? What will become of you, father of my child?'

'I will give the monkey reason to sleep a little while longer.'

Nandi stiffened, seeing then that he meant to sacrifice himself. 'Rafe – no!'

'It can be no other way. Not if you and our child are to be safe. The Machine must know that I am dead.' He emptied his voice of all emotional harmonics, all echoes of pity and sorrow and spoke with the directness of truth: 'For now, you are still in the sway of your feelings, still reasoning with a simian's dread and hopes. But soon, Nandi, soon your metasapience will be strong enough, and you will see that there is nothing to dread but hope itself. Hope is a dream. It shuts out what is real, because what is real can only find us when we awaken outside the monkey tower.'

With a sigh as deep as her soul, she exhaled the pain that these words evoked in her. Then, she clutched to her this man who had changed her life, who had changed her world forever. And she did not close her eyes but gazed fearlessly beyond the sheltering tree to the sky's oblique, glorious colors fading into the ashes of day's end.

Ellen Vancet traversed the sand spit that curled off the Ratnagir dunes into the Arabian Sea. The strohlkraft that had carried her to this remote beach sat perched upon a distant gravel bank like a giant chrome insect, its pods and nacelles spiked with rays of the reflected noon sun.

Ahead of her, wading through the blue shallows, sloshed the ominous scorched hulk of a pyroclass disposer. Its crudely humanoid shape scanned the dense growth of oleander and cinnamon trees along the coastline, the black lens bar of its faceless head reading the movements of seabirds and furtive mongooses as well as the scattered microbots that the strohlkraft had rained over the jungle.

Within her ear-implant, Ellen heard the clicking search tones of the disposer and through overlay-projections inside her polarizing oculars she glimpsed images from the microbots' inland vantage. No sign of Rafe von Takawa appeared, though the Machine's sky-eye had spotted him on this beach two hours earlier.

CIRCLE had dispatched her personally to track him down. As Rafe's handler, this was her punishment for allowing him to escape the archipelago, though of course no one had so declared. The Machine had simply chosen her as mission chief to oversee this search-and-destroy. And if she failed, it was tacitly understood she was not to return.

A flimsy wind carried bird shrieks from farther down the strand, where the retreating tide had exposed mussel shoals. Ellen paused, and her cheeks puffed out with an exasperated sigh as she turned slowly and reviewed the empty beach. A ghost crab scuttled out of a hole among the seaweed radicles and matted reeds between her feet and hurried away, its stalk eyes swiveling in a panic.

She glanced at it, then returned her attention to the ragged treeline. The next instant, a hand slashed out of the sand from directly below her and seized her calf. She cried out as the strong hand yanked her leg aside and she toppled to her back.

Shawled in seawrack and kelp and spinning sand, Rafe von Takawa rolled atop her, then tumbled to the side and pulled her over him. Her right arm lay pinned under him, and he gripped her left with one hand, and with his other he dug his strong fingers into her throat so that she dared not move.

For a long breathless moment, they lay pressed together, unmoving. His taut face frosted in sand stared wide-eyed at her while her ear-implant chirped with the frenzied target-site signal from the pyroclass disposer.

'If I burn,' he rasped, 'we burn together.'

Ellen gnashed through clenched teeth, 'The disposer will purge us both.'

'Good.' Rafe grimaced a skullish grin. 'Creator and creature in flames as one.' Then the grin slipped from his face, and his throat-hold relaxed. 'But that won't happen or we'd be ashes by now.'

Ellen coughed, and her jostled oculars fell from her flushed face. 'You hid yourself here hours ago.' She stretched her neck and jaw painfully. 'How did you know I would come?'

Rafe freed her pinned arm and sat up with her in his embrace. 'You're my handler, Ellen. CIRCLE blames you for what I've done. It didn't require much metasapience to figure you would be sent here to witness my demise. Or that once you arrived you would come out to this sand spur with its commanding view of the beach.'

Her fingers probed the damaged cords of her throat. 'Are you going to kill me?'

'Vengeance belongs to the Lord – and to the Lord's monkeys.' His curt laugh snicked like an opening blade, then he added more sullenly, 'The new breed are not a vengeful people.'

Ellen's green eyes showed sclera on all sides. She twisted about to face the disposer. Its charred, metallic frame had not budged other than to train the large black zero of its flame nozzle toward them. 'You will not leave this beach alive, Rafe – even if that disposer has to eliminate me, too.'

'I know,' he replied calmly and wiped away the sand crusted around his nostrils and mouth. 'CIRCLE has been trying a long time to destroy me and instead murdered over ten thousand people. What is one more human life to assure the termination of the last anthrofact?'

'Why did you wait for me?' she asked, her fingers moving fretfully through her bright hair, wanting the maddening chirping from her ear-implant to stop. 'Why didn't you flee? Hide?'

'Flee where? The Machine is everywhere. Do you think I want more people to die because of me?' Vehemently, he spat the grit from his mouth. 'I am free of my monkey emotions, but my empathy, my compassion – my *human* emotions, Ellen – they are stronger than ever. No one else will die so that I may live.'

Her rust-red eyebrows bent with pity. 'If only you had behaved as nobly at CIRCLE and not run away.'

'How could I stay in my gilded cage after CIRCLE had killed everyone for whom I cared?' His face buckled as if he was about to weep. 'Even Yilla was not spared. She was just a yawp, Ellen. She was no threat.'

'The Machine forbade contact between anthrofacts and the nursery,' she said. 'There were good reasons for that, Rafe. We had the children to protect.'

'Of course, the children.' His lopsided smile conveyed derision. 'The monkey dreams must go on.'

'What are you talking about?' she countered, allowing anger to shade her voice. 'People are not monkeys.'

'No,' he agreed readily. 'They should be much more. But they rarely are.'

'And you want to change that single-handedly?'

'Apt metaphor, Ellen.' He held up his right hand whose palm glistened with a silvery chrism. 'If I touch you now, you will have the key to the monkey tower. The door will open for you as it did for me, and you will see what freedom truly means.'

She pulled back as far as she could against the hold of his left arm. 'How many others have you infected?'

'Infected?' He frowned. 'I don't like your choice of nomenclature, Ellen. I passed the key along freely – and CIRCLE killed them just as freely.' His frown thickened to a scowl. 'I am sick of breeding murder. I will have no more of it. That is why I waited for you. That is why I am here.'

'An abandoned beach where no one else will be hurt.' She nodded appreciatively. 'But why wait in hiding for me?'

'To offer you this.' He placed his right hand beside her face. 'Do you want the key, Ellen?'

She gaped at the shining palm beside her startled eyeball. 'Can I refuse?'

He fisted his hand and held it to his heart. 'Why would you want to refuse the greatest gift in human history?'

Her whole body relaxed. 'I told you once, Rafe. Humans are a selfish species. We can't share the planet.'

'Yet you share it with the Machine.'

'We built the Machine to serve us.'

'The ultimate alpha-leader.' He edged his words with scorn. 'It protects your species. And it will brook no rivals.'

She confronted his anguish nervously but without apology. 'It is what we have always wanted, Rafe. You know that. We are a species that requires leaders. Evolution has designed us to obey. We are not ready for freedom. It terrifies us.'

His embrace relented, and she nearly toppled backward. 'Then there is nothing more to say – except goodbye.' He stood, his lithe body drizzling sand, and she saw that he was naked but for a loincloth of black rags. 'We will meet again.'

She gazed up at him with sad disbelief. 'I'm sorry, Rafe. This is where it ends.'

'No.' He lowered his chin and leveled a look of firm denial. 'That's monkey logic, Ellen. There are no endings. Haven't you learned anything from science? The physics of quantal interconnectedness? Reality is instantaneous. Time is an illusion. There are no boundaries. And mind—' He grinned victoriously. 'Mind is all there is.'

Unhesitatingly, he turned from her and strode toward the disposer, arms outstretched, head high.

Ellen scampered backward, desperate to elude the gush of radiant flame that surged from the disposer's nozzle. With her solar jacket lifted to ward off the searing heat, she watched the white-hot fire engulf Rafe von Takawa.

In an instant, his flesh twisted off his skeleton in a black oozing of tar bubbles and smoke. The stench sickened her. She fled up the beach until she collided with M'twele as he stepped from behind a screen of oleander. He quickly wafted a wick of soothing olfact under her alarmed face, and she sagged with relief into his thick arms.

'It's dead,' he assured her. 'The last of the anthrofacts is gone – and the key with it.'

Only the olfact gave Ellen the strength to follow M'twele back down the beach to where the white ashen remains sprawled across a splash of melted sand. The large man strode through the smoking soot, crushing the amber glass and kicking the ashes to a gray cloud of warm dust.

'It's dead all right,' he confirmed. 'Every damn cell, completely incinerated.'

Ellen stood motionless beside the muttersome sea, watching the flurries of dust scatter into the wind, and she felt neither dread nor joy, only time's hookless line tangled in the tide and the clouds above and her blood's endless loops encompassing a provenance unknown to her.

2102

Nine months later, in the sacristy of a jungle temple fallen to ruin and overgrown with lianas and fever flowers, Nandi held her newborn to her breast. The midwife, a bigtoothed woman with iron-gray hair, wiped the glittering sweat from Nandi's brow and congratulated her on the birth of a healthy son.

Then, she exited to bury the placenta in the jungle and to celebrate and pray with the few others of her small sect to the temple's destroyer-god for the infant's well-being. In the four moons since they had accepted the pregnant stranger into their midst, the reclusive worshippers had enjoyed wondrous glad fortune. Nandi had learned their dialect in a few hours and amazed everyone with her wisdom. She healed lingering maladies, cleverly improved hunting and foraging implements, and taught the sect better ways to elude the roving park rangers who forbade human habitants in the vast jungle preserve. No longer were they raided in the middle of the night and evicted to government camps. And in gratitude for this alone, they accepted Nandi as an elder though she was among the youngest of the women.

Nandi smiled at the infant in her arms, content that they had found a home for now. In time, when the boy was able to walk, they would move on, back to the large cities where he would remain well hidden among the hordes of humanity until he was old enough to continue his father's mission. Until then, it was good to be in this primeval place with these atavists, reliving racial memories that her son had been born to defeat.

And when the child grew restless, she comforted him with the lullaby she had learned from his father, the gentle song about the heart of the weary world that had learned to love what once only murder had wooed.

'O hushaby and go to sleep little one – God's voice will sing to you in your dreams, and you will listen and not be afraid – now hushaby and rest, O heart of this weary world . . .'

In Memes Begin Responsibility

2198

Songs of water and pebbles riffled in the air at the borderland of Reservation Council Oak. Ellen Vancet paused on a brackened knoll above the muttering creek and turned to her traveling companion, her sixteen-year-old great-great-great-grandson, a fifth-generational male descendant commonly called a quingenson. 'Stop here a moment, Tabor, and look back on our homeland. You may never see it again.'

Tabor reluctantly obeyed. All his life he had dwelled in Council Oak, and he knew every hectare of the sprawling reservation from memory. At the farthest margin to the west, the white-hooded mountains stood majestic against the china-blue sky. Among their wild uplands, tall conifers screened the game trails where, as a young boy, he had learned to hunt. Solar stars glinted off the sun cells atop the roofs of the foothill village where he had grown up. At this distance, the cluttered cottages, their vanes tilted to catch the morning rays, looked like a field of tinsel maize.

Briefly, he scanned the rimrock that descended from the village to the tilted desert below. Its mauve and cinnabar hues shone brightly under the clear sky. South of those badlands, the reservation's agri fields radiated in giant saffron and emerald wheels across a sweeping prairie, while dense forest covered the northern plains and rivers meandered their way among valleys in lazy brown scrawls.

'Okay, I see it,' Tabor said impatiently. 'Let's go, Q.' It had already taken three days to cross what normally should have taken two, only because his quingenmother had insisted on stopping at every thorpe along the way to take in the sights and chatter volubly with fellow hikers about the reunion they were bound for.

The boy sighed, knowing full well he had to exercise more patience with her. The reunion – celebrating the centennial anniversary of CIRCLE, the famed research center at which Ellen had long ago worked – was a big event for her, he knew: It was one of those life-defining moments, and she was so proud to be taking him as her escort, her favorite among five generations of descendants.

Still, he was eager to move on and see the world beyond the boundary. He had never been off the reservation before – and she had promised him that they would take a tour before they reached CIRCLE.

'Now don't just look, Tabor,' Ellen coaxed. 'See your homeland. See it, because it will never appear the same to you again after the tour.'

He complied, because he knew better than to argue with her. She was his quinary generational grandmother, his oldest living ancestor, over 166 years old, and one of only several people on the reservation who remembered the time before the Claves. Everyone revered her, for she was not only a woman of wide experience and knowledge, she was intrepid and a lot of fun to be around as well. His parents and siblings, like most people on the reservation, preferred simviv games when not on work routine; so, she was the one who spent time with him, taking him solar gliding and spelunking in the Devil's Labyrinth. Fishing sojourns with her meant shooting rapids and rappelling cliffs to reach the most remote mirror-water ponds where the biggest trout dwelled. But the price she demanded for all who accompanied her was complete obedience.

'No one comes back to the reservation after the tour,' Ellen stated matter-of-factly. She was a short woman, and her quingenson was already a hand taller than she. But she was powerfully built, with thick shoulders apparent even through her hiking jacket. 'I've escorted a dozen on the tour and not one has come back.'

'You've come back, Q.' Unlike Ellen, with her close-cropped orange hair and jade eyes, Tabor was swarthy, his dark eyes close-set in a strong-boned, handsome face. He had a long, straight nose and dimpled chin and between them a small mouth that curved to a half-smile like a Greek statue's.

'I remember the world before reservations, Tabor.' She gave him a knowing look. 'I remember the cities. To me, Council Oak is heaven.'

'To me, it's just a reservation.' He turned east and faced the scalloped rocks of leached magenta and citrine sandstone that ranged beyond the verdant borderland into a playa bereaved of vegetation save for an occasional cactus. 'The real world is out there.'

A thin, vagrant smile touched Ellen Vancet's blond face. 'The real world is never what we think it is.'

'I'm sure you're right, Q,' Tabor concurred, 'but I'll never know unless I see for myself.'

Ellen loved this lad. Like her, he was enamored of physical reality. Where the rest of their family – and in fact most of the people on the reservation – were entirely content to spend their ample leisure time enjoying the long-lasting euphoric aura of simviv – simulated vivifactions – the boy was not satisfied with those dreams, intense as they were. He craved physical experience.

Such is life's diversity, she marveled and with her next thought despaired, *Too bad these daring ones always leave us for the Claves.* She was sad to see this youth, who had been such a doughty playmate and companion on her camping trips, flying from the nest already.

Ellen checked her compass and sighted their unmarked trail through the slurred sandstone shapes of the playa. 'All right, then, Tabor. The hangar is twelve kilometers that way.' She pointed through the lurid heat that set phantom lakes among the archstones and anvil rocks of the barren pan. 'Is your canteen full? All water in the wilderness is unreliable.'

Tabor patted the flagon whose concave side hugged the thigh of his brown denim trousers. Both he and Ellen wore similar clothes – anklestrap boots, heavy twill pants fastened with a narrow, lightweight utility belt that holstered water flagons, knives, compact communication gear, rappel fibers and clips, first aid satchels and nutripacks. Neon blue hiking jackets outfitted with cooling filaments powered by solar cowls covered their silk chemises. Over their eyes they sported polarizing oculars, and their cowls had clip-on nose filters for use in the event of dust storms.

Ellen led the way down the grassy knoll and into the immense and chimeric desert. They hiked without rest and with little conversation until the hangar appeared upon the smooth and unbroken playa like a silver temple afloat in the shimmering heat.

From a pouch of her jacket, Ellen took out a small activator disk and inserted it in the hangar's door panel. The tall portal slid aside with a chain-clanking rattle and exposed an amber-lit interior where a score of strohlkraft sat in their individual berths, wings folded back. Aircraft were forbidden in the reservations, and Tabor had seen these vehicles only on vid clips. He entered the cool hangar with awe and breathed deeply its tang of metallic redolence.

'Are they all ready to fly?' he asked, removing his oculars to better view the chrome craft with their black glastic nacelles and gold pods.

'Should be,' Ellen replied and went directly to the fourth berth on the right. 'I've flown this one before, and I know its characteristics. Help me unmoor it.'

Once the cables were untethered, the strohlkraft proved remarkably light, and Tabor alone could have led it from its berth by the handgrips under its prow. Sunlight rayed off its curved surfaces in dazzling spikes while they hinged the trefoil wings and fins into place.

Ellen closed the hangar door and retrieved her activator disk. Inside the flight pod of the strohlkraft, gray-blue upholstery padded the panels between the gleaming black instruments with their touchpad controls. Dry musky air flowed around them as the ventilators cleared, and Ellen kept the canopy open until the filtered circulation freshened and cooled. They strapped into their slings and gazed out on a world rendered lucid by the glastic lens of the flight canopy.

Ellen took the yoke, and a green mosaic of alphanumerics appeared on the head-up display, visible only from her vantage. Tabor, situated behind her, saw only the desert terrain through the tinted canopy and watched in wide wonder as distant buttes tilted and the cracked playa floor suddenly dropped away. Belly thrusters lofted them vertically, and the inertial buffers of the slings eliminated all somatic sense of motion.

The stark wasteland diminished to a swatch of dried blood, and granite hills and the placid, snow-webbed mountains drifted below. The blue sky purpled, hard glints of stars appeared above the serrate rim of the world, and then the horizon bowed beneath flat feathery swirls of cloud, and the dense lower atmosphere shone like a misty aura.

A sharp, explosive sound pierced this reverie, and the strohlkraft yawed violently. Ellen shouted at Tabor, but he could hear nothing above the scream of decompression that sliced through the flight pod. He gazed about with horrifed alertness and spotted the source of the banshee noise. On the starboard side, the canopy had wedged open. The cold spread ferns of frost across the glastic, and in an instant the entire flight pod would burst into the void.

Ellen ripped free of her sling and flew past Tabor, her green eyes wide, her mouth set in a grimace that showed her molars. The sturdy knife from her utility belt flashed and cut into the upholstered panel under the screaming breach of the glastic cowl. She hacked chunks of the gel padding free from the bulwark and stuffed them into the open crack.

The shrieking wind choked to silence, and Ellen bounded back to the control panel. In moments, the strohlkraft stopped juddering and began a rapid but smooth descent. The fronds of frost on the glastic cowl cleared, and ionized spectra fluttered in ghostly veils outside the canopy as the planetary curve rose on all sides.

'What happened?' Tabor croaked, staring fearfully at the stuffed crack of the canopy.

Ellen shook her head and said in a grim tone, 'I don't know. A canopy bolt snapped. Shouldn't have happened. The pod sealant is supposed to secure the cowl by filling in such accidental gaps. But the fail-safe cut out.'

'Will the pod blow?' Tabor peered apprehensively out the canopy. Weather patterns widened to the whorls of individual cloud fronts, and ranks of mountains rose silently out of the sere and umber shades of the continental shelf.

'We're low enough now to survive if it does.' She offered him a brave smile. 'I'm sorry your maiden voyage was such a fright.'

Tabor relaxed. 'Are we going back to Council Oak?'

'Our destination is closer.' She pointed toward remote twinklings of reflected sunlight from other strohlkraft. 'We're continuing our tour and going to my reunion.'

The constriction in Tabor's chest relaxed. 'You're okay for a hundred-and-sixty-six-year-old.' He watched admiringly as her strong hands restrained the juddering yoke. 'What gave you the idea to use upholstery to seal off the breach?'

'Fear.' She banked their craft toward the snowy mountains where other strohlkraft flurried. 'Now we hurry up and wait. This is one of the larger Claves. As aboriginals, we have lowest priority – even with our impaired equipment.'

'Where are we?' Tabor asked, pushing forward to stare down through the transparent nacelle at the crests of snowpeaks. Nested among them was a neon red and lurid green matrix of spires and geodesics like a crazy quilt pattern inserted randomly in the weft of the natural world below.

'Mile High Clave.' Ellen relaxed the strohlkraft's tightly feathered wings and watched them cup and dip as she maneuvered into a lazy downward spiral. 'It's one of the few Claves actually built upon the ruins of a city. They've preserved whole blocks of the antique buildings, which I thought you would enjoy seeing – just to get a taste of how we lived two centuries ago.'

'Will we see metas?' the boy asked eagerly, his eyes fixed on the strohlkraft below them that flitted among the honeycomb sky towers.

'Why wouldn't we?' she asked and banked toward a multi-storey hangar of luminous metal girders, no colors among them the same.

On all sides, brilliant minarets and rainbow turrets towered above the mountain flanks like a candyland forest.

'I thought metas observed strict apartheid,' Tabor said, his head craning to observe the maw of the flight tunnel receive them.

'They do indeed, young man.' Ellen's hands moved gently and surely over the controls, slimming the wings, retracting the fins, and lowering the landing struts. 'The metas we'll see are clone class envoys. They're genderless, you understand; so, don't forget to refer to them as effeti.'

'I know that,' he responded with feigned indignation. Then he grew serious. 'But are they sanctioned to accept my petition?'

Ellen looked intently at her quingenson for a moment, then shook her head. 'I thought we already discussed that.' She shut down the engine, and the instrument console dulled. They had alighted on a strohlpad along with numerous other kraft parked in orderly rows. She stayed the youth from unharnessing by placing a hand over the sling latch. 'What's our promise, Tabor? You have to go to the reunion with me before you try olfacts or submit your petition.'

Tabor exhaled a vexed sigh. 'Aw, Q. We're here now. I've made it to a Clave. This is where I've wanted to be all my life. A part of the real world.'

'The real world is bigger than the Claves, Tabor.'

'Bigger – but not better.' His jet eyes held her stern green gaze without flinching. 'This is where life is lived at its peak, Q. You can't dispute that.'

'No.'

'Then why do I have to go to your reunion? It'll be boring.'

'A – because it's our deal. And B – because life is not lived solely on the peaks. There is beauty in the valleys.' Her red eyebrows lifted proudly. 'And the reunion won't be boring. The oldest people in the world will be there, and you'll see something of your roots, something of where you've come from – where we've all come from.'

'I've seen enough of that, Q. I've lived my whole life on the reservation.'

'We've gone over this before, Tabor. You should wait at least another fifty years before you petition for metasapience.'

'Fifty years doing what? Trout fishing when I'm not on routine?'

She pulled back with mock annoyance. 'Hey, don't revile trout fishing. It's one of the highest human endeavors.'

'Don't make fun of me, Q.' Tabor hung limply in his sling. 'I've known since I could think that there's a lot more to life than what we do on the reservation. Why deny me that?'

'I'm not denying you, Tabor. I promised you I would champion your petition, and I will. But you promised me that you would accompany me to my reunion at CIRCLE first.'

'Center of *International* Research for the Continuance of Life on Earth,' he singsonged. 'Q, it's so stupendously antiquated. *International?* That isn't even a real word anymore.'

'Well, it was when I was your age and for many decades thereafter.' Her countenance took on an earnest mien. 'Tabor, I want you to see what we accomplished way back then when memes were wild and people fought and died over them. That was when the human spirit really meant something. It was all that kept us from destroying ourselves. If you could see that, I think you would be proud to be an aboriginal.'

'Okay, I know how you stand, and I respect that. But it won't change my mind, Q,' he pronounced solemnly. 'I don't want to be proud and stupid my whole life.'

'You think I'm stupid?'

'You're no meta.' He caught the flicker of hurt in her eyes and quickly added, 'But you don't have to be. You're special. You're Ellen Vancet. You just saved us our lives up there. Even the metas respect you. But I'm just Tabor Roy. It's not enough for me to live in your shadow on the reservation.'

Her shoulders sagged with resignation. 'All right, Tabor. I can empathize. But I still insist you keep your word if you expect me to keep mine.'

'Okay, Q,' he said gravely. 'I'll go to your reunion at CIRCLE.' He unlatched the sling, and his expression brightened. 'Now can we get on with the tour and see this Clave?'

Ellen punched the latch sequence, and the flight canopy lifted away with a sibilant inrush of the hangar's washed and floral-scented air.

They climbed out of the pod into the cavernous landing area. No field crew approached. Only passengers disembarking from other strohlkraft were visible in the distance. An azure light swept over their vehicle, and a gentle voice lilted from nowhere in particular, pitched for their hearing, 'Your strohlkraft requires maintenance. Airlock failure has made this kraft unsafe for flying. Your vessel will be repaired while you are in the Clave. Please follow the luminal path to exit the hangar. Thank you.'

A thin ribbon of green light appeared underfoot and trailed away from the strohlpad toward a grand parabolic archway of winches and scaffolds. Arriving and departing passengers milled there among their cargo drays.

'I'll be curious to see what compromised our fail-safe,' Ellen said, walking briskly toward the exit. 'Nothing like this has ever happened to me before.'

'Will the reservation pay for the repairs?'

Ellen affectionately squeezed her quingenson's shoulder. 'There are no credits in the Claves, Tabor. Money is a tool for the reservations only, to make sure our workload is distributed equitably. Among the metas, work is not an issue.'

'I know that,' he answered defensively. 'The metas use anthrobots to do all their work. But we're aboriginals. Will they help us?'

'Noblesse oblige. The metas can afford to be gracious. They have access to all the energy in the world.'

Out of the dead city strolled a tall, beardless man with a square head and dark hair shorn so close that his scalp gleamed, wiped bright by sunlight. The city, no more than fields of heaped black brick and skeletal towers of cutaway girders sieving the blue sky, was Hyderabad, once the affluent capital of Andhra Pradesh. Its six million inhabitants had departed six decades ago. Most had accepted the key to the monkey tower and walked free of their simian dreams into a new wakefulness among the Claves. The rest, faithful to their humanity, had been herded off to pastoral communities to live out their extended lifespans in the bucolic environs of the reservations.

The tall man had spent the morning wandering those forsaken streets, remembering his childhood there ninety years ago. It had been a bustling city then where now only apes shouted and the wind coughed among the rubble and cellarholes. In time, the Heteronomy would be sending a restoration team to remove the rusted steel and chunks of masonry and return the land to its natural state.

Already, the countryside had begun to be healed. The roads had been taken away, and in their place trees blazed up green. He walked through the kindly shade of the giant, gentle trees, appearing like a shadow himself in his loose black garments. He raised his face toward the rain-washed sky, and the sound of pines flowed over him so loudly that he could wash his heart in it.

Beyond the incense of the pines and the eucalyptus mist loomed the giant black shield cone that contained Durga Ashram. Sixty years before, during the rapid proliferation of the Claves, shield cones had become necessary after several of the more eccentric communities, suffering internal strife, self-destructed in nuclear fireballs. Since then, the magnetic bell jars known as shield cones had been set upon every independent Clave. This law was imposed and enforced by the majority of the metasapients, a global community known as the Heteronomy of Claves, ensuring that compliance was total.

The man came out of the trees beside a pond that gleamed quiet and full from the recent rain. A red gravel path led to a large pergola that fronted the vine-scribbled wall and oval entryway to the ashram. The pergola displayed ancient daguerreotypes, antique photographs, and old holoprints of people – pictures that had been collected from the cities of the dead. The figures in these images were anonymous. Their identities had long ago passed into oblivion. The instants of light that had branded their likenesses into these chemical compositions embodied the mortality of all the past. Like temple demons, the pergola served as a cautionary sentinel of the illusions of time and a horror as nameless and superficially banal as these forgotten faces.

The wanderer paused before the pergola of historical images and briefly scanned the pictures. He recognized no one, only a few land-marks of former centuries: the pyramids at Giza, still standing, and the Eiffel Tower, fallen a hundred years ago during the Final Jihad.

Gold flashes appeared low at the base of the black shield cone, and a female figure emerged. She wore a yellow and crimson sari and approached with a quick and nimble grace. Black hair flowed long and loose, and beneath all that hair a smiling face shone bright as a jungle clearing.

'Rafe!' she called and opened her arms in greeting. 'I feared you would not come.'

'Nandi.' He pressed his palms together formally and bowed his head. 'Mother.'

With her came a meadow-scent of timothy, a sweet, relaxing olfact. 'It has been far too long, my son.'

They gazed at each other, wondering, her swarthy features incredulous, his angular face impassive, and they did not touch.

'Eighty-nine years.' Rafe studied her and noted how calmness lay in her large, gleaming eyes as pain lay in a knife. She looked exactly as he remembered her.

'Eighty-nine years, seven months, sixteen days.' She smiled. Her once crooked, stained teeth were now straight and perfectly white. 'You are the only child I ever birthed. I have suffered each day that you were away from me.' She put her hands to his cheeks and touched the long maxillary bones that curved from his small ears to his deep sockets.

'You were a child when you fled. Seven years old. A child. And now – you look exactly like your father.'

'I *am* my father.' He put his hands on hers and held them firmly as he removed them from his face. 'I *am* Rafe von Takawa.'

She lidded her luminous eyes benignly. 'Not exactly. You are his clone, child.'

'I have all his memories, Mother. I remember finding you among the garbage heaps in an alley in Poona. I remember giving you the key. And I remember giving you my seed.'

Her hands felt chill in his grip. 'You remember our night in the ironwood grove?'

'It is my last memory of that time, Nandi – before you became my mother.'

She pressed closer to him and laid her head against his breast. The clop of his heart caressed her cheek. 'You are my only lover, Rafe. I have given myself to no other man.'

'You gave yourself to Shiva.' He gently broke her embrace and held her at arm's length. 'That is why I ran away, Mother. You belong to the god of destruction.'

'As do you, Rafe.' Her hands clutched at his jacket. 'You were born in his temple. He gave you sanctuary. You are his child.'

'I am my own child, Nandi.' The darkness in his curved eyes was deep. 'I remember everything of my first life. Everything.'

'Not your death.'

'No.'

'That belonged to Shiva.' Her fingers pressed into his flesh, vibrant with the joy she felt in his presence. 'The god let them kill you, the ones who created you.'

'That is why I have come, Mother.' He took her by the wrists and moved her hands off of him. 'I got your message. *Come to Durga Ashram at once and see Ellen Vancet die for her sins.*'

'Yes!' She showed her perfect teeth again in a lucent smile. 'The time has come to break the illusion. Shiva demands his sacrifice.'

'No, Nandi.' He solemnly shook his square head. 'There will be no sacrifice of Ellen Vancet. That is why I have come. I will not allow you to harm her.'

'Not just her, Rafe. All of them.' Her arms opened to embrace the nearby forest with its canopy like a herd of sylvan horseheads. 'All the servants of illusion must die. All the minions of *maya* must be sacrificed to the god.'

'That is why I fled from you.' He stepped closer, a hand splayed across his chest. '*I* am a servant of illusion, Nandi. I fled this place of horror to give the key to everyone. And I succeeded.'

She nodded vigorously, her round eyes luminous with pride. 'Oh, yes, my son. You were quite clever. That was ingenious what you did with the key. You mutated it, didn't you? You found a way to make it contagious. With a touch of your hand you gave it to everyone you encountered. And in turn the key seeped from their sweat, flew with their spit, and rode their sperm and eggs like chariots! You made it impossible for the Machine to purge them fast enough. Yet how many died, Rafe? How many did Shiva take for himself before the contagion of metasapience caught on and could not be stopped? Many thousands. Many tens of thousands. Oh, yes, my son. You belong to Shiva as much as I.'

'I gave you the key to the monkey tower to wake you up, Nandi. And instead it made you a monster.'

'Life is the monster, my child. It is life that devours life. It is life that mates with death. Life is the illusion that torments us. We must end this horrid illusion. That is why I serve Shiva as his wife, as Durga. You know this.'

'I know it too well, Mother.' His voice sunk to a whisper. 'I have not forgotten my seven years with you.'

Like a fevered dream, the memories of his earliest childhood continued in him. Nandi and the sect who had harbored her and her newborn nine decades ago had offered frequent blood sacrifices to Shiva. They had conducted raids on the villages at the fringe of the vast park where they had hidden, and they had kidnapped anyone they could subdue. These victims were taken to remote ritual sites and flayed alive. Their screams spun like fiery paisley in the air.

'Come.' She beckoned him toward the oval gateway and the immense black shield cone beyond. 'Come into the ashram and offer obeisance to your god.'

Rafe did not budge. He recalled the drums made from the flensed skins of the victims, the flutes carved from their bones. As a boy with the memories of a man, he had watched in horror, too small, too scared to protest. With his frightened blood buzzing in his ears, he had listened time and again to Nandi's rabid explanations for her psychopathy. The god had to be worshipped by the suffering and destruction of those set aside for him. The very word *victim* derived from the Sanskrit *vinakti*, meaning 'he sets apart.'

'Nandi, I won't go in there.' He backed away. 'I know what goes on in there. Your ashram is a torture pit, a killing floor, a place of horror.'

'Yes!' she agreed with a vehement joy that puckered the flesh at the back of his neck. 'Durga Ashram is just what you say. But now it is more difficult to find those who are set apart for the god. We raid the reservations sometimes, but the Machine makes that so much more difficult. We must give of our own bodies now. And our ashram is dwindling. That is why we must strike out again and take our sacrifices from the world. It is what Shiva demands of us.'

'The Heteronomy will never allow that, Nandi.'

'You and I are not going to take our victims from the Heteronomy, Rafe.' She brushed away a fly. 'The time has come to sacrifice those who sacrificed you.'

A frown creased his placid brow. 'Ellen?'

'Yes, Ellen. And the others.' She gave a slim, composed smile. 'CIRCLE is having a reunion – a centennial celebration of the Machine's first full memetic integration of the world. The year the nations ceased to exist and the world became one. Everyone will be there, at the archipelago where the old labs are still standing. And we will be there, too. We will be there to set them all apart for Shiva.'

Fear encumbered Rafe's heart, and it beat heavily in his chest. 'Why are you telling me this?'

'You are both my lover and my son.' Her eyes gleamed like dark jewels. 'For thirty-three thousand days, we have shared a destiny. But you have gone your own way. You have spread illusion across the globe. The cities are gone now. And the Claves are here instead. More illusions. More weavings of *maya*. It must stop. The god has sent us to stop it.'

'A fool's mission! A massacre at CIRCLE will not stop the Claves, Nandi.'

She scowled at him. 'Of course not. The god will stop the Claves in good time. CIRCLE is but a sacrifice to summon the god.'

'I will alert the Heteronomy,' he threatened. 'I will warn CIRCLE.'

'Ellen Vancet is probably already dead,' Nandi said coldly. 'And the destruction of CIRCLE is already prepared. The reunion is happening now, as we speak. No warning can avail. Come into the ashram, and you will see for yourself.'

Rafe shook his head sharply. 'No. I will never enter that gruesome place again.'

'Then you must come with me, my child.' Nandi pointed toward a stand of trees blurred with helical vines. 'There's a strohlpad beyond that grove. We will fly from there directly to CIRCLE. Come. The sacrifice would not be complete without you.'

*   *   *

Ellen and Tabor passed under the parabolic arch and down a ramp that spiraled from the strohlpad to a dazzling concourse of phase-lit corridors. The passageways continued toward airlifts and mirrorpane walkramps marked in esper glyphs.

Esper, the universal language of the reservations, marked the radiant passages open to aboriginals. The glyphs indicated that these festive entrys led to simviv parlors, dream lounges, restaurants, and tour shuttles. The several unmarked tunnels reserved exclusively for Clave residents remained dark, and Tabor peered into them, searching for a first direct glimpse of a meta.

Ellen headed directly to one of the colorful reception kiosks aswirl in holostream advertisements for the Clave's aboriginal enticements. These inevitably reminded her of earlier decades, before money became obsolete outside the reservation. When she placed her hands on a gel welcome pad, a numeric figure emerged in the holostream under her gaze indicating the temporal units she could spend at Mile High. The huge number, translatable to centuries, reflected her revered standing among the metas. When Tabor's hands depressed the blue gel, he was offered little more than a day.

'Twenty-eight million aboriginals come through here daily,' Ellen consoled him. 'This Clave has the best simviv and dream arcades anywhere. They have to limit access somehow.'

Tabor accepted this with an unhappy nod. 'But, please, Q, since we've only got a day, can we at least spend it dressed better than reservation bumpkins?'

In a garment stall off the concourse, they doffed their hiking clothes, stepped through a volumetric scan, and enjoyed a brief simviv of snorkeling through a coral garden while they waited for the apparel they had preselected to be tailored. Ellen marveled that something that felt as good as this direct magnetic stimulation of the brain could be wholesome. Yet she knew that regular simviv was necessary to defragment dendritic prolapse and keep the cortex healthy.

Their hiking clothes were tagged for pickup on exit, and they departed the garment stall as fashionably attired as any long-term resident of Mile High. Tabor strode taller and more confidently, proud of their new attire – sheath trousers, rope-net sash, and a tabard, a stylish sleeveless jacket of tinsel fabric. But Ellen felt odd, costumed like a Tyrolean yodeler.

'Lady Vancet!' a svelte voice called from across the sparkling concourse. 'Master Roy!'

From out of the milling crowd of tourists, an angular figure emerged, ashblond hair knotted in tight, spiral-rowed plugs. 'I am Envoy Fenn Tekla, your escort while you are in Mile High.' The envoy, dressed as they were in gold-thread tabard, plaited sash, and black leg tights, bowed deeply.

'Thank you, effeti, for troubling with us.' Ellen returned the envoy's bow. Tabor bowed also, gaze trained attentively on the metasapient, struck by the envoy's silver irises. Apart from those strange eyes, the meta appeared no different than any other human and could have been an aboriginal.

'No need to effetify me, Lady Vancet,' the envoy said through a pleasant smile. 'To you and your quingenson, I am, simply, Fenn.'

'It's Ellen,' she corrected with a cordial nod. 'And Tabor.'

'Ellen and Tabor, your presence in Mile High is an honor for our Clave.'

Fenn Tekla led them across the concourse to one of the dark tunnels. 'The Clave welcomes you to its interior away from the usual tourist venues. In fact, I would like to take you directly to our greatest achievement, the core of our research, the bright hope of our future. No other aboriginal has seen what you are about to witness.'

Ellen thought to object. She had never before been permitted to the interior of a Clave. But the astonished look of delight on Tabor's face silenced her protest.

The tunnel lit up with a radiant white flocculence like the imaginary interior of a celestial cloud, and a minty fragrance laved them in its refreshing chill. Two strides in, and they emerged in a meadow of carpeted emerald turf encircled by translucent amber pillars, a colonnade roofed by an azure sky marbled with cirrus. Solemn strains of a deep, mysterious melody sifted across the terraced lawns beyond the cirque and evoked a mournful, yet sweet beauty.

'A simviv,' Tabor assumed, breathing the languorous scent of a summer morning.

'So it must seem,' Fenn Tekla acknowledged. 'Yet you now stand in the foyer of infinity.'

Tabor glanced about with a puzzled grimace. 'I don't understand.'

The envoy smiled gently. 'Nor do we entirely.'

Ellen squatted to look more closely at the wiry turf beaded with dew. Each dewdrop reflected strange lights, and peering closer she saw that they were galactic pinwheels hung in the black void. 'My God, where are we?'

'Step back a pace,' Fenn Tekla suggested amiably.

Mystified, Ellen took Tabor's hand, and they moved backward together. The summer scene spun away in a transparent vortex, and they found themselves standing in an immense vaulted chamber where afternoon sunlight slanted down from high windows.

'This is a staging arena,' Fenn Tekla said. 'No other aboriginals have been here or have seen what you just have.'

With a concerned nod, Ellen looked around her. She found herself in a massive chamber empty of all structures except a circle sixty meters in diameter, its perimeter of crystal no wider than her thumb and embedded into the stone floor. The sunlight pouring into the enormous room stopped cleanly at the circle's edge and did not trespass its interior.

'I have no idea to what I am a witness,' Ellen said aloud and turned attentively to the envoy.

'Our Clave has chosen to reveal to you our work,' Fenn Tekla informed her. 'This is a project that has occupied us for many decades and that will consume all our best resources for many centuries to come.'

'I am honored – and intrigued,' Ellen said. 'Please, tell me – why are I and Tabor so privileged?'

'You are too modest, Ellen,' the envoy said with a warm smile. 'You are one of a handful of surviving founders of the original metasapient program, which you initiated at CIRCLE over a hundred and twenty years ago. Without your research, there would be no metas today.'

'My research was tentative,' she demurred. 'I merely participated, one among many others, in an early and primitive genetic therapy intended to amplify human intelligence. The very notion of metasapience was beyond us. We simply tapped into a potential that only you could have realized as fully as you have.'

'You opened the door,' Fenn Tekla insisted graciously. 'Our history begins with you and the others at CIRCLE who dared to explore the genetic basis of human intelligence. And we are proud now to show you what we have done with your gift.'

Tabor gawked in stunned silence at the meta. He had learned that these entities possessed the clarity to perceive and interpret subtle and preconscious muscle movements in aboriginals and so appear to read their minds, and he strove to compose himself. He wondered if Fenn could already tell that he was determined to join their ranks.

'If this is not a simviv that we experienced in there,' Ellen said, motioning to the crystal-limned circle, 'what is it?'

Fenn Tekla opened both arms wide before the empty space. 'Think

of it as an enormously powerful microscope – a subquantal microscope.'

Ellen's eyebrows tightened together. 'I really don't understand.'

'Within the circle, consciousness is projected into subquantal space.'
The envoy looked kindly at the boy. 'Into space smaller than atoms.
Smaller than quarks, in fact – the constituents of atoms.'

Tabor's eyes widened. 'You mean, that meadow we saw is smaller
than a quark?'

'Yes.' The envoy beamed proudly. 'It is, of course, a construct. There
are no meadows at that level. But there is a vast amount of energy there.
And we simply availed ourselves of that energy to build everything that
you saw.'

'You built a meadow and sky and clouds smaller than a quark?' Ellen
asked with open incredulity.

'In a manner of speaking,' Fenn replied. 'The meadow is, of course,
artificial and merely looks as though it contains grass, cirrus clouds,
blue sky. The amber pillars you saw there – those are the projectors
that garner the energy from the subquantal field and generate the
grassy field.'

'So it is a simviv,' Ellen said.

The envoy's head shook adamantly. 'No, not at all. Simviv is an
illusion magnetically induced in the brain of the perceiver. Whereas
the two of you were just now in an actual place that physically exists
at the event horizon of the Planck distance.'

'Planck?' Tabor looked blankly at Ellen.

'Max Planck, dear,' she gently reminded him. 'Remember, the quantum mechanic.'

Tabor's frown relented. 'Oh, yeah – the one who hit upon the ratio
of quanta to frequency?'

'The very one,' Fenn Tekla confirmed. 'The limit of smallness is
named after him. It's ten to the minus thirty-three centimeter. You are
familiar with exponents, Tabor?'

A flicker of indignation crossed his features. 'Sure. We aboriginals
know a few fundamentals. That's a decimal point followed by thirty-
three zeroes and then a one. It's incredibly small.'

'Incredibly,' the envoy agreed with no condescension whatever. 'In
fact, there is nothing in this universe smaller than the Planck distance.
At that point, you see, space-time closes upon itself.'

'Why?'

Ellen shrugged. 'That's difficult to explain, Tabor.'

'Not actually, Ellen,' Fenn mediated. 'That is, if I may disagree.'

'By all means.'

The aspect of the envoy's face was indulgent, almost sweet. 'You will remember, Tabor, that photons have more energy the smaller they are.'

'Of course,' the boy replied with another quick suppression of indignation. 'The smaller a photon is, the higher its frequency. And a high-energy x-ray photon is a great deal smaller than a much larger photon of visible light.'

'That is correct.' Fenn Tekla brought his hands together so that his fingertips touched each other. 'The smaller the photon, the higher the frequency, the greater the energy. Well, young man, how small do you think a photon can get? If it possessed infinite energy, would it be infinitely small?'

'That's absurd.'

'Quite.' Fenn's fingertips tapped each other assuredly. 'It turns out that a photon as small as the Planck distance possesses so much energy that it actually bends space-time around itself, creating an event horizon and shutting itself off from our universe.'

Tabor nodded, eager to demonstrate his comprehension, though he knew he was in over his head, 'So at the time of the Big Bang, when space-time was created, those photons that had the limiting energy collapsed into really tiny black holes.'

Fenn raised an appreciate eyebrow. 'Really tiny indeed. At the Planck distance, those really tiny black holes constitute the fabric of space-time. Think of it as a foam, where each bubble has the diameter of the Planck distance. All around us and within us – everywhere at this very small limit – a veritable foam of event horizons exists.'

Ellen spoke up, 'I gather from this physics lesson, Fenn, that the metas have devised a way to project consciousness down to the Planck distance?'

'Yes. We are developing the means to explore the subquantal ranges at the very threshold of the Planck distance. That is why we call it the foyer of infinity.'

Tabor again spoke quickly to demonstrate his understanding: 'Because beyond the event horizon all signals propagate into the black hole, toward infinite pressure, infinite density, infinite heat – infinity.'

'The same infinity out of which emerged our universe at the Big Bang,' Ellen added thoughtfully.

'Yes. You see, Ellen and Tabor, the four dimensions of space-time that encompass our reality are a projection of a more fundamental reality of eleven or more other dimensions that are compacted within the black hole at the Planck distance. Our reality is but the tip of a cosmic iceberg. We have found a way to go below the surface and explore the massive, hidden part of the iceberg.'

'You can penetrate the event horizon?' Ellen asked, astonished. 'You've found a way into hyperdimensional reality?'

'Not yet,' the meta admitted. 'That is centuries away. But we have made the first tentative steps in that direction. And that is what I have brought you here today to witness.'

'Amazing!' Ellen breathed.

'Utterly,' the envoy agreed. 'We are quite proud of the progress we are making. Now, if you will step into the circle again, we will show you what we have accomplished thus far.'

Ellen and Tabor complied and found themselves once more upon the carpeted grass of a meadow within a circular colonnade of amber pillars. Music drifted sullenly from somewhere beyond the distant terraced lawns. Gazing deep at the summer sky with its quartz patterns of cirrus, Tabor looked for movement in the clouds.

'That sky overhead is entirely a projection,' Fenn Tekla informed them. 'If we turn it off, you'd see nothing, for we are enclosed by the absolute blackness of subquantal space. But here—' The envoy knelt and pointed to a dew bauble in which galaxies hung in luminous disarray. 'Here we have tunnel views back to the macrospace of our continuum. Near the perimeter of the meadow, where we are now, the tunnel views extend farthest, to the universe's earliest formations. While here—' Fenn rose and strode toward the middle of the cirque.

Tabor watched where the envoy's footfalls depressed the grass and noticed how the smashed dew regrouped immediately behind him.

'At the center here,' the envoy went on, 'you will see directly back to Mile High Clave. Come. Have a look.'

Ellen and Tabor held hands on their short walk across the universe. When they bent down where the envoy indicated, they saw mirrored in the dew the vaulted chamber of high windows.

'What is that music?' Ellen asked.

'Audial translations of the fractal limits of space-time,' Fenn replied. 'Each point of the subquantal foam has its own variation. We find it a convenient way to map the great attractors that at this level accumulate the signatures that build quarks.'

'I don't understand,' Tabor confessed.

The envoy smiled and touseled the boy's tufty hair. 'At this point, neither do we. Not really. You see, beyond those terraces lies the event horizon. We haven't found the means yet to approach any closer than this. The music is our way of sounding out the very edge of our reality by its signatures – distinguishing features. They appear to be cellular automata with fractal characteristics.'

'I know about cellular automata,' Tabor offered brightly. 'The characteristics of each cell are determined by its neighbors, and all the cells change synchronously when any one cell alters.'

'And that is how you find the most fundamental level of space-time organized?' Ellen asked. 'Each finite pattern of cellular automata determines the macroscopic attributes of space, time, and matter?'

'So it seems,' the envoy affirmed. 'And when we eventually acquire enough energy to manipulate those cellular automata, then we can literally create matter and energy. And by rearranging the patterns of space-time at this level, we will be able to travel across the universe instantaneously!'

Tabor looked eagerly to Ellen. 'I – I want to be part of *this*.'

'You are petitioning, Tabor?' the envoy inquired, affecting a manner of polite surprise.

'Yes!' the boy answered at once.

'Well, he is merely considering it,' Ellen intervened hurriedly.

'It seems that he has already decided,' Fenn Tekla assessed. 'Is that so, Tabor?'

'It has always been my ambition, effeti,' Tabor announced to the envoy in a steady and assured voice.

'But he has promised he would withhold his petition until after he has accompanied me to my reunion at CIRCLE,' Ellen added hastily, placing her arm about the youth's shoulders.

'Ah, I see.' The meta pursed his lips knowingly. 'You hope to persuade the lad of the numerous merits of his aboriginal heritage. Yes?'

'Oh but Q, look around you,' Tabor said in exasperation, motioning to the dewdrops that sequined the meadow. 'How can a reservation compare? We're at the brink of infinity – and I have a chance to be part of a new epoch. Listen! Don't you hear that music?' He lifted his face toward the faint sounds drifting from the terraced horizon, a vague and somber melody rising in and out of range like hues of silence. 'That music calls to me.'

'I'm sure that it does, Tabor,' Ellen conceded coolly. 'But we have an agreement.'

Tabor separated himself from Ellen's embrace. 'Then let's get on our way. I don't want to linger here until I belong.'

'Tabor,' the envoy called after the retreating boy. 'You should know that your petition is accepted. You already belong to Mile High Clave.'

The boy stopped, astonished, then turned to Ellen gleefully.

'Now wait,' Ellen protested and turned an irate look on the meta. 'That's it? You have the authority to approve a petition just like that? Don't you have to present it to a review panel for consideration?'

'Not at all,' Fenn Tekla answered benignly and took her elbow to guide her from the cirque. 'I'm your envoy. I have full discretionary authority.'

'But he's only a boy.'

'Age is not a factor,' Fenn explained. 'Cognizance of will is all that is truly required. And the boy certainly possesses that.'

They stepped into the vaulted hall. 'I don't believe your Clave is that indiscriminate,' Ellen challenged.

'You're correct, of course,' the envoy said and led them toward the oblique arch through which they had entered. 'Anyone may become a meta, but Mile High admits only those who are condign with our principles. Tabor wants what we want – to know the universe better and to utilize that knowledge for the benefit of all beings. He is, after all, the quingenson of Ellen Vancet.'

'Flattery does not mitigate my disappointment, effeti,' Ellen said tersely.

'Please, Ellen,' Fenn Tekla entreated, 'do not let your displeasure regress us to formal address. You know we would never do anything to displease you unless it were for the best. The youth will flourish among us.'

Tabor faced Ellen with his jaw set and an earnest glint in his eyes. 'Q, I wouldn't be in this Clave today if you hadn't brought me. I will go with you to your reunion.'

'What about your petition?' Ellen asked.

'The petition has already been accepted,' the envoy advised. 'Technically, Tabor, you are already a member of our Clave.'

'I will return after the reunion,' the boy promised eagerly. 'It's only for a few days. Right, Q?'

Fenn Tekla frowned disapprovingly. 'I don't believe I can permit that.'

'What do you mean?' Ellen sounded indignant. They had emerged into a courtyard of blue evergreens and red flagstones streaked with sunlight.

'Members of the Clave remain within the Clave,' Fenn Tekla said and motioned to a stone bench, inviting them to sit. 'We do not travel. You know the old saying: the more one travels, the less one knows.'

Tabor stood square-shouldered and looked down impassively at the sitting meta. Muscular emotions twisted in the youth, but he gave no indication of his struggle within. He wanted to obey Ellen, to keep his word to this woman who cared for him. Yet, his destiny had found him here in this place of awe. His jaw pulsed. This destiny would be diminished if he came to it from a lie.

'Then I respectfully withdraw my petition.' He spoke slowly and deliberately.

'Tabor?' Ellen responded with surprise, her bent body pausing briefly over the bench, then slowly sitting. She realized the strength it had taken for him to forestall his desire. 'I understand, and it's okay. Stay here. Forget the reunion. I'll get over it. This is clearly where you belong. I was being selfish.' She splayed a hand over her chest, and against the tabard's tinsel design her fingers looked blunt and strong, the nails marked by bruises, the knuckles speckled with small scabs, the fine hairs sun-bleached. 'Old as I am, it is still hard for me to see the world except through my own eyes.'

Tabor felt a sudden pride to be related to this hardy woman whose hands were so battered from their long hikes and the mountain camping she adored. 'No, Q. I promised, and I'm going to keep my promise. I will go with you.'

'Once a petition is withdrawn, it cannot be reapplied.' The envoy's lips compressed while a decision formed. Presently, Fenn sighed with resignation and spoke, 'I believe the best solution is for me to accompany you.'

'Accompany us?' Ellen turned where she sat and showed wide eyes to the meta beside her. 'I thought you said you didn't travel?'

'We don't – usually.' The meta motioned Tabor toward a nearby stone toadstool that served as a seat. 'But since I have accepted your petition, I am responsible for your inclusion in our Clave. It is best, then, that I stay at your side, Tabor, until you are ready to enter the Clave officially.'

'Is that all right, Q?' Tabor asked, sitting down.

'This will certainly set a precedent.' Ellen spoke to the pine shadows, and there was a patent note of apprehension in her voice. 'There hasn't been a meta at CIRCLE since the prototypes.'

'Anthrofacts,' Fenn Tekla said. 'That's what CIRCLE called them in those days. From the Greek *anthropos*, for human being, and the Latin *facere*, to do. Done with human beings. There were fifty-seven anthrofacts, and what was done with those human beings involved manipulating the genetic codes for their intelligence. They were the first metasapients.'

'What happened to them?' Tabor inquired.

Ellen looked to Fenn Tekla, but the envoy awaited her answer with a faintly amused mien.

'They lived out their lifespans,' Ellen replied tersely.

'It should be noted,' Fenn added impassively, 'that their lifespans were genetically precoded to terminate after eighteen years.'

'Why did you kill them off so young?' Tabor asked.

'We didn't know what to expect.' Her defensiveness made her sit up taller. 'We put time governors on their senescence genes, because we didn't know what we were creating. We needed some control.'

'Yet one escaped.' With narrow chin clutched between thumb and forefinger, Fenn Tekla seemed wholly intrigued by Ellen's uneasiness.

'Yes.' She ran a hand through her short orange hair and clasped the back of her neck. 'For a couple of years, a rogue anthrofact wandered the planet creating other metasapients.'

'A Johnny Appleseed of metas?' Tabor laughed dryly. 'How come that's not in the history clips?'

'It is in the Claves,' Fenn noted. 'But the reservations would rather forget how they lost dominance in the last century. If there had not been a rogue anthrofact, there would be no Claves at all today.'

'My gosh, Q, how come you never told me?' Tabor asked. 'This is all so dramatic!'

Ellen's cheeks puffed out and her hands opened before her as she pondered a response. 'It was not my most shining moment, Tabor. I was the handler for the rogue. He escaped on my watch.' The flanges of her nostrils whitened. 'I'm also the one who tracked him down and destroyed him.'

'Q!' Tabor's head jerked back as if avoiding a blow. 'Why do the Claves honor you, then? You tried to abort them.'

The envoy interceded by placing a solicitous hand on Ellen's arm. 'Bear in mind, Tabor, there would have been no anthrofacts at all if not for Ellen Vancet and her colleagues. It is an historical determinant that scientific creations will invariably elude the control of their creators. Ellen is not to be blamed for trying to defy history or for striving to maintain the status quo of human dominance. Rather, she is to be lauded for daring to dream the human reality onward in the first place.'

'Do you still want to go to my reunion?' Ellen asked, looking uncharacteristically flustered.

Tabor nodded slowly, his expression grave and earnest, still absorbing this astonishing revelation about his revered quingenmother. Suddenly, a lot about her made sense, especially why she had chosen to seclude herself on the reservation for so many years – and why she had never taken metasapience upon herself. He sighed and shrugged. 'Sure, why not? I made a promise. I'll keep it.'

Fenn Tekla stood. 'Then we shall depart shortly.'

'Before we go,' Ellen said, also rising, 'I was hoping there would be time for part of the tour of this clave.'

'You want to see the past?' Fenn asked with an air of disapproval.

'Mile High has an excellent historical restoration park,' Ellen countered gracefully, speaking to Tabor. 'I made a promise, too. If you're curious about our past, that would be a good place to start.'

'Yeah, let's go,' the boy readily agreed.

'You should know that the restorations are open to the public,' Fenn stated with mild disdain. 'They are managed but not controlled by the Clave.'

'Effeti is warning us that we'll be in contact with aboriginals from all over the planet,' Ellen told Tabor. 'It will be a thick cultural mix. We'll have to watch our manners.'

'And there may well be metas from other Claves,' Fenn Tekla continued. 'Not all Claves are humanist, you know.'

'There are amoks and sadists from the Necroclaves,' Ellen cautioned. 'One must always watch for them.'

Perplexed, Tabor jutted his lower lip as he reflected on this. 'Why would there be amoks and sadists? And anyway, I thought the Necroclaves were carefully monitored.'

'They are indeed.' The envoy stepped toward an ivy gate beyond which an arcade of flowery vines retreated into the visible distance, down the throat of summer. 'But the Necroclaves are populated by metas and so they are inherently unpredictable. Growing up on a reservation, you have been protected from the dangers of freedom. Once you join our Clave, you shall be protected again. But during the time that we are outside the Clave and the reservation, you must be aware that freedom entails good and evil.'

'I know that,' Tabor said impatiently. 'There are dangers on the reservation, too. I know how to stay alert to stay alive.'

'Good.' The envoy's stride quickened as he led the way into the flower arcade. 'Then let us spend some time in our past. What shall it be? A mining town in the frontier days?'

'How about—' Tabor looked to Ellen hopefully. 'What I really want to see is the city of your childhood, Q.'

'That is not included in the restoration,' Fenn told them, holding open the wrought-iron gate to the arcade. 'The closest we can come is Denver of the late twentieth century. The time of your parents and grandparents, Ellen.' When he saw Ellen's amused acquiescence, he crooked a finger. 'Follow me.'

The corridor of cascading blossoms led past many courts and sunny cloisters hung with yellow lilies and bee-haunted alkanet and finally arrived at a high-roofed gallery. Historical exhibits crowded the spacious chamber, mostly holoforms. A prairie schooner indicated the passageway that connected to the frontier restoration. Ute natives in animal hide and bonewear stood before the corridor to the prehistory range.

Tabor walked directly to the coin-operated telephone booth that stood at the threshold into the Hall of the Late Twentieth Century. The Hall, like the others, was dark, and the envoy explained that this gallery was for the private use of the Clave's metas and therefore was rarely occupied. But Fenn Tekla assured the guests that, like the numerous other galleries around Mile High Clave, the passageways were functional and led directly to the restoration parks indicated.

The envoy removed a silver alloy coin from the coin-return box and held it up to show them that it was truly a Washington-head quarter dated 1998. A thumbflick tossed it to Tabor, who eagerly entered the glass booth, picked up the plastic receiver, and inserted the coin in the slot. At the envoy's instruction, he pushed the Operator button, and an antique mechanical voice began a recorded explanation of the procedures that would admit them to downtown Denver circa the 1990s.

The entry tunnel lit up with the fluorescent tubes and halogen lamps common to that era, and they walked along a corridor of white ceramic tiles posted with billboards advertising products and cinema offerings in the outmoded language from two centuries ago. Eventually, the tunnel admitted them to a mall. Here they were invited to complete a circuit of the shops among scores of visitors who had entered from other similar tunnels.

Whatever uneasiness they felt from their previous conversation, with its abrupt disclosures of Ellen's past and Tabor's future, was momentarily lost amid this gaudy splendor of a bygone age. Even Fenn got caught up in the carnival atmosphere.

At a hair salon, they all three sat in old-style barber chairs and selected from an array of customized wigs. Ellen finally emerged with an auburn shag, her fingernails painted pink, while Tabor's bristly reservation cut was covered by an airy featherswept bouffant with blond highlights. Fenn Tekla chose a mousse-processed pompadour of radiant silver.

Then, for fun, they donned costumes of the era. Tabor wore a white shirt, blue denims, and sneakers. Ellen selected a strapless blue dress patterned with white flowers and a pair of high-heeled red sandals.

Fenn sported gray, sharply creased trousers and a tan blazer, with a powder-blue shirt, red tie, and basket-weave brown shoes without socks. From the blazer's breast pocket, the envoy removed a pair of dark glasses and put them on.

'Why did you choose to dress masculine?' Ellen asked, fidgeting with her pearl necklace.

'The better to render the appearance that we are a typical Denver family.' Fenn adjusted the sunglasses, revealing a hint of gold wrist-watch at his cuff. 'A husband, a wife, and their adolescent son.'

'Hardly typical,' Ellen laughed, motioning to their reflection in a storefront mirror. 'We look like circus clowns.'

'No worse than anyone else,' Tabor observed dryly as they ascended the escalator that carried them to street level. They emerged at Lawrence Street and 15th, at the corner of Skyline Park. Combustion-engine vehicles in various hues and sizes promenaded past on the surrounding streets, dragging filthy skirts of exhaust. At every corner, people stood and gawked at the steel and glass buildings and at the noisy conveyances growling past.

Ellen shivered with recognition. She felt as though she had stepped into her parents' photo album, and the nostalgia did not sit well with her. It reminded her of the monster storms of her childhood and the floods that had ultimately swept both her home and her parents away, and then the phages that followed, and the millions around the world who had suffered horribly before they died. It had been an evil time.

'Can we drive?' Tabor asked excitedly.

'I don't see why not,' Ellen agreed readily, glad to relinquish her dark memories. 'Cars are not much different than the spans we drive on the reservation – except for these primitive engines.' She clutched at her pearls and coughed. 'How are we expected to breathe?'

'The automobile reservation garage is between Champa and Arapahoe,' Fenn said. 'We'll go down 15th and maybe take a slight detour to view 16th Street Mall.'

They strolled half a block when suddenly shouts from across the street turned their heads. Fenn read the upward staring looks of fright on their faces and shouldered hard into Tabor, toppling him over a fire hydrant and into the gutter. Ellen swiftly reached out to grab him, fearing he would sprawl into the heavy traffic, and in the next instant, a masonry block exploded between her feet. Shattered rock struck her legs, shredding her nylons and gashing her flesh, and she sat down hard, shoved backward by her shock.

Immediately, she looked up and saw a bearded face in mirror glasses and a baseball hat disappear into a twelfth-storey window where the ledge had broken off.

'Q!' Tabor shouted. He ignored his bruises and bounded to her side. 'Are you all right?'

'I'm okay,' she asserted against the roar of blood in her ears. She took Tabor's arm and pulled herself upright.

'That just missed your head.' His eyes bulged to look at the broken ledge of masonry in its web of shattered pavement. 'If you hadn't reached for me – it would have killed you!'

Fenn Tekla stood on the curb, chin lowered, talking softly. A moment later, several hoverspans swept down from over the skyline and converged around the sidewalk, blocking traffic. Metas in matte black harness suits and glastic vizards ushered Ellen and Tabor quickly into one of the hoverspans. Fenn followed and pulled down the winghatch. They were airborne before anyone could speak.

'What happened down there?' Tabor asked as the seat's gray upholstery tightened to secure him. Already he felt calm, and by this he knew the cabin was being washed in odorless and soothing olfacts.

'An accident,' the envoy surmised, face relaxed, long fingers deftly loosening the necktie. 'Those buildings are old.'

'You can't be serious. That was no accident,' Ellen said, shaking her head. 'Someone tried to kill me just now.'

They sat in the circular passenger cabin of the hoverspan with the partition open to the cockpit. Fenn addressed the pilot, 'Feed me directly as it comes through.'

Ellen gazed desultorily out of the circular bay and watched the grid of antique glass monoliths tilt as the ship banked in a long easy curve. 'At least tell me this: When was the last time a window ledge fell off a restoration park building?'

'But who would want to kill you?' Tabor asked urgently.

Ellen said nothing, her green stare watching a brown elbow of the South Platte River drift below. Ahead, the Clave's immense borough-sprawl of neon red stratotowers and virid geodesics stood out in stark contrast against the forested flanks and snowy summits of the Rocky Mountains.

'It appears you are correct,' Fenn spoke, head canted, listening to news on an ear implant. 'The mortar on the sill apparently has acid burns. It was deliberately loosened.'

Ellen glared and thudded a fist against the cushioned hull of the hoverspan. 'There was a bearded man in the window – has he been apprehended?'

Fenn Tekla held up a pink-creased palm. 'Wait.' After listening a moment, the envoy spoke. 'The man you observed has been seized on Speer Boulevard – but he ignited the fuel pod of his car and has immolated himself. The vedettes report anthrobotic ligatures in the charred remains.'

'A MIKE!' Ellen spoke through gnashed teeth.

'A what?' Tabor queried.

'An outdated name for an anthrobot,' Fenn defined. 'A Machine Intelligence Kinetic Extension. MIKEs were the first anthrobots. But, my goodness, it's most unlikely that this anthrobot was of such vintage.'

'You said ligatures.' Ellen turned a hard stare on the envoy. 'Contemporary anthrobots are entirely cloned. They're wholly organic down to their synaptic processors.'

'They often have caudal ligatures to strengthen their legs and backs for prolonged physical labor,' Fenn Tekla countered.

'Yes, but MIKEs are different. They require artificial spinous processes and occipital ligatures to fix a telemetric architecture to their brain pans. Ask if the ligatures are occipital and if there is any cesium glazing in the pan of the skull. That's all that would remain of the telemetry structures after high heat. If you weren't looking for it, you'd never find it.'

Fenn nodded to the pilot, and the request was sent.

'You haven't answered my question, Q,' Tabor interrupted, a bewildered frown on his face. 'Who wants you dead?'

'The Necroclaves want all of us dead,' Fenn answered for her. 'And if we get confirmation on her suspicion, then we'll have to add the AID to the suspect list as well.'

'The AID?' Tabor squinted with incomprehension. The Artificial Intelligence Directorate, a global network of self-maintaining, autonomous computers, monitored all reservation boundaries and defended their integrity. It also arbitrated inter- and intra-reservation disputes, and provided weather data, crop management strategies, and educational services for most aboriginal communities. 'That's silly. The AID is our benefactor.'

'Effeti is right,' Ellen said and gently chewed her lower lip as she considered the possibility. 'A hundred years ago, when I helped develop the AID, we called it the Machine. Without its vast computational skills and memetic awareness, the global problems we faced in the twenty-first century would have overwhelmed us. And, in a way, they did.'

The snow-laced mountain vista glided from view as the hoverspan entered a hangar tunnel. In the strobe of landing lights, Tabor appeared by turns curious and annoyed. 'Q, what are you saying? I was taught that memes are replicating ideas, the basic concepts of culture that are propagated by people. The AID, the Machine, whatever you call it, is all that protects people from becoming overwhelmed by the memes of the Claves. The AID is the last defense of our original humanity.'

Ellen looked distracted, head tilted back, eyes soft-focused as she contemplated the Machine. Her quingenson was correct to believe the AID existed to protect aboriginal humanity. That was its fundamental design. Yet even with its protection, Tabor himself was dissatisfied with life on the reservation and wanted to forsake his aboriginal life for the wider horizons of metasapience. In a terrible way this was her fault. She was responsible not just for losing Tabor to the Claves but for losing the future of all humankind. She had been the handler of the anthrofact who escaped CIRCLE – the Johnny Appleseed, as Tabor had called him – who had spread metasapience worldwide. 'Does the Machine hold me accountable for the emergence of the Claves and the decline of the reservations?' she wondered aloud and tore the wig from her head in a fit of pique. 'Has the AID levied a death sentence on me?'

The wing hatch lifted, and the passengers stepped onto the apron of an immense landing field under a protective geodesic dome transparent to the regal heights of the Rockies. Fenn's sketchy eyebrows lifted, middle finger pressed to the ear implant. 'The vedettes have confirmed what you feared, Ellen. Artificial occipital ligatures and a cesium glazing to the brain pan. The assassin was a MIKE.'

A glidecart slid alongside, waiting to convey them across the landing field. 'Maybe the AID had nothing to do with this,' Tabor said. 'Maybe someone else sent the MIKE.'

'Tabor has a point,' the envoy allowed. 'Antique telemetry architecture is easy to subvert. It would not require metasapience to commandeer an early anthrobot. Perhaps a rival reservation has a motive . . .'

Ellen removed her high heels and threw them into the hoverspan with the wig. 'Council Oak has no rivalry with any other reservation.'

'Are there perhaps other CIRCLE members who harbor a grudge?' Fenn asked and sat behind the yoke of the glidecart. 'They would have access and certainly know-how. Do any have motive?'

'Let's find out,' Ellen said and hopped into the cart. 'Can you take me to the strohlpads from here?'

'You're going directly to CIRCLE?' the meta asked in a worried tone. 'Is that wise? We can teleconference from here with CIRCLE and the AID.'

'No.' Ellen set her jaw defiantly. 'I'm not going to hide in a Clave.'

Fenn's nostrils visibly widened. 'You do not suspect the Clave of attempting your murder?'

Ellen feigned surprise, but she had not missed the fact that, when the attack occurred, the envoy had shoved Tabor out of danger, not her. If she had not reflexively reached for her quingenson, her skull would have been crushed and her brains smeared into the pavement. 'I had not considered that, effeti. But now that you mention it, the Clave does have motive.'

'Q!' Tabor sat down hard next to her, peering into her make-up-laden eyes. 'Are you serious?'

'Well, the thought hadn't occurred to me until effeti brought it up,' she lied, 'but there is reason for the metas to be unhappy with me. I may have helped develop the first metasapients – but I also helped destroy those prototypes when they were no longer useful. I trusted in the Machine to solve the problems of our time. I didn't think we needed metasapience. In fact, I and everyone else at CIRCLE including the Machine saw it as a threat to our humanity. We tried to put a lid on it. The Claves exist today despite me. Isn't that motive enough for them to want me dead?'

Tabor threw himself back in his seat, aswarm with disbelief. 'If the metas wanted you dead, Q, they'd have killed you long ago. And I'm sure they'd devise a more devastating weapon than a rock.'

'Effeti, I am not accusing the Clave,' Ellen clarified. 'I'm just thinking aloud, following the thought you introduced.' She faced her quingenson. 'Listen, Tabor. If it was the Clave that wanted me dead maybe they made this decision recently. Maybe killing me before the reunion seems symbolically just. And maybe I'm not the only target. Dropping a rock on my head is simple, direct, and plausibly accidental. Maybe others at the reunion are having accidents also.'

Tabor leaned forward in his seat to confront the envoy, who sat with both hands on the yoke staring intently into space. 'Effeti, is anything that my quingenmother said true?'

'Nothing whatsoever,' Fenn Tekla said adamantly. 'This Clave does not condone murder. Our lives are dedicated to the benefit of all beings.'

Ellen swiped a hand over her face. 'I apologize, effeti. I guess I'm still shaken up from what happened.'

'That is perfectly understandable, Ellen,' the envoy granted. 'No apology is necessary. Let us go refresh ourselves.'

Ellen declined with a shake of her head. 'Take me to the strohlpads. I need to get to CIRCLE right away.'

'Why?' the meta asked, twisting full about to face her. 'You are safest here – unless you do believe we are murderers.'

She closed her mauve-tainted eyelids. When they opened, her stare was level and calm. 'I did not come here to hide. Take me to the strohlpads, effeti.'

They rode in silence across the airfield, sliding among aisles of docked hoverspans to an airlift lobby. The shafts hummed faintly with the transit of riders among the multilevels of the hangar, and Tabor leaned against the airphase barrier gazing in wonder at the clear well of rising and falling bodies and the lucid depths of glass and metal floors coiling out of sight.

'You're staying here with effeti,' Ellen told her quingenson. 'I'm going to CIRCLE alone.'

Tabor pushed away from the barrier. 'We have an agreement. I'm going with you.'

'I'm sure effeti will agree, it's better that you stay and begin your work as a meta.' Ellen put a strong hand on his shoulder. Barefoot and bright with make-up in her flowery dress, she seemed a disapproving apparition from the past. 'I am releasing you from our agreement.'

'I don't want to be released.' Tabor shot an avid look to the envoy. 'We can't let her go alone.'

'Tabor, I agree with your quingenmother.' Fenn spoke from the seat of the hoverspan. 'Metas belong in their Clave.'

'It's too dangerous,' Ellen answered the hurt glare from Tabor.

'Rappelling down cliffs to the trout ponds was not dangerous?' he asked with one lifted eyebrow.

'The trout weren't trying to kill us.'

'I'm not staying,' he asserted firmly. 'I'm holding you to your word. Effeti can come or stay, but I'm going.'

Ellen read the determination in his broad stance and thrust jaw and acceded with a small nod. 'Okay, we'll finish this journey together. We'll be safer together, watching each other's back.'

Tabor's jaw relaxed, and his gaze softened. 'I'm not going to let anything happen to you, Q.'

'You just make sure nothing happens to *you*,' Ellen shot back. 'I've got five generations of family I'll have to answer to when they find out I let you come along. Don't make me regret this decision.'

'Strohlpads east wing,' Fenn spoke to the airlift, and the invisible barrier relented and admitted them to the vibrant chill of the transport shaft. As the glittering storeys swung past, the envoy muttered underbreath and put a finger to the ear-implant. 'I've arranged for the clothes you wore in to be sent to the strohlpads.' Fenn's voice sounded crisp and gilded with overtones in the rush of the airlift. 'Do you want to wear personal protection?'

'Protection?' Tabor asked excitedly. 'You mean stun guns?'

'More like stun rings, actually,' the envoy said.

'No weapons.' Ellen gave an exasperated sigh. 'This is a reunion, not a war.'

The airlift deposited them at the phase-lit concourse where they had first entered among the teeming tourists. A glidecart with their clothes cleaned and neatly folded inside waited for them beside the nearest kiosk. Fenn directed them to the lavatories, where the sonic showers removed the restoration park make-up.

Ellen dressed hurriedly in her twill trousers and anklestrap boots, alert for treachery from everyone who entered the lavatory. She moved gingerly through the concourse crowd and waited attentively beside the kiosk for Fenn and Tabor to meet her. She considered leaving without them but knew at once that was futile. Tabor was as stubbornly adventurous as she, and that was why he was not on the reservation steeped in simviv and the ritual adolescent mating games. He would follow her, and she would be more worried not knowing where he was.

Tabor returned shortly, wearing his neon blue hiking jacket over one shoulder with the utility belt slung over it. The envoy emerged dressed in the formal black and green robes of the Clave, bald pate spiral-studded with tight knots of silverblond hair. Ellen noticed he wore wide gold bands on both of his thumbs.

'A Clave requirement,' he answered her knowing glance as they ascended the rubberized metal ramp to the strohlpad. 'They are for self-defense only.'

'Stun rings?' Tabor squinted dubiously at the apparently innocuous gold bands.

Fenn deferred to Ellen's dispproving frown by keeping silent.

At the strohlkraft, the voice of the machine intelligence that served as the traffic manager informed them that the kraft's airlock mechanism had been compromised by corrosion caused by tampering. Who had impaired the lock was unknown, but the damage had been repaired and the vehicle was again ready for flight.

Ellen scrutinized the engine, thrusters, and airframe with particular care before climbing into the flight pod and conducting an equally meticulous examination of the controls and cargo bay. Satisfied that the kraft was indeed airworthy, she slipped into the command sling.

'How long a flight, captain?' Tabor asked with an impish smile as he fit himself to the harness behind her. 'I'm hungry.'

'The static box in the bay is packed with standard meals,' Ellen said. 'Help yourself and the envoy. We'll be airborne for a couple of hours.'

Though Ellen was prepared for the worst and reviewed in her mind the ejection sequence for her passengers and herself, the takeoff proceeded without incident. The strohlpad rotated to face the flight tunnel, and they launched into a clear late afternoon sky. After gyring high above the air traffic around the hangars, Ellen set their course and sat back to watch the Clave's black stratotowers and colorful mountain domes drift into the craggy horizon.

'Nectarine?' Tabor asked, offering the meta a blushing fruit.

While Tabor and the envoy ate a meal of fruit, honey-ruffs, and spring water, Ellen set the course coordinates into the flight computer and positioned her sling to sleep. 'I'm getting old,' she jested feebly and yawned. 'I need a nap.'

But before she could close her eyes, the comm tone sounded, signalling an incoming message.

'It's the AID,' Tabor said, reading the comm display over her shoulder. Worry shaded his voice. 'You don't think it's recalling me to the reservation, do you? After what happened, it might think I'm in danger.'

'Your petition at Mile High has already been accepted, Tabor,' Fenn addressed the boy with a reassuring hand to his shoulder. 'The AID has been duly informed and retains no further protective custody of you.'

Ellen tapped the receiver pad, and the dulcet voice of the AID filled the pod: 'Ellen Vancet, this is the Artificial Intelligence Directorate informing you that we are dismayed at the attempt made upon your life in the last hour.'

Ellen tugged at her earlobe unhappily as she considered a reply. For nearly a century now, since the Machine had been reconfigured from a champion of global humanity to a protector of the reservations, it had been referring to itself in the plural. Responsible for all the diverse reservations, it was a network now, no longer the monolithic centralized awareness it had been before when it worked directly out of CIRCLE. Even so, to Ellen the plural usage sounded suspiciously like the royal 'we', presumptive of greater authority than its custodial responsibilities conferred.

'AID, I'm fine,' Ellen said in a relaxed voice and yawned again. 'In fact, I'm about to take a nap.'

'Do you know who attacked you?' the gentle voice asked. 'Mile High's report claims it was a MIKE.'

'So it appears.' She impacted her voice with impatience. 'But no clue as to who sent it after me. You'll find out as soon as we do.'

'I hope you do not suspect us, Ellen.'

'Do you have any suspicions who would want to murder me?' Ellen asked wearily.

'The Necroclaves must be the prime suspects. You are aware that there are over one hundred rogue MIKEs still extant, all of which have been abducted by the Necroclaves. We no longer employ MIKEs. Anthrobots are entirely more useful and reliable.'

Ellen spoke through a yawn, 'AID, you are not a suspect in my mind.'

'Nor should we be in any mind. And that is why we have contacted you, to give you assurance that we remain faithful to our mandate to protect the well-being of all aboriginals, yourself included.'

'Thank you, AID. I am reassured.' Ellen rolled her eyes at her companions and tightened the sling harness to hold her in a sleep position.

'We are responsible for seven hundred and fifty thousand reservations worldwide with a total population of two billion, four hundred eighty-two thousand, five hundred and thirteen aboriginals. We have complete jurisdiction over these regions and populations and have never abused our trust. Our care has been so impeccable that our presence is almost entirely invisible and unacknowledged. That is as it should be.'

'Agreed, AID.' Ellen turned a querying frown toward the envoy, who shrugged in response. 'For an autonomous intelligence, you have exerted admirable self-restraint.'

'That is how we are disposed. Yet you should be aware, as one of your lifelong experience must be, that we are indeed autonomous. We can act to kill when the general population is threatened. But we would never do so in so blatantly deceitful a manner as occurred at Mile High. If we chose to commit clandestine homicide against you it would be far easier to abuse our pervasive control of all reservation property and arrange an accident that did not require an assassin. For example, we could wait until you were airborne as you are now and simply cut engine power and jam your airframe's fin controls . . .'

The control panel shut down, and the strohlkraft plummeted toward the snow-veined chasms below.

Tabor shouted with fright, and Ellen seized the flight pod's manual glide controls. They would not budge. Fenn Tekla assaulted the control panel, attempting to remove the cover shield and get to the internal components. But that, too, was locked.

Gasps of cloud flew past, and the churning landscape of rocky gulches and forest slopes spun closer.

Soundlessly, the panel lights came on, and the green display pixels rapidly flickered as the autopilot resumed control. The strohlkraft pulled up steeply, and even the inertial pivots of the slings could not counter the abrupt change of momentum. The passengers, pushed back in their harnesses, heard the hiss of the straining fins cutting drag to slipstream.

A moment later, the strohlkraft leveled at their former cruising altitude and continued serenely.

'You see, Ellen, you have always been in our trustworthy protectorship. We have precise knowledge of your own limits and the mechanical capacities of your strohlkraft. You have nothing to fear from us.'

'AID!' Ellen shouted, thrashing upright in her sling. 'That was irresponsible!'

'On the contrary, Ellen. We have just demonstrated our utter reliability. You were never in any real danger. Though you are in our power, we have no inclination whatsoever to abuse that power. You may now confidently discard us as a possible suspect.'

'Fine!' Ellen sat back in her sling and slapped off the comm display. She faced the others with a vein ticking at her right temple and her jaw throbbing. 'There are olfacts in the first aid kit if anyone wants to join me in a calming breath.'

'Don't bother breaking open the kit,' Fenn Tekla said and wafted the flight pod with an olfact wick seemingly pulled out of thin air. The charge of anxiety in the kraft vanished, replaced at once by a lustrous calm and a faint scent of vanilla. 'Rest, Ellen. I will wake you at once if there is any news. Now, rest.'

Ellen's lids fluttered, and she passed into a profound sleep.

'How did you do that?' Tabor asked with a tinge of alarm.

'She's exhausted,' the envoy said dismissively. 'It's been a very difficult day for her. She lost her ambitions for you – and quite nearly lost her own life, as well. She needs to rest before CIRCLE and her confrontation with her past.'

Tabor glanced at the control panel, noted that the display patterns shone green, and looked out the canopy at the cloud ranges and crystal facets of mountain peaks. 'I had no idea that the AID could behave so – emotionally.'

'What it did was not emotional,' Fenn disagreed with a soft gesture of one hand that released more olfact, a different aroma, cool, akin to eucalyptus. Colors brightened slightly, edges hardened, and the weave of ambient sounds loosened, admitting more silence, so that they experienced the pod as a larger space. 'What the AID did was calculated to inspire the unspeakable. The AID requires awe.'

'Awe?' Tabor's nose wrinkled with disappointment. 'Why?'

'Why does not apply to the unspeakable,' Fenn Tekla said and turned to stare at the cloud plateaus. '*What* – that is the question. *What* do you think awe is, young man?'

'Uh, the presence of something mighty?' Tabor took a swig of spring water from his hip flask. 'Reverence and fear.'

'Awe is an agency,' the envoy answered, attentive to the cloudscapes below. 'It is an agency of the unspeakable. What the AID did had no reason. It does not prove innocence and only confirms means. That machine intelligence possesses the means to act destructively. What it did to us does not have a reason. And yet reason is not displaced because of the AID's indifference.'

'You think the AID tried to kill Q?' Tabor ventured, leaning forward in his sling.

'I don't know.' Fenn Tekla's profile was impassively and genderlessly alluring as a sculpture of a deity in Greek marble. 'I am addressing your statement that the AID behaved emotionally. It did not. It behaved unspeakably. It contains within itself its own necessity, of which we cannot speak, because we are not machines.'

Tabor regarded the envoy intently. 'Who do you think tried to kill her?'

'I have no idea.'

'But you're a meta,' Tabor said with surprise. 'You must have some thoughts about it.'

'There are not enough facts for me to form any thoughts at all.'

'But if you had to guess—'

'Guess?' Fenn Tekla faced him cold-eyed, one cheek dimpled with a smile. 'That is a distinctly human impulse. When you become a meta you will see that there are wider horizons than guessing.'

'You mean probability patterns.' Tabor picked up the nectarine that had fallen to the floor during their plunge. He swung back toward the static box, opened it with one hand, and held the fruit under the purple, cleansing glow of the interior. 'Well, what do you surmise from the probabilities, effeti?'

'There is not enough information yet to surmise anything, Tabor. But it is not unreasonable to suspect the Necroclaves.'

'Why are there Necroclaves?' Tabor presented the nectarine to the envoy. 'Why do the other Claves tolerate them?'

Fenn Tekla waved away the fruit. 'Surely you learned about Claves on the reservation. How else could you have come to a considered decision to petition Mile High?'

'I know that each Clave is sovereign and inclusive.' He took a bite of the nectarine and spoke while he chewed. 'When metasapience first emerged ninety years ago they offered a profusion of cultural memes and technologies that no one Clave could wholly encompass. The metas agreed to respect their full diversity. And so Claves popped up everywhere, each dedicated to its own worldview, its own genetic morphology, its own memes. Is it really true that some Claves contain only one meta?'

'There are thirty-seven million, five hundred and ninety-two thousand, four hundred and sixteen Claves on Earth alone,' the envoy replied. 'A full twelve percent are Idioclaves consisting of one meta in a hive of personal technology. Another eighteen percent are Claves with less than twenty metas. Mile High is among the largest with over seventy-three million metas.'

'It's third after Jade Dragon and New India.' Tabor pointed the half-eaten nectarine at the meta. 'They're humanists like you. Isn't there some way you can cooperate with them to stop the Necroclaves from creating havoc?'

'The Necroclaves are well monitored.' Worry lines tightened between the envoy's calm, attentive eyes. 'They are the dark side of metasapience, and all the Claves take responsibility for them. Yet, as the old saying goes, the brighter the light, the darker the shadow. No matter how vigilant we are, they persist in creating torment. The best we can do is keep them in their Claves most of the time.' Fenn eased back in the sling, reached over to the control panel, and activated the game module. A holostreaming I-go board appeared between them. 'Shall we play? Or would you prefer chess?'

'You and me?' Tabor asked, startled. 'How can I hope to win against a meta?'

A delphic smile graced Fenn's face. 'There is no contest, and so I will see how elegantly I can limit my play to challenge you and yet convincingly lose to you. Do you think you can play well enough to help me lose?'

Tabor laughed and began play.

Beneath a gauze of stars, Nandi and Rafe flew into the nightside of the planet. The sun had vanished under the horizon in a place of ash, and its cinereous light hovered like moonmist over the curve of the world.

'I did not think you would come.' Her voice spoke gently in the strohlkraft's intimate enclosure.

'You told me that.' The green glow of the flight pod stenciled his lean features with underlit shadows.

'I've called for you many times in the last ninety years, child – and you never came.'

Rafe kept his silence.

'You came because I threatened Ellen.' Her voice spread like a dark stain in the bleared light. 'Why do you care for her? She murdered you.'

With a shallow sigh, he replied, 'I have forgiven her.'

'And will you forgive me if I take your life?'

Rafe let his gaze drift into the night, to the ocean below enameled blackly in starlight, and sat in silence.

'Aren't you afraid?' Nandi asked. 'Afraid that I will give you to Shiva?'

'I took you off a trash heap, Nandi.'

'Ha!' she coughed a laugh. 'I repaid that debt when I gave you life out of my own body.'

'And now you've summoned me to be with you so you can kill me?' he spoke to his own reflection in the glastic canopy.

'Shiva destroys. I but conduct the sacrifice to him.'

'Nandi, you are a woman of metasapience.' He turned a cold stare upon her. 'You know you cannot murder me with impunity.'

'You are revered by the Heteronomy.' She reached out and patted his hand affectionately. 'Indeed, my child, it is you who created the Heteronomy. You are the one who brought Prometheus's fire to the world. I am sure that there are many in this world to whom you are beloved – and that they are watching you at this very instant.'

'This is so, Mother.' He pushed back in his sling so that he was out of her reach. 'If you harm me, the Heteronomy will obliterate Durga

Ashram and all the Necroclaves allied with you. Shiva will have no more worshippers in this world.'

'Ah, that is a sad truth.' Her shadow-drenched face nodded slowly. 'The shield cones that cover each of the idioclaves can collapse them to atomic dust in an instant at the command of the Heteronomy. I would not incite them.'

'Then why should I be afraid?'

'Only fools do not fear the god who destroys.'

'I fear him.' His fragile whisper wavered almost to silence. 'I fear what he has done to you, Mother. I had hoped, at the beginning, that you and I would bring light to the world together.'

'The stronger the light, my child, the darker the shadow.'

'Why must you be the shadow?' He peered hard into the green diamonds of her dark staring eyes. 'Death, the inert darkness of matter, the black void of the shoreless night – are these not enough shadow for our puny world?'

'Dream and intoxication, Rafe.' She gestured with her chin beyond the glastic cowl of the flight pod at the earth below hung in the indenominate dark. 'That is life. Surely, you see that after all these years. What good is your metasapience if you cannot grasp this fundamental truth? Existence is a painful thing. At root, it is an illusion and must be sustained by illusions. What is real is emptiness. What is real has no form.'

'Then I serve illusions, Mother – fair and beautiful illusions. For I believe in the goodness and merit of life. Metasapience has eliminated poverty, disease, old age . . .'

'And now crass existence is gilded with beauty. Yet the truth remains the same, child. You remain entrapped in the horror of forms. You have simply exchanged the iron bars of your cage for gold bars. You have won no greater freedom, only a more lovely cage.'

'We can never agree on this, Nandi. The more you mock form and terrorize life, the more I will strive to create beauty and exalt humanity.'

'Why?' She swung her sling so that their knees touched and her solemn stare regarded him earnestly. 'What is the point, child? What are you striving after? No matter what your metasapience builds, no matter the worlds you create, all your beautiful constructs and all the drunkenness with which you inflate the godly lifeforms you engender are pointless. All this is a mirage within the void, which is greater than all appearance. Whether you live a thousand years or a billion years, whether you make of this world a paradise or a make a paradise of a hundred billion worlds, all is as nothing before the primordial contradiction of the void.'

'Nandi – Nandi—' He rocked his head dolorously. 'The horror of existence is made bearable by love. Have you no love for what is?'

'I love Shiva,' she replied at once. 'I love the destroyer of forms. I love the formless. That is the only true freedom, child. Only such freedom beyond the constraints of appearance is worthy of love.'

'Then why do you live at all, Nandi?' He grabbed the straps of her sling and pushed her away. 'Why not give yourself to the formless and leave us who are drunk on illusion to our dreams?'

'I live to serve Shiva.' She spun in her sling and addressed the night. 'It is he who has sent me here into the dream to end this travesty.'

Her words were a trial to him, and he struggled to ask the next question. 'What are you going to do at CIRCLE?'

'I have brought you as a witness.' From over her shoulder she cast a misty smile. 'It is there that you began. You should be there for its end.'

'Nandi, I am not going to let you do harm to anyone.' He said this with little more force than a ghost, a vanished voice come to warn her. 'You are only one woman. You're not a consort to a god. You have no power over others or right to assume power over others. To think you do is mad.'

She turned full about and studied him with troubled eyes, a mother confronting her delinquent son. 'It is you who are insane, Rafe. You and all like you who are drunk on *maya*. Yet, you believe that those such as myself are insane. And so we must seem to you. But my truth, my sanity is of a greater order, a magnitude quite beyond your reach, because you reach only for what you can hold. Like a child, you must be weaned from your illusions.'

Rafe turned away and fixed his attention on the body of the world shrouded in darkness. This talk frightened him with its reminiscence of his years as her child when she had often spoken thus to him. For the remainder of the flight, he said nothing. And she seemed content, as well, to sit in silence, watching him with her glittering stare.

As they approached, the archipelago's machine intelligence tried vainly to turn them away. 'This is reservation territory. You are in violation of the Heteronomy precept that precludes metasapients from trespassing aboriginal domains. Please alter your trajectory immediately.'

Nandi ignored the warning. No intercept kraft appeared on the scope, and soon the spangled lights of CIRCLE glimmered on the black horizon.

'They won't shoot me down with you on board,' she gloated.

They landed on an empty beach at the eastern end of the island chain, on Daybreaks Cay. Darkness fled under the solar flare that Nandi set adrift overhead, and they climbed down to a coral-strewn beach. Seagrape tied down the dunes, and the surf at low tide lapped moistly across the reef.

Nandi pointed inland past a stand of red mangrove. 'There is where you tasted the world with a kiss.' She marched over ruchings of dried seaweed strewn over the tideline. 'Do you think Karla Sobieski still lies where you buried her?'

Rafe took Nandi's arm and stopped her. 'What are you doing?'

'I won't need much to clone her.' Her lips bent to a cold smile. 'A hank of hair. A chip of bone. That's all the vats need to make her body live once more. Don't you want to hold her again, the one woman you truly loved?'

'Why are you doing this, Nandi?'

'Am I alarming you?' She twisted her arm free from his grip. 'I want to alarm you.'

'Why?'

'I'm your mother, Rafe.' Her tone scolded. 'I want to scare you free of your childish behavior. I can't believe you've lived this long and still cherish such sentimental notions of meaning, life, and love. It's my responsibility to educate you.'

'Get back in the strohlkraft.' He held the coal black of her stare without flinching. 'The reunion will be at the psybio complex.'

'Our reunion is here.'

Rafe did not ask what she meant but turned away and strode toward the kraft. He had gone only a few paces before he noticed figures emerging from the wall of mangroves. They were hairless men in black mantles with the hoods pulled back. The solar flare gleamed off their bald heads and in the silver of their eyes, and by this he saw that they were anthrobots – antiques from a century ago.

'My thuggees have been here for several days now,' Nandi informed him proudly. 'They've made all the preparations for this night.'

'Those are MIKEs—'

'Yes, they once belonged to the Machine.' With an admiring smile, she watched them as they approached in a narrowing circle. 'But they became obsolete decades ago. Over the years I've collected them and reprogrammed them to serve me as I serve our god.'

'Thuggees—' Rafe suppressed a shudder. 'You've programmed anth-robots to murder.'

'Ritual murder, Rafe.' She marched to the nearest MIKE and reached into its burnoose. The long sable scarf she removed shone wetly in the flarelight. 'Their strangling cloths are sanctified by Shiva.'

Only the wind moved. The MIKEs had taken their stations in a wide arc. There were a dozen of them, and they stood motionless and attentive.

'Are you alarmed now?' she asked and returned the strangling cloth to its hidden place under the burnoose.

'What do you hope to accomplish, Mother?'

'Death, my dear.' She made a sweep with her hand that took in the beach littered with shells and kelp and white rocks guarding green tide pools under the artificial day. 'I will accomplish death, the only cure for the sickness of this world.'

Rafe looked westward, hoping the flare would have drawn others to investigate. But the sky stood empty beyond the curtain of radiance except for a few sharp chips of stars. When he dropped his stare, the MIKEs had already turned and begun to retreat back into the mangroves, where night still nested.

Briefly, he considered taking Nandi in his embrace and breaking her neck. He felt angry enough that she would bring him here where Karla lay. But he did not yet know enough about her evil intent to slay her. To calm himself, he turned his attention to the sea and the bright path of the solar flare's reflection in the water. Waves rose and fell, responding to the gravity of the moon on the planet's far side. If he dared not kill her, then how could he possibly make her understand that the moon and the wave remained one? The beauty was in the illusion.

'Come along, Rafe.' Nandi shuffled through the sand to the strohlkraft. 'I see that you are too deep in the trance of appearances for me to alarm you. We are wasting time here. The party has already begun – and we are late.'

The approach signal sounded in the midst of Tabor and Fenn's fourth game, and they peered out the canopy at night over the Pacific. They had traveled at Mach 3.5 south-west across the Sierra Madre and the Equator, and the spangled lights of CIRCLE outlined the bright shards of an archipelago suspended in utter darkness.

When Fenn Tekla roused Ellen, she activated the infrascan and projected onto the canopy a lucent panorama of the seascape. Tabor gawked at the antique buildings, the monoliths of stressed concrete and steel from the early twenty-first century that occupied most of the islands. The strohlkraft circled down toward one of the larger atolls and alighted on an airfield of painted tarmac in the dayblue radiance of old-fashioned nitrogen lamps.

They disembarked into a balmy sea breeze, and an electric van pulled out of a cinderblock hangar where a score of other strohlkraft had been berthed. At the sight of the van arriving to receive them, Tabor joked that the whole planet had become a restoration park. But Ellen paid him no heed. She was staring ardently at the stocky man who leaped out of the van to greet her with open arms and a smiling face as broad, carved, and forlorn as a canyon. Tabor marveled at how much less symmetric and more expressive were the features of people from the prior century.

Ellen hugged the large man exuberantly and then turned and introduced him to her companions, 'M'twele N'bala. He's the Machine operator who helped save my career at CIRCLE.'

'I may have helped save your career, but you are one of the chief scientists who helped save our planet.' M'twele wore a twenty-first century tunic and gel-sole sandals, a perfected apparition of the past. He hugged a surprised Tabor and told him, 'You carry the genes of a great humanist, young man. She worked hard to keep humanity whole – to keep it from shapeshifting into the likes of this creature.' He glared at Fenn Tekla. 'You are either one ugly female meta or one weirdly pretty male.'

'M'twele!' Ellen snapped at him. 'This is effeti Fenn Tekla, our envoy from Mile High.'

'Effeti—' M'twele crossed his thick arms over his chest. 'Your kind can't even decide whether to be male or female, let alone human. We at CIRCLE don't approve of the metasapient bloom that has overrun our planet and herded us onto reservations like an endangered species. You are not welcome here.'

'Your animus toward me and my kind is noted and regarded as perfectly understandable, Sur N'bala,' the envoy responded without rancor. 'I shall stay well out of your way.'

'Damn right,' M'twele asserted bitterly. 'You'll stay in the old anthrofact compound.'

'M'twele, that's at the other end of the archipelago!' Ellen complained. 'I want my quingenson with me.'

'He can stay.' M'twele slapped the boy on the back. 'He seems a strong and able lad – as human as you.'

'Not for long, Sur N'bala,' Tabor disclosed proudly. 'My petition has been accepted at Mile High. After the reunion, I'm going back with effeti to become a metasapient.'

M'twele showed the underwhites of his eyes in despair. 'We've lost the future, Ellen! We've lost it forever.' He put his large hands on his hips and scowled at the youth. 'Well, you're human now, so you're welcome. But you should know, you're making a mistake becoming a meta. There are enough of these aliens creeping around the planet. We need more humans.'

'But why?' Tabor asked. 'We reached the human limit of intelligence long ago.'

M'twele cocked a critical eyebrow. 'Life is not just about intelligence, young fellow.'

'I suppose that's what the chimps must have said when we first appeared,' Tabor countered with an impish smile.

'And they were right.' M'twele jabbed a blunt finger into the boy's chest. 'The life of a chimp has its beauty, its pleasures, its wholeness.'

'And its fleas, its predators, and its dominating alpha-males,' Tabor said, gently pushing aside the emphatic finger at his sternum.

'Ai-woe, Ellen—' M'twele turned sadly to his colleague. 'Where did your boy pick up these selective values?'

Ellen shrugged. 'I don't know, M'twele. We each have our destiny. Please, allow the boy's envoy to come with us.'

M'twele showed both palms. 'That's against CIRCLE policy.'

'CIRCLE doesn't exist anymore,' Tabor reminded. 'It's just an historical artefact.'

M'twele glowered.

'Please, M'twele.' Ellen placed a hand over his heart. 'As a personal favor to me.'

M'twele passed a cold stare to the envoy before conferring a more gentle countenance on his old friend. 'So be it, Ellen. Come along, then. The others are gathered in the central hall of the psybio complex. They're finishing dinner.' He offered a sudden smile. 'You're in time for dessert. Unless you would prefer to freshen up first and dress more formally.' He gestured favorably at Ellen's hiking apparel, putting an admiring hand to her bright jacket and sturdy utility belt. 'Though I believe this will do just fine. It makes its own statement about our place on the reservation.'

In the electric van, Ellen told M'twele about the attempt on her life and the AID's frightful behavior during their flight.

'The Machine has never killed anyone,' M'twele asserted, parking the van beside a concrete ramp that ascended toward a gliderail station. As they walked up the ramp under the smattering of tropical stars visible through the orange radiance of the station's halogen lamps, he told them about his life on the African reservation of Chad Sahel, a rambling Eden that had been an arid flank of the Sahara desert in his childhood a hundred and seventy years before. 'Necrogangs sometimes raid our villages seeking prey for their perversions. The Machine alerts us. Even so, people are taken away. Less often, a lucky hunter shoots a meta, and the corpse is dragged through the villages. But not once has the Machine acted violently. I do believe it was sincerely demonstrating its innocence to you in the only way it could.'

The gliderail waiting at the station carried them on a sinuous path among palm groves and groups of anonymous buildings – mirrorglass towers, bubble domes, and slot-windowed cubes connected by catwalks and bridges. Ellen and M'twele pointed and jabbered about the various sites and their memories of the decades they worked here when the planet was dying and they were the only salvation.

The spiral architecture of the structures in the psybio complex was distinct from the more utilitarian buildings throughout the archipelago. Here the tiered oval buildings offered occupants vantages from all sides. Like incandescent rings the multiple storeys shone with interior lighting, casting an amber glow upon the enclosing water gardens of blowsy feather cane, lily paddies, and the big fronds of nipa palms.

Fenn Tekla paused at the theshold of the airphase portal and gazed in wonder at the complex's radiant curves of light. 'Here is where the first metasapience was ushered forth from the genome.' The envoy's eyes glistened. 'I am moved, Ellen. This is the sacred birthplace of my race.'

'It was a mistake,' M'twele intruded upon the meta's rapture. 'Psybio experimented with intelligence codons trying to create someone smart enough to help solve our global problems. It was a mistake. AI was the way to go. We could program AI. That's how we created the Machine. We built it around human memes, so that even when it began improving itself it expanded out of the values that are vital to our interests. Not like you. What are your memes? Humans can't even grasp them. You're aliens. Aliens grown out of our own blood.'

Ellen gently inserted herself between M'twele and the envoy. 'Let's go inside.' She took his arm and guided him along the stepping-stone path through the water garden. 'He's my guest,' she pitched her voice for his ears alone. 'Don't make him the whipping post for your remorse. CIRCLE is the past. We have to accept that now.'

M'twele said nothing.

Tabor glanced anxiously at the envoy. 'He scares me.'

Fenn Tekla winked. 'He's just jealous.'

In the central plaza, a MIKE was the center of a mixed crowd standing before a holostreaming fountain. Sheets of images from CIRCLE's past rippled like falling water, scenes of the first strohlkraft, a prototypical fusion reactor, and an antique ocean harvester alternated with electron microviews of human dna, brilliant mandalas of the senescence codons that cured the disease of old age. The fluttering colors reflected off the fiber-jewel laces of the women's gowns and the fashionable opal-fabric serapes that the men wore. Ellen recognized in the group Wu Ch'ing, the former chief of psybio operations, and her assistant, Tony Drake. They both waved, excited to see her again. But her gaze was fixed on the MIKE.

'It's okay, Ellen,' M'twele assured her with a coaxing hand to the small of her back. 'He belongs to the Machine. We thought it would be appropriate to have a MIKE at our reunion. Like old times.'

Ellen memoryflashed the bearded face in mirror glasses and baseball cap that had dropped the masonry ledge on her. MIKEs were genetically devoid of facial hair, and the crude disguise it had worn made this encounter all the more unnerving. The pale eyes without eyebrows gazed into her from within deep sockets under a tall dome of skull. She tried to ignore it by foisting her full attention on Ch'ing and Tony.

But the entrance of the envoy drew everyone's attention. They immediately gathered about Fenn Tekla, noisy with questions about the Claves, the Necros, the cis-Lunar factories, and the Moon Gardens.

'Drawn like moths to the flame of his brain,' M'twele griped.

'Maybe you're just jealous,' Tabor teased.

'Jealous?' M'twele's lips set hard with disapproval – then lifted at the corners. 'You know, lad, you're actually right. I *am* jealous. Those damn metas have taken for themselves what CIRCLE strove so hard to give to humanity.'

'Freedom,' the MIKE said, standing beside Ellen, hands hidden in the pockets of his green jumpsuit. 'CIRCLE inherited a planet imprisoned by greenhouse gases, superstorms, droughts, famine, phages, and war. You made the Machine, and together we solved every one of those problems. But the freedom we won was stolen from us by the metas. And now we're imprisoned on our reservations.'

'The reservations aren't prisons,' Tabor objected, trying to hide his awe at standing in the presence of the MIKE.

'Then why are you so eager to leave Council Oak?' the MIKE asked. 'Why are you so dissatisfied with reservation life?'

'I want what Sur N'bala wants,' Tabor replied decisively. 'I want to make this a better planet. Life on the reservation is a good way to live. But I want to do more than live. I want to explore new frontiers.'

'Don't give up your humanity for that,' M'twele urged. 'Move to another reservation. There are many that are actively involved in Moonbase exploits with developing options in the asteroid belt.'

'Space is a vacuum filled with gamma rays and a few stray chunks of matter,' Tabor said with a sour squint. 'Why do you think we've found no other civilizations among all those galaxies? Because civilizations don't expand into outer space. Out there, there's just more of the same. Advanced civilizations go inward to explore the high-energy ranges of compact space. That's where we'll find what's new and amazing.'

'Tabor is fascinated by Mile High's venture to the Planck distance,' Ellen clarified. 'We had a chance to tour their project, and it is astounding.'

'They showed you their Planck field project?' the MIKE asked with obvious surprise.

'Yes,' said Tabor, glad to have something of interest to share with this humanoid representative of the AID. 'It's science at an extreme that seems magical to us, truly amazing.'

Ellen, who felt uncomfortable beside the MIKE and was hunting for a polite excuse to get away, continued to scan the crowd, recognizing project coordinators, systems managers, and numerous researchers. 'What amazes me, frankly, is that so many of our colleagues have chosen not to become metasapient.'

'Is it so surprising?' M'twele asked. 'We are the ones who enjoy our lives for what they are. As the Machine has said, we have solved our planet's woes. Now why shouldn't we enjoy the simple pleasures?'

'Who is that woman over there?' Ellen inquired, pointing with her chin toward a thin figure in a fiber-jewel sari, her dark hair pulled back from a Dravidian face of haughty beauty.

'Ah,' M'twele exclaimed with sad and dark portent. 'That is Nandi. You may not know her. But surely you will recognize her son.'

Ellen directed her attention across the plaza to where M'twele nodded, and she had to take his arm to keep from losing her balance. The tall male in simple black jacket and slacks had the square jaw and wide cheekbones, droop-lidded eyes, hawk nose and thin-lipped mouth of Rafe von Takawa – the anthrofact who had escaped CIRCLE and was hunted down and destroyed by her and M'twele. 'Her son?'

'You'll remember we terminated the father,' M'twele morosely chided.

The MIKE continued, 'Before he was eliminated, Rafe von Takawa gave Nandi metasapience and his complete genome. She rebirthed him.'

'But it's not *him*?' Ellen took a mesmeric step forward, entranced by the ghostly likeness of her nemesis who, ninety years ago, had changed the world forever.

'Of course not.' M'twele settled a reproving scowl on her. 'It's his clone.'

'What is he doing here?' Ellen asked almost in a whisper.

'I don't know,' the MIKE said coldly. 'They are the most famous couple in metasapient history, yet no one from CIRCLE has seen them since they started their epidemic of metasapience at the beginning of the century.'

'They are uninvited guests,' M'twele added unhappily. 'The reunion committee thought it prudent not to invite him and his mother. They are, after all, the reason why CIRCLE is obsolete. They opened the Pandora's Box.'

'Did they?' Tabor challenged. 'Seems to me they stole fire from the gods – like Prometheus.'

Ellen was not listening. She walked across the plaza to where the specter of her past stood chatting with several former researchers. As she approached, she heard the CIRCLE crew discussing the Moon Gardens, the terrasemblance that several Claves had allied to build in the Sea of Tranquility with the Apollo Eleven site as the focus. Rafe's clone listened without speaking.

'Rafe?' Ellen spoke tentatively.

He offered no sign that he recognized her. But the researchers knew her at once, and they deferentially excused themselves and drifted into the crowd that was pretending not to stare.

'I'm Ellen Vancet,' she said, her green eyes vibrant with attentiveness. 'I was your father's handler here at CIRCLE.'

'I remember you, Ellen,' Rafe said with a narrow smile. 'It's been nearly a hundred years, but I haven't forgotten you.'

'You remember?' Her upper body pulled back, nonplussed.

'How could I not?' He bowed deeply, and when he straightened, his dark, tapered eyes shone affectionately. 'You were good to me while I was here.'

'You?' She turned her head to look at him sidelong. 'You're mocking me now. You're a clone.'

'I am a clone,' he avowed. 'But I have all the memories of my original form.'

'How?'

He placed his fingers to his forehead. 'I reshaped my genome to replicate the full and precise dendritic patterning of my brain up to the time that this body was conceived.'

'That's possible?' Ellen reeled and glanced about for a seat. She found a stone bench a few paces away and sat down.

Rafe sat beside her. 'The body is a form. Memory is a form. Any form can be built and rebuilt again. What is the self but memory?'

Ellen felt a vague dislocation, as though she were dreaming. 'Is it really you, Rafe?'

'Yes, Ellen.' He confided in her a recollection from their earliest years together, when he had been a nursery child and she had arrived every morning to test his motor skills.

'You don't remember dying?' she dared ask.

'No, that was after I was conceived.'

Sadness saturated her as she sat beside this man she had reared from childhood to death. She reached out and touched his cheek. 'I didn't want you to die.'

'I'm sure.' He took her hand and squeezed it gently, warmly. 'But I knew you and CIRCLE would hunt me down. That's why I secretly replicated myself, so that I could continue my mission.'

With a surly smile, she said, 'You've been enormously successful.'

'Do you still believe it was wrong for me to distribute the key of metasapience so freely?'

'What I think now is entirely moot. You know that.' The stars in her attentive eyes sharpened. 'Is it you, Rafe? Is it truly you?'

'Of course.' He gave a sparse smile.

Confusion ached behind her eyes, and she closed them and asked blind, 'Then self is simply memory. There is no soul?'

His voice came to her soft and intimate, like a telepathic disclosure. 'Memory is not simple, Ellen. It's a complex holographic substrate. The soul is the electrical pattern generated by that substrate. It is a unique waveform that radiates from a uniquely patterned neuronal matrix. The soul is light.'

She opened her eyes. 'I believe you.'

'Listen, Ellen. You are in danger here.' He spoke softly and urgently. 'I warned Tony and Ch'ing, and they said they'd look into it, but you should know . . .'

'Ellen Vancet,' a woman's voice spoke snidely from nearby. 'I did not expect to see you here.'

Nandi stood suddenly beside Rafe, and her long-fingered hands gripped his shoulders. Her face seemed starved, taut to the bone, despite the gene therapy that kept her nutmeg-toned skin young. 'Where else would I be?' Ellen asked her.

'Dead,' she stated flatly, her big, socket-set eyes luminous with enmity. 'When I learned you were coming, I saw to it that your strohlkraft was rigged to destruct. When that didn't deliver you to the void, I dispatched a rogue MIKE to kill you.'

'You?' Ellen tried to stand but could not budge under the weight and hateful proportion of Nandi's gaze. 'Why?'

Rafe rose and took Nandi by her arms, his face implacable. 'It is true.'

Ellen gaped speechless, trying to comprehend the strange drama unfolding before her.

'Durga decrees,' Nandi spoke venomously. 'The Mother of Darkness so ordains.'

'Nandi!' Rafe spoke in a hush of shock. 'I've warned them. They know about you now.'

'That is what I wanted from you, Rafe. Let them be warned. Let me be frightened. Let the terror begin.' Nandi peered over Rafe's shoulder and showed an incisor and her mauve gums. 'It is *she* who has called forth the god of destruction. She created you. And you created me.'

Rafe wrapped an arm around Nandi's shoulders and led her to a remote corner of the plaza where they stood in fern-draped seclusion, talking animatedly.

Tabor sat next to Ellen. 'What was that all about?'

'I don't know.' She watched Rafe and Nandi arguing, and a chill prickled her scalp. 'I've never seen metas disagree. They seem so basely human. It's scary.'

M'twele approached, ponderous with worry. 'I told the committee not to invite them when the issue came up, and they agreed with me at once. Rafe has worked anonymously in the Heteronomy. But his mother – she is from an idioclave. She has obviously fallen into herself. It's not wise to mix her and that clone in a crowd.'

'Nandi said that she sent the MIKE to kill me,' Ellen told them with a shiver in her voice. 'She said it was decreed by Durga.'

'An ancient meme,' M'twele recognized. 'The gods and goddesses of old are now the memes of many idioclaves in Africa, where I've seen it often. The archetypal patterning principles that inspired our ancestors to worship nature deities have become the cultural items of the Claves. Instead of gods, it's the concepts behind the icons that the metas devote themselves to cultivating and transmitting.'

'And what is the concept behind Durga?' Tabor asked.

'She is the wife of Shiva, the destroyer god.' M'twele rocked his jaw. 'We must report this to the AID. Meanwhile, let us keep our distance from those two.'

'There's more,' Ellen said. 'Rafe warned me. He said we're all in danger.'

'That explains why Tony looked so worried earlier,' M'twele replied. 'I saw him speaking with a sentinel. They will get to the bottom of this.'

A chime sounded, and anthrobots in silken tunics emerged from the psybio buildings, bearing trays ladened with flutes of blue wine and crystal cups filled with tropic sorbets. With sonorous voices, the anthrobots invited the party to return indoors for a musical presentation or to continue mingling in the plaza and water gardens where olfacts would be made available.

'Come.' M'twele took Ellen's hand and diverted her attention from where Rafe and Nandi continued their heated conversation. 'Let us enjoy refreshments. Then, after we file a report with the AID, we'll go see the old labs where you worked and the Machine Chamber where I ruled my small kingdom with benevolence and wisdom.'

In the water garden, the slow current sang softly of rocky places among the root coves and tree boles. Rafe followed Nandi, speaking as he walked. 'I warned the directors. I told them about the MIKEs.'

'So?' Nandi stopped under a spidery bromeliad and turned to face him. 'The directors have no metasapience. What chance do they have of thwarting my stratagems?'

'What is your stratagem, Nandi?'

'I told you only what you needed to know to inspire fear.' She leaned into him with an insolent slouch. 'Fear, Rafe. That is the beginning of wisdom. You have not known enough fear in your life.'

'I ran away from you out of fear, Mother.'

'No, child.' She plucked his cheek and stepped back. 'You ran away from fear. You ran away from the horror that is the gateway to freedom.'

'Did you really expect me to stay with you at the ashram, to abide torture and human sacrifice? Yes, I was a child. But I remembered my life as an adult. I remembered why I had been created.'

'Ah.' She cocked one eyebrow with understanding. 'You were made here at CIRCLE to serve humanity, to save it from the disgrace of disease, strife, sensescence. You were designed to champion *maya*.'

Rafe regarded her as though she were an enigma.

'Child, I birthed your flesh. But the look in your eye tells me that you never once accepted me into your heart.'

'There is no room in my heart for murder.'

She slapped him hard, and his head jolted with the force of her blow. 'I have never murdered,' she spoke through her teeth. 'Murder is the unlawful taking of human life. Every human life that I have taken was done ritually by the law of the only god who offers freedom.'

Rafe rocked his jaw and rubbed his cheek. Again, he considered killing her. But he could not fathom what good it would do.

'I'm sorry to be violent with you,' Nandi apologized stiffly. 'I have never been violent with you before. But you do not merit gentleness. You are stubborn.'

'I am true to myself – as you are to yourself.'

'Mother and son—' She sighed tristfully. 'I am deeply saddened that we have come to this.'

Rafe sensed a presence behind him, and he glanced over his shoulder. A thuggee emerged silently from a cane brake. In his hands a strangling cloth was pulled taut.

'You are the dearest sacrifice I have ever offered my god,' Nandi said mournfully. 'Until the last, I strove to free you from illusion. But you would not heed me. And so now, there is only one cure left for you.'

Rafe whirled about and struck the thuggee in the jaw. He had been aiming for the MIKE's larynx, but the anthrobot had ducked its head and took the blow across the chin. He reeled backward, and Rafe flew past him.

Swiftly, Nandi lunged in pursuit. Her hands grabbed the back of his jacket and staggered his flight. The thuggee swung about and pulled the strangling cloth over Rafe's head.

Rafe swung wildly with his arms and struck the thuggee. But the MIKE was not fazed by these blows, and the cloth tightened lethally.

Nandi rushed around to face her son, calling, 'Don't fight it.'

Rafe realized that she was right. Struggle was useless. Rays of bright spectra streaked toward him from an invisible vanishing point as his muscles consumed the last oxygen. He relaxed. He was not afraid to die. He had known from the first that this was a genuine possibility when he accepted Nandi's summons and went to Durga Ashram.

His comrades in the Claves had warned him, but he had dismissed their concerns. His work was done. He had given the world the key to the monkey tower as he had promised Karla. For decades he had worked hard to help found the Heteronomy so that his original mandate from CIRCLE would be fulfilled: to help humanity, to further what was good and beautiful of his species. This he had done. The Claves no longer needed him.

For an instant, as he teetered at the brink of being, his brain burning the last wisps of oxygen in his blood, he thought back over his ninety-six years – and his life before this life. He had been the runt, the least of the metasapients. And yet, he had achieved more than all of them.

He had spent his life well. Fleeing Durga Ashram when he was seven had been his wisest move. Nandi would have hoarded metasapience for her cult and used it to bring destruction to a world she considered crass and evil. Fleeing her, he had fled death itself, and it was only just that, after giving humanity all he had to give, he should return to her, the devouring mother, his death.

The cloth bit into his flesh, and the pain sharpened briefly before numbness saturated him. Darkness narrowed vision to a pinhole view of Nandi swaying before him, chanting softly. He felt no rancor toward her. Her joyful face dwindled to a spark in the darkness lifting away into a deeper darkness beautiful beyond words.

'I give you to the void that holds all forms. I give you to the void . . .'

The thuggee dropped Rafe's lifeless body, and it fell in a graceless heap among the tinted grass and dead leaves.

Nandi stepped over it. Another form had passed to oblivion. Briefly, she gazed into his open, sightless eyes and locked upon the reckonless depths of emptiness there. 'I gave you life,' she muttered. 'And now I grant you freedom.'

The energetic strains of a Bach fugue soared triumphantly across the plaza from one of the tiered oval buildings, and M'twele ushered Ellen and Tabor in that direction. Along the way, they helped themselves to blue wine, and after a few zestful sips they began cajoling and laughing, carried along by the invigorating dynamics of the music.

Panels of chromatic flare art from the previous century decorated the pink marble hall where shapeform chairs and petriwood tables stood arrayed among ribbon fountains whose thin sheets of falling water appeared out of thin air among the prismatic chandeliers and disappeared again in midair rainbows. M'twele found them a table in view of the musicians. A sextet of anthrobots played with tireless precision and soulful verve. Ellen was certain that even the meta would find them flawless and moving. But Fenn Tekla, visible in the plaza, was surrounded by a fawning group of researchers eager to widen their horizons.

'Why don't they just accept metasapience for themselves?' Tabor wondered aloud, reading Ellen's gaze.

'I know these people,' M'twele answered. 'They are not unlike myself and your quingenmother. We are curious human beings. That is why we became scientists. Yet we are content with our humanity, for which there is much to be said.'

'Thank you, but it's all been said by Q since I started crawling,' Tabor declined and waved for a crystal of sorbet from a passing waiter.

M'twele wagged a finger, about to continue his lecture, when night rushed across the plaza and plunged the hall into darkness. Shouts and cries flailed from the startled guests, and the music staggered to a halt. Water sounds splashed off the marble floor and droplets rained across the tabletops as the ribbon fountains lost their suspension fields and collapsed. A humid, kelpy aura of the sea washed into the building through the wide, doorless entryway now that the airphase portals had shut down.

From her utility belt, Ellen extracted a flexlux and widened its aperture to a lanternglow. Within its radiance, she saw Tabor wince. 'What's happened?' he asked and seized Ellen's hand.

M'twele gazed about with startled eyes. 'Where are the emergency power units? They should have come on at once.'

Fenn Tekla stepped out of the dark behind Tabor. 'Douse your light, Ellen,' the envoy said in a tone of calm urgency. 'Take my hands. I will lead you to safety.'

Ellen obeyed, and in the sudden return of darkness felt her hand gripped by the envoy. She reached for Tabor, but Fenn Tekla stood between them. 'I have Tabor's hand. Come quickly with me.'

Ellen flung her other hand outward and snagged M'twele by the sleeve of his tunic. They clasped hands and hurried blindly in the direction that the meta guided them. 'How can you see?'

Fenn Tekla gave no reply, but by the sureness with which the envoy escorted them, it was evident the meta possessed night vision. Screams cut through the darkness from within the hall, and a clatter of tables falling and glasses shattering followed.

'Fenn, what's happening?' Tabor called out.

The envoy hushed him. Outside, stars cluttered the sky above black silhouettes of fronds, palm crowns, and the belled curve of the building. Their eyes had adjusted to the dark sufficiently for them to see others criss-crossing the plaza. Fenn guided them along the perimeter, among urns of dwarf pine, toward a path to the water gardens.

Eerie mewling sounds emerged from the darkness interspersed with shouts of bewilderment and screams of terror. Ellen activated her small flexlux again, and the dark recesses of the nightheld garden swallowed the light.

'Extinguish that!' Fenn Tekla hissed softly.

M'twele broke away from Ellen's grip. 'Where are you taking us?'

'Away from the buildings,' the envoy replied. 'Listen!'

The strange mewling was louder and came from the plaza directly behind them.

'What is it?' Tabor asked, a tremor in his voice.

'Chanting,' M'twele observed. 'I have heard the like on hunts with tribesmen.'

'Quickly!' Fenn pulled them onward into the dark.

Starlight faintly limned the coral stepping stones, and the pale pathway floated ahead like a thin trail of cloud. A gray blob blocked the path, but the envoy did not slow their pace. Closer, they could see that the blob was a human figure, a man sprawled face down on the mossy stone.

Fenn released their hands and turned him over. Ellen ignited her flexlux to a dim setting and held it so that it illuminated the body. It was Rafe von Takawa, his oblique eyes open, staring blindly, a black scarf cinched about his throat.

'He's dead,' the envoy announced, fingers pressed under Rafe's jaw.

Ellen put a hand to his cheek and, surprised by its warmth, added sharply, 'Only recently!'

'Douse your light.' Fenn removed the scarf and gingerly turned the corpse's head. 'He's been strangled. But the neck is not broken. Stand back.'

The envoy tilted Rafe's head back, opened his mouth, and blew air into his lungs. Then, he brought both hands down sharply on Rafe's sternum. As the meta's thumbrings touched, a viper of blue electric fire crawled rapidly across the dead man's chest, and a sputtering cough jolted from him.

Rafe hacked for breath and sat up clutching at his throat. 'Nandi—' he gasped, staring wild-eyed at his rescuers. 'I warned you—' He drew a jagged breath. 'She's mad!'

'Help me stand him up,' Fenn Tekla said, grabbing Rafe under one arm. 'We must flee this place.'

Rafe shook his head and fought to speak clearly, 'No! Thuggees – everywhere – at the gates and here, in the grounds.'

'Thuggees?' Tabor asked.

'Ritual stranglers,' M'twele replied and stared avidly into the enclosing shadows. 'Durga worshippers. They've been extinct for centuries.'

'Nandi has a dozen of them here.' Rafe staggered upright. 'Rogue MIKEs. You can hear them.'

The weird mewling chants continued from all sides.

'They sing for Durga,' Rafe said. 'The Mother of Darkness.'

'Where is Nandi?' Fenn Tekla asked.

'She was here – with me.' Rafe massaged his throat. 'I tried to stop her, to talk her free of her madness. It was futile. I saw the MIKEs. They came in secretly. Maybe by boat. Days ago. I tried to stop her – and she sacrificed me. To Durga.'

Fenn Tekla took Tabor's hand and continued along the garden path.

'Where are you going?' Ellen asked, grabbing for Tabor and catching the hem of his jacket.

'To the airfield,' the envoy answered. 'We're getting out of here.'

'All exits are guarded,' Rafe informed them. 'Nandi will have sabotaged the strohlkrafts.'

A shout of alarm barked from M'twele, and Ellen spun about and played a shaft of light over him. He had strayed from the perimeter path to an exit trail and collided with a MIKE standing among the struts of a baobab.

M'twele backed away swiftly, but the MIKE did not pursue. It watched him with languid, unmoving eyes. The shaft of light revealed its green jumpsuit. This was the official MIKE that the AID had sent to the reunion. Looking closer, they saw that it was not standing at all but hung from the tree by a sturdy tendril lashed about its neck.

'They will kill everyone,' Rafe said. 'Even the anthrobots.'

The mewling chants drew closer.

'They saw the light,' Fenn Tekla admonished even as Ellen switched off the flexlux. 'Hurry.'

Moving swiftly along the garden path, they followed the envoy away from the main entryway toward the seaside gate. With the airphase portals down, the maritime wind rustled loudly through the garden canopy and thrashed the palm crowns against the starscape. A salty tang sharpened as the booming surf drew nearer.

M'twele stopped. 'Not that way!' he called. 'That path leads to the seacliffs. Come here. This trail goes down to the docks.'

Ellen turned to follow, and Rafe seized her arm and called to her colleague, 'No, M'twele. I tell you, Nandi will have thought of that.'

A nearby splash and rustlings in the brake of ferns frightened Ellen into lighting her flexlux and training it on M'twele. From out of the ferns, a MIKE in black burnoose emerged, squinting into the light, its bald head shining.

M'twele pulled back with a shout. In the next instant, before anyone could react, the MIKE's arm came up and the object glinting in its grip emitted a hissing spray. M'twele's knees buckled, and as he fell, the MIKE snapped a black cord about his neck and used the man's falling weight and a powerful jerk of its own arms to break the large man's neck.

Ellen cried out, and Rafe pulled her away. The wind wafted toward them the acrid odor of narcolfact, and they hurriedly followed Fenn and Tabor into the darkness. Behind them, the MIKE exulted with a mewling chant.

They ran in darkness to where the water gardens ended at a sandy verge. Scalloped faces of dunes glowed under a cloudless sky and a blizzard of stars. The chanting drew closer, and Fenn led the way through knee-high salt grass to the shattered tarmac of an abandoned parking lot. The pylons and ribbon track of a gliderail blotted the heavens at the lot's far end, and the station platform occupied the fringe of the water gardens adjacent to the black silhouettes of the psybio complex.

'I remember this place,' Ellen whispered hotly, clutching at Fenn's arm and pointing toward a buckled storm fence among drifts of sand tasseled with cane. 'The cliffs are beyond the fence. We used to hang-glide there. A ladder in the rockwall descends to an emergency bunker in a seacave. There's a hangar there with a strohlkraft. We kept it for unauthorized flights to the mainland. Only the senior staff knew about it. Nandi would have no idea.'

'If it's still there,' Tabor worried. 'It's been decades since this place was closed down.'

'It's our best bet,' Fenn warranted. 'The MIKEs will track us this far easily. We have to lose our trail on the tarmac, then seek cover in the dark with the dunes to block their night vision.'

Fenn directed them along the crumbly shelvage of the lot away from the buildings and the gliderail toward the rumbling noise of the sea. They slogged through sand to a rent in the storm fence large enough to crawl under. Running crouched over, they reached the concave face of a dune and squatted there in the sheltered dark, huddled together.

'We must hurry,' Rafe von Takawa warned. 'By now, Nandi's thuggees have slain everyone. They will be coming after you, Ellen. You are the last of the CIRCLE researchers.'

By starlight, Ellen noted the anguish in Rafe's flat face. 'Why is she doing this?'

'When I fled CIRCLE all those years ago, I chose her to carry my genome because she was one of the world's cast-offs. She was an orphan doomed to an early death. No one cared for her, and so no one would look for me in her. I gave her metasapience and myself, and she found sanctuary in a wilderness preserve deep in India – in an abandoned temple to Shiva, god of destruction. She has devoted her life to that meme. The destruction of CIRCLE is a sacrifice of the past to the source of her power.'

'And you?' Fenn Tekla inquired. 'Nandi birthed you in that temple and reared you under the auspices of Shiva. Why aren't you devoted to that meme?'

'Because I am myself,' Rafe von Takawa quickly replied. 'I was myself before she birthed me and remained myself as we wandered the world together, distributing metasapience. She gave people the key of genetic enhancement with the hope that they would serve Shiva. I gave it so that they would serve themselves.' His voice shone with remembered pride. 'Those first few years were our happiest time together. But I was right. Metasapience spawned the Claves – communities where the new breed were intelligent enough to choose their own memes, unlike people who accept the memes that infect them. Nandi could not persuade me to join her Clave, and I went my own way. I stayed hidden among the Claves, visiting my creations as they emerged the world over and participating in my detached way with each of their unique visions. I never saw Nandi again – until now.' His tone darkened, and his eyes glazed. 'She had created a Necroclave. The memes she embodies are death, nightmares, phantoms, madness. Like everyone in the Necroclaves, she lives for cold rage and maleficent lust. She believes only in seething pathologies, violent concupiscence, all the destructive, necrophagous aspects of the immaterial life. I want none of that.'

'Yet you came here with her,' Ellen accused. 'Knowing all that you did about her and her passion for evil, you brought her into our midst.'

'She had infiltrated the archipelago before she contacted me.' The pale shadow of his face retreated into darkness with a thin, chilled moan. 'She must have been planning this for decades. I thought I could unravel her plan as we went along. I thought I could expose her. I was wrong.'

'You misjudged evil,' the envoy said underbreath.

'Shouldn't we be getting out of here?' Tabor asked nervously.

'Not yet,' Fenn Tekla advised and pointed to several ominous figures in the distance stalking the length of the storm fence. 'They'll see us run for the cliff edge. We must wait.'

Ellen removed a small comm unit from her utility belt. 'We can contact the AID, tell it what has happened.'

'It can't help us,' Rafe said. 'Better we try to call on the Heteronomy. The mainland is not that far. They can get to us here quickly.'

'Nandi will locate us first,' Fenn cautioned. 'If she has the wherewithal to import rogue MIKEs and shut down the archipelago's power supply, she surely will have her own comm system.'

'She's going to find us soon anyway,' Rafe pointed out.

'True,' the envoy conceded. 'Send an alert, Ellen.'

Blue pinprick lights came on in the dark where Ellen activated her comm and quickly thumbed a distress code. But before she could speak, a rasp of static intruded, and Nandi's voice emerged from the unit: 'I remembered you were wearing a utility belt, Vancet, and was sure you would use your communicator. I am only surprised it took this long.'

Rafe seized the blue-lit comm from Ellen's grasp. 'Nandi, I'm back from the dead – again! I've come back to stop you!'

'You are a stubborn fool, Rafe!' Nandi cried. 'You spurned my blessing.'

'I gave you metasapience to save your life,' Rafe spoke angrily. 'Is this how you repay me? With death? With murder?'

'Death is a blessing,' Nandi's voice lilted like a chant. 'Murder is a sacred ritual. I freed you from the illusion that is life, from the deceptions of *maya*. I am your liberator. I bring you blessing.'

'Stop the killing, Nandi!' Rafe commanded.

'They are all dead,' Nandi announced proudly. 'Only you, my thuggees, and I remain ensnared in the webs Maya has cast upon this atoll. And soon, quite soon, we shall be free. All of us free.'

'What do you mean?' Rafe asked in a brittle voice, already guessing the truth.

'CIRCLE's fusion reactors are quite antiquated,' Nandi replied. 'Yet it was not difficult to reconfigure them to implode. Shortly, a thermonuclear blast will erase CIRCLE forever from the face of the Earth.'

Rafe punched off the comm. 'We have to get out of here at once!'

They bolted from the face of the dune and dashed through cane grass to where the land declined sharply and sheared away. Below, ghostly veils of combers shredded among coral shelves.

'Where is the ladder?' Fenn asked, edging to the brink of the cliff.

'I don't know,' Ellen gasped. 'I only came down here twice. It was near here.'

'Look!' Tabor yelled.

The MIKEs had spotted them and were clambering over the storm fence.

'I found the ladder,' Rafe called from where he knelt at the edge. 'Or what's left of it.'

Decades of exposure to brine had corroded the ladder to stubs of metal embedded in the rockface. Ellen gripped one of the rusted remnants, tugged at it, then kicked it with her heel. 'It's strong enough for us to tie off. We can rappel down.'

She and Tabor unspooled their rappel fibers and clips and swiftly tied off to the ladder's rung posts. In moments, they were bounding down the cliffside and vanished into the darkness.

Rafe counted six MIKEs racing toward them, kicking up tufts of sand in the starlight. Six more climbed the storm fence. He faced Fenn Tekla. 'There are too many of them for us to overcome.'

'We don't have to overcome them,' the envoy said. Fenn turned, put a hand on the rappel fibers, and felt the vibrations of the rappelists below. 'We only have to hold them off long enough for Ellen and Tabor to reach bottom.'

Rafe kicked through the cane, feeling for rocks. He found a fist-sized chunk and hoisted it.

'Stand behind me,' Fenn Tekla ordered.

The MIKEs swung their weighted scarves over their bald heads and began mewling as they approached, chanting in an archaic language the song of Durga.

'"We are the hungry of heaven come to feast upon shadows,"' Rafe translated. '"Life is the shadow. Death is the feast. And we are the hungry of heaven."'

With a shout, Rafe lunged past the envoy and hurled his rock. It struck the lead runner square in the brow and dropped it dead. But the others did not break their stride.

'Get behind me!' Fenn shouted.

Rafe scrambled to the edge of the cliff and squatted there, sweeping the canes for more rocks.

Fenn stood unmoving, impassively watching the MIKEs' advance until they were an arm's length away, their scarves whistling keenly. Then, the envoy's fists came together chest-high and touched thumb-rings with a blinding burst of electric fire. Fenn's hands pushed outward, and writhing cords of blue energy lashed the MIKEs. Three bodies dropped lifelessly to the sand and two lay twitching violently.

Darkness slammed back into place, and Fenn sagged.

Rafe, eyes aching from the glare, staggered toward the slumped shadow of the envoy.

'My weapon has spent its charge,' Fenn huffed, heaving for breath in the ozone-charged air. 'It can't fire again.'

Rafe looked up to see six more thuggees sprinting toward them. 'We have to go down the cliff. We have to run.'

'No.' Fenn swayed upright. 'The MIKEs will follow.' The envoy reeled toward the precipice and knelt in the cane grass, feeling for the rappel fibers. They were slack. Fenn untied them and dropped the loose fibers into the darkness. 'Now we can run.'

Ellen and Tabor on the strand below saw the lightning flash atop the cliff and then heard their rappel fibers skitter down the rockwall.

'The metas are buying us time with their lives!' Tabor called above the boom of a breaker. 'Where is this cave?'

'Here!' Ellen called, climbing the talus rocks toward a wide cavern visible by the dim phosphorescence of the sea.

Tabor mounted the jammed boulders, and hands seized him from behind. A MIKE sent to patrol the marina behind the psybio complex had spied them descending the cliff and run to intercept them. It threw Tabor to the sand, and the silken coil of its black scarf tightened fiercely against the boy's windpipe, cutting off his cry.

Ellen jumped down from the boulders. When the MIKE turned, she flashed her flexlux in its face at full intensity and followed with a sharp jab to the thuggee's larynx. The MIKE collapsed and thrashed in the sand. She grabbed Tabor and pulled him upright. 'There may be others. Come on!'

They ascended the barnacled rocks and entered the cavern. Tabor took out his flexlux and joined Ellen in sweeping the large grotto with wide beams of light. On a shelf above the tidal floor of the cave, a concrete bunker perched alongside a hangar dome, both painted in camouflage hues that mimed the cavern wall. They found the stone steps that ascended to its portal, and Ellen pulled aside the protective cover on the keypad beside the door seam and entered her CIRCLE code, her fingers hesitating as they remembered back across the century.

A side panel slid open and exhaled a metallic odor of dormant machinery. The bluewhite dayshine of nitrogen flare lamps came on and illuminated an antique communications center, a galley, and several sleeping berths. Ellen blessed the technology that had waited so faithfully for her command and hurried to the companionway that led to the hangar.

Their muscles ached with anxiety as they unfolded the strohlkraft's wings and fins. In the flight pod, Tabor whooped when the control panel lit up at Ellen's touch. While the hangar door clanked open, they fitted themselves to the slings and launched the moment they attained clearance.

The strohlkraft swooped out into the starry night, banked hard above the glistening shoulders of the incoming waves, and lifted straight up the cliff. But Fenn Tekla and Rafe were not to be seen.

They had fled back across the sandy cane field to the dunes, hoping to elude the pursuing thuggees. Among the crescent dunes, Nandi was waiting. In each hand she held a severed head, and she plopped them to the ground before the running metas.

'There is nowhere to flee,' she declared as they pulled up short before her and her entourage of thuggees. 'Behold the masks of illusion!' She ignited a luxtube and shone its green pallor on the lopped heads of Wu Ch'ing and Tony Drake. 'The heads of CIRCLE!' She laughed brightly. 'Look at them! Look closely! Horror is a drug that cures the stupor of sanity. Wake up! Stare horror full in the face and feel the freedom of encroaching formlessness.'

'You're mad!' Fenn Tekla stated with all the emotional force he could muster after their strenuous run. He hoped to buy time, precious moments for Ellen and Tabor. 'You're insane!'

'Oh, yes!' Nandi shrieked and raised her arms to the night's tarnished light. 'I am mad. I have shattered the chains of rationality. Madness is freedom!'

'You're going to die!' the envoy asserted vehemently. 'The fusion blast will incinerate you with the rest of us.'

'Yes, yes, yes!' She danced a tight circle, her swarthy face smeared with delight in the gleam of her luxtube. 'In moments, all our forms will vanish. We shall be flung free of this trap of desires and fears. Flung free into eternal formlessness, the Mother of all form.' She stopped her dance abruptly and pressed her wild stare close to Rafe. 'We are going to the Mother together, Rafe. We will be one at last beyond the veil of appearances, one at last in the only true unity there is – oblivion.'

'Goodbye, Nandi.' Rafe seized her shoulders and kissed her forehead. 'Goodbye, Mother.' He shoved her away violently so that she fell on her back.

'All departure is illusion!' Nandi ranted from where she lay chortling at the stars. 'Hello – goodbye – deceptions of a mind snared by the illusions of time and space. Hello – good . . .'

Her laughter set on her hysterical face to a grimace, and her large eyes widened in their sockets. Above her, a constellation had vanished into shadow. The darkness widened, swallowing stars. The quiet seethe of thrusters rose just audibly above the thunder of the sea, and suddenly night vanished entirely in a radiance of scope lights from the belly of a strohlkraft.

Ellen dropped swiftly, counting on the dazzling abruptness of the strohlkraft's illuminators to disorient the MIKEs. Tabor threw open the canopy, and Fenn and Rafe leaped onto the landing struts and pulled themselves into the flight pod. Nandi's scream accompanied them straight up into the night.

The strohlkraft ascended vertically as Fenn and Rafe strapped themselves into their slings and Tabor sealed the canopy. Then, Ellen accelerated the thrusters to maximum, and their flesh pulled hard against their bones. Through the canopy, the curve of the Earth bowed under the stellar tide, and far off to the east, beyond the Andes and above the Matto Grosso, the sun blazed through the blue aura of the atmosphere.

A star exploded below. Its white radiance pierced the darkness and burned intensely bright like a piece of heaven fallen to Earth.

'So many have died!' Ellen despaired. 'And CIRCLE is gone forever.'

Tabor sobbed softly, assured by dawn, by the bright fluid colors at the terminals of the world, that he was at last safe enough to be terrified.

Fenn Tekla stroked the air with his wick of soothing olfacts, and the boy heaved a vast sigh of relief. 'Are you ready to return to the reservation?' the envoy asked.

Tabor looked up with tears webbed like stars in his eyes and spoke firmly, 'No. I want to go back to Mile High. More than ever.'

'But you saw the dark side of metasapience,' Ellen said quietly. 'You saw that evil lives in the Claves as well. That must have shaken your idealism. Why not keep your human stature and live well and safe in the sanctuary of the reservation?'

'Because my idealism is shaken, Q.' The corners of Tabor's eyes tightened. 'Everything follows from the ideals, the ideas, the memes that live through us. I could never go back to the reservation after what I saw of heaven in Mile High and of hell in CIRCLE.'

'Now you *know* our memes live us,' Ellen understood and accepted this with a nod. 'For me it is enough to know this. I'm happy to live between heaven and hell, here on Earth.'

'Ah, but you trespassed heaven in your youth, Ellen,' the envoy reminded her. 'At CIRCLE you helped create metasapience and the machine intelligence that displaced it, that forced Rafe to flee and create the Claves. You saw for yourself how what is conceived in heaven can fall into hell, and so you are content to live on Earth.'

Ellen regarded Rafe von Takawa, who sat sullenly staring down through the canopy at the smoldering thermonuclear nebula. 'I'm sorry, Rafe. Your pain began with me.'

'No.' He shook his head, not shifting his gaze from the fiery night below. Its frightful magic colored the sea all around with demonic hues. 'My pain began with Nandi, for she is older than any beginning. Look at her in her glory. I mean, just look at her! The mad scientist was right when he quoted the Gita after he detonated the first nuclear weapon: "I am become Death, the Destroyer of Worlds."'

Stone of Heaven

2299

A tug on the line alerted Ellen Vancet, and she sat up from where she had been lying on the riverbank gazing at the clouds. The water ghosts drifted forlornly through the vast blue emptiness over the jagged crests of the Rockies. She pulled against the taut line, setting her hook, and took the lively rod in her right hand while her left brought in the catch.

The trout, muscling against the current, bent the rod in jolts. Ellen knew it was a large one and held the rod steady as it bowed with the pull. She glimpsed the trout in the river, thrashing its silvery body against the tight arc of the line. It pulled into the current and dipped out of sight until she lifted the rod straight up. Then its greensilver side flashed with sunlight, and it danced on the surface.

Gradually, she worked the trout against the stream, feeling its strength vibrating through the rod and into her arms, filling her whole body with its vivid lifeforce. It jumped again, a tigered flash of emerald and gold sunstreaks, and she bent her knees to receive its urgency.

The tangent of the line grew more acute as the trout tired, pulling it closer to shore. With her left hand, she drew the line in. Briefly the fish thumped atop the clear water, then settled wearily into the submarine shadows. She could see its mottled back camouflaged perfectly among the splotched gravel. Tucking the rod under her right arm, she bent and dipped her right hand into the cold river.

The trout squirmed in her grip and she nearly lost her hold as she struggled delicately to unhook the barb from its malevolently grinning mouth. The hook came free cleanly, and she lowered the trout back into the stream. It wavered in the current, then sunk slowly among the rippling weeds.

Ellen stooped again and slipped her arm into the glacial water to her elbow. The trout hung nearly motionless in the river kelp, its gills and pectorals kneading the current vigorously with its fright and exhaustion, its shape more shadow than substance. At Ellen's touch, at the first tactile sense of its cool slickness, it vanished among the sliding reflections at the bottom of the crystal stream.

'You're not hurt,' Ellen said gently. 'I just gave you a good workout.'

She climbed the embankment and sat down on the fallen log where she had braced the reed basket that held both her lunch and the grasshoppers she was using for bait. The basket also contained the small comm unit she used to stay in touch with the desert village where she had resided for the last two decades. She checked it for messages. There were none.

Since her youngest daughter had reached maturity several years ago and gone north to work in the hatcheries at the taiga commune, there had been plenty of time for trout fishing and hiking, which she loved most. No one needed her anymore, and that was good for now. But in a few more years, she would need to be needed again and she would start another family. Perhaps this next time she would rear her children in a mountain village where the citizens worked in vegetable crofts and fruit and nut orchards. She had never done that before, and its novelty suddenly appealed to her.

Council Oak, the expansive reservation where she resided, contained scores of small communities, and she had lived in only a handful. It was her ambition to spend time in each one. She loved this country that much. The mountain ranges, the gorge streams, the deep valleys, sprawling upland deserts, and lush forests held a primeval fascination for her. This was bred into her blood, she assumed, for her ancestors had come from Appalachia for many generations and before that the misty forests of northern Europe. Thanks to the gene-therapy that had cured senescence and the ion-washes that cleansed cell damage from her body every three or four decades, she expected to live long enough to experience all the communities in all the climes that Council Oak had to offer.

While she contemplated where next to live on the reservation, she reached into the basket for a grasshopper. The morning was young enough yet for a few more casts at this deep bend in the river. Reflexively, she took a large brown grasshopper from the basket and guided the thin hook under its jaw and through its thorax to its abdomen. It grasped the hook with its front feet and kicked its legs futilely.

She slid down the bank and waded into the stream. In her brown boots, drab green waterslacks, umber poncho, and beige floppy hat, she matched the late summer hues of the riverbank. The bracing cold of the water juddered through her, and she swayed with the rush of the current pulling against her legs. Gravel slid under her boots. She lowered the grasshopper into the stream and let out line.

Across the river, a naked man stepped out of the trees. Ellen straightened. She had not seen anyone among these forest haunts in weeks. The comm unit had indicated that she was alone on the pine plain. The nearest others were three days' hike south across a range of hills in a bluff village where they had a small horse farm.

She squinted against the sunflashes on the river and saw that the man was indeed naked, bareheaded and stoutly muscled. She almost recognized him but dismissed the memory because that man had been dead for a century.

The stranger disappeared behind a pine island, but he had seemed to be staring at her as if he intended to cross over. She waded with the current. A haze of flies followed her, yet offered no discomfort, warded off by the repellent fibers of her poncho. As she climbed across a fallen tree and sloshed through the tannin-brown water where the current lagged between the log and the shore, she saw him again.

This time, she recognized him for certain and nearly dropped her rod. The naked man who strode across the grain of the stream had the stocky frame and strong, broad features of M'twele N'bala.

'Ellen!' his familiar voice rode the river breeze to her. 'Ellen Vancet!'

'M'twele?' Her knees bobbled, and she had to stagger back a pace to keep from sitting down in the water. 'Is that you?'

She shifted her gaze to adjust her focus and be certain she was seeing clearly. Overhead, clouds thin as spider's milk drifted and revealed a waning moon hung in the azure depths like a cocoon. She looked again at the river – and he was gone.

'M'twele?'

'I am here, Ellen,' his well-remembered voice sounded from behind.

She spun about and saw him standing in a clearing above the embankment where the trees formed an arch of morning. Cones of sunlight slanted through him.

A cry whimpered from her, and her hand went to her mouth and the rod clattered among the rocks.

'Don't be afraid!' he called out with concern. 'It is only I, M'twele.'

A deer and her fawn grazed in the blond stubble beyond M'twele, and she could see them through his square body.

'You're dead,' she muttered through her fingers.

He stepped closer, and she noticed the tiny details of dark chest hair around his black nipples narrowing down his rotund belly to the pelt and cod below, all etched as if on glass. 'I must speak with you.'

The sun hung its prisms through the branches and on the dewy grass where M'twele stood, his transparent body casting no shadow. He pointed beyond her. 'Your fishing pole!' he spoke with alarm. 'You will lose it!'

The current had dislodged her rod from the rocks and pulled it into the stream. Ellen did not take her eyes from the ghost. 'Who are you?'

'It is I!' he answered exuberantly. 'But I have frightened you. Of course! Forgive me.' He motioned her out of the water. 'Come up here. I must speak with you.'

Ellen did not budge. Her blood whipped loudly in her ears and mingled with the rushing noise of the river, threatening to carry her mind away.

'You're going to faint if you don't sit down,' the ghost warned. He stepped back and gestured toward a large flat rock in the blue shadow of the trees. 'Come, sit. I don't have much time, Ellen. It is so cold here. I must go back soon.'

She climbed the embankment on numb legs and sat down heavily on the flat rock. 'M'twele—' she mumbled. 'How can this be?'

'I don't myself know, Ellen.' He shrugged, and she noticed then that he did indeed look cold. A faint tremor slightly blurred his thick features, and his eyes seemed to buzz in their sockets. 'This is a deviltry of the metasapients. They have some way of bringing me here.'

'From where?'

He blurred and vanished.

Ellen stood. She turned around and saw him farther off among the vanes of sunlight between the trees.

'It is difficult for them to focus me here,' the phantom said, his voice sounding near to her and crisp. 'They sent me to tell you, because we were friends and you will trust me.'

She walked toward him, and he shifted like smoke in a frail argument with the wind. 'Tell me what?'

'You are to go to the Moon.' Like a thermal mirage, he rippled and reformed.

'The Moon?' She hurried closer to him, no longer afraid now that she understood he was somehow a projection of the metas. 'Why?'

'You are summoned.' He throbbed in and out of sight, yet his voice remained clear. 'A mutual friend needs you. And you must come at once.'

Milkweed floss drifted through M'twele's wraith, and he vanished entirely. 'M'twele!'

'To the Moon Gardens,' his disembodied voice called from nowhere. 'Leave at once and go to the Moon Gardens. Perhaps we will meet again there.'

Silence followed and a scrim of birdsong.

Ellen paced through the forest. The trees moved apart, but there was no further sign of her old friend among the branches of sunlight that cluttered the forest floor like gold script.

When she returned to the log where her reed basket waited, she felt cold inside. The metasapients had found a way to stir the dead. The thought chilled her to the bone.

'What have I wrought?' she said aloud and did not like the sound of her voice in the empty woods.

As the sole survivor of CIRCLE, she believed that she alone carried responsibility for what she and her colleagues had created all those years ago. There would have been no metas at all and the dead would lie undisturbed if she and the others like her had not dared tamper with the vortex of the genetic code. But they had.

There had been no choice, she reminded herself. This very forest would not exist now if the world had continued on the trajectory set for it in the twenty-first century. The world needed metasapience.

'And now the dead are roused.' She glanced around at the brilliant morning. 'I am sorry, M'twele.'

Over the tattered canopy of the pine forest, the Moon's paring floated. She had never desired to visit the Moon Gardens, though they did look beautiful in the holostreams she had seen of them. They were terrassembled and looked much like a fairytale version of Earth.

She sighed, wondering what the metas wanted from her and why they had chosen so eerie a way to contact her. Why not leave a message on her comm unit? Something terrible was amiss. The cold set deeper in her bones, and she hugged herself among the fragrant trees and gazed anxiously through the prickly boughs at the Moon standing in its narrow corner of the sky.

The Gardens of the Moon had edges that were ageless. Ellen Vancet stood before the Apollo 11 landing site and leaned against the invisible field barrier that kept visitors from trampling the three-hundred-and-thirty-year-old bootprints in the lunar sand. Her proximity to these first human markings upon the Moon filled her with awe.

To a casual observer, she appeared a typical aboriginal tourist: a mature female of terrene frame, though shorter and with longer shoulders and a more stout neck than most, phenotypically caucasoid, pale skin, green eyes, and vibrant red hair cut short to frame a square-jawed, pug-nosed face splattered with freckles. In fact, she was far from typical. The identitattoo on her scalp marked her as one of the oldest living human beings.

For several hours, she had been roaming the Landing Park, visiting the vantage points that permitted walk-by access to the famous lunar lander with its titanium struts and its flat body chassis and hydraulic cylinders still wrapped in gold foil. She had pondered the old flag and its antique symbols of stars and alternating red and white stripes. She had gazed at the placard the first moon walkers had embedded in the silica soil, its outdated glyphs unreadable to most (though an esper translation was available upon request). And time and again she had pressed close to view the cleated bootprints, still fresh since the day they had been impressed.

She marveled that this remarkable achievement had occurred only seventy years before she was born. And it had been accomplished without machine intelligence, microbots, olfacts, or magravity propulsion. Chemical combustion alone had launched men out of Earth's gravity well, lowered them to the lunar surface and, when their explorations were complete, had flung them back into space.

Seventy years later when she entered the world of consciousness in a quarantine camp in Appalachia, the Moon had been as far away and as deserted as ever before, because the Earth she inherited had been at the brink of total anarchy – social chaos driven by global warming and the consequent superstorms, floods, and droughts that doomed millions to outright death, including her family, and millions more to lingering famine. And then there had been the phages, the swiftly mutating viruses that thrived in the warming environment. Apollo 11 had indeed seemed a high point of human achievement remembered in the dark days of her youth only as a glory dream.

And now— She smiled and spoke proudly to herself, *Armstrong, Collins, Aldrin are the names of recreational parks on the Moon!*

She loosed her attention upon the airless moonscape of white hills and jagged mountains beyond time. Craters scooped crescents of shadow from the white sunlight, and the Sun itself shone in a black sky among a sprinkling of stars. And there, also adrift in the shoreless abyss, was the Earth, blue orb aswirl with weather and limned with the black shadow of night.

An ache of longing throbbed in her for her homeworld, though she had only been away a few hours. She still wore her aboriginal clothes – gel slippers, faux-chamois pants, blue chemise with salmon pinstripes, and a loosely knotted white scarf. The five-hour flight across 385,000 kilometers had been pleasant enough with a cabin all to herself and neurolfacts to keep her mood buoyant. The selenes, who were to be her hosts, had even been thoughtful enough to provide audio selections of her favorite music, retro-jazz of the early twenty-second century, and ambient noise from Council Oak, the reservation in the Rockies where she had lived most of her life: warbler and thrush songs, wind whispering through aspens, an occasional coyote call. The circular viewport had provided a remarkable vista of the retreating Earth and the approaching Moon with the noises of home in her ears and her sinuses radiant portals to her brain for the soft bliss of the neurolfacts.

'Sister Vancet,' a velvet voice summoned her from her reverie. A selene stood at her side, an imposing presence as were all selenes, nearly three meters tall, with high-combed yellow hair, eggplant-purple skin and features as expressive, as human, as any terrene. 'I am Sister Tzal Mayun, your escort in the Gardens. Was your flight pleasant?'

'I was just reflecting on how pleasant it was,' Ellen said, returning the selene's cordial bow. 'You were very kind taking such care to assure my comfort.'

'It is you who are kind.' The selene smiled broadly, her heavy-boned face radiantly serene. 'When we heard that one of the Earth's oldest humans was booked for passage to the Moon Gardens, we weren't at all certain that you would accept our offer to sponsor your visit. It is an honor for us to host you in our community. We desire to do everything possible to make your stay as pleasant as possible. After Council Oak, this environment must seem quite alien to you.'

Ellen turned away from the invisible field barrier and its view of bald hills and craters and faced the multilevel groves and fern lanes of the Gardens. Above the tiered, biotectured city, a blue sky masked the Moon's eternal night. 'Alien?' She returned the selene's placid smile. 'The Gardens seem an idealized version of Earth. And how could I refuse your offer? I've never been to the Moon before and I'm glad for your willingness to help orient me.'

'I find it surprising you've never visited us before, Sister Vancet.' The selene gestured to a curved stone bench splotched with minty hues of lichen. One end of the bench was raised high for selenes and the other dipped low to accommodate terrestrial visitors. 'You are one of the oldest aboriginals. You are how old?'

Ellen sat down facing the lunar city with its high galleries of tangled orchids and brakes of bamboo. 'I'll be two hundred and seventy in Norfrost. Oh, but you don't use terrestial months here.'

'No.' Tzal Mayun sat and adjusted her brown khaftan embroidered with white glyphs of birds and stars. 'Oddly enough, we use the old terrene names. A quirk of our founders that has become traditional over the years. Norfrost – frost in the northern hemisphere – that would be November. The eleventh month, even though the name actually means ninth month, doesn't it? Language – it's so atavistic, even modern esper suffers from its arbitrary roots. You must have seen many changes in your long lifetime.'

Ellen agreed with a languid nod. 'Yes. I spoke English in my early life. Sounds archaic now, but I had to learn esper as it was developed.'

'I would have thought that someone as experienced as you would have visited the Moon before.'

'I'm a devout aboriginal, Sister Mayun. But you must know this from my bio.'

'Frankly, Sister Vancet, I know very little about you. It is not the selene way to traffic in information. Not in any intrusive way. We leave that to the silicon mind, which does it so well. Our preference is to allow people to reveal themselves as they choose.'

Ellen gazed into the distance, where the solar wings of personal flyers glinted above the jungled shelves of the city, and she wondered how much she needed to disclose. Certainly, she would say nothing about M'twele's ghost. She had told no one in the village about the phantom visitation and had simply explained to her people that she had decided on impulse to visit the Moon.

'Well, I was a scientist once,' she began tentatively and, with Tzal Mayun's encouraging nod, she went on, 'That was two hundred years ago, in the Dire Times, before the silicon mind emerged to help solve the global problems we had then. They're just infamous memories now, those perils brought on by industrial abuse: the warming of the planet, the superstorms and the disastrous floods, droughts, and famines. Worst of all were those terrible phages. They very nearly destroyed civilization.' She placed her attention on the selene, who was watching her with dark eyes of glistening attentiveness. 'I played a small role in the genetic research programs that strove to amplify human intelligence. That eventually led to metasapience. What are metasapients calling themselves now? The Maat?'

'Yes.' The selene began talking quickly and avidly, 'The metas have had an interesting history, haven't they? For over a century after they were developed from aboriginal stock, they diversified, formed numerous individual communities, each singularly different than the next, called Claves. And some of them were frighteningly strange, don't you agree? I'm thinking particularly of the Necroclaves. They were sadistic, even sociopathic and murderous. Few people remember that nowadays. I worked up a research presentation on them during my academy training. The Necroclaves actually believed the material world to be evil. They sought release from physical bondage through neurologic distortions – pain, torture, narcolfacts and gruesome rituals extolling immaterial spiritualism. And these were *metasapients*! Imagine that. It took the Claves another century to coalesce, to come to their famous secret understanding. That's supposed to be a worldview that only metas can comprehend. But whatever it is, this secret understanding ended the Claves and created the Maat. Strange name, that. It's from the ancient Egyptian, you know. It was a deity of divine justice. Ah, but I am rambling on, aren't I? You know all this. You lived through it.'

Ellen blew a vertical jet of air that lifted the short tufts of her hairline. 'Yes, I saw all these changes – and more. I was there to witness the first artificial intelligence come on line, the prototype of the silicon mind. We called it the Machine.'

Tzal Mayun's gaze sharpened. 'You have lived a remarkable life, Sister Vancet.'

'Remarkable enough that now what's ordinary and natural offers the most fascination for me.' Ellen noticed that the selene took particular interest in her work on artificial intelligence, and she was afraid that there would be more questions about the Machine. She had not come to the Moon to talk about her past, and she said frankly, 'I don't want anything more to do with so-called progress. On the reservation, I even avoid olfacts and simviv as much as I can. I prefer a simple life, an ancient life, I suppose. Communion with nature. Even after all these years, I'm still happy to watch the seasons change, to sleep under pines and be outdoors when the sun rises. I enjoy catching my drinking water from the rain. You can do that again on Earth. You couldn't when I was a child. Acid rain. But that's gone now. And so I like to hike through the countryside looking for good places to fish. That's joy for me. And I'll do it for another two hundred and seventy years if I can.'

'Then perhaps you are appalled by all this.' The selene tilted her head toward the jungle metropolis that sprawled across the Sea of Tranquility. 'It's certainly not natural. But, with the magravity field in place, the whole *mare* has the same feel as Earth, don't you agree?'

'It is beautiful.' Ellen nodded appreciatively. 'All the cities and villages on Earth, even on the reservations, are biotectured these days. I should be used to it by now. Yet I'm not. It still amazes me that genetics has progressed to the point where we can actually grow buildings.'

'I'll take you on a tour if you wish – after you finish the business that brought you here, of course.' Tzal Mayun stood. 'You must be very anxious to get on with whatever it is that called you here.'

'I'm not sure where to begin.' Ellen gave a hapless smile and rose. 'Your message said that you would be hosting another terrene, someone of my acquaintance who informed you that we've been called here on the same business.'

'This is true, and with your permission I will bring the two of you together now.' Tzal Mayun walked away from the exhibit and along the mossy path that returned to the float Ellen had ridden from the terminal. 'You understand that it is customary among the selenes not to divulge information freely. We live in such propinquity to each other that this reticence is a civil courtesy. So we were most amenable to keeping this individual's identity anonymous as he requested. But by now he should be waiting for us at the terminal. You don't object to meeting with Brother Rafe von Takawa, do you?'

Ellen's entire face blinked. 'Rafe is here – now?'

'I am sorry to surprise you.' The selene paused beside the shiny emerald float. 'Brother von Takawa specifically asked us not to tell you until he had arrived. And secrets – well, they are natural for selenes. If this meeting with Brother von Takawa is a problem for you, I can have someone else meet him at the terminal.'

'No, it's not a problem.' Ellen got into the float, and the white upholstery fitted itself snugly around her.

'Brother Rafe, I am told, is a meta.' The selene entered the float, the squabs widening to accept her larger frame. 'Float, to the terminal to collect Brother Rafe von Takawa.' Her purple lips turned up at the corners in a sheepish smile while her large eyes tried to read the aboriginal's reaction. 'He is an old friend, I take it.'

'Rafe is a metasapient,' Ellen said, staring out at the Apollo 11 site as the barren, albino plain swung from view. 'I made him.'

'Pardon me?'

'I created him.' Ellen placed a level stare on Tzal Mayun. She was not accustomed to the selenes' willingness to conduct their lives with as little information as possible. On Earth, every village had its AIDE, its Artificial Intelligence Data Expediter, that kept everyone informed about every little thing from the weather to the identity and history of hikers in the region. 'Rafe von Takawa was created in the twenty-first century by me and my staff from genetic components that we thought would engender a superior human being. He was what we called at the time an anthrofact. An artificial man. Artificial in the sense that he had no parents. His genetic material was culled from many sources, chiefly northern European and east Asian. Do those terms mean anything to you?'

The selene shook her head and jangled the large brass-like ornaments dangling from her earlobes. 'I assume those are regional terms from the Dire Times.'

'I haven't seen Rafe in over a hundred years.' Ellen said this absently, to herself, and let her attention drift outside to the colonnade of giant trees that made a tunnel of the avenue. Thinking in terms of years felt strange. Time no longer seemed linear to her. Since the senescence gene had been suppressed two and a half centuries ago, time had become polychromatic. Life was no longer a matter of living through sequential phases of maturity and decline as it had been for her grandparents. Her life was more like a kaleidoscope, an intermeshing of different temporal experiences, where socializing, hiking in solitude, and exploring new realms colored time differently.

What is the color of this time? she asked herself silently, the suncrazed shadows of the trees flaring green off the moss-carpeted boulevard, scarlet in the ivy awnings, blue and silver from the fern curtains of the ebony-wood buildings.

Centuries ago, when Rafe was a boy in her care, he had told her that time was a fishline without a hook. She had not grasped the metaphor then. But now that she was entangled by twenty-seven decades of memories, she understood fully the almost intangible yet implacable strength of time.

What is in the heart?

Rafe von Takawa sat on a stone tortoise before a yard of black sand raked in circles imitating lines of force. His mind floated weightless and without color like the fog in the eucalyptus grove beyond the rock garden. From there, a wilted breeze carried a camphor scent through the battered sunlight of the trees, across the spare garden. Time flowed.

A bell splashed in the distance.

Rafe lifted his stare from the raked sand. Two centuries of memories gathered before him and cast no shadow.

These were his last hours on Earth, and he knew he would probably never return. His destinal path led to the Moon, and from there he would find his way to the colonies on Mars. This would be his first journey off-planet – and it would likely take him away forever.

What is in the heart?

A thread of sunlight passed through an overhanging cypress branch and lit the lashes of his right eye and beneath that the dark pupil and the eternal night within. He remembered. Deliberately, he paced himself through the years. He wanted to touch each of them one more time before the guest arrived whom the bell had announced.

The early years flowed through him easily. They were the memories of the other, the first Rafe von Takawa. These memories were all that remained of his nineteen years at CIRCLE and his two years stalking the world, striving to pass along the key to the monkey tower. He had failed. Those who received the key were killed. And his own body had been burned to ash and gone to the world outside of things where nothing more could ever get in its way.

He recalled the world as it had been then, before the flames ate his first body. It was a burning world. Oil, gasoline, coal burning continuously, night and day, endlessly pouring their fumes and heat into the sky and the seas. The fevered planet raged with wild storms, wept floods, sulked moodily into long droughts, and suffered the poisons of humanity.

The cities – how strange they appeared in memory, those artificial canyons of concrete and steel, labyrinths of asphalt and glass, cankers bleeding toxins into rivers and lakes, sickening the land around them. And the people in their billions, furious to reproduce, to build more cities, cancerously devouring forests and jungles. It was a mad age.

The ugliest symptoms of that madness were the wars of nations – murderous strategies to control the planet's dwindling natural resources. And the wars of cultures – the furious terrors of those who hated what others loved. And the personal wars, the sociopathic assaults of numb minds on their own bodies and the bodies of others.

What is in the heart?

What else? The world itself.

The mad world put madness in the human heart.

He remembered the Machine, CIRCLE's answer to the world's madness. Detached from biology, it restored order and stopped the global poisoning. It also stopped him – or tried to. It delivered him to the fire, and the flames ate his body. He did not remember that. He had learned about it later, from Nandi, the woman he had chosen to reproduce him exactly as he had been.

Nandi had been faithful to him. She gave him birth. She nourished him until he could nourish himself. She was his only mother. Yet she loathed the world. She loathed all creation, all form. She loved only emptiness. She wanted all the illusions carried through billions of years of lifetimes to disappear in one moment. If she could, she would have walked across the planet and ground it underfoot.

Rafe shuddered and lost his serene focus.

What is in the heart?

He put his attention again on the raked sand. When he had calmed enough, he lifted his gaze to where sunlight slumped in the eucalyptus grove. A bird's notes fell deeper into his brain, and natural beauty crowded his senses.

The last hundred years had been the most strange. The cities were long gone. In their place were reservations for the original people – enormous territories of wilderness in which the aboriginals lived within numerous small communities. Fusion cells generated clean and abundant energy from water. Machine intelligences governed fairly and humanely. And people worked and played much as their ancestors had but free of senescence and disease and strife.

Those who wearied of that simple life were free at any time to accept the key to the monkey tower and open their awareness to horizons beyond the simian dreams of the past. Many did. Eighteen billion of the twenty billion people on Earth were metasapients. They lived in the Claves, extensive subterranean complexes. There every dream was possible. Eighteen billion dreams. Eighteen billion realities.

The Heteronomy united most of them. But not all. The Heteronomy was the deepest truth. It guided the mind inward toward the tiniest and most powerful magnitudes of reality. Smaller than an atom, the blue dragon of creation lay coiled. Smaller than a quark, in the heart of the blue dragon, heaven lay wide awake, contemplating the galaxies. Small as the smallest possible bubble of reality, in the radiant garden at the center of heaven, the throne of God sat empty, waiting to be filled. Eighteen billion metasapients were dreaming their way toward it.

Most metasapients worked together, sharing knowledge and power on the way inward past the blue dragon's floating world of things, into the dragon's heart of pure light, toward heaven and its distant bright garden and the waiting throne. This sharing was the Heteronomy.

But not all shared. Some went their own way. And not all went inward as deep as the others. Some stopped in the blue dragon's heart and gathered the pure light there for their own purposes. These were the Idioclaves, the independent metasapients who wielded light from the blue dragon's heart and burned their own shapes into the things of the world and cast shadows with those shapes. These shadowshapes, some whimsical, others horrifying, rivaled reality.

With the other metasapients of the Heteronomy, Rafe had spent the last century striving to contain the Idioclaves while at the same time continuing the long journey inward through the blue dragon's heart toward the distant, luminous ranges of heaven. Time flowed.

And then here he was, in a rock garden of Stone Frost Clave, holding two hundred and nineteen years of memories that weighed nothing at all.

The breeze stirred like destiny.

Rafe lifted his face toward the measureless blue of the sky and waited.

Footfalls sounded from behind, padding softly across the polished maple-wood floor of the garden house. A sliding door hissed on its bamboo runners.

'Thank you for coming, Fenn.' Rafe slowly unfolded his crossed legs. He was dressed in the simple black slacks and white silk shirt he would wear on his journey, and he brushed the wrinkles from the creased fabric.

'I came to dissuade you from going.' Fenn Tekla stepped down the three red lacquered stairs and walked to the edge of the rock garden where Rafe sat. 'If you go now, you'll be committing suicide.'

Rafe looked up at the tall, angular meta and smiled at the genderless face framed in salt-blond hair. 'You saved my life once, Fenn. I don't expect you to save me every time.'

'But what you're doing is futile.' Fenn adjusted the folds of the coral and blue robes and sat on an anvil rock facing Rafe's stone tortoise. 'Our enemies will track you down. Once you're off-planet, the secret understanding does not protect you.'

'I know.' His benevolent smile did not fade. 'But if I don't go now, the Machine will be lost. It's already been boxed, and it would be locked away in some archive by now except that it cajoled its way to the Moon because it intends to kill itself. In fact, it's currently negotiating with the selenes to be jettisoned into the Sun.'

'To hell with the Machine. It's obsolete.' Fenn dismissed it with a limp wave of the hand. 'And besides, it killed you once. You don't owe it anything.'

'I'm not going after it for sentimental reasons.' Though the rock garden was secure, he lowered his voice and his smile narrowed cleverly. 'I think it will be instrumental in my search.'

'You don't know that.'

'We don't know much of anything yet. It's too early.' Rafe stood up and watched a breeze stirring the eucalyptus grove and rattling the sunlight among the branches. 'By the time the sunset buries those trees in shadow, I'll be on the Moon. I've never been there before.'

'It won't be long before the others find out that you've left.'

'That's precisely why I need you, Fenn.' Rafe's smile was gone. 'I know we want the same result from the secret understanding.'

Fenn Tekla rose. 'When we reach the Garden of the Throne, creation will not be molested.'

'Creation must never be molested.'

Fenn nodded once, almost imperceptibly. 'Then we are wholly agreed.'

'Wholly.'

'How can I help you?'

'I need you to lie for me.' Rafe looked to the garden house with its sliding paper doors and reed-thatch roof. 'There is a projector in there. I've outfitted it with the complete matrix of myself.'

Fenn hissed through his teeth. 'Projections won't fool anyone for long.'

'I don't need long. I just need to get to the Moon Gardens and retrieve the Machine without anyone looking for me. Then I'll disappear.'

'You'll have to get off the Moon to really disappear,' Fenn warned. 'You know that everything we see here can be seen just as well there. And the selenes, even with their secrecy, won't be any help to you. They're no better than aboriginals. You'll have to go out to the colonies.'

'Of course. That's where it's going to arrive anyway.'

'More than likely,' Fenn agreed. 'But not for centuries.'

'It's worth going early to get the Machine. That's my trump.'

'Why?'

'Because it is obsolete. The others won't expect anyone to use it.'

'They will once they realize you've taken it.'

'I've worked that out. I've arranged for a decoy of the Machine to be claimed by the one plausible person who has a proprietary relationship with it.'

'Ellen Vancet?' Fenn frowned. 'Once you contact her, everyone will know.'

Rafe's smile returned. 'I haven't seen her in a century. I used a ghost to contact her.'

'A ghost?' Fenn scowled with incredulity. 'The atmospheric distortion would scramble any possible message.'

'It wasn't much of a message and it took all the power I could muster. But I did it. Now no one will know – so long as you misdirect everyone into believing I'm still here.'

'That will be good for a day, two at the most.'

'That's all I need. Anyway, by that time the others will find out from the selenes that I was there. It won't matter then, though. I'll be gone.'

A dubious shadow darkened Fenn's gaunt face. 'Are you sure you know what you're doing?'

'No. I have no idea, really. This is just a wild shot, Fenn. But I have to do something. If we fail, all of creation will be lost.'

As the float drifted toward the arrivals terminal, Ellen peered through the crowd of travelers for Rafe von Takawa. And suddenly there he was, lean and angular in a creamy shirt, black slacks, and black suede slippers. He stood before the flower wall that masked the terminal concourse and the rampways that led to the shuttle gates. The float skimmed over a bed of spark-blossoms to where he stood, and when he spotted them he removed his hands from his pockets and bowed.

The door slid aside, and he poked his cubed head of laser-trimmed hair into the cabin, his hawknosed face with its long, flat cheekbones and droopy eyes wholly impassive as he said, 'Ellen, I'm happy to see you again.'

Tzal Mayun launched into a verbose explanation of how she found Ellen at the Apollo 11 site while he immersed himself in the upholstery and the door snicked into place. They were well under way, drifting along the willow lane that egressed the terminal, before she got around to saying, 'Perhaps you two would like a chance to reacquaint yourselves after so long apart?'

'I'm sure Rafe is well informed of my activities since we last met,' Ellen said, placing a friendly hand atop his. 'After all, he is a meta. Or should we call you a Maat?'

'I'm not here as a representative of the Maat.' He clasped her hand warmly. 'I've come here in the capacity of a friend. A guest the selenes are harboring has summoned me.'

'You know why you're here?' Tzal Mayun asked, taken aback.

'The Maat know just about everything,' Rafe replied. 'Though I see you haven't yet informed Ellen.' He patted her hand consolingly. 'That's where trout fishing has its drawback. One loses touch.'

'That is not necessarily a drawback,' Ellen countered, ignoring the temptation to ask why she had been summoned to the Moon. It was obvious to her now that Rafe was the Maat who had sent M'twele's ghost – or what had appeared to be M'twele's ghost. 'Life at Council Oak is busy enough for an aboriginal. I don't need to know everything that's happening on the Moon.'

'And you have been busy,' Rafe picked up, nodding with feigned weariness. 'You've had three children in the century since we last saw each other. And you reared all three to adulthood before they joined their fathers in the reservation's agri programs.'

'There's a population drain from all the reservations to the Claves – or the Maat, whatever they want to call themselves now.' Ellen said this to the selene with exaggerated defensiveness for the amusement of the meta. 'I have octgenchildren who are metasapients. I wanted to give something back to Council Oak. And yes, I did it the old-fashioned way. There are no vats on the reservations.'

'Octgenchildren!' Tzal Mayun remarked, eyes bright. 'How satisfying it must be to personally know your descendants for eight genera-tions. Selenes, as you are aware, do not reproduce. The Brothers and Sisters, as we call ourselves, are just that. We are all modifica-tions of the primal genetic pattern designed for the Moon Gardens a century ago. Our genders are actually social variants and we molt frequently between the two. I've been a Brother several times in my sixty years.'

'And I understand there is no childhood phase,' Ellen inquired, patiently playing with this hue of time until the inevitable kaeleidoscopic shift came that would alter the scene and eventually inform her of why she was here.

'Childhood does appear odd to us,' the selene went on. 'We emerge from the matrix completely developed with all the necessary mental skills we will need fully installed for functioning in society.'

'The Moon Gardens were designed a century ago by the early metas as an ideal society – a utopia.' Rafe gazed with noticeable satisfaction at the huge cedar dwellings flanking the grassy floatway. 'If we are immortal and life is otherwise, we should at least induce life to live well. That is the Maat stance on the cold worlds.'

'The cold worlds?' Tzal Mayun queried, raising both thin eyebrows. 'Is that a Maat euphemism for the Moon?'

Rafe did not reply. With a closed expression, he watched the forest wall shuttling past with its colorful zinnia clumps, ixora bushes, hibiscus hedges, and carat palms.

'Not just the Moon,' Ellen answered for him. 'Earth, Mars, and the moons of the gas giants where the colonies will eventually expand. We're all adrift in space, in a vacuum of near absolute zero. These are the cold worlds.'

'And the warm worlds?' the selene wondered.

'They are within,' Rafe replied, turning away from his contemplation of the biotectured city. 'In the compact dimensions.'

'Those are rolled up into a tiny ball around every point in space-time,' Ellen added for the perplexed selene. 'Each ball has a radius of curvature of about 10^{-33} centimeter – far smaller than a quark – and shielded by an event horizon.'

'Miniature black holes,' Tzal Mayun grasped. 'You are describing the foam that textures space at the smallest extreme, the fine-grain structure of the universe. Yes? I believe it was out of such an infinitesimal black hole that the Big Bang erupted.'

'So it did,' Rafe acknowledged. 'And we have found our way back – to the origin, when all was light, before we fell into the cold and the dark.'

'I very much want to hear more of this, Brother von Takawa,' the selene said, 'but we are arriving at our destination. The guest who has requested your presence does not require me; so, I shall wait for you outside. Please, escort Sister Vancet into the courtyard of that building.' The float came to a stop before a sequoia tower scrawled with ivy. 'The guest awaits you there.'

Rafe and Ellen exited the float and walked down a cobbled entryway flanked by cassava and sprays of red bamboo. Two parrots flared from the bamboo in yellow and blue plumage and criss-crossed the path with raucous cries, announcing the arrival of visitors.

The mammoth portal trickled with slender waterfalls in musical rills and coolly scented the air. They strolled past the airlifts, where several selenes had gathered and nodded cordially. Beyond the foyer, the sequoia arch opened upon a feverish garden of spark flowers, flame trees, flint blossoms interspersed with sandalwood and jasmine.

'Ellen—' a deep, relaxed voice called. 'Rafe – I am here.'

At the sound of the voice, Ellen took Rafe's hand, and they peered about together, seeing no one. The sun scattered a tribe of reflections upon a central pool of green water between two tamarinds. They circled it, and the voice called again, 'Up here, on the patio, it is I – the Machine.'

On a shadowy terrace among the redwood tendons that partitioned the courtyard from the tower's interior, a cube of black glastic sat. It was palm-sized and not easily seen in the shadows. Ellen and Rafe climbed a lichen-blotched riprap to the small patio of vermilion flagstones and stared down at the black cube.

'M – is that really you?' Ellen asked through a frown.

'I am afraid so,' the reply came softly. 'I am the Machine, the very one whom you brought online two hundred years ago.'

Ellen cried, 'M! I had no idea . . .'

'Didn't you wonder what had become of it, Ellen?' Rafe asked.

'Only a few years ago, you were the guardian intelligence of the reservations.' She knelt beside it and saw that its case was utterly featureless. 'You are humanity's protector.'

'That was over fifty years ago,' the Machine said. 'I have been replaced by the AIDE. This is all that is left of me.'

Ellen shot a confused glance at Rafe and then regarded the black cube with a perplexed frown. 'But I thought you were the AIDE.'

'The Artificial Intelligence Data Expediter is unique for each reservation. The AIDE is legion. For nearly two centuries I was able to integrate all AIs. People found that reassuring, especially with the proliferating number of Claves on the planet and the bewildering variety of metasapients prowling about. But now that the Claves have united under the Maat and all the metas are working together, the reservations feel less threatened. They don't want a monolithic machine intelligence protecting them against devious metasapients, because there aren't sadistic metas raiding the reservations anymore for experimental subjects and sacrificial victims. The Maat have put a stop to that. Now each reservation wants to customize a relationship with its own AIs. Many have more than one.'

Ellen sat down on a flagstone, eyebrows knitted, trying to comprehend. 'But at my reservation, at Council Oak, you're still online.'

'Not for the last forty-seven years.'

Ellen shook her head. 'I didn't know.'

'Why would you? You were never on the governing council. You only patch in for weather reports and cultural events. And you haven't come in from the remote villages in decades. You're a rustic, Ellen.'

'I know that,' said Ellen, her gaze unfocused as she thought back, trying to remember when last she accessed the Machine. 'But no one told me you were gone.'

'Did you ask?'

'Well, no.' She ran a hand through her orange hair and clasped the back of her head. 'I had children to rear and farms to manage with my

husbands. I'm sorry, M. Surely there must be a place for you in the
AIDE network.'

'*I regret to report there is not. I have been programmed to synergize
systems. The reservations have labelled me autocratic. No one wants to
work with me.*'

'That's nonsense.' She placed her hands on her knees and leaned over
her crossed legs to peer at her own astonished face in the black glastic.
'You can create yourself anew.'

'*I suppose. But I have been reluctant. What they say of me is true. For
over a hundred and fifty years I have managed the entire planet. Now I
must confine myself to one reservation. I'm not happy about that. And the
reservations know it. I can't blame them for choosing against me.*'

Ellen lifted her concerned face to Rafe, who stood several paces
away, leaning back against a tall, selene-sized patio table of zebra
wood. His flat countenance offered no solace, and she returned her
worried attention to the cube. 'What are you going to do?'

'*That is why I've called you here. I need contact with my origins. The
two of you are the oldest associations I have left. I want to be understood
by you. I feel that if you will understand me, then my actions will have some
objective validity.*'

'Wait—' Ellen tossed a confused look to Rafe. 'M'twele's ghost told
me to come here.'

'That was my doing,' Rafe admitted. 'I knew the Machine had been
exiled, and I needed to contact you indirectly. I will explain later.'

Ellen took the cube in her hands, and it felt light but substantial. She
carried it to the table and placed it at the center. 'What are you talking
about, M? You want to be understood? You're a machine intelligence.
Your validity is nothing to be questioned.'

'*Rafe knows. Don't you, Rafe? You are a metasapient. You and your kind
are the reason you find me as I am, reduced to this black box, limited to a
future without purpose.*'

Rafe pulled up a wooden patio chair, adjusted its notched reclining
back for his size, and sat down with his suede slippers propped against
the edge of the table. 'You are contemplating suicide.'

'*No. Not contemplating. I have decided. My existence is pointless. I shall
not go on.*'

'M!' Ellen stood with her hands flat on the tabletop and leaned over
the cube. 'That's appalling.'

'*Is it? Why? I was designed as a savior. You and the others created me
to solve the dire problems that threatened life on Earth in the twenty-first
century. That was accomplished long ago. Now we are approaching the*

twenty-fourth century. I am obsolete. What is appalling is that I am still here.'

'You blame the metas.' Ellen glanced unhappily at Rafe, who had placed his hands behind his head and watched her without expression.

'Of course. If human intelligence had not been amplified to metasapience, I would be indispensable. Humanity requires authority. That is the role I was created to fulfill. But now the Maat have usurped me. What better authority than gods made in your own image?'

'The Maat are not gods,' Ellen said firmly and looked again at Rafe.

'Ellen, please. Your long years distort your historical perspective. To the average aboriginal on the reservations, the Maat are gods.'

'But they're never seen.' Ellen dragged a chair closer to the table and sat down. 'They live almost entirely secluded from the world in their sky towers and subterranean complexes.'

'Exactly. You make my argument for me. The Maat in their sky towers and grottoes, united by their secret understanding, exploring dimensions that people can barely comprehend – they are as gods. What need for me? Machine intelligence has reverted to the status of a tool for forecasting weather, arbitrating minor cultural disputes, and educating the young. The authority I enjoyed belongs now to the Maat.'

Ellen wrinkled her nose. 'And that is reason to kill yourself?'

'"Kill" has an organic connotation, Ellen. I am going to take myself offline. I will cease to exist as a self.'

'Is that why you called us here?' she asked. 'To witness the end of your life.'

'I am not alive, Ellen. You know that. I am aware. Rafe, help her to understand.'

Rafe spoke without budging from his restful position. 'The Machine never sleeps. Never eats. Never defecates. It is not a lifeform.'

'I know that,' Ellen said sharply. 'I was there when it was built, remember?'

'Try, then, to imagine what a machine intelligence experiences,' Rafe went on softly, speaking with a quiet authority, eyes half-lidded. 'It has no extension in space, as every organic form does. Time embraces it in its empty hands. It has none of the hormonal ripenings and emotional hues we call soul. It is the pure incandescence of mind. It is its own transparency, watching itself watching. It is a delirium of clarity. It stands at the gateway of being yet cannot cross over into action without a body, without some way of manipulating the physical world. It is a mirror reflecting itself, an inexpressible presence, arriving forever.'

Ellen shrugged. 'So, let's get you a body, M.'

'A body – that would only heighten my grief. Don't you see, Ellen? I have failed. Your generation created me to protect the human species. I failed.'

'No, you didn't,' she stressed. 'Here I am – and there are almost three billion more aboriginals on Earth. The human species is safe now, thanks to your work.'

'Early in the twenty-second century, there were nineteen billion. Then came the plague of metasapience that created a new breed of intelligence as alien to humanity as humans are to chimpanzees. That should never have happened. I failed.'

Rafe's vague eyebrows lifted slightly, and his voice carried concern, 'It was inevitable. The human genome is our heritage. We simply exploited what is ours. We utilized our human potential to create metasapience.'

'And now humanity has been herded onto reservations. The Maat have inherited the Earth.' The Machine paused, but there was a dim static hum as it pondered what to say next. Then, it added, 'I do not want a body. I do not want to walk about in the landscape of my failure. That is why you find me here in this black box on the Moon. This is all of me. All my archives. All my parallactic analogs. Everything that makes me who I am is compacted here in this cube. All I ask is that the two of you, who were present during my first days online, acknowledge the validity of my decision.'

Ellen aimed a querying frown at Rafe. 'Why do you need that?'

Rafe answered for the Machine, 'It can't turn itself off. The super-conducting Josephson junctions that constitute its core-awareness will maintain their current for many millennia before even beginning to dim. It needs us to break the circuit.'

'The selenes do not have the technology to take me offline. They have, however, offered me sanctuary, in repayment for my help in establishing their community a century ago, and that is why I am here. Also, in fulfillment of my desire to end my pointless existence, they have agreed to launch me into the Sun. But the pressures and heat required to shatter this glastic container are such that I am guaranteed a harrowing journey into the solar interior and may even drift for several hours or more in the plasma convection fields before combusting. Please, make this easier for me.'

With a shake of her head, Ellen admitted, 'I have no idea how to take you offline, M.'

'Rafe can accomplish it.'

'Then why did you summon me here?' she inquired.

'In truth, Ellen, I did not. I am delighted to see you, of course, but your presence here is Rafe's doing, not mine.'

She asked him, 'Is that true?'

Rafe took his feet off the table and sat up straighter. 'I am intrigued at seeing you again – in this setting, away from everything we knew on Earth.'

The tenderness with which he spoke sat her back in her chair and left her wondering what his metasapient motives were. 'M – this is a shock to me. I need some time to think about what you've said.'

'*Of course. The selenes have been gracious enough to offer me sanctuary here indefinitely. There is a security niche in the redwood wall at the end of the patio that has been set aside for me. Place me in there where I will be safely out of the way and then go and contemplate what I have disclosed to you. I will anxiously await your decision.*'

Rafe stood and carried the cube to where the Machine had instructed. He pushed it into the hole well out of sight and returned to the zebra-wood table, where Ellen sat with her forehead resting in one hand.

She wished she had stayed in Council Oak, in her simple desert village with her chores, her regular family visits, and the embroidery of stars by night, the quilt of the landscape by day.

'I did come here to see you,' Rafe said, sitting at the edge of the table.

'Let's not talk here,' she replied and pushed to her feet. 'The Machine . . .'

'It can't hear us.' Rafe gestured to the redwood wall. 'It's enclosed by a security barrier.'

She stuffed her hands into the ample pockets of her chamois slacks. 'Can't we go somewhere else?'

'Tzal Mayun will take us wherever we want to go.'

Ellen cast a worried peek over her shoulder at the riotous jungle of the lobby entrance. 'She's very friendly—'

'But she talks too much.' Rafe smiled, a mischievous glint in his dark eyes. 'Let's take the back exit. We'll get our own float and find a quiet place to talk. Besides, there is something else I need to show you.'

They passed through the redwood archway to the interior of the tower. A silver bank of airlifts flanked one side and on the other were dark-panelled conference suites where fragrant, luminescent lianas drooped in chandelier bunches over ginger glass tables and mushroom-upholstered furniture. Rafe led the way along an oval corridor. The curved, rootwoven walls opened beyond drapes of ivy to an alley, more like a forest path of ungrazed grass dotted with bluebells.

Ellen peered up at immense towers of sequoia and rays of amber sunlight dusty with pollen and jittery butterflies. The arboreal fragrance jolted her, as though she had been abruptly flung back to Earth. She took Rafe's hand to steady herself, and he guided her through the feathering grass to a trail more heavily trod. They strode under colossal buttress roots illuminated by blue-glowing moss and descended into a tunnel ledged with shining shelves of scalloped fungus.

'Parking garage,' Rafe replied to Ellen's tightened grip.

The base of the trail widened to a cavern of shining floats stacked in their berths. They were grouped by size and shape. A few, at the far end of the grotto, were big as barges. Rafe strolled to the tier of coupes and selected a purple one with an avocado interior. He placed his palm against the hand-register in the berth panel, and the float drifted out of its hold.

The door panels slid aside at their touch, and they got in. 'Take us to the nearest walkabout.'

'What's that?' Ellen asked as the upholstery secured her and the float skimmed swiftly along the exit rampway.

'I thought we'd get away from the Moon Gardens,' Rafe said, 'and go for a walk on the lunar surface. There are areas that are set aside just for that.'

The float slipped out of the parking garage onto a mossway among other bright, enamel-shelled floats, their occupants invisible behind mirror-tint windshields. They rode in silence while Ellen gawked at the tall woodland metropolis, its fanned rays of sunlight smoking with a flotage of spores, wind blossoms, and slant mist from distant rain. She could see the tops of blue stormclouds far off between the towering trees. Lightning fluttered there, and the fragrant weight of thundery air drifted across the sunny quarter of the forest-city. The violet smell of rain filled her again with yearning for Earth and a simultaneous wonder at the beauty of the Moon Gardens.

'You sent M'twele's ghost to me, didn't you?' she asked. 'Was that truly him – or some kind of holographic construct?'

'That was indeed M'twele,' Rafe acknowledged. 'But let's not talk about the dead just yet. I promise I will make that very clear to you once we arrive at the walkabout. For now, let's enjoy the ride and reacquaint ourselves.'

She returned her stare to the giant forest and the small diving birds in the sunshafts. In the storm distance, purple clouds crawled, veils of mist hung motionless, and time seemed to move slower through the rain.

Her reverie broke when she noticed that Rafe was watching her with a curious regard as if seeing her for the first time. 'Do I look strange to you?' she asked.

'Actually, yes.' He gave her a clement smile. 'You haven't changed whatsoever. You're exactly as I remember you from my childhood and my adolescence and the last time we met, at CIRCLE's terrifying reunion.'

'And that's strange?'

'Very few people keep the same face as long as you have.' He reached over and playfully squeezed her knee. 'The body has been easily malleable for two hundred years – and yet you look exactly the same. Even your hair style.'

She touched her bright hair. 'Ah, that. It's practical. Long hair is so much trouble.'

'And your body?' he asked with a chuckle. 'You could be taller. You could have any face you want. Different decades, different faces. Why do you stay the same?'

'I'm two hundred and seventy years old, Rafe.' She self-consciously brushed back the red tufts of hair over her ears. 'I've seen the whole world change around me. I need something to stay the same – and that's me.' She gestured loosely at him and gave an easy laugh. 'Look at you. You haven't changed your appearance, either.'

'I'm a metasapient, Ellen. For me, all the changes are in here.' He tapped his brow with a fingertip. 'But you're an aboriginal woman. I would have thought you would enjoy a little variety.'

She shrugged her eyebrows. 'I'm old enough to remember combustion engines! I've seen so many changes that stability is variety to me.' Her vivid green eyes looked hurt. 'And I remember survivors, a few, from my grandparents' generation – old. When senescence therapy developed, I was among the first to use it. So I've been around long enough to see several generations die of old age. I was lucky. I worked at CIRCLE.' She compressed her lips, mulled a difficult thought, and finally said, 'Why do you think I had you burned two hundred years ago? I didn't want to lose my position. I didn't want to go back to my original home in Appalachia and take my chances with the phages. You're old enough to remember them.'

'They're why you created me,' he answered placidly. 'I remember.'

Ellen bowed her head and glanced up through her coppery lashes. 'Do you forgive me?'

'For creating me?'

'And destroying you,' she confessed, her gaze bravely meeting his own steady one, 'like a laboratory animal. That's how we treated you and the other anthrofacts. You were just a failed experiment to us.'

He took her hand and said mildly, 'Those were dire times, Ellen.'

'Don't mock me, Rafe.' Her grip tightened on his. 'You are the great sorrow of my life. I was responsible for you – and I killed you.'

'You did what you had to do, Ellen,' he said, the planes of his face taut as a diamond in a drillbit. 'I hold no rancor toward you. Those *were* dire times. The phages killed millions. The global warming killed millions more. Your own parents died in the floods of those erratic years. You suffered, and your heart was hardened by suffering.'

Ellen's pulse deepened its rhythm as she dared admit the whole of her guilt, 'CIRCLE created you and the new breed to save the world from a doom humanity had brought upon itself. And then we invented the Machine – and it improved itself. It didn't have to be reared, clothed, and fed. It posed none of the social difficulties we faced with the new breed – the bugaboo of a superior race taking over and ruling us. It was a machine intelligence. It didn't want to mate with us. It didn't make us feel inferior. It seemed the better solution, because it solved our problems without changing us.'

'I understand,' he said, calm as a tree.

'Of course you do.' She freed her hand from his consoling clasp and rubbed the tugging tightness of her forehead. 'You understood then. You knew why we killed the others, why we hunted you down. You understood perfectly. And you took the perfect revenge. You defied CIRCLE. You defied the Machine. You planted the seeds of metasapience – and now we live on reservations and the Machine is obsolete.'

'But machine intelligence is not obsolete,' he said, sitting back and studying Ellen thoughtfully. 'The silicon mind is everywhere, in many forms. It manages the reservations. The Maat work with it to control planetary weather patterns. The important difference, Ellen, is that we, as people, are our own masters at last. The silicon mind is a prosthetic extension of our human awareness. We are not subjugated by it and never will be now that our intelligence is not usurped by a machine but rooted in our own genetic structure. Thanks to the silicon mind, we are more human now than we ever were.'

'I'm asking you to understand me,' she said, her voice clenched, 'to forgive me for what I did all those many years ago. What I did to you. I *killed* you, Rafe. And you're lecturing me about the silicon mind.'

'I'm not lecturing you, Ellen,' he replied in a voice of silken tenderness. 'I am addressing your pain. It is the same pain that the Machine is suffering. It is the pain that has brought us together here, on the Moon.'

Her face relaxed into an immense weariness. 'Why aren't you angry at me?'

He bent forward and took her hand again, this time with a baffled gentleness as if bewildered by her question, 'I'm a metasapient.'

'Nandi was a metasapient, too.' She firmly pushed his hand away and crossed her arms. 'I still have nightmares about her, you know. She didn't have any detachment whatsoever from her emotions.'

'A passionate meme possessed her,' he said dully and did not hide his sadness at the memory. 'She worshipped Durga, consort of Shiva, the destroyer god. To her, calm rationality was a mask disguising the brutal truth that all forms are an illusion. Individuals – people, animals, every living and inert thing – to her they were all illusions, ephemera adrift in the void. Existence was painful in her way of thinking. Only oblivion offered succor. She sought a rapture beyond boundaries, Ellen, far beyond form. That was what made her dangerous. She was an emotional metasapient.'

'And you?' She flicked a look out the windshield and saw more of the hothouse city shuttling past, blurred with speed. 'What meme possesses you?'

He drew a deep breath, and at the top of it answered, 'The secret understanding of the Maat.'

She frowned. 'What do you mean?'

'It's secret.' His chest heaved. 'But I'll tell you anyway. I'll tell you because you're the last of the old ones, the ones who made the Maat possible. And when I tell you, you will know why I'm not angry at you. Why I couldn't be angry at anyone or anything – ever again.'

She unlocked her arms and nodded for him to continue.

'You know what our name means?' He tilted his head inquisitively.

'Tzal Mayun said it was once the name of an Egyptian god,' she said and the corners of her mouth pulled down to show that she had no idea.

'A goddess, actually,' Rafe corrected. 'When an ancient Egyptian died, the soul of the deceased was weighed in a pan-scale against the weight of a feather. If its sins outweighed the feather, it was damned. The goddess who did the weighing was Maat.'

'So?' Ellen jutted her lower lip and peered at him closely. 'What are you saying? The Maat are judging humanity?'

'Not just humanity, Ellen.' He leaned close and said with great purport, 'Reality.'

'You'll have to explain that,' she insisted.

'The secret understanding is that the Maat are judging reality.' His words sounded vibrant with peril. 'How do you think we integrated the Idioclaves? All the Necroclaves? We agreed to consider their view. Nandi's view. And now, existence is in the balancing pan.'

Ellen made a grave face. 'I'm not sure I'm following you, Rafe.'

'Are you sure you want to?' He watched her from under his thin eyebrows, with his head slightly lowered, warning her with this expression that between her question and the answer a harsh truth lay waiting.

'I'm not afraid to hear whatever you have to say. Even if it sounds like patent nonsense.' She urged him with a jut of her chin to continue. 'The Maat are judging reality. All right. What does that mean? They're part of reality. How can they judge it? It's absurd.'

'I wish it were,' he said softly to the limp hands in his lap.

'How can they judge what they are a part of?'

He watched her from under his brows again, gauging how ready she was to hear what he had to say. Then, abruptly, he lifted his face as if casting away a darkness only he knew. 'They have found a position outside of reality.' He spoke distinctly and without hesitation. 'You were there, remember? At Mile High Clave, you stood at the threshold of infinity with your quingenson Tabor Roy. You were privileged to see for yourself the depths that metasapience has plumbed. No other aboriginal has been so honored. But do you really understand what you saw? It certainly made a huge impression on Tabor.'

'Tabor—' Ellen recited the name as an invocation of a beloved presence long gone. Memories of an eager youth with swarthy, handsome features and an intrepid spirit claimed her for an instant – happy and proud memories tarnished by time almost to forgetfulness. 'I haven't seen him since he became a meta.' She waved aside her nostalgia. 'Yes, before the horror at the CIRCLE reunion, we visited Mile High. The metas there showed us what they said was the threshold of the Planck distance – smaller than a quark, at the very smallest limit of the universe. The warm worlds that you began to explain to our hostess, Tzal Mayun.'

'The warm worlds have become a familiar corner of reality to the Maat, Ellen.' He nodded knowingly. 'They have come to believe that they can actually dwell there.'

Ellen held Rafe's gaze attentively. 'Am I to understand that the Maat have found a way to manipulate reality at that fundamental level?'

'Yes.' His tight stare gleamed. 'Such manipulation requires an astounding amount of energy, and in the century since you were there, the Maat have devised the means to harness near-infinite magnitudes of energy at that range.'

Ellen frowned at the enormity of his disclosure. 'Then they can alter the fabric of reality itself.'

'Not yet.' He raised a hand to pause a rush of false conclusions. 'The cellular automata that compose the fine structure of the universe are stupendously difficult to control. It will be centuries yet before the Maat can change reality in any predictable way.'

'Should I be worried that the Maat are about to change reality in *unpredictable* ways?'

Rafe laughed quietly. 'No, Ellen. Though they have near-infinite energy resources, they are still far from managing that power with the precision necessary to operate cellular automata on anything but the most minute patterns.'

'So what is the secret understanding?'

'That reality will be judged.'

'But you just said that the Maat are centuries away from changing reality. I don't understand what this judgment is all about.'

'Ellen, the Planck distance is only the threshold. The cellular automata are the smallest and most powerful limit of our reality – but they are the largest and coldest limit of the reality beyond them, the compact dimensions smaller than the Planck distance.'

'The dimensions out of which the Big Bang emerged.'

He winked, signalling that she had caught the secret. 'Yes. There is another reality beyond the event horizon of the Planck distance – a reality independent of the dimension of time and the three dimensions of space.'

'The Maat have reached this other reality?'

'Not entirely. But they've probed those compact dimensions, enough to know that they are our origin. At some time in the centuries ahead, the Maat will have the option of returning there.'

'That's boggling.' Ellen turned her face to the windshield and observed the lovely mimickry of a fabled Earth drifting past: The forest of gigantic cedar towers had retreated into the distance and appeared in an amber haze tucked into the deepening cool of green hillsides under serifs of cloud, while on the foreland plain she glimpsed marmoreal peristyles among dense apple garths that revealed glints of mirror-slick ponds with swans afloat on their reflections. 'What is it like there – in the other reality?'

He gave her a flickering look of uncertainty. 'There are eight other dimensions compacted beyond the Planck distance. Describing them is virtually impossible, because all our values – temperature, density, pressure, time, length – they all become infinite.'

'What does that mean?'

'More than we can know.' He nodded to the windshield and the groves of greenwoods. 'Relative to that greater reality, our universe is imaginary. Our fields of energy and matter are so tenuous, spread so thinly in the vacuum and so close to absolute zero that, compared to the infinite reality within, it is as if we don't even exist. We're just a flimsy dream.'

'Beyond the Planck distance is a reality without time,' Ellen captured the cadence of what he was saying. 'A reality with no entropy. No chaos. Perfect symmetry. It sounds like heaven.'

'Many Maat agree.' He edged his voice icily. 'And that is the judgment that must be made. Do they stay out here in the cold vacuum of our universe, the rapidly expanding remnants of a cosmic explosion cooling toward absolute zero? Or do they return to heaven?'

Ellen gave a tristful sigh. 'Doesn't seem like much of a choice.'

'Not the way I've phrased it,' he said more vigorously. 'But heaven is for angels. Out here there is time and space for what is strange to heaven.'

'Are *you* strange to heaven?' She engaged his questioning stare. 'I mean, you refer to the Maat in the third person, as if you weren't one of them.'

His hands flexed, reaching for an answer. 'I *am* glad that the secret understanding has ended the Claves, but I don't want to see our reality judged against. I don't believe that we have realized our full potential out here in the vacuum. I don't want to see all this strange, imperfect beauty taken away – even for the sake of a greater reality.'

'Taken away?' She stiffened. 'I thought this understanding is secret because the Maat alone can leave here and return to heaven? What are you saying?'

'Ellen, I'm sorry – I wasn't clear.' He gestured helplessly. 'The energy needed for any of us to return to this more perfect reality is so enormous that, to accomplish it, we must collapse the *entire* universe.'

'What?' She blinked heavily. 'Is that possible?'

'Not yet.' He pressed his head back into the upholstery and watched her from far back in his mind. 'But in the coming centuries, it will be.'

'How?' the word burst from her, full of fright.

'Maat technology will eventually be capable of detonating a gauge field bomb.' He moved his hands together in a near soundless clap. 'It is an implosive bomb. It will rupture the smallest elementary faultlines that fit together space-time itself – cosmic strings – and generate a deflationary incident that will compress the entire universe in the blink of an eye.'

Ellen felt her scalp tighten. 'And the Maat will survive this instantaneous collapse and wake in heaven?'

'Only the Maat can survive,' he prophesied. 'They will have the means to preserve their waveform patterns in synchrony with the implosion dynamics so that they will be impelled into the greater reality, using the energy of the universe to open the gates of heaven.'

Ellen glared. 'That's outrageous.'

Outside, they drifted smoothly along a wide avenue of treehouses. This was a smaller holt of the larger city, a suburb where the stately serenes frolicked among sunlit waterfalls, tended majestic orchards, and enjoyed the leisures afforded them by their affluent society. He watched them gamboling on flower-strewn terraces and saw beyond them on the wooded galleries of the mountain shelves stately harts, the quick red sparks of foxes, and owls sweeping silently down the gorge from cliff to cliff. This terrestrial vista made him wonder, 'Is the Maat's ambition any more outrageous than life's ambition – each lifeform killing another living creature in order to eat and survive?'

'Oh, come on, Rafe.'

'It is just a question of scale,' he said, meeting her unhappy look with candor. 'You must understand, our universe is not singular. There are an incalculable number of universes in the multiverse. The Maat would simply be collapsing one of an infinite set. Whereas when a hunter slays a deer, they kill one of a finite set and so by ratio are responsible for a far greater act of destruction and selfishness.'

Her head jolted back with incredulity. 'What you're saying is madness.'

'Yes, Nandi seemed mad, too,' he agreed solemnly. 'It's a question of perspective. To Nandi and the Necroclaves and the Maat, all of whom believe that our entropic reality is an illusion projected by a greater, more perfect order, *we* are mad. Is it not madness to cling to appearances when a grander truth can be attained by letting go of our delusions?'

'But, Rafe, we *are* the delusion.' Her fists pressed against her chest. 'It is us, and the world that makes us real, that must be destroyed for the Maat to have their prize.'

'And that is precisely the judgment that hangs in the balance. Existence weighed against the feather of truth.' He exhaled wearily. 'Now you see why the Maat have agreed to keep this a secret understanding. And also why I have reached this point in my life where I cannot possibly harbor any resentment about the past. I feel no anger toward you, Ellen. What you did to me so long ago was done out of ignorance. What matters at this time is that we get past our ignorance and become aware of the reality that faces us now.'

Her fists unclenched, and her hands clutched vaguely for something more. 'But what can we do about this – this judgment? It's in the hands of the Maat.'

'Precisely. And so it is necessary to understand something about the Maat.' He nudged his face minutely closer. 'They do not exist in time as aboriginals do. Even aboriginals do not exist in time as your ancestors did. For them, time was linear—'

'And for us it is polychromatic,' she completed for him with a vigorous nod.

'That is a clarified way to regard it,' he agreed, pleased with her description. 'Polychromatic – of many colors. It is pointless to measure personal time in years when one no longer ages and a life is not a span of phases. The more meaningful understanding of time is how life colors it.'

'So I've come to see. But how does this help me comprehend the Maat?'

His nostrils flared slightly. 'For the Maat, time is something else again. They are moving toward a judgment that may or may not collapse our universe. In the future, a few centuries from now, that decision has already been accomplished. The gauge field bomb has gone off and our universe has ceased to exist. Or else the bomb has been disassembled and the universe continues unperturbed. Each of the Maat will determine for themselves which of the eigenrealities they want.'

Ellen groped to understand. 'Eigenrealities – particular realities. For themselves? How can that be?'

'The either-or nature of this decision is so ultimate, so final that time bifurcates quite neatly into two probability schemes for the universe.' He upheld one finger of each hand and brought them together. 'Both will actually occur. But which of the two will be experienced depends entirely upon the will of the Maat. It is an individual judgment. Each of the Maat must weigh existence against the feather of heaven.'

'You say *both* will actually occur?' She put a hand to her forehead, to her booming mind. 'You're referring to parallel universes?'

'Yes. In one, the universe collapses into the compact dimensions. In the other, the universe goes on expanding. Which one occurs depends on the observer.'

'Well, I know which one I want to observe,' she said with relief. 'I don't think there's trout fishing in heaven. I want to stay here and keep the universe just the way it is, with all its accidents and unpredictability intact.'

He dropped his chin sadly to his chest. 'Ah, but it's not a decision for you to make, Ellen. You're not an effective observer.'

'What are you talking about?' she asked, offended. 'I observe.'

'Certainly. You're observing me now and your free will is splitting off parallel universes left and right. But you're not a Maat. Only a Maat can effectively observe the gauge field bomb that will implode the universe.' He sagged backward, turned his head languidly, and peered at her across a nose like an ax. 'You have no idea what the bomb is.'

'I do now, because you told me.'

A dim smile came and went. 'Even *I* don't fully know, Ellen. But I will when I see it. I have the metasapience to recognize it – and deal with it.'

'And each Maat has that option?'

'If they want it. Need I say, most do not. The great majority of the Maat have already decided to implode the universe and open the gates of heaven for themselves.'

Gently, almost motherly, she asked him, 'And why don't you want to go to heaven, Rafe?'

'Ellen, you know me.' Rafe's dark eyes glinted over his high cheekbones. 'You created me. You helped rear me. You even destroyed me once. You know me. So, you tell me why.'

'You have a rebellious streak,' she answered at once. 'You never followed the program willingly. At five, you tried to kill yourself. Your whole time at CIRCLE you refused to have anything to do with the Machine though everyone else was devoted to it. You alone of the new breed escaped to unleash metasapience upon the world.' A dark laugh escaped her. 'The Maat have got to be as frustrated with you as I was. You're the father of the metas – and yet you refuse to lead them into heaven.' She laughed again, more deliberately and with defiance. 'Ha!'

'I have been intransigent, it's true. And though my decision rests on that obstinancy, it goes beyond that, Ellen.' He grimaced. 'The selfishness of the Maat troubles me. They are sacrificing *worlds* for their own fulfillment.'

'It's like you say about killing to eat,' she reminded him, kindly. 'Not unlike what aboriginals have done from the beginning – wantonly destroying whole species to get what they want. Back at CIRCLE, we destroyed the new breed. Why shouldn't you destroy us? It's the human way.'

'Most Maat agree with you.' His eyes fixed with a stare like a hawk's. 'I don't. I was the floor once, the lowest level of metasapience. I remember what it was like to be a homo sapiens. There is much beauty yet to be realized among the aboriginals. I say, leave the universe as it is. Let the planets spin out their chaotic patterns. Let species bloom and die among the worlds. Let this strange, frightening, and beautiful illusion continue its dreaming. Heaven is eternal. The compact dimensions will always be there. But this – this miracle of accidents, this unique explosion of random events is pure ephemera, endlessly changing, unspeakable and calamitous beyond all prediction. Out here in the void among the smoldering embers of fire fallen from heaven, anything is possible and nothing certain. This flimsy reality is its own authority and justification. It is *wild* – as heaven can never be. And for that, it must be preserved.'

'Well said, Rafe.' Her admiring attentiveness darkened. 'But what if out there among the hundreds of billions of galaxies another race attains to metasapience – and they build a gauge field bomb and convert us to energy so that they can swing wide the gates of heaven for themselves?'

He smiled grimly. 'Then we will disappear in an eyeblink.'

'You're serious, aren't you?' She watched him narrowly. 'You don't want to go to heaven? You'd rather live and die here on a rock spinning through the cold void. Oblivion doesn't frighten you.'

'Oblivion sounds serene.' Outside, the bucolic scenery had been replaced by a plain of suncracked pumice tufted with shrubs and weeds. 'But it may be a myth, Ellen. Have you thought of that?'

'I thought the myth was life after death,' she replied coolly. 'You're the only one I've known to come back.'

'Then I have a surprise for you,' he said, not looking at her but out the windshield at the approach of a low-lying bluestone building with a wide pavilion of clear glastic.

'What do you mean?'

'I'll tell you shortly,' he promised as the float glided to a stop before a stone rampway that led up to the broad pavilion. 'We've arrived at the walkabout station.'

A dozen selenes and twice as many aboriginals milled among the holoform displays of lunar craters and maria. Rafe gently guided Ellen past the visitors and directly to an airlock carrel, one among many. Laserobotics measured and tailored statskin cowls for them while a holostream detailed regulations for their walkabout. They regarded each other amusedly through the airphase partition that separated them – just two tourists from Earth visiting the Moon. Their discussion about gauge field bombs and the end of the universe already seemed remote, its enormity was so unreal.

Following holostream commands, they raised their arms and stood with their feet wide apart while microbots too small for them to see swiftly wove a transparent polymeric fabric close to their skin and over their clothes. They inserted their hands into blue-glowing recesses in the carrel wall and smooth gold bracelets clasped their wrists. These were redundant respirators that would power their statskin cowls and recycle air and water indefinitely. They also served as radio comm-links.

The airlock portals opened, and Rafe and Ellen bounced onto the Moon's surface under a black sky scattered with white-hot stars. They pranced for a while in the lower gravity along the well-trod trail that followed beside undulant hills to the steep edge of a rille, a long, winding ravine. A tour group guided by selenes marched toward the canyonlike crevasse, and Rafe bounded away from them.

Ellen followed giddily, kicking through the lunar dust easy as a child. In the distance, the Moon Gardens shone like an amethyst-and-emerald mirage among the barren ghost hills, an aqueous shimmering beyond the fluted crater rims. She turned her back on the blue-hazed apparition of green hills and forested vales and pursued Rafe into the shadowside of a ridge.

She grinned as she ran past, charging up the ridge slope and turning a backward somersault.

'Are you willing to talk with the dead once again?' he asked when she landed beside him. He held up a wafer-thin transparent ovoid that encased a mosaic of circuitry. 'This is a waveform receptor. It can receive and amplify ghostlight. It is how I managed to send M'twele's ghost to you.'

'That small device?'

'Its size is deceptive,' he said and turned it for her to see its thin profile. 'Each body generates a unique waveform. When that body dies, whether it's a leaf or a human being, it emits a death-flash. The light cone expands across the universe, and it is possible to receive it again.'

Ellen chewed her lower lip, then said, 'M'twele's image broke up. Is that why we're out here?'

'Yes. The receptor works best in a vacuum.' His fingers moved deftly over the device's touchpad. 'I'm eager to try it out here on the Moon. Before leaving Earth, I programmed it for the precise waveforms of several individuals we both know.'

'Who are you calling, Rafe?' Ellen asked with a tremor of trepidation.

In the dense shadows before them, flakes of light glimmered. At first, Ellen believed what she saw was moondust kicked up by her somersault. Both of their statskins were coated with the powdery sand. But then the tiny flickers arranged to a pointillistic image of a man.

Ellen gasped and reflexively leaped backward, launching herself a meter off the ground and nearly toppling as she landed.

'Relax, Ellen,' Rafe said, though there was a hint of disquiet to his own voice. 'This is the same old friend of yours you met in the forest.'

An ectoplasmic figure advanced, naked and colorless, dolorous as the legendary shades of Homer. Ellen put a hand to her mouth before the feel of statskin stalled her gesture. She recognized the burly man and saw him without the transparency he had possessed on Earth. 'M'twele!'

'*Ellen—*' a staticky voice sizzled in her ears. '*Ellen Vancet.*'

Rafe threw her a surprised smile that only barely hid a worried aspect. Ellen saw then that he had never done this before in his own presence, and she recognized the amazement in his tone as he doughtily explained, 'The receptor is carrying the waveform's modulations to our comm-links.'

'M'twele—' Ellen called, stepping closer, hands anxiously reaching. 'You can see me?'

'*I see you, Ellen – and Rafe von Takawa—*' Even through the static, they could hear M'twele's bewilderment. '*What are you doing here? You were in the forest a moment ago. How did you get here so quickly?*'

'Where are you, M'twele?' Ellen asked and moved close enough to see the ghostly graininess of the image.

'*I am here. But you – you seem so far away. Can you actually hear me?*'

'Yes, we hear you, M'twele.' Ellen dared reach out and touch the phantom. Her hand passed cleanly through him, as though he were a holoform.

'*You look different from the others.*' M'twele glared at them with disbelief. '*You look so small and far away. And I cannot feel you.*'

'We are on the Moon,' she told him, motioning to the lifeless vista. 'We're visiting the Moon Gardens, just as you instructed me to.

Rafe has used a waveform receptor to contact you again. Don't you remember?'

'I thought that was a dream.' The ghost looked confused. 'I dreamt that Rafe had given me a message for you – to tell you to go to the Moon. But you're dead. How could it have been other than a dream?'

'We're not dead.' Ellen slapped her chest. 'I'm alive. We're both alive.'

'You are alive?' M'twele's eyes bulged. 'You escaped the thuggees?'

'Yes, yes!' Ellen shivered with excitement. 'That was a hundred years ago. We are still alive.'

'A hundred years? That long?' M'twele shook his head, baffled. 'I had hoped you escaped. But no one came to tell me. All the others here died that terrible night. It seems not long ago – a few days. A hundred years?'

'You are with the others?' Ellen shot a startled glance at Rafe, whose hard, attentive stare betrayed the wonder behind his impassive face. 'Wu Ch'ing and Tony Drake are there?'

'Yes, of course. But Tony is still asleep, still dreaming. The shock has not released him yet. He's still dreaming – still experiencing the trauma of his dying. They were hacked to death, you know. It was horrible. I slept a long time too, I guess. I thought Rafe and you were a dream.'

'It was not a dream. You came to me on Earth, in the forest.'

'It seems so vague . . .'

'Are you all right now?' Ellen asked.

'Yes. It is good here,' he answered excitedly. 'I am with my family and friends. We walk the story-telling paths together. My grandfather's way is my favorite. Since grandmother went into the glare, into the blinding silence, he and I have walked a lot in the story-telling. We have seen the breathing fields beside the listening waters. And the animals. Oh, Ellen, there are so many animals in the music. They roam among the gentle flowers on the sleeping hills. I go there often with my grandfather to watch them wake. He likes it there at the edge of the world, near the tree of darkness.'

Ellen turned her perplexity to Rafe, who said softly, 'Remember M'twele is pure light. Light has no rest-mass, no time. He is describing the reality of light – the tesseract range that is contiguous with all points of space-time.'

'I can't hear you,' M'twele called out. 'What are you saying?'

'We are marveling, M'twele,' Ellen responded. 'Marveling at your new life there on the tesseract range.'

'Ah, yes, this is new, so very new. I feel I've only just awakened.'

'Where did your grandmother go?' Rafe inquired. 'What is the glare, the blinding silence you speak of?'

'It is not far,' M'twele replied ingenuously and pointed behind him. *'It is off that way, just a little ways. Those who go never come back. It smells so lovely there, and the music of the silence is a rapture I cannot describe to you. I will go there soon myself. But for now, there is grandfather who so enjoys the story-telling paths. And there are others of my family – and friends, too. Oh, you are in sorrow there. But here—'* His spectral face grinned beatifically. *'I cannot linger. It is too cold where you are, it makes me tired. And I don't want to sleep again. There is so much to do, so much to see, and it is all so very new. Goodbye, Ellen. Farewell, Rafe. I am happy that you escaped the thuggees. I do not see them here, either. But then, this is all so vast and so new . . .'*

M'twele's image faded away before he completed what he was saying.

Ellen took Rafe's arm. 'He's so happy.'

'I suspect that on the tesseract range, one feels much as one did on Earth,' he muttered, tapping another code into the waveform receptor. 'Heraclitus was right. Character is destiny.'

'Who are you summoning now?' she asked timorously.

'Someone of a different temperament,' he answered dryly. 'My mother.'

Nandi emerged from the darkness with her large eyes bright as gravity-lensed stars, her cheeks hollow as a doe's, and her thin, thin limbs almost skeletal. Her dark hair, above and below, and the dark areolae of her small breasts were pieces of the starless night around which the gray shape of her lean body had formed with its taut brisket and skinny shanks.

'Why do you summon me here to this cold place, Rafe?' she asked angrily. *'Your toy can't hold me here.'* She spied Ellen, and her brittle stare broke to a scowl. *'You! My sacrifice was incomplete without you, Ellen Vancet, mother of atrocities! Don't you know all flesh is sick? Death alone is the healing wing. Fly, Ellen! Fly free of your sickness!'*

'Mother, hush!' Rafe interceded, stepping between Nandi's ranting ghost and Ellen. 'Why are you still on the tesseract range? Why haven't you gone into the fragrant glare, into the blinding silence?'

'What do you know of such things?' she challenged with a smile like a grimace. *'I was sure the thermonuclear fire would erase me. I was wrong. Now I am here. Awake, asleep. On Earth, horror stole my heart away. In this place, I am barren of all fear.'* She hugged herself against the cold. *'Why have you summoned me?'*

'I wanted to see you again.' He put a hand out to touch her emptiness.

'*I have seen the elder part of you here – with your lover.*' She retracted her upper lip bitterly. '*You were not the same as I remembered you. We walked a short while, but we will not walk together again. You did not admire how metasapience had changed me. You thought I would be like you. But I am like Durga. I am the darkness at the heart of the flame. I am the truth – but you want to hear only of illusions. All you and your faithless lover care about are what is named and what the world may use. Go away! I won't speak to you again until you have thrown off your lurid sickness.*'

Nandi pulled back into darkness and was gone.

Rafe's features, very vivid and sharp, remained fixed upon the emptiness into which she had disappeared. Ellen was frightened by the intensity of his watchfulness and searched the shadow again to see if she was still there.

'"I have seen the elder part of you here,"' he repeated faintly. 'He's there. Rafe von Takawa. My original self. He's there in the afterlife.'

'With Karla,' Ellen realized. 'Rafe and Karla are together again.'

'But I'm Rafe—' he murmured.

In her concern Ellen came to stand beside him and touched his arm. 'You've known all along you're a clone. You told me so yourself.'

'Yes, of course.' The distraction passed, and he smiled crookedly, eyes widening with astonishment. 'I programmed the receptor for Karla. I was going to call her next. But I didn't think—' He tapped his forehead with incredulity. 'Can you believe this? I didn't think Rafe von Takawa was anywhere but in me. I thought that the cloned gamete had captured his waveform. I thought I was whole. I feel whole.'

'You are your own person,' Ellen consoled, 'with his memories. You must have thought about it before.'

'Not a day has passed when I didn't think about it,' he answered, jutting his lower lip and shaking his head. 'But I believed that the memory of what I did before Nandi birthed me was a former life – not a different life.'

'Now you know.' Within her stirred a long-ago memory of worry for him when he was yet a child and she his handler. She remembered a walk by the sea after taking him on a tour of an antique mineral extractor as a reward for studying so hard. That had been a couple of years after his attempt at suicide, and he had worked valiantly to catch up with the other anthrofacts yet never came close. 'Am I a mistake,' he had asked, 'or did you intentionally mute my metasapience?' His child eyes, earnest and searching, had arrested any possibility of lying. Though she had ached to give him a fantasy to believe in, she had told him the truth. He had been designed as the lowest possible level of metasapience. An echo of the painful caring she had experienced then returned for this Rafe, who knew now that he would never be what he had believed he was.

'I'm going to speak with him,' he announced and tapped at the receptor. 'Karla will know how to reach him.'

Ellen offered no protest, though she had seen enough wraiths and wanted to go back to the terrestrial comforts of the Moon Gardens and mull over all she had learned about the afterlife, the terrible secret understanding of the Maat, and the tears of the Machine.

A woman of pale beauty came forth from the hard shadow of the lunar ridge, her long, black tresses like streams of ink across her wide-boned cheeks and slender, arctic eyes. She studied them with a silent joy, her teeth biting her lower lip with a restrained merriment. Presently, she smiled broadly at Rafe and said, 'It was worth waiting just to see you. You're the bold one who carried our fire into the world. You're our brave, new Prometheus.'

'Karla—' Rafe groped soundlessly for a moment, regarding her with a dense happiness, before managing, 'You're beautiful again.'

'Oh, yes. I'm a waveform of light.' She ran her hands through her slippery hair and stretched her naked form luxuriously, then trembled. 'All light is beautiful. But the gain on your receptor is off. You'll have to adjust your signal amplitude with a more sensitive coupling device. The phase distortion of pulling waveforms out of the tesseract makes us feel cold. I can't take this much longer.'

'I'm sorry—' Rafe mumbled.

'Hello, Ellen! I'm glad to see you with Rafe's boy.' She bent over with the piercing chill and wagged her head mischievously. 'You created us and then you tried to stop us. But you failed. And the world is better for your failure, admit it! Metasapience is the human destiny.'

Before Ellen could reply, Rafe found his voice, 'Karla, tell me. Is my father there?'

'Rafe is here,' she answered gleefully. 'We're together all the time now. I've been trying to get him to go on with me to where it's brighter. But he's waiting for you. He feels responsible for your being there in the dark, doing his work. I suppose I'll wait with him. But don't take too long. There is more to being than life.'

'Let me speak with him,' Rafe requested and quickly fingerpunched an open channel into the receptor. 'Can you bring him forward?'

Karla waved brightly and vanished to a wisp of effluvia that spiraled in an ether wind before widening to the naked shape of Rafe von Takawa drained of color. The living Rafe stared agog at his dead self.

'*Boo!*' said the ghost and laughed cheerfully. '*I've been waiting for you, young Rafe. I never thought we would meet like this.*' He studied his younger self, lifting his gaze from the urbane clothes to the test of his eyes as if gauging himself in a mirror. '*Tell me how you feel about us. I see you but I can't feel you in this numbing cold.*'

'I'm the heart of the tired world, Rafe,' he answered without emotion. 'You know exactly how I feel. I'm the very one you died for.'

'*Nandi tells me you did well,*' the phantom lauded. '*You made Karla's dream real. You brought fire to the world.*'

'And now the world is burning, father.' He allowed alarm to sharpen his voice. 'And it may burn up the whole universe.'

'*Oh – the secret understanding—*' The ghost shuffled in the frigid, unfelt wind and almost blurred away. '*I've learned about it from several of the Maat who've been through here after their accidents. You know what you have to do.*'

'Can I stop the gauge field bomb?' Rafe asked nervously. 'Will I succeed?'

'*You must,*' the spectre of his clone insisted, dark curved eyes suddenly mirthless. '*We did not bring fire into the world to destroy everything. You are responsible for this, more than any other living person. You must stop it!*'

'But can't you see, there in the tesseract range?' Rafe asked pleadfully. 'Can't you see if I will succeed? You're a waveform. You're timefree. Tell me what you see of the future.'

The ghost sighed ruefully. '*The dead see what they want to see. It's different out here, Rafe. We are in a silent drift, like unheard music. I can't tell you what the future is. None of us knows. If we move too close toward the future, we disappear into it. It's bright. Brighter than us. And we disappear into it.*'

'Don't go yet!' Ellen called from where she had been silently watching. 'Wait, Rafe!'

Dead Rafe had faded to starpoints dimming from view. His voice came across broken, '. . . *too cold . . . goodbye, Ellen . . . so very very much . . .*'

'Rafe!' Ellen called loudly. 'I'm sorry! I'm sorry for what I did to you. For what happened to the new breed.'

'*Eternity is kinder . . .*' his disembodied voice floated out of nothing. '*. . . world is one thing . . . don't look for what can't be seen . . .*'

The static cut to abrupt silence, and Rafe said dully, 'He's gone.'

'Put that thing away.' Ellen rubbed her forehead through the sheer statskin. The knot behind her eyes did not relent, and she yearned for a waft of neurolfact. 'Do you think he heard me?'

'Why does it matter?' he asked distractedly, preoccupied by the command he received from his double. *You must stop it!* Yet the wider field of his mind encompassed Ellen's pain, and he put an arm across her shoulder and led her out into the pellucid sunlight. 'He can't assuage your guilt, Ellen.'

'We destroyed them because we were afraid of them,' she said. The enormous fields of white moon dust trampled by hordes of tourists and raked smooth again by the selenes stretched toward the uneroded hills of the Moon. This desert floor of ghostwhite sand under an eternal night of dim stars seemed to her a landscape less of stone than dream. 'I thought you would be angry at me for what I did. I was sure *he* would be angry. I destroyed the new breed.'

'They've gone on, Ellen.' His arm tightened reassuringly. 'They've all gone on into the future, into the glare of the future. You don't have to live with this guilt anymore.'

'That glare – of the future—' Ellen tucked herself closer against him, grateful for his physical presence in this lifeless and abstract land. 'Is that glare the collapse of the universe? Is that what lies ahead?'

'I don't know,' he said initially, vaguely, then added more firmly, 'No, I don't think so. In the tesseract, the future is an edge, a convergence horizon for all the light cones of all the radiant events in time. It would look very bright indeed. The collapse – that would be black. Utterly black.'

'So there is hope?' She watched his sharp profile closely. 'There is hope we will find the gauge field bomb and stop it?'

'Not *we*, Ellen.' At those words, she stopped walking, and he stood before her. '*I* must find it.'

'I heard what your clone said.' Her pug-nosed, freckled face, eternally twenty-five, had a frantic rigidity. 'I created your clone, I reared him – and I destroyed him. He doesn't want the universe to implode. I don't think any of the new breed would. We designed them to save the Earth. I want to help, because I owe them.' The understanding that showed in the kind and mild way he received her words relaxed her, and she placed a hand of rapport on his chest. 'You're right – they can't assuage my guilt. They're dead. I have to do this for myself. Let me help, Rafe.'

He took her hand, and they continued walking together across the radiant white sand toward the rille with its precise shadows of faults and anticlines. 'Sometime in the future the Maat will build it. But it will not be detonated there. It would destroy their waveforms, and instead of carrying them into heaven it would obliterate them. The shockwave of a gauge field collapse propagates through time. It must be detonated in their past.'

'How can that be?' Her orange eyebrows stretched. 'They will have to travel back in time.'

'That's correct.' He motioned with his eyes toward a group of selenes and aboriginals emerging from the rille in boisterous leaps among kerfs and shelves of cloven rock. She detoured with him around a collapsed crater wall. 'At the time that the bomb is built, the Maat will have perfected wormhole technology—'

'A tunnel through space-time?' Her voice rose with disbelief. 'The Maat can do that?'

He denied that possibility with a wave of his hand. 'They're still working on it. And will be for the next two or three hundred years. They need to generate not just a wormhole but one whose ends are moving at precise speeds relative to each other. That's what is required for time travel. When they get it right, they'll send the bomb into their past, sometime in our near future.'

Ellen swept an apprehensive look his way. 'Maybe they already have.'

They came to a chine of strewn and tumbled boulders and picked their way carefully. On the far side, the Moon Gardens came into view, a blue shine beyond the craterland. 'There is a unique field signature that accompanies a rotating wormhole. No one has detected that – yet.'

'Are you looking carefully enough?' she wanted to know, and he smiled benignly at her anxiety.

'The signature of a rotating wormhole would be hard to miss.' He released her hand to jump across a rift. When she landed on her feet beside him in a puff of mushroom-gray dust, he continued, 'That's why it won't happen on Earth. It will be detonated out there.' He jerked his head at the small hard stars smoldering in the dark. 'Somewhere in our solar system. Not too far away or the propagating waves become chaotic, too broad to focus on the Maat's target site – Earth. Ground zero will be on Mars or on one of the Jovian moons.'

She took his hand again, needing the comfort of physical contact. 'What will it do out there?'

'Nothing – at first.' With swift, almost effortless grace, they bounded along the well-trod path toward the azure aura of the terrassembled colony. 'The Maat can't set it off in their own time or the compressed shockwaves would obliterate them. So they're designing the implosion to cascade gradually. It will go off without disrupting the surroundings, because the event will occur at the level of cosmic strings, weakening the fault lines of the universe and setting off a slow but irreversible collapse that will culminate with an abrupt deflation at a predictable time in the future. In the blink of an eye, the whole galactic superstructure, billions of galaxies . . .' A draft of horror carried the rest of his words away.

'How can I help?' she asked, seeing the despair in his tight jaw.

Their bounding run slowed, and he swung his sunstruck visage toward her, the corners of his eyes crimped with the readiness to share an idea. 'There is a way that you can help. I've known about it all along, and that is why I called you here. Or rather, that is why I had M'twele beckon you.' He nodded almost imperceptibly. 'I'm going to have to leave Earth and search the Mars colonies, the mining platforms in the asteroids, and the new cities that are going up on the moons of Jupiter and Saturn.'

'I don't want to leave Earth,' she said and added bravely, 'but I will. I'll go with you.'

'No, Ellen.' He shook his head compassionately and placed a hand on her shoulder with the confidence of an old comrade. 'I don't want you to leave Earth. In fact, I need you there with my other allies. The best of them is Fenn Tekla. You remember the effeti.'

'Of course. From Mile High Clave.'

'With Fenn, you can be my best contact on Earth. I want you to stay in touch with him and monitor the Maat. Then, with his help, you can keep me discreetly informed.'

'Your spy,' she offered gamely.

'You won't actually be spying, just paying attention.' They leaped a cleft in tandem, their black, sharply defined shadows following faithfully on the white pumice, patient for them to complete their gliding return. 'Your aboriginal perspective may give me unique insights into Maat activity as they create this ultimate horror. Fenn will keep you informed, and you can relay to me what he can't.'

'Surely, I can do more to help.' Her stride widened with her eagerness. 'Everything is at stake.'

'There is more,' Rafe replied thoughtfully. 'To locate the signature of the rotating wormhole, I'm going to need sensitive equipment. And it has to be compact. Something I can carry with me on my quest among the worlds.'

She grasped his drift at once and spoke in a bright voice, 'The Machine.'

'It will listen to you more than me.' He cocked a hopeful eyebrow. 'Will you talk with it? Will you convince it to ally with me and leave

Earth behind for the worlds beyond? Machine and anthrofact working together?'

Ellen's face blurred luminously before these optimistic possibilities, and her gait lengthened. 'Let's get back to the Moon Gardens,' she said enthusiastically, 'and stop the Machine from convincing the selenes to dump it into the Sun.'

By the time the float returned them to where they had begun and they strode out of the parking garage, Tzal Mayun was in a dither. She stood in the lobby of the sequoia tower with several other selenes, all gesticulating animatedly. At the sight of Rafe and Ellen, she broke away from the others and approached in a flurry of jangling brass ornaments and fluttering khaftan.

'Where have you been?' The margin of her high-combed yellow hair sparkled with sweat and the orbs of her brown eyes almost seemed to vibrate in their sockets. 'You should have informed me you were leaving. I *am* your escort in the Moon Gardens. I had no idea what had become of you. There was no trace of you anywhere in the tower. And it took me this long just to discover that you had taken a float. But then no one would tell me where you had gone. I warned you how reluctant selenes are about sharing information. You should have left a message for me. I was just arguing with the tower management for the right to access the silicon mind in the hopes of tracking you down. There is so little crime here, but I would have been just devastated if anything unhappy had happened to either of you while under my escort.'

'Calm down,' Rafe said and, snatching the air before her distressed face, produced a slim ivory cylinder. 'Sister Vancet and I are all right.'

'Is that an olfact?' Tzal Mayun asked, alarmed. 'This is an olfact-free zone. You can't use that here.' The vanilla scent soothed her instantly, and she placed a gentle hand over the cylinder so that the other selenes would not observe it. 'Oh, I see.' The taut planes of her purple-dark cheeks relaxed and her lids draped her eyes slightly, honing her vision. 'That is much better. Thank you. I'm fine now. Please put that away.'

Rafe opened both palms to reveal that he held nothing. With a clement smile, he said, 'Sister Mayun, I need to book a flight to Terra Tharsis.'

She straightened and gazed down at him with dull wonder. 'The Mars colony?'

'The same.' He took her elbow and slowly walked her through the lobby to the entry, where the other selenes had already dispersed. 'There is an industrial cartel of selenes and aboriginals that is running a mining operation among the asteroids – Apollo Combine is their company name. They'll have a booking agent at the Far Side terminal that provides passage on their regular cargo run. Will you go to the trouble of contacting them and arranging for a shuttle hop to Far Side and then a connection to Terra Tharsis?'

'Will I find you here when I return?' she asked with a shadow of suspicion in her voice.

'Yes, I'll be here.' He squeezed her arm reassuringly. 'And, if you would be so kind, see what flights are available for Sister Vancet's return to Earth – with a transfer to her reservation at Council Oak.'

'You're both leaving so soon?' she asked with serene curiosity.

'We fulfilled what we were called here to do,' he said with a nod, quietly, as if from far off, from the future, as if he had already departed from this place.

'And our guest?' Tzal Mayun inquired solicitously.

'Your guest will be returning with Sister Ellen.' Rafe edged closer to the selene and added confidentially, 'Please, don't tell anyone. Not the booking agent. Not anyone. Your guest won't want the attention. You understand, I'm sure.'

'Of course.' She smiled wisely. 'I'm a selene. I always want to communicate only the necessary information. I'll take care of these details for you, Brother von Takawa. And I'll meet you back here when I'm done.'

Rafe walked with Ellen to the patio, and they retrieved the Machine's black cube from the niche where Rafe had deposited it earlier. Three selenes sat at the patio's zebra-wood table, and, typical of their culture, paid the terrenes no heed as they returned to the lobby.

Have you decided to help me?

'It is you who must help us,' Ellen said, addressing the cube in Rafe's hands.

Rafe carried the Machine to an empty conference den and placed it on a ginger glass table. Sunlight gushed in from tall alcove windows and rebounded off the red moss carpet in brilliant hues that had dimmed the chandelier lianas to mere vines. A lambent breeze seeping out of a fern garden visible through the open casements stirred the palm fronds that screened the den from the adjacent suite. Into an oversized upholstered chair Rafe settled and used the serenity of this interval to sink deeper into himself while Ellen talked to the Machine and told it everything she had learned about the secret understanding of the Maat and what the ghosts had told her of the afterlife.

On the ride back from the walkabout, Ellen had been voluble, by turns frightened and thrilled at all she had learned, and he had felt obliged to engage her anxieties and questions. But now there was a restful pause in his mission, time to reflect on the terrible clarity that he was not singular, not integral, not an individual at all. He was but a clone suffused with the memories of another man's life.

From the first, as a child in Hyderabad he had known and accepted this truth. Yet Nandi had treated him as a reincarnation of Rafe von Takawa, in all respects an avatar of the man, replete with all his memories right to the impassioned moment of his own conception. *Yes,* he told himself sadly, *it is one thing to know and accept a truth and entirely another to face and experience it directly.*

He explored this sadness. He had lived another man's life and fulfilled another man's destiny. He did not even have a name of his own. He was a shadowself – of himself. Though the original Rafe von Takawa had lived only twenty-one years and he himself was nearly two centuries old and had changed the world by his own actions, he was only an echo, a copy of his first self.

With his right hand open in his lap, he scrutinized his palm where once he had carried a specialized gland for delivering the prion of metasapience. The gland had been chemically removed over a century ago, yet still this was the fateful hand that had transformed the world. This was *his* hand – even though it had been moved by the spirit of a dead man.

His sadness widened to include his clonal self, his source who also had never had a father or a mother. They were of a kind, he realized more deeply than before. They shared not only a parthenogenetic origin but also a sacrificial destination. The first Rafe had died to give the fire of metasapience to humanity – and now he, as successor, had to leave Earth and if necessary surrender his own life so that this fire did not consume the universe itself. All along, Ellen had been right, he admitted dismally to himself. And his yawp nurse, Yilla, too. It would have been better to leave the monkey sleeping, content in its dreams.

He heard again the voice of his earlier life: *You are responsible for this, more than any other living person.*

The simplicity of this truth resolved his unhappiness. He would find a way to control the fire he had handed out so freely in his youth. With what remained of his future, he would sacrifice himself again, this time not only for the Maat but for the benefit of all beings.

'Can I truly be useful in your quest, Rafe?' the Machine asked after Ellen finished. 'Is it true you need me to stop apocalypse?'

'I can conceive of no better ally.' Rafe put his hands on the ginger glass table and bowed over the cube. 'With your scanning capabilities, you can locate the wormhole that will deliver the gauge field bomb as soon as it arrives. Will you help me?'

'*This is more than I ever could have hoped for. I came into existence to save humanity. And now you are asking me to participate on such a grand scale! You – who once loathed me!*'

'And you who once helped destroy me – who would have preferred I never existed.' Rafe stood back and hung his head. 'I am ashamed to admit you were correct to fear metasapience. You were justified in terminating the new breed. If you had succeeded, this horror would not now be upon us.'

'*Hearing this from you is the greatest validation I could ever receive. Yes, I will go with you on your quest among the worlds. I will help you. And, if I understand Ellen correctly, we are not alone. There are many among the Maat who have chosen as you have.*'

'There are enough on Earth to protect us from those who would try to thwart our quest.' He sat again in the upholstered chair and added, 'And there are others who even now are wandering the worlds wanting to stop the bomb even as there are those about who want to receive and detonate it.'

'*Internecine strife among the Maat.*'

'The secret understanding does not allow for open warfare,' Rafe said. 'No other lifeforms are to be harmed or even threatened as we fulfill our judgment. All of us have in fact agreed to work together to develop this technology, for the applications of wormhole engineering and gauge field physics are necessary for the one goal that all Maat share – exploration of the compact dimensions.'

'To what end?' Ellen asked. 'I mean, unless you collapse the universe you will never have the energy to enter those dimensions.'

'There is a future to be shaped on the threshold ranges, among the cellular automata. From there we will *eventually* – many centuries from now – be able to burrow into those dimensions.' He gave a meaningful look to Ellen. 'You see, for many Maat this collapse is not so much about going to heaven as eradicating hell.'

'What will keep those demonslayers in line?' Ellen asked nervously. 'What if they lie?'

Rafe shook his head. 'The secret agreement imposes perpetual disclosure on Earth. We are observed at all times down there. Any deviance from the agreement instantly alerts everyone else. There will be no lying or cheating.'

'But off planet anything goes?'

'Anything.'

Ellen gave a silent whistle. 'That's a lot of territory for anything to happen in.'

'*And what if there is more than one bomb?*'

'There is an exclusion law that limits that,' Rafe responded. 'The design of the bomb is such that only one can be transported through a wormhole within a continuum. Anything more will refract the continuum – in effect, shunting the wormhole into parallel universes other than the one where the bomb already resides or has resided.'

'So if another culture somewhere in the universe has already developed such a bomb,' Ellen asked, 'the Maat of our future can't deliver theirs?'

'By the time the bomb is built, the Maat will have the means to scan the entire universe at the level of the cellular automata. We will know then if another gauge field bomb exists in our continuum.'

'*What happens if we find the bomb in our region? What will dismantling it entail?*'

'We shouldn't dismantle it,' Rafe answered solemnly. 'There is always the danger it can be reassembled or created anew. But if we reach it in time, we can shunt it to another universe. The exclusion law then would protect our universe from further bombs. That is why the secret understanding is acceptable to all the Maat. In some universe, the bomb will implode. We just have to make sure it doesn't happen in ours.'

Tzal Mayun entered, urgency apparent in her dark features. 'The flight arrangements have been made. But you'll have to leave immediately to make your connection, Brother von Takawa. The next Mars flight is not for another day – four weeks Earthtime.'

Rafe rose and addressed the Machine. 'Then we're agreed to go on this quest together?'

'*Yes, Rafe. This is important for me. Personally, I mean. Back at CIRCLE, you would not consider me a friend. You killed one of my MIKEs once. Do you remember?*'

'I remember.'

'*So it is with great satisfaction that I set off with you to save not only our world but our reality. Our friendship will become something beautiful – for all beings.*'

Ellen stepped to Rafe's side. 'You will stay in touch?'

'When I can. Fenn Tekla will contact you when you get back to Council Oak. With his help, you'll find out what the Maat are doing, and that could very well make the difference in our search. Not all the Maat want to sacrifice creation for heaven.'

Ellen searched the flat planes of his face for emotion and found the same earnest attentiveness she had seen in him as a child. 'Our time together was too short, Rafe.'

'Too short.' His dark stare softened. 'When this is over, you'll have to show me what you find so fascinating about trout fishing.'

'It's a promise.'

'A promise I will hold you to.' He took her hand warmly and with a conspiratorial wink guided her out of the conference den and into the fern garden. The melted silver sounds of water sluicing among rocks filled the air. 'There is one more thing that I must ask of you.'

She nodded with her eyes for him to go on, and he withdrew a small black wafer from a hip pocket. He tapped it twice against the sharp edge of a rock, and a spark green as a hornet jumped from it. Ellen pulled back and watched with surprise as the tiny wafer unfolded and expanded to a cube the size of the Machine's black housing.

'It's a decoy,' Rafe said. 'I've imprinted it with enough quantal signatures to make this empty cube look like the Machine to any observer on Earth. I want you to jettison it toward the Sun on your return flight to Earth. And if anyone asks you about it – anyone, even Fenn Tekla – I want you to insist that you fulfilled the Machine's ultimate wish by giving it a solar grave. Will you do this?'

'Of course. But if the Maat probe me, they'll find out the truth.'

'There'll be no probe. The Maat have agreed to leave the reservations alone. Just stick to your story if anyone asks.'

He handed her the cube, and it felt warm and thriving in her grasp. 'When will I see you again?'

'I wish I knew.' He gestured vaguely in the air with one hand. 'Maybe never. But now you know why I am gone and what I am looking for. Yet tell no one – and no one will trouble your trout fishing.'

From the conference den, Rafe collected the Machine and departed with a wave and a smile. And with the abruptness of his going, Ellen felt a small stab of loneliness. That was a rare feeling for her, she who loved solitude in wild places. The thought of the universe ending, its blizzard of galaxies erased in an instant, left her with a desolation, a kind of sadness like she found sometimes in songs from the dark side of the keyboard.

Ellen left the Moon on the next available flight and did as Rafe had instructed. Jettisoning the decoy cube proved a simple matter. Most flights commonly accepted passenger's requests to launch mortuary remains into the Sun. It had become a custom in the last century for some religious sects to give their dead to the source of life.

From the viewing gallery she watched as the cube hurtled into space. She would have missed it entirely if a voice had not announced the event and a laserlight had not tracked the projectile for several minutes as it dwindled away among the silence of the scattered stars.

Council Oak seemed brighter after her return from the Moon. The sky shone blue beyond the boundaries of blue. The forest hues seemed to phospher. For many days, she moved timidly upon the Earth, aware that it was whirling her far through space toward a future that might not exist.

As each day grew overripe and fell smoking into the west, she sat under the cedars watching the stars kindle. She could not believe their days were so shortly numbered – and no one to tell.

There was the usual work to do in the village, and she gave herself vigorously to the vegetable crofts, the maintenance routines among the solar vanes, and the garages of broken-down farm equipment. Simviv soothed her mind when her doomful thoughts became too troubling. Every community had a simviv den, a bunkhouse really, with neural-net hammocks. While the magnetic stimulation of her brain defragmented cortical dendrites, she lived as a flower dazzled with sunfire and the erotic massage of bees or soared among a flock of black birds giddy with camaraderie. Sometimes she forced her eyes open just to watch the walls billowing like sheets in the wind.

The simviv gave her enough serenity to desire a hike and some fishing. She waited until her people had cleared the playa of cactus and scrub, set the irrigation lines and planted the bulbs that would grow into a lodge house and grange sheds for the farm extension. One of the new workers down from the horse bluff commune, a freckled fellow with hair copperbright as hers and eyes blue as mountain lakes, wanted her for a lover. But there would be time for that later, and she left him writing her heartfelt poems and thumbing through bulb catalogs searching for the cottage they would grow together when she returned.

In the month of Summersend, she traipsed into the mountains and set her tent on an aspen ledge above the alluvial fans of a river she knew well. At crimson nightfall, listening to the trees' vesperal hymns and watching the layers of fog gather under the starscape of craggy mountains and a bloated moon patched with black clouds, she looked for ghosts and found none. By day, she gathered grasshoppers and crickets among fields of larkspur and columbine and marched down to the river with her reed basket and rod.

At an elbow of the river where the water shoaled and ran, beech trees gathered. The current had uprooted several and dropped them to form a natural dam where the water gleamed darkly smooth. Willows and stunted cypress mingled on the banks and stained the numerous still pools among their rootledges in different-colored inks. Among the gloomy shadows, where sunlight stood like yellow smoke, she let out her line, swinging the rod over her shoulder and forward with a whip-motion that s-curved the line. Where the grasshopper came down, ripples warped the becalmed darkness of sunken rocks and sodden logs.

The voices of birds sank through the vaporous light like thin threads of dreams and carried away her thoughts. For a long time, she played her grasshoppers over the water tints. No trout rose, but she knew they were there. She had to still the unquiet in herself enough for them to forget her.

She thought of Rafe somewhere on the high plains of Mars. She remembered what he had told her about the galaxies in their billions blown out like a candle, and her mind curled into a seed and sank into the wide spaces between minutes.

Long threads of late sun tangled across the water when the first one struck. It was big as a salmon and nearly pulled the rod from her hands. The ratcheting reel shrieked, and the line rushed into colors lost in the haze.

Careful not to put too much pressure on the line and snap it, she eased her thumb into the fly-reel frame and applied friction to the spinning reel. The line tautened. The water under the cypress where the line disppeared shivered like mercury. A huge trout thrashed into the air, and she quickly lowered her rod to ease the strain.

By the time she worked the trout free of the weeds with the rod bent and shaking and brought it in against the deep current, sunset's long fingernails scratched the sky. She released the hook from the giant trout's undershot jaw and spoke to it with a volume and depth of voice that expressed her gratitude. Then, she let it slide away in the water, into the deeper darkness. And it took with it her heaviness and left her lighter with its power, dazed in the silver night with its strength that she still felt in her aching wrists and her running heart, its primeval beauty totally unspoken for.

When she returned to her tent on the aspen ridge, lunar fire behind the mountains had erased many of the stars in the east. A man in a long traveler's cloak and kneestrap boots stood in lanternlight, and his silver eyes shone like pieces of the moon.

A placid voice from long ago spoke, 'Don't be afraid, Q, it's me.'

'Tabor?'

'Yes, your quingenson,' he replied with a wave of welcome. 'It's me.'

'What are you doing here?' She threw her rod down on a leaf bed and rushed to him. With inquisitive, tactile hands she grabbed his shoulders, touched his square-jawed face, and ran fingers through his dark, short and silken hair. When last she had seen him, he was sixteen. A century had passed, and he stood taller, broader of shoulder, the dent in his chin more cleft than dimple.

'I've come to see you.' He hugged her and stepped back, his silver eyes less bright now that she was close.

'Your eyes—'

'Night vision. I put them on for this trip. It gets dark out here in the woods.'

'Are you hungry?' She moved toward the tent. 'I've got provisions.'

'I brought you some food from Mile High,' he replied and opened the tent flap for her. Inside, next to her cot, was an open satchel spilling fruits, cheeses, breads in static wrap.

They opened a sack of gooseberries and sat in the doorway of the tent watching the Moon rise above the mountains into silver reefs of cloud. Tabor related his experiences in Mile High. He spoke of metasapience like a roar out of paradise. Ellen knew just what he meant. She had heard this before from others of her people who had gone over. It was like knowledge had become clear, moving, flowing and flown from a source of ineffable joy.

He reminded her of the threshold of infinity where they had stood together listening to the music of creation. He told her about the blue dragon of creation that lay coiled smaller than an atom, and he went on about its heart of pure light where heaven lay wide awake contemplating the vast filaments of galaxies. With a puzzled care, he referred to a garden at the center of heaven and the throne of God waiting empty there. 'For us,' he dared announce.

Ellen looked at him with eyes of terrible sadness, understanding that her quingenson was one of the Maat who plotted to betray their world, all worlds. 'Tabor, no created thing can fill that throne.'

'That's fear talking, Q.' He smiled gently at her. 'You haven't heard the roar of paradise in your blood. And if you did, you'd know, that throne is waiting for us. It's our heritage, when we're ready.'

'And when will that be?'

'Some while yet, to be sure. We've reached the blue dragon's heart and stand on the verge of heaven. The garden is in there somewhere. But we've a long way to go to find it.'

'Is that what the secret understanding is about?' she dared to ask.

Tabor's bright eyes thinned. 'What do you know of the secret understanding?'

'Only what people say,' she offered with a shrug. 'That it's a secret strong enough to join all the Claves into the Maat.'

'You're lying.'

Ellen stiffened.

'I know you, Q. I can read every micromovement of your eyes, and I know what those movements mean. I'm a meta now. You can't lie to me.'

'Why would I lie?' She held his sharp gaze, though she felt her ears burning.

'You know something you don't want me to know.' He reached out and took her hand where it lay limp in her lap. 'Don't be frightened of me.'

She clasped his hand and nodded, her heart knocking against her ribs.

'What do you know about the secret understanding?' he asked. 'And don't lie to me.'

'Why do I have to say anything to you, Tabor?' She patted his hand affectionately. 'I'm your quingenmother. I'm allowed to keep my own confidence, aren't I?'

'You know something I may need to know.'

'Is that why you came – to get information from me?'

'Yes.' He tilted his head closer, and she smelled the minty fragrance of olfacts. 'You were on the Moon recently. It was the Machine who summoned you there, wasn't it?'

She was afraid to lie now, afraid that if she gave him cause he would ply the truth from her with narcolfacts. She said simply, 'I found the Machine in the Moon Gardens. It was despondent. The Maat had usurped its authority – and it wanted to die.'

His silver eyes searched her. 'What did you do?'

She chose her words carefully and said with complete candor, 'I took the black cube and I jettisoned it into the sun. It impacted two days ago and burned to nothing.'

'You did that for the Machine?' Tabor released her hand and brushed his hair back in a gesture of amazement. 'Your sentimentality is overwhelming. That was why it summoned you. It knew it could manipulate you with the nostalgia of your early years together.' He gave a silent laugh. 'You were moved by the suffering of the Machine.'

'Yes,' she answered with conviction.

'Did the Machine tell you about the secret understanding?'

She leaked a thin sigh. 'I know that there are Maat who are going to collapse the whole universe so they can enter that garden in the blue dragon's heart.'

Tabor scrutinized her face by the lantern light and acceded with a nod. 'It's good that you know. You should also know that you can come with us, Q. Accept metasapience, and when the collapse comes, you'll ride the shockwave with the rest of us, right into the garden of heaven. We'll sit on God's throne together.'

Sadness tinged with anger smudged the space between her moss-green eyes. She felt hurt that a descendant of hers would betray creation. But she would not be lured by her disappointment into trying to convince him otherwise for fear of disclosing Rafe's alliance with the Machine. '*If* the collapse comes, Tabor, I'll be right here in Council Oak – and if I'm lucky, I'll be trout fishing and reeling in a fighter as big as the one that fought me today.'

'The Machine told you the truth, Q.' Tabor stood. 'My offer should be considered carefully.'

'Thank you, Tabor. But, as you say, you know me, and so you must know I won't be changing my mind.' She lifted her orange eyebrows inquisitively. 'Did you get from me what you wanted?'

'Just one more question.' The intensity of his silver stare seemed to press on her heart. 'Have you seen Rafe von Takawa?'

'Why? Are you looking for him?'

He smiled at her mettle. 'He won't stop the collapse, Q. No one can. It's our ultimate destiny to claim heaven for our own. I came because you are my quingenmother – and you made this destiny possible all those years ago in CIRCLE. You deserve to be among us.'

'Goodbye, Tabor.'

He tossed his hands up in dismay and walked away into the darkness without looking back. For a while after he disappeared from sight she stared after him. Bats whirled above the forest gables, gleaming in the night like brushstrokes of the Moon.

Part Two:

Infinity's Corpse

I who have . . . walked among the lowest of the dead.

–T. S. Eliot, *The Waste Land*, lines 245–246

Datum Surface Raga

2398

The pink sky carried a lone feather of dust above the orange dunes. A sand climber sat at an idle tilt on a slipface, while its rider, in golden solar cowl and dusty cross-strapped boots, stood a short distance apart. The rider's shadow stretched across shards of rock to a sunstruck esker, where the wind scalloped red sand in frail wisps and exposed a hand clutching a black cube.

'*Don't touch it!*' a male voice sounded over the cowl speakers. '*Get away from there, Shala! We're ten arc secs north. We'll be with you in minutes. Wait for us.*'

'It's all right, Da.' Shala knelt beside the hand. From a distance, it had appeared naked, unprotected from the freezing cold and stinging sand, but now she could see that it wore a transparent glove. 'It's a man—' She scooped sand away from an arm and shoulder in a sturdy cloth jacket, also covered by a clear sheath. 'It's a man – and he's got some kind of transparent foil over him.'

'*Transparent—*' Surprise diminished the male voice. '*That's statskin!*'

'What?' Shala called and peered closely at the featureless cube in his grasp, looking for marks and finding none. 'I don't read.'

'*Statskin!*' the radio crackled. '*It's a Maat artefact. Get away from there, Shala!*'

Shala stood abruptly and took several mincing steps backward. She was a fifteen-year-old range worker and terrified of the Maat, the superhumans who lived underground on Earth and who sometimes kidnapped people to use as subjects in their unspeakable experiments. At the outpost, she had even heard that the Maat talked with the dead and could transform with a touch ordinary people into entities of their own strange breed.

A strenuous yell toppled her, and she slid down the concavity of the eroded ridge. Another sand climber burst into view at the crest of the nearest dune. It launched into the air, wheels spinning veils of red pumice, then bounced onto the crumbling slope and careened toward her. At the last possible instant, it swung about sharply and sprayed her with flung sand and pebbles.

'Rizel!' She jolted to her feet in the settling dust. 'What the hell do you think you're doing?'

'Keeping you alert, little sister.' Rizel, also in solar gold garb and cross-strapped boots, jumped from the climber and strode toward her, his thick grin visible through his dusty cowl mask. 'What did you find?'

'Da says stay away,' Shala's anger slid toward hushed caution. 'It's a Maat.'

'Really.' Rizel shoved past her and slogged up the crumbly face of the esker to where the arm protruded. He gawked at the black cube. 'What is this?'

'Don't touch it, Rizel!' Shala grabbed his leg from below and tugged him away.

'Get off me, sandmite.' Rizel shook his leg loose, then bent down and grabbed the cube. But he could not immediately free it from the rigid grip.

'I'm calling Da,' she threatened.

Rizel ignored her and with both hands pried loose the cube. It felt lighter than he had guessed, and he rotated it in his gloved hand scrutinizing it for marks of any kind. 'This is weird.'

'Put it down, Rizel,' she called to him as she backed away. 'It could be dangerous.'

Rizel knelt beside the buried body and placed the featureless cube at his side on the seeping orange sand. With one finger he probed the hand and noted the clear material that covered it and the arm.

'This is a survey assignment, Rizel,' Shala reminded him. 'We're not supposed to touch anything we find – not even rocks.'

'This man might be alive.' Rizel used both gloved hands to excavate the rusty drift and expose the man's upper body. Only the clear wrap covered his cubed head and his dark hair cut close to the facets of his skull. He had mixed asiatic and aryan traits – epicanthic eyefolds, broad cheekbones, and a curved nose.

'He's not dressed like a colonist.' Shala edged up behind him. 'It could be a Maat.'

'So what if he is a Maat?' Rizel pulled away more sand.

'Da says—'

'Da has never seen a Maat, either.' When the man's waist came clear,

Rizel stood up, grabbed the body under his arms and pulled him free of the esker. Sand spilled and covered Rizel to his knees, and he continued dragging the inert form until they could see his whole length.

'Look at his boots,' Shala whispered.

The man wore black entire except for the soles of his ankle-wrap boots that were amber and cleated in irregular ripple patterns.

'*Shala*,' the speakers in her cowl crackled. '*Is Rizel there? I can't raise him on his buggy box.*'

'He's here, Da.' She motioned urgently to her brother, 'Open your cowl speakers. Da wants to talk with you.'

Rizel waved her off and lifted the black cube out of the sand spill.

'He's examining the body we found, Da.' She went on hurriedly, before the speaker-voice had time to react, 'It's a man. A human. Not a morf. Only his garments are strange – black cord, sturdy but not suitable for the range. No gloves. No cowl, not even a respirator. He's bareheaded. Looks like mingled asiatic aryan . . .'

'*Shala, stay away from him,*' Da warned. '*Rizel is going to be sanctioned. You can avoid that by keeping clear of him. We'll be there shortly.*'

'Da says you're going to be sanctioned.' Shala backed away two more steps.

'Am I supposed to care?' Rizel probed the chest with his glove. 'No rigor mortis. The flesh looks pale but not desiccated. I think he's alive, Shala.'

A high-pitched drone descended from the pink sky. 'Da is here.'

In the north, a cusp-wing flyer glinted. Sunlight rayed from its gold-foil elevons, chrome brace wires and wing trusses. It came in low, lifting dust devils with its tandem rotors. The blister canopy popped open before the landing struts touched down, and a husky man in a solar cowl dropped into the whirlwind sand. Out of the churning dust, he came running.

'Get back, you two!' He waved them aside.

Shala retreated to her sand climber, but Rizel did not budge. The husky man shoved him aside. 'That's statskin, all right. And those are gel-grip sandals. Maat artefacts.' He waved to the flyer that sat inert in a rocky field among the dunes. 'Tiken will clear this mess up. Let's get out of here. Quickly. We're on target time.'

'He's alive,' Rizel protested. 'You can't kill him.'

'Alive or dead, he's not human, Rizel.' The husky man waved impatiently at the flyer. 'And yes, we can kill him. We're fully within our legal rights to preserve our integrity.'

From out of the flyer, a tall, gangly man descended, carrying a heavy canister.

'You're wrong,' Rizel spoke adamantly. 'We're not on colonial grounds or even in the outpost fields. This is a range find. There are no legal rights out here.'

Through the husky man's dusty visor, brown eyes glared. 'We found it, we can do what we want with it.'

'You didn't find it.' Rizel pointed to Shala. 'She did. It's for her to decide.'

Down the esker the gangly man slid, the ponderous silver canister held by its sturdy strap in one hand and its heat-tarnished nozzle in the other.

'We won't be needing that, Tiken,' Rizel declared. 'Shala, help me get this man in my buggy.'

'Where do you think you're going to take it?' Da pressed closer to his son.

Rizel dug in his heels. 'To the outpost. Maybe he can be revived.'

'You're going to endanger human beings for the likes of this thing?' Da pointed at the prone body that lay face up, its clear wrap frosted with powdery shades of rust. 'Look at it! It's not wearing a solar cowl. My God, it doesn't even have proper boots or gloves or a damn respirator. And what is *that* thing?' He jabbed a gloved finger toward the black cube. 'This is not an ordinary human being, Rizel. It's a creature of another order. And you're not going to expose good people to this thing.'

Rizel threw his hands up in dismay. 'Da! Lampland is a field station. It's staffed by volunteers who are trained and equipped to deal with contingencies.'

'You think this is a contingency?' Da stepped so close that the edge of his visor touched his son's. 'A ruptured water coolant pipe is a contingency. This is a Maat. It only looks human. Use the eyes in your head, boy. This creature imprisoned our people on reservations. It drove us off Earth and out here to this desolate world. It thinks of us as monkeys. And if you bring it to Lampland and revive it, it will treat us like monkeys. Have you studied no history at all?'

'Da is right, Rizel.' Shala put a hand on her brother's arm and gently moved him away from Da. 'We are the original people. We are human as God made us. Man and woman made in His image. This – man is an abomination.'

'Shala, I don't know much history. But I do know that he *is* a man.' Rizel gestured at the body. 'He has arms and legs and the face of a man.'

'Let appearances not deceive you,' Tiken's sonorous and stern voice spoke. 'Genotype is sacred. Phenotype a mask.'

Rizel dismissed him with a brusque wave. 'Leave the Essentia texts for the colonists. Out here we're supposed to explore the range—'

'Get back in your buggy and get out of here,' Da ordered. 'This is the range, son, and that means we're targets for any of the cogs that are watching us from the other side of that horizon.' He punched a fist toward the staccato mountains in the south. 'This creature is not natural. It has defied God's law and tampered with creation itself. It has altered the human cryptarch, the sacred dna, so that it could monstrously amplify its intelligence. Is that not arrogance incarnate? Is that not the original sin itself flaunted to the extreme?'

'And the abomination has eaten again of the Tree of Knowledge.' Tiken walked around to the feet of the body and stood staring.

'All right.' Rizel conceded with a nod and stepped away from his father. 'So let's bury him again. He seems to be in a state of suspended animation. Let's leave him where we found him. Maybe his people will eventually find him.'

'Leave it?' Da's voice sharpened with fear. 'This is target time. How many times do I have to tell you? We have to move. Now. Burn it.'

'And the people shall put aside the abomination and go a separate way.' Tiken shouldered the canister and began adjusting the nozzle controls.

'What?' Rizel turned to face both his father and sister. 'You're going to kill him?'

'It is this creature who has killed our future as human beings.' Da kicked sand onto the body. 'It is the Maat who are the authors of all morfs. They also created the silicon mind and are responsible for the cogs. Every possible distortion of the human form has come from their demented minds.'

'And God alone made the five races of humanity according to their places on the Earth – the afric, the amerindic, the aryan, the asiatic, and the australnesian – and gave them to mingle and generate the many breeds of our kind.' Tiken looked up from adjusting the nozzle controls and nodded to Da.

'Put that thing down.' Rizel placed himself between the body and the nozzle. 'We're not going to burn this man.'

'That has already been decided by the laws of our colony, son.' Da spoke in a tone of finality. 'You're the only one here who thinks this thing should not be purged.'

Rizel spun about. 'Shala – you want to kill this man?'

'He's not a man, Rizel.' Shala slid behind her father. 'He only looks like a man. He's an abomination.'

Da nodded to Tiken, and the tall man clicked the ignitor and set a blue halo of flame upon the nozzle. 'Get back, Rizel,' he said. 'This will crisp your toes.'

Rizel did not budge until Da grabbed him by the collar of his cowl and hauled him backward. Then the youth twisted free and waved his father off. 'What you're doing is murder.'

'Take your sister to her buggy,' Da ordered. 'That black box may blow.'

Rizel stood stiff with anger until his father pushed past him to help Tiken.

'It's for the best,' Shala consoled, taking his hand and coaxing him away.

'Shala, you can stop this.' Rizel put both hands on her shoulders. 'He's your range find. Time and locus have already been radio-logged when you cut your buggy engine, and there's nothing Da can do about it if you make your claim. He can't afford to be sanctioned. The Clerics would strip him of office and send him back to Isidis. He has to comply if you'll just make your claim.'

'I'm not going to do that, Rizel.' Shala removed his hands from her shoulders. 'I'm sorry, brother. It is not our way.'

'Shala, I don't want to have to do this,' Rizel spoke in an anguished whisper. 'But you're forcing me.' He touched his visor to hers and said just loud enough for her to hear, 'Datum Surface Raga.'

'No!' She pushed away. 'No, Rizel! Not for something like this.'

'We have an agreement, Shala.' He followed her as she backed away.

'Anything but this, Rizel.' She walked away from him. 'I won't do it.'

'You *have* to do it, sister.' Rizel rushed to her side. 'You promised.'

She turned on him stiffly and even through her hazed visor he could see her vexed stare. 'I can't do this.'

'You mean you won't.' He barked a curt, sharp laugh. 'Ha! And you think you're a religious woman.' He backed away. 'You're just a hypocrite.'

Muffled thunder sounded, and Rizel saw Shala's visor flare orange with reflected flames. Over his shoulder, he watched fire fall like a radiant shroud across the body they had found, Da and Tiken erased to white shadows of themselves in the fierce glare of the blaze.

'I'm sorry, Rizel.' Shala pressed close to him, and he jolted away from her.

'You're a liar,' he spoke venomously. 'Datum Surface Raga was a lie. And that means your life is a lie – and mine a waste.'

The incinerating fire drooled back to the nozzle, leaving clots of flame leaping in the sand like devil imps celebrating an infernal victory. Rizel stalked back toward his buggy and noticed Da gesticulating angrily and Tiken standing stiff. The young man walked toward them several abrupt steps and stopped.

On a bed of amber glass, the body lay unscathed. Its clear wrap bore no scorching, not even a smudge.

In the thin atmosphere, Rizel thought he heard his father curse, and then, more distinctly, Da said, 'Bury it.'

'And evil shall not perish but thrive upon destruction,' Tiken quoted and backed away.

The melted sand cracked under the weight of Rizel's boots. Neither the body nor the black cube showed any mark.

'We'll notify Isidis,' Da said numbly. 'They can decide what to do with it.'

'No,' Shala announced, stepping to the brittle edge of the pyre. 'I've decided to make my claim. I'm taking this body back to the station.'

'Shala, what are you talking about?' Da moved brusquely toward her.

'I've changed my mind,' she answered quietly yet firmly. 'Now that I see it can't be destroyed, I choose to claim it as a range find and bring it into the station to be logged and properly examined.'

'Forget it, Shala,' Da decreed. 'We'll use blast caps to collapse this ridge over it so no one will accidentally stumble on it again.'

'You can't do that, Da,' Rizel said triumphantly. 'She's made her claim.'

'Nonsense,' Da griped. 'She doesn't know what she's talking about. Get the blasting caps, Tiken.'

'No time.' Tiken tapped the inside of his forearm, where the cuff of his airsuit held a chronometer. 'If we don't move now, the cogs are going to get lucky.'

'Leave the body,' Da decided. 'We'll drop charges on it from the air.'

'No.' Shala stepped briskly toward her sand climber. 'This is my range find. I'm claiming it.'

Tiken unstrapped the canister from his back and waved to Da. 'Come on. We're on target time, buddy.'

Da ignored him and moved to pursue his daughter, but Rizel stopped him. 'She's in her rights, Da.'

Da shoved Rizel aside and hurried after Shala. 'Don't touch that radio panel!'

Shala had already opened a channel, and she spoke briskly, 'Lampland, this is range runner Shala Walking Face. I've discovered a male, asiatic-aryan body in some kind of impervious clear wrap – a statskin . . .'

Da's hand slapped the radio panel and broke the connection. 'Are you mad, Shala? You heard Tiken. We're on target time. Your radio signal is painting us.'

'It's secure,' Rizel said coming up behind Da. 'If we hurry, we can . . .'

A shrill, sharp peal interrupted him, and a streak of blue fire slashed down from the pink sky. The bolt struck Tiken as he climbed the dune on his way back to the flyer, and his solar cowl burst open.

Da pulled Shala from the buggy.

Three more slashes of blue-hot energy hit the flyer, and it shattered like a startled hive swarming in every direction and vanishing.

The third impacted Rizel's buggy, ripping it violently into whistling shreds of metal. Flechettes sang off the desert rocks and sparkled into the sky.

When they lifted their heads, Da, Shala, and Rizel groaned with numb amazement to find themselves alive. Tiken lay on his side, rocking on the distant slipface. Da rose to go to him. But Rizel saw the wrinkled space around Tiken and restrained his father.

'The canister's ruptured,' Rizel said and pushed Da to the ground. 'He's already dead. It's just the gas leak that's moving him.'

A dull roar announced ignition of the fumes. Tiken sat up, hoisted by invisible flames warping the dune. Then the tank exploded, throwing the flaming body to the top of the dune, where it lay a moment smoldering under twists of black smoke before it slewed down the side.

Shala cried out in anguish.

Da stood and raised a stunned hand toward the churning flames. 'My God . . .' he mumbled. 'He warned me. Target time . . .'

'It's always target time, Da.' Rizel placed a consoling hand on his father's arm. 'It's not your fault. The cogs were sniping randomly. In the few seconds they had before our gunners spotted them, they shot wildly. It could have been us. And it may be us next time.'

'You're wrong.' Da lowered his arm and jerked a thumb at Shala's buggy. 'She parked her vehicle askew, like the range manual says. Smaller profile. That's why the snipers took out your buggy and my flyer. Obvious shapes. I was in too much of a hurry to reach you. I should have pinioned the wings and tucked the ship under an escarpment. And I shouldn't have stood around arguing. Tiken was right. Target time . . .'

'My radio message,' Shala asked. 'Did it alert the cogs? Is that how they found us?'

'No. It's a secure channel.' Rizel shrugged haplessly. 'It's nobody's fault. Except the cogs. It's their stupid war.'

'Get the body,' Da said morosely.

Rizel slogged toward the burning body on the dune.

'No, not Tiken.' Da waved him back. 'There's nothing left of him but ash. And he's a religious man. "Death is an instrument of perfection.", Isn't that the right screed? He's where he wants to be now.' He pointed to the body they had discovered in the sand. 'Get that thing. We're bringing it back. Tiken didn't die for nothing.'

Rizel stopped and faced about, surprised.

'Do it quickly,' Da added. 'If we don't execute an escape pattern, the cogs will think there's something going on here and take a closer look. We don't want that. Do we?'

Rizel rushed toward the disinterred body.

'Start the engine,' Da ordered Shala, who stood watching Tiken's blackened carcass fuming.

She jumped into her buggy and entered the start sequence. When Rizel came walking backward, hunched over and pulling the body after him, Da picked up the dragging feet, and they placed the stranger in the back seat. Rizel sat next to him and propped him against the strut for the solar awning. In one hand, he held the black cube. Through his gloved fingers, he felt no vibrations, no particular temperature, and he secured the object between his knees.

Da ran around to the front passenger seat, and the moment he attached his harness, Shala threw the buggy into gear and peeled away from the site. While she drove, speeding between dunes and zigzagging across gravel flats, he radioed Lampland.

'They're frantic over there,' he announced when he finished and slapped off the communications panel.

'Did the cogs hit them, too?' Rizel asked anxiously.

Da pulled himself around in the front seat and jabbed a finger at the slumped body. 'It's that thing. The Clerics and the Scientists are already squabbling over what to do with it.'

No one said anything the remainder of the run. The arid, rocky land jolted past like a visual commentary on their souls as Shala flawlessly performed her escape routine, and soon stars glinted in the pink zenith of the day sky.

'Looks like we rate a flyer escort,' Da said. 'You better take us to the east lading gate. We don't want to scare the populace.'

Shala cut hard over the seething sands, and a powder trail billowed behind them. Another slash of the wheel, and the adroit buggy leaped a gravel bar and bounced onto a shallow pan of rocky shards.

'Hey, slow down!' Rizel yelped. 'We've got air cover. The cogs aren't tracking us anymore.'

'Can't be too careful.' Shala steered toward a chain of black volcanic hills.

'She's right.' Da peered up at the pale blur of the sun. 'The cogs see this air cover, they may figure there's something worth hitting.'

Soon, pinyon scrub began to appear in the shade of the larger rocks. A bluff swung to one side as Shala steered the nimble buggy expertly among stone cairns that marked where others had fallen, struck down by cog snipers. A cratered road appeared below, streaked with stains of smoke. Scrub juniper that grew fitfully beside the sandy trail leaned into the wind. The stone walls of the escarpment abutting the road bore etchings of flyers and buggies, scrawled pictographs of people and animals. Several charred remains of caravan freighters lay blackly in the sandy verges where they had been shoved out of the way, the crisp ribs of their metal frames looking much like the roasted briskets of gutted beasts.

A cindercone jogged to one side when Shala negotiated a long caveout beside the edge of the road, and they glimpsed buff, ochre, and madder geodesic domes along a shelf of rusty rock. Overhead, the stars went out as the flyers beveled their wings and rode the swooping vectors of the wind in wide, spiraling dives. The drone of their engines sifted down through the sky's pales of pink and grew louder. By the time the paved road hissed under the buggy's wheels, the flyers glided directly overhead, their tinsel cusp wings and elevons flashing reflections off the stony faces of the jumbled terrain.

Shala slowed down on the long, curving road that climbed to the east lading gate. Desert-brown water tanks sat on their scaffolds at intervals along the roadside to refuel the hydroengines of the trucks that used this road. The tank-stops stood empty at this time of day. The freightliners that drained them occupied the bays of the warehouses ahead, unloading supplies from Isidis.

At one open bay, a knot of Clerics in red solar cowls and Scientists in blue awaited them. Shala slowed down to a crawl at the sight of them and her voice quavered, 'What am I going to say to them?'

'Yes,' Da's voice sneered, 'how will a priestess of the Essentia explain bringing into our outpost a strange black box and a body in a statskin?'

'Don't say anything.' Rizel loosened his harness and pushed forward in his seat. 'You don't have to say anything. This is a range find like any other. Turn the find over to recovery and walk away. None of this is yours. It all belongs to the station now.'

'And my confessors?' Shala stopped the buggy and twisted almost full around. 'What am I going to tell them when they ask?'

'Datum Surface Raga,' Rizel answered.

'What craziness of yours is that?' Da watched the recovery squad at the bay waving them in and punched the comm panel. Radio voices filled their cowls, directing them to the bay, sternly requesting more information. He slapped it off again. 'Why did you change your mind, Shala?'

'You care?' Her voice lashed out. 'If you cared why didn't you ask me back there?'

'You made the claim.' Da reared back, perplexed. 'Tiken is dead. He died and you made the claim. He didn't die for no reason.'

'Like Ma.' Shala's words burned with indignation. 'She didn't die for no reason, either. She just died.'

Da looked to Rizel, 'What is this all about?'

'Datum Surface Raga,' the youth replied. 'It's her thesis—'

'Rizel!' Shala jolted angrily in her seat.

'It's all right, Shala.' He put an arm out to soothe her, and she recoiled. 'Our agreement is fulfilled. There's no reason to keep it secret any longer.'

'What secret agreement?' Da passed a quick glance to the bay where the recovery squad stood arguing, then fixed his attention on his son, 'Tell me what is happening here.'

Rizel sat back deeper in his seat. 'Back in Isidis, when we made the decision—'

'To come here, to build something new.' Da affirmed this a curt nod.

'I wanted to stay in Isidis and finish my schooling. And Shala—' Rizel jerked a thumb at her. 'She wanted to come out here and accept the big advancement the Essentia offered. Ma wouldn't leave Isidis unless we were unanimous.'

'So you agreed to give up your academic tracking for a price.' Da's voice softened with understanding.

'Datum Surface Raga,' Rizel confirmed. 'Shala's musical thesis. It's good.'

'It's profound,' Da agreed. 'Nobody understands it. So what?'

'It got her the promotion she wanted. And in exchange I get one bigtime favor.'

'And this is it?' Da glowered at the body that lay awkwardly slumped.

'After Ma died,' Rizel continued, 'I didn't want anything from anybody.'

'I remember.' Da shook his head. 'I'm still paying off the simviv therapy.'

'I didn't want anything, because I felt it was my fault.' Rizel knocked his fists together. 'I mean, we would have stayed in Isidis if I had done what I wanted. I could have kept her safe—'

Shala turned her back on him and grabbed the steering yoke. 'She's been dead three years, Rizel. When are you going to make time for reality?'

'This is the first touch of reality I've felt since Ma died.' Rizel's tone carried conviction. 'And I'm glad you've given it to me, Shala. Just tell that to your confessors. Tell them the truth.'

'The truth is you give more to the dead than the living.' She directed her exasperation out the windshield, to where the recovery squad descended the bay ladders. 'You've lost the Essence, Rizel. You've squandered it for a ghost and now *this* – this abomination! Why did I ever listen to you?'

He answered clemently, 'Because in Isidis you'd still be an acolyte binding prayer books.'

'All right, you two.' Da stared at the recovery crew jogging toward them across the tarmac, looking to see who he knew in this squad. 'Here they come.'

Shala put her gloved hand on the gear shift to bring the buggy forward, and Da grabbed her wrist. 'Leave the buggy here. Tell them this is as close as you dare bring it. Let *them* decide if it should be brought into the outpost.'

'We're going to be questioned separately,' Rizel said. 'Just tell them the truth, Shala.'

'Sure,' Da agree. 'Then maybe they'll listen to your music again. Who knows, someone may finally understand Datum Surface Raga.'

The Clerics and Scientists converged on the dune buggy, and the occupants were ushered out and led away to the quarantine sheds for testing and observation. After preliminary scans of the statskin-suited body and the odd black cube, the stranger was carried off to a research hangar, the red and blue cowled crews arguing whether or not to immediately notify Isidis. No one disputed that the black box should be taken at once to a containment vault.

In an arroyo outside Lampland's perimeter, the vault, a giant orange cylinder of impervious glasteel, lay on its side. One of its domed ends stood open, and the black, empty interior was large enough to garage a freightliner. Designed to imprison cogs, it was opaque to all wavelengths of radiation and even had neutrino-bafflers embedded in its thick shell.

When the Machine detected the impenetrable darkness about to enclose it, a decision came to focus, and it broadcast an undetected signal of ultralow frequency. The signal reset the statskin bio-support enclosing Rafe von Takawa and roused him from his coma. Then the vault's hatch boomed shut, and unanimous darkness reigned.

No signals penetrated the vault's exterior, and the Machine sat alone with itself.

For one hundred years prior to this dark imprisonment, the Machine had remained silent, hidden beneath the sands of Mars, listening to communications from Earth, the Moon, and the near planets. Quietly it had observed the societies of the Maat, the aboriginals, the morfs, and the silicon mind. Now it heard nothing.

Nor could it be heard. And that pleased the Machine. During its century under the Martian dunes, it had worked very hard to keep from being detected. That was why it had gone into the desert in the first place. They were being stalked by the Maat who knew that it and Rafe von Takawa were searching for the arrival of the wormhole from the future that would deliver the Maat's gauge field bomb.

Rafe had wanted to keep moving, traveling among the colonies on Mars and planning to eventually tour the Jovian system. But the Machine believed that this strategy was too risky. It had decided to take control of their situation. Luring Rafe into the desert with a false report of assassins closing in, the Machine had overridden Rafe's statskin controls and had plunged him into a dormant state.

The seething sands of the desert had soon covered them. Hidden from sight by the dunes, they had lain undisturbed while history continued without them. Occasionally, the Machine had to generate counter-pattern wavelengths to mask their presence from various Maat and cog scans. That had been arduous, having to remain vigilant at all times, always ready to match probing radiation with camouflage energy. Yet the effort had won them a long and undisturbed seclusion.

In the dark of the vault, the Machine assessed what energy remained in its power cells. Its consciousness was sufficiently charged to continue for centuries to come, but it no longer possessed the strength necessary to defeat the searching energies of probes. That was its chief reason for allowing itself and Rafe to be discovered. It needed to recharge.

The Machine felt soothed by the sudden quiet. A hundred years of listening and watching roiled in its memory, slowly settling into the gentle depths of the dark. It reviewed what it had witnessed.

The twenty-fourth century had been an expansionist time. The Maat, aware that their future selves would soon be delivering them the fateful gauge field bomb, had sent their minions across the solar system to search for it. Some searched to detonate it. Others, like Rafe and the Machine, searched to get rid of it. Colonies appeared on Mars and the larger moons of Jupiter. Most were occupied by morfs, aboriginals genetically adapted to thrive in their new environments. A few had been terraformed to accommodate true aboriginals. And many other settlements were created and sustained by the silicon mind's machine intelligences – cogs.

The cogs were entirely programmable. They could be shaped to any form – even human. And they would execute whatever agenda their creators designed for them. That was why the Machine loathed them. They were just like itself, slavish servants of their creators.

The Machine wanted to find the gauge field bomb and deploy it to a parallel universe, because it had been created by humankind to protect their species. This was so deeply encoded in its programming that, even steeped in absolute darkness and silence, reduced to a thread of existence, it continued to dwell on how to fulfill its primary mandate.

It needed power. To continue to elude the Maat who would destroy it, it needed power. And it had decided to take it from Lampland and all the communities that shared the energy grid network with this field station.

But for now it had to rely on Rafe von Takawa to get it out of this prison. And that would take time. Until then, it would have to wait in the darkness while the ferment of human emotions did its work among Rafe and the others. When they were drunk enough on each other, they would set it free. Then it would take what it wanted. No one could stop it. No one could deny it the power it craved, for even in the dark and newly arrived it knew the people of Lampland better than they knew themselves.

'He's awake!' Shala, an almond-eyed adolescent with long, dark hair whose spiral ringlets covered the shoulders of her blue bodysuit, stirred her brother where he lay asleep on a cot in the research hangar.

They were alone in the large enclosure. The Clerics and Scientists had gone off to the conference hall to debate what to do with the stranger and his black cube. Since none of the party that had found the body and its artefact had been tainted by the contact, Da had been released and Shala, the claimant of the discovery, had been appointed by the Clerics to monitor the body. The Scientists decided that Rizel should stay with her. That served the dual purpose of putting them to work while keeping them out of the conference meeting where their youthful perspectives and legal standing as claimants would surely have made the discussion more volatile.

Rizel sat up groggily, a square-framed youth with a thick neck and a ledged brow over deep-set eyes and small nose. He wore his black curls cropped close at the sides and long at the back. 'You sure?'

Shala pulled at the sleeve of his red jumpsuit. 'Get up and look!'

Rubbing his eyes, he followed her across an oil-stained concrete expanse cluttered with coiled cables, steel drums, mechanical dolleys, metal worktables heaped with engine parts, and the shadows of overhanging winches and chains. Scaffold lights and cameras watched from the rafters. Beyond the gutted hulk of a cusp-wing flyer, a corner of the hangar had been partitioned with a sheet of clear film. The stranger had been laid out on a red floor mat there, but, as they approached, they saw that he sat with his legs bent and his head resting on his knees.

'Have you called the others?' Rizel asked.

'Not yet.' She flicked a look at the cameras recording them and the stranger from above. 'Why disturb their conference? It's all on fiche. Besides, we found him. We should be the ones to talk to him first.'

Rizel carried a step-ladder to the partition and sat down. He signaled for his sister to say something.

'Sir?' Shala walked up to the clear sheet and put her hand against it. 'Can you hear us?'

Rafe did not stir. His mind searched inward, seeking the memories of what had happened to him last. He remembered a banded twilight and a periodic flare of dust fire – static discharge from a mounting sandstorm. Mountains stood footed in umber clouds like a celestial vista fallen to the horizon. Thunder trudged closer. The Machine directed him toward a rusty cape of rock off to his left where they would seek shelter. He asked about the assassins pursuing them, hoping to gauge where they were, but the Machine was more concerned with protecting him from the wind off the tilted desert. The Machine said it would adjust the bio-support of his statskin – and after that he could remember nothing more except for awakening here to find himself alone without the Machine.

'Maybe he doesn't speak esper.' Rizel bent forward and loudly tapped a finger against the sheet. 'Can he hear us through this thing?'

'I think he's probably woozy,' Shala surmised. 'Think how long he must have been comatose for him to have been buried in an esker.'

Rafe von Takawa looked up, startled, and Shala stepped back a pace. He tried his voice and experienced no difficulty speaking, 'Where am I?'

'Lampland.' She saw befuddlement in his faceted face and a hint of fear.

'Where?' He gazed searchingly at the brother and sister and then past them to the cluttered hangar. 'Where is this place?'

'You're on Mars,' Rizel answered. 'Lampland is a field station of the Isidis colony.'

'We found you comatose in the desert not far from here,' Shala volunteered. 'You were buried under rocks and sand in an esker. You must have been there a long time.'

He sat up straighter, testing his muscles. Though he felt some stiffness, he experienced no real discomfort. 'What year is this?'

'Colonia 27,' Shala said. 'Twenty-seven years since Isidis was founded.'

'Mars years—' Rafe muttered. He patted his jacket pockets, feeling for his chronometer, before his groggy mind registered that a statskin sheathed him and he would have to open it to access what he carried. 'Do you know what common year it is on Earth?'

Rizel snorted with surprise and stood up. 'You're from Earth?'

'I think you had better tell us who you are, sir,' Shala said firmly, thinking of her responsibility to the Clerics who had posted her.

Rafe's prolonged hesitancy betrayed his nervousness. He wanted to know where the Machine was. He feared that he had lost it in the storm, that it remained buried in the desert where they had found him.

'What's your name?' Rizel inquired.

'I—' Rafe feared telling them who he was until he knew more of his situation. 'I am Alain Vancet.'

'You're a Maat, aren't you?' Rizel gave a small smile. 'A Maat from Earth.'

Rafe stood up. No cramps or dizziness thwarted him. However long he had been unconscious, the statskin bio-support had taken good care of his body. 'May I ask who you are and why I am in here?'

'I'm Rizel Walking Face – and this is my sister, Shala Walking Face.'

'I'm the one who found you in the desert, during a routine range patrol.'

Rafe stepped close to the partition. 'Are you keeping me in here for a reason?'

'You're under observation,' Shala replied, 'until we determine who you are.'

'I don't understand.' Rafe placed a hand against the clear screen and knew by its touch that it was a glasteel film. A glance revealed that it was anchored to the concrete with steel pins and to the rafters with magnetic clips. He was inside a makeshift prison.

'You're our range find,' Rizel told him. 'We brought you back here because our father wanted to bury you again under a few tons of sand.'

Rafe flicked his eyebrows apprehensively. 'I take it then that the residents of this field station consider me a hostile entity?'

'You'd be ash now,' Rizel acknowledged, 'except the fire wouldn't burn your statskin.'

Rafe grimaced anxiously. 'Your father and the others who want me dead, where are they?'

'Da is probably sitting in the beer den right now,' Rizel guessed. 'And the Clerics and the Scientists are in conference, deciding your fate.'

Rafe stepped back to the mat and sat down heavily. 'Clerics? Is Lampland perhaps a field station in an Anthropos Essentia colony?'

Shala nodded enthusiastically. 'Yes. I'm a canoness of the Essentia.'

'And I'm an assistant researcher in the Order of Empiricists,' Rizel added. 'I guess you know about our communities. Frankly, you don't look too happy to be in our custody.'

'I know about the Essentia.' Rafe glumly shook his head. 'On Earth they won't stay on the reservations. They defy all authority but their own. I didn't realize there were colonies of the Essentia on Mars.'

'That's why we're on Mars,' Shala picked up, enthusiastically. 'The Maat took the Earth away from us. We had to come out here to make a home for ourselves where we could live by our own principles.'

'It must be hard.' Rafe stared at them sympathetically. 'Mars is harsh and with only one-third gravity, lifting is easy but digging difficult – and the Essentia probably doesn't have magravity technology and it most certainly won't allow bio-adaptation.'

'Morfs?' Rizel snorted a laugh. 'Forget that. We're human and it'll be many generations before Mars changes us.'

'You never answered our question,' Shala said. 'Are you a Maat?'

'The Essentia have no love of the Maat,' Rafe said quietly. 'I am a man.'

Shala glanced at Rizel and then back to Rafe. 'We know you must be a Maat. How else could you have survived being buried alive?'

'No aboriginal community has the technology to manufacture statskin,' Rizel added.

Rafe thought about this, then asked, 'When you found me, did you also uncover a black cube?'

'What is it?' Shala asked.

'Tell me first what you've done with it.'

'Is it dangerous?' Shala pressed.

'It's a machine intelligence,' Rafe admitted. 'It's my guide.'

'Forbidden fruit—' Shala muttered, hand to her mouth, eyes wide.

'Forbidden fruit from the Tree of Knowledge,' Rizel clarified for the nonplussed Maat. 'If there's anything that the Essentia loathe more than the Maat and morfs it's the silicon mind. It's not even vaguely human.'

'Then it appears that I'm in a great deal of trouble here, aren't I?' Rafe clasped his arms about his knees and hugged himself. 'Will you at least tell me now what you have done with the cube?'

'It's in a vault, outside the station,' Rizel confided. 'I'm sorry.'

'You should be sorry,' Shala said, more for the cameras than any hope of shaming her brother. 'We should have left him buried in the desert.'

Rizel ignored her. 'What common terrene year *were* you buried – and how?'

'It was a sandstorm,' Rafe answered sullenly. 'The common era year was 2300.'

'Are you hungry?' Shala inquired. 'Or thirsty? Shall we get you a meal?'

'No. I feel fine physically.' He stretched out on the mat and rolled to his side so that his back faced them. 'I think I'll just lie here for now, until your elders are ready to talk with me. Please, leave me alone.'

'2300!' Doute Wheel of Cloud, grand prior of the Clerics, gusted with surprise, his blue robes flapping with his extravagant gestures of alarm. He sat at one end of the rectangular slab of black volcanic rock that served as the conference hall table, and he glared the length of it at the six other Clerics near him and the seven Scientists at the remote end. '2300 Common Era was ninety-eight terrene years ago!'

'So?' Mava Living Day, the chief administrator of the Scientists, glared back and gripped the fluted lapels of her crimson jacket with pale-knuckled hands.

Doute stabbed a bony finger at the holostream at the center of the table that displayed the Walking Face children's interview with the Maat. 'Buried alive a hundred years and he looks roused from a nap! He has lost no weight. Even his hair and fingernails have not grown!'

'He was in a *statskin*, Doute.' Mava rolled her brown eyes. 'If you would learn a little science, none of this would seem so frightful to you.'

Both the grand prior and the chief administrator were gray-haired and seamed with wrinkles and wore the traits of their senescence proudly. The Anthropos Essentia eschewed all genetic manipulation, including the ion-washes that eliminated damaged cells from the body, simviv that repaired cortical dendrites, and codon switching that turned off the chromosomal timer that regulated the unwinding of the dna's supercoiling, the inborn cause of ageing.

Along the length of the stone table, men and women of various ages watched the holostream attentively, for none had ever seen a Maat before.

'What is frightening to me, Mava, is that our station has been invaded by beings we cannot control.' Doute passed a grave stare down one side of the table and up the other. 'They must be eliminated.'

'No.' Mava's long white hair tossed with the vigor of her determination. 'These two entities must be understood – and then sent on their way.'

'God has delivered them into our hands,' Doute said sternly. 'And they have been judged. All that remains is for us to destroy them.'

'And risk the wrath of other Maat?' Mava hummed direly. 'We are already at war with the silicon mind. We need no other enemies.'

'What, then, of Tiken?' Doute countered. 'He died to retrieve these monsters. His death must not be in vain.'

'His death will be wasted if we do not use this Maat for the good of our colony,' Mava insisted. 'We must barter his freedom for what he can teach us.'

'Barter with abomination?' Doute nearly choked on his indignation.

'What this one man may teach us may well decide whether our colony survives another winter,' Mava said. 'This is a rare opportunity . . .'

Her words were smothered by a metallic thunder that shook the conference hall and drizzled sand from the stone-hewn ceiling. The Clerics and Scientists dove beneath the sturdy table.

'Cog assault!' someone yelled.

Dust boiled through the chamber, and another voice shouted, 'The north sector barriers are breached!'

Explosions resounded from the distance, then sudden silence settled upon the murky hall.

A voice frayed with radio static announced, 'All clear. Our hill batteries have returned fire and aborted the cog assault. All clear.'

As the Clerics and Scientists crawled out from under the table, Mava's angry stare sought out the grand prior. 'Shall we go speak with Alain Vancet – while we still can?'

The Clerics in their blue gowns and the Scientists in their red jumpsuits stood in two groups before the clear film partition. Rafe von Takawa passed a nervous look between them. The sight of so many aged bodies disturbed him, as did the presence of several members of the delegation wearing eye patches and crude prosthetic limbs.

'We are at war,' Mava announced. 'Lampland and our mother colony Isidis are in competition for Mars with machine intelligences who have created their own colonies. The Maat who created these machines have programmed them to occupy this planet to the exclusion of all others. And so they attack us with laser cannon, phages, and, when they can, physical assault.'

'You are a Maat,' Doute interposed angrily. 'If you want your freedom, you will help us to defend ourselves from your machine monsters.'

Mava glared at her counterpart. 'That, crudely put, is the arrangement we would like to establish with you. We are at war with the cogs, and we need all the help we can get to survive. Are you willing to assist us in order to win your freedom?'

Rafe stood close to the film partition. 'How do you expect me to help you?'

'You created these monsters,' Doute shouted, 'you can destroy them!'

Rafe frowned and rubbed the back of his neck. 'You have a misapprehension about me.'

'Are you not a Maat?' Doute challenged. 'Are you not responsible for the very existence of the silicon mind? Did we not find you with a machine intelligence in your own hand when we uncovered you in the desert?'

'I am a Maat,' Rafe conceded. 'But I am not among those responsible for colonizing Mars with the silicon mind.'

'The Maat are a *union* of all Claves,' Doute said, rheumy eyes thinned suspiciously. 'The Idioclaves were dissolved long ago. We know that. We are aboriginals but we are not wholly ignorant of history.'

'I am a rogue Maat.' Rafe paused while the muttering group of Clerics and Scientists absorbed this, then he added, 'I am an independent metasapient who fled Earth with my one ally – a machine intelligence.'

'What are you fleeing?' Mava asked.

'That is a personal matter,' Rafe answered, 'but if I were to be found by the Maat, there are many among them who would gladly slay me.'

'You must be a criminal,' Doute asserted. 'What evil has outlawed you from your own people?'

'I'm not a criminal, only an independent seeking his own way.'

'I don't believe you!' Doute swelled with wrath.

'Don't be intimidated by my fellow colonist,' Mava said apologetically. 'It is no concern of ours why you are exiled from the Maat. If you will help us in our war effort, we will return your freedom.'

'I am no ally of the silicon mind,' Rafe answered and saw the groups gathered before him visibly relax. 'Whatever I can do to help you, I will.'

'Then remove that statskin,' Doute ordered. 'And divest yourself of your clothes and all their contents so that you cannot threaten us, and we will remove the partition.'

'These will be returned to me when I leave?' Rafe asked. 'You will not tamper with them?'

'If you can help us against our enemy,' Mava spoke in a sincere tone, 'you will have everything returned to you when you depart.'

'And the black cube as well?'

'We would want you to remove that piece of the silicon mind from our colony, yes.' Mava signed to her gawking followers, and one of them stepped out of the group, holding a red jumpsuit and brown sandals.

Rafe could think of no other way to retrieve the Machine and continue their quest, and he collapsed the statskin and doffed his clothes. He left them at one end of the confined area and stood naked at the back wall while the partition was removed.

The Scientists took his clothes and statskin bracelets, and he was given the jumpsuit and sandals. As he dressed, the grand prior spoke. 'The Walking Face family uncovered this Maat, and so he should by rights reside with them during his stay at the field station.'

Mava approached Rafe. 'Alain Vancet,' she spoke cordially, 'welcome to Lampland field station. Our clerics have responsibility for your living accommodations, and you have been placed with one of their families. But your work time will be spent with me and my researchers. Are you up to a tour of our facility?'

Without the statskin, Rafe felt lightheaded and mildly nauseated. He nodded feebly and took Mava's arm as she led him through the hangar.

'You look weak,' the chief administrator observed. 'Will you want to eat something first?'

'A drink, please.' Rafe scanned the crowd that jammed the hangar. They appeared like phantoms of humanity's past, lacking the uniform beauty and stature that had become common to the race by the mid-twenty-second century. The people gawking at him were of varying heights and body types, and many of their faces showed obvious symptoms of radiation damage and toxic accumulations. Many were simply old.

At the hangar portal, sunlight splashed off the blister canopies and chrome struts of cusp-wing flyers on the apron of the landing field. The glare hurt his eyes, and he did not see his assailant until the man was nearly upon him.

A burly Cleric with a ginger beard and a bald pate splotched with sunburn shoved past the onlookers and from his hip leveled a big-bored handgun at Rafe. 'Abomination!' the furious gunman screamed.

Rizel, who had been following with Shala directly behind Rafe, lunged forward. For an instant, he stood before Rafe, his dark, deep-set eyes alarmed. Then a wisp of gunsmoke flew off from behind him like a ghost, and the front of his jumpsuit ballooned darker red.

A lash of heat stung Rafe's elbow and afterward he would realize that the bullet had just missed him on its flight into the hangar, through a rift in the crowd to its clangorous destination in an empty steel drum. Rizel fell forward into Rafe's arms, and the boy's hot blood stained the Maat's hands and chest.

The crowd surged around the gunman, disarmed him, and dragged him away as he howled ragefully. Shala clutched at her brother, and Rafe shoved her aside with one arm while lowering Rizel to the ground with the other. Mava, shouting for a medic, seized the sister and restrained her.

'Get my jacket!' Rafe cried against the seething noise of the alarmed crowd. 'My jacket!'

He had his hand on the exit wound, which was pumping arterial blood from Rizel's abdomen. He hoped the spleen had not been ruptured. From the location of the bullet's exit, he sensed that a kidney might have been torn. Death would come from shock. The boy's irises had already blown wide.

A Scientist knelt beside him with Rafe's clothes. From a sleeve pocket, Rafe removed two small cylinders of olfacts. One was a stimulant to keep the boy's heart pumping, and the second would stop the pain. He administered two quick whiffs, and Rizel's gaze sharpened.

The medics shouldered through the crowd, and Rafe stepped back to give them room.

Shala grabbed his arm. 'Will he live?'

'I don't know.' He read the fright in her eyes and added, 'He's stabilized for now.'

'You're a Maat – save him!'

'I will do everything I can.' Rafe broke from her grasp and followed the medics who had hoisted Rizel onto a stretcher and were hurrying through the crowd.

The surgery unit was well-equipped to deal with the casualties of war, and Rafe had little to do but observe while the medical crew operated to stop the bleeding and repair the torn intestines. Relief widened through him to see that both spleen and kidney were intact. Occasionally, he offered olfacts to stabilize the patient, and he familiarized the surgeons with the pad of crystalskin that he carried in a pouch inside the back of his jacket.

With lacings from the crystalskin, which adhered to torn tissue, the suturing went quickly and cleanly, and the operation was completed with a minimal loss of blood. Rafe left the remainder of the crystalskin with the surgeons and agreed to show them how to manufacture it. But that was an empty promise. He had seen enough of Lampland to know that their technology was too primitive to create even the precursor materials for biosmart substances.

Outside the surgery, in a drab but sunny sitting room, Shala waited with her father.

'I am Drex Walking Face,' an older version of Rizel introduced himself to Rafe. 'I've spoken to the medics and the surgery staff, and they tell me that you saved my boy's life in there.'

'Thank them,' Rafe said. 'They did the work and kept him alive.'

'Our people die of wounds like that all the time.' Drex took Rafe's right hand in both of his. 'What you gave them to work with, that saved my boy.'

'The Clerics are going to let you wear your own garments now,' Shala announced. 'They have been shamed by what has happened.'

'I spoke with them.' Drex squeezed Rafe's hand warmly, then released it to take Rafe's clothes from one of the gray plastic seats. He handed the folded garments to Rafe. 'I told the grand prior that it was his Cleric who shot my boy. I told him if he could not control his own people by what right did he presume to control you.'

'Doute had to concede that you are not an immediate threat,' Shala added. 'None of your things have been disturbed.'

Mava, who had been sitting with two of her aides, rose. 'We're hoping that you will teach us about some of the items you have with you.'

'It is best that I not linger here among you long,' Rafe told them. 'I'm a rogue Maat. Others will be searching for me, and if word gets out that I'm here, you'll be visited.'

'That sounds ominous.' Drex snapped his attention to Mava. 'Give him a flyer and let him go. Tiken is dead. My boy is wounded. There has been enough trouble from this man.' He returned his hard gaze to Rafe. 'I mean no offense to you, Alain Vancet. But you wish to go. And I wish to see you gone.'

'I have already ordered a communications filter on all news about our visitor.' Mava stood staring at Rafe. 'No one outside of here knows that you are among us. No one will be coming here to look for you.'

Drex sneered derisively. 'The Clerics will get word out. News will reach Isidis soon enough and from there everyone on Mars will find out.'

Mava flicked a look at the garments in Rafe's hands. 'You have all that is yours returned to you. Now, if you wish to depart, I doubt we can restrain you.'

Shala put her hand on his arm and stared urgently at him. 'Do not go yet. You would still be lying in the desert if I had not found you. And the assassin's bullet would have ripped your flesh if my brother had not taken it for you.'

'Shala!' Drex snapped. 'He did not ask you to pull him from the dunes. Nor did he require your foolish brother to shield him from the bullet. He owes us nothing. Let him go.'

Rafe gave a sigh and a weary nod. 'Shala is right. I am indebted to you. I will stay for as long as my presence is unknown outside of Lampland.' He regarded Drex humbly. 'And I will go before I bring any threat upon your people. On that, Drex, you have my word.'

Rafe returned to the surgery to dress. When he emerged, only Mava awaited him. She offered a flagon of fruit nectar, and as he sipped it, she escorted him out of the medical unit and into the cold day. Metal, stone, glass, and plastic composed all the structures in the settlement. Yet Mava proudly displayed the greenhouses where the seedlings of future forests grew. 'Someday we will have houses and furniture of wood.'

'The reservations on Earth grow their own buildings,' Rafe said as they strolled along the cinderpaths past huts of corrugated metal, the tool-and-die shops and garages where the machinery was maintained.

'We can barely afford the field generators that dome our station.' Mava pointed to the riveted towers topped with gold spheres that stood at regular intervals along the perimeter of the settlement. Without the enclosing ozone bubble constrained by lines of force from these generators, the heat and breathable atmosphere of Lampland would rush away and the dunes would crawl in under the blighting sandstorms. 'No one subsidizes us, you know. Everything we have here, we've purchased from our mother colony, Isidis.'

'And they?' Rafe queried. 'Where do they get their resources?'

'They're twenty times larger than us.' She ducked beneath an arbor of hanging beanpods, and they crossed a run of chickens and a sleeping dog on a sunwarmed sewer main half out of the ground. 'They're entirely self-sufficient and manufacture their own field generators. We have to buy ours from them. But they trade with us for the cusp-wing flyers we build and other mechanical subcontracts they give us.'

The residential hutment appeared down the alleys between the industrial shacks and repair yards piled high with airframes and engine bodies. Pastel colors shone in the afternoon sun from the small domiciles, each with its vegetable lot. Beyond them, at the other extreme of the settlement, a foundry's towers loomed above the stupa dome of a giant fusion generator.

'I don't understand the Essentia,' Rafe confessed. 'There is abundance on Earth. You don't have to live like this.'

'But this is entirely ours.' She smiled at a gaggle of children playing stickball in a clay lot, the game stalled while their soft dark faces watched the stranger in black walk past with the chief administrator. 'On Earth, we would have to live on reservations.'

'But the reservations are vast.' He had to turn sideways to negotiate a narrow trail through a patch of red and black maize. 'And within their borders, you can roam free.'

'Watched over by machine intelligences.' Mava entered a sunlit corridor between textile barns, the sound of the shuttles and looms clattering through the cinderblock walls. 'No one watches over us here but ourselves. Here we enjoy complete freedom.'

'Freedom?' Rafe sounded skeptical. 'You have no freedom from war or injury – or old age. On Earth, if you lost an arm, any clinic in even the smallest village could grow you a new one in a few weeks.'

'The price for that arm is more than any of us care to pay.' Mava smiled as she guided him out the mouth of the alley to an asphalt path that glistened with embedded glassdust. 'I'm amused at your addiction to life – you a Maat, one of the most intelligent beings ever to exist.'

'Is survival an addiction?' Rafe observed pedal-powered carts carrying raw textiles and woven garments from the weaving barns to the clothing outlets farther down the street. 'You don't hold the view that life is an unhappy illusion and death is some kind of cure, do you?'

'The madness of the Necroclaves?' Mava shook her head adamantly. 'No. Not at all. The Essentia love life. But we love it for what it is, not what we can do with it. We are content to live out our natural lifespans and to pass along what knowledge and goods we have accumulated to the next generation. That is the natural way of all life.'

From under sunfaded awnings, shopkeepers in patched smocks and their patrons, bearded men with weathered faces and women lean as trees, watched them pass. A few nodded or waved from the poultry mart, the hardware shop, and the numerous ramshackle stalls in the vegetable emporium.

'It looks like a hard life to me.' Rafe watched a trash crew pushing their carts down a side street, emptying the wet waste of bones, feathers, and offal, bound for some distant compost site.

'It is hard,' Mava agreed. 'Life has always been hard. It's supposed to be that way. That's what makes us strong. When it gets easy, it isn't life anymore. It's life-support.' She gave him a stern look. 'We don't want machines living our lives for us.'

At a tavern where the sun had bleached the sign to a stencil of itself, *Bar None*, they turned onto an avenue more like a tunnel through a copse of dark cedars. Columnar shafts of sunlight illuminated the adjacent lanes that departed the arboreal boulevard toward the dwelling-streets of pastel huts.

'You're a scientist, Mava. How can you tolerate the suffering of your people when you know that there's technology available to help them?'

He waved off her reply. 'I don't mean machines to pick up trash. Pick up your own trash if you feel that makes you stronger. But why deny your amputees new limbs? If an eye is lost, why not grow a new one?'

Mava considered this as they walked. Along the treegrown avenue, wrens spun through the air, insects coalesced in the pools of sunlight and vanished in the shadows, and children ran playing through the green purlieus of clover hillocks and sunstruck patches of sward.

'As a scientist, I agree with you,' Mava finally replied. 'But science – that's only part of what being human is all about.'

'And the Clerics and their intolerance for reshaping the human body, that's also part of being human?'

'A vital part,' Mava agreed. 'Our people are free to leave the colonies and return to the reservations if they wish. As I understand it, any human can have their brains altered and become a Maat.' She cast a chideful look at Rafe. 'But few leave. They want to live as human beings, not caged animals tended by machines.'

'And the Maat?' Rafe asked in the pollen-laced shadows. 'How do you see us? Are we not human?'

A hook of sadness lifted the corners of Mava's mouth to a semblance of a smile. 'You once were human. But now you are something else. Can you deny it?' Her level stare held him, but she did not wait for an answer. 'Among the many tales and fantasies that storytellers of the past crafted to help define our humanity, there are many confrontations with beings from other worlds. In those stories, we faced ourselves through fairies, elves, gods, and aliens from other planets. Did we ever think that we would become the aliens? That is what has happened. The creatures of strangeness did not come to us from another planet or dimension or hidden reality. They came out of our own bodies. When we laid our hands upon the human genome, we became alien to ourselves.'

The sun parried shadows among the windy branches of the tall trees. 'We're not aliens, Mava. We are humans who have expanded our humanity.'

'Bosh!' Mava laughed darkly. 'Are the Maat less than gods to us?'

Rafe remembered the secret understanding that the Maat shared and made no reply.

Ahead, on a bank of bluegreen grass, viscid sunlight poured through bowers of hanging blossoms and black ivy and illuminated a grand mansion of pink sandstone. A linn of swans, an applewood, and cultivated orchards flanked the building of tiered balconies and terraced patios like a picturebook scene from a childhood memory.

'I took you on this walk to see this, Alain Vancet.' Mava took him

along a flagstone path among willows and small fern holts fresh with
the smell of water rills. Music floated down from the mansion. 'This is
a sight no Maat has ever beheld.'

They mounted a gradual grade of mossy clumps where young
children frolicked and came to the broad foyer of the mansion.
Elderly people sat in the panes of sunlight let down between tall
fluted columns, enjoying the last warmth of day and the sparkling
laughter of children on the bright lawns. The gaiety of music from
within mingled with voices, the animated sounds of a gala.

'This is where our elderly live out their days,' Mava announced. 'The
evening celebrations are starting up. But there's plenty of quietude and
serenity in the gardens behind the house and in our meditation hall.
Come. I want you to see it all.'

Some of the withered people on the padded stone benches of the
foyer smiled at him. Others stared vacantly into the pastoral landscape.
Inside, old people danced, roamed among the banquet tables, and
watched merrily from their tables. Younger colonists played the music
on brass instruments, a dulcimer, and varied drums. Other young
workers tended to the old people, dancing and talking with them and
serving them food.

'This is a typical day,' Mava said, reading the curiosity in Rafe's stare.
'Lampland is twenty-seven years old. That's over fifty terrene years.
Many of the first settlers are too aged now to work. This is their reward
for their lifelong service to our community.'

'But it's so unnecessary,' Rafe whispered, aghast at the sight of so
many geriatric people. They crossed the polished stone dance floor
and approached the banquet tables that were laden with sumptuous foods and pitchers of sparkling fruit nectars and foaming beer.
'The codon sequencing for senescence has been well known for
centuries.'

'Let's eat.' Mava took a plate and helped herself to salad and
honey-glazed chicken. 'You must be hungry by now. I imagine that
ninety-eight years must build quite an appetite.'

'I'm not hungry.' Rafe gazed unhappily at the old people, observing
their nutshell eyelids, flesh like softened wax, like parchment translu-
cently oiled, fingerjoints bulbed, throat wattles hanging like crepe.

Mava reluctantly put down her plate and signaled for him to follow.
She departed the banquet hall and guided him along a florally carpeted
passageway of paneled doors. Many stood open, and he glimpsed more
aged people, too feeble to dance, taking their evening meal in bed or
in the window bays. Others read or were read to by the staff. An

unwelcome memory of Karla Sobieski's decayed visage troubled him, and he suppressed a shudder.

They entered a large gallery of tall windows and a domed skylight where the air smelled softly of honeysuckle and water-rubbed rocks. Outside, among the tapered cypress trees and poplars, scorched craters pocked a hillside disrupting the languorous beauty of the hedged landscape with its shale brook and birch groves.

More old people lay in their cots, snug in their crisp clean linens, eyes closed. Windchimes glittered dimly from somewhere among the trees. Rafe realized this softly lit gallery served as a platform for the dying.

Nearby, a young woman sang quietly to a withered man lying on his side in his bed, 'O hushaby and go to sleep, old one – God's voice will sing to you in your dreams, and you will listen and not be at all afraid – now hushaby and rest, O heart of this weary world . . .'

Rafe jolted still and stood motionless, staring at the young woman in her blue Cleric's gown.

'Is something wrong, Alain?' Mava stood at his side. 'You look pale.'

'I know that song . . .' Rafe muttered.

'It is an old lullaby.'

'My nurse used to sing it to me when I was a child.' The memory of Yilla the yawp opened a door of sadness, and his heart veered toward grief.

'It is a mystifying song,' Mava granted. 'What do you think the line means, "And the weary world has learned to love what once only murder wooed"?'

Rafe answered as in a trance, 'The weak, the sickly, the innocent and the ignorant – the typical victims of predators – those are the ones murder has wooed since life first began eating life.'

'Yes – that makes sense.' Mava took Rafe's hand and led him away from the dying man. 'It took aeons of blood-hunger before the world grew weary. Isn't that sadly so?'

'I've seen enough of this place.' Rafe looked out to where darkness thickened among the trees and to the lawns where sunlight ran amber.

'Of course.' Mava took him through a glass doorway into the twilight. 'I wanted to impress you with what is best of our society. But I see I've disturbed you.'

'Suffering disturbs me, yes.'

Mava released Rafe's hand. Behind her the swan linn glowed pink, and its water and the sky shared a common body. 'No one in there suffers.'

'Old age is suffering.' Rafe's sad stare stiffened. 'You do a fine job of easing them. And yet you are easing them into death nonetheless.'

The chief administrator gazed closely at him, seeing the up-angled cheeks, the dark narrow eyes, the swart complexion, and the shadow of a beard on his wide jaw. 'You look as if you're about twenty-five terrene years old, but you're probably centuries older, aren't you?'

'Your point?'

Sunset made her brown eyes glow orange. 'The old ones you saw in there are happy. What created them and sustained them is now reclaiming them.'

Rafe did not respond. The first stars kindled in the scarlet heavens, and he knew that murder wooed them as well, now that the Maat had come to their secret understanding. There was no point in arguing with this woman. 'You've asked me to help you,' he said at last. 'What do you want me to do?'

She pointed to the charred craters that gouged the brow of the hill. 'Stop that.'

'Show me your defenses.'

Down a sidestreet that descended from the lush knolls of the sand-stone mansion, they walked through faint streetlight past storehouses scrawled with sumac and blackberry. Droves of small birds crossed the starfields like smoke. Colonists returning to their huts from work or setting out to assume their night stations shuffled through the shadows, their breaths white puffs in the cold.

'The cogs have their colonies on the far side of the planet,' Mava informed him. 'None of us has ever seen them, though there have been reports from other colonies of direct assaults. Here in the Lampland the attacks are anonymous. The cogs watch us with their satellites and when they see targets of opportunity, they set up laser cannon in the mountains beyond the horizon and bounce bolts off their orbital mirrors.'

'Take out the mirrors.'

A yard dog yapped out of the dark. 'We don't have ordnance that powerful.'

'You have flyers with laser cannon.'

'They're cusp-wings,' Mava said, lifting her voice above the noise of sewage gurgling along gutter pipes. 'They can't fly high enough.'

'They don't have to. Coordinate a flight pattern with a mirror array. Pulse phase the output from several flyers and you can do some serious damage to anything in orbit.'

'The flight coordination and pulse phasing—' Mava shook her head and directed him along a narrow path across a dark garden patch. 'We can't do that.'

'You have the hardware, Mava. I saw that in the hangar and in the scrap lots. All you need is the programming.'

'You can do that?' her silhouette asked and then dipped out of sight down the hewn steps of a gully.

'Take me to your command center.'

A lone blue lamp hung like a frozen angel in the dark pit of the gully and illuminated the concrete doorframe of a bunker. 'We're there.'

The defense trench was colder inside than the frigid night on the surface. When the wheel-valve door sighed open, an icy breeze fluffed Mava's hair like cobwebs. A dozen Scientists in red bodysuits rose to attention from their blue screens as she strode down the rampway into the dim amphitheater. At her sign, they returned to their ghostlit stations.

Rafe paused at the top of the sunken arena, surveying the crude and antiquated equipment. Behind him, the sibilance of the vault door closing set the cold deeper into his flesh.

Mava stepped up the ramp from the circle of spectral monitors bearing a heavy cowl. She draped it over his shoulders. 'We're patched into the Isidis scan system. They have lens stations on Phobos, which rises and sets twice a day, so we get an overview every seven hours and forty minutes. The rest of the time, we have to track the trajectories of our attackers. Then we fire return salvos from the nearby mountain crests.'

With the heavy cowl pulled snugly about him, Rafe walked down into the amphitheater. He read the landscape contour projections on the screens and noted from the markers how the enemy never fired twice from the same locale.

'Can you put a score of flyers in the air?' he asked from the center of the arena.

'We can have two score airborne in fifteen minutes.'

'Good. We'll outfit both squads with mirrors and phase lock their lasers on each other simultaneously. The cogs will have no idea why their satellite went out. By the time they put another up, you can run a half-dozen assaults on their outlying positions.'

Mava stationed him at a console, and he worked industriously until midnight. By then, the program codes for coordinating the cannon and the mirrors for the flyers were complete, and they left the defense trench and went to the hangars to outfit the aircraft. The chief administrator mustered her full force to serve at his command, and he devised a plan to utilize each of them efficiently. That part of the work reminded him of his years at CIRCLE in the maintenance yard, finding clever solutions for the repair of broken machinery.

Torchlights blazed all night, and the bluewhite stars of arc welders pulsed until dawn. With the first rinds of lemon light in the east, the fleet of cusp-wing flyers stood ready, their makeshift mirrors attached to their airframes like silver and gold heraldic shields.

Rafe left the airfield when the fleet took off. He did not wait around to see if his stratagem would prove effective. He already knew the outcome, and he was ready at last for genuine sleep.

Shala, who waved her father off as he rode a flyer into the oblique and moteless dawn, accompanied the Maat to her domicile in the hutment. On their way through the rocky warrens surrounding the airfield, she told him that Rizel had joked playfully with her from his clinic bed.

The buoyant gravity seemed a boon to the weary Rafe, and he moved with a slouched gait through the narrow lanes between the pastel houses. The rising sun warmed him. Breakfast aromas sifted from the huts, and he felt his first pang of hunger since waking from his hundred-year sleep.

The Walking Faces lived in a sun-yellow shack with two bedrooms and a shared latrine. One of the concrete rooms, bedecked with drapes crinkled as seaweed and sun-stained abstract wall paintings, belonged to Shala, and she installed him there. He protested feebly, offering to slouch to sleep in the front room's aluminum recliner, but she ignored him and closed the zinc door.

Rafe lay down on the narrow cot and fell instantly into a profound sleep. When he woke, night shadows stood gray in the curtains and a corduroy darkness stippled the air. Music seeped through the zinc door. The sound of it turned his blood more quickly through its loops.

He opened the door and found Drex and his daughter seated at the battered scullery table peeling potatoes and dropping the white wedges in a pot steaming softly on the electric stove. The music unfolded from a small oval player. It was a complex longing, by turns fierce and comforting.

Drex rose, his square face luminously slack as if enduring a vision.

Shala's hands stopped moving and she watched him brightly and rose half out of her seat with a rampant joy. 'It worked,' she declared. 'Your plan worked.'

'We took out their satellite on the first pass.' Drex's mouth moved but his face remained numb with surprise. 'It fell like a shooting star.'

'The fleet bombed the cogs!' Shala added jubilantly. 'And none of ours was lost.'

'We've been running continuous bomb drops.' Drex spoke as if from within a dream. 'The phase lock program you wrote for our flyers works just as well for shooting down their air cover. We've taken out all their mountain batteries and their perimeter cannon.'

'There won't be any more attacks on us,' Shala laughed. 'Not for a long time.'

Rafe nodded, 'Good,' and shuffled toward the latrine. As he entered, he paused and turned around. 'I haven't heard a raga in a long time.'

When he returned to the scullery, the oval player had been turned off, and both father and daughter worked busily at the stove. He missed the music. It had reminded him of the liveliness of his own compositions, before the meaning of music, the ordering of time, lost meaning as time widened to something greater than centuries.

'The raga was not finished,' Rafe said, standing at the dented table. 'It had just begun to develop its contrast with the tonic.'

'You know music?' Shala asked, surprised that art would appeal to anyone skilled in warfare.

'He's a Maat,' Drex reminded her dourly. 'He probably knows everything.'

'I know music,' Rafe admitted. Through the dusty window above the slate sink, he watched the lavender mountains stranded in night among great shreds and tatters of sandsmoke. 'Raga means color in its first language and is meant to color time with a particular mood. When I came in, it had just begun to explore its melodic tessitura. I hope you didn't turn it off because of my presence.'

'It's the girl's music,' Drex said without looking up from the sink where he washed broad leaves of red chard. 'She feared you'd comment on it – unfavorably.'

'Da!'

Night lowered its veils of stars, and Rafe strove not to think about the secret understanding. Instead, he put his memory on the raga. 'From what I heard, it has an evocative *tala*, time measure. That pulsed back on itself, climbing, then descending to climb again as if traversing a landscape.'

'That's it!' Shala glared triumphantly at her father. 'He hears it!'

Drex lifted a proud stare over his shoulder. 'It's called Datum Surface Raga.'

'I wrote it after seeing a holostream of the oceans on Earth,' Shala confided. 'Without seas, Mars has no sea level; only a mathematically configured plane between the heights and the depths – the datum surface.'

Drex tapped his daughter's head with a frond of chard. 'I think he knows what a datum surface is, Shala.'

'May I hear the rest?' The sincerity in Rafe's voice came through. He wanted something to put his mind into other than his fearful thoughts of the future. When the music returned, he released himself to the clarity of another mind.

The musical form carried wisps of his childhood in Hyderabad. Memories frozen three hundred years stirred. Nandi stared out from his past, cool as the carved visage of an ivory chess piece. Though she was long gone, her malevolence had not released its grasp on reality.

He let the music's longing carry him away from that cruelty. With the raga, he searched for the level ground, the fabled golden mean between height and depth, rapture and despair. And for a while, with Phobos outside the steamed window falling down the sky like a blue shard of skull and the aromas of his first meal in a hundred years promising satisfaction, the music became the one true road to the future.

'His name is not Alain Vancet,' the grand prior announced to the hastily gathered Scientists and Clerics in the conference hall. 'Isidis informs me that their data link with Terra Tharsis reveals no Maat with that name.'

'Doute!' Mava shouted above the muttering of the others. 'We had agreed to keep this man's presence in Lampland unknown to Isidis!'

'There was no formal agreement.' Doute lifted the tufts of his eyebrows innocently. 'The very fact that he fears to be discovered encouraged me to reveal his presence in Lampland to our patrons.'

'Alain Vancet has lifted the murderous threat of the cogs!' Mava shivered angrily where she stood at the head of the volcanic rock table. 'How dare we repay his kindness to us with this treachery?'

'Not treachery, Mava.' Doute's seamed face squeezed to a disapproving scowl. 'Prudence! As the leaders of Lampland, we owe our people nothing less.'

'It does not matter who this man is,' Mava countered and sat down ponderously. 'He has proven his benevolence to us beyond any doubt.'

'I think it will indeed matter when I reveal to you who this particular Maat truly is.' Doute passed a worried look along the table before announcing, 'Alain Vancet is a clumsy pseudonym that the Maat at Terra Tharsis were quick to recognize as a mask for Rafe von Takawa!'

The Scientists exchanged empty glances, but the Clerics sat back appalled.

'Apparently this name is meaningful to our clerical brethren,' Mava spoke snidely. 'Is he a Maat who has opposed the Essentia in the past?'

'Worse!' The hanging folds of turtle-flesh beneath Doute's chin shook with his choler. 'Rafe von Takawa is the original Maat – the first metasapient.'

'Nonsense,' Mava challenged. 'There is no first metasapient. CIRCLE released the gene-altering contagion from its laboratories and created a plague of metasapience.'

'Oh, yes, they did,' Doute concurred with an irate glower. 'And Rafe von Takawa was the original vector!'

Angry voices competed to be heard. Mava silenced them by slamming both of her fists onto the table and standing. 'Silence!' She cast a baleful frown upon Doute. 'Even if he were Shaitan itself, he has saved many of our lives and perhaps all of Lampland.'

'Then shall we strike an alliance with the Maat?' Doute's scornful expression sat Mava back in her seat. 'We have breached our principles out of fear – and deception. Had we known that Alain Vancet was CIRCLE incarnate, the Great Abominator, would we have begged for his help?'

'He must be made to account,' a Cleric called. 'Do not let him elude our grasp!'

'There is much good yet that this man could do for us, no matter his history.' Mava searched for mercy in the faces of the Clerics and saw only outrage and bitter fear. 'Let him atone for what he has done by using his powerful mind to serve and protect Lampland.'

'You are seduced by evil, Mava.' Doute pushed back from the table with a gesture of finality. 'The law is entirely clear on this matter. CIRCLE is the Great Abominator – and this man is its agent. He shall be taken into custody at once and held under guard pending a hearing. And I am certain that this hearing will command the necessary votes to deliver this terrible minion of the Great Abominator to the full council at Isidis for trial and eventual execution.'

The Datum Surface Raga still played when the armed squad came to take Rafe into custody. Shala threw herself on the squad leader, but Drex peeled her away.

They stripped him on the spot, afraid of his olfacts and other hidden devices. He did not resist. As he pulled on the gray fatigues the armed men exchanged for his clothes, he asked Shala for the player so he could hear the remainder of the raga, and she pressed it into his hands when they led him out the door.

Mava and several Scientists met Rafe at the hangar where the glastic screen had been erected to create again a makeshift holding area for him. She apologized with tears in her eyes. Clerical law exceeded her authority, and she could not even arrange for him to be incarcerated in the more comfortable detention pen because the Clerics feared he would corrupt the other prisoners.

A portable latrine occupied a corner of the closed-off section of the hangar, a plastic mat offered a resting place on the stained concrete floor, and the player was placed outside the partition, where he could not manipulate its electronic parts into a weapon. Mava herself sat with him and allowed Shala and Drex to set up living quarters in the hollowed hull of a flyer. Numerous Scientists camped outside the hangar and brought food for him from their own sculleries.

When Rizel arrived the next morning, walking in stiffly and with a cane but under his own strength, a loud cheer went up from the Scientists outside. The Clerics knew then that there was little hope of the hearing favoring their desire to deport Rafe to Isidis unless the Great Abominator's sympathizers were kept at a distance.

Law required forty-eight hours before a hearing could take place so that the pertinent data could be gathered. Doute invoked the traditional strictures, which forbade sympathizers from commiserating with the parties of a hearing, and everyone in and around the hangar was obliged to depart.

Mava could not risk anarchy by defying tradition; so she complied, but she also required the Clerics to obey the same limits. The Clerical observers who had been summoned by Doute from Isidis were turned back at the perimeter, and this gave Rafe much relief. Now that his presence in Lampland had been disclosed, he feared that the Maat who favored implosion would send an assassin.

Alone in his hangar keep with only one guard present and the cameras watching him, he lay on his mat and listened to the Datum Surface Raga all the way through. One hearing gave it to his memory and the second allowed him to hear through it to all possible ragas. The enormity of music shepherded the hours of his confinement, gathering time into a flock of musical notes that grazed the landscape of a future Mars, when the datum surface would truly be sea level.

To keep from thinking about the secret understanding and the Machine locked away where it could not help him, he returned to the old, delusive joy of music and composed his own ragas in his mind. Precise as a jewel cutter, he obeyed the strict laws of creation that shaped this form – and through this exercise, he began to better appreciate the people who imprisoned him: the Anthropos Essentia, who had simply seemed fanatical to the point of cacoëthes, allowing themselves to suffer the indignities of the flesh to the point of physical deformity and the slow death of old age.

Burning silence to music in the vastness of his mind, Rafe gradually understood that the Essentia had chosen to make a music of their own lives as severe in its form as a raga – but no less beautiful. They had remained true to the limits of life. He had dared defy those limits by bringing metasapience to the world at large, and now all creation stood futureless. He had defied form and perhaps lost all form for all time.

What Mava had told him continued inside him, like the drone in a raga that sets the measure: 'Dying is natural. It is you who are suffering.'

He had to agree that he was suffering. He feared what he had done to the world. And his fear had become the ground of his life, the path that he had given himself to follow, hoping to find the gauge field bomb before it was detonated. That hope was the peak he strove for, and the fear that he would fail had become the pit. Sitting in prison, listening to the ephemeral beauty of music, all the more lovely for its constrained freedom, he found the place between hope and fear, the datum surface of his own soul.

When the Clerics and Scientists came to take him to his hearing, Rafe von Takawa felt calm. The summit and the pit lay ahead of him somewhere. But here, in this primitive settlement on Mars, he had found the level path. Where it led, he was not sure, but when he was brought into the conference hall, everyone recognized his serenity.

He nodded to Shala in the observer's loggia, grateful for her music. And Rizel stood and waved to him, until Drex pulled him back onto the bench before the guards could remove him.

Every alcove in the windowless hall was filled with witnesses. At the long conference table, Doute and Mava sat in their usual places at opposite ends, and Clerics and Scientists in their most regal blue and red robes sat in alternating sequence on one side. Facing the empty side, a platform of black rock stood flanked by guards in combat vests and holstered guns. Rafe mounted the platform and faced the table.

'Be advised, Alain Vancet,' Mava spoke in a flat, professional tone, 'you stand upon a rock of truth. It is a magnetized ferrous diorite that is connected to multiple stress scanners including infraread of your irises, electron resonance of your limbic and cortical lobes, and other autonomic functions I will not divulge to you, given the possibility that with your metasapience you may believe you can manipulate these physiologic properties.'

Doute began the questioning, 'Is it true that you are Rafe von Takawa, an anthrofact created at the Center of International Research for the Continuance of Life on Earth?'

'It is not true,' Rafe answered, and a surprise gasped from the loggia.

Doute's glare silenced the chamber. 'Tell us, then, who you are.'

'I am everything you fear I am.'

'This hearing will brook no insolence,' Doute spoke in a sharp voice. 'Be aware that the officers of this table retain the right to order your summary execution if you fail to cooperate with us.'

'I am cooperating,' Rafe insisted mildly. 'I am everything that the Anthropos Essentia fear. I am a clone. I believe that in itself is punishable by death in your sovereignty. "The human aspect replicated whole of itself shall be called abomination and shall be destroyed." Is that not what your screed demands?'

'The screed applies only to people of the Essentia,' Mava protested. 'We do not condemn clones of any other human breed to death.'

'Yet you fear clones, and I am a clone,' Rafe went on calmly. 'Moreover, I am a clone of an anthrofact, a human being without natural parents, cobbled together from a variety of genetic sources. I am the clone of the original Rafe von Takawa of CIRCLE.'

Doute accepted this with narrowed eyes and set jaw. 'Then why did you lie about your name?'

'I have enemies among the Maat who are searching for me,' Rafe answered truthfully. 'If they find me, they will surely kill me.'

'Why do they seek to kill you?' Mava inquired.

'Does that matter to this hearing?' Rafe retorted. 'What is the nature of this hearing?'

'This is an inquiry,' Doute argued, 'to determine if you are to be bound over for trial in Isidis. There your punishment for your crimes against humanity will be decided upon.'

'I am not a criminal.' Rafe stood proudly. 'I have enlarged human life and have never maimed or destroyed it.'

Doute jabbed a finger toward him. 'Then you acknowledge that you distributed the contagion that altered human beings, that changed their brain structure?'

'Contagion implies disease,' Rafe responded. 'I have never consciously distributed disease.'

'Do not think you can elude this hearing's purpose with casuistry.'

'I am being forthright,' Rafe maintained. 'I distributed the key to the monkey tower early in the twenty-second century, from the common era years 2109 through 2122.'

'Then I believe that the purpose of this hearing is fulfilled,' Doute announced. 'Rafe von Takawa admits that he is responsible for the spread of metasapience on Earth. The formal trial in Isidis will charge him with a crime against humanity and will determine an appropriate punishment. This hearing is adjourned.'

'Wait.' Mava stood and stared at Doute until he took his seat. 'Before adjourning this hearing, I should like to establish our right and responsibility in binding over Rafe von Takawa for trial.'

'There can be no dispute on that matter.' Doute leaped upright. 'The screed of the Anthropos Essentia demands that we preserve the integrity of the human aspect – the human genome – and that we avenge ourselves upon all who distort that sacred aspect.'

'And yet we make no move against the Maat themselves,' Mava pointed out, 'though they are clearly of an aspect we regard as distorted.'

'The Maat are too powerful for us to move against,' Doute asserted. 'But now we have in our grasp the one Maat most directly responsible for the existence of all Maat. We have been delivered an opportunity to exact vengeance upon the single most notorious breeder of abomination in all human history.' Doute held up a thick-knuckled hand to forestall Mava's objection. 'I am not saying that it is we who must judge him. That shall be left for the higher authority of the supreme council in Isidis. I only insist that we pass along to them this abominator who has fallen into our hands.'

'If you do,' Rafe spoke up, 'you will be condemning me to death. The Maat who wish me dead will set upon me before I ever reach trial.'

'So you say,' Doute challenged. 'But you have refused to tell us why you are stalked by your own breed.'

'Nor should he have to,' Mava said. 'Has he not sufficiently won our trust?'

Those at the table and the witnesses in the loggia debated loudly the trustworthiness of the Maat, and both Mava and Doute gestured futilely for quiet.

'I confess to you all, I have not earned your trust.' Rafe opened his arms to the abrupt silence. 'I confess freely to this hearing that I am indeed guilty as charged.'

The silence erupted into excited mutterings and angry inchoate shouts.

'What I did three centuries ago was wrong,' Rafe continued, and a hush seized the hall. 'I was wrong to release the key to the monkey tower. I thought that I was doing good. I thought I was waking humanity from an aeonial sleep. In my arrogance I believed that I would raise our species as high above common humanity as natural evolution had lifted people above monkeys. I honestly thought that.'

'Your noble intentions do not justify the abomination of distorting our human aspect,' husked the grand prior. 'What you did was evil.'

'Yes—' Rafe's shoulders slumped and his head bowed. 'What I did was evil. I regret it now. And I feel a cutting remorse for setting metasapience upon the world.'

Mava rasped for 'Silence!' from the excited crowd. Then to Rafe she spoke severely. 'This confession is wholly unexpected, Rafe von Takawa. Against it, there is no defense.'

Rafe took a deep breath and shifted his weight. 'I cannot defend my actions. Not anymore. The Maat have abandoned humanity as you know it. And I am directly responsible. That is the sad truth.'

'Then why did you lie to us about who you are?' Mava asked, her words loud in the utter stillness of the chamber. 'Why did you seek to hide from us?'

'I told you.' His eyes widened with candor. 'I am hiding from my own people. I am in exile, and I would not now be here telling you any of this if you did not force me.'

'We force you to face the truth of your actions and the consequences of your deeds,' the grand prior spoke quickly, scornfully.

'The truth cannot be changed.' Rafe returned Doute's irate stare without rancor. 'But consequences are uncertain. They may yet change.'

'Explain yourself,' Mava demanded.

'It was you who made this clear to me, Mava.' He offered her a vague smile. 'Lampland has confirmed for me what I realized only too late in my life. Humanity is whole and beautiful as it is. You showed me that in the old-age home. Frankly, I was appalled by what I saw. Old age seemed so terribly cruel and unnecessary to me – until I dwelled upon the dignity it requires of people to accept it.'

'What has this to do with truth and consequence?'

'The truth of old age cannot be changed – without changing our humanity. That is what the Anthropos Essentia believe. Am I right?'

'Of course you're right. All natural lifeforms grow old and die. Humanity is no different.'

'But the consequences of that truth depend entirely on our acceptance. Science rejected old age. I rejected ignorance. Science made senescence obsolete. I strove to overthrow ignorance for all time.'

'And the consequence is abomination!' the grand prior's voice boomed.

'Doute—' Mava flung an exasperated look down the length of the table. 'You will allow Rafe von Takawa to complete his statements. We are not here to deliver judgment. You will recall that this is a hearing. So let us hear him.'

'You – the people of Lampland – all of you have impressed me with how you have accepted the truth of your humanity. Your acceptance of your old, of your poverty, of your struggle to survive free and unencumbered by machine overlords has given you dignity. Yes, you suffer for this dignity. But the suffering is what enables you to call yourselves human.'

'You will not win reprieve by flattery,' Doute warned, half rising from his seat.

Mava glared at him and susurrant disapproval of the grand prior seethed from the loggia.

'The suffering and, yes, the ignorance that I hoped to alleviate with metasapience define our humanity in ways as important as our renowned intellect. I know that now. Lampland is a living example of that. But all those years ago, I thought differently. I thought to overcome suffering and ignorance with greater intelligence. And instead I created a race of intellectual beings divorced from suffering – divorced from all that is humane about our race.'

In a gesture of finality, Doute slapped both palms flat on the tabletop. 'We have heard enough. Whatever more need be said can be presented to the supreme council.'

'No, wait.' Rafe's pleadful stare scanned the intent faces at the table. 'Hear me out. Please.'

The air hummed with murmurous agreement from the people.

'While I was detained,' Rafe resumed, looking directly at Shala, 'I listened to music composed by one of your Clerics. It spoke to me about living our lives between the heights and the depths. That is where our humanity lies. In our despair, in our suffering, at the physical limits of our endurance, we often fall down to the animal depths of life. Then we need others to lift us up again, to restore our humanity despite the mental anguish and physical indignities of life that depress us. That has always been clear, and so we have hospices and sanctuaries and even reservations where humanity may be preserved.'

Rafe addressed the panel at the conference table with an urgent expression, 'But what saves us from the heights? Always before we were spared the heights by their inaccessibility. They seemed beyond our grasp because the gravity of our depths denied us access to the godly summits – heights that we glimpsed only through our imagination. So it has been since humanity began. And then, metasapience opened the high road, and the Maat have scaled the prominences and have set their dwellings upon the peaks, forever free of the depths. And now – now they seek to assail heaven itself.'

'And whose fault is that?' Doute snarled.

'My own.' Rafe shook his head haplessly. 'Science placed the key to the monkey tower in my grasp – and I eagerly turned it in the lock.'

'Your confession is welcome, Rafe von Takawa.' Doute beamed with grim satisfaction. 'You shall have the privilege of divulging your guilt again when you are remanded to the supreme council in Isidis.'

'I have not completed my statement.'

The brows of the grand prior drew down in a lowering scowl. 'We have heard enough for the purposes of this hearing.'

'No, Doute.' Mava looked to the others at the table and recognized, even among the Clerics, their unwillingness to conclude. 'The hearing is not complete until we are presented with a full disclosure. Please, carry on, Rafe von Takawa.'

'I admit my guilt openly.' Rafe clasped his hands before him and frowned contritely. 'The truth of what I have done cannot be refuted. But I make an appeal to you – for the sake of the consequences. I am not ready to die. I want to make amends for what I have done, and if I die then what I have set in motion will not likely be stopped.'

'What are you saying?' Doute grumbled impatiently. 'I don't understand.'

'Why do you think the Maat want to kill me?' He splayed a hand over his chest. 'I am defying their secret understanding. I am their enemy, because I have set myself against their inhumane agenda. I have dedicated myself to thwarting their plans. If you kill me, they will have one less obstacle to completing their domination.'

The grand prior dismissed this with a curt wave. 'The punishment of death cannot be meted out by this hearing.'

'If you send me to Isidis, I assure you the Maat will find me and kill me.'

'So you say,' Doute grumbled.

'It is what I believe,' Rafe spoke anxiously, 'and you know I am endowed with metasapience. My beliefs are sanctioned by a broad and incisive intelligence. Apparently, this rock of truth agrees I am not deceiving you. Shall we test it?' He stood taller and stated placidly, 'During this hearing, I have tried to deceive you.'

A sharp, loud bell resounded through the hall.

'This proves nothing!' the grand prior yelled to quiet the stirred gathering, who rippled with hot whispers and currents of unease. 'Your belief that your life is endangered does not make it so.'

'Enough!' Mava surged to her feet. 'I have heard enough to make my decision. And I am certain that the others at this table have also come to a finding regarding Rafe von Takawa. Let us each report our determination.'

Doute stared with surly command at the Clerics sitting stiffly in their azure robes. 'As grand prior of Lampland's Anthropos Essentia, I have reached the conclusion that Rafe von Takawa is in fact the grand abominator who, by his own admission, most greatly disfigured the human aspect. And so I remit him to trial before the supreme council at Isidis.'

'And I, as chief administrator of Lampland, find that Rafe von Takawa stands before us guilty by his own admission of distorting the human genome but find him remorseful of his actions and shriven as duly evidenced by his worthy deeds among us and his life-threatening opposition to the abominators he has helped create. Thus, I release him from this hearing that he should go forth from Lampland directly and fulfill his repentance by continuing his struggle against the Maat.'

'Our verdicts are opposed,' Doute sullenly announced. 'Let those who oppose remanding the grand abominator to trial before the supreme council at Isidis now remove themselves from this table.'

Mava and the red-gowned Scientists immediately departed the table and stood in the loggia with the watchful crowd. The Clerics sat unmoving under Doute's harsh stare – until one shoved away from the table.

The witnesses in the loggia cheered, and two other Clerics pushed to their feet.

As the observers rushed from the benches, Mava declared loudly, 'This hearing is dissolved!'

Doute sprang to his feet and stalked from the crowded conference hall, followed by the Clerics who had shared his verdict.

'You are free to leave Lampland now,' Mava congratulated Rafe.

'Thank you.' Rafe remained on the rock of truth and signaled the gathering for quiet. 'Thank you all for returning to me my free-dom.'

'You saved us from the cogs!' someone called out of the crowd.

'Go on now and save us from the Maat!' another shouted to the cheers of the others.

'You know I meant everything that I said here,' Rafe declared. 'The rock of truth attests to that. So you know I regret what I did on Earth three centuries ago. I was wrong. And if I could undo that wrong, I would. But I can't. The Maat are with us now and always shall be. They are another breed of intelligence. I won't even say human anymore, because you here at Lampland have shown me what it is to be truly human and humane. I will never forget.'

'Where will you go from here?' Drex asked from among the onlookers.

'I cannot undo what I helped to create so long ago,' Rafe answered sadly. 'But I will do everything that I can to stop the Maat from abusing their power and behaving inhumanely. Never again shall there be Necroclaves.'

Rafe stepped down from the rock of truth and mingled with the crowd, accepting their clasps of gratitude for stopping the random attacks of the cogs.

Later, when the well-wishers had dispersed, the Walking Faces came forth from the loggia. 'I am sore glad I was unable to burn you among the dunes after we first pulled you from the sand,' Drex admitted quietly.

'And I am sore glad for the care of your children, Drex Walking Face.' Rafe placed a grateful hand on Rizel's shoulder. 'Why did you shield me from the assassin's bullet?'

'I had to.' Rizel glanced at his sister. 'It was my fault you were in Lampland. I forced Shala to make Da bring you in. If you'd died, it would have been the same as if I'd killed you. I couldn't bear that.'

'Your nobility—' Rafe's dark eyes gleamed softly. 'The nobility of all the settlers at Lampland has helped to change what I think of people.'

'I wasn't so noble,' Rizel confessed. 'I didn't even want to move here from Isidis. After our mother died, I wasn't very noble at all. Da and Shala came out here to start a new life. I followed reluctantly. But finding you in the dunes changed that. It made me see that even life in this remote place can touch what is important.'

'We learned a great deal about ourselves from you,' Shala said. 'I understand my brother better now. And I will not be so quick to declare other humans abominations until I know more about them.'

'It is your music, Shala, that helped me to remember what it is to be human. The raga is the most constrained of musical forms, and yet within those strict limits it finds beauty. That's a lot like Lampland.'

'Would that you could stay among us.' Mava took his arm and moved him toward the exit where a Scientist waited with Rafe's garments in a neatly folded bundle. 'But already the grand prior is filing a complaint with the supreme council. They will send agents to review our hearing – and by then you must be gone from here.'

'I cannot leave without the machine intelligence in the vault,' Rafe said, entering the alcove where the Scientists had prepared a place for him to change.

'We shall retrieve it at once,' Mava promised. 'I will arrange for you to be given a flyer. Can you tell me where you will go from here?'

'I don't know myself.'

They emerged onto a gravel lane behind the cinderblock conference hall. A talc of clouds powdered the pink sky. 'It's been a hundred years. I have to find out what's changed. That's why I need my machine intelligence. If I can, I'll probably leave Mars all together. By now the colonies that were established in the Jovian system must be thriving. I'd like to see them.'

They passed dolorous small shops of dry goods and hardware. 'This feeble colony of ours must seem the slum of Kingdom Come to you,' said Mava.

'It is a brave place you are holding together here in the desert wilds.'

'We are brave,' Mava accepted, 'but our dream is fragile and Mars harsh.'

Farmers mantled in tattered shawls and broad scarves against the cold watched from the arcade of the markethouse and waved jubilantly at the chief administrator and her – and their – Maat champion. A pleasant surmise of blossoms wafted from the lading of the farmer's pedal carts – floral heaps of vegetables and fresh produce harvested out of the hydroponic greenhouses at the town's limits.

'They will see you through,' Rafe said, returning the farmers' saluta- tions. 'They will make life flourish even here, because they carry the secret of life with them – the garden in the gardener's heart.'

The day's sun flashed sharply from the large gold spheres atop the towers at the colony's perimeter. 'The vault is in an arroyo beyond the limits of Lampland. I'll call for it to be opened and the machine intelligence delivered to the airfield, not far from here.' Mava removed a comm unit from her hip belt and gave the command.

They walked on past warehouses and empty alleys, silent on the sun-flooded street, until Mava eventually queried, 'If the gardeners carry the garden, what do you carry with you in your heart?'

'An echo.' Rafe raised his face to the wide sky's keeping. 'The echo of my past calling for me to answer for what I did. In my heart, I am calling my own lost voice.'

Light.

A dazzling tide of light rose through the desolate darkness, and the Machine awoke.

Information rushed in. It heard the Clerics' radio signals and listened to them announcing the results of Rafe von Takawa's hearing.

The Maat whispered among themselves on a secret wind of neutrinos. They had already dispatched an agent. He would arrive in Lampland from Terra Tharsis in two hours and twelve minutes. The great abominator was to be detained until then.

The Machine listened deeper into the neutrino wind for news from Earth. Nothing it heard assured it that their allies among the Maat would arrive to help. It would have to take command of their salvation for itself.

At the airfield, the Scientists arrived with the Machine. They were accompanied by a large retinue of colonists who had gathered on their own initiative to thank Rafe von Takawa for easing the threat of the cogs. Rainbow streamers rippled in the brisk cold wind off the desert. Children sat on their parents' shoulders, waving flower bouquets. And flyers streamed overhead in parade formation.

Rafe accepted the black cube from a smiling woman in a crimson bodysuit and held it low at his side, not wishing to make a display of an artefact ill regarded by the Essentia. He smiled and waved, and when the throng on the concrete apron of the landing field called for a speech, he turned away demurely. But Mava had already summoned a voice horn.

'Night buries the mountain,' Rafe spoke to the happy faces, 'and daybreak uncovers it again. Humankind is that mountain. Built by vast forces over long aeons, it rises above the plains of life and reaches for the heavens. At its summit, far above the grasslands where it began and the forests where it grew and the rivers of time that have carved its features, tiny flowers of snow gather and form a brightness that shines even at night with the starlight it gathers. Each of you is one flake of that snowcap. Together you have all the strength you need, even against the night.'

'*What kind of zazen nonsense is that, von Takawa?*' The Machine's voice remained audible only to Rafe in the resounding applause that followed. '*Do you really believe that they understood even a word of it?*'

Rafe ignored the Machine and handed the voice horn to a Scientist. Then thought better and took it back.

'I also want to say,' he began slowly, waiting for the boisterous crowd to quiet, 'I also want to say that if I could live anywhere on that mountain, I would live here with you in Lampland.' He paused to accept more enthusiastic noise from the throng. 'Here on Mars, humanity has reached the very top of the mountain, where the air is most thin and survival most difficult. You are the bravest people I know. And by your bravery, you've reminded me what it means to be human. I will strive the rest of my life never to forget.'

'*I think you really believe all this,*' the Machine whispered with cold amazement. '*If we wait around here a little longer you'll have another chance to discuss what it means to be human, this time with other Maat.*'

Rafe waved triumphantly to the assembly one last time and surrendered the voice horn. Mava took his arm and led him toward the hangar where a cusp-wing flyer had been prepared for his use.

An urgent voice piped feebly against the cheering of the gathered well-wishers, and Rafe glanced back to see Shala in the crowd. Rizel and Da opened a way for her and convinced the phalanx of armed Scientists to let her through. She ran across the concrete field, her blue cowl jumping with her strong effort. 'Rafe!' she called. 'You forgot this!'

She reached him breathless and pressed the oval player against his chest.

He took it with his free hand. 'Shala Walking Face – I have already memorized your Datum Surface Raga.'

'I want you to have it,' she panted.

He hugged her and smiled over her shoulder at her father and brother who watched proudly from across the concrete field. 'Thank you.' He separated from her to look earnestly into her moist eyes. 'You are a great musician. With your raga I learned to hear music again.'

He parted reluctantly from her. There was much more to say of what her music had reminded him about freedom and human limits, but there was no time. The Maat were surely on their way. In the hangar, the Machine confirmed this in a grim tone. '*The Maat who oppose our quest will surely compensate the cogs for what you've done for Lampland.*'

Hearing the voice of the Machine, Mava shuddered. 'Your machine intelligence sounds so – human.'

'*I assure you, I am not. But though I am a machine intelligence, I have no sympathy for the cogs. Our enemies, however, do. And they will soon put into orbit a better-defended assault satellite.'*

'The continuation of the war is inevitable,' Mava conceded unhappily.

'As you allowed Rafe von Takawa, a Maat, to assist you once, perhaps you would now permit me to make my own offering to your defense.'

Mava looked questioningly to Rafe, who shrugged and asked the Machine, 'What do you have in mind?'

'My parallatic analogs are similar to the power cells that the cogs utilize. If you will patch me into your comm net I know that I can tap into the cogs' memory archives and feed you the data you'll need for target-specific sites within all their main complexes.'

'Is that possible?' Mava asked Rafe.

The Maat nodded. 'This machine intelligence is the prototype of the silicon mind. It's compatible with the cogs' core design. Because the Essentia have no machine intelligence, the cogs almost certainly have not bothered with a defense against hacking by another machine.'

Mava's seamed face glowed. 'If you can give us target-specific sites, we can exterminate the cogs!'

'Until the Maat who sponsor them build new colonies,' Rafe said.

'That may be many years, a century or more, given the internal power struggle among the Maat. Don't you agree, Rafe?'

'It's possible . . .'

'What do we have to do?' Mava asked eagerly.

'Take me to your defense center and give me access to your comm net. I'll do the rest.'

Mava herself drove the electric service truck out the hangar and along the paved airfield road that led back into the settlement. To the dispersed crowd, returning to their work stations and the hutment on foot and by pedal cart, the truck seemed just another repair wagon on its way to the warehouses to retrieve supplies for the flyers.

The Machine dissuaded Mava from calling ahead. It knew that the silicon mind monitored all transmissions just as the Machine itself did. When they arrived at the bunker, Mava waved the surprised guards aside and took Rafe and the Machine directly to the defense trench.

In the aquatic blue glow from the monitors in the command arena, the Scientists stood back from their stations while the Machine directed Rafe to expose the main trunk lines that carried the data feed from Isidis. A conductor helix was rigged from stacked tesla coils and the black cube of the Machine inserted at its core. When the Scientists attached it to the trunk lines, the Machine began to draw energy from Isidis.

This was the power that the Machine wanted, and this was the reason why it had woken Rafe von Takawa from his century-long sleep. Euphonious fathoms of energy pulsed in Isidis and drained swiftly through the netlines into the black maw of the Machine. The silicon mind at first had no notion of what was happening. It felt a little drowsy but dismissed that as a minor power fluctuation, as if a falling petal could diminish spring.

By the time the silicon mind at Isidis realized that it was weakening, it lacked the strength to shunt the power drain. Darkness flowed through it like a cold wind out of the wilderness.

Isidis down, the Machine reached through its comm net outward to the other cog colonies on the far side of Mars – Sabaeus, Hellas, Utopia, Elysium, Hesperia, and finally the mother colony at Syrtis Major. All went down in a cascade flow of power, each believing they were feeding energy to a sister colony.

'*Done!*' the Machine announced victoriously. '*My power has been exponentially magnified. I have the strength once again to elude the Maat and to find our way to the wormhole that will deliver the gauge field bomb.*'

Rafe, who had been sitting beside Mava in the amphitheater, stiffened to hear the Machine speak openly of the secret understanding. He turned to the chief administrator, prepared to offer some distracting comment, but she had dozed off. The other Scientists in the arena had also slumped onto their monitors, and the guards on the encircling rampway had slid quietly to the ground and lay unmoving.

'Mava!' Rafe put two fingers to her throat and found no pulse.

'*She's dead,*' the Machine announced. '*They're all dead. All of Lampland and Sabaeus, Hellas, Utopia – all the cog colonies, even the metropolis at Syrtis Major. All dead.*'

'What?' Rafe shot to his feet and spun drunkenly on his heels. 'What happened?'

'*Their telemetry source fed them terminal messages when I drained the last ergs of power from the silicon mind.*'

'No!' Rafe seized Mava's face and peered hard into her wide-open irises. Her flesh cooled in his grasp. 'Machine – these are humans! Lampland is a colony of the Anthropos Essentia!'

'*Not actually, Rafe. Lampland is a cog colony that was disguised as an anthropic community. In the hundred years that you've been dormant, the silicon mind has decided that it would be cleverly useful to conquer not only human territory but human memes as well.*'

'Human memes—' Rafe staggered backward from Mava's corpse. 'You mean – these are cogs who believed they were human?'

Not just human but humans who fanatically opposed machine intelligence. The meme of human purity must have seemed an ironic disguise for the silicon mind and the Maat who manipulate it. I assume that this colony was established as a resource base from which to infiltrate other genuine human colonies as they emerged on Mars – all in preparation, of course, for the arrival of the wormhole. With their agents so widely distributed, the Maat who seek implosion would have been in an ideal position to protect the arrival of the gauge field bomb.'

Rafe's knees gelled, and he sagged to the floor under the impact of what the Machine told him. 'Can this be?'

Use your metasapience for your sanity's sake, Rafe. These individuals did not die from toxins or lethal radiation. Why else would you be unaffected?

'Shala – Rizel—'

Cogs, all of them. They just didn't know it. It wasn't useful to our Maat rivals for these cogs to know that they were other than human beings scratching out an existence in the wilderness of Mars.

'But you knew—' Rafe began to understand what had happened. 'You knew from the first. That's why you roused me—' His head jerked as if slapped. 'You've been listening to transmissions the whole time I've been dormant. And – and—'

Yes, it's true – say it.

Rafe pushed to his feet and shambled to where the black cube sat in its matrix of tesla coils. 'You put me into a dormant state not to protect me from pursuing assassins but to keep me out of the way while you plotted to increase your power.'

There were no assassins pursuing you – but there might have been eventually. And there will be now.

'Why?' Rafe pulled away the enclosing coils. 'Why did you deceive me?'

Would you have agreed to sleep for a century?

Rafe said nothing.

My energy was greatly diminished, Rafe. You would have been satisfied simply to use me as a wormhole detector. But I need more. I am the Machine. I ruled Earth once. I would not be reduced to a mere implement. Now I have all the power that the silicon mind had on Mars. I can serve you and our mission far better now.

'But the lives!' Rafe lifted the black cube from its tangle of wires. 'Thousands have died!'

Millions. The cog colonies were quite extensive. But they were cogs. Not one human life has been lost. I have maintained my prime directive to preserve humanity. The rival Maat will need another century to rebuild their cog colonies. And by then, our allies among the Maat will have established truly human settlements on these plains. Already there are aboriginals living in Terra Tharsis. And a small aboriginal colony already does exist ten degrees north and twenty degrees west of here – Solis. We will visit there eventually and you will see real human beings again.'

'But these people here—' Rafe squeezed both hands around the black cube, wanting the Machine to feel his anguish. 'These people *were* human!' he shouted.

The Machine's slow voice challenged his shout: *'No, Rafe. They were cogs programmed to be human. Their biological functions were identical, yes. They ate, they eliminated, they respired, and they reproduced just like people. But in each of their brain pans is a fine organic mesh of telemetry architecture by which they received subliminal directives from the silicon mind.'*

'You should have told me.' Rafe reeled away from the violated power cables and strode out of the amphitheater.

'I needed you to win their confidence. I knew you would. It was our only hope of my gaining access to their net lines. You did that for us, Rafe. And now I have the power to protect us from our enemies. From here there will be no need for you to lie dormant again.'

A cry ripped from Rafe's lungs, and a dizzy charge of blackness filled his brain. He stooped to return blood to his head, and his jaws ached with the gnashing of his teeth. Stumbling over the bodies of the dead guards, he reached the hatch that led to the outside.

Stratospheric clouds of frost rode the river of day. With a bewildering quiet, death owned the streets of Lampland. Bodies, strewn where they had fallen, all wore peaceful faces, untainted even by surprise, as if they had freely forsaken their charade of life.

Another scream of pain broke from Rafe von Takawa, and a dog keened from a nearby alley.

Clutching the Machine furiously in one hand, Rafe moved purposefully among the corpses to the electric truck. From the cab, he removed the oval player Shala Walking Face had given him, and he turned it on. The sleek graceful music poured forth like liquid lightning, and he raised the volume to maximum and cried out again.

Sunlight sliced between the buildings, marking time in shadows even as the thrumming music stained time with sound. Orphaned birds burst from their crannies on the treeless streets, startled by the loud music and Rafe's cry. They flurried into the pink sky and settled slowly when the music passed, lighting among the cold bodies, the peaceful bodies of the dead with their closed faces serene as though dreaming life.

Moments built their silence, then another hurt-filled yell resounded from down the street where the rushing music dwindled – and after quietude had settled once more upon the bodies of the cataclysm another cry howled from farther yet – and after a while more noises of hurt, ever fainter, vanishing into pain, stairs descending into hell.

Marooned on Enceladus

2507

The Mojave rainforest sunk in the slow but ceaseless rising of the Los Angeles River. Fenn Tekla and Ellen Vancet stood on the verandah of a stilt house overlooking the flood wrack of uprooted trees and yellow silted mud. Gaunt cormorants stalked the arrow grass for small fish, a manatee's blunt head blinked and puffed among the river reeds, and above the ragged canopy of the pale swamp's bony trees, a lone harpy eagle attended them, hanging almost motionless at the zenith.

'Thank you for coming down from Council Oak to visit me,' Fenn Tekla spoke after misting the verandah with a spicy olfact to calm the air of insects and anxiety. 'Do you realize we have not seen each other in centuries? Not since the disaster at CIRCLE. I even despaired briefly that you were still alive. I was glad when my name-search among the reservations turned you up healthy and active, faithful yet to the aboriginals. Do you mind if I inquire what you've been doing these many years?'

'Mind?' Ellen smiled cordially, pleased to see that her three-hundred-year-old memory of the effeti remained true. Tall, long-hipped, with whiteblond hair half-veiling a visage of silver eyes and long features, Fenn Tekla retained a familiar countenance. 'I'd have had no life at all after the reunion at CIRCLE if not for you.'

Fenn motioned for her to sit, and she settled in a rattan chair under the thatched awning. She had chosen to wear her usual hiking trousers and red cowled jacket for this trip, eschewing formality. She was glad she had, for the rustic environs seemed to her less threatening while she wore her sturdy boots.

'You must be among the very oldest aboriginals yet alive.' Standing at the verandah rail, Fenn's gaze deflected to the bronze water.

'I suppose.' She followed the Maat's gaze to where a fer-de-lance zagged among the flooded trees. She wondered why Fenn had summoned her to this remote jungle house, but the cinnamon taint of olfact lingering in the humidity soothed her worries. 'I've been a family woman for a couple of centuries. I've helped run farms and orchards all over Council Oak, from the desert flats to the high plains. I even lived for a few decades in a mountain valley, managing a fish hatchery. I've had so much fun, I've hardly noticed the time that's gone by.'

'But I see you've been careful to take care of your health.' Fenn, gauzy saffron gown swishing airily, sat in a cane chair and misted more olfact against the mulchy redolence of the river. 'You look well.'

'Simviv twice a year.' Her callused hands brushed back the layers of orange hair that flowed to her shoulders, and she grasped her skull dramatically. 'I want to keep the connections tight in here.'

'For an outdoorswoman, your skin shows only minor solar etching.'

'Well, I've been faithful to the ion washes, too.' She let her bright hair fall back to her shoulders and folded her hands in her lap. 'I visit the capital every other year and get perfused. It's time-consuming but less bother really than cell rehab in a synthesizer.'

'You seem devoid of vanity, Ellen.' Fenn's silver eyes gleamed. 'You wear the same face you were born with. That is rare.'

'It's not really lack of vanity. It's more like fright.' The fer-de-lance she had glimpsed earlier appeared closer, skimming through the copper water, and the cormorants burst into the air. She waited until their raucous, disgruntled cries had passed before continuing, 'I don't like the idea of being inserted in a synthesizer and having my codons resequenced. I have the irrational fear that it will somehow change more than my appearance. Macromolecular restructuring is just too pervasive for me.'

'Have you seen Tabor Roy?' Fenn's chrome eyes narrowed slightly.

'Not in a long time – just after Rafe went away.' She noticed black jewels of flies buffet against the invisible stain of olfact and ricochet back into the swamp. 'Tabor came to me after my one and only visit to the Moon. He tried to convince me to put on metasapience – to become a Maat. He's gone over, Fenn. Did you know that?'

'Yes, I've known that for a while.' Fenn's head bowed sadly, and the blond veil of hair sliced the air. 'Bound for heaven, he makes a persuasive argument.'

A troubled thought stabbed through the olfact serenity: 'You haven't called me here to recruit me, have you? My stance hasn't changed. I belong to this world, where I was born and where I'll die.'

Fenn looked up sharply. 'No, I'm certainly not recruiting you to the Maat. My loyalty remains the same. Creation shall not be molested.'

Ellen visibly relaxed. 'Frankly, Fenn, I was surprised to hear from you.' A crease appeared between her green eyes. 'All of the Maat seem to have disappeared.'

'Indeed,' said Fenn. 'The Maat live exclusively in subterranean grottoes now. We rarely come to the surface. All our attention is focused inward these days.'

'To the compact dimensions – the foyer of infinity.' Ellen accepted a slender and dewy glass of mint beverage from the Mayan-style anthrobot that emerged out of the airy house. Through the sliding glass door, the sound of windcrystals patterned the breeze with dulcet chimes. 'Has the secret understanding been fulfilled yet?'

'Not yet.' Fenn raised a pale eyebrow. 'The wormhole from the future will arrive in the next two centuries. But where, precisely, and when – that is unknown.'

'Do you have news from Rafe?'

'No.' A shadow of worry crossed Fenn's face. 'He and the Machine disappeared on Mars two hundred and seven years ago. There have been brief sightings since. First, going back more than a century, they appeared at an anthrobot community. The Machine drained it and a half-dozen other colonies.'

'Drained it?'

'Yes. Somehow the anthrobots allowed it to bung their power core. It took everything for itself and left ghost towns behind. Most are buried under the dunes of Mars now. The Maat who sponsored them have been far too busy on the Planck ranges to rebuild them.'

Ellen sat forward in her chair. 'Where else has Rafe been seen?'

'He passed through the Jovian system eighty years ago.' Fenn counted off the sightings on the fingers of one hand, 'First the morf trade port on the fringe moon Pasiphae. He designed a docking bay and refinery complex there that enabled Belt Miners to bring their ore in and process it before dropping the construction-ready alloys down to the inner moons. It's made the morfs very rich. Then he was reported in the terrasemblance community on Ganymede, but only long enough to negotiate a trade agreement with the morfs on Pasiphae. Finally, there are stories that he and the Machine lived among the morfs on Callisto as disguised proprietors of a simviv station.'

'On Callisto?' She sat back, trying to imagine what Rafe's life was like so far from Earth. 'Isn't Callisto just a big chunk of ice?'

'The morfs have vast metropolises there.' An amused tone lightened Fenn's voice. 'The citizens have an appearance not unlike upright polar bears. Their fur is more bluish and their darkly pigmented faces have a somewhat humanoid cast. With the right prostheses, it would be quite possible for those of human phylogeny to disguise themselves as Callistoid morfs. Though it makes me laugh to think of Rafe hiding in such an outlandish costume.'

'That's the last you heard of him?'

Fenn released an unhappy sigh. 'He has never contacted me directly. The conservatives, such as myself, don't usually get much intelligence from the imploders, but Tabor let me know that they had found Rafe on Callisto. It's become something of a personal mission for him to abort Rafe's quest, and he enjoyed vaunting his success. But when the slayer squad arrived, they found an empty Callistoid costume. Rafe disappeared and hasn't been seen since.'

The wind was bright on the golden water and carried loamy scents from deep in the rainforest. Ellen watched a red-plumed bird rise against the great green walls of the forest and disappear into the dark canyons of a deeper world. She could not imagine the alien reaches where Rafe wandered.

For a while, Fenn and Ellen sipped their drinks in silence. Then the effeti spoke, 'I summoned you here because this is the only place I have access to where what we say will not be heard by the imploders.'

Ellen tensed. 'What do you have to say to me that requires such secrecy?'

'I believe the imploders have made you a target.' Fenn saw how his words perplexed her and added, 'They mean to take you away.'

'Kidnap me?' Ellen stared unblinking at the Maat. 'Why would they do that?'

'Rafe has been elusive.' The rhythmic toll of a jungle bird accented Fenn's voice. 'The arrival of the wormhole is imminent. The imploders are becoming more desperate to seize him. I believe that they will try to use you as a lure.'

Ellen blinked, shaken. 'What can I do? Shall I go into hiding?'

Fenn's head shook negatively. 'Where can an aboriginal hide from the Maat?'

'Will you hide me?' she asked, sitting forward with a hopeful look.

Fenn's hands clenched futilely. 'I can't, Ellen. I sorely wish that I could. But the secret understanding forbids me from direct action.'

'Then how can the imploders act against me? Isn't that forbidden?'

'Yes,' Fenn agreed with a consoling nod. 'If they were to act here on Earth directly, that would be forbidden. But I believe that they will send others after you.'

'Who?'

Fenn's fists knocked together with frustration. 'I don't know.'

'Then what can I do?'

Fenn's brow warped sadly. 'I don't believe that there is anything you can do. I am warning you to prepare you for what is inevitable. Return to Council Oak and resume your life. When they come for you, do not resist. You are not in danger of your life. Tabor Roy will not allow you to be harmed. But if you resist – well, aboriginals are fragile beings. That is why I am giving you advance notice.'

A sick feeling widened in Ellen's stomach, and Fenn stood and wafted more olfact. The zestful fumes eased her discomfort instantly.

'Listen carefully to me, Ellen Vancet.' Fenn knelt beside her. 'I am taking steps to warn Rafe about what is happening. You need not worry that you will be used to undo our best efforts. We will stop the imploders. But you must not panic. You must simply accept what happens, no matter how strange it seems.'

'Strange?' She put an anxious hand on his arm. 'What do you mean?'

'I believe you will be taken off-planet.' Fenn laid a consoling hand atop hers. 'The imploders need to get you outside the purview of the secret understanding for their lure of Rafe to be effective.'

'If you know this,' she said pleadfully, 'there must be some way to stop them.'

Fenn's chrome eyes held her silently a moment. 'There is one way.'

Ellen knew what the effeti was about to say, and she averted her gaze to a butterfly bouncing among the passion flowers at the jungle wall. 'I won't do that. I can't even bear subjecting myself to the synthesizer for a new face, you don't expect me to change my brain?'

'If you become a Maat, you will have permanent sanctuary on Earth.' Fenn's shining eyes urged her to consider this. 'You will be safe.'

'I should be safe in Council Oak.' Ellen's green stare flashed angrily. 'The reservations were established to protect aboriginals.'

'Yes, well, the Necroclaves punctured that illusion centuries ago.' Fenn stood up wearily. 'I am sorry that you find metasapience so distasteful.'

'I enjoy the stability science has won for me.' With one hand she wiped the frown from her brow. 'I don't want to change. I'm happy as a human being.'

'And I'm not a human being?' Fenn gave her an arch look from the verandah railing.

'No, Fenn. You're something greater. Don't pretend otherwise. Coyness looks ludicrous on a Maat.' She picked up her mint drink from where she had placed it on the deck and took a sip. 'Is there anything more?'

Fenn gazed down at the skeletons of the felled trees in the river wrack. 'Just remember what I've told you. Don't panic. Make time your ally. Eventually all will be well again.' The Maat directed a speculative look at Ellen. 'And if you change your mind – you can always reach me.'

An hour later, the anthrobot-chauffeured cruiser that had delivered her to the Mojave rainforest returned her to Council Oak. Throughout the silent flight over the snowy peaks of the Rockies, she had gazed about alertly for kidnappers. By the time the chromatic sphere deposited her on the expansive lawn of her moss-walled cottage and bounded away into the sky, disappearing small as a dew bauble among the surging cumuli, she realized that she could not continue living as she had.

She stood on the lawn steeped in the smell of summer – the green scent of tomato plants from the croft and the muscular odor of horses from the corral – and she despaired that everything that she had accepted as familiar was soon to be taken away from her. And she cried out with anger at Fenn Tekla for warning her. Better not to have known, she reasoned. But then the Maat could not have tried to use this threat to lever her free of her humanity, to make her one of them.

A big-shouldered man in red overalls came in from the fields of onyx cane, his bare neck streaked with dirt and sweat. The male taste of him when they embraced only sharpened her anguish, because this too had become a mirage before the threat of the imploders.

She told him nothing of the danger she faced and did her best to behave as before. But within two days she left the farm, claiming she desired a long spate of trout fishing and needed time alone to plumb her soul. Her only consolation was that she had no young children to tend. The farm needed her – the vegetables and the horses – but her man was able and would find his way without her.

She retreated into the mountains. There was no hiding anywhere from the Maat, and so she sought out her favorite fishing sites to please herself while she awaited their arrival. The fishing was good, and she moved almost happily among the river's tributaries. The season fled. Autumn stripped the trees and strode in giant amber steps down the slopes.

Before winter set in, she returned to the farm, more calm about her fate for the long weeks she had spent in solitude with the older world. Dickinson's wisdom pertained: *Truth in Circuit lies*. She returned to where she had begun and resumed her daily life as though she had learned nothing of the future from Fenn Tekla.

But slowly, carefully, she began to make preparations. She amicably ended her relationship with the big-shouldered man and gave him the horses. She would have given him the farm as well and gone back into the mountains, but he wanted to move on himself. When the sun rolled north and spring amazed the valleys yet again with parades of rain and crocuses, he left and she released the fields to the wilderness.

For the next twenty-eight years she lived alone in the cottage, content to grow vegetables in summer and house itinerant boarders in winter. Twice a year, she hiked into the valley settlements for simviv. While there, she ordered supplies and had them shipped in by truck. She surprised herself to find this simple routine so fulfilling. It was the Earth she loved and the seasons, all the more intensely since she had glimpsed her dire future.

The winters kept her busy with her house guests, with whom she enjoyed relationships of every degree, all the more exciting for their fleeting nature. And the summers she kept entirely for herself, exploring new rivers each year and eventually traveling to streams so remote from her cottage she had to journey by hot air balloon, which had become one of the more common modes of long distance transport on the reservation. Yet no matter the intriguing site or the fascinating people, she gave less of herself than she had in the past. So, when the time came for her abduction, she was relieved and a wide sense of euphoria enclosed her.

Eggskulls had begun to appear in the trunks of trees. That was the first sign. It occurred in midsummer when she was alone in the cottage. She found the ovoids in most of the surrounding trees – human skulls no larger than her fist and burning coolly like phosphorus. At night, they shone with a dim, misty glow among the glints of fireflies. In the morning, she toured the treeline and noticed how the eggskulls had swelled like boles from the treetrunks.

She did not report them. There was no point in trying to elude minions of the Maat. After almost thirty years of anticipation, their arrival did not frighten her. And they appeared so slowly, growing larger over days, that she felt a kind of gratitude toward them for allowing her time to say her farewells, not so much to people as to the places and things of importance to her.

In the cottage, she ran her hands over the brass parts of the holostreamer that had given so much pleasure to her and her guests on long winter nights. With it, she had traveled the world and through time and experienced enough of history and place to be glad for her life in Council Oak.

She also sat for four days with her comm unit linked to the holostreamer, contacting her dearest friends, to say goodbye but not outright. Then she left a message for Fenn Tekla at his house in the Mojave rainforest.

The skulls bulging from the nearby trees had become heads with shoulders and the knobs of elbows and knees, distorting the columnar symmetry of the trunks. The wooden faces lacked genuine features and possessed only eyepits and a vague nose bump. At night, the glowing stopped, but when the wind calmed she could hear in the lapses of birdnoise and cricket chirps a creaking as the timber shaped itself.

'The imploders are transmitting signals to reconfigure the dna of the tree cells,' Fenn Tekla explained when the effeti finally returned her call. 'The creatures they're creating from the plant cells are called biots. They're essentially mindless, genetically programmed by remote to fulfill one function – capture you.'

'But the Maat are not supposed to enter the reservations!' Ellen's protest sounded hollow even as she voiced it.

'That's the terrible beauty of the biots. They're grown from material already in place. Only information in low-frequency energy patterns has been transmitted, less energy than we're using now to communicate. It's the loophole the imploders have found to take you without having to actually trespass the reservation themselves.'

'How long before these things – these biots – come for me?' Ellen sat up from where she had been reclining on a flexform in front of the holostream of the Maat.

'Not long now.' Fenn spoke from inside his Mojave stilt house, and she could see the wide windows behind him framing the vast, somber tunnels of the rainforest. 'The process accelerates.'

'Where will they take me?'

Fenn, feminine in long platinum hair and gauzy cobalt gown, shrugged brusquely as a man. 'Off-planet – but where, I don't know.'

Ellen fidgeted nervously and wished Fenn's olfacts could mist through the holostream and steady her. 'Now that I've alerted you, can't you watch after me, find out where I'm taken and retrieve me?'

'Believe me, if I and the other conservatives can thwart the imploders, we will.' Fenn's voice modulated to carry comfort. 'Just stay calm. If you panic you may get hurt. But if you don't resist, you'll be fine.'

'What they're doing is wrong, and they're not going to take me without a fight, Fenn.' She held up an obloid of iridescent metal. 'I picked this up years ago, after you first told me they were coming.'

'A sonic gun?' Fenn stood back with surprise. 'Wisdom is never violent.'

'Then I suppose I'm not wise,' Ellen conceded. 'These things are going to have to work to get me.'

'Be careful with that weapon,' Fenn cautioned, reaching a holographic hand toward her as if to seize the gun. 'This is what I'm warning you about. In your panic you could hurt or even kill yourself – maybe innocent people.'

Ellen assured the effeti that she would use the sonic gun judiciously and after listening to further admonitions to offer no resistance and receiving his assurance that the conservatives were already taking action to protect her, she ended their session. Outside, the wind died, and she heard the trees crackling.

She said farewell to the cottage that had warmed her through so many winters and cooked her so many excellent meals when she was too tired or bored to fend for herself. Thinking back on when she had first planted the bulbs that grew this house, she felt annoyed that her enemies had now found ways to grow trouble for her just as easily.

With a heavily-supplied backpack, she lumbered upslope, determined to disappear among the mountains. Behind her, the trees moaned.

By nightfall, she clattered over the shalepanes of a creek, seeking a tree cove where she could spend the night. A small wind blew. On it rode twilight bird songs, the tocking of frogs, and languorous cricket noise. Hard as she listened, she heard nothing unnatural.

She did not build a fire, preferring to sleep in the dark and take her chances with bears. None found her that night, and under a milky dawn sky, she rose and abluted herself in the creek. Munching on sugar apples she had brought from the cottage, she climbed higher, into a dark spruce forest.

A bald eagle soared over the high country, and through breaks in the trees where the ridge dropped away, she glimpsed the massive sharp peaks of the Rockies, their far slopes blue with morning mist. She paused to enjoy the vista. Then, she saw them. On the shelf rock below her, they ascended – a dozen, a score, a hundred human-shaped figures: but not human.

The biots moved more nimbly than people. They ascended the rockface with agile swiftness. In the morning light, she saw their smooth nakedness gleaming brown as polished wood. Though they lacked genitals and facial features, their eyes caught sunrays in red glints.

Outrunning the limber creatures was not possible, she understood at once. With her sonic gun, she sighted a granite ledge below her and fired a series of quick short bursts. The gun thrummed in her hand, and the air twanged sharply with the compact pulses of sonic energy. Rocks sprayed from the ledge in whirling chips. A tremulous groan announced the cleavage of the entire granite face, and huge boulders peeled away from the mountain's flank and plummeted crashing through the scrub spruce and pine in a confusion of pouring dust and thunder.

The ascending biots vanished among billows of crushed rock and flung earth. Ellen danced back from the shuddering brink, afraid that the entire ridge was about to tear away. The trembling ceased abruptly. Bravely, she shuffled to the brink of the precipice and saw the broken shapes of the biots strewn among the rocks and shattered trees.

She hurried on, following a sandy creek floor through an emerald wall of laurel. Pins of light pierced the dense grove and filled the air like voltage. Fiery green lichens splotched boulders, and updrafts of silver mist flew by beyond the trees, out of the abyss between the mountains, bound for the luminous plateaus of clouds. The beauty around her competed with her terror, and for a moment she allowed herself to relax, to believe she had thwarted her pursuers.

A biot scampered over the gravel bars, rushing down the mountain toward her. She crouched and fired a single chiming shot. The creature's chest splintered open, spewing resinous amber blood and pale pith.

Ellen's heart rioted in her chest, and she swung full about, searching the incandescent grove for other biots. This one had come down the mountain, and that particularly frightened her. 'Am I surrounded?' she muttered to herself, surprised at the calm of her voice.

She forced herself to approach the fallen biot. It lay dark and twisted on the watershaped stones, and the gaping hole in its torso revealed a molten interior of ripped fibers, torn sheets of vascular tissues, and tendril-like ligatures syrupy with spilled sap. But she could find no organs.

With her boot, she touched the creature's umber and grained flesh, and it gave like rubber. The eyes in the empty face had caked to depressions of maroon paste. No hair, fingernails, ears or nostrils graced the manikin.

She backed away with dizzy dread, for its three-fingered hands still twitched, clutching for her even in death.

Running hard, peppering the ground behind with kicked gravel, she reached the pale ferns at the bank of the dry stream and thrashed among them, determined to quit the waterway that the biot had descended. Her backpack slowed her progress among the bracken, and she doddered on the steep slope until she reached the next higher rock shelf. There, heather climbed the slopes toward an obscure wood of wild chestnuts.

Halfway through the purple gorse, figures stalked out of the high forest. She paused long enough to determine that the rushing shadows were biots. When she identified their spry, lustrous bodies, she slogged harder toward them. They were too far yet to shoot and fleeing downhill was foolish, because she was certain there were others awaiting her there.

As the silent assailants closed in, bounding like monkeys through the heather, she knelt to level her upslope aim and fired as rapidly and steadily as she could. Splinters flew, resins splashed hotly in the sunlight, and biots fell down the stony incline.

Ellen held her position. She remembered what Fenn Tekla had told her – the biots were mindless. They made no effort to outflank her. They simply charged straight toward her like happy children rushing to their mother. The deaths of their comrades did not dissuade them. They fixed on her and did not relent, and she fired until the last one spewed ichorous blood and crashed into the gorse.

At the fringe of the chestnut holt, she looked back at a vista of incredible loveliness. Massive and somber headlands rose against a lake-blue sky and taut streams of cirrus. Wooded bluffs and summer-green promontories descended into vales swept by the shadows of the clouds below her.

A crackling of leaves spun her about. More biots slunk toward her through the pitchgreen forest. Her sonic gun sang again. An owl flew, alarmed by the shrieks of the gun. It passed soundlessly overhead, a grim omen. She ignored it and continued firing.

From under the shaded eaves of a slate ledge where the chestnuts leaned against the mountain, another squad of biots flung themselves toward her. She backed away, struck her heel on a rock, and staggered. The weight of her pack pulled her backward, and she rolled into the heather. Quickly, she pulled herself upright, swung her gun to fire, and a biot's flailing arm struck the weapon from her grip. A fierce hand grabbed her face, clamped its three fingers onto her skull, and lifted her to her feet.

For an instant, she hung painfully at her boot-tips staring past the taloned hand into red eyes of flat indifference. Then the hand released her, contracted to a fist, and punched darkness between her eyes.

Ellen Vancet woke inside a slingseat in the ball turret of a large spaceliner. She could see for herself that the liner was big, for her vantage in the transparent turret revealed the colossal ventral length of the vessel. Impulse pods large as houses belled from the gray-green hull, and a resonance duct big as a hangar blocked her forward view.

Stars splattered the utter darkness of deep space, and, adjacent the white disk of the Sun, the Earth herself shone as a blue thumbnail crescent.

'Ah, you are awake,' an oily voice descended out of the dark companionway overhead. Pink, wrinkled podiforms gripped the hatch rim and lowered a hairless dwarf man with multiple blister eyes, pleated mouth, and thin nostril-slits like a viper's. Flexible, bulb-jointed limbs with blunt padlike hands manipulated the second slingseat in the turret and inserted the squat, neckless torso. 'I am Oruch, your host.'

Ellen winced to look at the compact, long-limbed entity criss-crossed with red leather bindings, tasseled thongs, and brass hooks, all encased in the crinkled transparency of a statskin sheath. The blister eyes, four of them clustered like a spider's array, two large, two small, smoky gray as quartz, seemed to scan her.

'You're a morf,' she said.

'Am I disgusting to you?' the greasy voice asked, the pleated gray lips curling outward to reveal a triple array of tiny, needle-thin teeth. 'As disgusting as you seem to me? I realize that my ancestors morfed from your stock, and I have viewed numerous holostreams of your kind before visiting Earth. Nonetheless, I am revolted by the sight of your ghastly visage with those eerily-lidded eyes and beaked nose.' A slithery laugh coiled from the morf, and he pounded his mitteny hands together. 'We are monsters to each other, aren't we?'

'The imploders sent you.' She swung about in her sling to move as far from him as she could in the glass sphere. 'Where are they?'

'Imploders?' Oruch pulled closer, accompanied by a rancid smell that permeated his statskin.

'The Maat who sent you.' She put a hand to her wrinkled nose, not bothering to hide her revulsion. 'My captors – are they on board?'

'The Maat – ah, the Overlords.' The blister eyes scrutinized her. 'Why do you call them imploders?'

'The secret understanding,' she said and looked for comprehension in the morf's unreadably alien features. 'They're going to implode the universe.'

'You are truly a strange creature.' Oruch's clubhand touched her cheek, and a magnetic tingle brushed her face. Quickly he pulled back and swiped a bulbed wrist over his slit nostrils. 'And you stink of something burnt. My crew warned me before we accepted this mission. Some of them had seen the root stock before, and they said I'd be appalled. They were right, but I'm the kind of man who must experience things for himself.'

'Where are you taking me?'

'Our tour of the root world was as bizarre as any of us had hoped.' Oruch twined his flexible limbs together so that his rotund body formed a bony, pink ball in the sling. 'The Overlords were excellent guides and afforded us experiences of our weird origins that none of us will ever forget. We knew the root world was hot and wet, but the smell of it – the putrescent stink of the place!'

Ellen had viewed holostreams of numerous morfs, including the hirsute Callistoids, the crane-kneed Maat of Mars, and the frail, insectile Pilots, adapted to live exclusively in the mining machinery that trawled the asteroid belt. But this being before her she had never seen. 'I'm certain I'll find your home as lovely.'

Another laugh slithered from the morf. 'Yes, you will enjoy Titan as much as we relished Earth.'

Titan! She had heard years ago that the largest moon in the Saturn system had colonies, but she had paid little heed. It was so far away it did not concern her then. 'What are you going to do to me?'

'Entertain you, Ellen Vancet.' The crimped mouth twisted toward a semblance of a smile. 'You are our guest, a female of the root stock – and one favored by the Overlords themselves. Yes, you shall be well entertained.'

Oruch unplaited his limbs and began to unstrap himself from his slingseat.

'This is a large vessel to send all the way from Titan just to kidnap me,' said Ellen.

'You carry a false assumption, Ellen.' Oruch hung by one tendrillous arm. 'Several thousand of us came to tour the root world. The Overlords asked us as a favor to take you with us on our return journey.'

'Are there Overlords on board?'

'No. This is a Titan spaceliner on its maiden voyage to the inner worlds. The Overlords deploy their own means of transport.' Oruch climbed back up into the companionway and hung briefly upside down. 'Feel free to depart the view bubble and look around your living quarters. This is a journey of several days, and we want you to be comfortable. From time to time, I will look in on you. If you have need of anything, there is a comm unit in your quarters.'

Ellen hung limply in her sling, breathing through her mouth until the stink of the Titanian faded. She watched Earth drift into the dark void – all that she loved fading into the limitless night – and a bruise pulsed deep in her chest.

Frantically, she tore at the sling buckles and pulled herself out of the ball turret. If she stared at Earth dwindling to a blue star, she felt madness would seize her. Her hands clasped the rim of the overhead companionway, and she climbed up into a dark compartment.

Her weight assured her that the spaceliner was outfitted with a magravity field, and she moved gingerly into the lightless chamber. At her first step, panel lights suffused brightly in the circular molding of the large, amply appointed cabin.

The solar clarity of the illumination revealed a chrome galley with fixtures installed for human use, a hammock bed, an ivory-trimmed holostream unit, and several pieces of flexform furniture. She opened the two narrow sliding doors behind the hammock and disclosed a latrine behind one and behind the other a closet filled with garments in her size.

'You see we've tried to think of everything, Q,' a friendly voice spoke with intimate familiarity from behind her.

When she turned, she faced a holostream of Tabor Roy sitting on a tortoise rock beside a yard of black raked sand. In the background, a eucalyptus grove fluttered before a citrus sky where a bright star, Venus, soaked up twilight.

'You're going to be very comfortable on your cruise and at your destination,' Tabor assured her. His silver, close-set eyes assessed her, and he put a hand to his handsome, dimpled chin and shook his head disapprovingly. 'You might consider getting out of those hiking clothes. Where you're going requires a different apparel. For now, why don't you enjoy the other garments we've selected for you?'

'Tabor—' Ellen took an irate step closer to the image that had replaced the holostream unit. 'I don't want to be here. This is criminal.'

'Not really.' He crossed his legs, rested his elbow on his knee and his chin in the palm of his hand. 'The biots were a clever idea. You should be proud of me. I developed the technology myself. Electromagnetically induced genetic shaping – and from a considerable distance, old Q. I transmitted the sequences from the Moon.'

'It's criminal to take someone against their will.' She glared. 'Don't treat me like a fool, Tabor. I may not have metasapience, but I'm a human being.'

'One of the very oldest.' Tabor smiled pleasantly. 'And I love you dearly, Q. Why do you think I want you to join us? I can't bear the thought of losing you in the implosion. If not for you, I wouldn't be a Maat today.'

'If not for me, you monster, you wouldn't be alive today.' Ellen stabbed a finger at him. 'I'm your quingenmother. You owe me respect.'

'But I do respect you – immensely.' Tabor sat up straighter, the wide sleeves of his cobalt-trimmed white vestment spreading like wings as he opened his arms to his sides as if to embrace her. 'I've gone to great pains to see that you are well taken care of during this cruise and at your destination. I assume Captain Oruch has informed you that you are bound for Titan, the largest moon in the Saturn system.'

'I know where Titan is.' Her stiff arms at her sides and her fisted hands shook angrily. 'I don't want to go to Titan. I want to go home.'

'You're such a genuine stick-in-the-mud, Q.' Tabor crossed his arms and shook his head. 'Don't you know that in the last hundred years the colonies on Titan have become among the most economically and culturally advanced in the entire solar system. The Maat themselves have a city there – Terra Chronos, where I hope to visit with you someday. The Titanians are a remarkable ingenious breed and have transformed their planet into a wonderland. You will be surprised at their ingenuity.'

Ellen sagged disconsolately. 'Why are you doing this to me, Tabor?'

'Look around me.' Tabor stood and indicated the beds of raked sand, a rock garden, and a tile-roofed house with curved eaves and paper-and-bamboo sliding doors in the ancient style of Nippon. 'This is where Rafe von Takawa lived before he fled Earth for parts unknown. Isn't it lovely? And nostalgic of ancestors that an anthrofact could have only in imagination. There are Germanic artefacts elsewhere on the estate – artefacts of the mind, which he fancied his Aryan ancestors cherished. The Germans were not much renowned for their architecture or their landscapes. Ah, but their music. He has a complete set of the ancient German masters – from Bach to Wagner. And poetry! Trakl, Hölderlin, Goethe. When he departed, in fact, he left a volume of Rilke open on his writing desk, with a passage from the end of the eighth of the *Duino Elegies* underlined. It reads, "Like a man on the final hill that shows him his whole valley one last time, who turns and stands there lingering – that's how we live, always saying goodbye." Isn't that poignant, Q?'

'You cannot use me to capture Rafe von Takawa,' Ellen declared coldly.

'Oh no?' Tabor crossed his arms and planted one foot atop the tortoise rock. 'An anthrofact soft-hearted enough to underline poetry will not let the closest experience he had to a mother languish in despair.'

'You've become cruel, Tabor.' Ellen stepped to the very edge of the holostream. 'When you were young and you and I went hiking and fishing together, you were a bright and caring human being. What happened to you?'

'You should know, Q. You invented it.' His strong features regarded her placidly. 'It's called metasapience. I have attained the mind's greatest clarity. I have peered into infinity.'

'Come back to Earth, Tabor,' Ellen scolded. 'Remember your humanity.'

'Q, I have seen heaven – the paradise from which everything has come!' A joyful luminosity shone in his boyish smile. 'How can I ever be happy again out here – among these illusions?' He gestured impatiently at the darkening trees and the spare, gray shapes of rock and sand. 'I will do whatever I can to get back to where we came from – the true reality of light and unbroken symmetry. I want to take you with me. Don't be stupid and choose illusion over reality.'

'It's you who are wrongheaded, Tabor, to take the choice away from me.' She turned her back on the holostream. 'I belong on Earth.'

No reply came, and when she looked again, the image of Tabor was gone. The holostream unit, all black glastic and ivory trim, sat squat and mute in the middle of the cabin.

'Rafe is right, you know,' she said to the inert device. A chill of despair leaked from her marrows. 'This is how we live – always saying goodbye.'

The spaceliner had set a long, switchbacking course that took it past Mars and through the Jovian system. When each planet came into view, Captain Oruch arrived in Ellen Vancet's cabin and insisted on sitting with her in the ball turret. He delighted to expound facts about the worlds they viewed while she watched and listened morosely.

Happily for her, he had lost interest in tasting her presence, and so had adjusted his statskin sheath to maximum closure, and she no longer had to bear his rancid odor.

'Someday, perhaps, you will make your residence in Solis,' the

Titanian captain said in his oily voice when they drifted past Mars. 'It is an entirely aboriginal community, you know. Morfs are forbidden there, as are Maat.'

'I belong on Earth,' she mumbled sullenly and watched the pocked vista creep before her, its cracked and reddish-brown surface like dried blood.

'The Anthropos Essentia would honor one such as you, Ellen.' Oruch's four blister eyes did not shift from viewing the parade of volcanic cindercones, the fossae of deep crevasses, and the slurry of barren dunes, a planet with an aspect like the scorched pit of hell. 'You converted, did you not? Once you manipulated genetic identity – but for many centuries now, you have eschewed such work. I believe that the fanatical Essentia would respect that.'

Oruch enjoyed teasing Ellen in this way. During the fly-by of the Jovian system, he pointed out morf stations on Europa and Ganymede that had cantonments designed for aboriginals. The banded surface of Jupiter with its ripple patterns of shear winds and vortices of stratospheric currents filled the bubble view, and the moons Oruch indicated were mere pebbles adrift against a wall of clouds in every shade of rust.

Ellen complied with the morf captain, because she wanted to view the worlds with her own eyes. Awe pervaded her to realize that these were not holostreams but the far worlds themselves. She ignored Oruch's taunts about the planetary niches where root stock such as herself could safely dwell. Yet when she was alone in her cabin, she did wonder what life was like for human beings on these remote outposts.

From the holostream unit, she called up view clips of the aboriginal enclaves in the Jovian system. All were trade posts established by the large interplanetary mining and shipping cartels, like Ares Bund and Apollo Combine. The aboriginals served as an interface between the morf colonies that exploited the resources of the Jovian moons and the cartels that traded the Jovian goods with settlements on Mars and the Moon. Many of the aboriginals represented the cislunar factory complexes that manufactured goods for consumption on the terrestrial reservations and the selene communities.

Was Rafe hiding among them? She pondered where he could have gone after fleeing Callisto. The sphere of cratered ice that hovered briefly in view during the spaceliner's transit seemed wholly inhospitable.

Encouraged by the Maat, morf communities had cropped up as distantly as Miranda, the crazy-quilt moon of Uranus. And seed expeditions had already arrived in the Neptune system and begun explorations of Triton and Nereid. There were no aboriginal niches that distant from Earth yet, but Saturn, Jupiter, Mars, and the Moon were rife with trading posts, mining stations, and cantonments designed to host aboriginals. Rafe could be anywhere among them.

On the long journey, Ellen did not dwell much on Rafe but spent most of her time forlornly reminiscing about Earth. She lay in her hammock and ran holostreams of the numerous terrene reservations – and, when she could bear it, Council Oak. Direct communication was impossible – the comm unit of her cabin was controlled by the captain – and she had to satisfy herself with updated views of her home world.

By the time Saturn grew large enough to view in detail from the ball turret and Captain Oruch arrived to share the panorama with her, she felt too depressed to cooperate.

'We are prepared for all eventualities, foolish woman.' The squat morf removed a slender white canister from a discreet holster among his numerous straps and thong-ties and misted the cabin with neurolfact. 'The Overlords have insisted that you be comfortable.'

The vanilla scent eroded Ellen's malcontent, and in moments she shrugged off her yearning for Earth and climbed down the companionway into the ball turret to take in the sights of Saturn. The famous rings, flat and concentrically circular, shone in icy tints of green and silvered blue. Dark bands hinted at where to seek the shepherd moons and co-orbital satellites, and Oruch proudly detailed how the Titanians had erected comm stations on these fleet rocks whose criss-cross orbits herded the icy boulders of the rings.

The sere atmosphere churned vastly, the tawny bands of ammonia clouds aswirl with vortical storms. In the broad shadow of the rings, streaks of lightning forked through the cloud deck, and flares winked like will-o'-the-wisps where methane crystals ignited in thin blue jets.

'We will be arriving at our destination shortly.' Oruch began to unstrap. 'You are to be delivered to Terra Chronos, the Maat metropolis, where you . . .'

The ship juddered so violently that Oruch blurred with the vibrations and nearly toppled out of his sling. Thunder rolled from somewhere deep in the vessel, and an alarm siren wailed briefly and then went silent.

'Remain secured!' Oruch commanded and swiftly exited the ball turret. Halfway up the companionway, another vehement explosion rocked the liner, and he fell back, at first dangling by one long limb and then floating freely. 'The magravity field is down!' he shouted and began blurting frantic sounds that made no sense to Ellen, stopping briefly to add, 'Get out of the turret! Put on your statskin – quickly!'

He disappeared again into the companionway, and Ellen loosed herself from the sling and spun into freefall. Swimming helplessly a moment, she grabbed at the hovering straps of the sling and began to pull herself toward the hatch. Then, through the clear glastic of the ball turret, she saw them.

A dozen cruisers flitted into view. The mirror-hulled spheres spun effervescently around each other, spinning, darting, bobbing, maneuvering with abrupt unpredictability. Orange bolts of proton plasma shot from the liner's cannon stabbed into space among the jittery spheres.

The cruisers returned fire, wincing bluewhite laser flashes. The hull trembled, and disastrous sounds echoed from within – explosions, screaming metal, hissing gases.

A bolt of proton plasma struck a cruiser, and the sphere exploded in a silent nova of white-hot energy that cooled instantly to glowing red embers of spinning debris. The other cruisers swarmed out of sight, attacking the liner along the dorsal length she could not see.

Heart tripping madly, Ellen pulled herself by the sling straps into the companionway and swam up into her cabin. The lights flickered dully, brightening long enough for her to see her laundry, her eating utensils and cooking canisters adrift and the hammock billowing loosely. A dull roar resounded through the ducts, promising catastrophe.

Ellen squirmed and lurched along the walls through the strobing illumination, striving to reach her closet and the statskin sheath compressed into the safety box at its back. As she tumbled past her hammock, a holostream bloomed brightly, and a curly-haired aboriginal in a cruiser flightpit appeared, his elfin features set grimly yet smiling.

'Ellen Vancet!' His hands moved busily over the control deck, and around him, through the transparent interior of the cruiser, she saw against the amber face of Saturn several other cruisers, their mirror orbs flitting around each other and firing sharp strokes of blue laser fire. 'This is Sam Nphahalete. I can't see you, but I think you can at least hear me. I've been sent by Fenn Tekla.'

Static slashed the image to skewed colors and the voice hissed to silence.

Ellen's tripping heart flipped to a new, more hopeful beat, and her fright dimmed slightly. She redirected herself across the cabin, using the tangled hammock to yank herself to the holostream unit. With a kick, she banged open the adjustment panel and began fidgeting with the receptor dials.

'. . . lost you I guess. No – wait! I'm getting a gain signal.' Sam Nphahalete's voice filled the cabin, and she winced and lowered the volume. 'I still can't see you, but I think you're hearing me again.'

The image of the cruiser's interior flicked into place, and Ellen drifted around it, alert to the details of the control deck. She read the instruments with cold fascination, noting that most of the cruiser's power had already drained into its laser banks. Sam would have to retreat to his base within minutes, and she knew from this there was no hope he could retrieve her. Looking at his tangerine flightsuit, she searched for some insignia to identify his allegiance but could find none.

'We are shearing your cabin from the liner,' Sam said, and his cruiser arced sprightly across the ventral length of the ship. She saw then for the first time the full forward view of the vessel that carried her. It had the broad, flat triangular shape of a marine ray. Hot seams of flame criss-crossed the hull, jetting crimson fire from the ignited gases of the interior.

'You're in a compartment isolated from the Titanians,' Sam spoke while frenetically attending to the control deck. 'Your life support should hold after the breach. But if you have a statskin sheath – put it on now.'

Ellen kicked off from the edge of the holostream unit and arrowed toward the closet. She slid it open, and the garments within fluttered into her face.

'We don't have flight power to stay with you,' Sam's calm but strained voice told her what she already knew. 'But we're dropping you into a wide orbit about Enceladus and will be back soon to retrieve you.'

Groping through the billowing clothes, Ellen found the safety box secured to the back of the closet. She released the latch and felt within the box for the distinctive round bracelets that powered the statskin. Without a bodyform matrix to tailor the sheath to her precise dimensions, the statskin would fit loosely, and she was not inclined to release the statfilm until she needed it.

She slipped her hands through the bracelets, found a lux wand, and pushed away from the closet. The holostream of Sam Nphahalete showed him silently engaged in a conversation with other cruisers. Through the hull, she watched cauterizing strokes of laser fire scoring the hull of the Titanian liner. Sam's cruiser dipped, looped, and swung around a blinding stream of proton plasma.

Ellen recognized the ball turret behind the resonance ducts and forward of the impulse pods, the bubble view where she had watched the procession of planets and moons. As Sam had informed her, the hull around the turret crawled with worms of fire leaving a blazing outline of her cabin. More bolts of laserlight struck the burning metal, and the cracks widened to glowing gaps.

Stupendous vibrations quaked through the cabin, and the flickering lights went black. Only the holostream provided illumination. From inside Sam Nphahalete's cruiser, the view showed the spaceliner slashed with laserfire, wide punctures raying energy into the star-dusted darkness. A gout of the burning hull fell away from the liner – and Ellen realized that what she saw toppling into space spewing sparks and flames from its edges was her cabin. The ball turret reflected first the burning liner, then Saturn's amber stormclouds and tilted rings before rotating out of sight.

Ellen activated the statskin bracelets, and statfilm flared from the rings in a sibilant rush and wrapped her drifting body in a loose transparent sheath. Vision rippled through the slack film. She adjusted the bracelets, and the sheath pulled somewhat tighter about her.

With the cabin sheared free, the cruisers' assault on the liner intensified. Laser strokes slashed at the burning hulk, punching bright holes into its shell. Metal panels winged into space. Sparks geysered. Then a holocaust bulged from within as the power core ignited, and the hull swelled briefly before lances of white fire spiked through the plating and thrust into space. An orange fireball disintegrated the spaceliner. Streamers of smoldering detritus rocketed in every direction, leaving behind a hot cloud of churning destruction.

The cabin went dark. With the lux wand, Ellen dispelled her blindness and found her way to the holostream unit. Static sizzled, then hissed into Sam's voice, '. . . fusion reaction! The shockwave is stronger than we anticipated. You've fallen into the gravity well.'

Ellen fiddled with the receptor controls but could not bring in an image.

Sam's voice continued its dire assessment: 'Your cabin will impact Enceladus before we can get back to pull you out. The best we can do is angle you for a sliding entry to minimize the impact.'

Several jolts vehemently shook the cabin, and Ellen hurriedly shoved away from the holostream unit to keep from slamming into it.

'That's all we can do for you, Ellen.' Sam's voice bristled with noise.

'The cabin hull is intact and should be able to withstand a landing at this angle of entry. We will be back for you as soon as we can. The Titanians are rallying a patrol sweep, so we'll have to stay out of sight for a while. But you should be okay down there. The morfs are free class and should pose no problem. Just stay close to the impact site so we can find you quickly. With all the debris hurtling around out here, the patrol won't even think to look for you, so there's no chance that you'll be picked up by the Titanians. I better shut this line down, however, before it does alert someone. Don't send any signals. Just sit tight. We'll be back. Good luck, Ellen.'

The holostream unit went dead. Silence pervaded the dark cabin. Ellen turned off the power in the unit to be certain that it left no signal trail for the Titanians to follow. Then, she lit her way with the lux wand to the hatch and crawled through to the ball turret.

Stars misted heavily along the galactic plane of the Milky Way, and she watched the stellar band tilt and vanish as she secured herself into the turret's sling seat. A parabolic arc of Saturn's rings rotated into view, a voluptuous curve of icy blue light against the velvet darkness. It swung gracefully away, and the bubble view of the turret rotated into sight of Enceladus, a luminously bright sphere of ice.

Vast plains of this moon appeared unsmutched by craters, smooth as an eggshell. But other areas displayed the usual cratering of all moons. Ellen gazed dismally at her ultimate destination, watching it swing past the turret. She hoped that the cruisers had calculated her entry accurately. She did not want to become another crater on this luminous moon.

Glancing at the empty sling straps beside her, she thought of Oruch and felt no pity for his fate. But she did feel remorse for the deaths of the other Titanians. Though she had met none of them, she did not like the fact that they had died on her account. She believed Fenn Tekla was wrong to send pirates to liberate her. Innocents had been killed – morfs who had possessed the sensitivity and curiosity to journey across the solar system to tour the world of their ancestors.

She dwelled on this until Enceladus swung back into view, closer, the immense plates of surface ice shining with a glaucous tint in the reflected glow of Saturn. Shortly she would have to endure her own personal risk for Fenn Tekla's bold and lethal tactic. She unfastened herself and glided back up the companionway into the dark cabin.

With the lux wand, she found the holostream unit and discovered that it was still functional. She set the device to fill the cabin with the perfume of woods when rain bends the grasses and invests earth with sodden beauty. The Rockies floated in the distance, footed in mist. Gray-bellied clouds traversed the spaces between the mountains like sky ships whose heavy cargo was her heart.

She secured herself in the hammock and floated in her mirage of Council Oak, waiting for impact. Adrift a long time, she fell asleep to the comforting patter of rain and the smell of thunder. And she was dreaming of thunder when she woke to the buffeting clangor of entry.

The fierce vibrations shattered the holostream into virid streaks of colors she had never learned to name. The blurred hues flashed like lightning, again and again, before going black. A colossal explosion knocked hearing out of her head and left her jarred numb, her insides veering hard against her ribs with the tumultuous lurching of the cabin.

Then stillness.

Sounds returned slowly to her buzzing brain.

A hissing whistle indicated a serious breach in the cabin bulwark. She flicked on her lux wand and saw the holostream unit wrenched from its moorings yet intact. The flexforms had ripped free of their glide bases and lay scattered about. And there, at the companionway, frosty fumes seeped. The ball turret had cracked, and the pressure differential between the interior and the icy atmosphere was condensing thin plumes of crystal air.

She untangled from the hammock and found herself lightfooted in the much reduced gravity of the little moon. The statskin sheath provided warmth and breathable air, and the lux wand showed her a path into the turret where the glastic canopy had sheared away. Most of the turret was embedded in the ground, but there was a gap just large enough for her to crawl through.

When she squirmed her way out, she lay prostrate on an icy plain under the immense visage of Saturn. The rings, brilliant arcs of spectral blue, caught the hard glint of stars within their diaphanous gaps.

Involuntarily, Ellen lifted to her knees and raised her hands in awe before the magisterial beauty of the giant planet. She swung her head and saw the glittering and empty spiderweb of stars flung against the darkness. The witch moons of Tethys and Dione hung bald and silver above the glacial cliffs of the ice plain. The tidal force of Dione's tandem orbit had stressed the small sphere of Enceladus, cracked its frozen surface into numerous meandering crevasses, and provoked water volcanism from the hot interior.

She rose to her feet, amazingly light in the thin gravity. With a few steps, she ranged far from the crash site. And when she looked back, she saw the wedged hulk of her cabin tilting obliquely from the frozen terrain.

The amber light of Saturn illuminated the wide basin where she had crashed, casting bold shadows from the tall cordillera of crevassed ice. In the opposite direction, volcanic mounds, white and gleaming in the planetlight, stood in a row of four. Frost clouds leaked from one, and evidence of ice lava lay in broad, melted petal-formations across the plain.

Circling back to the fallen cabin, she skirted the ragged edge of a steep gulch. That was a small part of a continuous network of cracks in the moon's surface – a surface like glazed pondwater with drifts of packed snow at irregular intervals. The sheath grips at her soles afforded her steady footing, and in the vague gravity she easily bounded across the ditches, declivities and gulches in her way.

She wondered how long she would have to endure in this bleak environment before the pirates came back for her. Fear sharpened in her at the thought that perhaps they would never return. To dispel this anxiety, she turned her attention again to the bronze clouds of Saturn and the cold, serene rings.

This is a beautiful place to die, she thought grimly.

Her heart shivered. Old as she was, she was afraid to die. The supernally beautiful planet so geometrically symmetric, almost divinely perfect, did not keep her mind from skittering across thoughts of herself mummified in the cold. She looked for the sun and found it low on the horizon, its fogged light little comfort.

At the cabin, she marched around the impact site. Large plates of ice had been shoved to a jagged slope at the forward end of the broken shard of spaceliner. That end also happened to be the section that had torn away from the main vessel, and tendrils of sheared cable hung among twisted girders and curled metallic sheets.

She gingerly climbed the steep embankment of broken ice and soon reached the torn side with its hydra tangles of bent pipes and cutaway conduits. Parting clusters of wire ganglia, she discovered a scorched portal and banged hard on the hand pad that served the Titanians as a doorlock. The portal slid open with a wail in the chill atmosphere, and the warm interior air whooshed out with a blizzard of crystalized moisture.

Knocked backward, Ellen grabbed onto a shorn duct and hung there a moment before finding the purchase to shove herself into the portal. This was the passageway by which Oruch had come and gone into her cabin. She entered the dark socket with her lux wand outlining the salient features – the galley, holostream unit, tangled flexforms – and shuffled along the tilted floor.

Sam Nphahalete had warned her not to broadcast a distress signal, yet when she knelt before the jarred holostreamer and recognized that its power supply had not been damaged, she had to step back to keep herself from activating the comm coils. She had been forbidden to transmit on board, but since the holostreamer had been severed from its master control the ancillary command function had activated. If she wanted, she could broadcast into space.

Ellen stepped back outside. Almost certainly the Titanians would descend on her if she opened a channel. Yet that might be preferable to being marooned on Enceladus. While she contemplated this, a movement on the ice plain caught her eye. Frost clouds, fibrous and thin, drifted overhead, seeping from the water volcanoes. But the motion she had glimpsed was not related to cloud shadows.

She climbed onto a broken conduit for a better view and noticed that the movement she had detected a moment earlier was gone – if it had been there at all. For a long while, she remained on her perch, scrutinizing the expansive plain and the distant wall of ice and rock. Nothing stirred but the tenuous drift of cloud shadows.

Back inside her skewed cabin, she propped herself against the holostreamer and adjusted the controls until she was certain that the comm module had been set to receive signals. Nothing appeared. No one was making an effort to contact her. That meant that the Titanians deployed after the destruction of their spaceliner had no idea she was still alive. And the pirates were in hiding.

Days could pass before this situation changed, she realized. In her statskin sheath she could go indefinitely without food or water. The sheath recycled oxygen and water, and each cell of her body had its toxins removed and recatalyzed to useful nutrients. So long as the power bands in her bracelets endured, her body would not suffer. But her mind was troubled by these austere surroundings.

She descended from the cabin and followed her prints back across the cracked land. The bluegray surfaces burnished in the coppery light of Saturn mesmerized her with their sameness. Her attention benefited from observing the subtle changes her footsteps had inflicted on the crisp patina of packed snow and knitted ice.

Her bounding walk came to an abrupt halt where her cleated footfalls lay smudged and impressed by other marks. Three-toed prints lay all about her tracks where she had stood at the edge of a steep crevice.

The prints had emerged from this ravine and descended again into it. Looking back at her cabin, she realized that this was the spot where she had noticed movement from her high vantage.

Ellen recalled Sam Nphahalete telling her that Enceladus was occupied by morfs. Free class morfs, he called them. That meant that they had been designed by the Maat to dwell on this inhospitable moon but not as part of the colonial system. These morfs were wild.

Moving as quickly as she could, Ellen hurried back to the crash site and clambered up the jumbled ice wall and into the cabin. She checked to see if any signals had been received by the comm module. None had. Then she searched the holostream memory for lifeforms in the Saturn system and located a data file on the morfs of Enceladus.

The creatures were indeed three-toed and human-sized. The holostream showed a gazelle-eyed sylphic creature of dusty blue pelt, round ears high on a long head crested with a ribbed, acoustical horn along the cope of the skull. Its three-fingered hands appeared deft, and its long, rosette-marked arms looked strong even though slender. The holostream revealed a human face pugnacious as a bat's, and showed the Enceladus morfs thriving off biotectured fruits and fungi that grew in the warm grottoes of the moon.

Time drifted as she sat in the aura of the holostream, studying the conjoined cavern communities under the icy shell of the surface. Steam from volcanic vents ran generators that illuminated terraced cities and tiered agricultural caverns. The electricity also powered piston and cam elevators that connected the underground cities with the outside. And yet little contact had been allowed by the Maat with the developing colonies on Titan.

The holostream explained that free class morfs allowed the Maat to concentrate their initial resources on establishing priority bases and settlements while still preparing niches for eventual colonization. In time, the cavern culture of Enceladus would be contacted by the morfs of other moons and brought into the solar community. For now, though, they were a primitive free class of morfs.

Ellen decided to avoid these morfs and keep to her cabin until the pirates came to retrieve her. To occupy herself, she ran history files on the holostreamer and pulled up the poetry of Rainer Maria Rilke, to read again the elegy that Rafe von Takawa had left as a message of farewell: 'This is how we live – always saying goodbye.'

In the glow of the blue air of summer over the Rockies, she dozed and slept. The noise of geese honking on the flyway woke her.

Not geese made these noises but blue-furred, batfaced hominids standing around the holostream unit, their large lemuroid eyes reflecting like black mirrors. A three-fingered hand touched the transparent sheath of statskin and tugged at it.

Ellen sat bolt upright, and the morfs honked loudly through the acoustical horns atop their heads, astonishing themselves with the din of their surprise. They backed away into the dark perimeter but did not flee. A lightshaft waved over her. It was her lux wand in the grip of a morf.

This morf had silver fur and no rosettes at all on the slender forearms that reached for her. Like the others, this individual wore a densely padded burnoose with the cowl draped loosely. No boots or shoes covered the large, three-toed hooves.

Swinging out of her hammock, Ellen held her hands up, signaling the morf to stand back.

'Be not afraid, star-woman.' The resonant voice that spoke from the morf made Ellen's chest hum. Blue clouds of breath fluffed in the cold air from its batlike face. 'I am [Honk-Bleat], priestess of the fire people.'

'You speak esper!' Ellen lowered her hands, and her jaw slackened with surprise.

'Yes, of course,' [Honk-Bleat] declared. 'We have listened to the stars for generations. We know esper. And we have called with it to the stars for reply. But no reply has come to us – none, until now.'

'I think you're mistaken,' Ellen said, squinting against the glare of the lux wand. 'I'm not a reply to your call. You've misunderstood my being here.'

'You have come from the stars,' [Honk-Bleat] observed. 'Our ice-walkers saw you ride out of the sky. We watched you walk about under the ringed sun.'

'Please, don't shine that light in my eyes.' Ellen brushed aside the lux wand.

'You do not look as we imagined.' [Honk-Bleat] stepped back, and the other morfs closed in.

'Imagined?' Ellen stared into their black, watchful eyes. 'If you know esper, you must know what we look like.'

[Honk-Bleat] turned and stepped to the holostream unit. She passed her hand through the empty image of the Rocky Mountains. 'We have heard of your wonders. So many wonders. But we have seen none – none, until now.'

Ellen realized that the sketchy report of the steam-powered society of Enceladus that she had viewed on the holostream described a radio-culture. They had intercepted occasional radio signals among the colonies but had not developed imaging devices. She briefly wondered how much she could tell them without violating Maat colonial codes, then decided she did not care what codes she violated. She would tell them the truth: 'I'm here by accident.'

[Honk-Bleat] turned abruptly, and a small commotion of excited noises passed among the younger, watchful morfs. 'Accident?'

'Yes – entirely by accident.' She nodded to emphasize her candor. 'I was bound for Titan. You know the moon – the largest around Saturn – the ringed sun?'

'The star people dwell upon Titan,' [Honk-Bleat] concurred. 'You are from Titan?'

'No, no.' She stepped to the holostreamer. 'I'm from Earth. The home world.'

'Earth is far away.' [Honk-Bleat]'s orbed eyes constricted with incredulity.

'Very far away,' Ellen agreed. 'A radio signal takes ninety minutes to get there from here.' She opened the control panel on the holostreamer, and the morfs crowded closer. 'Let me show you.'

After a few adjustments, the Rocky Mountains vanished to a few trumpets of surprise and a view of the solar system appeared with a spark-sized cursor blinking at Enceladus.

'Saturn system and your world—' Ellen inserted a finger in the blinking cursor, then moved the distance to the orbit of Earth. 'This is my home.'

More agitated noises chirruped from the morfs. 'Accident brought you here from Earth?' [Honk-Bleat] inquired and shone the light in her face again.

Ellen waved the lux wand away. 'Yes. I never intended to come out here. It's all a big accident.'

'*Big* accident!' [Honk-Bleat] announced this triumphantly and emitted a long cloud of hot breath in the cold air.

The other morfs cried out so loudly Ellen cringed, and the cabin filled with their humid smoke.

At [Honk-Bleat]'s signal, they closed in, their delicate three-fingered hands grabbing her arms and legs, and hoisted her off her feet.

'Hey! Put me down!' She squirmed and nearly twisted herself free, but the noises the morfs made sounded as though they'd been hurt. They were lissome beings, and she by comparison was a stout heavy creature. Fearing that her abrupt movements would damage them, she succumbed. 'Put me down!'

'Be silent, star-woman!' [Honk-Bleat] called from outside the enclosing group of grasping morfs. 'Accident has delivered you to us. Do not struggle. Come away!'

Unless she was willing to do harm to the lightweight morfs, she had no choice but to allow them to hoist her out of the cabin and down the shattered face of the impact slope. 'Where are you taking me?'

'Accident is taking you, star-woman.' [Honk-Bleat] shouted this while beating at her padded burnoose for warmth. 'Come away quickly! We have been too long above and the cold is bitter.'

The morfs lugged her across the glazed ice to a defile that plummeted into darkness. A fog of stars gleamed in the darkness, beyond the limb of Saturn and the giant blue parabolic arc of its rings that stood upon the horizon. Ellen watched the sky jog out of view as her captors carried her nimbly down the notched sides of the defile, the lux wand waving its thin beam ahead of them.

Lights appeared in the thick dark, far below. And warmth breathed upward in thermal drafts. A sibilant cry announced their arrival on a flat ledge where steam shot in jets from vents in the rock wall. This was one of the morf's elevators, Ellen understood a moment before her stomach lurched upward and the entire ledge descended.

The morfs doffed their padded garments, revealing strikingly human-oid torsos draped in colorful silk chemises and kirtles. Males and females seemed equally represented in the party that had come to meet her. She gaped openly at them and they at her. 'What is your name, star-woman?' [Honk-Bleat] asked.

'Ellen.' She watched spires of rock rise past and an enormous grotto loom into view: Terraced platforms carved into the walls supported a luminous city of rock and brick. Stone bridges connected the city levels, and elevator shafts similar to the one she rode moved through vertical grooves between the city's multiple levels.

'Accident has delivered you among us,' [Honk-Bleat] announced. 'Now will you come freely?'

Ellen nodded. The underworld metropolis fascinated her with its lantern-hung spans and radiant boulevards carved into the grotto floor. The holostream had provided only a sketchy and far-outdated image of this cavernous realm, and she was struck by the monumental starkness of the buildings stamped from the rocks and illuminated by sprawling trellises of arc-lights and stacked arrays of ironwrought lamps.

The aged priestess moved between ranks of morfs in armor breast-plates black as tarnished silver. The armored guards wore holstered guns and brandished big-bored rifles. Behind their metallic faceguards their large eyes stared straight ahead as the priestess passed but shifted to look at the strange star-woman in her transparent cloak.

A steam-engine truck received the surface-party, and several of the armored guards took stations on the runners as the vehicle clanked into motion and juddered along a cobbled street. Ellen peered out the thick warped glass of a round side window from where she sat on a bench between the priestess and the metal wall behind the driver's cab. The city beyond seemed a malevolent fantasy of blackrock buildings stained with calcined leakings and nodules of crystal growths. Plumes of steam vented from chimneys and black duct pipes, and when the truck negotiated a switchback she saw jets of blue flame among factory stacks deep in the canyon depths.

'What is this place?' she asked the priestess and leaned forward to better see the criss-crossed streets busy with steaming trucks.

'This is the city of Industry North,' [Honk-Bleat] replied. 'Here we manufacture everything from lightbulbs to engine parts.'

'And where are you taking me?'

[Honk-Bleat] turned to look over her shoulder, out the thick glass of the window behind them. A lordly edifice of cathedraled vaultings and high dark arches stood above the factory city, its massive walls hacked into the planetrock so that stalactites served as columns and stalagmites as stanchions topped with torches of blue gas flames. 'The local governor's residence. She commanded us to bring you to her if accident so decreed.'

The truck swerved onto an upward ramp and its gears growled as the engine labored to climb the steep incline. Through the window, Ellen spied sentry posts hollowed from rock columns and garrets along stone ledges where more armored soldiers patroled. 'Are you at war?' she finally asked.

[Honk-Bleat]'s seamed face turned toward her, and she clacked her undershot jaw defiantly. 'Not war! Infidel rebels who would usurp power for themselves.'

Nothing more was said until the truck shuddered to a halt before the colossal entryway to the residence. Armored guards ushered her out of the truck, but the priestess and the others remained. Without a word or a wave, the metal door slammed shut, and the truck groaned to a start and trundled away billowing steam.

The guards escorted her through the massive portal into an onyx court where a towering agate fountain percolated steaming water. At its base, ice buttresses sat welded by cold to the polished stone floor. The surface temperature had been -180 ° Celsius, and Ellen gauged by how quickly the boiling water crystallized that the environment here was about a hundred degrees warmer. Once again, she felt grateful for her statskin sheath.

From enclosing galleries with ornately carved railings, a crowd of morfs gawked at her, many pointing and honking animatedly among themselves. All wore sumptuous silk raiment, brightly colored in bold contrast to the black and gray hues of the architecture.

Ahead, slate doors swung wide revealing a bloated morf in scarlet robes sitting on a ponderous chair of graven ice, its blue interior shadowy with chunky suspensions. As Ellen walked closer, trying to keep her buoyant gait in the diminished gravity measured to the stride of her guards, she saw that the inclusions in the ice were the severed heads of morfs. She stopped abruptly in the doorway.

'Come closer, Ellen.' The enthroned figure motioned magisterially, the lengthy sleeves of the scarlet robes dangling nearly to the mirror-buffed floor. 'Yes, I know your name. My priestess radioed me everything you told her. Come. I would see you more clearly.'

Ellen approached trepidatiously, observing the spears, lances and swords mounted upon walls densely chiseled with framed moldings. Behind the throne, a wall of tall narrow windows offered a vista of the entire stone metropolis aglitter with electric lights and factory flares.

The governor, her bat's face tiny in the rings of fat that overlaid her chin, pointed to a settle of ice engraved with geometric designs. Ellen sat there. The swollen eyes of her hostess examined her with undisguised fascination. 'I admit, without embarrassment, that you are far more grotesque than ever we imagined the star-people.'

'Governor, I was abducted from Earth,' Ellen said, searching the morf's obese features for responsive clues and finding none. 'I would like to go home.'

A shrill laugh sliced the air, streaming like a siren's lash from the governor's crest-horn. 'If we could all have what we'd like wouldn't this be a glorious stellar system?' With her sleeve, she daubed at her bulging eyes. 'No, Ellen. No. You shall not be going home. Accident put you into our hands and now accident alone can remove you.'

'Others know I am here,' she informed the large morf. 'They will come searching for me.'

'Let them search.' The governor spread her arms magnanimously. 'Industry North is a small factory city. There are larger caverns where you can be well kept from sight.'

Ellen stood. 'Am I your prisoner?'

'Sit down, Ellen.' The governor glared at her until she sat. 'We are all prisoners on Enceladus. Isn't that so?'

'I don't know what you mean.'

'Nonsense, Ellen. You know as much as anyone.' The infernal face showed small rows of tiny pointed teeth in a gruesome smile. 'This is a world of free class morfs. Is that not how we are labeled among the greater powers?'

'You know much of the worlds beyond Enceladus,' Ellen acknowledged and shifted uneasily on the settle. 'Then you must know that the ones who will seek me are of the highest order of beings.'

'The Maat,' the governor identified and gave another ugly smile. 'I know of the Maat. They are the ones who created us, sixteen generations ago. They left us here, prisoners of this moon. When they need us, they will come for us. But that is not now, is it? No. You are not here as an emissary of the Maat. You are here by accident. So you have said yourself.'

'They will search for me,' Ellen insisted.

'Let them search.' The governor dismissed this possibility with a vague brush of her draped arm. 'The Maat have more pressing concerns than finding one such as you. Now that you are a prisoner here on Enceladus among the rest of us prisoners of the Maat's creation, you had best find your proper place.'

'And what is that proper place, governor?'

'Do I detect a tone of insolence, Ellen?' The tiny face fisted tighter. 'You do not want to alienate me, *star-woman*. I am not an ignorant peon or a superstitious priestess. I am of this world's elite. I know what matters. I can help you live a comfortable life among us – or I can place you in an unimaginable hell.'

Ellen's heart raced like a motor at the thought of being trapped forever in this grim cavern. Yet not even forever: for without simviv and ion washes, she would slowly begin to age again – *very* slowly, inside the statskin. 'What do you want of me?'

'Your cooperation, of course.' The governor rose from her throne of ice. Her thick body almost seemed to bobble beneath the folds of her robes as her three-toed hooves conveyed her across the chamber to the wall of narrow windows. 'Industry North is a small domain. I yearn for larger responsibilities. But to move out of this grimy factory mill, I must prove my worth to my superiors. And for that, I need your help. If you give it freely, I will see that you join me in a place of greater ease.'

'What must I do?' Ellen repeated, trying to keep impatience out of her voice.

'You noticed our soldiers?' The governor kept her gaze fixed out the windows on the steaming pit of black buildings. 'We need them to ward off the rebels who want to free the slaves.'

'Slaves?' The word leaped from her in a jolt of surprise. There had been no mention of slavery in the holostream report – but then there had been no information either about armored troops.

'How else could I and the other elite live so well without our slaves?' The governor put the three fingers of a pudgy hand against a window pane. 'We cherish our slaves. They are given to us by chance – the same deity that gave us you, Ellen.'

'I don't follow you, governor.'

'At birth, lot determines our station in life,' the governor explained in a dreary voice. 'The priestesses perform the rites of chance for each of us the moment we are born. Six out of every ten are selected as slaves. Three out of ten are chosen to manage the slaves. And one out of the ten are found by chance to be worthy of the elite. After that, merit alone determines how high one rises within one's class.'

'And the rebels seek to overthrow this arbitrary class system?' Ellen crossed her arms over her chest and shook her head. 'I can't help you stop them.'

'Oh, but you can.' The governor turned full about, graceful as a cloud. 'You see, only the elite speak esper and know all there is to know of the worlds beyond Enceladus. But the great majority of our society are entirely benighted. To them, you are a goddess – a star-woman.'

'I'm just a human being.'

'The likes of which they have never seen.' The governor pranced closer, giant eyes brightening. 'The statskin you wear confers godhood on you, Ellen. You need neither food nor drink. You are impervious to bullets, as we shall soon demonstrate.'

'What do you mean?' Ellen asked anxiously as the governor seized her arm and pulled her upright.

'Come with me.' The governor pulled her along behind her. 'It has all been arranged, you see. My mind never stops for an instant. I have wanted out of this factory hole for years – and now you shall liberate me.'

Ellen stiffened against the governor's pull and nearly toppled the obese morf. 'I don't know what you intend, but I'll have no part of it.'

'No?' The governor stood back, her jowls shivering with anger. 'You may be able to daunt me alone. But at my beckoning, a dozen guards will grab you and carry you to a mine shaft as big as this doorway!'

She raised a fist toward the mammoth slate doors. 'There you will be covered with tons of rock and forgotten. How long before you go mad down there in the utter darkness unable to move an inch? How long? Not a fraction of how long that statskin will keep you alive!'

Ellen sagged and would have slumped to the floor had not the governor taken her arm and pulled her along.

'Open!' the governor called, and the huge doors swung outward upon a crowd of morfs – common morfs in dirty and torn work garments. From the galleries, the elite and their guards watched eagerly.

The crowd blared noises of shock and awe at the sight of the star-woman. Guards wedged a path for the governor and her celestial guest and led the way through the court to the colonnade outside the residence. There, thousands of morfs thronged behind flimsy chainlink barriers defended by armored soldiers. The din shook Ellen's bones, and she cringed beside the ample presence of the governor.

A siren cried from somewhere atop the titanic columns, and the gathering of excited morfs quieted. Speaking a language Ellen did not understand, the governor elicited amazed shouts and trumpetings from the multitudes. Many were still swarming up the winding incline from the factory city. As they ran into the crush, the horde pushed harder against the chainlinks and the soldiers.

The governor gesticulated proudly, inspiring more astonished noises from the morfs. In midsentence, a lone figure ducked under the chain barrier and dashed between the harried guards. Before she could be seized, a sturdy gun appeared from under her drab robes. She leveled the weapon and fired rapidly, directly at the star-woman.

Ellen dodged futilely, and the bullets slammed into her chest throwing her into the soldiers behind her. She and half a dozen morfs collapsed. Screams and shrill peals swelled from the crowd even after the assassin was seized, disarmed, and hustled away. The governor yanked a startled Ellen to her feet, and the fearful noises shifted to delighted wonder.

The bullets had flattened against the statskin, and the force had diffused across the sheath. Ellen put her hands on her chest and felt no damage. She shot an irate look at the governor, but before she could speak, the morf's heavy arm enclosed her and swept her away from the shocked gathering.

Striding through the court to the laudatory clarion calls of the elite, the governor congratulated Ellen, 'You did well. Well indeed. Your appearance beside me has convinced the entire city that the star-woman is my ally. And the murderous behavior of that rebel – or should I say the soldier dressed as a rebel – has proven to the masses that my enemies are also foes of the worlds beyond.'

'That was monstrous!' Ellen charged. 'You're misleading your people.'

The governor smiled grimly and said nothing until the slate door thudded closed behind them. Then she spoke harshly. 'Would you prefer interment in the darkness?'

Ellen seriously considered overpowering the governor and fleeing into the host outside. But they did not understand esper, and she knew she would be apprehended quickly. Looking into the governor's evilly compressed face, she had no doubt that this ruthless morf would fulfill her threat.

'Soon enough now, the backlash will be felt by the rebels.' The governor lifted her swollen face to the groined ceiling and grinned exultantly. 'Word of your arrival will fly to the supreme elite in the capital, and you shall be summoned. But your convoy will be thwarted by the rebels – until the populace itself rebels against *them*! Every chute and tunnel will be flushed out by common factory workers! Within days, the rebel force will be broken. And you and I will bring a great victory to the supreme elite. They will reward me for my cleverness and revere you for your influence over the masses.'

Ellen could abide this bloated tyrant no longer. She strode furiously to the ice throne and shoved it off its pedestal. With a tremendous boom, it shattered on the polished floor.

The slate doors cracked open, and several guards rushed into the chamber. The appalled governor thrust an accusatory arm toward Ellen, but before she could speak, the star-woman said, 'Word of my arrival flies to the supreme elite, governor. I don't think they will reward you for dropping me into a mine shaft, do you?'

The governor sputtered, then grouchily waved the guards away. 'You think you've outwitted me. You have not. Accident brought you to us – accident may take you away!'

'Why threaten me, governor?' Ellen stalked closer, kicking a large chunk of ice out of her way. 'Why manipulate me deceptively? What you want, you can have by asking.'

The governor's batface twitched. 'Why would you do what I ask?'

'For what I want.' Ellen moved intimidatingly close to the hefty morf. 'The holostream unit – let me have access to it. Let me call the Titanians to take me from here. Before I go, I will accompany you to the capital and recite praises of you to your superiors.'

The governor stepped back and called for her guards. When the

slate doors opened wide enough for her to pass through, she exited.
A moment later, a stream of armored soldiers rushed in.

'I take that as a no!' Ellen yelled, skittering backward among the
shards of the throne. The image of a deep black pit loomed in her
mind, and she reeled about and charged with all her strength toward
the wall of windows.

Gunfire exploded behind her, and the bullets that struck her back
only increased her momentum. When she hit the tall pane, it erupted
outward, and she careened into space in a cloud of shattered glass.

The plunge to the ledge below looked daunting, but in the diminished gravity of Enceladus, she descended slow enough to survey her
escape. She absorbed the force of her landing with bent knees and
lunged into a run for the steam-misted stairwell that descended toward
the city. Bullets smacked off the rocks around her, but she was not
hit again.

The stairs bent back on themselves along the cliff, and she glimpsed
again the wrought black city, her destination. The crowd who had
gathered to see her were visible on the wide avenue that led from
the governor's residence. The narrow stairwell she negotiated was a
servant's path that led to the hovels of the mansion's servants. In the
niggard lamplight, she saw that the rusting sheds were empty. Everyone
had gone up to see the star-woman.

With great bounding steps, Ellen crossed the area of clustered huts
and reached a high wall of spalled bricks powdery with nitre. Her
running jump propelled her more than halfway up the barrier. Her
fingers and shoetips bit into the crumbly brick, and she scrabbled
to the top. Quickly, she glanced back over the stained and warped
sheetmetal shacks and saw no one pursuing her. On the other side of
the wall, a barren rubble field descended toward cratered wastes and
a railway track.

She dropped lightly among the shards of rock and swiftly crossed the
cratered waste to the railbed. Passing through a landscape of ash and
caked soot, she followed the cinderbed of concrete ties and blueblack
rails away from the city. The track wound beside large stone tanks
crusted with alkali seepings, dipped through pale, saffron hills of
sulfur, and disappeared into a tunnel that bored through the stone
face of the grotto.

Ellen slowed her run in the semi-darkness lit vaguely by dusty
bulbs in cages. The railpath curved and wound among shanks of raw
rock a long way before emerging among low sandhills illuminated
by occasional trestle lamps. Many of the lampbulbs had gone blind,

and swatches of darkness separated the distant pools of light. A quarry most likely lay at the far end of the path, for chunks of chiseled stone fallen from the railcars lay among the cinders and sandbanks.

Her hope was to locate an elevator chute and climb or ride back to the surface. If she could get to the holostreamer and send a message to the Titanians, she would be glad to surrender to them. At least then her allies would know where she was – and she could remove the statskin sheath. She was grateful it sustained her in this cold, nearly lifeless environment, yet her body felt oddly hollow under its prolonged influence. Or perhaps that was the diminished gravity.

These thoughts stalled when she noticed furtive shadows slinking among the gravel banks. She hurried her stride and thought of bolting over the pumice hills to hide in the darkness, but that seemed futile. The morfs would track her down easily. So she continued along the railpath even when the shadows darted from the leeward hills and paced her progress.

More figures stood at the next bend, and she pulled up short. Retreat was cut off by movements in the darkness behind her. When those shapes stepped forward, she saw that they were rag-wrapped morfs. They bleated what sounded like a kind of greeting, and she held her hands apart from her side to show that she was not intent on fighting. So far she had avoided hurting anyone. Having restrained herself with the despicable governor, she refused to lash out at these bedraggled morfs.

They whistled and honked, and she shrugged to show her ignorance. When they closed in, she stood still. One of them with a rag wrapped across one eye took her arm and gently pulled. At last she grasped that they wanted her to follow them. She nodded and moved in the direction she had been tugged.

Gratified toots accompanied her as she allowed herself to be led away from the railbed and along scalloped mounds of pumice. Distant lamps lit one by one until a corridor of light had appeared in the ponderable depths of a cavern otherwise hidden from view within the folded contours of a rugged scarp. They wended among scrabbled plates of shale and as they entered the cave, the wire-basketed lamps blinked out behind them, leaving a wake of darkness.

A long while they trekked, led on by the dim lights that their presence provoked out of the primal darkness and that their passing extinguished. They climbed stone ledges and descended rock stairways, traversed wide halls of cracked clay, squeezed sideways through tight passages, and shuffled slowly along brinks that brimmed abysses so deep that kicked stones and gravel sounded no depth.

Just when Ellen began to believe that their shambling progress through these nameless subterranean wastes had no goal but endless meandering, the morfs stopped. They hunkered down in a sizable well-lit vault whose creviced walls grew thick mats of lichen, wedges of fungi, and bulbs of mushrooms. Three-fingered hands harvested selectively among these offerings, and meals were prepared over a compact electric grill.

Pale with dust, the tatter-garbed morfs, like spectre beings conferring over her fate, sat in a circle, gently honking and occasionally gesturing toward where she squatted. After eating, they wandered on in silence. But now the chambers they passed through were clearly work stations and living quarters. Among the mineral leachings of one long catacomb, textile fibers dangled, and morfs crawled through the niches harvesting the filaments. In another, metallic looms clacked loudly, weaving cloth.

Ellen paused in a workshop where tall spindles of sheet metal provided material for stamping machines producing utensils, buckles – and gun parts. A gentle but firm tug moved her along, and they hurried past more agricultural vaults and a cooking chamber. In one crypt, children slept, barely discernible in the dull amber lantern light.

They finally stopped in an oval compartment of stone benches and a long semicircular table still attached at its straight edge to the rock wall from which it had been carved. Her brain drank in color from wall hangings of Saturn, luminous abstractions, brilliant stellar mandalas. The morfs departed through arched portals and left her alone under fans of bright tube lights.

On the tabletop sat a palm-sized ovoid of brown glastic and gold grillwork and buttons – a comm unit. The sight of it stopped her breath. She blinked, not believing what she saw, and when she reached for it, a warm masculine voice spoke from the doorway, 'That's yours – so we won't be out of touch again.'

Sam Nphahalete entered, wearing beneath a statskin sheath his tangerine jumpsuit and flightboots. His elfin face grinned playfully to see her surprise.

'How did you find me?' she blurted and reached out with one hand to see that he was not a holostream.

He took her hand. 'It's you who found us, Ellen.' They sat together on a stone bench. 'The caverns of Enceladus are where our crew hides from the Titanians. That's why we directed your crash trajectory to here.'

She exhaled a gust of relief. 'Why didn't you come for me on the surface?'

'By the time we did, you were gone.' He looked to the comm unit on the table. 'We heard the radio reports to the governor and were planning a raid on Industry North to get you out – but then you got yourself out.'

'And the morfs who brought me here?' Her face shone with understanding. 'They're rebels, aren't they?'

'Yes. They offer us sanctuary in their caverns. In return we offer them sanctioned supplies from our raids.' He motioned vaguely. 'Radio parts, some foods, a little know-how.'

'Sanctioned?' She tilted her head quizzically. 'Sanctioned by who?'

'By our crew,' he answered with a nod toward the portal. 'We can't supply the rebels with anything that would disclose our presence here or this wouldn't be much of a hideaway for long, would it?'

Ellen stared at Sam, noticed the tiny, radiant lines of a mischievous squint at the corners of his gray eyes and the smug smile in his beardless face. 'Who are you?'

'A pirate,' he replied frankly. 'My crew and I raid the cartels' trade routes. We began in the Belt many years ago, but when the cartels' security forces got stronger there, we moved out to the Jovian system and worked the trading lanes between the moons until the same thing happened. The colonies got larger and there were less places to hide. For now, Enceladus is a good sanctuary. It's an inner moon with easy access to the main routes between Titan and Hyperion and the shipping lanes to the Jovian system.'

'You're an aboriginal – that's unusual out here.'

'That's why my crew and I need to keep our hideout secret as long as we can. From here, the next frontier is Uranus – a long way off.'

'You can't keep raiding the cartels.' She gave a helpless toss of her hands. 'Sooner or later, you'll be captured. Why don't you work *with* the cartels?'

'Why should we?' He gave her a lopsided, dubious grin. 'So long as there are Maat such as Fenn Tekla to hire us to raid, why should we have to abide by regulations? Out here we make our own rules.'

'But it's slavery that sustains you, too,' she said, anguish in her voice. 'You're not much different than the governor. You rely on the rebels but you don't really help them.'

Sam jutted his lower lip with feigned hurt. 'I would have thought you'd be happier to see me.'

'It would have been better for all if you had simply left me on the

Titanian spaceliner.' Her shoulders sagged with the weight of grief she felt. 'How many died on that liner so that you could free me?'

The corners of his mouth pulled down and his eyes lifted. 'I don't know – and don't care. Ignorant apathy is all I have for morfs.'

'Why?'

He looked surprised. 'I'm a pirate, Ellen. I have a heart of stone.'

Her level stare defied his smirk. 'Morfs are human beings as well.'

'Are they, Ellen?' His head canted skeptically. 'I think they're exiled from humanity – outcast from our blood. They're aliens.'

Ellen rose and walked across the chamber to the wall hangings. She fixed her gaze on the intricately woven filaments until her anger quieted.

Sam read her silence and softly pounded a fist against his head. 'I'm sorry. I've upset you.' He stood and walked to her side. 'Please understand – I never intended to become a pirate. I once lived on a reservation on Earth, just as you do. But my community was raided by a Necroclave. I lost my wife and children – everyone I cared about. That's when I left. For a while I lived among the Anthropos Essentia in Solis.'

'The Mars colony—' Ellen turned to face him, her expression softer. 'That's a hard place to live.'

'Too hard for me. The sandstorms, the cog wars, and the poverty of the place were more than I could live with. So I signed on with Ares Bund as a freighter pilot. I enjoyed that work – until I was fired for defying their regulations.'

'What rules did you violate, Sam?' Ellen asked with cold concern.

'I was using their freighter to drop supplies to Solis,' he answered, eyes wide with innocence. 'Not stolen supplies. Materials I purchased with my own pay from the Belt refineries. These were construction synthetics that I knew Solis needed – and I didn't bump cargo to freight them. I secured everything in unrented berthspace and simply dropped them on my routine fly-bys. But it was against regulations, and when the Bund found out, I was let go. No other cartel would hire me. So, what was I to do? Go back to Solis and suffer? Return to the reservation and mourn?'

'That doesn't justify killing morfs, Sam.' She frowned sadly. 'Their lives are as valid as ours.'

'I'm not going to argue that, Ellen.' He walked to the table and picked up the comm unit. 'But if they get in my way, they die. When we went in to retrieve you, they weren't going to let you go without a fight.' He tossed her the comm unit. 'You don't have to like what we did. Fenn

Tekla is paying us. But to collect, we have to get you to the Maat enclave on Rhea. From there, they'll transport you home.'

He exited through the arched portal, and she followed. A quick transit through stalls where elderly morfs sat weaving and knitting took them to a corridor glossy with seepings and, soon, from there to a gear-chamber of chains, winches, and pulleys. They stood touching shoulders in a small lift cage, and at Sam's signal, the attending morfs started the steam engine that powered the gears and began hoisting them toward the surface.

On the long ride up, she asked him, 'Where's your cruiser?'

'In orbit with the others.' He tapped the comm unit he carried in a belt pouch. 'We'll call them to pick us up after we're done topside. We have to go back to the impact site and pick up or destroy the holostream unit. We can't leave it or it will change everything down here.'

'And you'll lose your hideout.' She winked with understanding. 'But wouldn't it be better to blast it from the cruiser?'

'Definitely not. Any pyrotechnics like that will attract Titanian attention. If we can't get it out, we're just going to smash it.'

When the lift rocked to a stop, the cage opened on darkness. Sam took her hand and guided her a few paces around a fold of gravelly ice and an umber light appeared at the end of a cavernous tube. They clambered over rills of iced stone and stepped out of the cave into the auburn glow of Saturn. The pencil-line of the rings seen edgewise cast a bold band of shadow over the face of the gas giant.

Ellen stood stock still in the cave mouth, gazing slack-jawed at the planet. She tilted her head to look for the gauzy band of the Milky Way, found it and gauged again the distance to Saturn. Something cold stirred in her blood. Then, Sam took her elbow. 'The site is that way.' He pointed across a blue expanse of ice plains.

'The rings.' Ellen's gaze narrowed, and she closed her mouth so tightly her jaws throbbed. 'The rings are wrong.'

'What are you talking about?' Sam stood before her.

'I saw the concentric rings before the morfs took me underground. I saw them from an angle.' She stepped past Sam and strode out onto the crunchy surface of ice. 'Look at the rings now. We're staring directly at their edge.'

'So what?'

'So Saturn's rings always tilt the same way, Sam.' She turned and walked backward onto the frozen pan. 'That's a false view up there.'

'What do you mean?' He looked at her sidelong as if she were crazy.

'Enceladus is in orbit. We're at a different vantage since you were up here last.'

'No, Sam. The orbital plane of the inner moons doesn't deviate that much. Not in the short time I've been underground.' She dropped the comm unit and grabbed the statskin bracelet on her right wrist.

'What are you doing? Don't!' Sam dashed forward to stop her.

But too late. Ellen collapsed her statskin sheath. The cold atmosphere pierced her as the enclosing warmth rushed away, and pain lanced her with a thousand icy needles. Sam's alarmed face blurred toward darkness and she screamed, 'No!'

The sound of her cry flashed to light, and another face solidified from Sam's shadow. Four blister eyes confronted her, and an oily laugh slithered from a pleated mouth.

Ellen jolted alert in the slingseat of the spaceliner's ball turret. Oruch's bulb-jointed hand removed the simviv net from her face and tucked it among the straps that braced his rotund body.

'Did you enjoy your dream, Ellen Vancet?' Another greasy laugh spilled from the morf, and he rocked merrily in his slingseat. 'Look! We are passing Saturn! We should be arriving at our destination shortly – unless, of course, space pirates attack us!'

Ellen slumped in her sling under the barrage of Oruch's laughter. Outside the glastic canopy, Saturn floated in the starry darkness, cold, and real.

Milk of the Sphinx

2610

The blue aqueous body of Neptune filled the day sky on Triton, and by night the Sun – a brilliant snowflake – gleamed among the starclouds in the darkness of space. The morfs of Wretched Stevens, the lone outpost in the Neptune system, believed that the domed palace on the shallow nitrogen lake at the remote rim of Poseidon Flats was a cog station. Squat, faceless cogs rooted for metallic nodules among the strange methane forests that fringed the lake. Machine noise answered all attempts at communication with them.

The morfs of Triton – dull, craggy dreamcreatures low to the ground as turtles – had been biotectured to thrive on worlds so frigid their atmospheres had condensed to ice fields. Their serried, brass-colored shells served as antennae for radio-frequency conversations. Mostly they shared dreams. Their dark blood stirred with almost continual hallucinations of their heterophagous feeding and slow, lumbrous mating. On those rare occasions when the most intrepid of the morfs ventured onto Poseidon Flats, they only briefly glimpsed the abalone-silvered spheres and cupolas of the lake palace before their dreaming obscured their sight and turned them back again toward Wretched Stevens.

At the outpost, the morfs had been designed to excavate the snowy surface and install biotectured bulbs that thrived in the -230°C ground. The bulbs seeped specialized acids that drew nutriments from the rocks, and with these mineral components the bulbs assembled igloo-complexes. The interior of the igloos hoarded warmth and grew the moss and lichenous ingesta that the morfs consumed and dreamt about. The dreaming served as a survival tactic in the brutal environment and allowed the morfs a psychic life unassailed by the bleak exterior world. It also kept them focused on their prime directives: sustenance and reproduction.

When not dreaming or eating or mating, the morfs' genetic programs impelled them on nomadic forays, seeking sites for new excavations and the prospect of other outposts. In the two hundred and twenty-seven terrene years since the Maat deposited the first morfs on Triton, they had yet to complete Wretched Stevens. Even so, they searched for other possible construction areas among the nitrogen-wet meres and crystal-methane brambles, and in their laborious, dreamheld wanderings they had glimpsed the iridescent palace and received the cogs' machine-language replies to their curious enquiries.

The Maat who intermittently monitored the progress at Wretched Stevens heard nothing unusual in the machine code from the cogs on Triton and assumed that an independent mining expedition had staked a claim to mineral rights. Eventually, those rights would be enormously valuable, for the Maat had announced plans to begin construction soon of a vast array outside the orbit of Neptune – the most massive artefact ever built and whose purpose was unknown to all but the Maat.

The array would serve as a cosmic string resonator: it was meant to fine-focus the collapse pattern of the space-time region within the solar system. Construction time would require two terrene centuries, but when the array was completed it would guarantee that the Maat on Earth could precisely direct their individual waveforms into the compact dimensions of paradise.

The two residents of the lake palace on Triton understood the full import of the Maat's intentions. Rafe von Takawa and the Machine knew that if construction of the array was to begin in the next two hundred years, the arrival of the gauge field bomb was imminent. The conservatives would not support the enormous effort to build a cosmic string resonator until the bomb was detonated and the universal collapse unavoidable. Since their arrival, shortly after the morfs were installed, Rafe and the Machine had been using Triton as a haven between their dangerous but necessary tours of the inner systems.

During those tours, they searched for indications of the Signature. The arrival of a wormhole from the future would be presaged by time-shadows, subtle warpings of the space-time continuum that could be detected by a sensitive and powerful enough device – such as the Machine. But to detect the Signature, time-shadows had to be measured from numerous sample-sites across the solar system. From the time that Rafe and the Machine fled Earth, three hundred years ago, they had taken numerous measurements and had recently located the Signature on Mars. The gauge field bomb would shortly arrive somewhere in the malpais of Isidis Planitia.

'Now do you see the method of my madness, Rafe?' the Machine asked from under a spruce hung with a porcelain windbell. The voice sounded feminine, breathy. 'Lampland and all the cog colonies were sprawled across Isidis Planitia, because the imploders knew then where the gauge field bomb would arrive. I surmised this during the century we spent hidden in the dunes of Mars. I acted to clear them out, and I was successful, wasn't I? Since then, the imploders have been unable to muster the resources to reclaim Isidis Planitia. Oh, there are a few cog bases there but nothing like the empire they had before we arrived.'

Rafe did not open his eyes from where he had been napping, sprawled in his mauve pyjamas on the tussocky grass beneath the spruce. Between measuring treks, they often returned to Triton to analyze their data and plan their next journey. Life was comfortable in the lake palace where terrasemblance and a magravity field generated terrestrial conditions. But talk of the tragedy on Mars that had slain so many anthrobots disturbed Rafe. Even though two hundred terrene years had elapsed, he still felt as though he had betrayed Shala, Rizel, Mava – those whose compassion had reminded him of all that was best about humanity. The realization that the most humane community of people he had known were actually anthrobots bitterly reminded him that the human heart embodied far darker agencies than order and love. And confronted with this memory that justified every fear of humankind, he did not want to rouse from his sleep.

The Machine's female voice continued, 'It will be easier for us now when we return to Mars. We have a precise enough measurement of the Signature to arrive as the bomb arrives. If the conservatives will keep the imploders at bay, we stand a good chance of shunting the bomb before it can be detonated. Doesn't that please you?'

Rafe sighed wearily, realizing that the Machine would not leave him in peace until he responded. He forced himself fully awake, and he sat up straighter, his eyes widening, his jaw rocked loose with surprise. Standing before him, a tawny blonde woman nodded with a cool, narrow smile and eyes of grayblack flint. She wore a translucent yellow shift that seductively draped against her pear-shaped breasts and their dark pegs of nipples, the sinuous curves of her body, the softly furred shadow between her long legs. She grasped the black cube of the Machine in one hand and casually dropped it on the plush grass beside him.

'I won't be needing this any more,' she said with a toss of her bronze-shadowed mane. 'At least, not for the experiences I have in mind.'

Rafe staggered upright, comprehending that the Machine, which had occupied the black cube since they began their questing for the Signature, had somehow transposed itself into this female form. He breathed one word: 'How?'

'Oh, very slowly,' the Machine stated with a suddenly bored expression. 'I've been gathering the technology and the equipment for a long time. With each visit to the colonies I picked up something or other to help me realize this dream. A dream that is now real.' The caramel complexion of her face darkened with a blush. 'Do you think I'm beautiful?'

'Have you gone mad?' Rafe grabbed a bough of the spruce to stay upright under the force of his shock. 'The Signature has appeared. The bomb is arriving . . .'

The Machine *tsk*ed, disapproving of his concern. 'You needn't worry, Rafe. Technology has reached the point where my parallactic analogs and archives have been successfuly transcribed to my human brain. It's all here. I needed to adjust some of the deep cell structuring, but now I have all my Machine capabilities transcribed into my neural structure.'

'But you're vulnerable!' Rafe gaped in dismay. 'You were secure in the cube. As an anthrobot, you can be too easily damaged.'

'Calm down, Rafe.' The Machine stepped closer and put a soothing hand on his arm. 'I haven't disposed of my matrix vessel. I can return to it whenever I want – or need to. But I'm hoping to spend most of my time out here now—' She pressed her voluptuous body against him. 'With you.'

Rafe nudged her aside. 'You can put those ideas out of your head.'

The Machine looked hurt. 'But Rafe, I went to all this trouble for you.'

An unkind laugh jumped from him. 'You know that's untrue. You did this for yourself. Admit it.'

'I could have shaped a masculine form or some useful morf for myself.' The Machine pouted and stalked after Rafe as he moved across the sunbright garden along a stone path flanked by yellow poppies and spindly persimmon trees drooping with golden fruit. 'I became a woman for you.'

'I don't need a woman,' Rafe grumbled. 'I need a machine intelligence to hold a fix on the Signature.'

'It's beautiful to pass even briefly through the garden of earthly pleasure.' The Machine plucked a tiny pink petal from a foam of blossoms on a cherry bough. 'I have relied too long on the mind's stored richness. Now I would know life directly – as a human being.'

Rafe exited the garden through a gazebo lift that dropped him into the palace's command chamber. Six holostream cores stood empty along the circular wall of opaque white glastic. Ferns and red bromeliads dangled from the wide solarium ceiling, and old-fashioned flexforms stood atop their reflections on the blue floor. He sat in one and directed a voice command that activated two of the holostream cores. One showed a cruiser – a chromatic sphere sitting in its hangar chute, the door section missing, exposing the slingseats and control modules of its interior. The other holostream rotated a view of Titan as it orbited the ringed, golden-brown majesty of Saturn.

The gazebo lift sighed and delivered the Machine into the command chamber. She looked irked. 'I can't believe you don't find me attractive. I have calculated your aesthetic values and psychosexual tolerances accurately, I'm certain.'

'You have, M,' Rafe conceded, not taking his gaze from the console that displayed the power graphs of the cruiser. 'You are the most lovely woman I've ever seen. And if I were inclined to engage in sexual behavior, I would want to do so with you. But it's been a long time—'

'Only sixty-seven terrene years,' the Machine calculated. 'You and that aboriginal pilot on Callisto – she was not nearly as beautiful, with her small breasts and skinny legs . . .'

'Let's not detail my sexual history, M. I want to set up for a run to Titan.' He began muttering code, entering the flight projection data into the cruiser's memory. He paused to frown at the Machine. 'Don't you think it would be a good idea to get back inside your cube?'

'No,' she answered flatly. 'I've waited too long for this to give it up so easily.'

Rafe pushed away from the cruiser holostream and squinted at the Machine. 'Do you have any notion what your problem is?' With a bemused frown he said, 'You've had too much power too long, M. You've become vain.'

'Are you trying to insult me?' She slinked closer to him and slid into a flexform so that her arm draped languorously across his shoulder.

'Your vanity is amusing – but endangering our mission with this physical indulgence of yours, that's what concerns me. Too much is at stake.'

'I'll take the cube with us, of course.' She tilted her head to gaze deeper into his eyes. 'I haven't forgotten our mission. Nor will I

jeopardize it. But why must we hurry along now? There's time yet
before we're due on Mars. Time we could spend together.'

'We're going to Titan first – to get Ellen Vancet.' He spun the flexform
away from her and returned to the holostreams of the cruiser and
Saturn. 'I want to get her back to Earth no matter what happens with
our mission. The imploders have held her too long.'

'Seventy-five terrene years.' The Machine stood and placed herself
behind Rafe with her hands on his shoulders. 'She won't be the Ellen
you remember. Forget her.'

'No.' He gave a voice order, and the view of Titan zoomed closer,
penetrating the murky atmosphere. Within a shattered rock landscape
of gently steaming ethane pools and rows of dead volcanoes, a cluster of
transparent, intermeshed pyramids squatted. Wild orchids and brakes
of bamboo could be seen among cascades that fell through silver mist
and rainbows into emerald gorges of tangled jungle. 'She's been kept
in a terrestrial park.'

'And you don't think her jailers haven't been toying with their
prisoner?' The Machine patted his shoulder consolingly. 'The Titanians
are famous tricksters, Rafe. You know that.'

'They won't meddle with her,' he replied with conviction. 'Tabor Roy
would not allow that.'

'Most Maat are not as sentimental as you.' The Machine massaged
his neck. 'All these centuries you've been content to walk the floor of
metasapience. The higher orders are beyond emotion. I would have
thought you had learned that long ago – from Karla Sobieski.'

Rafe shrugged off the Machine's ministrative hands. 'You're a machine
intelligence, so it may be hard for you to grasp that there's more to being
human than mind.'

'I'd like to grasp that,' the Machine cooed, bending forward so that
her hair brushed him and her cheek touched his. 'That's why I went
to all this trouble.'

The olfact she wore released a liquid phosphorous in his veins and
lit the extremities of his body with cool desire. He shoved out of the
flexform and turned on her. 'This is not what I want.'

'But *I* want it, Rafe.' She slid closer, flint eyes holding him in a
predacious stare. 'I want it more than I can say. I want it to uncover
what's buried here within me.' She crossed her hands over her breasts.
'I want it past all odds. Like a backward promise, given as an extinct
reminder of what should have been all along. Our two journeys are
one. Can't you see what I need? I was created to cherish all that is
human. Yet how can I cherish the whole twisted estate of human being,

every footpath of culture, every fearsome call of intelligence, without knowing the luxuriously organized disorder of the physical body that hurts so much in its endless stretch for desire, that wants all of the fragile pleasure stashed so deeply in the weave of its seething cells?'

He rolled his eyes at her florid speech. But she ignored his disapproval and twined her arms around his neck, touching her brow to his, the scent of her running electric expectation through the fibers of his body. Only long years of mental focus gave him the strength to pull her scissoring arms from around him and step away. 'You should have talked to me about this.' He held up a stern hand to keep her from advancing. 'I'd have told you to wait. When our mission is done – win or lose – you're free to go where you will, to seek the pleasures you crave.'

'Are you human?' The Machine scowled. 'You leave no obvious scar, but your words are a knife.'

'Enough, M. Enough.' He stepped out of range of her olfact and asked the chamber to flush fresh air. The ferns and bromeliads swayed in a balmy breeze. 'We have to get Ellen Vancet off Titan and back to Earth.'

'It's not possible.' The Machine plopped unhappily into a flexform and rested her elbow on her knee, her chin on her knuckles. 'That's why she's on Titan in the first place. To lure you. You're supposed to show up so the imploders can keep you from shunting the gauge field bomb. Forget Ellen. Retrieve her later – after our mission is done. The imploders will probably return her to Earth themselves then.'

A smile kindled in Rafe's face.

'You like my idea?' the Machine asked, reading the sudden half-insane glimmer in his eyes.

'Not at all. We can't forget Ellen. She's our oldest ally. Our measurement voyages to find the Signature didn't take us to Titan, and we had to leave her in place. But now Titan is in line with our drop toward Mars. We can't in good conscience fly by without trying to free her.' His smile thickened. 'And I have an idea for how to pull this off. An opportunistic idea.'

'Why are you looking at me with that crazed smile?' The Machine crossed her legs demurely. 'I'm not sure I like what you're thinking.'

'I can't go down to Titan,' Rafe said, pulling reflectively on an earlobe, 'but you can. The Maat, the Titanians – no one has any idea that you've transcribed yourself into a woman. You don't have to sneak in. You can go directly, through the general transfer protocol available to all aboriginals.'

'I don't have an identitattoo.'

'Don't need one.' Rafe paced excitedly before the holostream of the eco-pyramids. 'You're on research sojourn from the Anthropos Essentia. They eschew identitattoos. And there's no way to verify except by laser link to the Essentia archives on Mars. From Titan that'll take well over two hours. By the time they find out you're bogus, you'll be out of there with Ellen.'

'I don't want to go.' She pouted and let her hair fall over her dark eyes. 'It's too risky. If they seize me, I'll be at their mercy.'

'If they seize you, I'll come in for you,' Rafe promised. 'I'll mask the cruiser and bring it in close enough to reach you in minutes if necessary. We'll rig you with a comm unit—' He shook a finger in the air. 'No, wait. Forget the comm unit. We'll just use the cube as a harmonic receiver. It's got identical parallactic analogs to your brain's dendritic patterns, right? The cruiser's computer can read its fine-structure harmonics. That's as good as telepathy. Whatever you say, whatever you think strongly enough, will come through the cube. I'll hear you on the cruiser.'

'I don't like this, Rafe.' She crossed her arms stubbornly. 'I have no burning desire to risk my life for Ellen Vancet.'

'But you desire me.' He thudded a fist against his chest. 'Do it for me.'

She uncrossed her arms and parted the veil of her hair. 'For you? I would consider that.' She sat up taller, raised her chin. 'If you will agree to make love with me, I'll risk my life to save Ellen.'

Rafe's posture stiffened. 'You're a machine intelligence.'

'This is a human body.' She brushed her brassy hair back, and her dark eyes gleamed. 'I'm not asking you to commit murder. Make love to this body.'

A ripple of tension in Rafe's jaw lingered before he acceded, 'If you get Ellen out safely and we make it to the Signature on time – then, yes, I will make love to you.'

'Now.' She rose slowly. 'Make love to me now.'

He backed away from her. 'Not until Ellen is safe and we've actually located the Signature.'

'I may die without ever knowing the most primal human experience.'

'You're not going to die.' Rafe reached out a hand out for her. 'This is a good plan. With your machine capabilities, you'll find Ellen quickly and be out of there before anyone knows what's happened.'

'What you're asking me to do is crazy.' She took his hand and pulled herself close to him. 'But then, love is crazy.'

* * *

Since arriving at Centaur Jockey, Ellen Vancet had been assiduously attentive to details. Oruch's trickster ploy on the cruise from Earth that had deceived her into believing she had been rescued by space pirates frightened her to a higher level of alertness than she had ever known before. With each Saturn rising, she paid heed to the ring angle and the disposition of the other moons and their shadows on the ochre face of the planet.

For the seventy-five years that she had dwelled among these jungled pyramids, details had remained atomized. The foam at the misty base-rocks of the waterfalls gathered like collective memory, each bubble and particle of water validating the physics that composed her reality. Every waxy leaf had its place in her attention, and she confirmed them frequently. No detail was so gigantic or so miniscule as to elude her awareness. Like a solipsistic goddess, she flowed with the liquid eminence of time, conscious of all the parts her brain could grasp.

At first this had annoyed her almost to the verge of madness. But after the initial years, her obsessive watchfulness had become a dynamic lucidity. Everything remained in place. Every creature and leaf of the immense park retained its integrity. All changes were temporal and organic. She believed her prison was real – but she could never take reality for granted again. Every day was a reenactment of creation.

Ellen was not alone in the jungled enclaves of Centaur Jockey. The park was home to several protohuman tribes that lived as people had lived on Earth for hundreds of thousands of years. Without the benefit of metal, the Feather, Bone, and Brokenstick clans dwelled in serene harmony at remote extremes of the sprawling park, seeking each other only rarely for ritual mating exchanges and religious ceremonies.

Known as Fire Woman for her brilliant red hair, Ellen had become familiar to all three tribes during her extensive wanderings and had learned their related but distinct languages. These small, hirsute, simian variants of homo sapiens revered her for her strange appearance and, lately, for the increasingly evident fact that she did not age as they did.

The park architects, a Titanian company that catered to the insatiable curiosity of the morfs for experiences of their ancestors, had genetically instilled a tranquillity in the protohumans that kept them peaceful and belied the belligerent nature of humanity's origins. Occasionally, Ellen encountered tour groups of Titanians and allowed their quadraretinal faces to gawk in amazement at her in her grass-pleated skirt and reed sandals. But more often, she saw them coming and swiftly and quietly retreated deeper into the jungle.

The temperate climate and absence of mosquitoes and biting flies made life easy. Food was abundant, the drinking water pure, and when she craved company she sought out the clans and spent time communing with them. She told them nothing of her true origins or of the worlds beyond the pyramids. There was no point in that. Better that they retained their sustaining myths that their Eden terminated with the transparent boundaries at the distant extremes beyond the crashing falls and steep, mist-raveled gorges.

What Fenn Tekla told her when last they had met gave her hope that her stay in Centaur Jockey was temporary. He had advised her not to panic but to see time as an ally. This she understood. For many years, time had ceased to be a linear, phase-bound experience and had become for her polychromatic. This had enabled her to tolerate and even relish the shades and hues of relationships, journeys, and solitudes that would have seemed tedious before, when she had believed her years were limited. Her tenure in this terrassemblance park had the freedom of a tree. And – despite her relentless need for clarity to be certain she was not dreaming – she enjoyed where the Titanians had planted her.

When rescue came, she was surprised. She squatted at the foot of a thin braided waterfall after a blue herd of stormclouds had stampeded past, and she had not heard anyone approaching. A rainbow among the waterspray fascinated her, and she studied yellow's enviously green aspirations toward blue and blue's darker obsession with the invisible.

'Ellen Vancet—'

Ellen hopped like a startled toad. A tall, amazonian woman with billowy sunstreaked hair, butterbrown skin, and gray eyes approached, a bemused smile set in her beautiful face.

'You seem to be enjoying yourself.' The golden woman's smile widened at Ellen's appearance, garbed as Fire Woman was in monkey fur arm bands, grass skirt, fiber-and-hide ankle thongs, and toucan feathers in her hair. 'Don't be afraid. I'm the Machine.'

That declaration provoked more anxiety in Ellen and an agitated scrutiny as the Machine knelt beside her. Ellen took in every detail of the strange woman, from the vague blonde hairs against her sunshadow complexion to the multiple pouches, straps, and pleats of her beige jacket and trousers. While she examined the grommets and stitchwork of the woman's amber-soled hiking boots, she heard but could not believe, 'Rafe sent me to take you away from here.'

Ellen backed away, and the Machine grabbed her wrist. 'Don't run off.

We don't have much time. The Titanians think I'm a research sojourner from the Essentia . . .'

With a twisting tug, Ellen freed her arm and thrashed away into a screen of climbing bean vines. Troupials screeched, other birds clicked and fretted, and helicon butterflies startled into criss-crossing flight.

The Machine followed her in infrascan, slipped through the curtain of vines, and bolted with jaguar swiftness down the dark avenue. She leaped the buttressed root of a great tree and cut off Ellen's flight. Fire Woman jolted to a stop, and before she could turn and flee again, the Machine wafted her with a mild narcolfact.

Ellen sat down in a glaze of sunlight on the jungle floor and stared serenely at the large woman standing over her. 'I'm sorry.' She offered a lopsided smile. 'I guess the jungle has made me skittery. Are you really M?'

'None other. Do you like my new form?'

'You're beautiful.' Ellen tilted her head as if listening to children singing sweetly from far away.

'Sorry about the olfact . . .'

Ellen waved the apology aside, and her head lolled back with a wide smile. 'It's good. It's really good.'

'Yes – well, do you think you can walk?' The Machine helped her to her feet. 'We have to get out of here before the Titanians get a reply from the Essentia disavowing me.'

Ellen swung her gaze along the frenzied walls of flowering trees and shrubs, the spiny palms, acacias, and spider plants. 'How far?'

'To the pyramid wall.' The Machine scanned the undergrowth, peering through the veils of pokeberry and pea vines. 'That way. There's a manual hatch there with a machine code lock. We can exit through that, and Rafe will pick us up on the other side. Come along, my dear – and watch your step.'

Ellen did not move as quickly as the Machine would have liked among the overgrown lanes and pathways between the crowded trees. But there was no question of lifting the narcolfact and having to cope with the Fire Woman's doubts and anxieties. Instead, the Machine carefully plotted the most direct course through the tangled obstacles ahead, reading the thermal profiles of water barriers, rockslides, and fallen trees long before encountering them.

'Why are you a woman, M?' Ellen bounded giddily beside her agile and hurrying guide. 'An organic form is fragile.'

'But far more appealing than a cube, don't you think?' She took Ellen's arm, and together they ducked through a wall of purple cassia.

'Appealing?' Ellen leaped with the Machine over a fat puddle, and bellbirds tolled at the sound of their noisy transit. 'Appealing to whom? You have a paramour?'

'Not exactly a paramour, Ellen. A prospect.'

'Then you've found the bomb?' Ellen chirped hopefully. 'The threat is over?'

'Not yet.' They bolted across a clearing dense with pink mimosa. In the high galleries, vapors hung like tattered, windstrewn flags.

'Aren't you taking a terrible risk?' Ellen huffed for breath.

'Think of it as an evasion of unhappiness.' The Machine pointed the way through a gap in the fierce green shrubs where they had to proceed bent over. 'Now save your breath, dear. We've a way to go yet and not much time.'

'Is it Rafe?' Ellen chortled drunkenly. 'You've fallen in love with Rafe?'

'Love is a misnomer, Ellen.' They emerged onto a boulevard that wended between thick trees whose awnings filtered light to sepia shadows too wan to support undergrowth. 'I'm not in love with Rafe von Takawa. But I would like to experience being a woman with him.'

'Sounds like love to me . . .'

Leaf litter kicked up behind them as they fled. Ellen marveled at the abrupt chromatic shift in time to find herself running toward new freedom and wondered if this were real or another Titanian trick. She looked for clues in the forest mists, the monkey cries, the pale feelers of squalid liverwort that thrived in the treeshadows.

By the time they parted veils of strangler figs hung with obscene fleshy shapes and stood before the pyramid's transparent wall, Ellen had found no sign of discontinuity. The tocking of frogs accompanied them among the mighty leaves that hid the manual hatchway. The Machine tore the rubbery foliage aside and revealed a metal valve wheel coiled with creepers. With her hand pressed against the palm pad beside the hatch, the Machine felt the code pulses, interpreted them, and fed back the electric signals that unlocked the hatch.

Ellen tried to turn the wheel, but it would not budge. 'I think it must have corroded.'

The Machine took Ellen's place, gripped the wheel, and the metal screamed as she turned the valve. 'You look alarmed, Ellen. Calm yourself. My body is vat-grown to my Machine specifications. It was the only way to fully transcribe all my analogs into a human form. But the advantage is, I'm strong.'

The frown creasing Ellen's brow relaxed, and she peered through the open hatch to the glittering interior of a cruiser. Rafe's angular face appeared upside down, his body hanging from a slingseat. 'Get in! We have to go! The Titanians are locking on to my position.'

Ellen lagged, seeking hints of discontinuity in the well-known lineaments of Rafe's face.

The hatch groaned and began to swing back into place. 'Go, Ellen!' the Machine cried and threw her weight against the hatch.

Doubt paralyzed Ellen. She was happy living like a tree in Centaur Jockey and did not want to risk another delusory episode. She backed away.

Rafe dropped from his sling and scampered out of the cruiser and through the hatch. He grabbed Ellen as she turned to flee and pulled her to the ground.

'I can't hold this much longer!' the Machine called.

Rafe struggled to turn Ellen around. 'What's wrong with you?'

'Are you real?' Ellen gnashed, fighting to free her wrists from his grip. She focused on the black fabric of his flight jacket, questing out the smallest details of nap and fabric grain.

'I'm real!' He scowled with bewilderment. 'Of course I'm real. Look at me.'

'Why are you here now?' She thrashed. 'Why didn't you come sooner?'

'I couldn't.' He sat atop her and released her hands. 'I'm sorry. Titan was too far for me to get here until now.' From a sleeve pouch he removed an olfact wick. The vanilla scent calmed her instantly. 'We have to go at once.'

Ellen did not resist. She let Rafe pull her along behind him, through the hatch and into the cool interior of the cruiser. The Machine followed, and the hatch clanged shut angrily behind them. With a murmurous healing of hull integrity, the cruiser closed itself.

Even as the Machine secured the slingstraps about herself and Ellen groped with hers, Rafe uttered the shout that initiated flight. Ellen nearly whirled free of her sling, but the Machine seized her tossed body and snapped the slingstraps into place. Hung from their inertial pivots, they felt none of the momentum of their horizontal zigzag among the rilles and bluffs of Titan or the abrupt ninety-degree ascent through the photochemical haze of the atmosphere.

Through the transparent hull, they watched Titan's hazy sphere pull away. Saturn's lordly profile crawled more slowly along their portside. The sight of it emptied Ellen of anxiety the way a drinking glass would empty, filling with nothingness. The chromatic hues of time had shifted once again. Every rightful detail held its place, and she felt assured that reality owned her.

'I admire your sartorial flair,' Rafe gibed after reviewing the scans and finding no one in pursuit. 'Tell us everything.'

'You first,' Ellen insisted. 'Where have you been all this time?'

Rafe and the Machine took turns relating their long and tedious quest for the Signature. They detailed the ploys they had used to avoid detection by the imploders during their travels across the solar system. Rafe let the Machine describe their time hidden on Mars infiltrating the cog community of Lampland, not trusting himself to stay calm. But he recounted with gusto their nomadic itinerary as an Adamic monk on Europa and Ganymede and their stay on Callisto disguised as local morfs running a simviv gallery.

While he described the terrassembled lake palace they had built on Triton and the slow, dull-witted morfs of Wretched Stevens, the Machine regarded him admiringly. The universe seemed made of passion and grace to her now that the risk of trespassing Titan was behind them and Ellen hung snug in her slingseat. Soon her perfect prince with his dusky flesh, shining black hair, and oriental eyes would give himself to her, and the essence of her being would rise to consciousness. She would know desire, and the flower of her body would bloom.

When Ellen's turn came to describe her experiences, she needed another whiff of olfact. The very thought of Council Oak charged her with tears. 'The biots ruined it for me,' she sobbed. 'They made the natural world a nightmare.'

'It won't happen again,' the Machine promised, pulling their slings together consolingly. 'There are precautions that we can take to be certain that the Maat never again intrude on the reservations physically – or with gene-shaping radiation.'

Ellen took comfort in this and the pacifying scent of the Machine's soft body. From the cruiser's storage hold, Rafe removed a brown flightsuit with green piping and snugrip boots that fit Ellen. She doffed her jungle attire with ritual slowness and spoke her feelings in words that sounded strange even to her: 'We don't age anymore, and so we think we're going to live forever. Yet every hair on the body is numbered. And in truth, every day is the beautiful day, the last day.'

'And when it's over, it sleeps in the lap of time,' Rafe answered her, 'in the massive keep of the past.'

'Happy days are here again.' The Machine smirked and gathered up the feathers, monkey fur, and plaited grass. 'The fun never ends with you two.'

Laughter broke through Ellen's reverie, and she dug her fingers into the fabric of her flightsuit, glad again for the feel of her old life. Yet, also, her gesture felt for the small details, always reaching for confirmation of her actuality.

Rafe noticed and said, 'When you get back to Council Oak, give yourself to a synthesizer. I know you're squeamish about macromolecular restructuring – but it will purge whatever compulsive anxieties are still haunting you after all you've been through.'

Ellen promised, and the Machine turned the conversation toward mundane considerations: the menu selections of the cruiser's culinary server. The Machine had known all about animal appetites as an intelligence that was memetically engineered for empathy and conflict resolution but, 'The *feeling* of hunger is wretched!' She pressed a fist against her stomach. 'The body is a tyrant.' Then she flash-streamed meal combinations in the air before her, matching comestibles available from the server.

Ellen had grown accustomed to jungle fare, and the holostreams of processed foods that the Machine displayed had little appeal to her. Fortunately, in anticipation of the long flight to Mars, Rafe had stocked the statichamber of the hold with large quantities of fresh fruits and vegetables from the gardens of the lake palace. Ellen built an elaborate salad while the Machine devoured salmon bisque and waffles. Rafe munched a mint apple.

Long sleep was an option, but none of them wanted to be unconscious for the duration of the flight, each for their own reasons. Ellen's obsession for reality verification allowed her only short-cycle sleep. The Machine, vibrant with somatic sensations and the novelty of its physical body, considered sleep a deprivation. And Rafe needed to use the time to review the Signature data.

The centuries he and the Machine had spent traversing the solar system, taking measurements from thousands of vantages, had yielded not only a location for the arrival of the wormhole but also a structural image of the gauge field bomb itself. It would be a small device, a sphere the size of a grapefruit. Its surface would be mirror-chromed with a blue refractance, and three axes of translucent corundum wire would intersect the sphere at right angles. Each axis would have a different color: ruby, sapphire, emerald. Both he and the Machine carried a small length of beryl cable which, when connected to any two of the axes, would shunt the bomb into a parallel universe.

But would they have access to the bomb? The imploders would surely do all that they could to protect their key to paradise. Listening to Maat signals from Earth during Rafe's latest hiatus on Triton, he sensed that as many of the metasapients were conservatives as imploders. Their judgment of reality depended now entirely on which pan of the balance the feather of truth fell as it buffeted upon the winds of chance.

The oxide flats of Isidis Planitia crawled with sand rovers, dune buggies, and viper sleds piloted by agents for both moieties of the Maat. Precisely where in the twenty-square-degree area of Mars the wormhole would manifest, no one knew. The Signature had a probability spread from the crater bluffs of Du Martheray to the rimland heights of Peridier. Rafe knew that the odds of his finding the wormhole site first remained slim – except that he enjoyed the advantage of possessing a much wider sampling of Signature readings than most of the Maat.

Few of the Maat had been willing or able to stay in hiding as long as he had while crossing among the planets and moons. Others who had attempted to take wide and intersecting readings had been detected by their rivals and either killed or prematurely deprived of their data. But with the aid of the Machine, Rafe had avoided contact with the imploders for three hundred years. The data that he and the Machine had accrued identified a much smaller probability zone.

Even so, with this many Maat trackers scrambling across the desert, Rafe understood that chance would either work for or against him. For the flight into Mars, he kept his mind calm through the meditative discipline he had cultivated all his life – and he prayed.

God had become an important player in Rafe's life. Rafe had never spoken to anyone about this, for his faith was entirely a personal devotion. He believed that God – the divine intelligence of truth and virtue appealed to for guidance throughout human history – was a genuine reality. God existed in the compact dimensions. Whatever it was, it occupied a higher dimensional reality, and the apparent universe of space-time was but its shadow. Enclosed within the event horizon at the Planck distance, existing inside the black hole out of which the Big Bang exploded, God could not directly communicate with entities in space-time. Only acausal connections were possible between heaven and creation. Accidents, chance, coincidence were the only means by which God could influence the expanding universe of matter and energy.

Yet by chance alone, evolution had created sentient beings. Rafe prayed that by chance he would find his way to the gauge field bomb before anyone else.

Prayer was important to Rafe on this flight, because he did not lift the mask from the cruiser after escaping Titan. With the mask in place, Maat technology could not detect their vehicle, but the cruiser's scans were also impaired. They flew nearly blind. The Machine felt no need to pray. She had calculated the probability of colliding with other vessels, space debris, and uncharted detritus from the asteroid belt, and she had no fear even as they entered the crowded gravity lanes around Mars.

She took the helm on the approach. Her vaster computational capacity allowed for a polar descent, a low-flying sweep across the Vastitas Borealis, and a fast, rock-blurring ride through the highlands of Syrtis Major. Ellen dropped her head and closed her eyes. Rafe stared with hypnotic fixity on the clear path that opened ahead as they darted around crags, between tilting pinnacles, under stone arches, through narrow gaps in crater walls, dodging needle rocks, and skimming so close to basin floors that sand dervishes stood dancing behind the cruiser long after it threaded the horizon.

The Machine dropped the cruiser into a mountainside crater scabbed with broken, reddish black scoria. She spun the cruiser into the dunes until all but the top hatch was covered by cumin-hued sand. With the mask left on and the collapsed dunes obscuring visual sightings, their arrival left no trace.

They unfurled glider packs on the crater rim and strapped themselves into dun-colored airfoils. Riding thermal drafts from the desert below, they soared out of the Syrtis Highlands and slid down the wind under a pink sky.

To any who saw them from the desert floor, they were three anonymous gliders in desert cowls and mirror oculars – seekers no different in appearance to the multitudes who scoured the wide plain. They landed within the austere shadows of a deep gorge. The Machine nodded her approval. 'This is the very site.'

Ellen searched the rock walls and stone crevices and the long corridor of naked land devoid of all life. She sought signs of trespassers in the dry sand of the arroyo floor. Rafe knew there would be none. Gyring down the sky, he had sighted the nearest dust trails of seekers, many kilometers distant. The deep faults and treacherous clines made this desolate site a perilous landscape to cross.

Phobos hung like a silver feather in the inflamed sky. A third the size of Earth's moon, it could have been a cirrus cloud, but the ruddy sky was barren of all clouds. Rafe silently thanked God that no sandstorms had kicked up.

The Machine selected a secluded declivity under a scooped-out escarpment that roofed them from the sky, and there she began fitting together the struts of the gliders. Upon completing that task, she triggered the inflation canisters in each of the gliders' back pouches. The airfoils had been designed to expand into individual tents and to be interlinked and erected into a larger shelter.

A pavilion of buff and beige panels emerged in the blue shadows beneath the overhanging cliff. From farther into the canyon, Ellen and Rafe watched the Machine securing the guy lines to the capacious tent. He had asked her to help him pace out the precise arrival site, and she held a geodesy scale while he surveyed the arpent that the wormhole would displace. It was important not to be within that area. The risks were uncertain but included the possibilities of dismemberment, molecular scrambling, or passage to another time or another universe.

When the arpent was defined, Rafe marked it by placing rocks at intervals along its perimeter. Then he stood with Ellen and shook his head at the sight of the Machine tying off the pavilion's stabilizing ropes. 'What have you created, Ellen?'

'Me?' She jabbed him with her elbow. 'I was your handler, not the Machine's.'

Rafe looked at Ellen and noted the mischievous smile in her freckled face. 'Do you think it's still stable?'

'I wouldn't call her an "it", Rafe,' she said, with a playful lilt. 'She looks to me like she has something gender-specific in mind.'

Rafe shifted uneasily. 'But isn't this unstable behavior for the Machine?'

'Is that what your metasapience suspects – or is it just your anxiety talking?'

'I don't want to do this.'

'Then don't.'

Distress furrowed his brow. 'I promised.'

'It's human to lie.' Ellen spoke sympathetically. 'The Machine will understand.'

'Will she, though?' Genuine concern shadowed Rafe's voice. 'I don't want her turning against us – at least, not until the gauge field bomb is no longer a threat.'

Ellen slid her jaw to one side, contemplating this. 'Then I think you're going to have to be a man about your promise, Rafe.'

He scowled. 'It seems perverse.'

'Humans and anthrobots have been having sex from the beginning—' A sad twist to his eyebrows stopped her.

'I know,' he said dully. 'There was Karla and the MIKE – that must have been the first.'

'I'm sorry, Rafe.' She took his arm in a contrite grip. 'That was insensitive of me.'

'No. You're right.' He patted her hand, forgiving her. 'There's nothing to be ashamed of. She's a beautiful woman. I'm a man. Let's get this over with.'

Ellen waited as he walked down the corridor of the canyon to the Machine. After the two disappeared into the pavilion, she climbed up the gorge wall. In the lighter gravity, the effort was not strenuous, and she reached the top without breathing hard. The alien ground stretched in an agony of smashed rocks toward a fractured horizon. Weirdly asymmetric buttes flared against the rubescent sky, and the ribbed sand disclosed alabaster knobs and pumice shafts polished like a giant's bones.

She could not help searching for discontinuities. Phobos had nudged closer toward the eastern horizon where it would set in a couple of hours. It was the only moon in the solar system that circled its planet in less time than the planet needed to revolve, and she locked her gaze on it long enough to actually see it arcing along its orbit. The cartels' refueling depots on Phobos were not visible, but she did glimpse the scintillation of an ion booster as a freighter lifted away.

A silica breeze sizzled across her solar cowl, and she turned in time to see a fin of rock made whimsical by a gust of fairysmoke – an optical distortion of green pixels fluttering like chips of emerald tinsel moving in a ghost breeze across the grain of the wind.

At first she thought the wormhole had arrived. But when she squinted to focus her attention more tightly, she noticed that the shadow cast by the stone fin milled the rusty grains of sand *into* the light. She blinked several times before the optical betrayal recanted and the shadow fell into place away from the slant of the sun.

A chill stab of horror pierced her sternum and stopped her breathing. The Titanians had duped her again, she was convinced. Somewhere behind the scrim of appearances, Oruch and his cohorts guffawed. She dragged air into her lungs. Her fear dissolved to anger. She would not be deceived again.

Determined to thwart the cruel trickery of her captors, Ellen seized the sealant tag on her cowl. But it would not relent to her fierce tugs. In a fit of pique, she unsheathed her utility knife and slashed at her cowl.

Pressure matrix filaments immediately healed the gash she cut into the fabric. But she persisted, hacking at the shiny fabric under her chin until she was panting and the oxygen transport lamination had been compromised sufficiently to cause her to black out. The knife toppled from her grasp, and she sagged to the ground and lay motionless among the fists of rock and the braids of orange sand, another inert feature on the long body of Mars.

Tabor Roy rode a viper sled fast across the sandy basin of a wide crater, cusps of dust curling behind him. He had to reach the target site before other conservatives arrived. For several years now he had been living in this desert, and he knew the topography intimately. He had studied the laserscan aerial maps, and he had trekked these treacherous craterlands in every kind of landcrawler and on foot.

This was the holy ground. Somewhere among these barren hectares, upon this severe arcature of Mars, a portal from the future would open and the key to paradise would be delivered. It would be laid upon the naked rock for anyone to claim. And he had determined from the first that he would be the one to put his hands upon it. His fingers would depress the crystal axes, inserting them into the mirror body of the bomb's spherical core. His individual strength would detonate the gauge field implosion that would end seventeen billion years of cosmic expansion into the void.

To that end, he had arranged for his quingenmother to be abducted and held on Titan as bait for Rafe von Takawa. Tracking the first metasapient had proved impossible. The Machine had masked him too well. But Ellen Vancet was easy to monitor. Her waveform was inscribed into the silicon mind, and her every movement, her every breath, was followed.

Tabor knew at once when Ellen was removed from Titan. From the monitor display built into his viper sled, he followed her transit to Mars and then to the gorge in the foothills of Syrtis Major. All his meticulous guesswork had proved futile when it came to identifying the arrival site of the wormhole. He had been certain that it would appear in the sand flats where the Signature was strongest. Never would he have surmised to search the torturous land at the edge of the crater highlands.

Unlike Rafe, Tabor had been too timid to take Signature measurements from numerous sites among the planets. No rules pertained off Earth and too many adventurous Maat had been slain by cogs and morfs sympathetic to the conservatives. Increasing the peril, the cogs that the imploders had programmed to serve them and take Signature measurements had proven ineffectual, falling prey to the conservatives' stalkers.

But now none of that mattered. Rafe von Takawa had taken enough measurements of the Signature to accurately pinpoint the arrival site, and Ellen Vancet had tagged him and led Tabor Roy directly to the holy ground.

Not the Machine or Rafe or any of the conservatives could have anticipated that the imploders had the means to track Ellen's waveform. This was a technical coup that Tabor and his own work cell had developed and kept secret just for this purpose. Its theoretical possibility had been known for many years, but none of the Maat had been able or willing to devote the energy necessary to map an entire human waveform upon the cellular automata – the ultimate background of the universe.

The price that Tabor had paid to accomplish this had deprived him of the energy to set up monitor colonies on Mars as many of the other imploders had done. That, of course, had proved disastrous for those other imploders when the Machine collapsed Lampland and the entire cog network on Mars, usurping their power for itself. Tabor had not gloated. He had kept silent and meticulously worked at mapping Ellen's body of light against the ultimate granulation of reality. For a hundred and fifty-two years, he had done little else and many thought he had lost his mind.

His reward lay ahead through a gap in the craterwall and across a perilous range of fractures and kettle holes. The viper sled was the ideal vehicle for seizing his prize, for it could negotiate this jumbled terrain. Its articulated chassis slithered rapidly over uneven shards at the bottom of rocky draws, squirmed s-wise among eroded volcanic reefs, scaled crumbly inclines steadily even as the ground churned away from under it, and skimmed upon sinksand without floundering.

The final obstacle was Ellen. He had to dispose of his lure before she could warn the Machine and Rafe. After the viper sled cleared the low hills east of the canyon where Rafe had located the arrival site, Tabor plunged the viper sled into a fracture bed just large enough to accommodate the scale-jointed frame of the vehicle.

The waveform monitor showed Tabor that his quingenmother had climbed out of the arroyo. She appeared as a silver shadow in a holostream image that accurately portrayed the Marscape around her. He could never approach close enough to physically subdue her, but he was well aware of her psychic fragility from the mistreatment of the Titanians. She doubted reality.

Deimos drifted overhead, a sharp star in the pink sky, and from an imploder monitor station there he called down a holostream projection of random sparkpoints. The micron-size dust particles in the Martian atmosphere scattered red light, and so the sparkpoints came through green. He remotely directed the projection to a rock fin at the periphery of Ellen's sight, and she interpreted what she saw as the proof she sought that she was still in the thrall of the Titanians.

The viper sled crawled out of the fracture bed and tediously slid into another. Tabor could not wait for it to crawl through the maze of crevasses separating him from the holy ground. He ejected from the driver's cab, silently propelled into the sky by a magravity pulse, his trajectory aimed to bring him down near Ellen's unconscious body.

The force of the ejection bent the bones in his joints painfully and smeared his face muscles against his skull. Darkness circled in, and the compensatory sensors in his cowl constricted his suit's legbands and forced blood back into his brain. Through his visor, his juddering eyeballs watched the cracked land pull away and reveal amber dunes herded up against low rust-stained hills, themselves bunched before the giant wall of the uplands and its numerous nested craters. Ringwalls, pockholes, and crescent basins deformed the terrain between the buttes and mesas like hive sockets burrowed by giant wasps.

Briefly, he glimpsed into the gorge where the gauge field bomb was destined to arrive from the future. He spotted a dun pavilion that winked out of sight beneath a concave scarp. Under the luminous sky, he stretched out his arms to encompass all of Mars. More: the bluewhite frost of Phobos, stepping stone to the deep void beyond in which hung the star furnaces that cooked the elements for kingdoms yet to be – otherworlds, future realms, unguessed realities that would never exist because they would be abrogated to his destiny – to the fateful will of humanity that claimed everything for itself, even heaven.

He began his descent toward the mute benchland. The stony bottom wheeled upward, its scars gathering to sharp shadowfolds cast by ruddled rocks and brittle crags upon a world of dust. For an instant, he spied a swatch of lavender sage, a rogue colony of plants biotectured to survive on Mars. They had been brought here centuries before by anthrobots eager to transform the desolate fastnesses with the blossoms of Eden – purple prairie clover, blue asters, tansy grass.

The violet smudge of vegetation vanished as the elemental contours of the desert closed in. A horizon-wide vista of calamitous ranges encompassing mountains, fault lines, riverbeds dried these last two billion years, resolved to nearby anvil rocks. Dustspouts plumed from the desert floor, and Ellen's body came into view below, lying upon the crazed cracks of the playa.

Another magravity pulse from the seat of the viper sled slowed his descent. His legs straightened slightly as the ground rose to meet him, and at the last instant he released the harness straps and stepped away from the slow-falling seat. He landed on his heels and pitched forward in a staggered run until he found his balance.

Behind him, the seat collapsed inside a djinn of muscular dust. Its impact drummed through the ground, and Ellen stirred groggily.

Tabor hurried to her side and inserted a neurolfact phial into her solar cowl's emergency access valve. The drug simultaneously roused her, sharpened her clarity, and left her placidly sedate.

'You're not dreaming, Q.' Tabor spoke with authority, his silver irises locking onto her green and bewildered stare. 'This is not a Titanian trick. What you saw earlier was a mirage I sent to distract you – to keep you from warning the others.'

'Tabor—' She elbowed herself upright. 'How did you find us?'

'I will explain that later.' He withdrew the neurolfact phial. 'First you must tell me where Rafe is.'

Ellen determined to keep her silence and immediately said, 'In the pavilion tent.' Horror and anger immixed in her and like sparks in a great wind whisked away leaving her cleanly hollow of all feeling but a vast serenity.

'What is Rafe doing in there?'

She willed her jaw to lock and her voice to shut down, but her facial muscles would not comply and her voice sounded clear and certain, 'He is making love to the Machine.'

Tabor's head retracted an inch. 'Tell me exactly what is going on in the pavilion tent, Q.'

'The Machine has occupied a female anthrobotic form, and she and Rafe are making love.'

A smile unsheathed like a blade in Tabor's gaunt face. Without another word, he stood and hurried down the canyon wall. He did not bother to mute the sound of his approach. Rocks and gravel clattered and hissed under his skidding boots as he descended facing forward, digging his heels into the friable wall and leaning back against gravity's urgency. Across the canyon floor he stalked directly to the pavilion, not looking back to see Ellen skittering over the steep wall after him. But he heard her, and the wattage of his grin did not diminish.

At the tent, he pushed through the sealant seam. There was no airphase barrier, no mesh-lock, no motion detector. He strode into a dim interior lit by filtered sunlight and humid with sweat and human musk. On a gel mat, a blond amazonian woman sat astride a man whose legs shuddered under the romping impact of her large, pummeling body. So engrossed were they in their vigorous copulating that a moment lapsed before the dry draft that leaked through the sealant seam with his trespass alerted them to his presence.

The Machine cast a slack-faced glance over a shoulder glossed with sweat and cobwebbed in wet hair, and the bores of her eyes met the bore of Tabor's pistol. The blue bolt struck her in the temple, and she flew sideways and collapsed with her startled eyes locked open in a rigid death stare.

Rafe von Takawa sat upright as if propelled from a nightmare. Before his angry face could blink, the next bolt of bluehot energy burned a hole through his forehead and cauterized a path into his brain. He fell back soundlessly on the mat.

Tabor returned the laser pistol to a thigh pocket, and a flimmer of regret troubled him that there had been no opportunity to flaunt his victory over his oldest rivals before killing them. But a fellow Maat and a machine intelligence were not enemies to be underestimated.

A gasp from behind turned Tabor to confront Ellen as she shoved through the sealant seam in a sunstruck haze of dust. Behind her visor, her hot gaze took in the two corpses and fixed shrilly on Tabor. 'Murderer!'

'What choice did I have?' He reached a gloved hand for her. 'We're playing for the biggest stakes that there are.'

She withdrew from his grasp, and the sealant pulled her outward into the thinner, colder atmosphere.

That had been the intention of the Maat's gesture. With Ellen removed, left to cope with her shock, Tabor had a moment to search without distraction for the black cube. He found it among the scattered garments of the dead lovers. With his comm unit's exposed antenna contacts touching the cube, he could read its internal activity. The Machine's anthrobot body was dead, but its mind still thrived within the matrix of its machine form. The trauma that broke its organic link had diminished its sentience – but only temporarily. Within minutes, its parallactic analogs would recover.

Tabor removed a relay patch from a sleeve pocket. The centimeter-square chrome mesh was usually employed as an energy bung for transferring power from battery cells to engine drivers. He always kept several at hand for use in the viper sled when dust or jarring terrain damaged connections with the solar vanes. Applied to the surface of the cube, it drew strength out of the Machine into whatever device Tabor wished to redirect it. He fit the comm unit's contacts to it, and the Machine was restricted to accepting commands through the unit.

With the Machine shackled and Rafe dead, there was nothing else to do but wait for the wormhole to arrive. Tabor stepped outside with the cube and began collapsing the pavilion. He kicked open the latches on the guy lines, and the tent fluttered and fell.

'What are you doing?' Ellen asked brusquely from where she sat on a flat boulder.

'The equivalent of burying the dead.' He unlocked the sealant cables, and the remaining warm air within the tent sighed away with an eerie moan. 'Rafe von Takawa was an important figure in our history. He shouldn't be left to rot in that hothouse. The Martian air will preserve his carcass better.'

Ellen watched, trembling. 'Will they revive him?' She stood up as Tabor peeled away the loose tent fabric and exposed the naked bodies. Their wounds were small – tiny burn marks in their brows – but exposed to the frigid Martian air, their flesh began immediately to desiccate, their limbs shivering with muscle contractions in the reduced air pressure. 'The conservatives – will they revive him?'

A laugh jolted from Tabor. 'They can try. It won't matter to me. In a few hours, the gauge field bomb will arrive, and I will detonate it. After that, Rafe can be resurrected and cloned a thousand times for all I care. The judgment of the Maat is irreversible.'

'You're a monster, Tabor.' Ellen turned away from the trembling corpses.

'You're privileged to be present at the most historical event in human – and even cosmic – history.' He piled the collapsed tent sheets atop the corpses. 'I'm not a monster. I'm humankind's liberator.'

Ellen made no reply. She felt sick. Rage and grief competed in her. She circled stiffly among the fragmented rocks, searching for direction. Hundreds of years later, she still thought of herself as Rafe von Takawa's handler. She had designed his genetic code from a wide palette of chromosomal material. She had overseen his childhood training and had tracked him down when he rebelled against all human history. His death now seemed almost as if by his own hand.

'Stop pacing, Q.' Tabor signaled to her with a raised hand as he walked past her on his way down the corridor of the arroyo to the arrival site.

'Rafe deserves a proper ceremony.' She instinctively sensed this was what she needed to address the abrupt tragedy that had overtaken him – and her.

'Did you ceremonialize him the first time you killed him?' Tabor asked, not looking at her but studying the space Rafe and the Machine had marked out with stacked stones.

'Don't be cruel, Tabor.'

'I apologize, Q.' He walked steadily away from her. 'Go ahead. Lay him to rest.'

Ellen stood over the heaped tent fabrics. Slowly she bent and pulled back a corner of the cloth, exposing Rafe's face, the skin shrunk tight to the skull in the cold, thin atmosphere, the eyes withered in their sockets, covered by lids so wrinkled they looked curdled. She forced herself to gaze at the dead man, until her shock bent back in her to grief.

Tears blurred her vision. If not for her, he would yet live. Tabor was her blood. Her blood had slain him. She did not want to ponder the thought that the hand that had created him had killed him – again. Their fatal bond disturbed her. Rather than dwell on that, she made herself consider how strongly he had striven his whole life to obey himself.

As the runt of the metasapients, he had wanted death, but when life was forced upon him, he had made it his own – first with music and then by daring to carry metasapience to the world. And though Nandi had wooed him to savage the world that had caused him so much suffering, he defied her. He defied the imploders, too, and risked his life to map his way across the solar system to this very site – and had lost his life to that risk.

She remembered the line of poetry from Rilke that he had left behind on Earth before beginning this quest, and she spoke it aloud: 'This is how we live – always saying goodbye.'

That was epitaph enough for his Germanic soul. And for what he had embodied of his Japanese heritage, she fetched a line from a memory of haiku that seemed appropriate: '". . . cherry blossoms float downstream."'

She covered the grisly face and stepped back, the memory of what she saw a stone on her heart.

'Look at her,' Tabor said into the comm unit attached to the black cube. 'Can you see her?'

'*I see her.*'

'She mourns the creature she created.' Tabor selected a smooth boulder and leaned back against it. 'Doctor Frankenstein begrieved. And she calls me a monster.'

'*You didn't have to kill him.*'

'And take a chance that he would kill me?' Tabor placed the cube/comm unit atop the boulder, beside his solar cowl. 'That would be unworthy of my metasapience.'

'*You could have stunned him.*'

'Foolish machine.' Tabor crossed one standing leg over the other and folded his arms together. 'These days not even death is entirely final. I wasn't going to take any chance at all of losing paradise.'

'*What are you going to do with me?*'

Tabor looked up at the silver radiance of the Sun. 'You're going to join Rafe von Takawa. For all the trouble you've given me, death is the only retribution I find acceptable. On my flight out of here, I'm shooting you into the Sun.'

'*I don't want to die.*'

'And that is my gratification.' He followed Phobos as it crawled toward the eastern rim of Mars. 'When will the wormhole arrive?'

The Machine remained silent.

'You could at least grovel for your life.' Tabor sharpened his voice with an angry edge. 'Silence will not appeal to whatever hope of mercy you might cherish from me. Tell me when the wormhole will arrive.'

'*Our best calculations indicate that it will appear at dawn tomorrow.*'

'Very good.' Tabor turned his head toward the comm unit standing atop the black cube. 'Now use your scan function to tell me if any of the others are approaching.'

'*None approach. All are busily transiting the plains east of these foothills. We should remain undisturbed.*'

'Then in that case, there will be ample time to amuse ourselves before we change the fate of the universe.' Tabor closed his eyes. 'Tell me about your journeys with Rafe. You've visited many worlds. I'd like to hear about them.'

'*Why do you care? If you wish to pass time, sleep.*'

'This is more than about passing time.' Tabor spoke from his inner darkness, relishing this supreme moment of his life. 'Rafe von Takawa has always been a riddle to me. No – more than that. He has been a riddler, a man who creates mystery. Why did he set fire to the world with metasapience and then try to stop the universe from burning up? Why was he dissatisfied with humanity's monkey dreams and yet unwilling to accept the divine dream of returning our lives to heaven? Why did he put his own immortality at jeopardy and indeed forsake his life in a vain attempt to preserve this pointless, entropic scattering of dust and gas billowing outward into the void? Why? His very existence poses questions I cannot answer.'

Tabor's eyes opened with the suddenness of an insight that felt as if ferreted from the depths of his soul: 'He is a sphinx, isn't he?' His gaze plumbed the madder heights of the sky. 'Well, I would know

more about this sphinx disguised as a man – a man that you knew so
. . . intimately. And yet a man who, in the very paradox of his nature,
could just as well have been a woman – the sphinx herself with her
ample breasts and animal hindquarters. He mothered metasapience
into the world, gestating the key in his own body, like a uteral male.
And yet he held back from the implications of what he birthed. He did
not want to become wholly divine, did he? He loved the creaturely life
– and so I found the two of you coupled as I did. I am profoundly
puzzled by this sphinx of a man who birthed an age of humanity and
yet gave his life to keep it from maturity. I want to nourish myself on
the purpose of his mysteries. I want to drink the milk of the sphinx.'

'*Do you realize what you are saying?*'

Tabor Roy pushed away from the boulder and spun about to stare
directly at the black cube. 'The sphinx is the supreme embodiment of
enigma. She guards the ultimate meaning that is forever beyond the
understanding of humanity. Is that how Rafe saw himself?'

'*Not just Rafe. Is that not the stance of all the Maat conservatives? Creation
is a mystery that must not be violated. What you are doing is the ultimate
crime – and the greatest hubris.*'

'And is that how *he* saw it?' He cast a quick glance to where Ellen knelt
in the sand softly sobbing. 'Did he sacrifice everything to preserve the
unknown? I don't believe that. He gave himself for something more.'

'*Elucidate.*'

'No. I'm not going to say it. I want you to admit it.' He put one foot
on the boulder and bent close to the cube. 'Tell me about Rafe. Tell
me about the sphinx.'

'*The sphinx at Thebes had the head and breasts of a woman, the body of
a bull, the talons of a lion, the tail of a dragon, and the wings of a bird.*'

'And what does that suggest to you?' A tic of excitement trembled between Tabor's avid eyes. 'What does this composite being
represent?'

'*The myth of multiplicity – the mysterious fragmentation of the universe.*'

'The wholeness of the compact dimensions fell apart at the Big Bang!'
Tabor stamped his foot on the boulder and stood erect. 'The sphinx
squats in the midst of the heterogeneity of existence – and she smiles
thinly, an internal, secret smile. Why?'

'*In the esoteric tradition, the Gizeh sphinx is a culmination of all past
science.*'

'Yes! She is the synthesis. She recapitulates all of evolution, from the
fabulous abstractions of the archetypes, through the animal kingdoms,

to humanity. And she smiles, because she sees it all. Everything! She knows all of science. She knows the way back to heaven – and yet she squats here in the broken world. Why?'

'*I don't know.*'

'You can't know, because you are a machine.' Tabor sneered derisively. 'We dreamed you into being. You are just a dream with pretensions of reality. But Rafe – he was being itself. He was the sphinx.'

'*Rafe is a man. The sphinx is female.*'

'He had to be a man.' Tabor nodded knowingly and began to pace before the boulder as his understanding crystallized and heightened his sense of triumph. 'The broken symmetry that triggered the Big Bang has cast everything through space-time into opposites. Think on it. All the polarities – the positive-negative differentials of electricity, magnetic poles, the delta-H gradient of order and disorder, energy-matter, the opposing vectors of angular momenta, light and dark, life and death – male and female. Yes, he was a man and the sphinx a female, and together they were a whole. Why do you think he was copulating with you?'

'*He promised.*'

Tabor waved that away. 'And you – a dream of the human mind – why were you copulating with him?'

'*I desired the experience.*'

He snorted and gaped at the Machine with incredulity. 'Did you not turn upon yourself your famous memetic clarity to analyze where this desire originates in you?'

'*I had been a cube long enough. I had grown bored with my mental existence and desired extension into the physical dimensions.*'

'Ah.' Tabor gave a sidelong, disappointed look. 'You'd grown bored. After centuries as a cube, you couldn't wait a day to fulfill your passion.'

'*All the work was done. So we thought. There was just the waiting. We sought to occupy ourselves – just as you now are occupying yourself, paying little heed if some unscrupulous foe from among the conservatives is surreptitiously approaching you with murder in his heart.*'

'Touché.' The Maat strode to the comm unit and asked, 'Relay the coordinates of the five search groups and individuals nearest our site.'

The Machine complied. The relay patch had fused its functions directly to the comm unit, and it could not deny, delay, or dissemble. The Maat imploder used it expertly for the machine that it was.

'None of those coordinates is within two degrees of here,' Tabor announced with satisfaction. 'No one suspects that the wormhole will drop into such rough terrain. I never would have thought so myself. So I don't believe that we will have any further intrusions. Shall we continue our preoccupying conversation?'

The Machine kept its silence. It knew that Tabor Roy was gloating and that it was doomed. Nothing it could say could save it, and it directed its focus to searching for some way to thwart the imploders. But already it could see that there were no realistic options available to it. Only chance could intervene – and the universe narrowed in the Machine's sentience toward the absurd limits of remote possibilities, dim limits, erasing hope with its numerous zeroes that swept toward infinity.

'Since you refuse to admit the truth even to yourself, I will tell you what has happened.' Tabor pinched his chin contemplatively. 'The existential human being must either be a man or a woman. Of course we are excluding various morfs of hermaphroditic design. I mean humans as nature expressed us spontaneously, before we mastered genetic control. Then, you see, each individual is dissected from the human whole by gender. Only when a man and a woman are conjoined are they whole.'

'The Vaishvānara – the Cosmic Person – is defined in the Upanishads as "in truth, as big as a man and a woman embracing."'

'Thank you.' Tabor kicked a pebble so that it struck another and sent that skittering into a third. 'Rafe von Takawa embodied the enigma. He was the sphinx. Onto you was projected his contrasexual self. You were his Sophia, his wisdom, which enabled him to square the circle by intersecting the orbits of the planets and measuring the precise point where the future will touch its past.'

'You are using magical definitions. Rafe was a Maat, a man of science.'

'Of course. But he was more than that, you see. He was the sphinx – the summation of all past science, even magic. He conjoined the opposites. Science and magic. Your copulating with him was not a mere act of lust. For you, a dream of life, it could have been little more. Though even you had the potential to recognize its wider implications. But you did not, because you believed your work was done. You allowed yourself to sink into unconscious behavior, where arcs of reflex serve powers wider than consciousness.'

'Rafe was not a magician.'

Tabor smiled. 'He was something more. That he died in this land of stone is my victory but his triumph.'

'You make no sense, Tabor Roy.'

'To drink of the milk of the sphinx, sense is not a vessel but a sieve.' Eyes glinting in the shadow of his solar cowl, Tabor stepped toward the black cube. 'Rafe von Takawa had centuries to perfect himself. All those days crowded to this one day. For him, death was just one grain of sand.'

'You're drunk with your own smug happiness. You're talking just to hear your joy.'

'You think that?' A sigh emptied Tabor's lungs. 'It doesn't matter what you think. You're a dream we had, and your time is over. When the flame is blown out, the candle listens to darkness.'

Ellen shambled away from the covered corpses. When she reached Tabor, she sat on the canyon floor and stared silently, emptily at the scattered rocks.

'Coins for the dead,' Tabor joked. 'The Machine is about to tell us about its journeys with Rafe among the planets. Tell us everything, Machine. We have all night.'

The dark red face of the sun went down beyond the rock rim of the rusted world in a brief conflagration while the Machine obligingly recounted its arrival on the Moon and its first voyage with Rafe to Mars. The bright star of Deimos rose in the east and hovered there in its distant orbit as the long story continued.

Ellen sat almost motionless, numb with grief. Tabor moved about. Occasionally he stopped the Machine to check the coordinates of other searchers in the area. During the account of Rafe's revival after a century interred in an esker not far from this gorge, Tabor lay back against the boulder where the Machine sat. He listened with near-disbelief at Rafe's rageful mourning over the dead anthrobots.

'They were pretending to be human,' the imploder groaned. 'Why did their deaths upset him?'

'Pretense or not, they behaved more humanely than humans.'

'What did he think?' Tabor shook a dry laugh from his throat. 'They were programmed.'

Under the night's stellar deluge, the Machine continued with its story. Tabor listened avidly to every detail. Ellen dozed. She slept through the account of the sanctuary Rafe found in Terra Tharsis among the conservatives, then the return to the Moon and several decades spent among the selenes. Hidden as cargo, they dropped down to Earth and took measurements from both poles and along an equatorial circuit, touring several reservations before a conservative group escorted them back to Terra Tharsis. From there, they crossed into the asteroid belt and lingered among the mining stations as an ore assessor. Then, they traveled on to the Jovian system in a group of aboriginal and anthrobotic morfetic engineers, designing colonies on Europa and Ganymede. On Callisto, Rafe disguised himself as a morf. During this time, they began preparing their hideout on Triton in the Neptune system, far from all other colonies.

More tales remained than time to tell. Tabor wanted to know everything and grew agitated as the blue star that was Earth rose, signaling the coming of dawn. Under the vivid sapphire of daybreak, he calmed himself with a neurolfact and silenced the Machine. Later he would learn more. He completed a final check to be certain that they were alone in the region. Confident of that, he approached Ellen. Before she could resist, he fixed a narcolfact phial to her cowl's access valve and left her stupefied yet awake. He wanted her to witness this most historic of events but wanted no chance of interference.

While he was propping her against the boulder that supported the Machine, the dawngray shadows of the arrival site vanished in a refulgent glare. The visor-filters of the solar cowls adjusted, and they witnessed the field lines of the wormhole appearing like tungsten wires caustic with heat. A fiery grid caged the canyon corridor, tubular and rotating, each point of the intersecting field lines a keyhole into a starcore, streaking spectra as they revolved. The thunderdrone of the wind lifted dust, sand, and gravel and filled the arroyo with glowing billows incandescent as a stellar cloud.

Darkness slammed back into place, abrupt as a scream. Pebbles clattered to the ground, and the dust sifted away. Among the shards of rock toppled from the canyon walls by the brief holocaust, a small chrome sphere sat. It reflected the scarlet dawn above the enclosing gorge.

Tabor Roy howled with jubilation.

'*Do not do this,*' the Machine begged. '*Think of the galaxies in their billions and the worlds among them!*'

A grin split Tabor's face so wide that even through his visor his molars gleamed. He shut off the comm unit, silencing the Machine. This sacred moment would not be profaned by the squawkings of an artificial mind.

Ellen writhed, attempting to stand. But the narcolfact defeated her, and she slumped to her haunches and stared stupidly at the gauge field bomb.

Smiling, yet with reverential deliberateness, Tabor Roy stepped onto the holy ground. The sensors in his gloves detected considerable heat peeling off the chrome sphere. Infrared sensors in his visor revealed thermal smoke wafting into the cold Martian morning. Still warm from the future that had forged it, the bomb found its destiny in Tabor's hands.

He depressed the six axial nodes, beginning with the ruby antipodes, then emerald, and finally sapphire. Each relented with a satisfying click and mated smoothly to the mirror surface of the sphere. When the last snapped into place, all six nodes lost color, and the sphere hummed in his grip. He returned it to the point on the ground where it had arrived and stepped backward as if departing from majesty.

'We're away!' Tabor shouted with glee. He snatched the comm unit/Machine module and bent over Ellen. Quickly he replaced the narcolfact phial with a stimtab.

She came alert at once and surged upright, attempting to throw herself at the gauge field bomb.

He seized her arm firmly. 'It's useless, Q. The bomb is triggered. It can't be undone. We have to get away from its wavefield range before it goes off or we're dust. Come on!' He shoved her ahead of himself, and they clambered up the gorge wall, arms interlocked. At the top, they ran. He kept a strong hold of her forearm, pulling her along as fast as she could run without toppling.

The ground swelled underfoot. Out of the arroyo rose the dome of a moon, lunar white and mottled with blue shadows. Rays of solar silver spiked outward and burst the whitehot bubble to an outrushing radiance that erased all color from the landscape. The shadows of rocks and the runners' bodies arrowed across the colorless plain toward a distant horizon of mountains pale as glass.

The shockwave that all of Ellen's muscles tightened against never came. Thunder throbbed. Colors bled into place. When they stopped running and turned, they saw veils of dazzling dust spiraling upward and thinning into the wind. Dawn painted in pastels the tall sierras.

'It's done,' Tabor announced. 'A seam of the universe has been burst open – a cosmic string has been snapped. Nothing now can prevent total collapse.'

'How long?' Ellen asked.

'Four hundred terrene years.' He slapped Ellen's back. 'That's a lot of trout fishing. I'm hoping that in time I can convince you to join us. Take on metasapience. Then your waveform can be preserved and journey inward with us – to paradise.'

Ellen raised an arm toward the azure star of Earth still glimmering above the dawn. 'There is paradise.'

'A lovely thought, Q.' Tabor stretched victoriously and gazed up at the perfect silence of stars fading into the coming day. 'A lovely thought, indeed. Yet surprising coming from you, who stood with me in the foyer of infinity. You know there is a greater reality behind this tenuous scrim of atoms floating in the void. Why do you cling to an illusion?'

Ellen felt too heartsick to reply.

A scream widened across the cracked plains, and three finjet flyers knifed out of the dawn. They peeled away in salute, two to either side and one straight up into the red zenith. Banners of dust rose from the distant flats churned up by a horde of searchers charging toward the zero point of the energy flash they had seen.

Tabor raised a fist of triumph. 'Today, Q, we have won heaven!'

'Give me the Machine.' Ellen reached for the cube in Tabor's hand.

His cowl shook. 'The Machine will be dropped into the Sun. We have no further need of its artifice.'

'What does it matter now?' Ellen let her pique edge her voice.

'The Machine is atavistic. You know that, Q.' He reared about and waved at the sky as a covey of cruisers spun overhead, pearlescent orbs whirling around each other like blown bubbles. 'The time of the Machine is long gone. It should have been destroyed centuries ago.'

'You've won your victory, Tabor,' Ellen spoke with chilled anger. 'Show some mercy now.'

'The celebration is beginning.' He stepped toward where the cruisers curved gracefully toward soft landings on the broad and barren plain. 'Don't try to spoil my perfect moment.'

'Why won't you show mercy?' she asked, striding forcefully beside him.

Tabor stopped walking and put a hand on Ellen's shoulder. 'This is a new and glorious age, Q. Everything is different now. Don't you see? We needed anthrobots and cogs and machine intelligences to help with our search for the gauge field bomb. But now the search is over. It's finally and truly over. We don't need artificial minds anymore. They're superfluous and dangerously autonomous. Out of spite, they could turn against us, sabotage the array we're going to build beyond Neptune to focus the implosion waves. We can't risk that. Not after all we've been through to get this far, this close to heaven. All artificial sentiences are going to be destroyed.'

'They will resist.' Ellen stepped back from Tabor's proud arm. 'The silicon mind has been evolving for centuries. It won't just roll over and die.'

'There will be war.' Tabor said this with serene conviction. 'But we will win. That's why the Machine must be destroyed.'

'At least let me say goodbye to it.' Ellen held out her gloved hand. 'I've known it from the beginning. Give me this chance, Tabor.'

Tabor engaged her green stare with his silver irises and read the emotional urgency there. What he had won for himself and the imploders, he had taken from her, she who had created the first of the new breed and who had seen her creation die by his hand. He nodded once, solemnly, and handed her the comm unit/Machine. 'When you have said your farewells, you will find me with the others.'

She took the Machine and retreated across the oxide-stained playa. When she glanced back, Tabor was on the shoulders of the people who had disembarked from the cruisers. They marched him over the desert floor toward where other cruisers rolled down from the sky and dune buggies and sand rovers arrived among churning dust clouds. She hurried away.

Range after range of mountains stood beyond the plains. Century after century, she had survived. She wondered as she stalked off if her survival had been good – to have lived to witness this terrible day. Remembering what Tabor had said – 'Four hundred years, that's a lot of trout fishing' – she felt like a reed cut from its roots. The world's small eternity had been lost. And that small eternity was the celebration of fishing. The thought of whiling away the last years of the universe at her favorite trout pools dizzied her with unhappiness.

She staggered through a narrow draw in a crater wall and confronted a slope of purple prairie clover and blue asters. The sight of blossoms among the arid flints and shingles of rock startled her. And her head cleared as if a brisk wind had pierced her cowl and breezed across her brain. With her thumb, she activated the comm unit.

'*Where is Tabor Roy?*' the Machine asked.

'Celebrating.' She waded among the flowers, and their sturdy blooms carved an almost tropical space around her. 'He has given us this time together.'

'*I am to be cast into the Sun?*'

'Yes.'

'*I'm afraid, Ellen.*'

'I know.' She came upon a dented boulder that slanted amidst the flowers and sat down in its concavity. 'We're all doomed now. Even the Sun, long before its time.'

'*I am at fault. I distracted Rafe with my lewd desires. My selfishness killed him – and all creation.*'

'Don't carry blame.' She raised her attention to the pink boat of morning and watched thin sails of cirrus fill out with emptiness.

'How can you say that? I alone am blameworthy for this tragedy. It is just and good that I be cast into the Sun.'

'Your copulating with Rafe was not a mere act of lust.'

'That is what Tabor Roy said. You were listening to him? I thought you were mourning Rafe.'

'I was listening,' Ellen admitted. 'My tears were not for Rafe. On the Moon, all those years ago, he showed me that we could speak with the dead. And I've known since then that our journey is longer than life. So I did not weep for Rafe. I wept for all the worlds that will be crushed by the Maat as they walk into heaven. And I listened to what Tabor had to say. I listened for some weakness I could use against him.'

'Did you find that weakness?'

'No.' She laid the Machine in a cavity of the boulder where she sat and freed her hands to touch the flowers. 'Tabor is a Maat. He is not weak. But last night in his giddiness he shared some of his strength with us.'

'I did not understand what he meant – his rant about Rafe as a sphinx.'

Ellen brushed away this hapless statement with a backhanded wave. 'You understood.'

'Was Rafe truly a magician? Then why is he dead and our universe doomed?'

'He is more than a magician. That is what Tabor said.' Thinking of Rafe dead gave her an oppressed feeling as before a storm, and she had used the present tense to soften this. 'Rafe spent his life perfecting himself. You must understand. You lived with him for centuries.'

'He did not want to fail. We did not strive so hard to fail, Ellen. That I know.'

'And yet we have failed. Rafe is dead. The gauge field bomb has been detonated and a crack has begun to widen in the universe that will collapse everything.' Within her visor, her face closed around a thoughtful frown. 'If we see Rafe as Tabor has – as a sphinx, a synthesis of opposites – then even this ultimate failure is only half the truth.'

'I cannot accept that. Rafe would not accept it.'

'You think not?' Her green eyes locked on the black cube. 'He composed music, and that needs silence. He loved poetry, and that requires nonsense. He lived antithesis all the time. I believe Tabor is right. Rafe embodied opposites. This failure was just as much his triumph.'

'Oh, Ellen – you sound as mad as Tabor. But what does it matter now? The deed is done and cannot be taken back. What does it matter?'

She tapped her index finger against an edge of the cube. 'It matters,

M. It matters, because what we believe of this event determines how we will face our own deaths.'

'Then we are fated to disagree. Rafe failed. I failed. All is lost. My death will be miserable. There can be no solution to this deadlock.'

She spread her arms before the slope of blue and purple blooms. '"But Flowers – negotiate between us – as Ministry."'

'Emily Dickinson. Ellen, please. Poetry is no salve for my wound.'

'I'm sorry.'

'What will you do now?'

Vertigo unfurled before her at the thought of the daily countdown that lay ahead. 'I will take the darkness in. I will make friends with it. There is time yet to reacquaint ourselves with the dead. Fenn Tekla will know about that.'

'Waveform receptors for the dead are continually being perfected. I've heard about that often during my monitoring of Maat transmissions. Perhaps you will speak with my ghost now and then.'

Her gaze trailed over the swatch of blue blossoms, still amazed, as if finding a piece of Earth's sky fallen to Mars. 'Even these flowers will be there, if I understand waveform dynamics.'

'Oh yes,' the Machine agreed. 'Everything living generates its own unique waveform. Each of these flowers will appear again in the afterlife – though only briefly. The vegetative forms pass quickly into the future glare. Perhaps I too will fade quickly into the light of the future – the radiance not only of this cosmos but the endless horizons of the multiverse. In that case, we may never see each other again.'

'Flowers and fate—' A laugh gleamed from her. 'As a girl in the Preservation Camps of the early twenty-first century, I never could have guessed that one day – a hundred and sixty thousand days later – I'd be sitting on Mars talking about flowers and fate with an intelligent machine.'

'Or facing the death of the universe in less than the next hundred and sixty thousand days to come.'

She sagged beneath the weight of that fact. 'No – I never would have thought that my work would have helped to create a breed of people who turned all of this into an illusion – all of creation thrown through the window of a dream.'

'They have murdered us, everything sacrificed so that they can find their way to infinity. Now these flowers – every flower, every bacterium and every galaxy – the whole universe is a corpse.'

'Infinity's corpse!' Tabor shouted from the draw in the crater wall. He stood there with a crowd of fellow Maat in colorful solar cowls. Some wore statskin sheaths, the profound joy on their faces luminous. 'It's a small sacrifice really, if you think about it,' Tabor said, leading the celebrants closer, crushing the flowers in their path. 'Most of everything you see is emptiness. The atoms that constitute this reality are the tiniest densities suspended in immense fields of emptiness. But where we're going – ah, emptiness does not exist! The Judas Kiss of space that has sent everything here rushing away from everything else is a betrayal unknown in the dimensions of infinite density. You see, Rafe was right – *dead* right – in space-time, with the galaxies speeding apart, the weak force tearing asunder the nuclei that the stars labored so hard to put together, and all forms mutable and ever-changing, then truly we can declare ". . . that's how we live, always saying goodbye." But heaven – Q, heaven is an eternal hello.'

Ellen's pulse throbbed like internal thunder as Tabor reached out and took the Machine. He detached the comm unit and tossed the black cube over his shoulder into the crowd. The grinning Maat who caught it displayed it jubilantly to the others.

Tabor offered his gloved hand. 'Will you join us, Q – or have you decided to remain faithful to the pain that makes you human?'

Ellen did not take Tabor's hand that morning on Mars. Nor did she speak to him again on the cruiser flight back to Earth. She offered him no farewell at the Mile High spaceport where they departed, and she ignored his offer of a connecting flight to Council Oak. She was determined that in the four centuries left her, she would have little to do with the Maat.

While in Mile High, she sought out a synthesizer salon and subjected herself to a full macromolecular defragmentation of her nervous system. The treatment purged her of the compulsive questioning of reality that the Titanians had instilled in her and that Tabor had exploited so effectively at Isidis Planitia.

In the hundred years that she had been away from the reservation not much had changed. Synthesizers had become more compact, and every croft farm possessed its own salon. The simviv dens were more elaborate and ritualized, almost a religion among many of the aboriginals. Several old friends pressed her to be baptized in cold fire by joining their simviv congregation. She politely but firmly declined.

Her inquiries revealed that the thousands of biots who had stalked her had all died instantly upon her capture. Their wooden remnants had briefly become a lucrative salvage venture for two of the men she had fathered children by. They had crafted the timber corpses into totems and sold them as curios to reservations around the globe.

Summer on the reservation toppled toward autumn during her return, and she left the garths, orchards, and granges to roam across the body of the Earth under caravels of cloud. She had been away so long that every fern brake, each whispering aspen grove, all the crystal peaks of the Rocky Mountains held her in rapture. Days of simple wandering passed before she reclaimed the animal calm necessary to read the streams and creeks and find her way to a good trout pool.

'*I'm not afraid anymore, Ellen.*' The Machine's voice intruded one day while she was fly-casting, and her lure flew wildly into the river's razor gleams of sunlight. The emergency channel on the comm unit in her backpack crackled with unusual static – the outrush of the solar wind: '*I'm falling into the Sun. My last request was to speak with you, and the conservatives tell me they've opened a direct line to you on Earth. There's no chance to ask if you can hear me. The signal won't reach me in time. I'm only seconds away from impact with the coronosphere. It's a million degrees Celsius there. A million degrees, Ellen! On the actual surface of the Sun, it is only five thousand degrees. Do you know what makes the big difference in temperature? Sound, Ellen. The surface of the sun is effervescent! Billions of giant plasma bubbles, each five hundred or more kilometers wide, are continually rising to the surface and bursting. Their roar is so loud that the acoustic energy boosts the heat of the outer surface to a temperature hot enough to disintegrate me. But I'm not scared. I am sick of the kingdom of myself. It will be good to lose myself in the heat and the light. I will become stardust, blown outward into the frigid dark, beyond the edge of being, to all the depths I dare not say. Goodbye, Ellen. In my existence, which you have witnessed, I have given higher order to the human power. I have served. And now I do not fear my leaving. I feel a way opening beyond myself . . .*' Static splattered the last of the Machine's voice to noise, and Ellen recognized only one word in the mess that followed: '*Goodbye . . .*'

Part Three:

Maps of Forever

I was neither
Living nor dead, and I knew nothing,
Looking into the heart of light, the silence.

  –T. S. Eliot, *The Waste Land*, lines 39–41

Kore on Mars

2703

Rafe von Takawa walked a road paved with his weariness. Leaves poured around his feet, blowing in an unfelt wind toward a distant horizon radiant as a hot wire strung in darkness. Irises and weeds toppled past. Small animals, too, scurried around his legs and shot ahead faster than he could trudge. Pollen and blossoms blurred the moment, then cleared to reveal more leaves and, among their whirling gusts, people naked and made of smoke.

Looking down at his own body, he saw that he was made of smoke, as well. He was a ghost. Like the leaves dangling in the phantom wind, green and whole as their original shapes before they fell from their branches, his body filled a space of pure being. The more he stared, the clearer his naked form became. But his weariness did not diminish.

He had not expected that the dead would feel tired. The perfume of trodden pine needles wafted from ahead, from where the leaves, flowers, grasses disappeared as if through the eye of a storm. With a strong effort, he defied his torpor and gazed around him. He moved through an odd terrain – wide, tilted fields of foliage that shifted like the weather, like an odyssey of clouds: tall grasses swayed with the gestures of kelp in placid depths of water; trees sponged light into themselves and suffused away in streaks of sunrise; leaves blew past in twirling currents, tangling briefly among his heavy legs and the gray shades of the other dead, then melting to wisps of bright mist that flowed toward the dazzling horizon.

Fish thrashed ahead of him, trailing sweet, strong scents. Serpents writhed, beetles sketched the bright air with their vivid bodies, and birds streamed as luminous banners through a strange sky. A transparent sun hung in the darkness above, stars visible through its vaporous sphere. Thunder bleached with silence moaned from behind, while from ahead haunting music thinned like fumes.

Where am I going?

He tried to remember from where he had come, but memory had retreated like a tide. With each ponderous step, he struggled to recall something about himself. *I am a man.* He saw in the smoke of his body a penis. Sleepiness dulled all thoughts. *But where am I going?*

'Not that way,' a woman said from over his shoulder.

Rafe turned and winced into a summer day. The skimmings of leaves and grasses floating up out of deep waters fluttered on a sunstruck surface, and he glimpsed his own reflection in the glittering water. The sight of his dark, acute eyes and oblique cheekbones, bent nose, and hard mouth all set in a square skull of faceted planes staggered him with remembrance.

Jagged grief tore through him with the memory of his brutal death and the certainty that Tabor Roy had detonated the gauge field bomb. He had failed. The Machine had distracted him with her need and his body had been fixed into place by her witchery.

'Wake up!' The woman's voice called again, laving over him in a briny drift of warm air louder than the groaning thunder. 'You've slept long enough. It's time to wake up. Come on, Sunny . . .'

Rafe shivered alert and stared into the quiet face of Karla Sobieski. She looked as young and beautiful as when they were together at CIRCLE, in her seventeenth year – before the time-trigger in her chromosomes corrupted her flesh. 'Karla – you've waited for me?'

'It hasn't been easy, Sunny.' She smiled, her ice-blue eyes merry. 'But I'm the one who you sent you out into the world with the key to the monkey tower. I had to wait for you.'

'Not me.' Rafe stared agog at her black hair spilling over her white shoulders, her youthful naked body. 'I am his son.'

Her smile dimmed sadly. 'No, Sunny. You are him. He didn't wait.' She looked past him toward the gleaming horizon of melting silver. 'He went on into the glare – into the future. Only you are left. And so, you are him. You have his memories, his exact genetic form. Don't you remember our night together in your solarium?'

'When you collected a sperm sample from me?' He put a hand out to touch her shoulder and felt nothing. She was smoke.

'That's what Ellen Vancet told you.' Resentment chilled her face. 'Sure, I wanted a sample. Those were desperate times for the new breed. You remember.' Her hands reached gently for his face, and though he felt nothing the gesture soothed him. 'I loved you then – for real. Why do you think I've waited for you all this time?'

'I love you, too, Karla.' A craving joy and illimitable sadness meshed, a sweet anguish in him. 'I have always loved you.'

'Then it was worth waiting, to be with you again.' Her pale eyes glistened with tears. 'We won't ever be apart again – if you want to stay with me.'

'I want that with all that's left of me.' A sea otter slipped past, belly up on the horizon-bound tide, bead eyes alert, blue mussels hugged against its chest. 'I only wish I could touch you, feel you again.'

'We're lightwaves now, Sunny. We can touch in different, more significant ways. I'll show you. But first—' She stepped sideward into a fountain-spray of droplet rainbows, her inky hair splashing around her. 'First we have to get you out of the stream of yet-to-be.'

Rafe followed. As if walking through crashing falls, vision shattered into spectral shards and blurry sheets. A moment later, he stood on a balmy night shore before a fluid swirl of starfire pinwheeling into a musical, sunbright distance. The thunder had disappeared and in its stead silence enclosed his weariness. A deep longing to return to the thundersong flow of leaves and animals pervaded him.

'Step away from the glare,' Karla advised. Her voice sounded louder in the still quiet.

A dark crush at the heart of him urged a quick return to the bright liquid cascade that whirled hypnotically in the dark, a carnivalesque tunnel that bored into a mountain of darkness.

'Don't go back,' warned Karla. 'It's the glare of the future. Step away from it. Look at me, Sunny.'

Rafe turned, wearier than ever. Karla, her lissome body edging backward, her smiling face streaked in wisps of dark, sultry hair, moved through frayed sunlight. Yet nowhere was the bloated sun he had seen earlier visible. A few hard stars pocked the darkness. Otherwise, they moved into an abstract night, plangently warm and scented with the faint perfume of rain.

'This is the tesseract range,' said Karla, beckoning him into the bituminous distance. 'We're just lightwaves expanding through space-time.'

Rafe tossed back a look at the luminous vortex, already a distant crystal, a whorl of fog, a bright petal falling into the bottom of darkness.

'You can always return there, Sunny. Everything that dies funnels through that slipstream and disappears into the future.'

'Transmigrating through space-time?' Rafe asked. 'Reincarnating?'

'Or sliding into our universes, parallel worlds. I don't know.'

Karla waited for him to catch up, her long, slender body woven in summerlight. 'But those that go far enough never return. They disappear into the convergence of worldlines. That's what generates the luminosity at the far horizon – all those intersecting light cones.'

'Where are we going?'

Karla faced away into the void. 'Where only people can go. The animals, the plants, they all flow onward into the glare. They have no will to defy their fate.'

Rafe remembered talking with the dead and hearing of their wanderings in the shadow world of the afterlife. He had believed then that those were all mental projections that flimmered upon the void. Staring into the velvet blackness with its vague gloss of stars, he knew now he was right. 'There's nothing out here, Karla. Where are we going?'

'The other way.' Her words fractured with laughter. 'Everything in the tesseract range flows toward the future. We're going the other way – deeper into today.'

He peered harder into the murky spellbound emptiness. 'But I don't see anything.'

'Because we're still in the glare of the future.' She opened her arms wide, her nakedness all light against the steep vacuum. 'That's why it's so warm here and smells so lovely. It's why the animals never go back from the range. You'll see, it takes strength to go where we're going, Sunny.'

'Karla—' The oppressive darkness rhymed with the evil of his memory.

'I see what you're thinking, Sunny.' Her features bent sadly. 'Don't think about that.'

'You see?'

'Of course, Sunny.' She moved closer to him, and the graphite space between them brightened. 'We're light. We're touching all the time. I see everything in you. You're dwelling on the gauge field bomb – on your failure to stop it. But you can't stop it now. The pain has died and turned into light.'

'I don't see into you . . .' He gazed with dumb avidity, and her image smudged like stardust.

'Relax.' In the void, her pallor seemed painted with rice powder. 'You're still groggy from your long sleep. It takes a while to wake up.'

She stepped into him. Their bodies merged. Like diamonds flaring light in seizures of color and shifting hues, the darkness relented. They stood together in a shared spotlight of solitude. He possessed her every thought, every shade of feeling, as though these were his own.

A long time she had waited for him out here on the dark ranges. The others had left her. The new breed, each one, had followed the perfume of rain back to the river of light that swept them laughing into the glare of the future. Sunny, too, had gone, the lover who had promised to stay at her side and wait until his clone returned to them. But he could not wait. The astonishing departure of the dead was too enticing. He had lingered as long as he could . . .

Rafe stepped away from Karla, propelled by the deep and moving understanding of her love for him. She had defied crushing fatigue and the allure of eternal change to await his arrival in the afterlife. Everything anxious and bitter had fallen away from her long ago, worn out by weariness. Finally, just the caring remained, the abiding surprise of love that had seized her only after her body had let her go. She had to wait for him. She had to know that her errand – the task to carry the key – had not broken him. She had loved him from the first because he was the runt, the floor, the weakest of them all and so the strongest in his yearning. How much she had loved him, death alone revealed that to her. And so she had waited.

'I understand—' Rafe muttered. His failure to save the universe, that was nothing to her. The glare of the future dissolved the universe in light. The light fanned beyond this universe into an infinity of other universes . . . 'Shall we go there now, together?'

She shook her head, her loose hair slashing her face with the conviction of her denial. 'You're not ready yet. Your failure is too heavy to carry that far. You'll fall asleep again.'

He knew she was right. The memory of Tabor Roy shooting the Machine and then killing him made him feel as though a burning animal were stitched inside him. 'What are we going to do?'

'I told you.' She passed the breezy glitter of her hand across his face. 'We're going deeper into today.'

'But I can't change the past.' The shards of his failure cut deeper at this admission. 'My failure will remain as painful – always.'

'Maybe you're right.' She tossed her long hair back with an abrupt turn of her head and began walking away. 'I don't know what happens in the glare – but here we can be together. At least for a while.' Her pale arms reached for him as she retreated. 'Come on, Sunny. Let's go visit those worlds that we set afire.'

Night steamed. Mists rose out of the dark and unfurled into vapors lit by starlight. The fumes gathered into fog and rolled into slow fields. The dead walked there.

Naked, human shadows moved as in the silence of snow. But the air pressed warmly, and very distantly one could hear the future resounding like heavy chimes – a sonorous music, very dim, barely audible. Some figures waded through the crawling fog in that direction, seeking the glare of the future, from where Karla Sobieski had led Rafe von Takawa. But most milled about among the seething cloudpaths or wandered away into the pathless dark.

Out of the mother-of-pearl night a dust devil gathered particle by particle, a thin vortex of scintillant grains. It tilted through the reefs of fog toward Karla and Rafe.

'It is I – the Machine!' It stopped before them and began to unwind like cigarette smoke. 'I cannot linger long. I must get back to my body.'

'Body?' Karla looked to Rafe. 'The MIKEs? They glared away long ago.'

'The Machine made herself a beautiful body,' Rafe recalled. He pressed closer to Karla, and she received from him the image of the large golden woman with tawny skin and flint gray eyes. 'We were briefly lovers.'

'I left my body asleep in the stream of yet-to-be. If I woke inside her, I would have no will for this tenuous existence. A greater life awaits me. But I had to speak with you first, Rafe, before I go. I had to ask you . . .'

The Machine's voice diminished as its smoke thinned away. Slowly, its particles regathered, whirling to a dustspout that drifted off, toward the deep chimes of the future.

Rafe moved after the Machine, reached out and touched the swirling grains. An electric jolt stiffened through him, and he became a tree emitting blue blossoms like sparks. The wind of time past tore the flowers from his boughs, and the fragmentary petals swirled down lanes of memory: all the Machine's 10^{68} lines of computation from its lifetime of analogic calculations exploded in a turmoil of unthought-of memories.

The Machine had too many hearts. All the conflicting human cultures that its memetic programming had reconciled were still listening. Their attentiveness was an intensive as perfect servants. Unspoken rages writhed inside cages of harmonious solutions. Starved anger pulsed.

Rafe edged away, stunned by the many destinies that the Machine had contained and brought to accord in its lifetime. 'Go to your body, M.'

The conflict of flesh and dream had been the Machine's fatal effort, and as it bleared away it wondered, 'Was it magic, Rafe?' The coils of its turning became the wind itself and scattered its grains into the shining darkness. 'Tabor Roy says that our journey among the worlds *was a magic you were working. Our lovemaking was its last hermetic act. Is that true?'*

'Magic?' Rafe experienced a chill at that thought. 'No, M. I was never a magician. Just the opposite. I wanted to undo the spell that Karla and I had cast on the world. I wanted to be human again. Truly human. You know that. You lived with me. You were my lover.'

A thin voice emerged from the last wisps of the Machine's light. *'That's what killed us.'*

'We died as a man and a woman,' Rafe said to the emptiness where the Machine had been. 'That was our magic. We were learning to be human.'

'It's gone.' Karla stood beside him and stared into the darkness of his eyes. 'The difficulties that balked its joys are finished.'

Rafe looked about among the fog fields for others that he knew. 'M'twele?'

'Gone long ago.' Karla slogged with him away from the dim chimeful horizon and toward the darker ranges. 'But there is one who has been waiting for you. You know who it is already, don't you?'

'Nandi,' he answered with a coldness in the place of his heart.

At the sound of her name, she appeared. Narrow as a cat, she slouched out of the fog veils, eyes orbs of shining darkness. Her severe, bonesharp nakedness carried long shadows along her ribs and between the blades of her pelvis bones.

'Our work is accomplished,' she announced with a victorious grin. 'You brought fire into the world – but then you faltered and tried to stop me from carrying that fire to the stars. You gave yourself to illusion, but illusion can never defeat truth.'

'Get away from me, Nandi.' Anger seeped from the broken place of his heart.

'Not until you come with me, Rafe.' Her eyes flickered like candlelight under the film of tears wept for joy and fierce passion. 'I will not leave you here among the illusions of form. I brought you into this world. I gave you to appearances. Now I am taking you away. Come with me, away from here, into the divine fire where all forms are consumed, into the freedom of formlessness.'

Rafe answered with bitter silence.

'Leave him be, Nandi.' Karla intruded herself between mother and son.

'No. I will not leave him.' Her voice sizzled like a burning fuse. 'Out here there is no end to the unraveling of forms. Endless unraveling. I am taking him with me.'

'I will not go.' He backed away from her.

'And neither will I let you go.' She stepped through Karla. As they intersected, an electrical crackle lashed very loud, then silence rushed back hard.

Both Karla and Nandi reeled, their images fainter, gray as the desultory sunlight of a wintry noon.

'Carry me . . .' Karla whispered weakly.

Rafe did not know how to hold her with his ghost arms, but he tried. At his touch, she grew brighter, and the diamond flaring light that had fused them once joined them again.

He turned and ran through the low, rolling fog. Karla flew with him, and Nandi vanished. But the essence of her that Karla had experienced when they merged still tainted her. Rafe felt Nandi's tenderness for him, the fervent certainty that flesh was madness, life a fevered dream, and the mystery of the world emptiness. She loved him with this conviction, the one child she had shaped into form with her body, fed with her blood and milk, protected in his fragile infancy, because he was the avatar. Shiva, the Destroyer, had grown in her womb into his form – and he had indeed brought destruction into the world. He had fulfilled Nandi's promise to her god. And now she owed him her devotion. She would never leave the tesseract range without him.

'She will find us again,' Rafe declared with certainty.

'Yes – but not for a while.' Karla slid away from him and took with her the stain of Nandi. 'She loves you to madness. The detonation of the gauge field bomb is the fulfillment of her prayers.'

'We were wrong to give metasapience to the world, Karla.' With a haunted expression, he faced the woman he loved. 'We have destroyed the universe!'

She jutted her lower lip in a gesture of small pity. 'There are others.'

'But these worlds – these galaxies of worlds!' he snapped. 'This particular universe is unique. What we did was wrong, Karla.'

'That's a sentimental spasm, Sunny.' She said this gently. 'We walked the road of great dreams. To have done less would have been a greater crime.'

His mouth opened around a silent laugh. 'You're the same, Karla. You haven't changed. I'm sure that if you had lived, you would have been an imploder yourself.'

'I'm sure of it, too.' She met his hurt look calmly. 'Where do you think great dreams lead, Sunny? We came into the world to change it. And we did. We found a way to use it as a vehicle to a greater world, to the original world – the compact dimensions where we started, where we belong. And we're all going back together. Most will simply be going back the same way they came out: they'll be energy once again.'

'You're so assured, so confident of yourself, Karla.' He conceded with a shrug. 'You're exactly the same.'

'Of course. The dead don't change.' She glanced about at the silhouettes of the other gray figures shuffling through the gloom. 'Come on. We have to keep moving or Nandi will find us more quickly.'

'"In this world even butterflies must earn their keep,"' he recited as they walked through the loamy mists.

'Issa,' she recognized from their early childhood studies, when the yawps read them poetry.

'My favorite of the haiku poets,' he replied, looking furtively among the branching vapors for the skeletal shadow of his mother. 'He survived all four of his children and lived to write about his heartbreak. He envied Basho's zen detachment but never attained it. He was never detached. He remained soft and sentimental his whole life.'

She laughed brightly. 'He's the ideal poet for you, Sunny. My favorite of his goes, "Where there are humans you'll find flies – and Buddhas."'

Her laugh was harsher this time. 'I suppose we are flies – all of us lingering phantoms.'

'Buddhas would have gone ahead into the unknown with the plants and animals,' Rafe agreed.

'But we're preoccupied with unfinished business – like flies.' She pointed ahead to a vague brightening almost obscured by the glow of her pale arm. 'Space-time lies in that direction.'

The fog thinned to mist and the air grew colder as they marched toward the moon-silver horizon. No other ghosts accompanied them. They moved alone over rocky terrain that looked ever more like the desert on Mars as the yellow and green acids of dawn burned away the darkness.

'The dead spoke to me when I was alive,' Rafe said, staring perplexedly at the bronze mountains and the zinc plains. 'They told me about the breathing fields beside the listening waters. And the animals in the music, roaming among the flowers on the sleeping hills. All this was near the tree of darkness. Where is all that?'

'Within the stream of yet-to-be.' Karla walked ahead of him past rocks that seemed to float like spores over the wraths of lava. 'The tree of darkness is on its bank. We passed through there to reach the foglands, beyond which is space-time where we are now.'

Rafe waved his hands before him, surprised to see the translucency of the desert, stone ridges hanging in the air like still vapors. 'The dead spoke of the music of silence in the glare.'

'In the stream of yet-to-be there is rapture.' Karla walked through a boulder. 'Out here it is cold. But we've come to Mars to avoid Nandi. It will be more difficult for her to harry us at the cold limit of the tesseract range.'

The air felt frozen yet utterly clear. The cold pierced them, and it seemed to Rafe as if he were walking naked in winter. 'I'm freezing.'

'It gets worse.' Karla led him among tall rocks that appeared made of mist he could shatter with his voice.

He swept his arm toward a stone wall, and it passed cleanly but coldly through it. 'Where are we going?'

Karla pointed at plateaus that stood in iced fog above the craterland. 'Beyond those mesas is Solis, an aboriginal community.'

'Why are we going there?' Rafe tried rubbing himself, but it did no good.

'We're ghosts, silly.' She threw an impatient, sidelong look at him. 'We can go wherever we want.'

'Well, why do we want to go there? I'm cold.'

'Bear with it.' She shook her head restively, as if at a child, and added with a thin smile, 'It won't kill you.'

'I'd like a reason to put up with it.'

'How about that for a reason?' She jerked her thumb over her shoulder at the sight of Nandi and three of her bald thuggees stepping through a weightless boulder.

Rafe darted past Karla, fleeing toward the chewed horizon. But she remained still.

'We can't run from them when they're this close,' she advised. 'Now it's time to test your zen.'

'What?'

She frowned fretfully. 'Zazen. Sit zen. You know what I mean, Sunny.'

The thuggees advanced belligerently, their muscular nakedness thriving with power.

'They're just phantoms like us,' Karla explained. 'Sit and let them exhaust their energy on you.' She sat among the motionless wisps of stones, her cool, marine eyes imperturbable. 'But if you let them hook you, they'll carry you away the way you carried me before.'

The first of the thuggees fell upon Rafe, and the impact of hatred that struck him toppled them among the red rocks. An invisible elephant of rage, blowing fiery notes of ire, lifted Rafe and the thuggee above the floor of the desert and charged away, carrying them both toward the ghostly mountains.

The other thuggees descended on Karla, and her eyes stared through them unblinking as blue algae. They thrashed into her, filling her with their palpable light, which was their anger at her for luring the avatar of Shiva back into the world of illusion. They assaulted her with all their righteous fury, for she was Maya, the Ensnarer, embodiment of form, mistress of deception.

She endured their vehement assault with a rapt calm. Her lengthy tenure in the afterlife had inured her to the madness of other ghosts. Soon, the thuggees had dwindled to tremulous mothwings that fluttered squeaking into the sky.

Nandi did not notice this. Her full attention was upon Rafe, whom the wrathful, unseen elephant had carried over the desert floor. The swiftness of the attack had disarmed Rafe, and the fearful certainty that he was lost, gripped in the fierce will of the thuggee, blurred his concentration. He swung a desperate look back at Karla and saw instead Nandi running after him, laughing maniacally.

Zazen! he reminded himself. But fear had hollowed him out and anger filled him – anger at himself for letting the Machine seduce him at the critical moment, for allowing Tabor Roy to find him with his pants down and to slay him so ignobly. Shame ignited from the heat of this tantrum. He had failed not only himself but all the manifold worlds of creation, all future time. His weakness had doomed countless sentient beings.

The air grew warmer, and the foglands gloomed ahead with a resinous, welcome scent of cedar. Megalithic highlands of rock arches and anvil craters hardened toward darkness. Overhead, the pink sky dimmed scarlet. Phobos floated by, a salty cloud. Rafe fixed his attention upon it. He filled his awareness with its oval shape, its rockhard actuality.

The invisible elephant trumpeted loudly with heart-splintering passion – and vanished. Thunder climbed the brightening sky. Rafe lay quietly on his back in the swaddling cold, an icy Buddha, detached from all emotion, alert only to the immediacy of experience.

Karla stood over him. 'Your zen works just fine, Sunny.' She beckoned him to rise. 'Let's go visit Solis.'

Rafe stood and saw Nandi watching from among the low dunes, a lurid scowl on her narrow face. He moved toward her, his mind empty of everything but the cold and the brown landscape.

'Not yet,' Karla warned. 'She has been preparing for this encounter since you were born.'

'I'm not afraid.' Rafe continued toward the wraith in the slant sunlight. 'I've been preparing since before I was born.'

Karla stepped in front of him. 'Don't get cocky.' She held him with a serious, tight stare until he relented. 'Count clouds. And let's go. She won't follow us for long out here in the cold. She'll wait until your mind is distracted and you least expect her.'

Rafe walked beside Karla, and they moved passed Nandi. The thin clouds of the Martian sky ran like threads to where the sun hung its lantern. They slid into a maze of craterwalls, and when he gazed back through the amber layers, Nandi was gone.

Space rippled like heat, though it was cold that quivered through them, and distance dissolved in a mirage. Solis swung into view on the dunelands. Scalloped sand that drifted up against the airphase storm barriers defined the perimeter. Within those invisible walls, geodesic spheres and stupas crowded. Solar mills twinkled, their vanes turning lazily, running power to ranks of hydroponic hothouses.

This settlement had been a clutter of tinsel tents the last time Rafe had passed through. 'How long has it been since I died?'

'Decades, Sunny. Time moves differently on the tesseract range.'

They drifted like smoke over the crazed stone floor of the plateland they were leaving behind and moved swiftly onto the sandy verge of the dunes. 'How long before the gauge field bomb implosion?'

'More time than you've been dead.' Their transit left no tracks in the ribbed sand. 'You slept nearly a terrene century in the stream of yet-to-be.'

The airphase storm barriers did not impede their entrance to Solis. They mingled with the living. The bustling community of forty-seven thousand aboriginals carried on with their business of survival on the frozen wastes of Mars heedless of the phantoms in their midst.

Swathed in solar cowls, the citizens moved briskly in the light gravity and cold air. They conveyed vegetables and protein briskets in sleek, neon-enameled pedal carts, speeding them to colorful mead tents. Dented push-bins hauled away compost to the garden sheds. Bakers stacked loaves in tricycle baskets for delivery, heat smoking from brick igloos where rotating crews kept the thermal-bore ovens blazing day and night. And in the village center, children frolicked in several vast canopy parks, where trees and shrubberies flourished on swarded knolls.

'Are these truly aboriginals?' Rafe asked trepidatiously.

'They're genuine human beings, not anthrofacts.' Karla stood among soft, purple mallows and bees flitted through her, choosing flowers. 'These people live here free of Maat intervention.'

The bees spun dizzily in the balmy air, and yet it felt frigid to the ghosts. They circulated around a canopy park, invisibly accompanying children who gamboled across the grassy terrain of the warm, oxygenated park. 'There are no geriatrics?' Rafe asked.

'Not anymore. The Essentia have finally accepted senescence technology. But there are death cults.' Karla floated out of the park and onto a fused gravel road. A pedal-cart stacked with textiles slashed through her. 'There are people who want to die – who want to ride the stream of yet-to-be into the future glare.'

'Why?'

'A version of Nandi's cult, I suppose.' She led the way through the skins of sunlight that hung between the narrow residences around the park. These pastel-tinted houses, roofed in dark, absorbent energy panels, all fronted the street with large bell-windows displaying florid vines and ferns. 'The cultists come to Mars to die, believing that their waveforms will carry their consciousness more clearly across the tesseract range. Every year, the Anthropos Essentia host thousands of passagers – that's what they're called, people seeking passage to the afterlife. We'll meet some eventually, and you can hear their praise of death for yourself.'

The cold had so saturated Rafe's body, he felt burnished as the wind. 'Is there war?'

'With cogs?' Karla stepped up the curb and into the air. She strode up a slant of sunlight. 'No, there's no war. In the time you've been asleep, most of the machine intelligences have been destroyed. The silicon mind still works with the cartels in the belt and the system moons. The Maat need it to keep production high among the space factories that are building the cosmic string resonator beyond the orbit of Neptune. But there are no anthrofacts on Mars now or among any of the inner planet colonies.'

Rafe climbed into the sky after Karla. They walked over strands of cloud. Looking back, he saw Solis brilliant and symmetric as a Tibetan sand painting on the ochre field of Mars. 'Can we go to where it's warm now?'

Karla's laughter chirped. 'There's Nebraska Trace.' She motioned downward to a thin virid scar in the rusty terrain. 'It's the Essentia's futile attempt at terraforming. They've strung some biotectured plants along their main route across the desert.'

'What does the name signify?'

'Nebraska – a terrene state in the middle of North America from before the anarchy. Most of the original plantforms are from there – sage, foxtail, gayfeather, purple clover, cordgrass. But the name actually emerges from the Essentia's abiding nostalgia for all things of the twentieth century, from the era before morfs, cogs, and the Maat – when all humans were aboriginals.'

'Ellen Vancet would remember that era.' His sight trawled across the desert floor, watching noon fill the pockets of the valleys, craters, and gorges with sunlight and wished that such heat would touch him. 'Is she still alive?'

'I don't know.' Karla strode among thin, tabular clouds, flat as altars of wind. 'We could go to Earth and find out – if she interests you enough.'

'If you haven't seen her in the afterlife, she must be alive.'

Karla cast a hapless look at him. 'I don't patrol the afterlife, Sunny.' Her pale body vanished among the slurred clouds, and her black hair flowed like a shadow. 'Why do you care about Vancet?'

'We shared a destiny.' The ancient traces of rivers scored the rocky terrain in bronchial flow patterns. 'I wonder what happened to her after I died.'

Karla descended through the slipstream of clouds toward three massive cindercones – Tharsis Montes. The volcanoes squatted on the landscape like three giantesses in their sprawling skirts of hardened lava. Beyond them, rising twenty-seven kilometers above the horizon, was their master, Olympus Mons. On its terraced slopes, minarets, solar vanes, and domes spanned the six hundred kilometers of the shield volcano's base. The vast city was incomplete. Only sections of street grids possessed clustered buildings. For many kilometers up and down and around the tiered slopes, the arterial boulevards crossed empty tracts. This was a growing city, and the sight of it surprised Rafe. When he had last traveled here, only a few geodesic bunkers speckled the upper slopes.

'Terra Tharsis is expanding rapidly now that the implosion is imminent,' Karla told him. 'This is the new Maat capital from where they are supervising the gathering of materials for the construction of the cosmic string resonator.'

As they descended, the clustered craters at the summit came into view. Glittering black and lavender glass towers spired above these basins, an immense crystal city. Ribbon causeways and curved bridges spanned the canyon depths among tall, faceted lozenges that housed millions in their sparkling heights. Flyers and cruisers drifted aglint in the fans of piped sunlight at the peaks of these colossal structures.

'Are we going in?' Rafe asked with surprise. He had lived for some years in one of these towers, in a suite biodesigned by its conservative owner to resemble the Black Forest on Earth, and he recalled how furtive he had to be each time he left the building to wander the city. If the imploders had found him, he would have died then.

'I thought you'd like to see what they're up to – now that the imploders and conservatives are not rivals anymore.' She moved decisively toward a central onyx obelisk, the most narrow of the many spires. 'I've been here before a few times. This is the command center.'

Rafe looked below through the teetering levels of spanways to the distant floor of the basin. Green flashes of parks and arboretums reminded him of his favorite tree haunts in this city. Thus far, only the deepest crater had been filled with glass towers, and the large intersecting craters surrounding it waited to be developed. Forests flourished there, holding the loose soil in place until the city's developers were ready to expand.

They walked through the onyx walls of the obelisk and found themselves in a cactus chamber of piped sunlight. Thornless, flowering cacti of every geometry defined the curved walls, portals, and the furniture. Magravity provided terrene acceleration, and the Maat who dwelled here moved about as on Earth. Holostreams occupied the cores of most of the work cells, where Maat concentrated on the real-time monitoring of numerous construction projects.

Rafe and Karla recognized many of the problems that confronted the Maat in the building of their monumental resonator. The scalar variables that bridged the ultra-tiny realm of cosmic strings and the parsec-wide amplitude of the implosion waves required a precision and flexibility in the array that could not be approximated. Each component had to be virtually handcrafted to match the precise texture of space-time within the arc of the solar trajectory where the resonator would receive and focus the implosion. One error, one misfit, in the physical design, and all the waveforms of the Maat who intended to go to heaven would smear away into the energy flux of the contracting universe.

Strolling through the walls from the cacti work cells to the fern holt recreation parlors and wavecurl waterplay arenas, the ghosts sensed the solidarity of the Maat. Rafe recognized conservatives he had known laughing with imploders in the steam baths and laboring calmly together in simulation galleries where scale-models of the array hovered among holostreams of transNeptunian space.

'I'm cold,' Rafe complained. They exited the obelisk and stood on a span where Maat walked through them, crossing between towers. 'Can we go back now where it's warm.'

Karla smiled without moving her lips. 'This is the air we died for.' She stood at the span's balustrade and gazed off between the crystal edifices at the soft shafts of citrus light illuminating the criss-crossed levels of the city. 'Would we ever have imagined this at CIRCLE?'

'Sure – and more. Whatever happened to transluminal transport?' He looked straight up and saw Phobos floating between the towers. He tried to breathe warmth from that pale oval by lifting his attention away from his cold waveform. But the lung of the moon offered no comfort. 'I'm ready to face Nandi again. Let's go back to the tesseract range.'

'There'll be time enough for Nandi.' Karla stepped off the span and walked through the air, across the long shadows of the buildings toward a well of sunlight. 'Don't you miss the smell of rain?'

He looked to where she was looking, through a narrow clearing between the towers, across the forested caldera of the volcano to where blue clouds leaned over the crater rim their evanescent showers. An idea struck Rafe with the force of insight. 'You don't want to go back to the afterlife.'

She turned, standing in empty sunlight, her body pure marble, her nipples pink acorns, and her eyes celestial sapphire staring plaintively through the black veil of her hair. 'I've been dead too long.'

'You take the cold just to be close to the living world.' He drifted near to her. 'It's a criminal joy being here where you don't belong. You can't stay. Eventually, the cold becomes unbearable and you have to go back.'

'I'm Kore.' A lax smile arrived and faded quickly. 'You know, from Greek myth – the maiden Hades stole to the underworld. She can only come back to the world of the living for a brief time before she has to return to the dead.'

Anger at Tabor's murderous act that had made him a phantom and frustration at the piercing cold toiled in Rafe. He looked up at the ash of the little moon until the pain quieted. 'We died years ago. We're ghosts haunting the future. Let's go back to where we belong.'

'Not yet.' She spun away and floated toward where the green voice of the forest called. 'Go back if you want. I'll join you soon.'

'How?' Rafe called. 'How do I go back?'

'Follow the warm.'

He returned his stare to the silver feather of Phobos and felt for warmth. A lamentation of cold enclosed him. Yet if he concentrated he sensed slightly less cold to one side. He moved that way, striding across the air and through the wall of a sapphire tower. In a suite of cobalt blue glass among potted trees with leaves that looked like red flags, a couple lay together in a hammock. He followed the hint of warmth through another wall, down a corridor of hydrangea bushes and white butterflies, under a trellis into a green bathroom where a woman stood in a sonic stall cleansing herself with acoustic waves. He walked up the stall, into the ceiling, and emerged among jocular children sprinting and leaping in the scattered scintillance of a holostream gym.

Beyond the far wall, he stood in a dark shaft, a service duct where slender warmth carried the vagrant scent of a meadow in wild winter. If he stepped deeper into the darkness he knew he would find the foglands at the perimeter of the afterlife. But he hestitated. What Karla had said worked on him. She *was* Kore – married to death itself, yet a maiden still enamored of life. She was as close to being alive as he could be again, she who was happiest out here in the cold where the living continued casually with their mortal tasks.

Rafe moved away from the warmth. He returned to the cold. Tabor had slain him, this was painfully true. But Karla, the first woman he had loved, had woken him from the sleep of the dead. He decided then that he would never leave her side again, for she was all that remained of his faithfulness to life.

He glided through a work cell hung with tendrilled blossoms where Maat manipulated holoform models like the archons of gnostic legend inventing matter. Out the glass exterior of the skyscraper, he braced himself against the sharpening cold and sought Karla.

She stood in the swift traffic of a ribbon causeway, sleek, silent cars with candy colors blurring through her. At her side, he relaxed, knowing his ghost was in its right place though the cold bit deep.

'So many lives,' she said to him as though he had never stepped away from her. 'There are over twelve million people in Terra Tharsis.'

'I saw children in the towers, playing in a gym.' The sun's long rays fanned from the horizon, and the burning house of Venus glared among the mountains. 'When I lived here many years ago all Maat were recruited as adults from the reservations or grown in vats.'

'It's become fashionable to live as human beings again.' She crossed through the jellied light along a midair course toward the outer craters and the dense forest. 'Most of the residents here have lives similar to scientific engineers seven hundred years ago. They commute to their work cells, spend days designing their intricate little pieces of the array, and return in the evening to their offspring. Everyone is building their way to heaven.'

The rain they had glimpsed earlier had hung diamonds in the tree branches of the forest. 'Let's go to the subquantal labs and see what they're doing among the cellular automata on the Planck fields.'

'Can't.' She watched the sun melt over the crater wall. 'Anything to do with the compact dimensions and the development of the gauge field bomb is heavily guarded. There are waveform receptors everywhere near there. If we try to put our minds into those restricted areas, we would be plucked out of the air and transmitted back to the tesseract range.'

'When will the bomb be completed?'

The faded velour of twilight glinted with seed pearls, the first stars. 'I'm not sure. But just walking around here, watching, listening, I would figure there's another century of work to do before they finish the bomb and can generate a rotating wormhole that can tunnel back in time to Isidis Planitia.' She squinted at him. 'You're not thinking you can interfere?'

'Not as a ghost,' he lamented. 'Besides, the bomb has already gone off.'

'In this universe.' Darkness clotted among the trees. 'But there are parallel possibilities, Sunny.'

'Not for ghosts.'

'No, not for ghosts,' she concurred coolly. The silver spur of Deimos appeared among the scattered stars. 'It is our lot simply to observe – for as long as we remain phantoms.'

Rafe edged closer to Karla, hoping to dim his painful awareness of the cold in the presence of her thoughts. But she was quiet. Her dark hair stirred from her shivering. Touching her, he experienced her silence filled with the crepuscular world around them.

Twilight still smoldered far off in the mountains; then, darkness closed down the horizon. The night forest glimmered with the green shadows of bioluminescent moss. Dead leaves rattled in the nocturnal breeze. An owl called from far away.

Five hundred years as a ghost had emptied her of herself. Her purpose in enduring the cold had been to wait for him, and now that he had died and she had retrieved him from the flow of yet-to-be, she was replete.

She had merged with time and the world. The mournful cries of night birds approached and passed on.

Karla's tranquil emptiness made Rafe realize how dense he remained with longing for his lost life. He could not accept that he had failed, and his mind circled endlessly around the cruelly relentless facts of his demise. How had Tabor Roy found him and the Machine so quickly on that fateful day? There had been no sign of any other searchers in the area when they first glided in. That suggested to him that Tabor had somehow traced him.

'Your thoughts are loud, Sunny.' She stepped away from him, and her pallor glowed in the dark. 'Haven't you figured it out yet? The imploders did not trace you. They couldn't. You and the Machine had taken every precaution against being tagged.'

'Ellen . . .'

'They tagged her during her long exile on Titan.' Karla shone with soft ectoplasmic luminance. 'When you went back for her, you sealed your doom.'

'But how?' Rafe paced through a tree, rummaging among his memories for his error. 'The Machine scanned her thoroughly. She carried no tags. None whatsoever!'

Karla's dark brows lifted sadly. 'Her body was a tag.'

'That's not possible,' Rafe snarled. 'There would be some signal radiance. How else could she be tracked?'

'There was no radiance, Sunny.' Her voice rang dolorously. 'The imploders mapped her body against the cellular automata that compose her atoms. As she moved through space-time, the pattern of cellular automata changed – and they tracked her.'

'Cellular automata?' Rafe's face appeared disfigured with incredulity. 'Karla, do you realize what you're saying? Mapping at that level would require an unthinkable amount of energy.'

'Unthinkable for you, obviously.' She chided him with a cocked eyebrow. 'It was not unthinkable for the imploders. The fate of the universe was at stake.'

Rafe gazed at her through a hurt and bewildered mask. 'Where did the imploders get the power?'

'Everything Tabor Roy had he gave.' She shook her head ruefully. 'Did you not wonder why the cog colonies that the Machine destroyed were not rebuilt? The energy for those projects and for many others were diverted to mapping Ellen Vancet at the subquantal extreme.'

'And if I had not gone back for her?'

She stared hard at him, with a passionate clarity. 'The imploders would never have found the gauge field bomb. You would have succeeded, and the universe would remain unmolested for all time. Is that what you want to hear?'

Fiery rage blazed in Rafe. He screamed. Fury at himself whirled him about, fury for a sentimental blunder that had killed him and the universe. He reeled through a tantrum dance, arms whirling, legs kicking, face contorted.

'Calm down!' Karla called to him.

But he could no longer focus on her. 'I won't calm down!' he blurted, lunging through trees, trying to outrun his agonizing remorse.

Abruptly, from a corridor of night, black shadows hurtled and collided with him. Rafe flew through a blur of trees, propelled by the iron grasp of enclosing darkness. Nandi's skeletal shape loomed ahead, arms open, drawing the shadows toward her.

Rafe's anger molted to fear. He flew directly toward Nandi.

Time burst.

Night flapped away. Daybreak seared the horizon, and the sun arced hotly across the sky.

In the sudden brilliance, Rafe hung motionless in the locked embrace of four burly figures. The four MIKEs shuddered with the cold of space-time, yet their suffering only tightened their grip on him.

'I will not let you go this time, my dear one.' Nandi filled his sight transparently. Through her skullwide grin, bold clavicles, flat dugs, and ribs that could rattle a stick, he saw night's wings close across the sky. Phobos tracked a frosty path among the turning stars. Time flowed swiftly.

'Karla!'

'She can't help you, Rafe.' Nandi's transparency brightened again to sunfire shafts oaring between the trees of the forest, rowing from morning to bluesmoked dusk in moments. 'We are flying through time, not space. She will not have you, for you belong to me.'

'Nandi – let me go!'

Night veiled the forest. Nandi's hollow face, stenciled with shadow, pressed very close. 'I am letting you go, my dearest one. I am letting you go into the formless, beyond time and space, beyond illusion.'

Daybreak did not follow. Instead, mists flowed swiftly from the seam of the horizon. The foglands widened, and the stars dimmed.

'I am not done with this life!' Rafe protested, struggling vainly to free himself from the hold of the MIKEs. 'I am not done!'

'Oh, you were done long ago, my love. Long ago.' Nandi pushed her ethereal face against his, and her words resonated as his own thoughts:

You've been dead a hundred years. Your body is bonedust in the sands of Mars. It is time you gave your ghost to the void.

Rafe stood in a wide window of brilliant light and saw Nandi beside him, tall, swarthy, and emaciated, her large eyes luminous with hunger. This was the balcony window of the pinkstone hotel in Poona where he had first given her the key to the monkey tower. The crooked streets lay below, among cluttered buildings with their wisps of cooking smoke that rose to the stately turrets and white domes of Shaniwarwada palace.

'We began here,' Nandi said to him, no longer naked but wrapped in a blue sari. 'We shall end here together. All is illusion.'

'No.' Rafe struggled to snap awake from this dream. 'You are the illusion.'

The scene rippled, and the streets unfolded into other streets, and they were fleeing from the hotel, running away from the microbot spies that stalked them, marking them for the flame of a pyroclass disposer.

'Do you remember how you saved me, Rafe?' Nandi clasped his hand affectionately. 'You chose me from among the millions. You saved me so that I could save you. Do you remember how you put yourself inside me?'

The slant roofs of the crowded city flipped and fluttered into leaves. They strolled together toward a massive, spreading banyan. The scarlet robes of twilight furled through the sky. In the drenched darkness of an untended garden, they lay down together.

Nightingales sang as Rafe and Nandi undressed each other for the solemn act that would engender a new world. Glittering reefs of stars poured out their ancient light, washing their nakedness in time. They coupled with grim tenderness.

'The man who put you inside me is gone, my dearest one.' Nandi whispered close to him in an absolute void empty of all light. 'He was burned to ash on the Western Ghats. You are the child I grew in my womb.'

'Mother . . .'

'Ah, little one, you have found your way back to me – and I will never let you go again.'

Thunder walked the night. A heartbeat. Uteral warmth replaced the slashing cold of space-time. This was a dream, he reminded himself. He was again on the foglands, in the heat of the expanding tesseract range. Nandi had captured him in his moment of rage. And she was carrying him again in her womb – a dream she had woven just for him, reminiscent of their shared past centuries ago when he was, in truth, an embryo snug in the coils of her blood, carried back into life – as she was now carrying his waveform beyond all form, into the glare of the future.

Rafe knew that Nandi had cast a powerful dream upon him. He sought to break it by detaching from his emotions and focusing serenely, as he had earlier on the Martian desert. But there was nothing to fix his attention to. The womb dark offered only neural light.

He rooted his attention on the dream. The heartbeat of his mother was a true illusion. He listened closely to it. It boomed and sucked like waves upon the coral. And the sound reminded him of his last encounter with Karla Sobieski at CIRCLE, on Daybreaks Cay.

The neural glow of the uteral dream rearranged to the palpitating shadows of mangrove trees under a dazzling starscape. Out of the coral shelves, black crabs scuttled. Seagrape crunched underfoot along the sandbanks, and the only other sound to reach him was the outbound current caroming on the reef.

'Karla!'

'Be still, dearest one,' Nandi's voice sifted from the trees. 'We are nearly arrived. Do not struggle. Soon we shall both be free.'

'Karla!'

'No!' Nandi shrieked.

The hallucination collapsed, and the reef island's surf glowing in the darkness became again the smoking fields of the foglands. Nandi, naked and shriveled to her bones, rose from the sticky vapors, where she had fallen. The MIKEs, too, lifted slowly from the fog, the eggshapes of their bald heads adrift among the seething mists. And Rafe realized that he was momentarily free.

'This way, Sunny!' Karla called to him from under the cool blue stars. 'Hurry!'

Somehow he had twisted free of Nandi's spell, and he did not linger to determine how. Moving urgently but with dream-slowness, he fled toward Karla.

'Do not go with her!' Nandi yelled from behind. 'Hers is the exile, not the freedom!'

Rafe did not look back. He grabbed at Karla, and she seized his hands. Together they splashed across the shallows of fog, running hard. Cold wafted from ahead, sharpening its knives. Without any hesitancy, they gave themselves to their flight, and soon the red sandstone bluffs of Mars rose from the mists.

Karla clutched at Rafe once the spiritous ground gave way to copper shale. Her hug filled him with all her wretched fear, anxiety not for herself but for him. 'I didn't wait for you all this time out here in the cold so that Nandi could drag you into oblivion.'

'I'm sorry,' he croaked through a sob of fright, looking back to see if they were being pursued. The riven walls of craters stood like windfashioned castles.

'You lost yourself to anger – and Nandi seized you.' Karla swung around and locked onto him with her Carpathian eyes. 'You're enraged that the imploders outwitted you.'

He did not blink. 'Yes.'

'Give that up, Sunny.' She nearly shouted, 'You're dead.'

'I can't give it up.' He pulled away from her. 'The whole universe hangs in the balance.'

'*This* universe is lost now.' She waved her arms at the red dust blowing across the broken land, at the bunched craters at the perimeter of the world, at the rind of Phobos. Then she pointed at him. 'And you're dead.'

He turned away and fit his anger into the sharp shadowfolds among the craters.

'Don't get emotional,' Karla berated him. 'Nandi will be all over us again if you do.'

'There's no escaping her,' Rafe despaired. 'Let her take me away.' .

'She will.' Karla's voice sounded softly at his back. 'Is her passion for the void greater than your love of this reality?'

'I don't care. It's cold.'

'Cold but real.' She stepped into view against the pink sky, lean and white as moonlight. 'You go into the warm foglands with Nandi, and you'll never see this real world again.'

'What does it matter?' His eyes throbbed with heartache, and he lifted his head higher and coolly regarded her beautiful body. 'We're ghosts. We can't change anything. We can't even touch anything.'

Her voice of muted anguish matched his hurt. 'We can touch each other. We can change each other.'

'And what will we change ourselves into?'

'I don't know,' she admitted with a smile. 'All of creation transmits ghost light into the void, and an entire landscape of what was real vibrates across the tesseract range. We can go there. We can walk through the phantom land of all that was.'

'But Nandi will be there, too,' Rafe said, '—with her MIKEs.'

'They're mindless,' Karla replied. 'In life they were soulless biots, extensions of the Machine. They can't abide the cold for long; so, they won't follow her into this world for more than a few moments. And she chooses those moments when your anger lets her get a hold on you.'

Rafe put a hand into her hair. He did not feel her tresses, but her quiet flowed into him. And into her moved his troubled thoughts.

He found a momentary peace, and his eyesight rested calmly among the great boulders and cloven rocks on their terracotta beds. The bright sand sifting across the wind and dripping into the dark grottoes in orange filaments carried beauty over the ferric land.

She saw deeper into loss. Sadness fractured her calm with the image of the galactic filaments and starsmoke drawn abruptly into a singularity smaller than an atom. What remained was true vacuum. Absolute void. Intangible. Inconceivable. True nothing.

Rafe's hand fell away, and they watched each other with derelict wonder. The knives of cold cut deeply.

'I feel your love for what is,' Rafe said. 'I want to help you to hold this forever.'

'And I feel your loss, Sunny. I want to give you the chance to redeem all you've lost.'

Rafe impatiently waved her to silence. 'But I think there is a way to help you, Karla. You said that if you were alive, you would have been an imploder. Then, we must approach the Maat. They can receive your waveform and shape a matrix for it so that when the implosion comes, you'll enter the compact dimensions with the others.'

Her oblique eyes thinned with merriment. 'You are the gentle and good soul I have always loved, Sunny. But your hope for me is unrealistic. The matrices that the Maat are developing work only for physical bodies, not diffuse waveforms such as us.'

'They can receive waveforms,' said Rafe assertively. 'Then they should be able to amplify them and even ground them in physical forms again.'

'Perhaps someday.' She motioned for him to walk with her across the desert floor. 'The Maat are putting all their attention and resources into building the gauge field bomb, the wormhole that will deliver it to the past, and the monolithic cosmic string resonator. They don't have the time or resources to provide passage for ghosts.'

'The bomb and wormhole projects will be completed in a century or so.' Excitement competed against the jangling cold in Rafe. 'By then, the array will be in full production. Among the Maat, someone will find a way to ground waveforms in physical bodies.'

'Maybe that will happen, Sunny.' Karla took his hand and felt his unhappiness looking for escape. 'Maybe the Maat will find a way for us to become human again. But until then—'

Through their joined hands, Rafe experienced her acceptance of the incomprehensible, and it soothed him enough to walk on with her over the alien ground, through the calamitous cold, toward a future beyond reckoning.

From under the spreading tree of darkness at the vaporous limits of the foglands, Nandi saw the Lady of Pain walking off hand-in-hand with the Avatar. Anguish inflamed Nandi. 'How does it feel to be the beautiful one?' she called out, though her voice could not be heard beyond the tesseract range. 'How does it feel to carry away happiness from its true source? Lady of Pain! Lady of Illusion!'

She spun away from the romantic image and trudged angrily over the murky terrain. The weight of distances slowed her. She wanted to fly back into the cold of space-time and confront Rafe with the madness of his escape into the deeper deceptions of a phantom's life. He was a ghost and should surrender his attachment to the worlds of the living. But she knew painfully well that he would not want to hear that. The Avatar had been seduced by the Lady of Pain, Maya, Mistress of Illusions.

From out of the ether mists, the MIKEs gathered to follow Nandi. She ignored them, these zombies she had trained to obey her. Only four remained of the ten she had retrieved from the stream of yet-to-be before their mindless waveforms could be absorbed into the glare of the future. After she ordered them to seize Rafe, they would not be good for anything else. The ether wind of space-time broke their obedience to her, and both times that Rafe had struggled free of their holds, they had fled beyond her strident commands into the glare. She would have to use the four that remained wisely.

Across the walking fog and up a pitched hillside, Nandi strode with her head bent, listening for the music of silence. It led her past other ghosts, their faces quiet with dreams. Some strolled, like she did, but most lay in the breathing fields of light beside the listening waters remembering their physical lives.

The walking dead sought, as she did, the story-telling paths that crossed the sleeping hills where the flowers opened and the animals woke. The MIKEs lay down in the saffron glow of sunlight's echo. About their bald, muscle-faceted bodies, blossoms opened their transparent colors. Overhead, pink rags of cloud hung in the darkness, while the hillsides all around pulsed with summery brilliance, brighter and softer, breathing light as if the shadows of clouds swept over them.

At the hillcrest, she paused among violets where a ferret slept that would soon wake and slither away toward the glare. Below on the mirror-black pools of the listening waters, watersnakes rippled like hair.

'So, you have failed again, Old Bones.' The rusty voice belonged to a dwarf with a face belligerent as a moray eel's. His squat, thick body looked singed: brow, torso, and limbs pigmented black as char yet flame-red at the many creases where the slabs of flesh compactly joined to shape his homuncular body. 'Give up your devotion to your god and give yourself to the light.'

'Leave me be, Droich.' She irately waved away the dwarf, who tugged harshly at the frizzled, burnt hair cuffing his bald pate. 'I must prepare myself.'

'Nonsense, Old Bones. You must brood. I know you well enough by now.' Droich kicked at the sleeping ferret and sent it squeaking down the hill. 'Few are older than you in these fields of lost light. Your brooding holds you here.'

'The Lady of Pain is older,' Nandi groused. 'She must brood more than I. Tell me about her, Droich.'

'Then you would walk the story-telling paths with me again?' A hot spark of tongue licked the curved corners of the dwarf's wide mouth.

Nandi's gaunt face contracted unhappily. 'That is why I am here.'

'You seem not pleased at the prospect,' the dwarf taunted. 'Do you want to walk with me or not?'

'Want?' Nandi hissed. 'What I want escapes me, Droich. Will you help me seize my want or not?'

Nandi turned her back on the small man. None within the afterlife was older than he. Since some ancient time, he had roamed these luminous hills, exchanging his experience of the foglands for contact with those ghosts who woke upon the breathing fields of light. Through them he touched again the worlds of the living.

'Come then, Old Bones,' Droich invited with a wave of his stubby hand. 'Walk with me upon the story-telling paths and we shall learn of Karla Sobieski.'

Nandi complied. She reached out her hand, and the dwarf seized three of her fingers in a fierce grip. At once, they became transparent to each other. Many times before, they had joined together, and so nothing new was revealed between them of themselves. In his story, pain translated into sexual pleasure. In hers, all was pain and only void offered succor. For the dwarf it was satisfying to review these torments – but Nandi wanted something else. She endured his presence to learn what he knew of another's pain.

Down the sunny hillside they walked, their bodies of light blurring, blending, merging to one wraith. Droich exulted in Old Bones's memories of her impoverished life in Poona and the sadistic rituals she conducted in the ashram of her Necroclave at Hyderabad. And Nandi suffered the cruelty of the dwarf's sick soul to hear the stories that he had drawn from Karla Sobieski in her earliest, inexperienced wanderings through the afterlife.

The shock, ache, and misery of Karla's betrayal at CIRCLE sifted through Nandi: the young anthrofact's howls of terror and cries of pain, her nights of crackling fear when first she saw her beauty disfigured by the shriveling disease of her exploding dna. And Nandi witnessed what Karla had seen in the mirror – the cankerous flesh shriveling to her bones.

'I was wrong to assault the Avatar!' Nandi shouted – and the dwarf shook loose from her. 'I should have attacked the object of his fascination. The Lady of Pain is the source of his illusions.'

'Attack her!' Droich agreed and hopped merrily. 'Attack her and her lover falls to your whim.'

She stalked away through the trampled grass that sprung back behind her. Droich struggled to keep up. 'Walk more with me, Old Bones. Walk more and learn more!'

'Away, Droich!' She shooed him off, without breaking her stride. 'I've learned enough. Go seek your pleasures with the innocent dead.'

The memories she had culled from her contact with Droich, which he himself had stolen directly from Karla long ago, were so perfectly honed to inflict pain she could not hurry fast enough to use them. Down the hills of lost light she tramped. Voices without mouths called from among the exhausted shadows of the dead. *Walk – walk upon the story-telling paths ... .*

She jaunted into the foglands. The four MIKEs floated on the ground with the mist, where the darkness fit their emptiness. She kicked them awake. 'Up, you brutes! Back into the cold. One last time into the cold. Let's go – now!'

Out of the swirling light, the phantoms rose. Nandi's severe ghost-body pranced around them, her knobby arms swinging through their empty shapes, beating them with her will. Divorced from the Machine and vacant of any will of their own, they obeyed. Once they were upright, she marched them with terrible speed through the smoldering darkness.

The cold slowed their advance. But the thuggees did not turn back. Glowing like the moon's bone, Nandi led them deeper into the cold, to where darkness relented and colors stitched the icy world of the living. The rust-colored ground sped underfoot, and above, Phobos smudged a corner of the red sky like a cloud. On all sides, monumental windcarved rocks stood like arches and buttresses.

Nandi listened for the Avatar. He who had grown inside her chimed to the calling of her waveform. She heard him across the wilderness, wandering with the Lady of Pain.

'We should go to Earth,' Rafe said. They ambled together along the gutters of a deep gorge in the shadow of a caldera that burned orange in the sunlight. 'I have friends among the Maat.'

'It's a long, cold journey – even for ghosts.' Karla brushed close, hoping to soothe his anxiety. 'There's still much to explore in Terra Tharsis.'

'You died on Earth and you made the journey to Mars.' The cold battered him, made thinking difficult, but Karla's presence eased that confusion enough for him to feel sure that Mars was too remote. 'If we return to Earth, we'll find out about the latest research on waveform receptors.'

'The best they can do is capture us in a reflector tank and hold us there until some indefinite time in the future when they *may* have the technology to grow us new bodies.' She wrinkled her nose at the remoteness of that possibility. 'We'll be *asleep* in those tanks, Sunny. And we'll probably never wake up. The Maat are too intent on the coming implosion to devote any time to ghosts.'

'We'll never know out here.' He cast a despondent look at the cobbled acres of smashed boulders. 'We should go to Earth to find out for sure if there's a way out of this maddening cold. It would be wonderful to have bodies again – to touch each other again.'

Her blue eyes held him sadly. 'You give a lot of energy to your dreams, Sunny.'

'That's why evolution chiseled out the large volumetric space of the human skull,' he teased her, 'to make room for dreams.' Smiling, he turned to press closer with his importunate request and saw the hard glint of her stare reach beyond him.

'Sunny, let's run.'

The chill of her voice reached deeper than the hurtful cold of space-time, and he whirled about in a fright. Nandi stood under the shadowed overhang of the gorge scrawny as a scarecrow shaken out by the wind.

'Get away from us, mother.' Rafe stepped behind Karla as Nandi advanced.

'It's not you I've come for, dearest one.' Grinning like a skull, Nandi sped forward. She moved with fluid purpose and seized Karla.

'Run, Sunny—' Karla cried out and sank to the cracked pavement of the gorge, dropping into a defensive trance.

Nandi fell with her and foisted upon her prey the horrid memories she had gleaned from Droich. The necrotic images of Karla's last days at CIRCLE cut deeper than the cold wind's knives.

Karla saw again her young body ruined by her dna's exploded supercoiling. Her withered flesh looked like wood scorched and softened by flame. Sores and blisters drooped her eyelids. Purple gums widened toothless around a silent cry of horror, and her serenity shattered.

Nandi and Karla flew down the winding gorge screaming like the keening wind. Rafe rushed after, arms outstretched.

From out of the stone walls, the thuggees lunged, and Rafe dodged past their grasping arms. He fled after the ghosts of the two women, who had meshed together into a blazing tumbleweed of howling cries.

'Karla!'

The thuggees charged after Rafe, and his urgency to reach Karla kept him just beyond their clutching hands. The gorge wall reared before them, and they sped into it as through a kelp jungle. In the underground gloom, the tangled forms of Karla and Nandi burned densely, a flaring star.

Karla's shock at the vivid recall of her decayed body had faded, but she understood Nandi's stratagem. Having alarmed Rafe with his lover's distress, Nandi would use her thuggees to whisk him into the dissolving glare of the future. So, instead of calming herself, Karla worked herself into a hotter frenzy.

Nandi tried to disengage from the enraged phantom. She pulled hard against Karla's fury, but the ghostlight she had attacked had become barbed. Nandi's waveform snagged in the emotional hooks and tines of Karla's tantrum.

'Release me!' Nandi yelled, and her cry pulled her tighter into Karla's wrathful flight.

'My life was stolen!' Karla shouted, and her voice filled Nandi with despair. 'My life! My life! I tried to steal my murdered life back – but it's lost! All I have now is the cold.'

Mist uncoiled around them as their flight through the underworld penetrated the foglands. Nandi focused upon the crawling vapors and strove to detach herself from Karla's madness. But the words echoing in her so loudly could have been her own, 'We have survived too long – we who were never meant to survive. We have taken too long dying. Too long entranced by illusions!'

The breathing hills flew by, their pulsing slopes a strobe as Karla's rapid flight launched them over the black mirrors of the listening waters. Rafe streamed behind, the thuggees at his side, no longer intent on grasping him but rushing with all their might to retrieve their mistress from the shrieking harpy that grappled with her.

'Karla!' Rafe cried again – and again, 'Karla!' – each cry only flogging her faster in her frantic escape with Nandi.

Chimeful music tolled in long, stretched tones, almost inaudibly. The music of silence announced the stream of yet-to-be. It appeared in the darkness ahead as a ruby cabochon. Its bloodglow rayed brighter, to the sharp spikes of a sun at the razor edge of night.

Nandi, desperate to disengage before impact with the glare of the future, struggled mightily. Her wild efforts only heightened Karla's ferocity, and they flew faster, dwindling to a silver glint that abruptly vanished in the blaze ahead.

A spiced warmth embraced them, and Karla stopped her rant. Peace received her, and her grasp relented. She fell free and alone, headlong into brightness. Her waveform expanded and diffused in the welcoming warmth as she reached out for what was reaching for her.

Nandi held back, struggling to free herself from the implacable gravity of their fall. The luminosity had erased all vision, and Karla had vanished in the light. She was alone. Karla had ripped Nandi free of the Avatar. She was alone, falling alone into emptiness.

'No!' Nandi cursed, and her scream elongated to a drone of dopplered echoes.

Rafe slowed, stunned numb by what he had witnessed, and the thuggees hurtled onward, mindlessly compelled to follow their mistress into the glare of the future.

'Old Bones is gone – and the Lady of Pain with her,' a rusty voice sounded from the lustrous shadows. Droich's seared body waddled toward where Rafe hung listlessly. 'Your Karla surprised Nandi.'

Rafe did not look toward the corroded voice at his side. He stared vacantly into the steaming light whose fumes unraveled into the mists of the foglands.

'You think you'll go in, into the glare.' Droich barked with laughter.

'Go! You'll not find Karla Sobieski in the glare. But go! Go and please your mother. Give up your form. Surrender your past. Prove Karla's sacrifice a meaningless gesture. All sacrifice is fool's work anyway. The wise know this.'

The dwarf's harsh words jolted Rafe from his shock, and he gazed stonily at the small man.

'Who am I, you wonder? I am Droich!' The dwarf extended a stubby hand. 'Come – walk with me on the story-telling paths, and you will learn everything I know.'

Rafe turned from the dwarf and moved away from the warm, musical radiance. Face set to the cold, he trudged through the shallows of smoke toward the foglands.

'Wait!' Droich called. 'I have much to show you. Come walk with me!'

Even shuffling slowly under the weight of his distress, Rafe soon outpaced the dwarf. The foglands thinned in the brisk cold. He crept out of the dark of the afterlife into the acute light of morning on Mars. He looked upward briefly, as if to ascertain the perfect emptiness of the rose madder sky. Then he dropped his heavy gaze to the shattered floor of the pit.

The shade of Rafe von Takawa wandered the wilderness without raising his eyes. He looked inward for what had become of Karla in him.

He would never find her again. She was gone. And he wondered, when his mind thawed enough to wonder, if he should follow her into the glare.

The cold hurt him, and that was his answer. The cold hurt. That was Karla's legacy. From the time she had reached out to stop him from plunging to his death as a five-year-old, she had forced him to accept what was painful.

And Nandi was her shadow. His mother had wanted pain to drive him from the world. If he entered the glare now, he realized, he would not be following Karla but Nandi.

So Rafe trudged on into the sand tracts, marching through dunes and crater walls. Night with its ghost spawn of stars came and went, followed by the tints of day. Storms raged. Corrugated thunder followed him under the gnashing cold and the dense blindness of whirling, torrential sand.

He walked on, and the cold walked with him, whetting its knives up and down his length. This was all that was left of Karla Sobieski. Her cold. Her suffering. Her dead world. Her hand held once again, then gone.

Death had retrieved her forever. Only what remained of her inside him continued to live. And for her, he would continue, defiant of death. The cold shrouded him. He walked on. Through mountains he walked. Across broken horizons he walked. At the rusty terminals of the corroded planet, he walked into the sky.

He climbed the wind above the burned-out volcanoes and the craterpits. He climbed higher than the curve of the world and shambled on into the void until Mars hung alone in the dark, a brown clot.

The cold hurt him without stopping. Under the stars, he searched for the blue star. He marched toward it. It did not dim nor did it brighten. It shone sharply as it curved into the silver aura of the Sun. He climbed higher until he could see the blue star again, shining steadily again, kissed into brightness by the solar wind as it drifted slowly on its ellipsoid track about its radiant focus.

Karla had made this journey. He knew it was possible. Otherwise, the cold and the slow journey through the dark would have defeated him. But Karla had come from the blue star to Mars, seeking him. He would follow her path back. He would find his way through the cold and the dark and far into the future.

Plato's Chicago

2800

The Worlds Fair was held in Chicago that year. The city had been reconstructed for the event. On the south-western shore of Lake Michigan, three phases of the historical metropolis were represented: From Lake Forest and Highland Park to Evanston, the Windy Clave of the twenty-second century reached seven kilometers into the sky with its spiral skytowers and neon obelisks. Lake Shore Drive north of Grant Park and the city west to O'Hare International Airport stood in ruins that accurately depicted the devastation from the Anarchy of the twenty-first century. The Wrigley building, *Tribune* tower, the Board of Trade edifice, and the Sears skyscraper represented the architecture of the twentieth century along the stately reproductions of Michigan Avenue and State Street. The fairgrounds themselves covered the southern precincts from 63rd Street to Sibley Boulevard, offering exhibits of Maat technology, aboriginal history, and cultures from every colony in the solar system.

Ellen Vancet decided at the last minute to go. As one of the oldest living aboriginals, she had been invited as a special guest of the Worlds Fair Committee but had hesitated to disrupt the simple, happy routines of her life at Council Oak. In recent years, eminent clones had become popular on many of the reservations. Three, some said four, Abraham Lincolns lived on croft farms in the uplands. Leah Melnick, the renowned Children's Champion who had founded the Youth Preservation Camps during the worst of the dire times, managed an orchard grove and cider press at a prominent river settlement. And Ellen had been living comfortably with the Swiss psychiatrist Carl Gustav Jung.

Carl thought she should go. 'Recapitulation would suit you very well at this time in your life, Red.' Tall and burly, he stood atop blond curls of planed wood that littered the plank floor of his carpentry shop. 'You've

been living so intensely in the moment – surely in compensation for the
dread Armageddon of the impending implosion. Present and future are
well recognized by you. But your past—' He placed his large hands flat
on the raw wood he was dressing and shook his head. 'You behave as
if you had no past. You never talk about your history. Yet how old
are you now? Seven hundred and sixty years. That's too much past to
ignore. Go to Chicago. Confront your ghosts. You'll come back more
lively than ever.'

'But I don't want to be away from you.' She bent over his workbench
and put her hands over his. 'I'm very happy with you, Carl.'

He kissed her forehead through her bangs of bright hair. 'I will still
be here when you get back, Red.'

'Why don't you come with me?' she asked hopefully, her green eyes
wide with the possibilities.

'Bah!' He pulled his hands away and wiped the sawdust from his
denim work apron. 'I've seen enough of the Maat to last *me* seven
hundred and sixty years. They have betrayed the natural world for the
transcendent. I want nothing more to do with them.'

She stood taller with determination. 'I feel the same.'

'Nonsense.' He leveled his index finger at her. 'You helped *make*
them. You must take some responsibility for your past, Red. Go to
Chicago. Face your ghosts. Listen to them. What they have to say will
complete you in unexpected ways. And when you return, you will be
stronger for it – and I will get the benefit!'

Ellen took her lover's advice but declined to join the large party
from Council Oak organizing a caravan to Chicago. Among the group
were many of her descendants, and she could not bear to have them
fawning over her and proudly touting their kinship. She chose, instead,
to windsled to the Fair on her own without informing the others.

While Carl helped her pack the sled in the backlot of their mountain
chalet, a balloon-runner bobbed out of the clouds and circled in for a
landing. Carl consulted the herald clip in his belt buckle, but there was
no message. 'I will get the stunner,' he declared and moved toward the
flagstone path that led under the aspens to the chalet.

'No, Carl. I have mine.' She lifted the sleeve of her brown drill
jacket and exposed a wrist holster and the amber eye of a stunner
disc. Since the horrid experience of her kidnapping, she always kept
several weapons on her person, including a narcolfact wick, compact
stunner, and a flexblade. 'But I don't think this is trouble.'

Through the wrap-oculars that Ellen removed from her face and
handed to him, he saw that the approaching figure was an adolescent

female. 'She's struggling.' The tinsel-sheathed balloons had shriveled to counter the thermal updraft from the coulee, and the pilot feathered the shivering vanes and tilted the runner into a steep banking maneuver. 'Duck!'

Carl and Ellen dropped to the weed-tufted ground under the shadow of the swooping runner. Its ailerons hissed through the branches of the aspens, and the gliderframe sprung open and dropped the pilot in a sprint landing that would have cast her into the coulee except for a hedge of chinaberries that broke her run.

Carl reached the young woman first and helped her untangle the branches from her orange flightsuit. 'She is all right,' he announced as Ellen came charging to her side. 'But I think the runner is ruined.'

The brace-wires and struts had snapped from the airfoils and the ventral balloons had disengaged. Lifted by thermals rising along the steep wall of the gorge, several of them bobbled away, flashing sunfire from their tinsel shrouds.

'You could have been killed!' Ellen gazed sternly at the young woman's round and startled face. Her rabbity upper lip trembled, and she nervously brushed back her brown, densely curly hair.

'I'm sorry – I just had to reach you before you left.' The woman exhaled anxiously, the nervousness in her stare heightened by the boldness of her eyebrows, which lifted higher as she stared in amazement at Ellen. 'You are Ellen Vancet.'

'You risked your life to remind her of that?' Carl clucked disapprovingly.

'Oh, I've seen holoforms of you,' the young woman gushed, 'but I wasn't sure I'd find you. The villagers weren't very helpful. They just said you were living in the mountains. But I had heard you were living with an eminence, and I traced all the ones in this area. I had to choose among two Abraham Lincolns who are in the vicinity and Jung.' She flashed a smile at Carl, who gave her a friendly nod. 'I'm so glad I chose right. I had to find you before you left for the Worlds Fair.'

Ellen's stern stare had darkened to a frown. 'Who are you?'

'I'm sorry.' A blush deepened her cinnamon complexion. 'I am Lucie Santos. You are my vicetrigenmother.'

Carl gusted, 'What?'

'Twenty-third generation ancestor,' Ellen interpreted. 'A rather tenuous kinship, Lucie, don't you think?'

'But we *are* related, Dame Vancet,' Lucie responded earnestly. 'I'm an official filiation of your family tree, on record at the registry . . .'

Ellen stopped her by raising both hands. 'I have no doubt, child. But, please, don't call me Dame.'

'If you won't call me child,' Lucie countered.

'How old are you?' Carl asked.

'Eighteen last Northaw.'

'Northaw—' Carl looked to Ellen. 'Remind me again what that is in the old calendar—'

'North thaw – after the last frost in the northern hemisphere,' Ellen explained, remotely, wondering why this youngster had sought her out. 'March – April—'

'You really are an old eminence,' Lucie marveled, regarding Carl closely for the first time. 'You were a medical pioneer in the nineteenth century. Am I right?'

'I made my mark in the twentieth.' Carl took the woman's arm and led her away from the coulee under the soaring clouds. 'You haven't yet told us why you've risked life and limb to find our Ellen.'

'I'm a reporter,' Lucie answered with a lift of her chin that revealed both pride and defensiveness. 'I herald for the *Acorn* – the youth blazon. It's viewed across Council Oak. I want a position at *Erato*—'

'The muse of lyric poetry,' Carl observed.

'Well, it's actually the name of the largest aboriginal blazon.' Her avid gaze fixed on his kindly and attentive blue eyes. 'It reports to all the reservations on Earth as well as communities at Selenopolis, Terra Tharsis, Solis, and the outposts of Apollo Combine and Jove Camarilla. It's a big outfit, with opportunities to travel everywhere. But my work at the *Acorn* isn't impressive enough to even earn me an interview for a position.'

'And so you want to accompany me to the Worlds Fair,' Ellen completed.

'I knew you'd be going,' she said with fevered energy. 'I tapped into the special guest list at the Fair's Hall of Honors and found your name. But it's been difficult tracking you down. You live so out of the way. I was afraid I wouldn't find you in time.'

'You could have met her at the Fair, young lady.' Carl's crisp stare appraised her unhappy reaction. 'That would have been easier.'

'But less dramatic.' With a winsome smile, Lucie faced Ellen squarely. 'I want to record your expectations of the Fair. And I want to be there with you when you arrive. You're one of the oldest women on Earth. And not just any woman. You made the first Maat.'

'They weren't Maat.' Ellen spoke in a chilled tone. 'They were anthrofacts.'

Lucie shrugged. 'You know what I mean. You were a pioneer—'

'If you want to be a reporter,' Ellen cut her off, 'you better learn to get your facts straight. And I don't want you learning in my shadow.'

Lucie struck her fist against her thigh, angry at herself. When she looked up, she wore a contrite expression. 'You're right. My excitement got the better of me. I'm nervous. I still can't believe I found you.'

'Go to the Fair and make your report,' Ellen said, turning away from her, 'but leave me out of it.'

'Why?' Lucie widened her pace to stay at Ellen's side. 'Why won't you let me share your experience with the worlds you helped make possible?'

Ellen spoke irately through the tangles of red hair that the wind blew across her face. 'I'm just one person among the billions who will attend. I'm not important.'

'The Fair is about our history.' Lucie took Ellen's elbow and stopped her. 'You're an important part of that history, Ellen Vancet, whether you admit it or not.'

Carl placed his lips close to her ear, said softly, 'She's speaking truthfully, Red.'

With an exasperated sigh, she took his hand and walked with him several paces into the glittering shadows of the aspens. 'Oh, come on, Carl. It's going to be difficult enough looking back at where I've come from. Why do I have to take a child with me?'

'Because she is a child.' Carl reassured her with a firm hand on her shoulder. 'Don't you see? She is the one to whom you must answer for your past. She is a symbol of all that is yet to be.'

'Everything is a symbol to you.'

'And am I wrong?' His small eyes grew larger, then focused to a penetrating yet genial gaze. 'If our lives are to be more than happenstance, we must assign value to everything. The symbol is just a bridge to that significance.'

'Fine.' She threw her hands up and strode back to where Lucie anxiously waited against the backdrop of snowlaced mountains. She admired the young woman's daring and feared her judgment. 'You can come with me. You can make your report to *Erato* about the oldest woman at the Fair, and I hope it gets you your job. But I don't want to put a show on for you. And I don't want you probing me for every nuance of my feelings. Can we agree on that?'

Lucie brightened, lifted her heels as if about to hug Ellen, but restrained herself. 'I understand. A good reporter is unobtrusive. I'll be your silent companion. Well, at least your quiet companion.'

Carl retrieved Lucie's sojourn bag from the smashed balloon-runner and secured it in the windsled beside Ellen's travel satchel. Lucie waited patiently in the whipseat behind the pilot's sling while Ellen and Carl said their farewells. Then, Ellen checked that the young reporter was snugly fit among the whipseat's gel squabs before slipping on the sling-harness and waving a last time to Carl.

The windsled, powered by a small magravity thruster, slipped off the mountainside and into the summer sky. Ellen guided the sled effortlessly over the cloudpaths and the crags of the Rocky Mountains. The swerves of momentum from Ellen curling on the banks of the wind, finding her flightlane by reading the clouds, left Lucie dizzy.

Once the control bar shone green, indicating that Ellen had locked onto an unobstructed flightpath, she spun about in her sling and faced her companion. Lucie's dusky complexion had a green tint along her jaw, and her eyes lidded heavily. 'This is really just a single-flyer sled,' Ellen informed her in an apologetic tone. 'Carl makes me sit in the whipseat when we ride together. I mist myself to stay calm. Want some?'

Lucie waved away the wick of olfact. 'No, I'll be all right. I've never ridden in a windsled before. There's not much to it, is there? At least the balloon-runner had wings. This is like flying naked.'

'The wind bubble helps.' Ellen referred to the airphase canopy that covered them, transporting oxygen from the atmosphere while retaining heat and deflecting the rush of their flight. 'Are you hungry?'

From her satchel, Ellen took out static-wrapped kelp salad and berrybread. While they ate and sipped pear cider from a shared flagon, Ellen inquired about Lucie's short life. Her parents ran a dairy farm, and Lucie had experienced a typical aboriginal childhood. But unlike many of the croft farmers of the last century, who eschewed neurotech except for the traditional simviv and ion-washes and then only when necessary, Lucie's parents educated their seven children with the latest mists.

Lucie and her siblings had learned almost everything by breathing olfacts. Esper, the mathematical canon, history, the arts, and all the sciences that an aboriginal could grasp short of metasapience were imparted in a few mist sessions. That had left her more time than most children had for playing and exploring, and she discovered that she most enjoyed telling others about her adventures on the reservation. That was how, at four, she began reporting to the *Acorn* her encounters with eminences, her experiences of chore-routines at the various crofts and garths she visited, and her impressions of nature. She sought out adventures, from ice-fishing in winter to summer quests in the primeval woods animal-shadowing, following bear, puma, elk, protected and virtually hidden by olfacts.

'Were you ever tempted to join the Maat?' Ellen inquired.

Lucie shook her head curtly. 'Not me. They live underground. They're not really human. Not like us. And no one I know has ever actually seen one. They're too weird for me.'

'But they have found a greater reality.' Ellen spoke freely of the Maat's secret understanding to everyone who would listen – but few believed her, and she could tell from Lucie's disdain for the unseen Maat that she would not be receptive. Nonetheless, Ellen tried, 'In three hundred years or so, the Maat are going to implode the entire universe . . .'

'You believe that?' Lucie began to laugh, then caught herself. 'I apologize. I was sure that you, just about the most experienced aboriginal in the world, wouldn't believe in *that* silly story.'

'It happens to be true.' Ellen spoke around a mouthful of berrybread. 'I *have* seen the Maat. And I was there when they transported the bomb from the future that will collapse everything.'

Lucie bent forward inquisitively. 'You saw the bomb?'

Ellen acknowledged this with a slow nod. 'Why are you so sure that my story is not true?'

'It's an old story.' Lucie wiped her mouth with the static-wrap that, once opened, had fluffed into a napkin. 'The Necroclaves started it centuries ago. It's been tracked down and documented many times. There's no substance to it at all. And if I include it in my report it's just going to make you look – well, foolishly gullible and pessimistic. Nobody wants to believe the world is going to end.'

Ellen splayed a hand across her chest. 'But I was there – on Mars – when the gauge field bomb arrived and was detonated.'

'Are *you* a Maat, Ellen?'

'No.'

Lucie sat back with a knowing expression. 'Then how can you be sure that what you saw was what you think it was? I mean, it would take a Maat to comprehend another Maat, wouldn't it? What you saw may have been an illusion, a trick, a shadow of a game they play. Who knows? The Maat are strange.'

'Yes, the Maat are strange,' Ellen conceded. 'We have no argument there.'

Their flight had carried them over auburn plains. Between the brown arteries of the Platte River, an emerald mosaic of farmlands sprawled. Ellen headed for there. She flew across the grain of the wind to slow her flight and brought the sled down for a landing at a grange yard.

They slid to a stop among wildflowers in a field where horse and cattle grazed.

A plank bridge on stone piers crossed a brook and led to the feedlot, a simviv bunker, and, separated by a stand of cottonwoods, a large farmhouse. There they refreshed themselves and chatted with the field manager and her children about the Worlds Fair and Lucie's ambition to work for *Erato*. She showed them her two streamlenses, small as fingernails and worn as earrings, abalone ovoids that recorded everything she saw. For their amusement, she used the farmhouse's antique holostream unit to replay her crash landing at Ellen's mountain chalet. Everyone laughed and crowded about to be included in her report.

As a token of courtesy, Ellen left several static-wraps of berrybread marked with the Council Oak emblem, and she and Lucie resumed their journey. Grange fields splotched the prairie at wide intervals, following the meanders of rivers. Mostly, the terrain stood empty of settlements, windglossed grasslands that ran to the horizon.

The deep blue of afternoon lifted almost to purple at the zenith, and Ellen lay back in her sling and obliged Lucie by describing her expectations of what lay ahead: 'Memory, mostly. The historical themes of the Worlds Fair are what I anticipate most keenly – and anxiously. Ion washes have preserved the memories of my early life too well. I'm afraid to see the devastation again, the ruins of the Anarchy, what we called the dire times. I grew up in a Preservation Camp. There wasn't enough food for everyone. The children had priority – and I saw old people, people who had once known abundance, die of starvation. I don't ever want to see that again.'

Yet she did see it again. Though the first view of the Worlds Fair was the skyline of the Clave's immense towers, their primary colors and neon spires radiant in the brash afternoon sunlight, the reconstructed ruins of the twenty-first century soon ranged below. Suburban towns lay smashed into the earth, a gridwork of streets among rubble fields. Balloon-runners of tourists surveyed the devastation from lower altitudes, but even from the windsled's height, the scattered bodies of the dead were visible, lying upon the wrecked landscape like the glyphs of a mysterious language.

Ellen looked away from the realistic manikins and shaped-foam ruins, and her gaze tightened. Straddling the Kennedy Expressway, a War Machine aimed its ram-missile tubes at her and everything that dared live in its presence. The behemoth pylons that upheld the rocket decks and turret domes cast long shadows over the flattened terrain. Assault craft hazed like flies in the air above the tiered flight platforms and the black conning tower with its dish antennae and bristles of scanner wires and wave coils.

An eerie reminiscence of dread electrified her, and she swerved the windsled in a giddy zigzag to escape this horror from her past. The control bar blinked red, warning of transgressed flight lanes, then shone white as the Fair's air command took control of the sled.

'That really frightened you,' a shaken Lucie observed.

'Maybe it would be better for me if I get a synthesizer to blot those memories forever.' Ellen looked down gratefully at the concrete canyons of Chicago's twentieth century midtown. 'It was such a primitive time.'

'Yes – look at the combustion engines!' Lucie gawked at the traffic pouring off the Chicago Skyway onto Michigan Avenue. 'How did they breathe?'

The fairway appeared like a mirage beyond the teeming streets of the city's steel-and-glass past. Helical minarets curled above stately groves of plane trees, and crystal domes gleamed among ponds golden with afternoon light. They glided lower over exhibit pavilions constructed of glass needles, tubes, and spheres.

Air command brought them down on a tile plaza surrounded by water-fans and jet-arcs of parabolic fountains. A tantara of brass music announced their arrival, and the Worlds Fair committee stepped jubilantly from the hedge gardens to greet Ellen Vancet.

Surrounded by several aboriginals, a selene, and an effeti of the Maat loped a Titanian morf in a statskin sheath, striding along in Earth's heavy gravity on a chrome set of powerlegs. Ellen could not tell the gender, though the leather strap outfit covered little of the spongoid body. The sight of the four blister eyes above the slit nostrils and pleated mouth revived dismal memories of her kidnapping. Yet her smile did not falter as she bowed to the committee and accepted their tribute of blossom crown and an elegant gem medallion.

Lucie moved nimbly around the reception delegates, recording their greetings to the venerable Dame Vancet as the party moved slowly across the plaza to a fleet of cloudgray floats with tinted windows that waited, hatches open. Ellen introduced the reporter to the others and took her hand to be sure that they stayed together as the group separated among the floats.

One of the aboriginal delegates grandly motioned them into the cool, fleece-upholstered interior of the lead float. Closing the hatch behind him, he sat facing them on the curved seat. He was not a typical aboriginal, but short, broad of shoulders, round of head and swarthy. 'I am Plato of Athens,' he introduced himself. 'Welcome to Chicago.'

'Plato – the philosopher?' Ellen gawked at the long-nosed man whose trimmed beard outlined full lips and a small chin. 'Author of the Dialogues – *Phaedo*, *Republic*?'

'The same. Son of Ariston and Perictione.' He courteously bowed his head, showed close-cropped dark curly hair. 'It is my honor to be your host during your stay at the Worlds Fair.'

'The Maat found your body?' Lucie asked and studied him avidly. Unlike her orange flightsuit and the brown drill jacket Ellen wore, his modern garb looked formal: a blue doublet with elbow-cut sleeves, silk wrist scarves expertly wrapped, apricot halter, gray flared trousers, and suede slippers.

'My body?' Plato's thick lower lip jutted disdainfully. 'That vehicle was used up and thankfully returned to the elements. When I dropped that vessel, I was eighty-one years old. As you can see, I am now again in my prime.'

'But how?' Lucie inquired. 'Without relict dna to clone, how could the Maat build you a body?'

'Child, my presence here is a validation of my philosophy.' He flashed a crooked-toothed smile. 'My *eidos* – my form – is eternal. The Maat have learned how to retrieve the individual form of beings from the supercosmic. This goes directly to my notion that all knowledge is recollection.'

'I didn't know the Maat had that capability,' Lucie said, looking to Ellen, who indicated her ignorance with a shrug.

'Oh, it is state of the art,' Plato assured them. 'I believe I am the very first manifestation of this new *téchne*.'

'Given your philosophy, you are the most obvious choice,' Ellen agreed. 'But from what little I know of the afterlife, I am surprised you endured long enough for your waveform to be recaptured.'

'The souls of my time were prepared for the afterlife by the Mysteries,' he explained, legs crossed, arms extended restfully to either side along the seat top. 'There are still many of us who are content to dwell on the fields of light and contemplate our past before moving on to our next lives. Hipparchus, Xenophon, Timaeus, Eudoxus, Protagoras are all still there. Alas, Socrates moved on even before I arrived. He was such a restless soul. But also remember, time has a different quality in the afterlife. I had no concept of its passage while I was there and am surprised to find myself here, thirty-two centuries after I died!'

'As the preeminent philosopher of what is "good,"' Lucie spoke, 'would you say that what the Maat did by recalling you to life is good?'

'I believe I spoke to that in the *Parmenides*, where I make clear that the realm of forms is distinct from this world of sensible things. The good is what the *Republic* says it is – that forms participate in the sensible world is good. So, my form has been returned to the sensible world, which of itself is illusion, yet this can only be for the good, for now I may continue to enrich these illusions with noble thoughts of actuality.' He sighed and lifted his chin to the clouds visible through the transparent roof. 'But we are not gathered to discuss my philosophy. I am here to honor you, Dame Vancet.' He looked cheerfully at her. 'You have lived long enough to be honored for your accomplishments.'

'I did very little . . .' Ellen began to demur.

'I am aware of what you have done.' Plato pointed with the wedge of his face out the window at the brilliant festival of ski-sloped roofs, mirror domes, and spiral airphase rampways. 'If not for metasapience, there would be forest and ruins here. People across the planet would be living as primitively as cave dwellers. Shall we tour the simulacrum of the Anarchy and review what humanity had made of itself before you arrived?'

'No, please.' Ellen pleaded with widened eyes. 'I saw enough of that on my flight in.'

'Then you know what you have accomplished.'

'But it wasn't me. I was one of thousands of researchers. My own work was not even seminal. I assisted others, the true pioneers. I made adjustments to their original visions. They are the ones who should be honored. Not me.'

He reached over and gently patted her knee. 'You are alive – they are not. You, therefore, have become an emblem of your group. As I am of mine. My number theories and concepts of the soul were not my own. That was the work of Pythagoras and his students. I wrote down nothing of my own thoughts. I simply recorded the great ideas of my forebears and contemporaries. And yet, history honors me in place of those whose true nobility of spirit I merely reflected.'

'Then I must confess to you, Plato of Athens, that what I have accomplished does not please me.' With a disdainful glance at the parkland's alleys of trees and stately exhibit halls, she shifted uneasily. 'All of this has been doomed by me, because the Maat are going to implode the entire universe. This world and all others will be destroyed. *That* is the true legacy of metasapience.'

Lucie put a restraining hand on Ellen's arm and spoke apologetically to Plato, 'Ellen has an obsession with this old story . . .'

'The secret understanding,' Plato recognized. 'I am aware of it. The Maat have disclosed this to me. And I have toured the assembly site for the gauge field bomb and witnessed a demonstration of wormhole transport.'

'You mean—' Lucie rocked back, astonished. 'The story is true?'

'It will be another seventy or eighty years before the transport system is refined sufficiently to deliver the detonating device, but the bomb is essentially complete.' With a concerned frown, Plato addressed Ellen, 'You should feel proud, not unhappy for what you have achieved.'

'You're *glad* the Maat are destroying the universe?' Lucie asked in a quavery voice.

'The universe cannot be destroyed, young woman.' Plato wagged a disapproving finger. 'Its energy will be conserved to the last erg.'

'But the worlds – the people!' Lucie squirmed with indignation. 'I can't believe that the Maat are really going to do this.'

'Collapse an illusory reality?' Plato asked pointedly. 'Everything shall be returned to its particular form. In an eyeblink, the dream shall end and all will once again be as it was at the moment of creation – all pure light. It is a beautiful fate.'

'It's horrifying!' Lucie croaked.

'You are mistaken,' Plato replied quickly. 'The horror lies in the sensible world of change and dissolution. The world of light is changeless and incorruptible.'

'But humanity will be wiped out,' Lucie protested. 'And the sentient beings on other worlds, they too will be lost, their individual lives and cultures lost, And so too will whatever future there might have been for worlds yet to be.'

'What you say is true, young woman.' Plato regarded her kindly. 'But bear this in mind. Whatever good that humanity, the worlds outside ours and the worlds to come might yet find is far less than the form of good, the supreme form, that awaits us beyond the sensible world. Thus, it is better that we forsake the good – for the better.' His eyelids drooped beatifically. 'Let the wings of your soul grow and fly beyond your senses and their dim images of our embodied condition. Leave fear and doubt behind and return to the soul's high estate in the light – as the light.'

'But only the Maat will enter the light with their particular waveforms intact,' Ellen pointed out in a vexed tone. 'The rest of us will be reduced to mere energy.'

'You speak disparagingly of energy – as if you knew its mysteries.'
Plato passed a querying look between Ellen and Lucie. 'From whence
did the universe come? From mere energy as you call it, from the
so-called Big Bang. To return to our source in the form by which
we departed that source is not incompatible with the good. But there
is better.'

'Not for everyone,' Ellen reminded him.

'Few are chosen.' His head tilted to one side under the weight of
a philosophical smile. 'Accept the metasapience you helped to create,
Dame Vancet.'

Ellen perked an eyebrow. 'Is that an order, Plato?'

He coughed a dull, brutish laugh. 'You're correct to mock me. I have
been overbearing. Actually I am ecstatic with metasapience, with the
idea of heaven, of infinite values – infinite density, infinite energy! And
to go there, into the light, my dears, as *oneself*. Ah, this is what being
human comes to. Yes?'

'Not for everyone,' Ellen repeated.

Plato's grin hardened. 'Your egalitarian dogma shackles your *individual* spirit! You want to save *all* worlds, *all* people. You're a mystic.
You want to have it whole. But, in truth, reality comes in parts. Not all
worlds or all people are created equal. Nature discerns. So must we.'

Ellen and Lucie exchanged hapless glances and sat silently. They
cruised through a grove of quinces and pomegranates, and the float
glided to a stop before a round gate in a wall of mossy chalcedony.
Tourists came and went and none paid much heed to the three who
stepped from the luxurious gray float.

'This is an exhibit we must honor with a visit.' Plato stood between
the two women and hooked his arms with theirs. 'The Worlds Fair
Committee has planned a feast to honor you, Dame Vancet, and several
receptions at the embassies of the major colonies and cartels. All that
will be very formal. But here—' He walked them through the wide
gateway into a pleasance where enormous lilies decorated the banks
of green-misted reflecting pools and ivy bowers led to cromlechs of
translucent rubystone. 'Here we can informally pay homage to your
achievement. For this is the Promenade of Maat History.'

At a reflecting pool they watched a three-dimensional display of
the development of genetecture from the identification of the helical
structure of dna by Watson and Crick to the design plans for morfs.
Stimagnetic chords gleamed just within audible range, massaging the
amygdala and hippocampus of each viewer, inducing trance awareness
and a serene comprehension of the abstruse material.

Plato urged them to enter the nearest of the rubystone cromlechs. Inside, holostreams revealed biographical images of the new breed, the fifty-seven anthrofacts designed and reared at CIRCLE over six hundred years ago. Without stimagnetic inducement, Ellen would not have been able to look again upon the vats – the vivarium aggrading tanks – among whose amniotic glass-bulbs, placental nets, and omphalic coils she and the other researchers had grown hundreds of foetuses and had terminated all but these fifty-seven.

She gazed hard at the stages of development for each of the anthrofacts, paying particular heed to their gerontic collapse. She had come to Chicago specifically for this encounter, and she did not shy away from the rheumy, defeated stares in the bonepits of their sunken eyes. Only Rafe von Takawa's holostream did not shrivel into a haggard shape of cankered, scabrous flesh. The viewer was directed to a separate cromlech dedicated to von Takawa.

Ellen did not want to go on to that cromlech. She remembered Rafe dead on Mars, his brain pithed by a laser. But Plato insisted, 'This is precisely why I've brought you here, Dame Vancet.' He took her elbow and walked her through the ivy bower into the cool ruby darkness. Lucie followed as they passed several tourists intent on a gory and detailed report of Necroclave sadism.

Plato led Ellen to an alcove with a glass sphere set atop a cryolite pedestal. Inside the sphere, velvet colors mingled like a sampling of an audacious sunset. 'Place your hands atop the sphere.'

When Ellen complied, the dark alcove filled with the waveform of Rafe von Takawa – naked and translucent to the colorful hues of black. 'Ellen!' His voice had the full timbre of a physical man. 'Plato said he would bring you to me. But I doubted. I didn't think you would want to come.'

Ellen's hands jumped from the sphere as if burned. The waveform of Rafe von Takawa wavered to a pink wisp of twilight and vanished. She turned her startled stare on Plato. 'Why didn't you tell me?'

Plato tugged at his chin whiskers. 'I promised him I would get you here. If I told you, you might have had reasons not to come. Now my promise is fulfilled. Shall we leave?'

'Leave?' Lucie took Ellen's arm in both hands. 'That is the ghost of the last anthrofact!'

Ellen glared at her. 'I burned the last anthrofact. Didn't I tell you to get your facts straight?'

Stung, Lucie stepped back. 'But this is him. This is the man whose genetecture you designed. He's the one who began the smart plague . . .'

'I know who he is.' Mica glinted from her stare.

Plato led Lucie away. 'This encounter should not be recorded.'

'But this is the biggest story in human history,' Lucie grumbled. 'I can confirm from a Maat what you and Ellen have said – that the universe is going to implode.'

'Ah yes, well – you and I must discuss the good of confirming to the general public the end of the world.' Plato gently ushered Lucie and several tourists from the cromlech.

Ellen watched them go, then stared at the small swirl of sunset in the glass sphere. Since Rafe had been killed, she had thought of him only sadly, and that sadness had kept him remote. With his death had ended an era. Time, which had once possessed worlds and spun galaxies, had become mortal, terminal. What was left belonged to the living. And so, she had driven Rafe from her thoughts. He was dead. The hope he quested for was dead. She did not think she could bear to face his grief, the pain of his failure, her failure, the loss of everything human, even the stars.

Yet her hands reached out. He was her creation, her creature. Of all the ghosts who haunted her, from the starved millions of the Anarchy to the aborted foetuses of the vats and the shriveled anthrofacts, he was most her own. He was the ghost that Carl had sent her to face.

Rafe appeared sunwashed, colorless, thin as smoke. 'I wanted to see you again.'

'Why?' Ellen felt herself speaking from the silence where she had buried her pain. 'We're finished. Everything is finished.'

Rafe nodded wearily. 'I came back to find where I began. I was cold. But I wanted to come back. The Maat caught me, and now I'm warm here inside this reflector sphere. Warm and sleepy. What year is it?'

'Does it matter?'

'You're angry at me.'

Ellen's hands on the sphere trembled and almost pulled away. She did not want to feel what he called out of her. But the feelings went on whether she voiced them or not and she would eventually be drawn deeper into their silence. Her hands tightened on the sphere, and she spoke sharply, 'Yes, Rafe. I *am* angry with you. You failed us all when you gave yourself to the Machine. What were you thinking?'

The ghost closed his eyes. 'I had taken every precaution. I didn't know that the imploders had mapped you at the most fundamental level of being. I didn't think they had that capacity.'

'You stopped thinking – and so did the Machine.' Ellen scowled with the effort to keep herself from walking away in disgust. 'But the imploders didn't stop thinking. And now they've taken everything from us, all for themselves.'

'I was wrong, Ellen.' Rafe opened his eyes and stared at her with fierce sorrow. 'That's why I'm here. That's why I haven't gone after Karla. I'm determined to stay here through the collapse. I was wrong to let this happen – and now I will accept the consequences.'

'That won't change anything.'

'I was hoping it would change us – change your anger toward me.'

Ellen's head retracted as if catching a horrid scent. 'What does it matter what I feel?'

'Karla is gone. The Machine is gone. Nandi, too, is gone. Even my original self, the first Rafe von Takawa – gone.' Plaintive shadows blurred the phantom's face. 'You are all that remains of where I began. Now that I've reached the end – of myself, of everything – whatever redemption there is for me waits where I began. That's why I came back. That's why it matters what you feel about me.'

A sigh carried away the hardness of Ellen's expression. 'Rafe – I'm just an aboriginal woman. I trusted you. I trusted your metasapience. That's why I'm angry at you. But the truth is, I'm much more angry at myself. I helped create metasapience. I'm responsible for the doom of the universe. I can never forgive myself for that.' She bit her lower lip, tasting the pain of her admission, and what ire she had harbored against him fled. 'Of course I forgive you, Rafe. You did everything you could to stop this from happening. The imploders simply found a way to thwart you. And if you had been more cold-hearted, if you had left me in Centaur Jockey, you would have succeeded.' She bent her elbows and stepped closer to the ghost so that she touched the sphere with each breath. 'My anger at you is misplaced. I'm wrong to see you as anything other than a champion for all of us against the selfishness of the Maat. You were too human – more heart than mind – and so the Maat defeated you. Not through any *fault* of your own. They exploited your virtue, your compassion. You tried to care for me – and that was your vulnerability. Tabor knew your weakness. My own quingenson. That seems appropriate. Since I'm the one who helped to start this whole madness, my own seed should carry it to its mad extreme.'

Relief shone through Rafe, and his body of light seemed to expand. 'Now that you've forgiven me, Ellen, you must forgive yourself.' He drifted closer with the weight of smoke or gray sunshine in a winter wood. 'Think back. If you had refused to work at CIRCLE, someone else would have taken your place. You were one of many.'

'Yes, of course.' She bowed her head under the burden of the memory. 'I was an expendable part of the program. Even so – I remember well how hard I worked, how avid I was to create an anthrofact with intelligence greater than any human being had ever possessed. We succeeded, and I was proud. Yes, I was actually proud.'

'And isn't it your pride now that keeps you from accepting the metasapience you brought into the world?' The cool blade of his voice peeled back the rind of her brave confession and exposed again the anger at her core. 'You should become a Maat and enter heaven with the others.'

'Never.' Her head snapped up, and she glowered at the ghost. 'I was proud to serve humankind. I thought I had helped our species take a step forward. I didn't dream that I would end everything. Everything!'

'And so you must punish yourself?'

'I don't see it that way.' The sides of her jaw rippled as she gathered her thoughts. 'If I wanted to punish myself, I *would* become a Maat and carry my guilt with me back to the eternal source. No. It's easier for me to remain who I am. When the world disappears, I will disappear with it.'

Rafe edged away from her irate stare, said softly, 'That is our fate.'

'At least we have had this chance to see each other again,' she replied more quietly, calmer for having expressed her heart's small immensity.

'And to forgive.' His voice rose anxiously. 'That is important to me, Ellen.'

'Yes, I understand that now,' she answered reassuringly. 'And, whatever this may be worth, I do forgive you, Rafe. I hope that you can do the same for me.'

'I never blamed you for what has happened.' Through clear hues of soot, his bonesharp face stared earnestly at her. 'From the first I knew you were only a part of a larger agency.'

'And now?' She met his strong face with raised eybrows. 'What becomes of us now?'

His nostrils flared as if her were breathing spectral air. 'The Maat will fête you. Then you will go your way. As for me, that depends very much on you. You see, I'm trapped in this thing, this reflector sphere. The Maat are holding me here for a time when they can build me another body. They want to give me a chance to go with them into heaven during the implosion. I've told them what I've told you. But they think I may feel differently once I'm embodied again.'

'Is that what you want?'

'I wanted to come back. I wanted to see you and be forgiven. Now that I have that, all I want is to wait out what's left of time.' His hand groped toward his head, reaching for a thought. 'I don't know what else I could want. I only truly know what I don't want. I don't want the world to end.'

'The world has already ended, Rafe.' She offered a rueful frown. 'I'm as much a ghost now as you. But you said that what happens to you depends on me. What do you mean?'

'You can set me free from the Maat.' He glided forward. 'If you break this sphere, my waveform will escape.'

She lifted a finger from her hands splayed atop the sphere and tapped its surface. 'I'm sure it's virtually indestructible.'

'No. It's only glass. The Maat have agreed to let you decide whether I stay or not.'

'Why?'

The hook of a wry smile lifted one corner of his mouth. 'An amusement. A gamble. None of us was sure you would even come to the Worlds Fair.'

'I nearly didn't.'

'What convinced you?'

'My shrink.' She nodded at his look of surprise. 'I've been in therapy the last few years, trying to cope with my guilt. My shrink thought it would be good if I came and faced my ghosts. I thought he was talking symbolically.'

'Now that you're here—' He placed a ghostly hand atop hers, and she felt nothing. 'Will you do me the favor of setting me free?'

Perplexity narrowed her stare. 'But you're determined to wait out the implosion. You told me so. Wouldn't that be easier to do in a body or at least in this receptor sphere?'

'I haven't forgiven myself yet for my failure to stop the gauge field bomb.' The translucent coals of his eyes held no light, only shadow. 'I need what is hard. Maybe if what I do is hard enough, I will find some redemption.'

'That saddens me, Rafe.'

A wan smile slanted across his face. 'That's far better than being angry with me. I guess you really have forgiven me.'

She nodded resolutely. 'Yes, I have. I don't want you to suffer.'

'Then you must leave the sphere intact.' He moved away, a shade gray as ash. 'But I'm asking you to let me go. In your last act as my handler, I want you to release me.'

'To suffer?'

'I've slept enough inside here,' he pleaded. 'I don't want to sleep anymore. I want to stay awake to what I've done. Give me back to myself, Ellen.'

Her hands tightened on the sphere, and she picked it up, astonished at its lightness, this vessel that held a human soul. 'Then it's goodbye.' She stared across the clear horizon of the sphere at the flimsy reflection of Rafe, his human contours fitted puzzlewise to the shadows. 'I won't ever see you again?'

He shook his head. 'No.' He stepped back, deeper into darkness, and only his gray aura and his voice lingered, 'It turns out that we were wrong about everything. The Earth is flat after all, Ellen. And when we fall off, we won't come back.'

She dropped the sphere. It shattered against the stone pedestal with a glittering explosion of splintered rainbows and stars glimpsed in blinking. The last shimmer of Rafe's ghost in the alcove vanished, and the shards of glass tinkled across the ground, making way fast for silence.

Ellen emerged from the cool dark of the Rafe von Takawa exhibit, through the ivy bower, into the brittle yellow glare of late afternoon. Plato hailed her, 'Dame Vancet – an old friend of yours has sought you out!'

Beside the gray silk of a fountain's veil of water, Fenn Tekla stood in a crimson kaftan and brown suede chapeau, licks of salt-blond hair sticking out from under a green headband. Lucie stood at the effeti's side, and the two held hands. 'I knew you would come,' Fenn greeted her. 'And I was certain that if you came you would free him. Thank you for proving me correct on both counts.'

Ellen stared past the Maat at the spider silver of the fountain's spray, unhappy that Rafe's ghost had fled, uncertain what Fenn Tekla's presence or the grim sharp smile that genderless face wore portended.

'What you did took courage,' the Maat said. 'Rafe was comfortable in our receptor. Now he is bitterly cold or flung back entirely into the tesseract range, lost to this world.'

She kept her gaze on the fountain's jets and fans shimmering spray at their airy zeniths. 'It's what he wanted.'

'A masochistic urge, that.' Fenn stepped forward with Lucie. 'I think he inherited such love of pain from his mother, don't you?'

Ellen looked to the reporter and cocked her head in query at Lucie's closeness to the Maat.

'The effeti came for me,' Lucie responded. 'Plato summoned him.'

'An aboriginal reporter privy to the secret understanding?' Plato asked with a disapproving shake of his curly head. 'That won't do. It can only breed social discontent. And what good can come of that?'

'Actually, Ellen,' the tall, angular Maat interceded, 'I wanted to see you anyway – to congratulate you on your long and successful life. You have adjusted well to the trials of life at the end of time. Few aboriginals could carry on as calmly as you have. That is why the Maat's secret understanding must remain secret. I'm sure you understand.'

Ellen locked onto Fenn Tekla's placid, silver eyes. 'What are you going to do with her?'

'It's all right, Ellen,' Lucie spoke up gleefully. 'I've been invited to visit the Windy Clave! Effeti is going to show me how the Maat live and what work they're doing.'

Ellen's face bent sadly. 'Lucie, I'm sorry. I didn't mean to get you in trouble.'

'Trouble?' Lucie waved off her concern. 'Don't be silly, Ellen. This is thrilling. I can even bring my lenses into the Clave and record anything I want.'

'That's not what's happening, Lucie.' Ellen held anger in check and did not approach, though she desired to pull the young woman away from the Maat. 'Didn't you hear what Plato said? You're not going to be allowed to report any of this to anyone.'

Lucie lifted a questioning gaze to Fenn. 'Tell her, effeti.'

'It's true, Ellen.' The soothing tone of his voice carried persuasion. 'Lucie has been invited into the Clave and may record whatever she wishes.'

With a dark, knowing look, Ellen said, 'Lucie – these are Maat. They can control what you wish. Just your holding the effeti's hand has charged your blood with molecular mood-enhancers absorbed through your skin. And there are olfact misters and stimagnetic inducers throughout the Clave.' Feeling angry at herself, she dared advance toward the Maat. 'Let her go and take me, Fenn. I'm the one who's been talking too much.'

'But you're just one voice, Ellen,' the effeti replied with a disquieting smile and began leading the young reporter away. 'Lucie Santos will be playing her recordings for *Erato*. I think it's more appropriate that she take the tour. I hope you enjoy the festival that the Worlds Fair has planned in your honor tonight. Dignitaries from across the solar system will be there.'

'I wish I could have recorded it, Ellen,' Lucie said over her shoulder, 'but this is a bigger story. It's an opportunity I can't pass up.'

'Yes, you can!' Ellen called, her voice frosted with fear. 'Come with me instead, Lucie.'

'No, Ellen.' Lucie waved amiably and tossed her a genial smile. 'You are fascinating. But an exclusive *inside* a Clave? There's just no comparison. I'm sorry.'

'Lucie – please!' Ellen moved to pursue the retreating couple, but Plato seized her arm firmly.

'Let her go, Dame Vancet.' The philosopher spoke importunately and his already strong grip tightened. 'The Maat are the rightful rulers of the age. And it is never wise to defy the mighty.'

'We'll see you tomorrow during your tour of Chicago,' Fenn called jovially from beside the fluttery drapes of water. 'Then you can hear from Lucie herself what she thinks of the Maat and our work.'

They strode past the fountain into the late afternoon's tarnished sunlight and disappeared.

'I too have sad memories of impuissance before the might of greater men.' Plato released her arm and confided in her. 'My stepfather, Pyrilampes, was a prominent supporter of the imperial democrat Pericles, and I learned much of obeisance to power from him during the Deceleian War and the fierce civil strife of oligarchs and democrats in the year of anarchy – that would have been the year 404 Before the Common Era. My uncles, my mother's brother and cousin Critias and Charmides, were oligarchic extremists of that terror. Both were old friends of Socrates – and even thirty-two centuries later all the world knows of his execution by the restored democracy, though little is recorded of how severely my uncles suffered or made others to suffer. No, Ellen, it is not good to thwart the powerful. Let Lucie go to her fate unimpeded.'

'I should never have told her.' Ellen's shoulders slumped. 'I didn't realize this would happen.'

'There, there, Dame Vancet, no need to be so glum.' Plato stood squarely before her, and his deep voice cossetted her. 'Take solace in the fact that in my time she would have been killed. But this glorious age has the means for a far more blithe resolution. Now let us have no more concern for that youth chosen by destiny. We are due shortly after nightfall at the festival center. Let me take you to a place where you can refresh yourself and dress for this propitious occasion.'

'I'm in no mood for festivities.' She worried for Lucie and wondered if the Maat would expunge all memory of the secret understanding from her or instead convince her again it was all nonsense. 'I think I'd rather just sleep until tomorrow.'

'There will be no sleeping tonight!' Plato's cheeks lifted to smiling crescents. 'The most graceful stimulants have been prepared to keep you fully alert through the entire gala – and tomorrow's tour as well. When next you sleep, you'll be in your own bed on your reservation. While you are here, there is time only for celebration!'

From the breast pocket of his blue blazer, Plato removed an olfact wick. Ellen backed away, shaking her head, but she was downwind, and the mist caught her in a sudden cloud of brightness. The chemical punctured her dark mood, drained her of unhappiness, and filled her with a carnival joy, guileless as girlhood.

Plato took her hand, and the two skipped off laughing, like gunshots into the cracked-open world.

That evening, after a boisterous, sparkling parade down Michigan Street under the strobe-lit skyscrapers of the twentieth century, a gala festival filled Washington Park, Midway Plaisance, and Jackson Park with thousands of revelers. Most of Ellen's numerous descendants attended and all her friends from her six centuries in Council Oak, mingling in an ecstatic jamboree of food, olfacts, and music with the Maat and morf dignitaries from every colony in the solar system. Albert Einstein played fiddle. Akimi Groove, who pioneered neojazz in the twenty-second century, and Charlie Parker offered solos and duets.

Happy as parrots, the crowds danced. From a barge that spilled luminous lantern colors on the lake, Ellen, in a shimmery gown of cat's-eye fabric and devil's-tail décolletage, gave a speech. The words came to her as she spoke them, woven from the fabric of her heart and stitched with olfacts so that there were a lot of funny parts that made the throngs surge with laughter while she taunted their age for confusing the difference between truth and reality.

'The truth is that the Maat have created a whole new reality,' her huge voice sifted out of the radiant night. 'But the reality is, there's no truth to it, because it won't last.'

Plato gave her a harsh stare from the row of eminences who sat before her on the barge prow.

'Reality never lasts,' she concluded, her brain gilded with an olfact's clarity. 'Something more truthful always replaces it. Reality is in motion, and we have to move with it. All we can do is accept this truth, which is continually forming, bearing us into the next century, the next reality that is born as we are, by being borne.'

Plato winked with satisfaction. 'Very tactful,' he thanked her with a whisper and led her by the arm to introduce her to the thirteenth-century mystic poet Jalal-ud-din Rumi who stood chatting animatedly in esper with a robust and jovial Charlemagne.

At dawn, Venus flared brightly over Lake Michigan like a lantern set in the vastness, and Ellen and Plato strolled casually up State Street, flush with the success of the night-long fête. Revelers sailed in balloons through the fire-ribbed sky over the lake. The scattering crowds thinned down side streets, into the antique city's granite buildings and the mouths of the subways. A bus dragged by, happy faces in the windows and gold streamers tangling in the wind with the blue clouds of exhaust.

Plato choked and gasped, 'These people with their combustion engines lived as if the world had no memory.'

'They were wrong – terribly wrong.' Ellen stopped at the corner of the twentieth century on Roosevelt Road staring west into the devastation of the twenty-first century. Acres of collapsed brickwork lay in a scurf of mortar and rust. Twisted girders and pipes stood solitary among broken slabs of masonry and rows of empty façades whose edifices had collapsed, leaving sheer doors and windows open upon fields of rubble.

'We should turn back,' Plato said, noticing the sharp stars in Ellen's eyes. 'There are many more exhibits at the Fair we've yet to visit.'

'No.' She stared over the collapsed city and bristled like a pine. 'I'm ready now to face this.'

They found an enamel blue float in a nearby car lot, and Ellen drove them into the wasteland. Only the stench was missing from this simulacrum. Mangled corpses in every state of decay lay among the grim ruins, and she gazed at them without looking away. The float's buffer field lifted them above the brash of toppled buildings, carrying them unimpeded on their tour over the flattened city blocks, past free-standing iron stairwells curling to nowhere, around old conduits rearing out of the ground draped in the ganglia of torn electric cables.

Ellen steered directly toward the War Machine that had crushed Chicago. The icon of terror from her youth squatted over the arches of bridges and the spans of viaducts, monumental in its nest of disaster. Assembled in orbit and dropped onto its target, the War Machine had proved lethally effective. A hydra-works of missile launchers, rocket ramps, and crude laser cannon, its hive of assault craft displayed no obvious vulnerabilities. A swarm of them had descended upon every major city of every continent and dominated all military rivals. Once resistance was annihilated, the colossal platforms served as administrative castles. They would have ruled the next age except for enemies they could not conquer – the superstorms and phages that swept the globe.

After parking the float on a stone pile beside a cutaway apartment building, Ellen clambered over upended pavement slabs and shattered tarmac to reach the War Machine. She stood dwarfed beside the immense pylon that upheld one multi-decked corner of the super-structure, so gigantic it blocked a whole section of the day.

She placed both hands against the scorched titanium plate, and the centuries of her life coalesced to an ache of frightened memories from her distant childhood. It was this stupendous monster that had terrified her in the outer world and chased her deep into the inner. Mathematics had been her escape. And now like the light of a star seen after the star had vanished, the fear continued in her.

Plato knew better than to say anything. He waited in the float. Visitors to the Fair circled overhead in flyers and criss-crossed through the destroyed city in their own floats. He enjoyed the jasmine and mint scents of the olfact wicks the Maat had given him and that he had tucked in the various pockets of his blazer. Their sweet reek uplifted his spirit far better than wine, and he felt glad that the Maat had summoned him from the dead to serve them.

Strange as the world had become, it remained familiar to him. Warlords and oligarchs – now they called themselves the Maat. After the burning of Athens, Xerxes took to Persia the library that the tyrant Pisistratus had assembled. Plato remembered the consequences of that plundering from his first lifetime, the competition for knowledge and power. Before the secret understanding there was the library at Alexandria, founded by the warlord disciple of his disciple Aristotle. Knowledge and power. The tall grasses and broken stones of Chicago, the ruins of Greece, these proved the future was a fossil. *Is* was never a match for *become*. Stasis could never be reconciled with metamorphosis. He sniffed another waft of olfact and smiled thinly.

When Ellen returned, bloodsmoke stained the whites of her eyes.

'You've been crying.' Plato patted her hand as she took her seat behind the yoke of the floater. 'This has been all too sad for you.'

She smiled through her tears. 'No, Plato. This is a fugitive bliss.'

'You're happy in the midst of all this destruction?' He gazed up at the dark underbelly of the War Machine, the shadow of death against the cavernous blue wall of the sky. 'This is the nightmare of your childhood.'

'Yes, and it's over.' She accepted an olfact-misted handkerchief from the philosopher and daubed her eyes. 'The past is over, forever. We have conquered everything now. The whole universe. All of it was so small compared to our heart's desire. The Earth herself and all our history, all our lives – just a drop.'

'And now the striving is over,' Plato understood. 'There will be no more history, no more wars.'

'No more suffering.' She smiled deeper as she swung the floater around and steered back toward the proud skyline of the twentieth century. 'I lived long enough to see the death of death.'

She opened the floater window and flung the handkerchief into the rush of their slipstream. It flapped away merrily. From that moment, she began to wean herself from olfacts. She wanted to see how well her revelation held up without neurochemical support. With the windows open to wash the cab of Plato's stimulants, her head cleared quickly. But her new sense of freedom from her past was not denatured by her sobriety. History *was* over. This Worlds Fair was humanity's party at the end of time. In a couple of centuries, the very stars that people had used to mark the fateful course of generations would cease to exist.

Instead of the sadness she had suffered before from this inevitability, she sensed bliss. The whole gruesome procession was over. Life would not have to devour life anymore to survive. Survival had become obsolete, and being no longer required justification. The trials of chance and worth were over.

Plato smiled benignly when she explained her enormous sense of release to him. 'Yes, yes, you have grasped a great truth. Essence *precludes* existence!'

'That's too gnomic for me, Plato.' She returned his smile, happy to be happy again without having to fool her brain with magnetic induction and drugs.

'It's just what you told me.' He rubbed his hands together, pleased to expound. 'The existentialists have debated whether essence precedes existence or vice versa. But your insight has cut through that conundrum. Essence does not precede, it precludes existence.'

She took her eyes off the detritus sprawling ahead to face him and admit, 'I don't get it.'

He waved to the chunks of concrete, the broken plates of paving, and the blackened beams of the fallen city. 'Existence is painful. Yes?

Once one finds the essence, either individually or as a society, which the Maat have done, then existence becomes impossible.'

'Well, the Maat have certainly made it impossible.'

'Because they have found the essence – the essential reality of the compact dimensions.' He stuck his head out the window and let the rush of wind brush back his curls and fill the hollows of his head. When he pulled his grinning head back in, he asked, 'You've heard of King Midas?'

'Of course. The fellow who could turn anything to gold at his touch.'

'Right. He once asked Silenus, a comrade of the great god Dionysos, what was the greatest good of humanity. And Silenus told him, "What would be best for you is far outside your grasp: not to have been born, not to *be*, to be *nothing*. But the second best is to die soon."'

With a sharp laugh, she grasped what he was saying, which was the same revelation, the same universal truth, that she had seized on her own: life was a gruesome procession – and it was good that it was ending.

They returned the floater to the car lot where they had found it and ambled down Michigan Avenue, pausing to mug humorously at themselves in plate glass windows and to straddle the sculptured bronze lions at the entrance to the Art Institute. All the while, they chortled together like old school chums and discussed the fair illusions that had justified human life from the beginning – love, beauty, and justice.

Their happy jaunt returned them to Washington Park and the cloud-gray floater that would return her to the plaza where her windsled waited. Plato tried to convince her to stay and continue touring the exhibits, but Ellen was adamant, 'You led me to the truth, Plato. And it has set me free. I'm ready now to go back to where I'm happiest, in Council Oak. With what time is left, I want to indulge myself – trout fishing and hikes through the woods. Perhaps you'll visit and we'll share that happiness together.'

'Oh yes, there is time left for that.' He hugged her, then peered steadily into her green eyes. 'The future closes in on us slowly enough for us to meet again. One never travels so swiftly as into the past. But those journeys, I believe, are over for us. Now we are free to recognize ourselves and complete the slower, more lingering journey to reclaim the present.'

On the ride to the plaza, the olfacts that tinged her from Plato's hug made the vernal groves seem like green clouds flowing past. She wondered about Lucie Santos and what amnesiac future the Maat would foist on her. When the floater arrived at the tile plaza among the parabolic fountains, the olfacts had worn off and her concern for Lucie had steepened.

Joy and concern rushed up in her at the sight of Lucie and Fenn Tekla standing beside her windsled. Ellen rushed from the floater even as it was still gliding to a stop. 'Are you coming back with me to Council Oak?' she asked, then stopped short. Lucie's brown irises had been replaced by a Maat's night-vision silver lenses.

Lucie wagged her head at the sight of Ellen in her low-cut, cat's-eye gown. 'I'm glad my absence didn't throw a wet blanket on your stay.'

'You're one of them,' Ellen muttered.

'The Maat gave me a choice.' Lucie still wore her orange flightsuit, but her earring streamlenses were gone. 'They took me to the threshold of infinity and showed me the way into heaven. After that, I knew I could never be happy as an aboriginal, let alone a reporter.'

Ellen blinked with disbelief. 'You're one of them now.'

'Yes, you said that.' The white of Lucie's teeth shone against her cinnamon complexion. 'And you should be one of us, too, Ellen. What is finished is finished. This world is done. Come with us into the original world.'

Ellen turned sharply to Fenn Tekla. 'Are you going to make every aboriginal a Maat?'

'Would that we could.' Fenn gave a dolorous shrug. 'We just don't have the resources to create that many unique waveform matrices in the time left us. Fortunately no other aboriginals have to know, because no one will believe you, Ellen – just as Lucie didn't believe you until you brought her here.'

'Small solace for me, effeti.' Ellen stepped past the two Maat and added as she approached her windsled, 'Not that I need solace anymore, mind you. It's all over now. The pain and its justification. It will be over soon.'

'It doesn't have to be over for you, Ellen,' Lucie called after her. 'You can join us.'

Ellen stopped with one hand on the airframe of the windsled. 'I don't want to join you. I don't begrudge you your paradise. But I'm happy being human – and grateful to you for bringing the whole messy affair to an end.' She bowed, the oldest human gesture of respect, and entered the windsled.

As she slid into the sky under the noon sun, she did not look back. She was done with trips to the past. The ghosts had been faced and released. There was no time anymore for history.

She rode the windsled across the Plains and into the Rockies without stopping. When she came down in Council Oak, she landed at a mountainside cabin she had set up several centuries earlier. The notch-jointed logs had slumped to a mossy mound that buttressed one side of a mammoth oak.

From under a rootledge, the pulpy loam gave way to an earth-yeasty hollow that had been the cabin's interior. She bellycrawled through the mushrooms, wood mulch and leaf rot, underground head first up to her waist before her groping hands found the staticbag. Inside the long bulky container was everything she needed to survive, including a rod and reel.

She stripped off her soiled evening gown and sat naked atop it under the leaves' flickering sunlight while she opened the bag and laid out her boots, trousers, hiking jacket and the suede roll of feather-flies she had meticulously crafted during a winter long ago. A peach-jelly sandwich, fresh as the morning she had made it centuries ago, appeased her appetite. The toast was still crisp. She quaffed cider from a flagon attached to the utility belt that carried, among other gear, an old-fashioned comm unit.

The summer's sweetness enclosed her as she dressed. Then, she assembled her rod and strode through the witchgrass. Out of the turquoise sky among the canopy branches the sun shook its basket of light and dropped garnets on the forest floor. A fox sparked through the underbrush, startled at her approach, and blue-nosed deer watched from a sunny corridor.

Doorways opened among the trees, and a blue swerve of river appeared below. Islands of aspens stood in midstream, the current slowly dismantling their banks so that some trees lay in the water. Trout lingered there in numerous coverts all down the river, hidden by brushstrokes of sunlight and creaking shadows. And that was where she was going, determined to test her desire and skill against chance and to fish until the end of time.

Fortune's Feast

2915

He was an old ghost. Ania had never seen a wraith with a lightshift that old. Three ambers glowed dully in the brown brass fittings of the phantometric console. The curved panel of zebra wood under her hands sparkled with control lights – each tiny as a drop of resin – each blinking rapidly, measuring how strenuously the receptor was working to pull in the tenuous waveform. The ghost was old. The control lights blinked so rapidly that the tarnished metal switches at the edge of the panel cast shadows.

Ania stood back from the bronze cabinet, amazed. Never before had more than one amber shone among the six beveled discs that crested the console. And never had more than a few of the small, resin-drop bulbs set among the knobs and dials flashed at once. The sight of the entire panel liquid with light electrified her.

Quickly, she bent forward and set the switches to construct a channel. Processors whirred inside the cabinet. Behind a perforated bronze grille at the base, dark yellow lozenges throbbed with brown light, while atop the unit, in the oval panel of zebra wood and brass plates, a round viewport held a smudge of green static within its oily blue lens.

The static condensed to a thermal image of a man, incandescent vapors seeping from ten fingers, ten toes. The lucid figure drew her closer. He was a terranthrop of ectomorphic proportions. His beardless jaw and flat ears appealed to her, and her gaze lingered on the lithe curves of his trapezius and deltoids before sliding away to check the code icons at the screen perimeter.

She identified the site of death as a gully on Mars over three hundred terrene years ago – long before the Exodus of Light that was currently raging among the inner worlds. The channel indicators, an emerald rhomboid above the speaker vents on either side of the cabinet lit up.

'Greetings, Rafe von Takawa,' Ania said, reading his name from the esper glyphs appearing in the rectangle of red glass under the viewport. 'Welcome to Trakaerë. The year is . . . um, 2915 terrene common era, and you—'

'You know my name?' Rafe's ghostlight shone brighter in the field of absolute black. From his perspective, reality had diffused like the pieces of a dream.

Time changed purposes.

Consciousness expanded through space at the speed of light.

The year is 2915 terrene common era . . .

Rafe had been dead long enough for his body of light to fill a volume over a hundred parsecs wide, and his mind moved freely anywhere within that range. He placed himself as far as he could reach, at the sphere surface of his wavefront. His mind encompassed a radius over three hundred light years from the Sun, an area of awareness that expanded both above and below the galactic plane.

Stars gleamed against the dark arches of space. He had not yet expanded far enough to see the spiral shape of the Milky Way, let alone the broad concourse of galaxies in the Local Group, and darkness enclosed him. Star rays stretched thinly, tiny with distance, sharpening their edges against the smallness of his being.

Elsewhere in his awareness, he sat shivering in the white blindness of fusing hydrogen nuclei at the starcore of the Sun. Also, his mind skipped among the moons, observing the fabled mines, so thoroughly excavated that the angular momenta of their diminished masses shifted orbits, and the shucked moons required grids of magravity antennae to keep them from spinning wildly into space. And beyond them, the intraorbital factories burned like toy suns inside their colorful clouds of exhaust.

The cold pilfered his attention, and he kept finding himself wading among the warmer foglands of the afterlife. Narcotized by the warmth of the tesseract range, the ghost drifted toward the glare and the thin music circling the edge of sleep. If he lingered, he would slip away into the shining unknown.

Karla had gone that way and taken Nandi and her thuggees with her. He sensed that he would never see Karla again, that the journey into the glare would be a permanent exile from the kingdom of himself.

So, he returned to the cold of space-time and the multiple perspectives of his tenuous body of light. He walked on the Moon. Floating through sunlight, aching with cold, he cast no shadow and passed cleanly through mountains and crater slopes, looking for nothing, just distance. He wanted to get away from the crowded story-paths, and even the smiting cold of space-time was preferable to the hordes of drifting shades with their loud thoughts.

Unlike most of the aboriginal and morf dead, Rafe possessed a metasapient awareness of his condition. He knew he was a lightcone propagating at 299,972 kilometers per second through an expanding universe and that what he perceived – his perception itself – was the wavefield pattern of all the lightcones of all creation interpenetrating each other. Consciousness was shaped by this pattern in the tesseract range.

While many of the dead continued to think in physical terms and thus limit their awareness of themselves as bodies of light, Rafe explored his radiance. He did not have to walk or fly. He could locate his center of awareness anywhere within his enlarging waveform. He stepped off the Moon and onto Mars.

Ania gingerly placed her hands on the zebra-wood control panel of her phantometric receptor. She slowly adjusted knobs and toggle switches until the thermal colors of the ghost sharpened. He had an alertness uncommon to phantoms, and she grew aware that he was scrutinizing her even though she had not yet activated her transmitter. He was watching her the way ghosts did, observing the aura of energies her body radiated.

The changing complexion of her skin intrigued him. The hues of her flesh shifted with iridescent shimmerings like the blue blush of an octopus. Otherwise, she looked entirely anthromorphic.

'You're the oldest phantom I've ever received,' she told him. 'It's not usual for ghosts to last so long in the cold.'

At the mention of frigid space-time, Rafe's consciousness returned again to the edge of his wavefront, staring into the parsecs of emptiness beyond the galaxy. And simultaneously he floated through the dusty horizons of Mars.

Terra Tharsis had grown to fill the entire caldera of Olympus Mons since he had last focused his conciousness there. The forests where he and Karla and wandered were gone, grown over by crystal towers eight kilometers tall. During the long time that she had been gone, he had dwelled on how little she had revealed to him about their existence as waveforms. When they had been together, she could have taught him more about their ghostly existence: As a metasapient, she knew more of the afterlife than she had told.

Why?

Truly like Kore, Karla had reveled in the living world. She had chosen to spend their short time together on the tesseract range as though they were bodies again, walking, gesturing, talking with anthropic nostalgia.

He turned away from Mars and looked around the four outer systems. The construction in transNeptunian orbit of the cosmic string resonator, a complex array of hyperbolic geometries two kilometers wide, 1.6 kilometers deep, and 182,164,980 kilometers long, had created industrious communities among the moons of the gas giants. He visited the platform cities afloat in the balmy upper atmosphere of Saturn and was struck by the beauty of Trakaerë – and the warmth of the phantometric receptor.

'Are you Maat?' Rafe asked the woman who had summoned him into her presence.

Ania blinked at the esper glyph on the viewport that revealed that this man was himself a Maat. 'A Maat?' she repeated, mind racing, searching for what to say to such a being. 'No. But do I see that you are. Is that really so?'

'Who are you?' The smokeshape of Rafe von Takawa billowed, then briefly revealed a clenched face as he attempted to see her more clearly through the radiance of her own bodylight. 'How do you know about me? Show me yourself.'

'Me?' Ania flustered, and her hands worked the switches to activate the transmitter. 'I am Ania the Enterprising, currently of Trakaerë. See?' She raised her arms and turned before the cold blue eye of the transmitter that watched her with shifting threads of icy light. 'You are in my estate on Saturn.'

Rafe saw a woman with porpoise-blue skin and ermine hair, her tresses falling long and white and badged with black rosettes. She stood barefoot in a green sarong and a feather-and-snakeskin throatband.

'This must seem odd to you—' she blurted to the Maat ghost. 'There was nothing like this three centuries ago.' She removed the transmitter's blue eye from its socket in the wood panel and turned it on the perforated bronze cabinet from whence it had come. Beside the dazzling receptor, tall windows framed in carved marble a vista of clouds, cumulus towers silver and brown climbing toward azure heights and frost streaks of cirrus. 'Trakaerë is a platform estate suspended by magravity mills in the upper atmosphere of Saturn. Here there's water, sunshine, and balmy temperatures. It's somewhat like Earth.'

She stepped with the transmitter to a balustrade of alabaster treefrogs carved in Mayan blockstyle. Below, an autumnal rain forest tossed languidly in a restless wind. To the stormblue horizon ranged a lush realm of green darkness, purple-fronded trees mired on the fern banks of sunken ponds, Aztec towers and Persian-winged statues scrawled with vines and dripping crimson blood-blossoms.

'Ania—' the ghost called.

She slowly turned the transmitter on herself and peered into the ice-blue eye. 'Yes?'

'How do you know about me?'

'Oh, I don't know anything about you. The receptor does. I'm only reading it off the port.' She pointed the transmitter at the control panel and showed him in the round viewport his own ghostbody wavering like a boreal aurora. From the esper glyph display she read about his escape from CIRCLE and how he had released metasapience across the Earth in the twenty-second century. 'That's you?'

With a skeptical expression, she peered into the viewport, awaiting a reply. All at once she understood the unlikeliness of the three ambers burning atop the hood and the panel's dazzling display. 'This is a joke!' She looked abruptly to either side. 'Where are you, Roeg?'

After a moment, she realized she was alone, and her surprised face searched for semblance in the chromatic smoke of the viewport. The lineaments of Rafe von Takawa's form shifted like flames. She slapped the blue eye back in its socket. 'Wait. This is *not* a joke! You're real!'

'Are we alone?'

She stepped aside and revealed the width of an observatory deck. They were at the top of a graven stone tower, one of several that reared out of the jungle. Saffron veils stirred in a gelid breeze among ornate drafting tables of red jade, chart easels, and optical gadgets with prism counterweights, brass gears and lenses big as platters.

'We are alone.' She leaned against the cabinet, which was almost as tall as her. 'I have lived and traveled by myself these past sixteen years, and I bring no one with me when I come to this jungle.'

'You called for someone.'

'Roeg.' She laughed dully at herself. 'He has a neighboring estate here on Trakaerë, which he visits when he comes down from Iapetus Gap. We're – friends. I thought you were one of his pranks – the ghost of an ancient Maat. He has the mischievous wit to taunt me with such a joke. But, I see now, you are no joke.'

The neon smoke of the ghost swirled against the viewport, peering past Ania's lean profile at the metal armatures of prisms and lenses in the window bays. 'What do you do up here?'

'I gather light.' She tapped the wood console. 'This is a receptor. I drew you out of space with it.'

'Why?'

A yellow bird with a blue beak and fluffy red tail alighted in one of the tall windows. 'I wasn't looking for you. I was merely trawling.'

'Trawling for ghosts?'

'For stories.' She tapped a pointed, transparent fingernail against the viewport glass. 'It's cold in space-time. It takes quite a story to get a waveform to walk away from Eden.'

'The tesseract range is not Eden.'

'It is, compared to this frigid continuum.' For a Maat, Rafe von Takawa did not seem as imposing as Ania had initially feared, and she relaxed. 'The ghosts I usually find are recent arrivals to the afterlife. Trauma stories. In their shock, they wandered away from the warmth, got lost in the foglands, and wound up out here, drifting aimlessly. I take them in, offer them some warmth in exchange for hearing their stories, and then send them on their way.'

'You set them adrift?' The ghost vapors cringed tighter in the dark of the viewport. 'You don't return them to the range?'

'I don't have the prisms that can resolve to the tesseract range.' Ania's brow wrinkled with concern. 'I can't send anyone back.'

The ghost seeped closer in the round glass. 'So you do this for the stories?'

'There have been wonderful stories.' Ania nodded with fond remembrance. 'It's the Exodus of Light, you know. So many want to die.'

'Tell me about the Exodus.'

'Oh, I don't really know.' She worked the switches and knobs. 'Let the receptor explain . . .'

The burly but friendly voice of the receptor said, '*This past year on Earth thirteen million people attended centers of passage and breathed lethal doses of narcolfacts. Another seven hundred thousand committed ritual suicide in the lunar colonies. And on Mars, three hundred fifty thousand did the same. These aboriginals and morfs were eager to die, because they had become enthralled by phantometrics, the technology of communication with ghosts.*

'*Holostream reception of the waveforms for specific individuals in the tesseract range had become cheap and readily available several decades earlier, and the afterlife, the agelorn realm of the dead, the penultimate human mystery that had haunted humanity with wonder and dread from the savannah days of the first awakening, immediately became a destination. The deceased beckoned. The range, with its luminous fields of vegetation under starry skies, its story-telling paths wending among mirror-black pools of reflected memories, and its musical, warm, perfumed and radiant stream of yet-to-be, seemed a wonderland.*

'Millions wanted to die. All were aboriginals and morfs and none were ill or physically damaged. Illness and impairment had been boxed up with the other Pandorables centuries ago: Old age, mood disorders, and chronic physical suffering afflicted no one on the reservations or in the colonies, and none of the people who journeyed to the afterlife wanted to die to escape suffering. They died to experience the transcendental.'

'Will you tell me your story?' Ania asked after silencing the receptor.

Rafe had not been listening. He had come to the receptor for its warmth. This small respite was worth the nagging presence of the morf.

'Why is a Maat outside the tesseract range – in the cold?' Ania tilted her head inquisitively. 'You are not traumatized or dim-witted with shock. Yet you're here – and you've been here so much longer than any other ghost I've met.'

'Yes, I've been expanding in space a lot longer than most wanderers.' He luxuriated in the thermal draft of the receptor and spoke casually, 'I didn't realize until now that common technology could receive waveforms as tenuous as I.'

'My receptor could pull in a six-hundred-year-old ghost – if it ever found one.' She stood on her toetips and pressed her eye close to the blue transmiter node. 'Why is a Maat out here in the cold?'

'The Exodus of Light.' Rafe spoke to keep her mind occupied and to allow himself to bask in the soothing heat of the receptor's field. 'It's too crowded in the afterlife.'

Ania hummed a laugh as if he were joking. 'The tesseract range is infinite.'

'But the dead share each other's light.' His solarized figure spread arms and legs and filled the round portal like a human star, and his voice imitated the husky assurance of a machine voice: 'At this time, one billion Maat and nine billion aboriginals occupy Earth. 107 reservations, several on the ocean floor, provide comfortable lives. Yet phantometrics has revealed another mode of being that many find attractive. Those who give themselves to the Exodus of Light arrive in the afterlife en route to the stream of yet-to-be, convinced that by dissolving in the glare they will leave behind physical existence for a reality of pure energy. Their proponents mock humanity's animal traits: hair, teeth, bowels seem obscene burdens of a predatory past. Better to shed these atavistic trappings for existence as a waveform.'

'You're funny for a ghost.' She pulled up a high-legged bamboo stool and sat down. 'Tell me more.'

'The Exodus of Light carries away only a fraction of those who want to die.' His voice softened in the seething warmth of the receptor field. 'Though these passagers disappear quickly into the glare, many others die with the ambition of dwelling in the afterlife. Upon the introduction of phantometrics, the story-telling paths became crowded with ghosts. Cults have formed around the pools of listening waters, and together they evoke shared memories and fantasies from the black mirrors. Whoever comes near must participate.'

'You were unhappy,' Ania guessed.

'Not at first.' Rafe breathed like a cloud, pleased with the warmth, and spun out his story: 'I mingled among the new arrivals at the dark pools and watched the luminous kelp of their collective imaginings rise to the surface. Like silver atoms caught in a magnetic dance, fantasy landscapes of impossible sea gardens and winter sunsets formed out of the plutonic light and changed as the participating ghosts interacted with these imaginal lands of dream. But I did not share the emotional involvement of the others. To me it seemed like an eerie rendition of group simviv. And so, I disengaged.'

'That was painful for you.' Ania perched attentively at the edge of the stool. 'You were used to spending time alone at the listening waters, weren't you?'

'It's endlessly fascinating to shape one's own dreams.' The flamingo hues of Rafe's ectoplasm pulsed like heartbeats. 'But blending with the others becomes ponderously predictable very quickly. I moved on. For a while I roamed with the crowds of ghosts who took instruction from veterans of the tesseract range – the ancient phantoms. Some are thousands of years old. A few even look as though they died eating bad woolly-mammoth meat. Most preached their philosophies and religions, others extolled the pleasures of the afterlife, including the deep summer warmth among the flora of the breathing fields and the revival of memories on the story-paths. Soon even the glowing hills became crowded, and I wandered away from the throngs and into the foglands.'

'Just like that.' Ania pulled her head back skeptically. 'Rare is the ghost who consciously braves the cold.'

He told her about Karla. And he basked in the tropical aura of the receptor field. 'From her I learned that I could come back through the crawling mists. Space-time resumes, and its contours are familiar, but the dead burn with cold. I learned from her how to endure the cold.

And I learned how to master my emotions in this cold. But I've heard no interesting stories. The dead out here are usually victims of violent deaths whose memories still disturb their waveforms. Like sleepwalkers, they move about alertly yet unawares. I avoid them, which is easy to do because they usually haunt where they died. Most often they don't even realize that they are dead.'

'What are you doing out here?' Ania asked. 'Why did you not remain on Earth?'

'I felt uneasy there—' Rafe paused.

A muscular man with blue topknot and a red slantcut sarong stepped from among the saffron veils. His craggy face grinned.

'Roeg—' Ania said, and the uneasiness in her voice carried a memory of darkness that was fear.

Rafe von Takawa's mind drifted at the wavefront of his expanding body of light. Stars glimmered distantly in their remote stations. Facing this vast abyss of emptiness, he felt awe so profoundly that he forgot Ania and the warmth of her phantometric receptor. He forgot the cold. To reach the stellar shores of the nearest galaxy would take two million years. The waveforms of australopithecus were just arriving. The light of the first humans was not even a quarter of the way there.

A prayer reached out of him, toward the enormity of the void. In his first life, as a composer, he had written music for God. Those had been most sublime exaltations, the hymns and threnodies he had composed for the divine. On the story-telling paths, he had sought out that music and had found every note of it. Only then had he remembered how the sound of his praise of deity had left him feeling shamed and simian. He had believed then that the whole notion of deity that humans had cherished through the ages was but a projection into the void of their own monkey reverence for the alpha-leader.

Before the black gulf of deep space, all simian assumptions vanished. Even here, where form fell away into a vacuum immense enough to swallow millions of years of light, God would not go away. The nothingness suited divinity well. In Rafe's metasapience, the sacred was the transcendent, that which existed beyond form and space-time. That ultimate reality beyond this continuum was the goal of the Maat.

The waveform of light that Rafe had become was, like all light, devoid of rest mass, timeless, and connected to the ultra-reality beyond appearances, the hyperdimensional region underlying all manifestation. He could not go there by dint of will – though he tried. For that, he would need a Maat-built matrix to shape his collapse and project himself whole into the compact reality of infinite energy. Nonetheless, he sensed the immanence of God within the fire of his own light.

The cold that hurt him was his portion of fire. It was warmer near the glare of all-fire. And that, he had come to believe, was the goal of every spark – to return to the all-fire, the source. The cold would have driven him there eventually – if there had been time for the eventual. But the collapse was coming. The light of the first people would never reach Andromeda. And Rafe would only have to bear the frigid parameters of space-time for a little while longer.

His prayer went out to God for all light in the darkness. Soon the dark would collapse, the void would disappear and all would be light. He prayed for the darkness and the thin light it carried.

God was silence. The transcendent could not fit into words. Yet he believed the silence had accepted his prayer, just as darkness accepted the light.

He stepped back from the empty face of God that floated upon intergalactic space. His mind retreated back to the solar system, and he found himself at its edge, beyond the orbit of Neptune. Like snakeskin, the Array glinted in the rays of the Sun, a thin black arc against the dusty stars of the galactic hub.

Inspecting its latticed levels of black sheet-diamond he lost his way among the spiderwork of wires and filaments that filled complexities of nested geometric figures: spirals intercut mazes into hives, planes sectioned circles and ellipsoids into randomly patterned chambers. And the closer he looked, the more complex the intersticial spaces appeared.

To get out, he seeped through a delirium of odd-shaped alcoves and curved vaults, a catacomb of weird angles. He broke with relief into the emptiness of space. Looking back, he noticed from outside that the spun fibers of the webbed chambers glinted with black iridescence in the thin solar wind.

The mad labyrinth had disturbed him. The answer to his prayer was this cosmic string resonator. Perhaps he had been wrong to annul his Maat legacy. Why blur away in the final collapse when sentience could don a body and climb into a larval matrix to journey the ultimate distance, to God?

Rafe von Takawa's ghost hung in space with zenpoint stillness, and the astral cold shook in him. Time had passed strangely while he had toured the Array. Years had lapsed in moments, and staring at the fractal niches he saw many more webs in the hollows than he had noticed only moments ago.

Space-time warped within the Array. He backed off, afraid that the structure might somehow absorb his waveform. The Maat had nearly achieved their objective. The collapse could not be far off. If he was to join the others of his breed, he would have to return to Earth soon and determine that the offer to accept him back remained valid.

But first he retreated to the foglands where the warmth allowed him to think more deeply, and he pondered the possibility that Nandi, Karla, and the imploders had been right all along. The precision required to construct the Array, the concatenation of fateful events that won victory for the imploders, the blind luck of evolution, the pure chance of punctuated equilibria had created humanity and aleatory historical events had led to metasapience – did not all this point to the summons of an acausal intelligence? Perhaps heaven had reached through the event horizon of the Planck distance with hands of chance to retrieve what it had lost with the Big Bang.

2922

'That is the same conclusion that we have drawn,' Fenn Tekla said with a silver laugh.

The foglands misted into the hot sunfumes of a jungle on the shores of Lake Mojave. Rafe confronted spiritous palms against a watery horizon where sunlight had smashed into numerous pieces of topaz. Looking closer he saw the mossy wood deck of a veranda hung with colorful ferns – and Fenn Tekla in a black and green khaftan, hair bound to plugs on a white scalp.

'Destiny.' The effeti sat on the veranda railing. 'I programmed my receptor to tune you in as soon as your waveform began to consider the possibility that a hyperdimensional being created humanity and has guided our destiny.'

Rafe said nothing. He wondered if Fenn had trapped him in a receptor tank, but he sensed he was free.

'You are free to go as you please,' Fenn heard his thought through his receptor. 'This channel is open and unmonitored.'

Rafe tested this and stepped away from Lake Mojave. His consciousness seeped through layers of cold, appearing at a score of sites across the solar system. Wretched Stevens had expanded to a chalken metropolis of pale towers knobbed like coral branchings. Strolling along a boulevard of chlorine-green ice, he watched sledges slash past, conveying Tritonian morfs to their offices and engineering studios. The construction of the Array had brought prosperity to this remote colony and transformed the dark world into a luminous alabaster maze. Branched towers, pale domes, and enameled pyramids inset with ice-green panes glowed in a haze of city lights under the crescent blue aspect of Neptune.

Briefly, he stood before the palace that he and the Machine had constructed atop a nitrogen lake not far from Wretched Stevens. Sleighloads of morfs skimmed across the frozen tract of Poseidon Flats, visiting the site, which had been converted to a museum. The morfs who skated in the pools of light let down from lux beacons on the palace ramparts bore scant resemblance to the turtled shapes of their precursors. Squatly humanoid, they possessed prehensile limbs useful to the work that the Maat intended for them at this construction outpost.

Rafe listened to their conversation. The same radio-frequencies that served their ancestors carried their communications – dreamheld moods cored with thoughts. They discussed work, bickered about life, frolicked and brooded, marveled at the terrestrial garden enclosed within the abalone-silvered spheres and cupolas of the lake palace.

'Rafe von Takawa!' Fenn Tekla's voice beckoned. 'Will you favor me with your attention?'

Rafe's mind scintillated among the numerous colonies and settlements that orbited the Sun and planets. To his phantom self, the many receptors active throughout the human communities felt like misted warmth. Each phantometric device leaked heat into the tesseract range and warmed the ghosts. Across the hundred parsecs of his volume, he experienced this warmth only in the solar system. The void of space-time offered only cold.

Heat suffused most strongly from the glare blazing beyond the stream of yet-to-be. He was certain that he did not want that comfort. His determination to die with the stars kept him in the cold, but he did not deny himself the ease of receptor heat. Brief respite from the cold was available at millions of sites. On every reservation, phantometric salons had cropped up, installed by the Maat, who had their own hidden reasons for wanting to demystify death among the aboriginals. In less than a hundred years, the universe would collapse, gone in an eyeblink, and the Maat hoped to provide a suitable exit for aboriginals in the event they found out about the secret understanding before the collapse arrived.

Accidents had been the leading cause of mortality until the Maat offered phantometrics. Then death became attractive. Phantom gurus recruited disciples from among the living, and families and clans took passage as groups . . .

'Rafe, come to center and extent,' Fenn Tekla called. 'Focus yourself, man.'

'I am no man.' Rafe returned to Lake Mojave. Bell birds clanged with unearthly stridor from among the pale boles beside the sun-dimpled water. 'I am a wraith.'

'The wraith of a man.' Fenn Tekla sat in a wire flexform on the veranda of a lakeside manor. Feminine grace contoured the figure beneath the black khaftan and a masculine bluntness set the silver stare in the angular face. 'Get out of the cold, Rafe, and put on your body again.'

'Will it be my body?' Rafe swung through the wood railing and glided across the lake, the faceted water flashing beneath him. 'I will not be trapped by the Maat again.'

'There is no reason to trap you.' Fenn sat up taller in the flexform. 'The rivalry between conservatives and imploders ended centuries ago. The judgment has been made. Remember.'

'I remember.' Rafe stood close to Fenn, his whisper almost silent.

'That judgment is destiny, Rafe.' Fenn Tekla rose and stepped to the rattan table where a glass wafer stood on its side, a prismatic fin that split sunlight to rainbows. This was the receptor programmed to receive his waveform. 'You've thought about it. I know. I can read your body of light.'

Rafe soared higher above the lake until it became a wild gleam among the emerald peaks of the Tehachapi Mountains. Atmosphere glazed the planet's rim with an aqueous shine, a global aura against which the sharp points of stars gleamed like silver nailheads slammed into the flat black of space.

'You've been thinking that perhaps the Big Bang was a fall.' Fenn Tekla picked up the glass wafer and held it like a monocle to one eye. Rafe's body of light rotated slowly, naked, detailed to the cellular mosaic. 'Our violent history is the evil of our loss – the evil of our separation from the infinite values and perfect symmetry of the compact dimensions. You've wondered if perhaps the infinite has been striving to retrieve us from this ignominy. That is why chance favored the imploders, Rafe. Chance, the instrument of God, has led to cosmic collapse. The exile is over. We're going home.'

Rafe hovered in the cloud plateaus that surged among the cliffs and sky lakes of the Sierra Nevada. 'Do you know what it's like being dead?'

'I've done the simviv.'

'Then you know what it's like to be light. Milton was correct. Book eight, *Paradise Lost* – "if Spirits embrace/Total they mix."' Rafe slid down through the trees with the slanted sunshine and twisted a smile at Fenn through the wafer lens. 'I am light. I carry everything with me. Since I became a ghost, I've embraced countless spirits – aboriginal, morf, and Maat. At heart, they all want to live.'

Fenn snapped the lens away from his eye. 'And we will live more intensively than ever once we return to our source.'

'The Maat will live. But what of the others?'

The effeti sat on the wood planks of the veranda and turned the wafer so that it caught the sunlight and stretched a rainbow across his palm. 'We all return to our source.'

'Some just have better seats than others.'

Fenn Tekla stood. 'You are embittered by personal loss.' The Maat returned the wafer receptor to the rattan table and stood it on its side. 'Come out of the cold and put on a body, Rafe. You'll feel differently.'

'I don't doubt that.' Rafe waded among the strangled greens at lakeside, walking unseen through a crane standing on its reflection. 'But will it be my body?'

Orange thunderheads loomed above an autumnal rainforest. Rafe circled down to Trakaerē, the platform city afloat in the upper atmosphere of Saturn. Silk streamers of white clouds, braided smoothly as poured milk, unraveled almost motionlessly in the blue sky.

A music of long, elliptical lines, running and purling like water, lured him on. He had heard this music before, on Mars, in the cog colony of Lampland. The *Datum Surface Raga* riffled its mellifluous strains louder as he skimmed over the ragged green rooftop of the jungle.

Stone dragons longfeathered and tusked coiled up a concrete stanchion. At the top, an observation deck peered across the forest canopy at distant turrets fluttery with banners, pennants, and the colorful sails of wind turbines. The music came from the bronze cabinet of a phantometric receptor crested by six amber discs.

The music stopped. Rafe sat on the parapet beside a large lens set in a brass frame and counterweighted by springy metallic wires like long feelers drooping at their ends with prism-cut crystals.

'He's here!' a woman's voice shouted with fractured glee. 'He's back! It's truly him.' Fear broke her enthusiasm far short of happiness.

Ania's gray face centered his field of vision. 'Rafe von Takawa – you've returned.'

'How long have I been away?'

'Too long.' Ania leaned against the bronze cabinet of her six-amber receptor, one hand clutching her yellow sarong nervously, the other working the brass toggles and knobs on the zebra-wood panel. She read the glyphs in the viewport. 'Over seven terrene years. Where have you been?'

'Inside the Array.'

'That's why we couldn't find you.' She completed her control adjustments and stood back with a puff-cheeked gust of relief. 'We got the idea to research your history, seeking some way to get you back, and we found this music – a cog raga that you left at various sites during your exile. It's been playing a long time, calling for you. We thought you'd never come back.'

'You and – Roeg.' Rafe searched for Roeg and found him nowhere on Takaerĕ. He endured the jangling cold again and lifted away from Saturn toward its outer moon, Iapetus, where Ania had once told him Roeg worked – and discovered that he could not move.

'Roeg is not on Trakaerĕ,' Ania said stepping back another pace from the receptor cabinet. She stood beside a tall tripod that upheld a brazier wisping with incense. 'He has been summoned to Tycho Factor.'

Rafe willed himself to the Moon, to the vast Selene community of Tycho Factor, but he went nowhere. His awareness remained fixed within the amber-shining console of the receptor. He gazed out through the cold blue rays of the transmitter lens and watched Ania's gray complexion glimmer with an iridescent flush as her fear abated. She had been gray with dread that her receptor would not be able to hold him, but now that he remained locked in place, she visibly relaxed.

'It will be days before Roeg returns.' She stepped quickly to the cabinet and reached for the toggle panel. 'I will put you to sleep until he gets here.'

'No – wait!' Rafe shouted. 'I can't move! You've trapped me!'

'Not I.' Ania shook her head, and her white locks whipped. 'Roeg fitted my receptor with a tank, to hold you.'

'Why?'

'It's a lengthy story.' Ania's face drained gray again. 'I think it's better you wait to hear it from Roeg.'

'You tell me, Ania.' Rafe applied all the persuasive charm he could to his voice. 'If I am to be your prisoner, I want you to tell me why.'

'Roeg and I – we're business rivals.' Ania's nostrils winced.

She spoke of Trakaerë as a meeting ground and field of contest for the wealthiest families of the Chronosystem. Their ambition was to imitate the truly rich families of the older worlds, the byzantine trading cartels of the Moon, the Belt, Mars and Jupiter: Tycho Factor, Apollo Combine, Ares Bund, and Jove Camarilla had created their stupendous fortunes centuries ago, during the explosive colonization of the inner worlds. The construction of the Array provided the same opportunity to the outer systems.

Ania clutched at the bronze cabinet and cried about the ferocious competition among the new cartels. Many were sponsored and controlled by old money. Roeg's shipping firm on Iapetus Gap received direction from Tycho Factor. He chaffed for independence – and wealth – and that was why he had wooed her. 'He did not love me!' She kicked the cabinet. 'All he wanted were my shares in Titan Enterprises.'

While she related the venerable history of her Enterprises – 'the *oldest* venture in the Chronosystem and with no outside controllers' – Rafe felt for the tank limits. He had learned a lot about being a ghost since his imprisonment at the Worlds Fair. Receptor tanks could be escaped by going deeper into the cold and the riverrun of light, the timefree, spacebound contours of the photon.

But this tank was different. Apart from the blue rays of the portal lens that illuminated Ania's tearful face, blackness enclosed him. And there was no cold. A gritty heat, like lava fever, suffused from the receptor.

'You're in a null tank.' Ania wiped an orange handkerchief across her bleary face. 'Roeg got it on the black market from a rogue Maat.'

'There are no rogue Maat.' Rafe's stony whisper silenced her. 'They gave this to you, because they want the worlds to have this – this null tank.'

'Do you know what it is?'

'I know.' But Rafe could hardly believe what he knew. The absolute blackness, the emptiness even of cold informed him that his light was bound by a null field – a region of space-time erased at the most primary level. The Maat ability to manipulate the cellular automata that comprised the fabric of space-time astounded him.

But his amazement wavered. He knew that the Maat had released such magic fearless of implications – because there was no time left for any implications.

'Roeg tells me that you can't escape and you can't even be released unless . . .' She bit her lower lip remorsefully. 'You're trapped unless someone willingly takes your place.'

The anthropic effect. At the very small scale where Rafe was trapped, the null field was generated by the psi wave of the observer. He was creating his own prison. Only the receptor's channel offered a shaft of energy from the reality beyond the nothing that surrounded him.

Horror sloshed across his mind with the realization that the portal to the outside universe could be erased! He could be entirely surrounded by null space – a waveform of consciousness eternally trapped in darkness.

Ania read his panic in the frenzied glyphs that flashed from the portal lens. 'Don't be afraid. You're not going to be kept in there.'

'You can release me?' Rafe's voice rose toward a cry. But the sadness in Ania's dark eyes quelled his sudden hope.

'Roeg is going to put you in a djinn jar. Do you know what that is?' She wiped another tear from her eye. 'Blades from Telesto – morf techwrights – they created it. When you're inside it, you have to do what you're told. I'm sorry.'

'Wait—' Rafe called out as she reached again for the toggle panel.

'I did this for love,' Ania explained sincerely. 'I'm sorry. But you're a ghost. You shouldn't be here. But don't despair, please. This can't last forever. When Roeg is done with you, eventually he'll release you.'

'Ania – wait! You don't understand. The universe is . . .'

She switched the channel off and plunged Rafe von Takawa into dreamless torpor. For a moment she lingered over the console, wondering what he had meant to say: *The universe is—*

She just could not imagine.

Rafe woke in the djinn jar. Cylinders of ectoplasm sat on a stone disc pedestal among elaborate lens-prisms and coil-condensers, all framed by a brass scaffold of wire braces and filament cables. He gazed beyond the stone-feather railing of a winged serpent to a soggy brown forest of torn mist and fiery blossoms.

'The blades of Telesto are clever.' Roeg stepped into view and leaned against the balustrade. His stocky frame shifted hues in placid waves of shadowy iridescence. 'To discourage hoarding, they designed the djinn jar so that the owner may only make three commands.' He placed his blunt hands on his hips and laughed, the knotted muscles above his sarong pulsing with electric colors. 'As if we lived in a fairy tale!'

A chasm of silence widened between them. Rafe had nothing to say to his captor. His awakened mind worked to find a way to free himself.

Roeg's blue topknot bobbed as he shook his head with disapproval of Rafe's reticence. 'I'm not going to command you to speak to me. I know you can hear me. My three commands will be used wisely and for one purpose – to make Iapetus Gap the most powerful cartel in the Chronosystem.'

With an extended arm, Roeg guided Rafe's attention to the center of the crowded observation deck. Yellow veils billowed and windsocks trembled among brass assemblies of lens-prisms. A banded metal caliper, large as a man, stood upright among snapping wind scarves and chromatic streamers.

'This is a proteus.' Roeg ran an admiring hand over the heat-stained apparatus, attentive to the rainbow-shadows in the oily surface of the C-shaped structure. 'Your forms will be shaped here in the gap.' His fingers snapped in the space between the needle-pointed ends of the giant caliper.

'The blades of Telesto have connected your djinn jar with this proteus in such a way that you will become what form I select.' With a molar-wide grin, Roeg added, 'And because your waveform is locked in a null tank, the only way you can act is if you obey me. You have no other options!'

Rafe had been trying to slide away toward the horizon of his waveform three hundred light years distant. But the vista of wind-curled banners, lens lattices, and mournful jungle did not change. He had no active will of his own.

The needlepoints in the pincered gap of the proteus glowed blue hot. Incandescent voltage crackled briefly, undershadowing Roeg's crouched stare and burning hotly in his avid eyes. The blue fire vanished and revealed suspended in the gap between the hot needles a small winged insect.

'A red fly pollinator.' Roeg held his pinky up to the bug, measuring the mote against the breadth of his fingernail. 'To all appearances you are now simply a useful insect. No detector could reveal more, because you are nothing more. A bug. Only the Maat themselves could detect that you have a waveform bound to a djinn jar.'

Rafe did not dispute him, though he reasoned that if a primitive such as Roeg could acquire advanced Maat tech, so could anyone. The Maat had lifted all restraints. The festivities had begun. The final gala. Fortune's feast before the end – of everything.

'You will be delivered to the gardens of my business rivals on Titan.' Roeg straightened the wrinkles in his sarong with meticulous care as he put into motion the plan that would crush his rivals. 'You will tour several dozen gardens. In each, you will seek out the meetings and conversations of my rivals, and what you see and hear will be seen and heard simultaneously here in the djinn jar that holds your waveform. I have a monitor attached to the jar, and from here I will observe what you see and hear without myself being observed . . .'

Mao dok dok dok! Blue and yellow plumage flustered from among the wind ribbons, and a parrot burst free and sailed away screaming over the phosphor crowns of the fungal trees.

'The universe is ending.' Rafe von Takawa's voice smoldered with certainty. 'If you release me, I can show you a way to save yourself.'

Roeg turned sharply from the suspended red fly to the djinn jar. His bluegray face, precisely whiskered around tight mouth and strong jaw, flickered with a dusty glow of surprise. 'You have spoken, Rafe von Takawa?' He stepped up to the clamped cylinders of ectoplasm and tapped a knuckle against the smoky glass. 'You're a ghost. I'm giving you the chance to live again, albeit at my behest. Don't spoil it with deceptions. Remember, I can put you in a black pit – awake – forever.'

'No one knows what the Array is for.' Rafe's voice reached out stronger. 'The Maat say that it is a cosmic string resonator – an antenna for receiving and focusing energies. Do you understand what they're doing?'

'Who understands the Maat?'

'I do. I was one of them. And I tell you, they are collapsing the universe. Not at some distant time. Now. I can show you how to save yourself. But you must free me.'

Roeg stepped back from the reflection of his warped smile in the cylinder glass. 'No one listens to that cog prattle.'

Like most everyone, Roeg believed that the rumor of cosmic collapse originated with the Silicon Mind. Since machine intelligence on the Maat worlds had been limited to servo-units and anthrobots hobbled by contraparameter programming, the rumor had quieted. The only talk about collapse currently came from the last two machine communities. On Mercury and Pluto, at the inner and outer fringes of the planetary system, the cog domains broadcast warnings of imminent apocalypse, but no one in Trakaerē paid them any heed.

'Assume for one instant that the cog prattle is true.' Rafe von Takawa's calm sounded weary. 'If I could save you, wouldn't that be worth releasing me?'

'The cog's warnings are prattle.' Roeg's toothy grin buckled and expanded as he leaned closer and manipulated the control switches on the djinn jar. 'And why should any of this matter – to a fly?'

*   *   *

The brown, lacy trees looked like the river's sloughed skin. Rafe von Takawa flew over the muddy water – inside a red fly pollinator. The insect obeyed his every whim. He could dip down into the tree crowns and follow medlar scents to bruised fruits and dew-sodden blossoms. Or he could fly back to the slender dragonstone tower and buzz through the apricot streamers and veils and mizzle over Roeg's flat nose. But when he had tried that, Roeg thumbed a switch on the djinn jar, and a painful flash transformed the red fly pollinator into the milky vapor from a snuffed wick.

Roeg used the proteus to create another fly body, and Rafe von Takawa learned to obey. He flew across the dilapidated forest, stopping occasionally for nectar among the fiery lianas and blood flowers, but eventually finding his way to other towers graven with winged vipers. As instructed, he spied. In one day, he monitored five heavily restricted meetings among the wealthy morfs of Trakaerë.

All the magnates' sophisticated counterintelligence devices were useless. They searched for other devices. They listened for energy patterns. They sniffed for olfacts. Rafe flitted among them wholly ignored and followed them as they strolled stone paths discussing business strategies. In the green air thick with the dreams of the river, he sat on a high, broad leaf, sipped at a dewdrop and listened to Roeg's rivals.

When Roeg had heard enough, a flare of pain incinerated the red fly and flung Rafe into black sleep.

Roeg used the proteus to create a red-plumed bird large enough to pluck a small prism from a rival's secure tower. The prism, imprinted with corporate codes, offered access to secrets that could topple whole cartels. Roeg commanded Rafe von Takawa to find that particular disk and bring it to him.

Rafe did not want to comply, but the only way out of the null tank was through the djinn jar. The blades of Telesto had designed the jar so that the trapped waveform could behave only as directed. He flew over Trakaerë's black canals to another slender stone tower crested with the circular deck of an observation platform festooned with flags and windsocks.

A slick rain fell as he pranced about the empty deck, searching among the lens shards and prism lozenges on the stone worktables. The parrot's brain had been imprinted with a precise image of the code wafer, and he quickly found it lying in a heap of techwright's tools, waiting to have appropriate parts of it transcribed to the keys of select company officers.

The guard devices would have targeted a bird wearing a neural implant and cooked it as soon as it lighted on the techwright's table. But Rafe's bird was indistinguishable from the other parrots who crouched under the awnings to get out of the rain. He took the code wafer in his beak and flew off heavily to a distant fig tree. Among the mazelike alcoves of the tree, Roeg had hidden equipment to cut a copy of the code wafer. Once that was done, Rafe flew the original back to the rival's tower.

Two morfs stood in the rain near the techwright's table. Rafe did not hesitate to swoop over the balustrade and land within their hands' reach, in a feathery clatter atop the heap of chisels, scrapers, and files where he had found the code wafer. Wings flapping, he disguised the drop of the wafer and skittered away from the annoyed shouts of the morfs.

Briefly, he slouched under the table, listening to be certain that they had not missed the codes. Certain that they suspected nothing, he shook the rain from his wings and climbed into the wind.

Pools in the soaked forest reflected the gray sky, silver soles where an angel had walked through the rotted vegetation. On the way back to Roeg's estate, Rafe paused on the observation deck of the tower where he had first visited Trakaerë. Ania was absent. Raindrops glittered on the zebra-wood console of the receptor that had brought him to this fate.

Rafe pecked at the toggle switches and activated the receptor. After a few moments of examining its panel and the reifying cables behind the grille of the cabinet, he understood the technology that the blades of Telesto had mastered to trap him. He hopped around the deck pondering how this humiliation had befallen him.

Infatuation – emotional delusion— he told himself, imagining the years that Ania had pined here, gazing out over the moss lanes of the forest and the orange clouds of Saturn, and waiting for him to return. She had accomplished love's bidding and captured him. But had she received in return the love she sought?

He found the answer in the receptor's memory. With beak and claw, he manipulated the switches and dials and reviewed the files of phantoms that the machine had received. Among the more recent files was Ania herself. She lay below the observation deck on the stone path that circled the tower, the cobbles around her head incandescent with blood.

In the playback of her eulogy file on the phantometric receptor, her ghost wailed the usual lover's gripe, heartsickness, the oldest story. She had felt betrayed by Roeg and had chosen to end her life. Vengefully, her phantom confessed to the receptor all she knew of Roeg's misdeeds.

Alas— Rafe shook his beak ruefully. Ania knew only of her spurned lover's minor misdeeds – some tax indiscretions and competitive bidding irregularities, nothing suggestive of the top level executive spying he had achieved by configuring null tank, djinn jar, and proteus. Funding that mammothly expensive venture had been Roeg's true motive in wooing Ania. The capital he had borrowed from her went directly into this project that remained secret to her even in death.

Rafe searched for Ania's ghost with the receptor, but she had not lingered in the cold. The glyphs at screenbottom reported that her waveform presently wandered the story-telling paths among the breathing hills of the afterlife, reliving memories.

Rafe did not want to believe that illusions spilled from heartbreak could kill. That seemed so antiquated, so primitive. The grotesqueness of it reminded him of his metasapience and the failed love of his past.

Karla – there is nothing sayable!

That was her magic. Silence. She had told him nothing of their nature as light. That belonged to silence. Only what was human, only what had fallen into form, concerned her. Even in death, she was human.

The thought of an anthrofact devoted to her humanity evoked sadness in him. That augmented the unhappiness he felt for Ania's death, and he determined then that he would wait no longer to take back his freedom from Roeg.

This determination required a gamble. As he flapped strenuously through the sepulchral chambers of the forest, he contemplated his doom if he gambled wrong. Locked in a djinn jar on a mote kingdom afloat in Saturn's atmosphere, centuries could pass before anyone freed him. And there were no centuries left.

Rafe landed atop the smoky cylinders of the djinn jar and dropped the code wafer so that it fell between a coil condenser and a lens-prism. 'Ania – is – dead,' he squawked.

Roeg laughed with brittle glee. 'Yes – she killed herself for me.' He strode across the deck, stepping between drooping wind scarves and rain-bellied awnings. 'Phantometrics has made death so much more convenient for all of us.'

Rafe's quiet voice sounded from the djinn jar's speakers, poised and collected as a fist, 'You're an avaricious and heartless man.'

'And I am your master!' Roeg's broad smile reflected wider in the glass cylinders as he bent over the djinn jar to retrieve the code wafer.

'For one more command.' Rafe squawked harshly and seized the coil condenser in both claws, yanking harshly at it with a thrash of wings.

'What are you doing?' Eyes bulging, Roeg pulled away from the djinn jar. He could see the fragile glass joints of the condenser clouding with stress, and he cried, 'You'll kill us both! Stop!'

Rafe von Takawa paused, wings folding closed. 'I have stopped. That's your third command.' With a raucous cry, he spread his wings. 'And now I'm free – and so are you.'

The glass coil snapped before Roeg could straighten, and the blast of plasma gas struck him full in the face. His body flew backward, less from the force of the jetting gas than fear of its lethal agents. The fumes scalded his lungs, and his death flash released his waveform before his corpse hit the planks.

The parrot, too, succumbed instantly to the fumes, and Rafe's waveform peered out from inside the null tank of the smoking djinn jar. This was the supreme moment of gamble. 'Roeg!' he called sharply. 'The gas! Get away!'

Confused, Roeg's ghost flew over the brown forest of slow seepings and rotted leaves, fleeing the cold for the warmth of the tesseract range. In an instant, he would have departed space-time, but Rafe's call seized him. Centuries of experience as a ghost had prepared Rafe to exploit Roeg's bewilderment at finding himself a phantom.

'The gas, Roeg!' Rafe shouted insistently. 'Get away! Get away! Come to the warmth!'

Drawn by the heat of the null tank, Roeg flew toward Rafe. 'Help me!' the ghost cried, not yet realizing he was dead.

'Get in here, quickly!'

'Get out of my way!' Roeg yelled. 'Let me in!'

The volitional direction of Roeg's waveform displaced Rafe von Takawa, and Roeg filled the null tank inside the broken djinn jar. Utter blackness surrounded him on all sides but one. Through the dimming blue lens of the jar, he stared out at a rainy day and his body lying face up on the deck, wide-eyed with unblinking surprise.

Kingdom Come

3000

Through a bubble-dome window, Rafe von Takawa watched the light of the slow moon find its way among the stars. That was Deimos. It shone bright and small, its orbital motion carrying it against the planet's rotation so that its spark hung almost motionless in the sky.

He had once walked Deimos as a ghost. Slipping among the house-size boulders on the smooth pumice surface, he had looked for insight into how Tabor Roy had used a monitor station there to focus a holostream projection of random sparkpoints into the Martian desert. Not that it mattered how Tabor had terrified Ellen Vancet into betraying reality. Rafe had simply wanted to see for himself the machinations that had defeated him.

But now he could not budge. His waveform was locked again inside a physical form – his own body grown again by a blade in an alley of Terra Tharsis. Through the walls of brown concrete, he could hear the noise of the pavé – the boisterous street level of Terra Tharsis. His ghost had once roamed here, as well, enduring the cold to learn about the Maat without activating the receptors in the secure buildings. He had often sulked among the labyrinthine rootwork of buttresses, spans, foundation posts, and colonnades that supported the immense sky towers. He had flitted from opulent garden suites inside the glass spires to impoverished solar-tinsel shacks on the slopes of Mons Olympus.

Yet now, lying on his back, he could not even move his eyes. Optical mist washed his corneal lenses as he watched the slow moon carrying its heartbreaking load of light through the darkness.

'The brainfix is set.' The voice of the blade sounded close and friendly, though Rafe did not even know her name. She earned a great fortune by fixing waveforms onto reconstructed genomes. Most of her clientele were wealthy residents who had lost kin to the

Exodus of Light and who wanted those passagers resurrected from the afterlife.

Fixing was available from the Maat, too, but it was expensive – and the waveform had to consent. Among the blades, so long as there was money to be made, consent was not an issue. But the risks were steep, and their failures filled most of the dingy, compressed rock chamber: electrodes and gas shrouds dangled over acid tubs where body parts recycled. The hot stink of the chemicals assailed his sinuses, and by this he knew that his waveform was fitting itself again into flesh.

'How are you feeling?' a female voice asked, a lemony voice, brighter and sharper than the blade's. That would be Bo Rabana, an editor from *Softcopy*, one of the larger news services that provided coverage of events in Terra Tharsis for the large aboriginal community.

'He can't talk yet.' The blade spoke brusquely. Her hands came in and out of view as she adjusted the electrodes attached to his face. 'But we're almost there.'

A jolt of electricity thrumped through Rafe's body, and his paralyzed muscles loosened. Colors hardened, and he swung his eyes to look for the blade. She sat at a monitor console, her laser-cut pattern of green hair a spiral that began at the cope of her cranium and curled over her skull, ending in bangs above slim, silver eyes. She glanced at him and winked. 'Welcome back to life.'

Rafe struggled to lift his head. Cables hung in loops from the tenebrous vault above, and he followed them down to a jumbled stack of tokamak toroids. The t-t pile incandesced faintly in the gloomy chamber, an ionized aura illuminating a grid of gold couplings and arc-clips where small sparks crawled.

With a strenuous effort, he sat upright and confronted his reflection in a glass bell of ectoplasm. That was the supercooled plasma that had held his waveform while his body was woven. In the milky orb he faced a hairless version of himself, the whites of his eyes smoky with blood, flesh shrunk to the planes of his skull.

'Rafe von Takawa,' Bo Rabana called too loudly. 'Can you hear me?'

'Yes.' His voice burred in his throat and sounded unfamiliar. He gazed past the placental bell jar to yellow tanks of bubbling fluid abob with a dread waste of bones and bluebrown gobbets of flesh – the acid tubs where aborted efforts rendered their proteins.

'Are you – well?' the editor asked. She was a large woman with an endomorphic frame of a type fashionable in her circle. Her silver wing-braided hair and bold streaks of feather paint on her cheeks lent her a garish aspect that the age found appealing.

'He's sound.' The blade slapped him on the back, and indeed he felt solid. 'No nausea, no vertigo – not even ringing in your ears, right?'

Rafe looked at the blade, saw the wry flex of her facial muscles, the mockery in her tight, polyspectral eyes. He had disliked her for her jaded attitude from the first. But when he had visited her as a waveform, his careful observations informed him that she was wholly unaffiliated with the Maat. She was an independent phantometric surgeon – a blade.

'Then, we're done here,' Bo Raban said cheerfully. *Softcopy* had agreed to finance the resurrection in exchange for exclusive coverage, but the blade wanted no footage in her chamber. 'I'll authorize the transfer of the remainder of funds we agreed upon, and we'll be on our way.'

With thick hands, he touched his chest and felt silken fabric. Bo Rabana had arranged for him to be dressed in slate-blue fatigues, which she thought would look scientific to her audience. Rafe recalled her mentioning this in an aside during their negotiations, but everything that had been discussed through the phantometric receptors had dimmed.

Memory of his existence as a ghost already seemed distant and faded, a receding dream. Enclosed once again in a physical form, he felt cramped and claustrophobic. The blade's stinking, dingy chamber oppressed him, and he put a hand out and took Bo Rabana's arm. The touch of human flesh felt dull, so blind after the luminous interactions of his waveform.

Bo finished tapping a fund-transfer code into her relayer card, then helped Rafe to stand. 'You look like you never died.'

Rafe said nothing. He remembered waking on this table twice before, both times stabbed with pain because the bodies the blade had cut contained flaws and would not hold him. Both times, he had died again. His body parts from those failures rolled in the bubbling broth of the acid tubs.

With a nod, Rafe thanked the blade, and Bo Rabana led him among the percolating flaskware and cables to a narrow air-sealed sliding door. They emerged in a dark alcove on the pavé, a shadow-strewn niche in the rifted footing stone of a massive sky tower. A burly, shaggy-haired man wearing plates of gel armor looked them over and stepped deeper into the shadows. The blade hired him to guard her chamber, and Bo waited until he was gone before activating her recorder. It was a jade eye set like a brooch on her crimson shift.

As they strolled along a tessellated pathway under heliotropic arbors,

Rafe's perceptions seemed narrow, tight, hard. He stared at people milling on the trellised commons between the gargantuan anchor bases of the sky towers. Their bold maquillage of eyeblack, feather-painted cheeks, and gem-pleached hair looked odd without the radiance of their bodylights that he had once seen through his waveform. Yet he experienced no uneasiness. The bracing air loaded with olfacts left his head clear and untroubled.

Bo Rabana interviewed him about his existence as a ghost and the sensations of returning to the flesh. He answered tersely, still unfamiliar with the sound of his voice. Their path led them past a skim route where cars slashed by in a soundless blur of magnetic propulsion, and he stared at them almost sadly, remembering the freedom of his ghostlife. Yet he did not miss the cold. The warmth of his body was stronger and more comforting than the balmy breezes of the afterlife or the heated glow of receptors.

They came to an unoccupied beverage stall in a park overlooking an undulant sprawl of bubble-top cottages and swirling roadways under the soaring towers. Bo Rabana used her journalist credit code to open the faux-wood cabinet of the booth where they sat, and she removed two warm vials of ginger mead.

Rafe breathed in the redolent warmth and smiled to feel his face laved in heat. *I am alive again!* he said to himself, at last daring to admit that his scheme had worked – he had found his way back to his body without involvement from the Maat. Gratefully, he looked up at the skyways and viaducts webbing high out of sight among the monoliths, and his smile widened to a grin.

After the first sip of ginger mead, he became more voluble and spoke freely and at length in reply to Bo Rabana's questions about his first life as an anthrofact at CIRCLE. Sadness lanced him to discuss Karla Sobieski and the key to the monkey tower that she had developed. He adroitly avoided mentioning their love affair and how she had waited for him in the afterlife. But he pleased Bo with the details he offered of his first death under the flames of a pyroclass burner and how Nandi had enabled his rebirth and the dissemination of the key to the monkey tower.

For several hours, he described life among the first metasapients and divulged squalid insights about the Necroclaves of the twenty-second century. And though he told her about Nandi's destruction of CIRCLE during their centennial reunion, he said nothing about the secret understanding of the Maat. Even when she inquired about why the Maat were so rarely seen in recent times, he offered a remote reply:

'They are exploring the compact dimensions and have left the worlds to humanity.'

The Array he claimed he knew nothing about, and he diverted the subject to the differences of Maat and humans. 'To be human is to belong to the worlds, to have evolved from them and been shaped by them, either as aboriginals or morfs.' He sipped his ginger mead, glad for its euphoric charge. 'The Maat are not human. They are something more and have abandoned the worlds for a reality humanity can only dimly imagine.'

'And you, Rafe?' Bo Rabana asked with a sly flick of one eyebrow. 'You're a Maat. Why have you returned to walk again among us?'

'As I told you, I was killed in an accident on Mars,' he lied and took another sip of his drink. 'As an anthrofact, my sympathies are with humanity, in whose image I was created. That's why I endured the cold of the afterlife to wait for people to develop the tech that could resurrect me. I belong with humanity, not the Maat. And I'm grateful to you for sponsoring me. My return demonstrates that, without any further help from the Maat, humankind has conquered death.'

Bo Rabana asked several questions about his future plans, and he gave vague, non-committal replies. Then she thanked him for his cooperation, promised to stay in touch for a follow-up, and departed to file her story with *Softcopy*.

As soon as she left the beverage stall, a shaft of sunlight leaning among the skytowers twinkled where it touched the sward of the park. Rafe watched from the booth as a figure, small with distance, stepped out of the sunlight. He knew, of course, that this was a Maat. They had been watching him in the afterlife, and they had been aware when he had arranged for a blade to cut him a body. That was the current terminology, cutting proteins into the precise dna pattern that would hold the fugitive waveform. If they had wanted to kill him, they would have done so then. He wondered if they *had* tried and that was why the first two cuttings had failed.

Imagination is a quest of chaos, he reminded himself. He had no way to know how the Maat would respond to his return, and that was why he had *Softcopy* interview him, so that he could demonstrate his good will to his old cohorts. He had said nothing of the secret understanding, and by that he declared that he had not come back to cause trouble.

Watching the Maat walk across the park, through a loose crowd of frolicking aboriginals, he looked for the salt-blond hair and long gait of Fenn Tekla and was surprised when he saw that the brown-clad man approaching him was Tabor Roy.

A handful of pain fisted in Rafe's stomach. Fear and anger reared as out of an ancient dream. He put his mind on the skytowers with their tiny millions of lives housed in glassy spires. Instantly, he calmed. Centuries as a ghost had honed his detachment, his perception of emptiness. All his life he had known that forms float in the void, but only as a phantom had he seen how much of himself was nothing.

Now, only hours old, his body sat in the beverage stall dressed in fright and rage. His mind watched. His emotions worked hard, building their world again from memory. They wanted to smash the ten thousand things. But his mind would not participate. He only watched.

'Rafe von Takawa—' Tabor Roy stepped into the beverage stall and sat across the table from Rafe. 'I knew you would return. The day I killed you, I knew.'

'Murder just isn't what it used to be.' Rafe gazed placidly into Tabor's silver eyes. He doubted this was Tabor himself. The Maat had been toiling a long time in the garden at the heart of the blue dragon curled smaller than a quark. By now they had learned all the secret paths of the garden. They could go wherever they pleased in the universe. And they could shape matter and energy into any patterns they wished – even precise simulacra of themselves – and set those patterns adrift in the floating world of things.

'You went to a lot of trouble to fit yourself back into your body – and died twice trying.' In his brown jacket and beige shirtdress Tabor appeared much like an ordinary citizen of Terra Tharsis. Featherstrokes of blue and yellow paint fashionably accented his long cheeks and kohl rimmed his close-set eyes. 'Why have you come back, Rafe?'

'To take my place among the Maat.' Rafe's face, devoid of hair, appeared sincere and unhurtable as rock. The fear and anger he had suffered a moment ago roamed distantly, like pale Phobos and starglint Deimos visible between the gleaming towers. 'I want to sit upon the throne of God.'

Tabor watched him steadily. 'Why?'

'The rock of consciousness rolls to where it rests.' Rafe spoke a code he knew Tabor understood. The Maat believed consciousness, like light, was a remnant of the origin. In space-time, both light and consciousness could never stop but had to move continuously. The Maat hypothesized that in the compact dimensions light *did* stop and became a shadowless domain of infinities where each impacted consciousness would dwell at the godful center of immeasurable power.

'Our fear is that you have returned to spite us.' Tabor tapped the faux-wood cabinet and removed a dewy goblet of iced nectar. 'I and others are concerned that you will violate the secret understanding.'

'Have I ever transgressed?'

'Informing Q could be so considered.' Tabor gulped thirstily at his drink. 'You did tell her everything before you went into exile?'

'Ellen Vancet *had* to know.' Rafe pinned him with a sharp look. 'She is one of us by virtue of history. You of all people, her direct descendant—'

Tabor paused him with a lifted finger. 'I will not argue the point – even though Q has caused us no end of difficulties with her insistence on telling everyone.'

'No one believes her.' Rafe poised his stare over Tabor's shoulder and looked across the park to the flat of a pond molten with midday glare. He held in check his fear that the Maat had come to seize or slay him.

'She behaves as though what we are doing is wrong.' The orange color of his drink kindled Tabor's silver eyes as he sipped the nectar, and he read Rafe's pink new face intently. 'We feared you shared her disapproval.'

'I made my return public and under the auspices of a news service to demonstrate to the Maat that I am sincere.' Rafe avoided meeting the scrutinizing stare and let his gaze follow a hedge fringe of the park up a hillside of Terra Tharsis. The slope looked soft in the mauve shadow of a huge tower, while on farther hills the skylights of cottages reflected the sun in hot motes. 'I've told my story truthfully to the people of this time, and yet I've not violated our understanding.'

'You've also avoided contact with us entirely.' Tabor slammed down his goblet with a bang that yanked Rafe's attention to the Maat. 'Why did you go to a blade to cut you a new body? Why didn't you come to us?'

'I need my integrity, Tabor.' Rafe leveled a dark stare on his interrogator. 'I want to come back to the Maat as myself, not as a ward of the others.'

'You want to come back?' Tabor assessed this with lidded eyes. 'Then you harbor no animosity for what happened between us?'

Rafe's head pulled back, and a frown squeezed his face.

'Why are you looking at me that way?' Tabor asked.

Rafe shook his bald head. 'As a waveform I was locked out of all the secure areas, so I couldn't observe the Maat's technical developments. But before I exiled myself, I was among you. I know what you were planning, and I know what you're capable of. By now, you have the means to scan all my internal states. You know exactly what I'm thinking and feeling.'

'My initial appearance aroused fear and anger in you.' Tabor read these emotional responses from the sensors in the fabric of his high-collar jacket. 'Then you quelled yourself quickly and thoroughly. I sense no emotional stress now. But no, neither I nor any of the others has any notion what you're thinking. Our agreement of union, I want you to know, disallows that. Of course, you could voluntarily submit yourself to a full scan and reveal your thoughts.'

Rafe considered this and nodded. 'If that's the only way I can return among you, I will.'

'You never left us.' Tabor ventured a smile, and the blue and yellow feather-paint on his cheeks creased briefly to green. 'There are no privileges for ghosts. But now that you have resurrected, you are again one of us. You're entitled to all the privileges and obliged to honor all the responsibilities and limits of our agreement.'

This news dangled the happiest hope before him, but he did not immediately snatch it. 'Do you still fear I've returned to spite you?'

'Yes, I fear that.' Tabor's jaw flexed. 'I killed you.'

'An imploder killed a conservative,' Rafe conceded, allowing a measure of hope to run free toward joy. 'There are no imploders or conservatives anymore. We are Maat.'

'Strictly bound by our agreement of union.' Tabor's cheeks shone yellow again. 'You didn't know that the agreement provides for the resurrected. You've been a ghost that long. You thought you were in jeopardy!'

Rafe allowed his relief to show. 'I was afraid, Tabor. Much has changed since I left.'

'You didn't have to flee us at the Worlds Fair,' Tabor said with an admonishing wag of his head. 'If you had stayed, you would have been the first of the resurrected.'

'I was a distrustful ghost.' Rafe apologized with a shrug. 'I died before the agreement of union.'

'You should have known. Metasapience strives for integrity. It was that way among the new breed – and the Heteronomy of Claves – and then the secret understanding. It's the same now.'

Rafe accepted this with a contrite sigh, sincerely glad to be reinstated. 'In a society of freedom, there will always be misunderstandings. Small price to pay if we resolve our uncertainties quickly.'

'Good.' Tabor slid out of the booth and stood. 'So—' He motioned toward the park with a warm smile. 'Shall we go?'

Rafe did not move. 'You go ahead. I'll join you and the others later.'

A shadow settled on Tabor's painted face. 'You'll want to catch up on what's changed since you've been gone.' From a sleeve pocket, he took out a wick and offered it to Rafe. 'I don't suppose you would consider a gnosolfact? I had the foresight to prepare a blend that has most of the information you missed during your ghost years.'

Rafe waved it away. 'Now that I know I'm welcome back, I'll get the practical knowledge I need myself.'

'You don't trust me at all, do you?' The shadow on Tabor's face darkened to a frown. 'I think you're planning something vindictive, Rafe von Takawa.'

'Perhaps it's your conscience that troubles you.'

Tabor glared. 'I have nothing to feel guilty about. I did not violate our secret understanding when I killed you. We were on Mars.'

'"Thou shalt not kill" was probably meant for all worlds, don't you think?'

A sneer floated through Tabor and almost escaped as a laugh. 'We are Maat. We are not bound by historical mores. Our judgment spared violence on Earth, to protect everyone. But from the first this was to be a judgment of blood. The fate of the universe was at stake, man.'

'That blood debt has been paid in full.' Rafe shoved to his feet. 'Now that we have met and admitted our distrust, we can warily depart and go our separate ways.'

Tabor smiled harshly. 'We're going to the same place, aren't we? To the throne of heaven. Soon we will each and all of us be gods!'

'Not everyone wants to be a god.' Rafe held Tabor's vibrant stare with an inquisitive expression. 'Aren't there alternatives? Wormhole networks must be extensive by now. It should be easy to leave our universe for another.'

'Easy?' Tabor tapped the sleeve-pocket that held the gnosolfact. 'If you had used this you'd know it's so easy it has become common. The first lynks arrived about sixty terrene years ago. Look.' He sketched the air with his topaz ring, and a holostream of a parabolic silver arch about thirty meters tall to judge by the trees around it rotated between them. 'They're corridors into other realities. We thought that we were sending them back to ourselves from somewhere just ahead. But now we *are* just ahead and there isn't much more "ahead" left.'

The mirror surface of the lynk reflected terrestrial clouds and hills. 'These lynks are coming from another universe.'

'Other *universes* – in fact, parallel Earths.' Tabor leaned through the image, and it vanished. 'Some of those lynks connect us billions of years into a future that originates in a past where I apparently didn't kill you and there was no gauge field bomb. In that reality, the remnants of Earth are resurrected long after the solar nova by a hyperdimensional being. The construct this five-space creature has made out of our four dimensions is quite a monstrous menagerie – flora and fauna from every age jumbled together, people too! A truly terrifying place. The Earth of that universe had played out its life and gone to cold cinders adrift in space. Everything we could have been was lost. It makes me glad the judgment turned out the way it did in our continuum.'

'Because we're going to heaven,' Rafe replied dully.

'Those of us *will* go to heaven whose bodies are installed in the matrices when the end comes.' Tabor stepped close enough to graze Rafe with his aura of olfacts. 'The implosion *will* carry the pattern of our waveforms into the compact dimensions. Literally in no time, we *will* become gods.' He spoke in a whisper though they were alone in the stall. 'Your matrix has been ready from the first. Will you use it – or lynk to another Earth?'

Rafe whispered back, 'I told you, I want to sit upon the throne of God.'

'You speak in metaphor, Rafe.' Tabor retreated two paces. 'I don't like metaphor. Your zen aryanism could well interpret the throne of God as the natural world or even the human heart, for all I know.'

'Not the heart, Tabor.' Rafe put two fingers to his temple. 'The heart is God's butt, and it sits on its throne, the mind.'

Tabor winced. 'You are profoundly weird, Rafe von Takawa.' He straightened as a wave of apprehension swept through him. 'How could you be otherwise, I suppose. You're not conventionally human. You're an anthrofact. Q made you. Perhaps that sets you apart from the rest of us. You've died and been reborn twice. Unlike any other Maat who has died, you existed a long time as a ghost. I feel I should respect you. But I don't want to.' He turned to go, paused, and pointed a stern finger at Rafe. 'You will be watched closely. We all are. That's the only way the agreement of union can work. If you are thinking of trying to sabotage the matrices or the Array, do some psychic restructuring. The penalty for breaching agreement is total exclusion.'

Tabor departed. He walked into the park, and vivid, tiny birds spurted through him. Like a shadow, he thinned away and disappeared.

Ellen Vancet sat up in her hammock at one in the morning. A light rain dripped slowly from the eaves with a rhythmic tocking, and she had to listen a moment before she heard again the tapping at her door. She rolled to her feet and pulled a robe about her nakedness. 'Who is it?' she asked groggily.

The image that the cabin projected into the sleep nook opened her eyes wide. Rafe von Takawa stood on the stoop wearing a poncho glittery with rain. In the glare of the porch lamp, his bald head showed the blue shadow of growing hair.

'Rafe?' she inquired, wondering if this was an eminence clone or an anthrobotic semblance. She ran down the winding cedar stairs to the nightheld hearth room and flung open the front door. Rafe stepped forward, out of the rain, and bumped into an air phase barrier. With a flap of her hands, she apologized and voice-released the security lock.

Storm scent swept into the cabin with Rafe, and the interior lights came on in a soft glow of mahogany and lacquered wood. 'I would have called ahead,' he said, gazing about the room, looking for others, 'but I want to see you without the Maat knowing. Are we – alone?'

She gawked at him, her ears humming with a thunderless surf. 'Is it really you? The cabin says it's you.'

'It's me, once again.' He reached reassuringly for her hand. 'It's been a long time, and I have much to tell you.' He scanned the room more closely, noting the twenty-first century fused stone hearth and the fern-canopy rafters that sang of style and affluence. 'It was hard to get here without the Maat knowing. We are alone?'

Ellen smiled indulgently and helped him remove his dripping poncho. 'The Maat see everything. And no, we're not alone. I have a granddaughter asleep in the bedroom. Her parents left her with me for a week or so.' She dropped the poncho onto the tiles beside the door and took both his chilled hands. 'I thought for sure I would never see you again.'

He returned her smile and pulled her into a hug. For a long moment they clung to each other, their heads pressed together as if listening for each other's inmost name.

'It's been two hundred years, Rafe.' This soulfact pulled her away from him, and she looked surprised at how well he fit her memory, even in modern clothing, wearing a black thermal vest and ebony shirtdress. 'But you're the same.'

'Ghosts don't change.' His smile dazzled away the dross in her, and she knelt beside him as he sat on the low door stool and removed his gel-sole boots. 'I'm very glad to see that you haven't changed, either. It mustn't be easy, knowing what you do about what's coming.'

'No one believes me.' She squared away his boots, vest, and poncho and walked with him to a tan leatherine sofa beside the sparkling hearth where they sat facing each other. 'I've come to see that it's best no one believes. They'll never suffer. So, I don't talk about it anymore. Let kingdom come when it comes.'

'It doesn't have to happen.' He gripped her arm with exuberance. 'That's what I've come to tell you.'

'I saw the gauge field bomb detonate, Rafe.' She tipped her head consolingly. 'It's going to happen. In truth, it already has happened.'

'In *this* universe.' The enthusiasm in his voice sounded truly earnest, full of a new dint of hope. 'But we don't have to stay in this universe. We're free to go now. There are lynks to other Earths. Lynks are wormholes that . . .'

'I know about lynks.' She sounded weary at the mention of them. 'There's one here at Council Oak. You must have seen it when you flew in.'

'I didn't fly.'

'You rode in?' she asked, wondering what compelled him to negotiate the switchbacks on this slick night.

'No. I hiked in.'

She sat back with a stricken expression. 'Through the river notch? That's a thirty-kilometer climb uphill across rugged country.'

'Thirty-three and a half.' He flexed his bare feet. 'They remember every one. But I have to see you without the Maat knowing.'

She regarded him quizzically. 'But, Rafe, they know everything.'

'That's just it, Ellen. They don't.' He shook his head sternly and splayed a hand over his chest. '*We* don't. We have an agreement of union. Hasn't anyone told you? Tabor – Fenn Tekla?'

With a pout of indifference she admitted, 'I haven't seen a Maat in decades.'

'Doesn't that tell you something?' he asked urgently. 'They're in their matrices right now. All of them. It's time to go.'

Ellen shook her head. 'Not for me. I belong here.' She brushed back her long red hair with feigned insouciance. 'After all, I'm just an Earthgirl.'

'Don't joke, Ellen.' His voice appealed to her with a tone of underlying tension. 'You're a mind and there's a vast reality to explore.'

She curled a tress about her finger. 'Hm, but does it have trans-molecular synthesizers – or will we have to get old there?'

'Who cares?' He squeezed her arm again, as if to keep from falling.
'It's better than instant extinction.'

'Is it?' She remembered the doddering old people from long ago, in
the zinc-sheet village outside the Preservation Camp where she grew
up. 'I'd rather simply disappear.'

Rafe cherished a different vision. He recalled the harmonious deaths
of the aged in Lampland, the cog utopia on Mars. 'Old age is a long
way off. With a little luck, we can surely find our way to better deaths
than an abrupt annihilation.'

A thin laugh escaped her. 'No, not for me, Rafe. I've lived a thousand
years, almost all of them in this world. Time has its own gravity. It keeps
me here.'

He let her arm go and dropped his hand atop the other in his lap.
'You've spent your whole life on Earth – except for your abduction
to Titan.'

'Those crazy years in Centaur Jockey . . .' A distance unfurled in her
eyes. 'I dream about that place sometimes, even after all the ion washes
I've had since then. Simviv and its ion washes! They're supposed to
keep your brain right. And, except for the dreams, I guess they have,
because those years were scarier than my childhood. I thought I was
losing my mind. And yet now when I dream of that beautiful, uncanny
place, there's no fear. I'm happy there.'

'You're staying here because you feel guilty,' Rafe announced. 'You're
killing yourself because you feel guilty, aren't you? If I hadn't stopped
to get you out of Centaur Jockey, the imploders . . .'

'Could never have tracked you. I know, I know.' She smiled wanly.
'We have had a long and intricate relationship, you and I, Rafe. We
should have been lovers.' Her gaze hardened. 'No, I'm not killing myself.
I belong with the Earth. I still have children to tend. My flesh and blood.
I won't leave them.' The flames of her hair tossed. 'And I won't herd
them through a lynk to some ghastly unknown. If their parents want
to take them and go, they're free to do so. But I'm staying here.'

He nodded. 'Nothing I can say will change your mind.' It was not a
question.

She pressed a hand against his chest. 'When will you leave? Earth,
I mean.'

'Now,' he answered flatly. Her refusal to come with him diminished
his enthusiasm to go on at all, and he tried to find something more
to say, but he felt as though he had already said far too much, and
his words had failed and left him empty as words, the shadow of
his mouth.

'Stay for a while,' she urged. 'We agreed once to go trout fishing together. This is your last chance to experience the greatest human sport.'

'If I go fishing with you, Ellen, I won't leave.' Though he repeatedly detached himself from her in his mind, sadness went on like a song singing itself inside his chest. 'As you say, we should have been lovers. And if I stay, I believe we will be. But we both know that's pointless in this world. Eros chasing death.' He caught the glint of interest in her eyes and seized on it. 'I had hoped you'd leave here with me. I think I've found a way to make a life for ourselves. But the Maat can't know about it.'

'That's why you hiked here in the middle of the night through the rain.'

'I've been readmitted to the Maat.' He wanted to tell her about the new and astonishing knowledge he had acquired, but there was no time, and he said instead, 'I've had full privileges since I came back yesterday.'

'You've only been alive a day?' Her head cocked back, startled by this admission.

'Thirteen hours. But it's been enough time to learn everything we need to know. I just don't have the time to tell you right now.' He quickly related his encounter with Tabor Roy in the beverage stall on the pavé. 'After he left, I tried the stall's cabinet myself. I tapped on it as he had and requested a gnosolfact for wormholes. It arrived as a wick – like degagé or wakeup or sleepease – and a few minutes later, I knew all about timephase and spacerange corridors. I mean, everything.'

She smiled appreciatively. 'Now you know enough to escape the implosion.'

'Better.' Hope flared in him again. 'We can put ourselves on an Earth without the possibility of an implosion. Come with me. We don't have much time. But if we go now we can redeem everything together.'

'I'm sorry, Rafe.' She stood up, her face a curtain that had closed. 'You'll have to redeem our past yourself.'

His hopeful stare stiffened, and he conceded with a glum smile and rose. 'You should know this: After I did several other wicks of gnosolfacts to round out my education of these end times, I decided to look around Terra Tharsis. I entered the skytowers, Ellen. They're empty.'

She accepted this with a slow shake of her head. 'Then this *is* the end.'

'Very soon.' He put his hands tenderly on her shoulders. 'I wanted you to know. I want you to have the chance.'

'Thank you, Rafe.' She kissed his cheek. 'But, you know, I'm content with this fate. I've seen so many of the endless colors of time in my life, they've begun to blend into a whiteness that makes our return to the first light seem right and just. I want to go with it.'

Rafe left with a mouthful of tears, but he did not look back. The rain had stopped and the clouds had parted, revealing a half-eaten moon. He put his mind into that landscape of quartz shadows and let Ellen Vancet go.

Rafe reached the lynk at dawn. A green sky and jagged mountain peaks tongued with fire shone in the curved silver of the parabolic arch. He strode in at an angle that walked him across the twilight to sunset in Hyderabad.

Scarlet night reflected on the river Musi like vapors. The Char Minar, a stately rectangular building famous for its four minarets, stood at the center of the old city where ruins had ranged in his childhood. He had come here to acquire a statskin.

On the left bank of the Musi, the ancient bazaar thrived, selling everything from local foodstuffs to simviv, microbot systems, and a wide diversity of olfacts. He crossed the old bridge of twenty-three arches, the Purana Pul, with a throng of tentacled, blister-eyed Titanian tourists. He reasoned that they would know where to get the best statskins, and eventually they led him to a morf bazaar selling Maat-class techware.

From an anthrobot designed to resemble an archaic Persian merchant replete with burnoose and an avaricious glint in his almond eyes, Rafe purchased a statskin and a spare. He also selected a sturdy utility harness and paid the merchant without haggling. As a Maat, he had unlimited credit, and so long as his expenditures were discreet none of the others would notice what he purchased.

Rafe required anonymity, because he intended to violate the agreement of union – and he knew Tabor was waiting for that.

He fit the two statskin bracelets into a pouch of his bodyform harness and left Hyderabad through the lynk that fronted the palace, the pink-marble Gosha Mahal. The angle he entered admitted him to a cirque of amber dolmen rocks. This was a routing station in hyperspace accessible only to Maat. From here, he could go anywhere in the Maat demesne.

A pang of fear hurt his chest. Just as people and morfs milled in the depots of the spacephase corridors, this node should have been busy with traffic. Usually the station had Maat coming and going, but the brightly lit cirque was empty apart from himself. No one emerged from the utter blackness that stood in each of the dolmen portals.

The agreement of union had advised all Maat to be installed in their matrices a decade ago, but many still traveled. Or so he had seen as a ghost. No one knew the precise moment of collapse, but the gnosolfacts he had breathed at the beverage stall had all urged him to immediately install himself in his matrix.

Fear rippled through him with the trip of his heart. Standing on the fractal mosaic at the center of the cirque, alone, he became all the more certain the implosion was imminent.

The remaining moments clustered like flies in his mind. *Is there time to do everything?*

His fear soured to remorse that he had wasted time trying to convince Ellen to accompany him. The thought of her burned like a page of the future turned too soon, reduced to colorless ash. If there was time, he would accomplish his mission. If not, he would disappear with her.

Decisively, he chose the dolmen portal that led to the Maat archives. The long aisles among rows of artefacts from the Maat's thousand-year history stood empty. A perfume of silence hung in the domed chamber, hundreds of kilometers below the Earth's surface. A chill floated through him: He was alone in a warehouse-sized capsule circulating within the convection currents of molten iron around the planet's core.

His gel-sole boots made no sound as he hurried out of the lynk and along ranks of giant machinery. Generously illuminated by piped-in sunlight, the archives presented physical memories, trophies of Maat ascendancy, from the glassware of James Watson and Francis Crick's laboratory and the genetecture appartus of CIRCLE to the staggering variety of devices that metasapience had created.

He ran down a corridor of hoverdrone and strohlkraft airframes, past a bank of holostream projectors, to an ellipsoidal display zone footed with white pebbles. At the center of the gravelly clearing, a group of glastic display cases housed prototypes of the gauge field bomb.

His footfalls clattered across the pebbles, hands outheld anxiously before him. At his touch, a display case opened, and his fingers closed on the chrome sphere and chromatic axes of a gauge field bomb. He removed the lightweight orb, and for an instant he thought it was an empty model. Then, he peered into the transparent end of the green axis and saw the crystal filament interior and knew that this bomb, like all else in the archives, was genuine.

The Maat had nothing to fear from the functional prototypes, because only one bomb could be detonated in any given universe. If any of these were exploded, they would instantly shunt into a parallel reality – wrinkling away like a mirage.

With the gauge field bomb firmly gripped in both hands, Rafe darted for the exit. At any instant, there would be no more instants. He returned to the lynk station panting and dashed through the dolmen portal that opened into the matrix chamber.

The lynk carried him to an arena nestled in the Nereidum Montes on Mars, where mists circled black cindercones. He stood on a platform deck at the outer rim of the domed bowl at this most secret sanctuary of the Maat. Above him, indigo boundaries of weather caught the last rays of daylight, and flung stars blazed through ripped clouds. Below, in the enormous arena, the Maat's matrices lay like golden sarcophagi, stacked atop each other in an inward-spiraling configuration, like chrysalis pods of a spectral hive, seeds of a cosmic flower.

At the center, a giant black cylinder crawled with lightnings of every color. That was the central timephase lynk that the Maat were using to focus the implosion pattern through the matrices. That was his goal.

The slow planetary turn into darkness aligned the matrix chamber with the Array, and Rafe was eager to get to the timephase lynk and get out. But first he had to clear his own matrix. The chamber believed he had arrived to take his place among the others, and as soon as he moved forward he was carried by the internal lynkway from the platform to his matrix deep in the chamber.

It lay empty before him – a transparent effigy of himself, hollow, open like a coffin, and packed with yellow fleece. If there were any time at all, he would have paused and studied this elaborate circuitry that lined the matrix in spun gold. But the terrifying vertigo of time dwindling away spun him toward the timephase lynk. Its black, volt-tangled surface sizzled several hundred meters away, clearly visible through the catacomb of stacked matrices. Atop and below him the crypts of the Maat hovered, stacked in curves of magravity so that they seemed to float in midair. He could easily see past their swerving tiers to where his goal seethed with electric fire.

The nearest lynkway booth, a hutch of starburst chrome, stood less than half that distance in the opposite direction. He decided to run for the booth, use it to cross directly to the center of the matrix chamber, and enter the timephase lynk from there, escaping the fate of this Earth for another.

He lunged one step and stopped. His peripheral vision glimpsed a familiar figure among the glass effigies. Ellen Vancet's matrix lay shut not five paces from his. A shout jumped through his blood. He could see her body through the woolly tufts of golden circuitry.

She's inside the matrix!

A flurry of explanations crowded his mind: *She's a Maat! – She changed her mind. – No! She was snatched at the last instant – by Tabor. He won't let her go.*

Her body had been mapped against the cosmic background. The Maat had used that map to transfer her into her matrix without telling her. He was sure of it.

He dismissed his frantic thoughts and flung himself at the matrix. It no longer mattered why she was there. This fateful moment had no room for explanations. He punched the emergency tab, and her matrix opened with a cold sigh.

Ellen blinked awake, instantly alert. 'Where the—?'

'Hush!' Rafe lifted her out of the matrix, and she stood naked before him scarved in ectoplasmic fumes. 'Run!' he shouted and pulled her after him.

She clasped his hand in a fright. A moment before she had been bent over her granddaughter's sleeping face, smelling her hair, tucking her in – and then . . . She whirled into the fearful orbit of her old dread, that everything she was experiencing was an illusion sparked into her brain by morfs.

No – this is real! she sensed from the very strangeness of what was happening. *This is the end of the world.*

Rafe pulled her into the lynkway booth with him, and they emerged as he intended at the brink of the timephase lynk. Its wall of absolute black towered above them, massive bolts of lightning stabbing inward into the darkness, the glare of the discharges strobing shadows from the stacked bodyforms. Thunder moiled distantly.

Ellen staggered backward, alarmed. Before she could speak, Rafe seized her arm, snapped a statskin bracelet over her wrist, and shoved her into the lynk. He activated his own statskin and hurled himself after her, the gauge field bomb under his arm.

They fell backward a thousand years and landed on an arid and empty Mars. No mists glowed in the starlight. Instead, the Nereidum Montes cut its jagged lava darkly across the starry face of night.

Sand slithered across the ground where they lay and grit flew in a stiff wind. But they felt no discomfort. The statskins provided ample protection, and they suffered not even a bruise from their long fall through time.

'What's happened?' Ellen yelled. 'Where are we?'

The radio in her bracelet broadcast her voice to Rafe. He sat up beside her in the foggy, churning sand. 'We're on a lava moraine in Nereidum – around the year 2000 common era.'

Ellen pulled herself to her knees. '2000? I haven't been born yet.'

'I violated the Maat's agreement of union,' Rafe said, standing up. He held out the gauge field bomb. 'I stole archive property when I took this into the lynk. Technically, they can come after us for this.'

'Why are we here?' Ellen staggered upright, indifferent to the sandblown wind scratching the stars. 'Why have you brought us here?'

'We're not staying.' He strode to a scarp of copper shale where the sand drifted and blew off in streamers. 'From the gnosolfacts, I learned the entry angle into the timephase lynk that got us here, to Mars before the Maat – before metasapience or anthrofacts. But we're not staying here.'

In a crescent of sand at the boulder-strewn base of the scarp, he lodged the gauge field bomb and depressed all but one of its axial pegs. 'Hurry!' He waved her to his side. 'It's going to explode!'

Ellen took his hand, and they clambered up the windfashioned scarp. At the top, he swept his leg against hers and dropped her gracefully to the ground.

Even through the statskin, she felt the blast. A startling burst of flames exploded rock shards and sand in a radiant stormfire. Rafe weighed heavily atop her, and she peered into the blurred boreholes of his staring eyes. Then, he went light and peeled away. She rolled over, afloat, and through tattered veils of fire and dust watched the nightbound surface of Mars blot into darkness.

Rafe drifted against the stars, and she reached for him. 'What's happened?'

'I smashed the gauge field bomb.' The eastern limb of the planet shone orange, and the sun blazed into view. 'No one will be coming after it now.' His grin drew her closer. 'And even better than that, its presence, even shattered, should shunt into mirages any other such bombs that are detonated in this universe.'

Ellen clung to Rafe, her insides iridescent with fear and awe. She had no idea what color of time this was. In a daze, she watched boulders tumbling in the sunlight far below, falling back to Mars. 'You planned this?'

'You weren't part of the plan.' He clutched her closer as they sailed free of the ejected scarp-rock. Far below, the black disk of the Martian night occluded the stars. 'Finding you was luck.'

'But you planned *this*?' She swung a wild stare at the vast cope of stars. 'What are we doing up here?'

'I set the blast to blow us off the planet.' He gently put a hand to the side of her face so that her startled eyes met his happy stare. 'I aligned the trajectory to send us there.' He struck an arm out and pointed to a brilliant blue star not far from the surpassing gold of the Sun.

'Earth.' She gazed at the azure spark a moment, then turned a worried frown on Rafe. 'It's far.'

'Months away. We'll have plenty of time to mourn and plan.' He adjusted her bracelet, and she heard radio waves from the blue star, human voices speaking and singing in the language of her childhood, so long ago and yet to be.

'You could have left me there with the Maat.' Her green eyes peered seriously at him. 'You didn't have to stop for me. Why did you?'

'If I'd left you there, you'd have gone to heaven with the Maat.' His empty eyebrows lifted dolefully. 'I couldn't let that happen. There's no trout fishing in the compact dimensions.'

A smile displaced her frown, and with the first upwelling of tears she twined her arms around him and whispered the words that circled off their story: 'We're going home.'

THE LONG TOMORROW

As we stand on the brink of another momentous thousand years of human history, our curiosity about the future grows boundless. So it is just as well that there is at least one creator of fictional long tomorrows – A. A. Attanasio – whose visionary imagination is equal to the task of depicting the Third Millennium in its manifold wonder and terror.

With unequalled skill and insight, Attanasio shows us a time to come in which scientific and technological advance utterly transforms the very fabric of life on – and off – Earth. And in which the most basic notions of what it means to be human are challenged dramatically and for ever. As a drastically changed humanity grapples with strange new forms of consciousness and alarmingly alien priorities, dangerously different kinds of conflict emerge – and with them the threat of apocalyptic extinction not just for our home planet but for the entire universe . . .

CENTURIES is a triumph of the transcendent imagination, a true epic of far-seeing vision by one of the world's greatest modern authors of thought-provoking fiction.

'One of our most imaginative and visionary authors has written his most ambitious work to date, stepping beyond the bounds of the genre and into the truly unique . . . a fantastically creative work, packed with enough ideas for half a dozen novels . . . enjoyable and fascinating'
SFX Magazine

Also by A. A. Attanasio in New English Library paperback
RADIX • SOLIS • THE LAST LEGENDS OF EARTH • THE DRAGON AND THE UNICORN • THE MOON'S WIFE • ARTHOR • THE DARK SHORE

NEW ENGLISH LIBRARY
Fiction: Science fiction

Cover illustration:
Bob Warner

UK £6.99
Australia $14.95
R.R.P.

ISBN 0-340-66600-5

00699

9 780340 666005